For more information visit: *https://sfarda.carrd.co* & *https://larrpress.carrd.co*

ALSO BY SFARDA L. GÜL

The Hypostasis of Dissent Duology
Non Serviam (I)

Earth Hagiography
Feed the Forest and Never Choose Death

POETRY PUBLISHED IN:

Musing Publications
From Heart to Stomach
Mollusk Literary
Metachrosis Literary
Full House Literary
Qafiyah Review
HyeBred Magazine
Split Pomegranate
The Malu Zine
and others

SHORT STORIES PUBLISHED IN:

The Globe Review

Content Warnings

Political oppression.
Lethal human experimentation.
Mass disabling and eugenics.
Death and executions.
Graphic violence and gore.
Graphic murder.
Police brutality.
Gun violence.
Riots.
Classism and class apartheid.
Genocidal rhetoric.
Discussions of sex trafficking.
Scenes of sexual harassment.
Slut-shaming and abuse/rape apologism (*from villain character*).
Descriptions of sexual violence (*retrospective; additional warnings issued before the scenes in question*).
Chapter sections from the perspective of a misogynist and rapist (*no acts of sexual assault portrayed*).
Mentions of sexual mutilation.
Suicide (*on- and off-page; attempted and successful, including a child*).
Suicidal ideation, depression.
PTS nightmares.
Panic attacks.
Psychosis and hallucinations.
Eating disorder behaviours.
Descriptions of food.
OCD.

Religion, religious fundamentalism, religious abuse.
Violence against women and trans people (*including implied transphobia; challenged*).
Implied homophobia (*negative portrayal*).
Internalised lesbophobia and queerphobia (*challenged*).
Internalised ableism (*challenged*).
Partial healing of a disability.
Allusions to body integrity identity disorder.
Implied Romaphobia (*challenged*).
Implied Orientalism (*challenged*).
Discussions of a murdered Armenian-coded female character.
Deaths of POC characters (*on-page*).
Death of a child (*on-page*).
Discussions of child abuse.
Implied ephebophilia (*antagonist; off-page*).
Mentions of divorce.
Smoking (*tobacco*).
Drug use (*opium*).
Alcohol.
Discussions of intravenous drug abuse (*including depictions of side effects*).
Surgical procedures and needles.
Fires and fire injury.
Consensual sex (*open-door; non-graphic*).
Blood- and knife-play (*brief; non-graphic*)
Strong language (*including misogynistic and classist slurs*).

Take care of yourself, reader; your wellbeing is of utmost import~♡
If you find throughout the reading experience that a content warning
is missing, *please do not hesitate to reach out to the author.*

DISCLAIMER

This novel is <u>not</u> intended to be a true-to-life representation of any languages or cultures coded, mentioned, or alluded to in any degree of detail throughout the novel—text proper or footnotes—appearing in approximately this order: Venetian, Sardinian, Izwawen (*Kabyle; Algerian Amazigh*) and Algerian, Etruscan, Roman, Western Armenian, Erromintxela (*Romani*), Basque, Kalbelia, Ḥijāzi, Turkmen, Polonè-Ayisyen, Aragonese, Georgian, Northern Sámi, Balóch, Friulian, Maltese, Greek, Mongolian, Yamato, Nama, Milanese, Norwegian, Ovimbundu (*Angolan*), Danish, Sephardi (*Haquitía*), Nicaraguan, Irish, Albanian, Pontian, Tigrayan, Zunda, Scottish, Assyrian, Neapolitan, Sicilian, Palestinian, Bámáná, Cypriot and the Eteocypriot language, Lebanese, Persian, Chuvash, Sumerian, Lydian, Ilmen Slovene, Khmer, Welsh, French, Northern Kurdish (*Kurmancî*), Xi'an Han Chinese, Luoravetlat, Sicilian, Senegalese Fula, Telugu, Norwegian, Andamanese, Avar, Emilian-Romangol, Griko, Ryukyuan, Tibetan, Afghan Hazara.

While SWANAn, Eastern European, and Central Asian, with this book being in part *Own Voices* for multi-ethnic representation, the author does <u>not</u> fall under all of the aforementioned identities. The author does <u>not</u> subscribe to any of the religions underpinning the inspiration to those featured in-text. One pivotal in this novel is inspired in part (*though not entirely*) by Gnosticism. Certain aspects of Gnostic theology have at times been appropriated by a violent alt-right subculture of USAmerican conspiracy theorists. This practice is rooted in Antisemitism, Orientalism, and anti-Mandaean racism by proxy. The author condemns <u>all</u> alt-right conspiracy theories, as well as any form of bigotry therein or elsewhere.

Some characters' internalised descriptive prose in this novel may read like a romanticisation of cigarette smoking. *Please* <u>do not smoke</u>.

<u>Do not</u> take any of the material featured in this book as unaltered cultural, theological, linguistic, or historical fact. That was <u>never</u> its purpose.

If you find issue with the portrayal of subjects, peoples, *etc.* in any capacity, *please reach out to the author.*

This is an adult book. 18+

NON OMNIS MORIAR

The Hypostasis of Dissent
Book II of II

SFARDA L. GÜL

for those who search for hope,
for a better world, against
all odds, against hope itself;
the fight is worth it

BALINOR
GETHLEN
MAANAAT
AVALLA
VILGES ISLAND
POHMAPERA
o'COLLARSAIDH
DAL LISHIR
WHILWEN
WATERS OF THE FALLEN
CURSED GOLD
PROPHETEN SEA
SEA OF SOLITUDE
TIR LINTHAR
AURELI
VTHELM
TYRAGWLAN
IRON MOUND
GETTUM
CAPE ESTREK
THE TENDER SEA
SLEEPING STONES
KYCLINTH
ARESA
YEGRIKA
THMURTASF
LERRKIT
DILIJANA
AD-DIMARD
KUDTRAA
NAANGDI
SH'OVVA
ARELECH
KIDHO PLAINS
PETRO
ONTOLELA
OMANIYA
SA'AHDA
THEMISTORLIS
YEWADA
HART SEA
THE AGNOSIS
THE SPIDER GARDEN
DAYARABAD

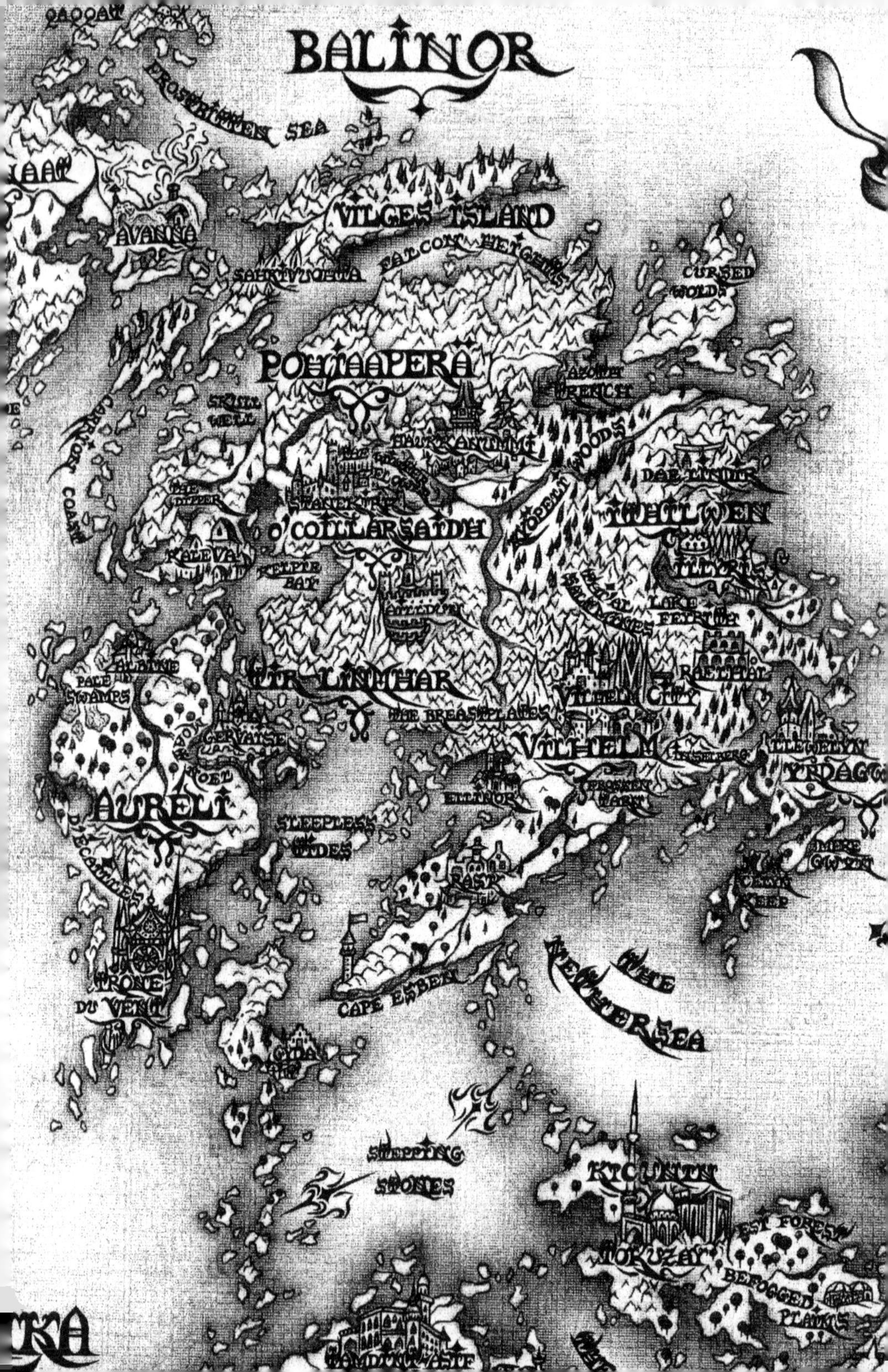

BALINOR
FROSTBITTEN SEA
VILGES ISLAND
AVANIA
SAERTINGUA
FALCON HEIGHTS
CURSED WOLDS
POHTAAPERA
AZOTH
REICH
SKULL WELL
HAUT AUTUMN
NOPETT WOODS
DAE LINDIR
THE DIPPER
WAKERTH
WHITWEN
O'COILLARSAIDH
KALEVA
KELPIE BAY
WEST OF LAKE FEIRTOR
UIR LINMHAR
RAETHAL
PALE SWAMPS
ALBINE
THE BREASTPLATES
VILHELM CITY
GERVAISE
VILHELM
ILLEWELYN
NOET
TESSELBERG
YRDAGG
AURELI
ELINOR
FROSTEN VALE
MERE GWYT
SLEEPLESS TIDES
CLIFF KEEP
THE NETHER SEA
TRONE DU VENT
CAPE ESBEN
SLEEPING STONES
KICUXIN
MORUZAY
EST FOREST
BEFOGGED PLAINS

GULF OF
MIOKAH
DRAGON'S BIGHT
RUSTEITTA
SLOTOH
SALVATRICE
BATOLA CHAPEL
ZARGOSA
DU PRAVIA
DU ERRETICA
SNOPPE
SANCTA MARTA
MINUCA
REPUBLIC OF
FAUSTINA
SIERRA
THE BASIN
VELENCA
LOS INCARNE
SEA
VALLEY
OF
FACES
PROSCENIUM
KURT ISLANDS
CORAL
THE TEMPLER
SHPOKE
OCUVA
REVERIE
SEA
VODARTO
DREAMING REEF

Weekdays in Faustinian

Monday	*díem auróra*	'dawn day'
Tuesday	*díem sóle*	'sun day'
Wednesday	*díem zenítis*	'zenith day'
Thursday	*díem tramòne*	'eventide day'
Friday	*díem crepúsca*	'dusk day'
Saturday	*díem lunéra*	'moon day'
Sunday	*díem stelláre*	'star day'

MONTHS IN FAUSTINIAN

January	*Acásce*	'Creation'
February	*Cechásu*	'Binding'
March	*Velcítna*	'Healing'
April	*Aprésa*	'Consecration'
May	*Ampíles*	'Thriving'
June	*Acále*	'Refinement'
July	*Tranéa*	'Ratification'
August	*Ermìus*	'Kindling'
September	*Celí*	'Glorification'
October	*Sàref*	'Assurance'
November	*Capéni*	'Harnessing'
December	*Màsan*	'Realisation'

Vencenzani Masks

Faustinian Military Sigils

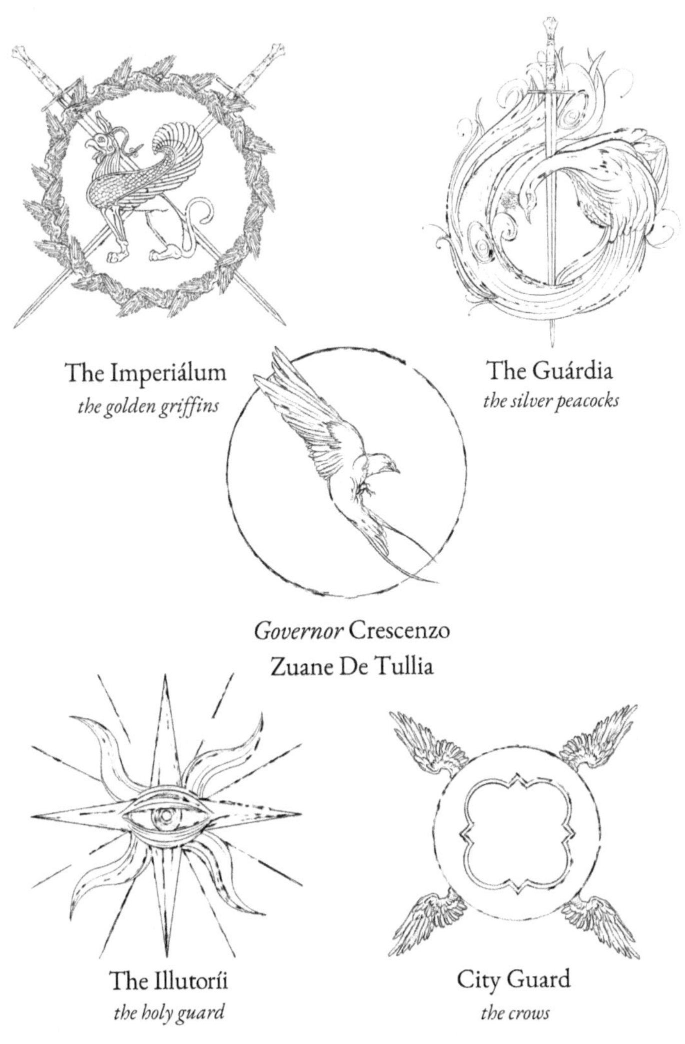

The Imperiálum
the golden griffins

The Guárdia
the silver peacocks

Governor Crescenzo
Zuane De Tullia

The Illutoríi
the holy guard

City Guard
the crows

DRAMATIS PERSONAE (FAR FROM EXHAUSTIVE)

Giorgianna Damiani

The heroine of our tale. A wrathful woman scorned—a deranged maenad hellbent on revenge for the murder of her beloved childhood friend in an attack by three men, and her dissident father's execution by the tyrant of the city-state of Vencenza, Governor Crescenzo Zuane De Tullia.

Cesare Ramiro Agostini

The revolutionary of the city state; a myth hiding behind the mask of The Bauta. At the end of *Non Serviam*, he was stabbed in the eye by Davide, a bandit blackmailed by the tyrant to bring The Bauta to "justice".

Eligio Liwạr Commegno

The elder twin. The caretaker and the sweetheart. Painter.

Lissandri Sardûk Commegno

The younger twin. The sardonic and sour one. Clockmaker and bookworm.

Rosalia Trine Dalgaard

A foreign girl taken in by the twins' late parents (*killed by the state*) after her own parents' arrest by legionaries for laughter during their visit to Vencenza. Had strongarmed her way into living at *The Sunrise* theatre with Cesare and the twins before it was burnt down by the Governor's men (*informed by Davide*).

Basilio Lanuza

A wealthy aristocrat and current owner of *The Crescent*, one of Vencenza's "six hearts", or its six theatres. Giorgianna's ex-employer who framed her for treason, resulting in her banishment from the city-state.

Ygạl Najm

The Dóminus of The Boars and Hounds—condottiére parties ruling districts of the Antrum, a subterranean city beneath Vencenza which had once served as the innards of a pagan temple and has now been repopulated with the outcasts of society.

Lucrezia Montefiore

The former cosmetics artisan at *The Crescent* and a sleeper agent for Ygal's condottiéri. At the end of *Non Serviam,* she was shot non-fatally by Basilio in the torso. Ygal's basically-wife.

Isaia Caruana

Once a member of The Hounds before its subsumption into Ygal's Boars. Now the head eavesdropper and Ygal's right hand.

Fabio Amadi-Spýros

Captain of The Salt Hydras smuggler band and former playwright and owner of *The Sunrise.* Long-time close friend of Giorgianna's late father, Ludovico.

Emanuela Vehanush Airaldi

Giorgianna's childhood best friend and the initiator of her vengeful wrath. A strangeling. Murdered by General Manuele Dioli during her and Giorgianna's attack by him, Erminiu Matracia[†], and Abramo Sessa two years prior to the commencement of *Non Serviam.*

Abramo Sessa

A former employee of *The Crescent*; once an Imperiálus of the Governor's elite soldiers.[1] The one who broke Giorgianna's fingers during the attack.

Irene Falco

The sadistic Madáma of *The Arum* "brothel" (*it is not a true brothel*) where Giorgianna had at one point been "employed".

---

[1] It is important to note that 'soldiers', 'legionaries', *etc.*, isn't used here in quite the same context as the army. Their jobs in Vencenza are more akin to police officers.

An Abridged Glossary

Óssium

Literally "bone". A euphemistic way of referring to the city-state of Vencenza.

Córpus

Literally "body". The outer structure of a theatre.

Víscera

Literally "flesh". The interior of a theatre.

Ossíi

Literally "of the bones". The citizens of Vencenza (*i.e.* the óssium).

Vìtae

Literally "souls" (*archaic*). Multiple theatre staff (*e.g.* "three vìtae").

Vìtus

Literally "blood" (*archaic*). Either one individual theatre staff member (*e.g.* "that vìtus over there"), *or* a theatre's staff as a whole (*e.g.* "the vìtus of *The Nox*").

Court of Secrets

The slum district of Vencenza's oldtown. Strange magic lurks there.

Antrum

A secret subterranean city built beneath Vencenza into what had once been an underground pagan temple. Only accessible via the Court of Secrets and by the very few in the know.

Carnesíi

Literally "of the innards". The denizens of the Antrum.

Azoth

The life force within each fleshbearer (*living being*), as well as the source of a magus' magic; expenditure of azoth for magic shortens one's lifespan.

Take note that this book is very heavy
on *worldbuilding* and *conlang* and is written in
poetic, *metaphorical*, at times *archaic-esque* and *abstract*
language, something which some readers may find detracts
from immersion for them. This is the author's *stylistic
choice*, as she deliberately writes in English the way she
would in her first language, and is reflective
of her *authentic artistic voice*.

Artists whose works are featured in this book (*who are not
the author*) are credited in the Acknowledgements.

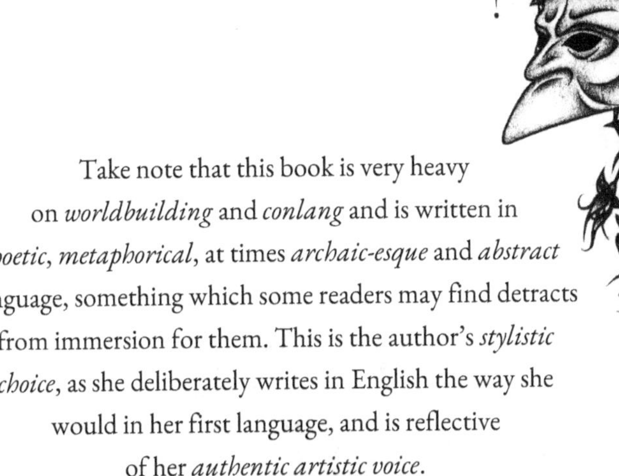

READING IS POLITICAL

ACT I

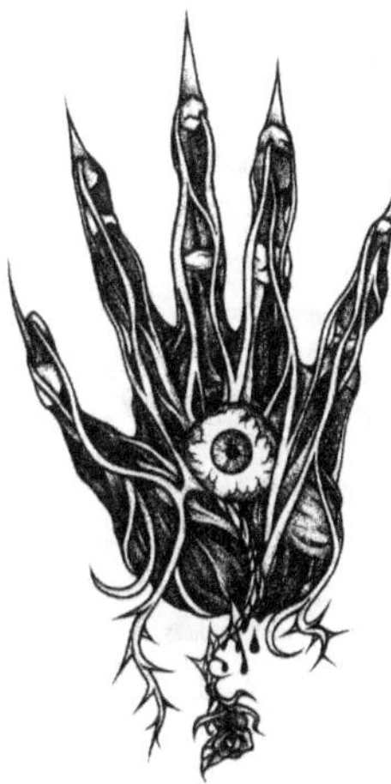

<table>
<tr><td>rather than
devastating,
enslaving
«social</td><td></td><td>see this
cankering,
system you call
order» go on…</td></tr>
</table>

"It must be considered that there is
nothing more difficult to carry out,
nor more doubtful of success,
nor more dangerous to handle,
than to initiate a new order of things."

—*The Prince*, Niccolò Machiavelli

PROLOGUS

DUES

FAUSTINA, VENCENZA, 1762, 18TH CENTURY,
9TH CENTIMILLENNIUM ZE (ZEPHYRUS EPOCH)

autumn

A FACE WITHOUT A NOSE WAS A MOUNTAIN WITH NO PEAK—it gushed sweltering red ichor like nobody's business.

But in time, the ruption peters out. Ichor coagulates to viscous tar. Hardens into the obsidian of volcanic rock.

Or the pasty ivory of Abramo Sessa's physiognomy.

Lightning fulmined across a weeping sky swollen as a beat-up eye, striking the desilvering mirror, and into view of Abramo's cerulean gaze swam a face perforated with a pair of holes where an up-turned nose had once crowned a rough-hewn terrain of features.

The sky clapped stridently enough to set Abramo's ears a-ring.

He skimped on his bills over the past three weeks, so the landlord cut the alchemy to his dingy upper óssium apartment, leaving celestial light his only illumination.

Concluding the expedition to explore his scabs wasted, Abramo swayed for his bed, eager to pass out for the night. With a swig of water from the chipped cup on his nightstand, he slumped on the creaky mattress without disrobing.

The clock ticked. Lightning stabbed through belluine thunder's hide. Rain bucketed beyond the lidless eye of the window.

Snarling, Abramo went to turn onto his side.

But he could not.

Eh?

His limbs from the neck down weighed a mountain each, nerves tingling with a revolting buzz.

He flung his head leftward, vision centring on his cup.

Shooting a gaze into the darkness of his dank room, he found his mark in a black silhouette perched atop the iron footboard. Levin kindled the sky, illuming the apparition into a female form. Hair whiter than snow streamed in a glossy avalanche to what must have been her calves.

Alarm spiked Abramo. "What the—?"

"Smite," the intruder spoke in a voice dim and lulling as autumn dusk. "Of the genus *Prasinum*. An unsightly flower, but insidious."

As she tipped her head, that howlite-pale hair coiled into an endless mane of spirals, darkening to caramel, and recognition pleated Abramo's brow into a contemptuous scowl.

"What'd you want, *harp*—?"

A yowl cleaved his sentence short as splintering agony ruptured through the knuckles of his hand—its middle and index fingers bent grotesquely out of shape.

"Don't interrupt me." Giorgianna unfurled her fist into slender fingers. *Flesh tailoring…* "Three species fall under this genus: *goldarus, angustia, accidia.*[2] *Accidia* numbs every nerve. Every muscle, cell, turns

---

[2] *ahch-CHEE-dee-ah*

lifeless; insensate. Torpor. *Angustia* numbs all but the eyes; no speech or somatic movement is possible. Yet you feel everything. Harrow."

Abramo went to retort.

"*Goldarus*—"

The man's throat loosened another shriek as a rib snapped. The tartness of blood spritzed his tongue.

"What did I say?" Giorgianna's blacked-out eyes crucified Abramo. "*Goldarus* numbs from the neck down. And yet... you feel... *everything*."

Snap!

Abramo gave up a full-bellied wail. Serrated shin bones protruded from torn skin and cotton.

"A *smite*, for instance." A simper slashed Giorgianna's lips—almost equally indented on the bottom as the bow.

Abramo gulped. "The fuck d'you need, harpy?"

Giorgianna rested her elbows onto her knees. "Enlighten me, Abramo Sessa. Was your employment at *The Crescent* merely a means to finish the job you and your friends failed two years ago?"

"You don't know *sh*—"

Splitting pain cracked open his kneecap.

"I know it was you and Erminiu Matracia who restrained me that winter solstice night. Who forced me to watch as General Manuele Dioli murdered my friend. Emanuela Vehanush Airaldi." Her jaw flexed in the levin-graced darkness. "You remember, I'm sure. How could you forget? How could *I*, when I have every mark to remind me?"

Abramo scoffed. "You want an apology or something?"

"I want an admission of guilt." Giorgianna's tone tempered when she added, "And your dues will be repaid."

"Fine. Have it," groused Abramo. "It was me and Matracia who mangled you."

Black ink washed the night. Yet, even beneath its grime, he saw Giorgianna's eyes burn blood-red. "Why was Emanuela murdered?"

"I don't know; I was doing a job! Weren't briefed—just how that shit goes. Figured they wanted you both dead and just happened to kill her first, then you got away which wasn't planned, *obviously*, and 'cause you were so bloody nosy and cussed with getting answers, the Governor decided to bump you off another ways. Hence me and *The Crescent*. That's all I gathered. Wouldn't trust what fuckers tell *me*, though—lying every chance they get, cunts."

"Oh don't fret. I'm beyond accustomed. What of *The Sunrise*'s burning?"

"Not on me. Arsonists were sent by Davide to blaze up the place if he didn't come back from Smugglers' District by a negotiated time."

"And you know these arsonists?"

"Blokes called Alphaeus, Mircea, and Cataldu. Supposedly fucked off to the District someplace after Davide got done in. Part of his gang."

"*Commegnos' Curios*?"

"*There*, I *was*. With Imperialíi. Davide's orchestration, more or less."

"Basilio?"

Abramo's eyes spun hard. That pampered little oofy man had brought him nothing but grief. "I pitied the snivelling bastard, so I hauled him to a medic. He's all back together. Heard he's useful to the Governor, by some miracle." A begrudging chuckle. "You made a righteous mess of the twat, gotta hand it to ye."

Giorgianna waited out the clap of thunder. "Any more admissions I should hear?"

Abramo attempted to jerk free. "Let me go, harpy!"

Hopping off the footboard, Giorgianna stood to her considerable height, sweeping heavy curls down her back. A velvet jacket trimmed with ruffles dressed her slim torso and broad, angular shoulders in red, her long legs and wide hips sheathed in tight black trousers and knee-high boots.

"A shame indeed that, of all people in this slaughterhouse of a world, *you* were the one willing to answer my questions." She neared, halting at Abramo's middle. "I'm eternally indebted." From the harness at her thigh, she unsheathed a baselard, its tarnished gold hilt encrusted with a pair of garnets—an eye at the pommel and a teardrop as the crossguard. "I am rather the proponent of retributive justice, you know," she added.

"You said my dues'll be repaid!" Abramo cried out.

Her blade glistened as she angled it to catch the lightning's flash. Then thunder clapped, and Giorgianna impaled it into Abramo's navel.

She stepped closer. *Squelch. pop! pop! pop!*

Hot agony radiated through him, morphing into a scream to the tune of every bone making his skeleton snapping. Ribs distended from his abdomen, twisted vertebrae skewering the bed as she sawed through him as if he were meat.

Cracking open his sternum like a glittering scarlet geode, Giorgianna stopped by his chest and leaned closer. Bloodthirsty pupils devoured her eyes, the scent of roses on her person bitter as funeral flowers.

"And they will be," she cooed, then yanked Abramo by the collar and hauled him onto the floor—a boned, gutted fish of a man, his opened stomach spewing entrails across mildewed floorboards.

Giorgianna mounted him, dagger in a reverse grip. Lighting silvered her face in time with her blade impaling his throat.

"Blood—" thunder knelled "—does not wash off."

And she tore his head from his neck.

Scene I

Kybalion

Cesare | Giorgianna

SIX.

A throwing knife, sharp and slim as a willow leaf, glinted in Cesare's long fingers.

Training his left eye on a target etched upon a wall decorated with sailor flotsam and jetsam, he angled his arm and swept it in a swift arc. The knife slipped free.

Steel cleaved the salty air, burying three rings from the bullseye.

Agitation nipped Cesare's fingertips.

Five.

He sipped the blood off his teeth and swallowed dryly, retrieving the knife from the wall and returning to his position.

Centring his one-eyed gaze once more, he repeated his ritual.

Four.

Four hundred hours on díem lunéra and Cesare had only just returned from his shift at Iyad's docks, skull a-clang with tinnitus.

Fourth straight day of no sleep and barely a bite of food effected the grottiest sensation, and Cesare's ruinous ways spiralled only deeper each turn following the massacre at the *Curios* and the burning of *The Sunrise* over a month prior.

He retrieved his throwing knife, restless fingers fiddling with the strap of his square eyepatch.

"Bastard's been wailing for weeks," Ygạl's smoky voice shoved Cesare from the oubliette of his ruminations into the captain quarters upon The Salt Hydra's galleon.

The amazonian woman's carob-brown eyes appraised with distaste the storm beyond the heavy teal curtains half-swathing the sweeping aft window. In her gold-beset fingers, tipped with filigreed zhǐjiǎtào nail guards, sat a tumbler of Ziliesu rum. An ankle-length thawb of black cotton embroidered with agate and sequins adorned her sturdy frame.

Cesare aimed for the target. "Weather tends towards autumn this time of year."

He released a dagger.

It skewered the target two rings from the bullseye.

Three.

"Damn right!" Scraggly Eyepatch Dan, with his bandana and dark blue rattail, sat on Korneli's massive shoulders—the one-handed, black-bearded quartermaster reclining on a sofa—and picked grains of sand and dried tatters of seaweed from the quartermaster's tricorn. "Started growin' mould in the hold." Danilo clapped his knuckly hands, one tanned fist pumping the air and the other smacking his ribbed chest. "Lyrical maestro, I tell ya!" His shoulders swayed in a dance.

Cross-legged on the floor beside ver sword and sharpening whetstone, first mate Risten fixed Danilo with pale pink eyes. "You disgust me." Ve stroked ver fingers along the grains of a waist-length platinum braid, the rest of ver hair cut into a short bob round the ears.

Danilo pulled a mocking gurn at Ren, prompting ver eye roll and Korneli's deep snicker.

Cheek between his teeth to hinder his jaw's grinding, Cesare swung his arm and flung a knife.

Two.

He retrieved it.

Across the window from Ygạl stood Fabio, hands pocketed in his turquoise greatcoat. "Likely some of the last good rain of autumn, this is." Greying chin-length curls curtained the stern lines of an ageing face anointed with a seafarer's tan. "Getting cold early this year…"

Lissandri, hands folded on Fabio's cluttered desk and chin resting on his knuckles, roamed exhausted eyes along the pages of a hefty book standing upright on the table. He was usually fast asleep at this hour.

Cesare's gaze snared on Eligio who sat across from his twin, his brow creased and a colombína in the process of being painted gripped by his fingertips. His fluffy halo of brown coils had grown to his shoulders much like Cesàre's own dark waves, now pulled into a loose tail at the nape of his neck. Eyes like polished acorns, lined by somnolent darkness, regarded Cesare with acute worry.

Over the preceding month, Lissandri's cynical demeanour soured, bittered to anger, whilst Eligio withdrew, quietened, every shadowed smile of his hiding tears. Meanwhile, Rosalia had taken a liking to the undertaker's work—much to Libitina's endless vexation—and opted to spend her nights at the mortuary to observe the embalming of bodies set for cremation or burial.[3]

Shaking Eligio's fretting eyeline off his own, Cesare aimed for the target and swung.

"Can you cease?" Ygạl reprimanded.

The throwing knife skewered the target three rings from the bullseye, wood spitting splinters.

One!

Cesare pivoted. "*Make* me, Najm!"

The Dóminus of The Boars and Hounds scrunched their face. "What's your problem, Agostini?"

---

[3] Given Illutèri beliefs regarding the material form (expounded upon later in-narrative), bodies intended to be buried *or* cremated are fully embalmed, as it is viewed as a 'cleansing' process. Additionally, the only people buried are criminals who died in prison or on death row. Everyone else is cremated due to the conviction that the latter is a destruction of the hylic whilst the former is a confinement to the physical plane.

Cesare's eye flung wider. "Are you fucking kidding me?"

"Enough," Fabio interjected. "Much remains to be discussed by way of band affairs, but best have Giorgianna here for it." He paced to his desk, tracked by Eligio's condemning scrutiny. The artist opted to sit beside Korneli and Dan when the captain neared. "As it stands now," continued Fabio, "only a couple smuggler bands are willing to ally against the legions, though I remain to receive confirmation—should do in the coming days, with hope. Convincing anyone else holds a tenuous chance at best, or is an outright impossibility, what with most amicable bands asea for the foreseeable future and the worst bunch left around."

"Worth an attempt," said Cesare. Adviser Clario Barsotti had sent for him and Giorgianna a week ago, requesting they convene on the night of the turn yet to commence at *Stalker's Barge* in oldtown. The one to approach them named herself Ioana De Rege,[4] Centúrion of the Adviser's Guárdia. "We need The Morettae." He stifled the urge to scowl.

Korneli shook his head. "Can't believe we oughta cooperate wi' '*em* menaces."

"*You're* not the ones forced into verbal negotiations." Kel-Kech was at least agreeable, albeit wavering, but Lorita remained stubborn to the point of irrationality, and Cesare was yet to be convinced she wasn't playing that game with intentional malice.

Korneli whistled. "Bless your soul, dzamiko.[5]"

Cesare retrieved his throwing knife for the final time and slipped it into the inner pocket of his waist-length leather jacket. Thus concluded his besetting knife-throwing ritual for the day, awaiting to be commenced anew to-morrow. Six uninterrupted throws, three with his left and three with his right, or he felt as if something cataclysmic would happen. And *every* throw reminded Cesare of his maimed eye. *If Etenesh doesn't receive that ano-apozem shipment soon, I'll entirely madden.*

"Regardless," he fidgeted with his eyepatch, "communication demands establishment within the city and Antrum both, and The

---

[4] *ee-oh-AH-nah DEH REH-jeh*
[5] *'Brother'* in Damtani enay.

Morettae further the former." Try as he might, he couldn't recover the light in his voice, but a revolution was due to be carried out.

"Still finessing the latter," admitted Ygal. "Isaia should be sending word soon." She sipped alcohol, pursing her scarred lips. "I dispatched an envoy to Lucanus."

Cesare's brow rose. "Shall I retell what befell your last envoy?"

"Strung up on meat hooks, dismembered, disembowelled."

"And those members and bowels strewn upon your district's territory."

"Holding out for Lady Luck's smile this turn."

"All right, that's it." Lissandri slammed his book shut with a profound thud and swept it into his arm, standing. "Off to bed." His voice rang sharper, tetchier, angrier. Cesare's stomach tied up.

Eligio frowned. "It's four hundred? The sun will be on the ascent soon and our shift starts at seven."

"*I* didn't sleep, because *lyrical maestro* over here decided to serenade the moon with his mouldy accordion."

"Ya know ya love it!" Dan cheered along to his tumble onto the sofa as Korneli rose with a complaint of a sore neck.

Lissandri levelled a withered gaze at master gunner. "Not as much as beauty sleep."

"Would you like my valerian?" offered Eligio.

"Not *that* desperate."

"Cesare." Fabio materialised beside him. "Step outside with me."

The two sheltered from the autumnal downpour beneath wide eaves. Silver shards of rain forked the night, the moon's ghostly sickle futilely fighting to cut through thunderclouds.

"What is happening with you?" asked Fabio.

"Well…" Cesare crossed his arms. "I *am* only recently recovered from a blood infection an entire month later considering the whole butchered spleen fiasco." At least he was no longer bedridden. *Rot, Manuele.*

"That's far from all of it," correctly noted Fabio.

Cesare replied with silence.

Fabio sighed. "You didn't kill Lập̣ẹn and Micheletto."

"Didn't I?" Cesare returned fire. "I may not've swung the blade but I was the reason for their targeting; they wouldn't *be* killed if not for their connection to me, you *cannot* refute that. I've caused this before." *Bringer of death just like Chiara said.*

"Don't be ridiculous!" reprimanded Fabio. "You are not the reason sick, depraved people *choose* to commit sick, depraved acts. No one blames you for this but *you*."

"So they're mistaken."

"You are impossible."

Cesare clicked his tongue. "I *have* been called a prideful bastard."

Fabio snorted. "Running through your head without rest, that one."

A frown. "I'm sorry?"

Lips nudged by a furtive smile, the captain produced from the inside of his ocean-worn greatcoat a box of sigaréttae, taking one before offering Cesare. "Always soothes the soul."

Inclined to agree, Cesare accepted and reached for the trusty lighter always carried within his jacket. Holding it to Fabio's sigarétta, he struck open the flame.

Boom!

IN ALL MY LIFE, I had never conceived that I'd one day scour journals from my father's youth for answers to political riddles.

Years and maritime elements had not been kind to those dossiers. Hardened paper, ink faded upon its stained canvas, crinkled against my cello-callused fingertips, some documents all but destroyed by the fire Davide had set, or the rain that had beaten through the tear in the ceiling which Korneli and Danilo were kind enough to help mend.

Placing a quire of miscellaneous court records onto an oaken desk, I trawled deeper through the bookshelf's uppermost slot, brows meeting when my fingers brushed something silky. I pulled free a sheaf of six letters bound by a thin ribbon of sapphirine satin.

Curiosity eagerly pushed my hands to unbind the sash and open one of the envelopes. Candleflame flinched at my movement; distorted my silhouette upon the star-chart-wreathed walls.

Unfolding the note, I yet again beheld father's studious hand.

My brow softened as I traversed the tiny letters, heeding the way my father's 'c' often looked like an 'i' with no crowning dot, or his 'v' tending so thin it resembled an 'r'.

A line snared my attention.

'Deathless sleep is a
heart's undying melody.'

My stomach kicked as more prose floated into my grasp.
Love letters… And they were unsent.

'In life and death, I love. For tides
ebb and flee. Flames diminish with
their tinder. Winds are eternally
ever-changing. And you
are the moon.'

The moon…

Father's features—my near-exact simulacra—would always ignite at the sight of the planets. He seemed to know everything about the inhabitants of our Seren system. To the stars he put a purely analytical mind, dark erudite eyes and lips pressed into a stern line, treating the sun no differently. But it never escaped me: the dimness upon him when he gazed at the desaturated nighttime luminary. Was *this* why? Did the moon remind him of my mother? *My mother who reviles him. Reviles* me.

Sorrow reclaimed its hold on my heart, so I folded the letter into its envelope and slipped it among the shelves.

On the desk, beside the boundless documents, lay a jacket I'd discovered among my father's old clothes. Belted at the waist, its hem sat at the pelvis in the front, dropping to the knees as it snaked around to the back—trimmed with frills. A quartet of tarnished gold clasps fastened the torso and one pinned the frilly neck from which a miniature cut-out looped down, shaped like a teardrop and adorned with lace. Long sleeves puffed at the shoulder and cinched tight to the arm, flaring to long pagoda sleeves. Blood red. I never took Ludovico Lounès Damiani for a wearer of the heart's crimson, and I supposed the pristine state of the jacket adjudicated in favour of that assumption.

Lightning slit the storm and thunder lashed out angrily. The waters of the firmament drew my eye to their plummet. I pulled a stool to the south-gazing window and sat on my haunches on it, folding my hands on the sill into a cushion for my chin.

The lazulum hadn't ceased weeping over the last forty turns, the city's aqueducts racing with nature to tap rising water from the canals.

I traced my fingers along the glass. A gentle frost of azoth gusted through my veins, behind my eyes, as I spoke to the water swilling the windowglass, catching a droplet wandering the pane and guiding it in swirling motions down.

My front door swung open, pulling me from the edge of the abyssal chasm that was pondering.

"Whatcha doin', girl?" Sarnai stood in the doorway, a soaked black sentinel jacket held over her head and snow-white hair plastered in wet bands on the wide cheekbones of her tanned face. Grinning ear to ear.

I smiled; slid off the stool and crossed my legs on the floor. "Paging through notes."

Sarnai wrung out her hair and discarded the daggers she kept dulled, joining me on the ground. "Amidst committing bloody homicide?"

I cocked my head. "One more name struck off."

Her monolidded eyes widened. "You got him?"

"Earlier to-night." My smile dropped. "Yet the dues owed to me remain unrepaid."

Hours following Abramo's execution, my heart still fluttered with the thrill of a bloodhunt, yet those in deepest debt—Basilio Lanuza, Grand Judge Giordano Veronesi, General Manuele Dioli—still walked, living their soulless lives. The blood on their hands would never wash off. *And I shall avenge.*

"Careful," Sarnai pointedly warned. "Revenge is a narcotic. It turns you just as ravenous for another hit."

My eyes flickered to the armillary sphere standing by the desk, the astrolabes adorning the walls like earrings, father's old cello lounging in the umbrous corner—one I hadn't dared touch yet. "Our inherent agenticity leaves so little of this world *not* a narcotic. And yearning in a human's soul can never be abated, no matter by what instrument, for it is the ache of absence which begets it." My gaze fell to the scars on my left hand, the pale tears along my knuckles. The grim reminders of the day everything aborted. *Blood promised to myself.* To Emanuela. To my father. My fingertips brushed idly over the gold-and-garnet bleeding eye necklace between my collarbones.

Sarnai giggled. "How funny when you get like that."

My brows touched when I met her gaze. "Meaning?"

"All intense and…" she bunched her mouth to the side, "romanticist."

I laughed. "Not just 'romantic', I see!"

She tapped a finger on her lips, eyes swerving ceilingward. "Figured a person like yourself called for something more apt."

I propped my elbows on my knees and cupped my face. "What *is* such a person like?"

Sarnai leaned so close our faces nearly touched. "Murderously vengeful." She shrugged. "Not bad on the eyes."

And maybe *I* was the crook for wishing she would reply in likeness to the things I said, but Sarnai wasn't that sort of person, so I wondered if we were ever destined to be one another's beloved. We were neither together nor otherwise, still exchanged no more than kisses, and each day her affections towards Itxaro[6] grew more apparent.

Yet my wretched heart longed for love the way flesh longed for its skin. A burn longed for salve. A blade yearned for blood.

So maybe I *was* the crook—

Boom!

My heart juddered at the crackling explosion.

---

[6] A reminder that the letter '*x*' is pronounced as '*sh*' in Zargòsian.

"Gunshots?" Sarnai asked.

I fired to my feet and shot for the window, peering through the rain towards Buccaneer's Landing. Towards the commotion on the wharf between *Antigone* and *Hangman's Dowry*.

Knots twisted my vitals. "Stay." I grabbed my jacket, sheathed my rapier and baselard, holstered my revolver.

"It's bucketing down!" protested Sarnai, but the threshold was already behind me.

SCENE II

SOVEREIGNTY

Cesare | Giorgianna

"WHAT IS GOING ON?" Ygạl exclaimed once the first gunshot drew everyone out on *Antigone*'s deck.

A good dozen Morettae attacked *Hangman's Dowry*—masked, guns blazing and daggers drawn as they clashed with infuriated Blood Dahlias on the berth beneath the unrelenting rainstorm. Enraged Dahlia shouts pealed from the deck as Morettae clambered their way onto the dark caravel and charged at the crew.

Cesare bound his too-long hair, checking for the twin stilétti strapped into his thigh harness. "Ygạl, on me! We're breaking this."

"Quartermaster, first mate: with me." Fabio emerged from the captain's cabin with a cutlass and revolver. "Master gunner: on range."

"¡A'*right*!" Danilo hauled his pair of massive muskets from the cabin. "Babies 'ave been missin' target practice!"

Cesare's chest bundled. "Fabio—"

"Don't be a hypocrite, boy." The captain passed a dry regard and made for the gangplank.

Blood was quick to stain the white ruffle of Cesare's shirt as he cut into the dark throng of Dahlias and Morettae, stilétto in his left hand and revolver in his right, cautious to guard his sightless side. Immediately, he recognised both parties as foes.

Clinquant lòthmir opened a spewing gorge down an attacking Moretta's neck. Whirling swiftly around his axis, Cesare shot another point-blank, narrowly avoiding a stab.

A step to his left, Ren—Fabio shielding ver back—skewered a Dahlia onto ver bident like a trout, Korneli decapitating them with his sword-arm before first mate sent their spurting champagne bottle of a husk tumbling off the pier.

Danilo shot down the Moretta Ygal had gone to finish. The woman brandished a vulgar gesture at the gunner, leaving their lines open for a slinky Dahlia to swing her uchigatana in a broad arc for their head.

Cesare shot the Dahlia.

"Even with the *eye*," Ygal's saif spiked a Moretta through the gut, "you're not half bad, for a trim twat."

Cesare thrust off the wharf a Dahlia, misjudging his range and crying out when cold metal razored his blind flank. The grip of a double-bladed polearm knocked his revolver from his hand.

Springing sidelong, Cesare swiped his stilétto at his attacker—Moretta—slicing their mask from their scarcely-freckled face but losing his foothold when they swung their polearm.

His head bashed hard against the wooden pier; the Moretta's polearm bound with Cesare's stilétto to pin him down.

Cesare grasped the polearm's grip with his free hand. "What's gotten into you people?"

"Not all of us are complacent like Kel," the Moretta hissed. "We will *nev*—"

The Moretta spewed blood. The tip of a blade protruded from the base of their throat. Cesare shoved them off with their polearm, thrusting its bladed end through their chest and propelling their corpse into the frigid sea.

He met copper-bullet eyes. Petering raindrops ran down heart-shaped cheekbones and dangled from long curls of lashes. Giorgianna huffed, "Another due you owe me, bàuta," tossing Cesare his revolver.

"We can negotiate the terms later." He stood, the gun coming in good use when another Dahlia made a pass at his life. Giorgianna ran them through with her rapier and hauled them into an oncoming Moretta whom Cesare likewise shot.

"*HOLD IT*!" An indistinguishable voice roared.

All fighting on the wharf ceased.

Every eye trained onto *Hangman's Dowry*.

On the caravel's dark deck, a stocky older woman in a greatcoat black as squid ink embroidered with rubious veins of thread rigged up a squawking Moretta upside down with one of the innumerable ropes draping the masts, a misericorde in her fist. Gouged eyeballs cast in glass hung in baubles from Blood Dahlia's ears and a string of torn-out teeth garlanded her waist. A black bicorn crowned blacker hair streaked with silver; a fringe cut straight across her brow.

"You think you can crawl aboard *my* ship," Dahlia bellowed, her misericorde sawing open the Moretta's stomach, "antagonise *my* crew," she shoved her hand into the slick orifice of the man's belly, hauling out ropes of intestines and heaping their gory mass over the edge of her ship; blood disgorged from the Moretta's mouth like a broken faucet, "and get anything more than what you *asked* for?" Eyes blacker than nightmares hurled at Ygạl, at Cesare, threatening to devour. "You cadre tapeworms are *parasites* to our District. Waltzing onto territory that isn't yours, thinking you have *any* right to it and *any* sway upon its operations? You have *no* place here." She slit the Moretta's throat. "No *place* to assume pleasantries from people you've only *ever* seen as beneath you just 'cause we don't have cushy homes and disposable coin!" She pointed her blood-sheathed knife at the Dóminus, gore too thick upon it for the rain to sluice off. "Crawl back to the festering pits of your filthy fucking home and leave Smugglers' Cove out of your worthless politics."

As if a denouement to her grand performance, she slashed cloth from the Moretta's crotch and castrated him, throwing his penis down to the wharf beneath Ygal's feet who regarded the captain with abhorrence.

"Feed it to your dogs," sneered Blood Dahlia and cut the rope suspending the Moretta's mutilated corpse.

She left her final glance with the tight-jawed Fabio, spitting in his direction before departing.

SCENE III

IGNORATIO ELENCHI

Giorgianna

THE MORETTAE'S HIDEOUT WAS AN ABANDONED ARMOURY tucked at the base of an eight-hundred-year-old military barrack—a relic of the Empire days—not far from the bridge into Smugglers' District and entirely gutted of the weapons it once housed. Most Morettae occupied one of the two storeys above the ground floor of the complex, its stone-carved walls gnarled by centuries.

It was in a ground-floor chamber once dedicated to melee weapons we gathered: the *Sunrise* vìtae, Kel-Kech and Lorita, Fabio and Ren, Ygạl with Isaia and Sarnai.

"This shouldn't've happened—*couldn't've!*" Kel stammered. Her eyes, limpid as aquamarines, darted from Fabio to Lorita to Cesare.

"Shouldn't've; couldn't've; *did.*" Fabio glanced sternly between the Moretta women. "What do you have to say for yourselves?"

Kel ran twitchy fingers along her close-cropped hair. "Truly, *I*—we do not und—"

"Don't grovel, Kel," Lorita heckled, small arms, draped in loose khaki sleeves, folded at her chest. Her dark honey eyes dripped poison at Cesare and Fabio. "We do not answer to you. *I* say those Morettae showed some spine in standing strong by their aims."

Ygal snorted. "Of *what*? Being odious pests?"

"*Rebels!*" bit Lorita.

"Against what?" Cesare fired. "Their own supposed cause? We need everyone with us if we want a chance at abolition and your inability to keep your people in check made negotiations even harder—we *need* the smugglers."

"Quit acting like we'll succeed with politicos and pirates beside us."

I nocked a glare at Lorita. "Once more, I will question how far you have gotten *without* us. You self-admittedly have no organisation."

"*And* no strategy following the overthrow of De Tullia," Lissandri pitched in, coldly eyeing Kel.

"Your rogue Morettae made an assault on smuggler territory," Fabio steered us back to the original contention. "You do *not* come there to provoke us, no matter whom you choose. How *dim* do you have to be to assault *Hangman's Dowry*? The Blood Dahlias are *the* most territorial band—your people signed our death warrants."

Lorita's fair brow writhed with serpentine vessels. "Pray tell, did *your* people not sign *our* death warrants when your cadre buddies shot them upon that dock as if bloodsport instead of 'cooperating' as preached by your intellectualist—?"

The blonde woman flinched mid-earful when Cesare's knuckles drove hard into the table. Its rattle struck an arrow through my gut. Cesare's temper was welded of steel, his patience seemingly a bottomless crucible. But his fuse had been burning shorter and shorter over the recent weeks, flames of discontent bringing his anger to a boil.

In the breathless silence, I considered his insomnia-bruised eye, sunken and bleak, his too-lean jaw. Tension tautly bound his shoulders, bones protruding beneath the jacket where the passing month had mercilessly stripped his frame of flesh.

A frown etched deep into my brow as my gaze slipped along the gaunt curve of his high cheekbone. My innards cooled to ice.

Cesare was a dark mirror—unbearable grief had devoured me the same way, once.

He shut his eye and dragged a deep breath, rubbing his knuckles. "This will get us nowhere," he asserted. "Communication within upper and lower óssium is vital, which *includes* The Morettae." He flung a cursory glance at Lorita who received it like a dart. "A certain amount of class consciousness is missing among upper ossíi, owing to the Governor's intellectual insulation—by design. Remaining ignorant of injustices only weaves them deeper into the fabric of society. One begins to unravel such a history by direct confrontation alone."

Lorita snorted. "And I suppose you want *our* aegis?"

"Would *sure* be helpful," sniped Cesare.

"All right, Agostini," Ygạl swept in, "lay it out. How *shall* you unravel such a history?"

Elbows on the tall table, Cesare leaned against it. "The government keeps secret on secret stowed away. The higher those secrets stack, the more difficult they grow to hide, the more heavy-handed must become the government's means of protecting them. Thus, demanded grows the employment of repression—an integration of ignorance directly into societal structure. We know this, we *see* this. Intellectual insulation by design, as aforementioned.

"De Tullia's aim is to keep people ignorant to ideas he deems insubordinate. To do so, he instils fear of revolutionaries in the masses, and enacts tyrannical laws which dictate what 'correct' conduct is. However, keeping such an immense amount of information hidden is a volatile endeavour. Try as they might, secrets are prone to discovery, and ignorance is fragile."

Cesare, with his honey-sweet voice and pianissimo Zargòsian lilt, spoke the way might read the ink-splotched pages of a philosophy book scribbled feverishly by a dialectician in the dead of an insomniac night, and somehow it seemed that I had begun describing *him* again.

"Thy *point*, yā scholar?" Ygạl's sardonic urging spirited me back to earth.

"First." Isaia's flint-black eyes found me, his mouth and aquiline nose masked by black cloth and bronzen face shaded by a loose hood. "Your father's documents?"

"Cover-ups of legionary-perpetrated crimes, liquidation of citizens on no basis, threats of violence against senators on condition of silence, private executions." I folded my arms. "By hook or by crook, De Tullia wishes full autocratic control. This would grant him access to Grand Judge Giordano Veronesi's court documents. De Tullia, Governor or not, has no right to said documentation, and Veronesi is essentially untouchable, for our Lord of Bless'ed Dominion holds nothing to earnestly blot the Grand Judge's escutcheon. Through De Tullia integrating Veronesi into his Ministry as the Minister of Justice, Veronesi is similarly barred from political endeavours not concerning the judicial tribunal. Notwithstanding, Veronesi *must* hold a degree of freedom compared to the other Ministers, and could no doubt be a threat to De Tullia if he chose to be.

"Father never kept the information he gathered cohesively. Everything is disjointed, but there *is* a pattern to it. Like a cipher." I beheld Fabio. "That which he took to the grave with him—a revelation so grim he couldn't utter even to you, or whatever it may've been—I'm yet to uncover, at least I think, but this riddle I sense convinces me I near it. That it's *there*. Somewhere."

"What's the pattern you note?" asked Cesare.

"Frequent mentions of High Priest Benetto Abelli." I frowned. "Eye and trinity motif."

Sarnai's face scrunched. "Eerie."

"I wouldn't put it past the High Priest and his Clergia to be far more woven with the state than we fathom." Morning sun streamed into the armoury through the clerestory windows I gazed toward. The battered armies of thunderclouds beyond retreated. "Votaries of the Order flock upper óssium streets," I added. "It's like a sea of blood."

Yet it had nothing on the military checkpoints now erected at the mouth of oldtown. Them and the strappado together, the Solar Square was grim. With soldiers scouring for identification documents, contraband, fugitives, it wasn't rare that lower ossíi were denied passage into upper óssium or vice versa (though vice versa was seldom a presented case), and reports of humiliation and abuse at the hands of soldiers grew by the day. As such, a few citizens in the vicinity permitted folks to traverse their living quarters to bypass the legions. Some took the approach of hopping rooftops, or climbing fences followed by lengthy detours. In the end, the checkpoints served only to further fragment and stratify the ossíi, and to further dehumanise the subjugated.

"So the *point*," Cesare returned to Ygal's impatient and half-forgotten inquiry, "is that we utilise the fragility of ignorance and the volatility of secrecy to our advantage by disseminating our *own* 'propaganda'. My primary contacts in city-proper are yet to cooperate, which I glean to be *quite* the pattern." Lorita studied her gilt-coated rings in counterfeit obliviousness. Cesare clicked his tongue. "Nevertheless, they can help enlighten the people as information surfaces. No rumour flies better than upon the whisper of the common man."

"What of the aftermath?" queried Isaia. "Once we've assembled?"

"Glad you asked." Cesare cocked his head, standing to his full height with a glint of long-lost glee in his eye. "Donatello informed me that plans of a prison break stir in The Trabeculae, organised in part by one calling themselves 'Laútni', though they don't claim a leadership title."

I peered curiously. "Go on…"

"Donatello maintains contact with inmates confined to the southeastern wing of the prison: political dissidents and people who earned their jail time via a misplaced chuckle."

Sarnai frowned. "How's he communicating with *inmates*?"

"Donatello has a frightening way of cajoling gears." Cesare rapped his over-long nails on the desk. "The prison break is scheduled to take place three months from now, give or take. We need arms, the support of the working people, *and* control of the government building if we want victory. *So*, with Giorgianna aiding to weaken the government from the inside, the rest of us watering the seeds of insurgence from the *out*side, condottiéri working the Antrum, and Morettae *not* fucking with our efforts, the prison break can be our decoy. All attention will be on the acropolis."

"What of the smuggler bands?" Kel-Kech questioned Fabio.

"Most asea. The ones remaining are…" he pulled a face, "a *bunch*. The Black Tongues are out. Besides being nebulous allies with The Blood Dahlias, Sten detests intruders more than she and, un*like* Dahlia, is absolutely willing to hunt them himself. The one thing about Sten is that he is completely sightless from birth. However, he is a blood singer, and a damn good one—can tune into the finest body movement through your blood flow and is almost impossible to sneak up on or away from. His quartermaster is Visolela. The White Lotus are just as unlikely to cooperate. Raffaele serves solely his own ends and convincing him to potentially jeopardise the affluence he's accrued is a tall order. He's in the same boat as Dahlia and Sten by way of tender mercies."

"So no luck?" Lissandri grumbled.

"Cooperation of The Brass Teeth and The Grey Pearls is foreseeable."

Light suffused Ygạl's features, a smile tugging the scar running through their lips. "The Grey Pearls?"

"Fēngnà is willing to consider the offer, yes—her band is large and strong. Şirîn and her Brass Teeth are as good as a promise."

Cesare expelled a sigh. "We meet Adviser Clario Barsotti to-night."

Ygạl flourished his zhǐjiǎtào at him and me. "I'd like the pair of you at the Antrum to discuss Leone."

Lorita nailed an iron glare to her, to Cesare, to me. "Go on and clear out, then." She stormed for the door. Kel's hand darted to touch her wrist but she recoiled. The slamming door announced the blonde's exodus.

"Follow after your girl," Lissandri hissed at Kel-Kech. "Since she's not fucking neutered like the rest of your boorish herd of cows." For that, he received an elbow from his eldest and a reprimand from me.

A storm obnubilated the turquoise sea of Kel's eyes as she gazed at the door, as if her eyeline could reel Lorita back to her. Then she marched off without a word our way.

SCENE IV

UNA RONDINE NON FA PRIMAVERA

Kel-Kech | Giorgianna

LIQUID VIVID AS AMBER strained through gauze, hot and perfumed with lemon for tang as it poured into an old metal tea pot.

Discarding the cloth, Kel-Kech poured chipped porcelain cups of the rooibos tisane for herself and Lorita, bringing them over to the creaky bed where the blonde lay blank-faced.

When Kel offered, Rita shook her head.

Kel-Kech staved off a sigh and sat beside her strange lover, sipping the tea of her lost homeland. Uncle Tsui ignited her love for rooibos. She had never been partial to it in her parents' home, but she hadn't been partial to much in that east-facing western |haru oms[7] within those transient settlements of theirs.

---

[7] A bee-hive-shaped Nama hut constructed of reed mats. Renowned for highly-effective engineering against the elements.
|: a lingual ingressive dental click like a *tsk*.

Lorita's eyes veered to Kel. "His creepy insurrectionist character killed our Morettae."

Kel swallowed a sip and cleared her throat. "Well… They hindered our cause, no?"

"*Did* they?" argued Lorita. "They were unwavering."

"But also stubborn."

"And they *shouldn't* be?" Lorita buttressed herself on her elbows. Thick tresses, blonde as hammered gold, tumbled around her hard brow.

Kel eased the tension of silence with a gulp of tisane. "Not when they negate the goal of liberation, I don't think…" her voice came out quiet. Halting.

Lorita sat up, beholding her with round eyes, doe-like and syrup-sweet. "But you hear me, don't you, Kel?"

How could Kel-Kech tell her that she did not know? "I hear *him*, too."

A frown reclaimed Lorita. "How can you hear *anything* over the sound of his altiloquence?"

And, once again, Kel-Kech couldn't answer in any resolute way. She couldn't *answer*, for she did not *know*—a vestige of a childhood spent holding a guiding hand. Instead, she set aside her cup of rooibos and reached for Lorita, entwining her slim fingers with the petite ones of the blonde. "I hold out hope that we will endure." She went to press a kiss to Lorita's knuckles.

"No." Rita wiggled her hand free. "No, just stop."

"Why?"

"Because *it*—" Lorita's jaw quivered, her nose dragging in a stilted breath. She leaned back in and lowered her voice like someone might listen in. "Because it's repulsive."

Kel-Kech jerked back, affront piercing her heart. "What, my touch?"

"*No*! This…" The blonde wrung her fingers. "This *urge*."

"I don't understand you." Kel's cheeks burned. "You love me, no?"

Lorita's lips hovered ajar for a pained heartbeat. "I *love* you…" *But?* "I just cannot abet… *this*."

Kel-Kech crossed her arms. "The Lord does not speak on it," she quoted Uncle Tsui—the words he would repeat against his brother Aemûs' self-begotten bigotry.

"My *church* does," retorted Lorita, launching to her feet and approaching the opposite window: a paltry thing perforating the stone wall, empty of glass. Beyond rolled oldtown rooftops and rose walls of adjacent edifices, all weathered and forgotten.

"The one which kicked you to the streets of Salvatrice and damn near forced your departure from that city altogether?" contended Kel-Kech, voice crescendoing.

Lorita whirled. "Watch it, Kel!" she bit, eyes flashing.

Kel-Kech's brow smoothed. Her shoulders loosened with dejection. "Don't you think Cesare speaks some reason?" she quietly raised.

"He reasons with extremism. Id est: not at all."

"Well, what is *your* reason?"

All that outward zeal, and yet did *Lorita* know? Could *she* name where she stood? Did she stand for *anything*?

The golden girl stiffened to a statue, pallid as if carved of alabaster, her eyes glinting, jaw tense, unyielding, before marching for the door and slamming it behind her.

Kel-Kech loosened a breath heavy as a conscience, gazing into the warm darkness of her rooibos tisane.

Her father, Aemûs, had rejected her identity, not out of principle, but given his entrenched hatred for his younger brother Tsui whom he blamed for the death of their mother—a woman who died giving birth to Uncle Tsui—and waited with bated breath until he could out from the tribe. Kel-Kech's love for the femme-akin proved enough for Aemûs to justify the expulsion of his eldest late into her sixteenth year, too. Her thirteen-year-old sister, Nū-Ûn,[8] chased her down in the night, claiming she wouldn't stay if Kel-Kech couldn't, so the pair embarked on a journey to Uncle Tsui's settlement.

While Aemûs' tribe practiced the old tradition of nomadic cattle herding, Uncle Tsui's remained mostly sedentary, rendering them far easier to locate, even for a pair of adolescent girls with little tracking expertise. Uncle Tsui welcomed them with open arms, and their lives started tending towards near-idyll.

---

[8] ǂ: a palatal dental click similar to snapped fingers.

It always seemed to Kel-Kech as if *Nū-Ûn* was supposed to be the older sister, not she. The girl never dithered, never sought guidance, never fled a fight. That's what got her killed at that assembly riot Davide tricked The Morettae into assailing. The pair had sought adventure in novel lands—largely on Nū-Ûn's imploration, given Kel appreciated tranquillity—so they'd found themselves in Vencenza, only to be trapped with no way out, and roped into rebellious schemes.

Kel-Kech took a sip of tisane to soothe her throat, and wondered what Uncle Tsui thought of their lengthy absence, or how she could ever explain to him what happened to their little Nū-Ûn should they see each other again.

THE TWINS HEADED OFF TO IYAD'S DOCKS whilst Cesare and I followed the condottiéri to the Antrum. Luckily, we had taken to keeping spare clothes at the Boar estate, so were glad to not be shivering in our rain-soaked garb.

I'd planted myself on a stool by the intarsia coffee table, massive swathes of hair draped down my chest and sprawled across my thighs, as Isaia's tattooing needles finished inking the scarred lines of the dagger stigma branded in between my shoulder blades at *The Arum*.

My body was mine. And so my Malefactor's Mark too would symbolise that I survived. Even if the body and mind I reclaimed were left with scars, with grim reminders, I had *lived*.

Isaia completed the tattoo on my arm two weeks prior: a cut rose branch, a half-bloomed bud reaching vainly towards my shoulder and the full, lush blossom beneath it cradling an eyeball. All illustrated across my *Bedlamite* scars.

Another symbol. Another memento mori.

Yet, equally, a memento vivere.

Ygal set onto the intarsia a platter of white rice salīg, a bowl of dainty ball-shaped çakçak dough sweetened by apricot sugar, and a decanter of tart camel milk alongside fig pekmez, the air within their office a mélange of spicy and saccharine perfumes. "You have your uses," they quipped at me and Cesare, kissing Lucrezia's cheek and stirring a spoonful of molasses into their snifter of milk, the latter seemingly to their inamorata's revulsion.

My tattoo patched up, I stood with thanks to Isaia and plopped onto a gold-trimmed sofa of rubellite velvet, legs bent towards my torso and chin perched on my palm. I chased Aengus' feet out of my way—the man previously claiming the whole sofa whilst sipping Línmhar fuisce. An olivaceous shirt bared a slit of his freckled chest sprouting red hair.

Across the coffee table was a matching sofa on which Ygạl lounged in a billowing black çyrpy embroidered with sparkling tangerine threads, and a magenta bisht,[9] her hair wrapped into a citrine ommah. Supposedly prepared for a cadre assembly later. In her heavily-ringed fingers was a Dülúyan cigar she was trying losingly to acquire the taste for, and on his lap sat Lucrezia, a glass of limoo amani tea in her dainty white hand. Her loose ebony waves were trimmed into a pixie around her ears, a sheer fringe curtaining her brow and a silk peplos pouring down her buxom figure like molten smaragdine. After the gunshot she'd sustained at Basilio's hand, Lucrezia hadn't worn a single tight article of clothing.

Cesare's eyeline flickered to me from where he sat smoking at the opposite end of Ygạl's sofa. A gossamer shadow of a smile flitted in the corner of his lips as he leaned his temple onto his slim knuckles. Aurous alchemy melted into the silken dark waves of his shoulder-length hair. "Quite the allure, too." He looked Ygạl's way. A tongue-click. "You wished to speak of Leone?" He inhaled sigarétta smoke.

Even with the confectionary before him, even with his own white ruffled shirt grown too loose upon his willowy frame, he refused to eat.

Ygạl coughed, pulling a face and discarding the cigar into an ashtray, and opted for the camel milk sweetened by pekmez. From a drawer in the coffee table, she produced a decorated envelope wrapped in pale pink silk. "The Serpent requisitions we make an appearance in his district to-

---

[9] A floor-sweeping, long-sleeved, flowing cloak especially worn in Saudi Arabia on special or ceremonial occasions, and often by clergy or officials.

morrow night for one of his 'consultations'. Valentina is promised to be present." He tossed the letter onto the intarsia. "No guards."

Cesare knocked his head back with a sigh. "Joy…"

Lucrezia's rainstorm eyes slitted behind her gilded pince-nez. "What's the issue?"

"He's a pervert."

"*Every* time you claim that."

"And *every* time, my claim holds water."

Ygal imbibed. "The slippery wanker would rather eat, fuck, and make merry than keep his district leashed."

My eyebrows gathered. "Why should we rely on his aid, then?"

"His Serpents have always been allies."

"One swallow does not make spring."

"But it *does* bode warmer skies."

Isaia sat beside me, a plate of salīg in hand. Aengus stretched his legs across the eavesdropper's muscled thighs. "The Serpents are tight with The Hyacinths.

"If we have Leone's backing," Ygal took Isaia's prompt and carried forth, "we'll have Valentina's. That's two out of the four other cadres on our side and therefore increased reinforcement for the Antrum should legions try anything. Leone has… longwinded ways of hosting conclaves. If a single change with him slips through our fingers, we'll never grasp another. *So*, whatever he asks for, just play along and look alive." Ygal reached for alcohol. "Now what's all this about contacts failing to cooperate?"

"Their affection towards one another is simply none," explained Cesare, tone flighty. "Donatello and Iyad are prone to friction, and I'm astonished Anukka hasn't taken her sickle to Donatello's throat yet."

Lucrezia *tsk'd*. "How *is* Tello? It's been a while."

"I doubt *Donatello* could answer such a question."

"Glad to hear he's well."

Aengus urged Isaia to hand him his own portion of rice, asking, "So which one's a Centúrion for, 'gain?"

"The Guárdia," I clarified. "The Minister of Emissaries'—the Adviser's—personal faction of legionaries. I believe there are about one hundred in the ranks?" I wordlessly consulted Cesare.

He adjusted his gold nose ring in contemplation. "Closer to seventy, by now. General Dioli isn't partial to not holding absolute command over all soldiers, and Ioana presents an issue on that front."

"I cannot imagine the likes of *him* being thrilled that a woman wields authority, either." The thought of him, the man who stole from me my most beloved friend, was like a shucking knife to my skin. *You will pay your dues in blood, scum.*

Cesare clicked his fingers. "Wouldn't be surprised if he keeps a close eye on her in court, just as well."

"Another potential dimension to examine?"

"How fortuitous that you should be so well-versed in riddles then, vólto."

I plucked and bit down on a çakçak. "I'd extol your contribution if it were not also a scourge."

"I *do* think of myself as something of an enigma."

"A *liar* that I now see him for, one means."

"That's my girl."

"I beg your pardon?"

"How do you know the Adviser won't try anything?" Lucrezia broached, striking me with the mortifying realisation of mine and Cesare's raptness in each other.

"As I have *said*," Cesare's eye at long last diverted from me, and a coldness seized my body as if I were deprived of firelight, "he knows his secrets are at stake: his journal remains in my possession. One skewed move, and that little notebook finds itself on De Tullia's escritoire. If a trap is what we are destined to walk into, it will not be to-night."

Lucrezia's face screwed up. "What kind of answer is that?"

"My point is that we have loopholes. We need to get inside the government building. *So,* an appropriate intermediary is called for. Barsotti presents an adequate solution."

"In theory," I murmured.

"And to-night, we shall learn if said theory holds practical functionality."

Isaia put down his cleared plate. "Araya will be stationed by the apothecárium from twenty hundred until midnight. It's close enough to *Stalker's Barge* for him to swing by."

I clasped my hands at my heart. "Thank you."

Isaia nodded, stone-faced as per his wont. He never failed to offer aid, and I couldn't be more grateful.

Ygal topped up their snifter with more camel milk. "Bit the bullet and sent an envoy to Vitture whilst the one to Lucanus takes her sweet time."

Discarding his filter tip in the ashtray where that cigar was relegated, Cesare rose and shrugged on his blazer. "Anything else?"

The Dóminus lifted his drink, tapping a zhǐjiǎtào against it with a crystalline *ding*. "I'll relay what my envoys report."

"If they have the tongue and hands to do it with."

Before I could breach the threshold of the Dóminus' office, Lucrezia pulled me aside. "Remember what I said of my surgeries performed by the High Priest at the behest of my father?"

I crossed my arms. "Unfortunately, the atrocity is not especially forgettable."

She bumped up her pince-nez. "Well, alongside everything, I'd like it if you could keep a look out for Magister Ilenia Farnese, the Minister of Scholars, given she was rumoured to attend those sessions. I'm wondering if she knew something."

"If you think it might be enlightening," I agreed, admittedly intrigued. "Has '*Spagyrism and Spellwerk*' been useful, at all?" I couldn't fathom what divinity made it so Nashǐgostu Kurilit Gostiata's magnum opus didn't perish in the fire at *The Sunrise*. I resented the tome for it, and was content with Lucrezia holding onto the wretched thing.

Lucrezia beamed. "You don't know how much I appreciate that. And yes, it's been... a slog, frankly, but illuminating."

I glimpsed the empty doorway. "Before I go, I'd like to request a small pouch of çakçak." A smile found my lips. "I'm quite keen on the sweet."

The Antrum's mechanical not-sun basted the thrawn stacks of buildings and the colossal arms of ancient colonnades in the greasy glow of icteric serum, the lucifugous underbelly of Vencenza every inch an abstract painting.

Cesare tied up his hair as the two of us started down an alley leading away from the estate. "Etenesh will be expecting me for Bloodletter upkeep," he half-muttered.

"When is her apozem shipment expected?"

"To-morrow."

Cesare's taciturn replies irked me arguably more than his incessant talk, but the past five weeks steeled my tolerance enough.

We proceeded past the yellow egress into the umbrous hallways within. Alkalinity soaked the dank atmosphere, bleak alchemy illuming dark brickwork. The ascending passage branched, dripping, rippling water a ghostly echo haunting the warrens.

The spirit of inquiry, my faithful familiar, compelled me to ask: "What *is* the deal with Leone?"

"He likes to put his hands where they're unwanted." Cesare's starlight voice collided with a vaulted ceiling wrought with grotesques and ouroboroi. "Leone seeks out peoples' hurt regarding touch and intimacy, and exploits it."

"And why is *that* whom Ygal trusts enough to approach directly and bend over backwards to appease?"

"Ygal is a creature of habit."

We turned a bend.

I kicked a chip of brick into the poppling duct. "I'm wondering to what extent the cadres are unlike the Ministry. The Boars are an oligarchy on paper; in practice, I'm yet to see Ygal truly consider outside input by way of district rule." Isaia's authority was a ruse—he was demoted to a lieutenant-equivalent the day The Boars absorbed The Hounds.

Disengaging the latch on an iron door at the end of the final corridor, Cesare and I ducked through, finding ourselves in the innards of an oldtown canal terminal.

"In the end," Cesare addressed me as we passed solomonic columns guarding the abandoned station, "Ygạl is a politician. As is every Domíne. They will look out for their own ends first, and the ends of the politicians will never be to the benefit of the masses."

"Then what use are they for our means?"

He slipped his hands into his pockets. "Steel is one of the Court's only currencies."

My eyes lifted to the skirmish of clouds gyrating in the firmament. "And when it turns on *us*?"

Cesare walked a half-pace ahead and revolved on his heel, continuing backwards along the unpeopled flagstone whilst fixing me with a wearily amused look. "Knife tricks serve us all, princess."

The switchblade lines of his lips slit into a smile, and my gaze deserted his as indefinable tension pushed in between my ribs.

"*Um…*" I tucked fugitive curls behind my ear, hastening my pace to walk beside Cesare. "I noticed you didn't have anything at Ygạl's—of food, I mean. So, I held onto some çakçak for you." From a pocket, I plucked a small organza pouch, handing it to Cesare. "It's very little, and hardly real food, but I know you like sweets, and…" I silenced at the recognition of how my every word sounded more and more juvenile.

Cesare's tongue clicked. "You *know*…" In the thump of silence, he wreathed his long arm around my shoulder, the silver cufflink cinching his ruffled cuff glinting like a tanzanite star. "You secretly enjoy my company, vólto."

My cheeks nipped, heart baltering. "Really, *you* are the one who flatters *himself*."

His features creased in counterfeit rue. "Must you add insult to injury when I am *so* defeated by melancholy as it were?"

"You are nothing if not a melodramatic diva."

"You are nothing if not willing to shoot me through the heart." His fingers grazed the curls swirling around my temples, quickly snapping shut as he snatched his hand away.

"You need not trouble yourself." I frowned at the stained-glass mosaics of vermeil Şahmaran and cyanic Leviathan decorating circular windows within the sgraffito façade of a building we passed. "Providing to-night bears fruit to our tastes, I shan't be around to bruise his majesty's ego for a while."

Arm still around me, Cesare didn't answer. *You are a coward.*

Scene V

I Saw the Devil

Giorgianna

MYRRHIC AROMAS OF MEDICINAL SALVES and herbal tinctures anointed Etenesh's apothecárium, humidity weighing the ether.

'*Venomcraft*' by Imetsáli[10] toxicologist Tsíra Paloúriou Tanailídis lay open on the cypress counter in front of me. Etenesh had supposedly spent absurd money on the thing in her first year at the very institution that was my own alma mater, only to never once open it for it was barely relevant to her curriculum. She'd gone back and forth between Faustina and Ṣh'ovvā for years, working in damn near every major city of both countries, yet her copy of '*Venomcraft*' followed her every step of the way despite everything.

In a halo around the tome arose a measuring cylinder of distilled water; two small ceramic bowls, one holding clear, sticky birch sap and

---

[10] Minority ethnic group from Eagle's Vigil in northern Themistóklis; genetically related to the southwestern communities of Usaz'khili.

the other heaped with ferruginous bloodroot[11] powder; a box of matches; a metal spatula. *To-day, I unsnarl this mystery.*

Across the counter sat Cesare, his bloodwork being examined under the scholarly auspices of the forty-one-year-old apothecary. An ankle-skimming shemma ḳemis the colour of eggshell adorned her tall figure, embroidered with yellow around the yoke and elbow-skimming sleeves. Her fluffy hair wove into albaso braids to reveal shield-shaped gold earrings, the back left unbound as if a cloud settled on her broad shoulders.

"Well, your infection *is* resolving," the woman appraised, "but I will ask you to continue taking ínyan[12] for the next two weeks to ensure no recrudescence."

With the spatula, I heaped four lots of bloodroot into the birch sap, stirring them as I asked, "How did it ever progress like that?"

Etenesh went about tidying. "See, the klis[13] is a common environmental dweller around still, brackish water, and the vast majority of people—*especially* in Vencenza—have at some point been infected with it, usually in childhood." I scooped up a generous dollop of the bloodroot-sap and stirred it into the water in the measuring cylinder, tinting it to rust as the viscous substance dissolved. "The klis' sole tropism in the body is blood," Etenesh continued, "but with a functioning spleen, the protozoan is destroyed, and most people experience only short-term symptoms, unpleasant as they are. The difference with *Cesare* is that he *has* no spleen."

Cesare snorted wordlessly, resting his cheek against his hand and toying with his earrings.

He'd expressed joint pain so acute he felt crucified, and his fever had once reached such a height that we'd feared his organs might boil inside him, his state of mind driven to the point of amnestic delirium. The twins'

---

[11] *Sanguinaria canadensis.*

[12] Tablet or dissolvable powder made from the starch of Ínyangatí leaves ('*moon tree*', named on account of its moonstone-coloured foliage and silver trunk, endemic to southern Yewada and The Spider Garden). Treats a range of protozoal infections.

[13] A colloquial portmanteau of o'Coillàrsaidh [*oh-kyoh-LAHR-see*] words '*klee*' and '*wolis*'; literally '*filthy blood*'.

polarised sleeping tendencies proved favourable, for there could always be someone looking over Cesare. Eligio always kept Fabio at an arm's length. Unlike Lissandri, he couldn't bring himself to forgive the old man for letting Cesare stay at *The Sunrise* by his lonesome. However, there remained a stretch of deepnight when nobody was awake, so I'd slink into Cesare's room and sit at the foot of his bed. I stopped doing it when his sickness began to abate, when he grew cognisant. I didn't know how I would explain myself had I been questioned. I didn't even know my own reasoning.

While Etenesh sanitised her hands, I finished mixing my concoction.

"The shipment is due at approximately five hundred to-morrow," she informed. "I've reserved a one-hour timeframe at seven for you."

"Thank you, Etenesh." Cesare stood, tightening his bound hair and brushing back the loosened bangs. The upward movement of his arms bore starkly the alarming wane of his form. His collarbones protruded like twigs; the already slim column of his neck lay bare each tendon and vessel as if grooves of a moribund tree. Yet, the transient flicker of light in Cesare's eye did not evade me, as if his soul sought to ignite again— that unbearable burn his sole sustaining force.

I swapped out the spatula for a matchbox and struck a match alight. *Here goes nothing.*

"I apologise in advance." Remorse softened Etenesh's brow. I touched the flame to my concoction. "It mightn't prove wholly restorative, but half is better than nought."

The meniscus fizzed and sputtered, bubbles surging along the sides of the cylinder like magma up a volcano's conduit only to plummet back down and peter out. A growl broke from my throat.

"What *are* you doing?" Etenesh questioned.

"*Trying* to work with Myrabella." *Why won't it work with me?*

Etenesh frowned. "The what?"

"An amalgam of bloodroot and the sap of whispering birch."

Etenesh's eyes widened. "*Sanguinaria* is an escharotic!"

"So one avoids skin contact with raw Myrabella, yes." I dipped my chin. "When dissolved in water, a near-undetectable solution is formed, one *purportedly* flammable as paraffin and which emits a scarlet yet innocuous vapour." I hunched my neck so my eyes were level with the meniscus. "The trouble *is*, I cannot ignite it. I've tried every ratio, every volume, temperature, concentration, yet all that I get is *this*." I repeated the attempt. The liquid only hissed at me.

"Give that here." Cesare beckoned for the matchbox.

I made a face. "What would *you* know?"

"Resident pyro."

Etenesh crossed her arms. "You people are *not* setting fire to my apothecárium."

"Do you have a rock and a trough?" Cesare asked strangely.

Etenesh blinked, "*Y*—yes…?" but retrieved the items.

Cesare poured water into a brass basin, half an inch in depth, and positioned a palm-sized chunk of basalt into the centre. Using a transfer pipette, he doused the rock in Myrabella.

My curiosity peaked as the igneous surface absorbed the solution.

Cesare struck the match on the side of the table with skilled swiftness and touched it to the basalt. The stone ignited in rutilant flames, breathing plumes rich as alizarin into the air.

I gawked. "How did you know?"

Cesare raised one shoulder. "A Vyrl'iša'i[14] bloke once helped me decipher a cuneiform slab I nicked from The Encephalon."

Etenesh snatched her netela and wrapped it around her shoulders, clutching the shemma to her face. "And you're *sure* this smoke is innocuous?"

"Yes," I reassured. "The hue is for the dramatics."

Cesare tucked his fingers under the stone and upended it, unflinching when his cuff almost caught ablaze. The flame drowned.

Etenesh puffed. "Well, many thanks for compounding my stack of dishes." She walked the basin towards the back of the chamber. "I shall see you to-*mo*—" She jerked to a halt at the slender window; the deep brown of her sculptural cheeks blanched. "*The General*!" she whispered harshly.

My heart dropped like a deadman.

---

[14] *vyrl-ee-SHAAH-ee*

"With an Imperiáli entourage." Etenesh scrambled to clear away the benches, Cesare whisking on his jacket and tricorn whilst I shoved my rapier under the front counter.

Light glinted across the treen facets of walls in a ghastly presage.

I threw myself in front of Cesare.

Chin tucking to my collarbones, I screwed shut my eyes and projected azoth from the crevices between my lungs into my bloodstream.

Hideous pain gored my eyes as if jagged lancets slowly scraped off my corneas. Tears burned down my cheeks. I clamped on a whimper, nails sinking into the soft cloth of Cesare's sleeve.

When the transmuted azoth expended, I dashed away my tears, every blink abrading my eyes as if sand lay trapped beneath their lids. From my scalp cascaded an outpour of tarnished gold waves. The colour of my eyes mattered not, only that it was not amber.

The doorknob twisted.

Etenesh tugged her netela over her head on instinct, folding its border over her right shoulder and smoothing her ḳemis. "Just customers," she hissed at us.

Three Imperialíi forwarded in, their immaculate armour wrought of gold filigree, eyes cold and void behind gilded colombínae and elegant helms. Hernias of pauldrons boated their wide shoulders from which draped heavy flavescent capes inaurated with intricate wing detail. Cuisses tapered up their powerful thighs. Spathae and pugiones hung sheathed at their hips. The emblem of The Imperiálum—a pair of crossed swords within a nimbus of wings all behind a glorious griffin—embossed their vambraces.

At the centre prowled the golden lion General Manuele Dioli, his half-obscured face itself as if moulded of gold—a sharp, masculine jaw, sculpted lips, a tan gracing his cheek only just. The sides of his ornate helm fanned rearward into golden wings, and every inch of his herculean body seemed stripped of fat, only honed muscle burgeoning beneath a resplendent uniform. At his colossal back I sighted the hilt of an equally titanic flamberge, effulging the celestial light of a luminary. *Lòthmir...*

I took a backward step. The bandage concealing my Malefactor's Mark tattoo pressed into Cesare's shoulder.

Etenesh bowed. "General Manuele Dioli, officéri del Imperiálum, bon merìdi.[15]"

"Apothecary Etenesh Asmeret?" Manuele's voice was dark molasses and smooth bordeaux, its husky rumble reverberating through my bones until I wanted to empty my guts and rend my skin in crazed, vile hatred.

He was the genesis of my pain, the one who stole from me my dearest friend and left me with purulent wounds where festered wrath and its vengeful progeny. Where teeth grew serrated and hungry.

You will die, Manuele. Even if I die with you.

"Correct, signóre.[16]" Etenesh tethered me to the material.

Manuele ambled closer, too graceful for someone so mighty. He regarded Etenesh with a disdain vivid as the haüynite of his eyes. "I have been directed by High Priest Benetto Abelli, illúxito am issúsu ramnúna,[17] to communicate to you that your name has been drawn up among Vencenzani apothecaries. You are expected to report to the basilica at sixteen hundred this eventide to assist in the conduction of a surgery on an injured Illutóre." He handed her a neat scroll belted with a rubineous ribbon. "Bless'ed be the poor sod subjected to vivisection at the crooked hand of a female." Manuele's dulcet voice grated against the disgusting words his mouth spewed at Etenesh, and I wanted to claw his tongue out for her.

His eyes shot me a sickening once-over, briefly flicking to Cesare where they stalled. I unhanded his ruffled cuff and grasped his wrist.

"Am I to be escorted," Etenesh swept in, "or shall I make my way to the basilica on my own accord?"

"Report to where set forth by the designated time and hand the document to an Illutóre. Illuteríi will direct you therefrom." I sensed Manuele's mounting impatience in his clipped tone, in his tightening fists where gold claws stood proud of his gauntlets' knuckles.

Etenesh dipped her head in falsified reverence. "Many thanks, Minister."

---

[15] *'Good afternoon.'*

[16] The usage of the gender-neutral address here denotes higher respect.

[17] *'Enlightened be their name'*; an honorific used when referring to the High Priest in their absence.

The piercing azure of Manuele Dioli's eyes centred on me, and dread scuttled down my skin as if ticks looking to feast. His lip twitched, gaze feeling down to my chest and hips. "They really do cry so much."

Slender fingers entwined with mine. *His hands are never so cold…*

As if noting the fine movement, Manuele looked to the dark-haired man he had already seen. Already heard speak. Already almost murdered.

"Pity about the eye," he jibed, and my grip steeled. *I swear to the Gods, Cesare, do not open your mouth.*

With a lecherous leer thrown in my face, Manuele and his entourage departed.

I clasped my hands to my eyes, enduring the agony of tailoring until the revolting tension loosened from my irises and my shoulders bore once more the weight of a coiled mane.

But the tears streamed even when the pain receded.

"Gods…" A breathy sob ripped from my chest. The edge of the counter rammed into my spine as I staggered backwards and sat up onto the bench with reason abandoned. Only hot, consuming panic endured. "Gods, Gods, *Gods*, he was too close *he was too close nonononono I can't do this* please *Faces I cannot do this*—"

"Vólto!" My cheeks seethed against cold skin as hands grasped my face. "Vólto, listen to me. He is gone. You are safe, you are present, there is nobody here to hurt you anymore."

My ribcage lurched with a sob, fingers cramping as I latched onto Cesare's forearms. "I'm sorry…" *I will always be too afraid.*

"What?" Cesare shook his head, careful hands tucking curls behind my ear. "This isn't your fault."

I gasped arduous breaths, stomach in nauseating knots.

"Do you need to leave?" Etenesh's sturdy hands soothed my shoulders.

I nodded. "I want to see *The Sunrise*."

"Ḥafti," wariness underscored Etenesh's voice, "are you s—?"

"I want to see *The Sunrise*," I repeated and, with a shuddering inhale, wiped my cheeks, blotted my eyes, hopped to the floor.

"Do you know why they chose you?" Cesare asked the apothecary.

Etenesh sighed, netela fallen across her shoulders. "They do a luck-of-the-draw of all Vencenzani apothecaries—standard *Códice Erudíti* practice." She snorted. "I suppose this round brought *my* 'luck'."

"Let Araya know."

"Will do."

Scene VI

Butterfly Effect

Giorgianna | Ygạl

AFTERNOON CHASED THE STORM AWAY, the sky already painted with ruddy aquarelles where the gilden disk of Seren's sun descended for the eastern horizon. Quiet oldtown streets scintillated with the distant hubbub of checkpoints as we turned into the shadows of familiar warrens under the paperweight of silence.

"Are… you certain you want to go through with this?" Cesare tentatively asked.

"I'm fine." A terse retort from me.

"I mean the government building. You will be close to Dioli."

"This time around caught me off guard." Irritation crackled down my nerves. "I will be prepared when I go inside."

"When it does *that* to you?"

"This isn't *about* me!" I snapped.

"What are you *saying*? Yes, it is."

"It's about Ema." Pique shoved me into a brisker pace. "Dioli will pay for her death."

Cesare halted behind me. "How much will your surety amount to if he kills you as well?" His whetted tone shot through me.

I stopped. Pivoted. "You really do think so lowly of me, don't you?"

He flinched. "*No, I*—"

"*Forgive* me," I sauntered closer, "that my prowess with *sword*play, or my *aim*, aren't up to par with his *majesty's*."

"Vólto, that's not my *point*—"

"Stop." Fury lashed me. "*Calling* me that!" It took me everything to keep my voice hushed in these streets where the walls were living flesh. "I have a *name!*"

"I am being serious!"

"And *I* am not?" I chided. "You spent an entire month treating me like I was *dead*, and you cannot even do so little as refer to me by *name*? Am I an inanimate object to you, Cesare?"

"*Fine*, fine!" He raised his palms. "You're right. I'm sorry."

I crucified him with flaying scrutiny, waiting for him to keep talking, to say something—*anything*—else. Yet I was met with null. *Prideful bastard like no other.*

Gaze plummeting with my heart, I wrapped my arms around myself, "Perish the thought," and walked on.

The crumbling carcass of *The Sunrise* wrung within a cavitation of charred sandstone, its gutted superstructure echoing as we paced through its ash-sown halls, our silence splintered only by the groans of the córpus' scorched skeleton and the crunch of crumbled concretions beneath our boots.

My ribs clenched unbearably tight with recollections of the glimmering etchings of faces and salt seas upon rustic wooden panels once dressing the winding corridors. The rose and yellow gold twirling hand-in-hand across the ornate balusters of the auditorium's mezzanine, its balconies. The illusionistic fresco with its gold quadratura oculus gazing into a rosolite sky awash with clouds of ouro. Those elysian curtains sewn from blushing dawn.

Black-brown cinders and pallid rubble were left.

Items fashioned of metal survived the conflagration—weapons and Cesare's cufflinks too, some of his earrings—but most were surrendered in exchange for some measly coin. Cesare held onto his tanzanite cufflink, the twins keeping a dagger each, Lissandri his brass knuckles and chamkạli. Most Vencenzani vendors refused to take worn earrings, so Cesare couldn't sell all of his, whilst Lissandri was forced to relinquish most of his remaining tools. All of his beloved books perished just like Eligio's art supplies and masks. *Commegno's Curious* was immediately seized by the state, so the grieving twins weren't permitted to retrieve a single item of their parents'.

Cesare's footfalls shuffled to an abrupt stop. "Do you see that?" His attention affixed the terminus of an offshooting capillary.

I sighted among the ruins… *an arm?*

We cleared the narrow hallways and rounded the bend.

I clutched a gasp in my palms. *"Gods…"*

Two bodies lay battered and livid. Bullous scabs of caramelised sanies puckered around their throats—dealt by strangulation.

"Nara and Eluisa…"

The lavìre from *The Arum* who'd been my first clue to finding *Stalker's Barge*. The nursemaid from the vicinal slums.

Veins slithering in Nara's emaciated arms still ran dark and bulged with pollution yet her auburn hair gleamed even in death, her skin sun-embraced. Cinders soiled Eluisa's pistachio-and-buttercream empire gown and freckled skin, glaucous eyes gazing sightlessly at the paunched ceiling. *They were innocent…*

My chest tore. I wanted to scream. *You are always innocent!*

Coldness grazed the back of my neck. *Elenedda.*

There was no explaining how I knew, but she was in danger, and despite everything, I couldn't let her be. I couldn't let her die.

"Call on Libitina," I ordered, "then wait for me at *Three Suns*," and ran towards the àtrium.

"Where are you going?" called Cesare.

"My mother!" Heart in my belly, I dashed beneath the nimbus of smiling faces weeping golden tears, and bolted from the oldtown.

THE TRANQUIL AMBIENCE OF YGẠL NAJM'S BOUDOIR and a glass of fine amaretto always soothed her spirit after a meeting with the cadre. Being the Dóminus of the largest district in The Antrum came with a price, and sometimes that price was peace.

Ygạl sat at an escritoire tucked into a corner perpendicular to the wood-carved door and mulled over misdemeanour reports from the district, köz earring rolling between the pads of her fingers. Decorated columns flanked the nook, rugae of muqarnaṣ wheeling above and tulle the orange-magenta of an imperial topaz swathing it.

At the opposing wall, away from the satin-draped bed, a cusped window opened to a turquoise natatorium assembled of coral and ceramic. The balmy humidity overhanging the water drifted with its orange blossom perfume into the chamber.

Kilims stretched across the stone floor, calligraphies and miniatures adorned the hand-painted walls, and within the geometric patterns, Ygạl at times descried echoes of her parents. Annagül Yạrınuya and Laḥīn ibn Hābīl u-Jāzbiyya Najm al-Imlāq. Both tall and proud with those dark eyes and strong roots they cultivated within their children: the eldest Narjis; the twins Gunça and Lawāḥiẓ; the youngest Döwran—the sole boy; to this day only twenty-three. And Ygạl. Tucked between Narjis and the twins, yet no less loved.

At thirty years of age, twenty-four years had passed since Ygạl last laid eyes upon the rolling verdure of Kıcunın, or the volcanic sands of Sa'āhḍa which stretched beyond the window the night of her birth— when an asteroid shower streaked the sky in a rain of stars. It was not without woe that they looked on their forced disconnection from ancestral land, from beloved family and mother tongues. What no artefact could replace. Yet Ygạl sought to try, mithering any merchant they came by for pieces of her two-blooded heritage: textiles, tchotchkes, recipes, raiments. Though she toiled tirelessly to accrue the coin for it, far more instances than not called for barter. Notwithstanding, most furniture in The Boar estate came to either be of Kıcunınese or Sa'āḥḍi make—Ygạl had traded all the Faustinian items he could for a slice of his lost homelands. The homelands she travelled between throughout childhood, and all their neighbours just as well, sailing up and down Sofía River by Themistóklis and ad-Dīmarḍ and Lerrḳir and Akésa, marvelling at them and, sometimes, immersing within.

Across from Ygạl's desk stood a provincial chaise divan, its shiraz-coloured velvet patterned with rosettes. Within the divan's curve nestled a glass table arrayed with amla murabbā and leftover çakçak, a crystal decanter of limoo amani tea standing beside Lucrezia's pince-nez.

Having concluded her soak in the natatorium, the petite woman in question stretched across the divan with that '*Spagyrism and Spellwerk*' tome Damiani had given her, chewing on some of the gooseberry fruit preserve. The emerald bathing robe wrapping her buxom curves gleamed beneath the honeyed alchemical glow of ceiling lights.

Maybe Ygạl had a different family, now.

She rose from the desk. Over her çyrpy she sported a bidi aba cloak the likes of which wore her father—woven of sturdy cream goat wool and embroidered along the front and shoulders with orange twitching. "What do the grimoires speak of, söygülim?[18]" Ygạl slid carefully behind Lucrezia on the sofa, gentle with their inamorata as if she were woven of glass threads, allowing her to lean into their body and tuck her own shoulders beneath the bidi aba.

Plucking a doughy little ball of apricot-sugared çakçak, Ygạl tossed it into the air and caught it in her mouth to her own vocalised surprise, igniting Lucrezia's effervescent delight.

A grin tugged the lip scar Ygạl won in a knife fight—merely sparring—against the old Boar Dóminus Carcan. She'd lost, that day, but hadn't so much as flinched at the slash, and walked away with dignity.

---

[18] '*Sweetheart*' in Koşatlen.

At once, Lucrezia's black brows met, eyes narrowed, lips pursed at the meticulous script on the tome's old pages. "This…" she dithered, *"Nashĭgostu Kurilit Gostiata.* The one Giorgi seems so fascinated by. Truly a basket case of a bloke, I tell you what!" She tapped her cleft chin. "He seems a sort better suited for writing stream-of-consciousness memoirs and verse, not scholarly material, with how fitfully he hops topic to topic." A scoff. "Not to mention, I've *never* seen an author carry on in such verbose, flowery gabble. You'd think somebody would've told him along the lengthy way! I'd wager that head trauma did a *little* more than grant him illimitable use of azoth."

Ygạl poured herself limoo amani tea into a handle-less white finjān patterned with leaves, thinking how Lucrezia never drank on account of liver issues since childhood, so the dried lime tea hailing from Faryâ— one she'd always drink on her family's visits there—never failed to be of use. Giorgianna, another one to spurn alcohol, had from the very start taken a liking to the sugar-and-rose-water gahwa bayḍā, a recipe Ygạl learned in the cedar-crowned mountains of northern ad-Dīmarḍ. "Elaborate?" she volleyed back. "Regarding this head injury and its relation to azoth, I mean."

Lucrezia expelled a '*hmmm…*', noisily flicking through pages before finally halting at a dog-eared chapter, a thick circle of bloodink at its number. Seven-hundred-twelve. "From what I understand… In our bodies, the humour that is azoth, or our 'life essence', concentrates in the pericardium, the frontal lobe, the liver, and, in residues, in the wrists. There, it's almost… *encapsulated*, right? When a magus accesses it, the azoth sort of 'filters' through this occlusion, this *sieve*, of sorts, into the different forms of magics we know—like Giorgi and Sarnai's flesh tailoring…" A pause. "And the water speaking Giorgi's been dabbling in." Gloom gripped Lucrezia's tone. "That filtration is dubbed 'transmutation'."

Ygạl chased gooseberry murabbā with lime tea. *Absurd affair, thaumaturgy.* Why did magi ever risk consequences as punitive as aneurysms and organ failure just for a couple incantations?

"As for *Gostiata*," Lucrezia carried on, "I still cannot understand *what* his injury was. A skull fracture, an orbital intrusion of some kind, a heavy concussion—honestly anything, with how vaguely he writes! Never matter, but what *does* is that whatever occlusion once existed in his frontal lobe was rendered ineffectual, and he could essentially syphon pure, untransmuted azoth right into his blood. He called it a 'transfusion'. What happens is that azoth is almost…" A gesture of the hand. "Sticky. It *grabs*. That made it very useful to Gostiata as a blood singer because what he'd do is slash his wrists, and void his *whole* body of blood which he then used as weapons."

Ygal covered his mouth, gulping down acid as their gut roiled. "How does that not kill you?"

"It's almost this 'phantom blood' sort of effect, I suppose? Your azoth is still engaged, so even though your blood is external to your body, because of your azoth, it's made so that your body still functions…" Lucrezia trailed off, dragging in a breath through the nose and leaving the sentence with a shrug for a full stop.

"Did you manage to find anything hinting towards… whatever may've been transpiring with the High Priest's operations on you?" A sharp gnash edged Ygal's tone, her blade-shaped fingernail guards *clacking* together. Domínie Benetto Abelli was lucky she still respected religious institutions and their leaders.

A weighty sigh departed Lucrezia. She shut the tome with a muffled *boom* and hugged the titan to her chest. "It always *feels* strange. You know? Like I'm close but not there." She kissed her teeth, kneading her glassy nazar ring between her fingertips. The charm Ygal gave her as a promise of forever. "I asked Giorgianna look into it for me, if the chance presents itself. I want her to be my ears. My eyes." She grew silent again, then her tone duskened, "I want her to pursue something fruitful in this suicide expedition Cesare has sent her on."

Ygal snorted, then gave way to a melodious bout of laughter. "*Please*, the fool is practically smitten with her!"

Lucrezia knocked her head back to look at Ygal, her gaze flat. "He is smitten with freedom more."

Ygal's brows nudged together a tad even as a hesitating smile held on. "You hardly know him."

"What is there to *know*, Ygạl?" Lucrezia sat up abruptly, book still held. "He is unwavering; he does not change."

"But *love* changes," urged Ygạl. "Love transmutes people, Luce."

Lucrezia shook her head, then stood and forwarded to the exit. "By his own admission, Cesare is not a person. He is an instrument. A tool. A weapon. An idea, or somesuch fucking nonsense."

"Tools dent." Ygạl sat up. "They bend, they *break*—"

"Not the ideological sort." The mercury of Lucrezia's eyes churned—millions of grey ripples gleaming and calid. "And so the taste of loss does not repulse him from his hunger for greater calamity." And somewhere deep within, beneath that steel armour of his and the incongruous sweet pudding of a heart it concealed, Ygạl couldn't help but comprehend the tragic keenness in Lucrezia's observations. She had watched the earth split open and her world collapse, after all. "And so forgive me if I harbour little hope." Lucrezia pirouetted to the door.

It swung open before she could reach for the knob.

On the threshold stood Isaia, black working satchel slung over his shoulders. He nodded to Lucrezia as amicably as the frigid stone slab of him could accomplish before shooting a flinty regard for the Dóminus. "Get up." He marched towards Ygạl's desk.

"What is it?" Ygạl approached.

Isaia hoisted his satchel to the desk and dumped out its contents.

Lucrezia yelped, Ygạl thrusting back as across the sumptuous oak rolled a severed head.

Cavernous craters of crimson-black pulp congealed where eyeballs had once swivelled. Chunks of vermilion-dyed hair torn out at the blonde root exposed poultry-pale patches of a bruised scalp. With the tatters of lips lanced off by a razor, the toothless gums puled bloody pus onto a severed tongue. *Mair.*

Isaia dropped onto the desk an envelope rattling with what Ygạl assumed were Mair's teeth. "Lucanus' respects."

Her gut turned over and over. "Wonderful…"

Scene VII

Mother!

Giorgianna

I CAREENED OFF THE SUNSET-LAVED *AEGIDIUS BOULEVARD* into the golden sandstone of my mother's apartment building and up the circling staircase to its apex, dashing across the sharp-armed sun transposed by the skylight onto the etched tiles of the foyer and bursting through the unlatched front door.

Azoth blistered my flesh as I snapped the knife-wielding arm of a man within the schematics-clad architecture studio. Elenedda shrieked and crawled beneath her drawing board. The hilt of my unsheathed rapier swung for the intruder's head.

Blood splashed across his eyes at the splitting collision of skin and metal. His unmangled arm swiped a dark stilétto at my ribs.

I volted, thrusting my rapier into his thigh. He cried out and lunged with a stab.

Blocking his reprising attack, I flicked my wrist to disengage his handle and kicked him in the abdomen when he moved to rise, punting his blade across the room.

I pinned him down, baselard skewering his arm to the floor and my rapier thrust in an open reverse grip against his bobbling larynx. "Talk."

"Fuck off."

Pain engorged my sinuses as I splintered the bones in his flailing legs. His screams rent the air. "*Fuck*! Shit, *all right*!"

Azoth receded.

He gobbled down air. "Fuck do you need?"

"What is your name and why are you here?"

"Alphaeus. I'm—"

"Of Davide's troupe?"

He gawped. "How—"

I drove my rapier into his neck. "Why were you sent?"

"Finishing some jobs," gritted Alphaeus.

"Besides yourself, the remaining living members are Mircea and Cataldu, correct?"

"And Abramo."

I cut a cruel smirk. "My condolences."

"You—"

"—was informed that Mircea and Cataldu fled to a location in Smugglers' District following Davide's death."

He blinked in place of a nod.

"Give it to me."

His lip twitched. "Something in it for m'self?"

"A swifter death." I pressed harder. Red rivulets branched down his neck.

Alphaeus' dark brows bunched and buckled. "Die, bitch."

My blade split a gorge down his arm. Veins gushed. He screamed horridly through my question: "Are you aware Davide stuffed childrens' corpses like trophies? That he violated them in vile ways?"

The bandit's face drained to a greenish pallor. "*5 Kraken Avenue 13/7, East Fin, Smugglers' Cove.*"

"Why did you flee to Smugglers' Cove?"

"To be safe from legions."

"Did you have a hand in the burning of *The Sunrise*?"

A blink. "We all did—"

"Morphera," I snapped. "Did you use it on the young girl in the theatre?"

"Aye. We knocked her out b'fore Imperialíi helped us light the place."

"No…" I drew my words out to painful slowness, "*qualms*…" and stabbed him through his shoulder, "about burning a child alive?" His belly gave up that scream it clutched so tightly. "A lavìre and a nursemaid were left in *The Sunrise*. Your doing?"

"Aye…"

"How did you know whom to target?"

"W'en ya worked at *The Arum*, d'ya notice blokes tryin' to kill ya?"

No… "That was your little gang, wasn't it?"

"On top o' a few fellas we paid off." *A hit out on me all along…* "We 'ad a list—Davide wan'ed to tie up loose ends, and ordered we leave some time 'fore comin' to mess wi' yous 'gain. Mircea, Cataldu and me 'pproached ya ol' keeper."

"Madáma Irene Falco?" That moniker tasted revolting on my tongue.

"Aye, 'er. We thre'ened to off 'er. She told us… do in the druggie girl, 'en showed us directions to Spottie's place. 'en we dumped 'em both in ya ruins."

"I'll be sure to repay your cooperation in kind."

With a lengthwise thrust of my arm, my rapier's blade opened Alphaeus' throat. His bulging socket ruptured with thick fluid when I plunged my baselard into his skull to sever clean in twain the gossamer string of his pitiable existence.

Claret warmth slid between my finger, under my nails, a frisson thrilling down the shivering ridges of my spine as iron perfume laid heavy and wet upon the heady air I dragged into my pleading lungs.

I shot to my feet and tottered back, my vision doubling and unifying. Heartbeat pulsed in my ribcage. My neck. My blood-drenched fingertips.

"Giorgianna…?" A woman's dusky voice stitched my ripping mind back together. My eyes found their perfect mirrors—vivid as magma. Yet cold as copper.

Her pupils cinched to tiny specks as she stayed hunched under the drawing board.

Fear.

Of *me*.

I strode towards the centre of the room to leave a comfortable distance between us. "Salúdi, Elenedda." Wiping my baselard against my black trousers, I watched as she who was once 'mother' to me climbed out. A redingote dress adorned her tall frame, sapphire *like the satin ribbon binding Father's letters to you.* Thick caramel ringlets perched on its wide lapels.

Her nose sloped like a high, narrow buttress of gothic monasteries, a dainty flattened peppercorn of a mole dotted above her budded lips whereas mine marked the skin beneath my left eye. High cheekbones carved deep into her slender face.

Nothing of me sculpted into her architecture.

Everything of me painted upon her tapestry.

"Who was...?" Elenedda stammered, lips bleaching at the sight of Alphaeus' corpse.

"A member of a gang led by a man who had once been father's..." sickness probed the back of my tongue, "comrade? I was led to believe the two never got along."

Elenedda clutched a hand at her chest. "Davide?"

I started. "You know?"

Pressing her lips into a stern line—*just like me and father*—she waited out several breathless ticks before her head pitched into a hesitant nod. "Only by name. By person, I knew Fabio." Her eyes welded to me. To the blood on me. "How much do *you* know?"

"Enough. Though you could enlighten me further, I'm sure."

"I take it you're no stranger to your father's collector proclivities?"

If only you knew. "I happened to cast my eye on his compendium."

"So what is it you seek?" Elenedda's pin-straight spine steeled as she shed fear from her slender shoulders.

I sheathed my weapons.

Some wretched premonition, perhaps divine, perhaps honed by The Court, compelled me to rush to my mother's home. It could mean nothing, but coincidences did not simply happen. That cruel lesson had been taught to me almost better than Fear.

I racked my brain as my scrutiny tethered to Alphaeus.

If Abramo came into employment at *The Crescent* almost a year before all of this set into motion, it could mean—"The government was aware of my father's identity and, undoubtedly, whereabouts for potentially far longer than either of us know, and yet it still took *all* of that time for them to arrest him." My behold reconvened with Elenedda's. "Did the Magister's *Códice Erudíti* play any role in that?"

"Yes." Her throat bobbed. "There came a time when Ludovico essentially lived at the observatory, granting himself indemnity."

"But they got their hands on him still, did they not?" I bit.

When I was forsaken to the foulest of places, memories of my father had been the few shards of light to stave off the darkness. Even if his echo had been little more than a flame's candent flicker, ephemeral as time, it was my lullaby when I feared the black maw sleep, when my only heat was the blood pouring from my putrescent veins. The six of faces and sun goddess he gifted me never left my side, even to this moment.

Elenedda's groomed brows slanted. "After you… disappeared… I believe Ludovico could no longer stand to remain in hiding." She rubbed her lips together, and my ribs corseted. "He demanded an audience with the judgement tribunal and was granted it—you and I both know why. That is… when their saw-tooth snare snapped shut."

I couldn't breathe. *No…*

Nonono, Gods, why would you do that? Not for me…

Anguish poured from the cracks in my maimed heart.

All this time… it was because of me…

I barely swallowed, biting as painfully as I had to on my sorrow before asking, "And you?"

"They called upon my testimony during the private trial. '*Trial*' holding a significance of next to null—their decision as to your father's fate was predetermined." She grasped her own elbows, gaze evading me. "I tried to speak to him prior but, of course, they would never allow such. So, in the end, I told all."

"How did you escape unscathed?"

"Ludovico took a plea bargain." I could have promised under oath that Elenedda's eyes silvered. "He would confess to every accusation bar none, and in return I would be let free, bound to never speak a word of the arrangement to a soul." Her shoulders bobbed with a scoff. "It seems we both sported an inclination towards sharp practice."

And so my mother lived at my father's expense.

She remained transfixed by nothing, features locked away behind a porcelain mask, yet her jaw wrung tight, and as much as Elenedda would hate me for it, I pitied her. To live trapped in a dominion which decried emotion, *humanity*; to internalise that poisonous pedagogy for fear of persecution or death… It was a hideous reality. One I *knew*—had *lived*, once. And each dawn brought with it the reminder that humans, given the faculty to do so, would be willing to break themselves or one another in the worst ways for power. For avarice. For warped and fallacious ideologies. *For vengeance.* Even for love.

"Why did you not tell me when I asked all those months ago?"

"I was *afraid*, Giorgianna." Elenedda's mask cracked. "Do you not recognise that?"

"And I *wasn't*?" I couldn't believe her. "My life was destroyed. I was wanted—*framed*—for treason because, *all* this time, they wanted to be rid of me. *You* called me a misbegotten harlot. Do you know that I was trafficked by monsters just to barely survive? Do you know how afraid *I* was?" My voice faltered. "Perhaps it can give you some peace of mind that you shall never be cursed with blood grandchildren." Elenedda flinched whilst I pushed on: "Father was the *only* person I had left who'd *ever* cared for me and they *took* him, and *you* didn't even have the *Godsdamn decency* to tell me the truth!"

Her cheeks flushed. "You were *not* the only person hurt!"

"Yet *I'm* the one to impart empathy?" I snapped back. "You couldn't so much as not treat me like a leper yet here you are demanding I weep with you?" I thrust a condemning finger at her. "*You* spat on my father's grave, and you *never* afforded me the kindness a mother should! After *everything* you put me through, how *fucking* dare you?"

Elenedda stared back. Silent.

I tread my bloody fingers across the dales and wolds of bloodier knuckles. "It scarred, you know." The molten iron of my tone tempered to a cutting edge. "All of those times you put your hand fan to my knuckles for the most infinitesimal cello recital mistake." I pinned that *mother* of mine with a glare. "Why did you do that to me?"

Elenedda's eyes momentarily cast heavenward before plummeting back to the seething crucibles of mine. "Ludovico and I met in an oldtown tavèrna where he dealt. I had been curious about the goings on of The Court of Secrets, hence my visitation." Her scrutiny cowered beneath a thick curtain of lashes. "He used to play the cello, and sometimes he would play it for the tavèrna. Sometimes, he would play it for me."

I grew ill with budding cognisance. *No…*

Elenedda's hands tore at her gloves as if she vied to scrape off her own nails, the gesture an ugly mirror of myself. *"One…"* her eyes flickered into oblivion for an instant, "of the reasons he departed from his old life was on account of *me*, hence Fabio never found me agreeable. As you grew older, the realisation that your father and I were not nearly as alike as we'd thought dawned. Perhaps I'm equally culpable." She wove her fingers together, resting them beneath her pointed chin. "There was no bite in him. No singe or talon. He was soft-hearted, doting. Even *I* admit to my coldness, my distance. It harmed *you* most of all." I wanted to scoff, yet I wanted equally to weep until there was nothing left within me. *Why did my cards fall so?* She shook her head. "As I was saying, your father played the cello throughout his youth. He was never very good, so… each time you made a mistake, it reminded me of nights at the tavèrna, and of nights together."

I blinked. *Surely not…* Surely *that* couldn't be her reason.

"And you thought it was acceptable to take your misery out on *me*?"

"I know," Elenedda admitted, guilt-ridden eyes finally bearing to look upon mine. "I am sorry, Giorgianna. It was wrong of me to do such a thing to you."

"Does your apology mend my near-motherless childhood?" I snapped. "You treated me like *dirt* just to expel your anger at my father unto someone. Gods forbid you be forced to confront yourself!" My stomach dropped. *I almost became this woman's hideous simulacrum…* "And I cannot believe I nearly fell victim to the same trap." I had never wanted to beg for Cesare's forgiveness more than at that moment. "Your compassion would have been worth far more had it not been spurred by this castigation of you in retrospect." My voice no longer cared to rise above a sneer; she had drained me of too much for far too many years. *You deserve nothing from me.*

"You are right," Elenedda stated simply and sat at her drawing board.

The clock *tsk'd* an elegiac rhythm through the silence which settled between us.

"A part of me wished to be Ludovico." Her pitch rose hardly above a murmur. "I wonder what would've happened had I entertained that curiosity, if I followed it into the depths of his world instead of merely loitering on its doorstep." Her eyes looked up at me, more sorrow harboured within their depths than I had ever witnessed upon her visage. "I loved your father." My heart winced. "And I wonder if, at the moment of his death, he loved me too."

"*You loved my father,*" I jibed. "*I* loved my father." Heat puddled in my eyes. "*You* called my father a crook and a reprobate!"

"Perhaps I stand by my words." She gazed at the hands folded in her lap. A tear dropped down her cheek and mine followed. "Perhaps *I* was, too." She shot a glance at Alphaeus. "You had no reservations about doing that?"

"Why should I?" I wiped my face with an unsullied sleeve. "His troop destroyed my home and irrevocably hurt the people I love. Be thankful I didn't wash your pristine fucking floors with his guts."

Her house always smelled of nought. Clinical. A blank slate. *Have you always been this way? Or did they erase everything that you were? And how easily I could have been her…*

Elenedda's eyes, dry once more, returned to me. "Will you kill *me?*"

Though the thought had flitted past my mind, it no longer demanded me to look at it. My rage towards her, my resentment and bitterness, burned itself out, disdain and abhorrence erecting amid the ashes in eternal coldness.

Lifting my chin and pinning straight my spine—*like mother like daughter*—I approached Elenedda, halting knee-to-knee with her.

"You don't deserve to die." My sneer jolted her. "You deserve to live knowing you destroyed everything you ever had. May the agony gnaw at you even half as voraciously as it did me."

Azoth bolstering my bones for strength, I slung Alphaeus' cooling corpse across my shoulders and quitted my estranged mother's abode once and for all.

Vencenza wore dusk like a saturnian veil, and beneath those swathes, I cut open Alphaeus' torso and sunk his body in an oldtown canal.

Blood blackened the water and drenched the breeze as his thorax flooded, the current's weight dragging him into the depths of his final resting place.

How many had I already killed? How many more was I destined to condemn to the Everlasting Null? *They deserve it. So let them suffer.*

But had *I* not developed a taste for slaughter? For violence?

How deep was a cut too deep?

Rinsing my hands and blades, I skulked into the alleyways towards *Three Suns*, acronychal Nereida twinkling in the dusk.

Living shadows danced with mine, every detail of passing architecture the daliesque haze of a waking dream.

"SHE SHALL WEAR MANY FACES," drones of oracular apparitions possessed my thoughts, tugging my step and breath to a cessation.

I whirled.

Avascular sclerae, punctured with hungering cosmogyral entities of irises, gazed into me from behind vólti white as fear, the masks' temples moulded into spirals of ram horns and lips painted aurous. Misshapen vinaceous triangles hung off The Rams' torsos. Pantaloons circular as lanterns dressed legs in white stockings and cerise winklepickers.

"WHEN HER SKIN IS TORN," the dainty woman commenced, "STITCHED LIKE A MARIONETTE, HAIR WEAVED INTO THREAD ANEW, WILL SHE, UPON THAT SILVER LOOKING, SEE HER FACE?"

The living shadows linked fingers, danced a roundelay around my gravity, bloated, ruptured like amnions, their membranous forms obscuring the drowned light of gloaming.

Blood beat at my brain yet thrummed in such shallow, head-whirling pulsations within my ribs. Powdered diamond a wintry breeze flurried along my skin. *Azoth!*

"*You.*" I lifted a forefinger at the woman. "You are a mind scourge."

The writhing of cold worms through my brain, the lucid, distorted visions and psychological warfare. She was *inside* my mind, rifling through my memories, my thoughts. Conjuring up scenes of her own construction. And with each fragment she broke off my sanity, she fractured her own irreparably.

Yet scourging was not so easy unaided, for her mark could flee her field and render her impotent.

I turned to the man. "And *you* are a shadow weaver."

Darkness spindled in threads at his fingertips, slunk like black cats by his ankles, spinning into a cobweb to trap his prey and vanish them from the eyes of the world.

"SO SHEDS THE CHRYSALIS," they intoned in unified speech.

And yet, still, something *more*.

"For such powerful azoth," I addressed the man, sinking my fingers into the whispering oblivion of caliginosity; it rippled like water against my touch, "you should not be able to see me. That is your deficiency as a weaver—a potent spell blinds you with darkness upon its casting, just as a light bender is blinded by their light." My eyes narrowed. "Yet you *see* me."

His masked face tilted earthward.

"How?"

"WE ARE THE MAGNUM OPUS OF THE GODS' CHILD."

"You say that…"

Slowly as rusty mechanisms, his head canted. "WHAT KIND OF LIGHT KEEPS YOU IN THE DARK?"

Blackness blotted out my sight.

My boots squelched against a fleshy floor; I found myself in a cavity streaked of blood, thick air redolent as putrescence. Pink tissue stretched the soaring walls into cords, a windy murmur swirling through distant chambers. *Right heart ventricle!* I'd been there before.

Lustrous sinew of the shut tricuspid valve to my left gleamed with sunlight conducted through the pulmonary valve yawning open above.

A mind scourge's vision.

Before me arose a throne wrought of seven skinless hands. Within their flensed palm sprouted a bulging eye each of distinct shades:

Deep oak.

Pale as ice.

Bright azure.

Black like blindness.

A murky wash of grey and green.

A chimeric smear of viridian to cerulean.

Dark brown shot through with a blue streak.

"FIND HIDDEN WORDS SPAT BY THE BLEST TO THIS PLANE FROM THE CELESTIAL LAZULUM," The Rams' whispers echoed through the ventricle, walls distending with a shallow pulse, "SENTENCED TO QUIETUS BENEATH THE SOFFITS OF A SUZERAIN'S KEEP."

From within their pupils, the eyeballs began to weep scarlet, each orb deliquescing into grume.

Each orb but the night-black singularity at the throne's centre.

"THE THIRD EYE BLINKS."

And it did, membranous lids peeling shut.

When they slid back, the singular iris had split into three, each with their own pupil. Own muscle. Own gravity.

The pupils constricted in unison.

The walls pulsed, rattling the floor and knocking me off my kilter.

I gasped the putrid air as blood seeped through the fleshy floor.

The throne was gone.

'*RUN!*' shrieked a far-off voice.

I screamed and darted for the tricuspid as the heart continued to shudder.

The valve flung open.

A tidal wave of crimson gushed into the ventricle.

I caught my final breath before warm humour drowned me and the world plunged into an abyss.

SCENE VIII

LA RIVOLUZIONE
È LA MORTE

Cesare

AT NINETEEN HUNDRED HOURS ON DÍEM LUNÉRA, *Three Suns* lilted with anachronistic Ahărla kesle and Dīmarḍi mijwiz, the warm tavèrna perfumed with strawberry kompot and clandestine revelry.

Cesare arrived from the mortuary recently and sat around a table with the twins who had only just gotten off work. Iyad finished up at his docks outside. The fourth chair at their table awaited Giorgianna's arrival.

Anukka circled the tap room—a raven in her embroidered cotton çerşçitti[19] which concealed her from the neck down. A mosaic of silver coins like fish scales draped her head and neck to resemble a mail coif.

Attentive as she was to her patrons, Anukka's son exerted no effort at all to snare her away. Perhaps thirteen years old, Yason was—certainly

---

[19] *chehr-sh-CHEET-tee*; a long Chuvash dress (generally of *white* linen), worn with an apron or pinafore, featuring elaborate embroidery. Alternatively known as a '*sappun*'.

younger than Rosalia—with dark eyes and black hair like both his parents.

Anukka and Yason conversed in a macaronic jargon of Ahărla-Dīmarḍi, a smile slipping upon the woman's face as easily as if across sleet at something the boy said.

She kissed her son on the forehead and ruffled his hair, the boy accepting her touch entirely before sweeping into his arms the black cat trotting along the tavèrna floor and running off upstairs.

A tender childhood. Such a notion evanesced into nothing within Cesare's mind, a fragment of a past life he was no longer convinced belonged to him.

His fingers fidgeted amidst themselves, with his nose ring, his earrings, his eyepatch, his hair. What they sought were throwing knives.

A hand caught his shirt's cuff.

Cesare met insistent eyes. "Ces," Lissandri voiced firmly but gently. "I don't think you're alright right now."

He felt the hurtle of his own heart, then—desperate as a hunted hare, the twitchy, light sensation of hunger pinching at his hands and gnawing its way through his vitals. "Don't worry about me." He tugged his sleeve from Lissandri.

Eligio leaned forward across the table. His brows dented, drooping in time with the corners of his lips. "You *know* we do." His voice fell low— almost a whisper. "You hardly eat or sleep, you're just about never home," the word nicked Cesare's skin, "you're always… *moving, and*-and repeating the same actions. It's like watching someone descend into madness. But it isn't *madness*. It's *hurt*."

Cesare teeth grinded.

He despised this. The concern. The burden of his dismal existence upon his famìlia. He didn't deserve it when he was supposed to be the untouchable one. When he never made oversights and nothing ever stumped him. He could never let himself lose.

And yet there he was.

"Please," silver illumined Eligio's eyes, "*please*, know that you are not blamed for *any*thing." Cesare's stomach began to rise. "You're torturing yourself. It's punishment, isn't it? Punishment that's unearned. You cannot save others if you sacrifice yourself."

Cesare swallowed the singe in his throat.

"You're wasting to nothing," Lissandri asserted. He sat cross-armed, holding Cesare with a frowning regard, yet Cesare *saw* it in his eyes once more, clear as cut glass. *Fear.* "You were seventeen last time this happened," he added darkly, and Cesare's stomach keeled.

Seventeen was when he stuck needles into his arms within the valves of Vencenza's slums. Cesare still hadn't a clue what'd been in those syringes but, in all its harlequin glitter, injustice ruled this callous world. Narcotics accentuated the colours, dulled the edges of agony, *left you beaten to near-death and begging for mercy once petered out.*

After getting clean—those crushing months when every day ached worse than bone-scarring burns—Cesare promised himself and the twins he would never, *ever* again repeat such self-obliteration.

In the end his '*never*, ever *again*' had been a lie.

He'd never once felt a belonging to his body, to this plane of existence. He clashed with it—a force trapped in skin; an abstract concept chained to physics; a wraith possessing an effigy of itself. Far too often did he entertain the wish of those needles filthening his flesh and ridding him of an arm. Of cutting from his body his own limbs just to be lighter, *less*, closer to the immaterial idea he felt himself to be.

He judged himself sick in the head for such thoughts—a contradiction to the instrument, the weapon, he had made his being into for this revolution's sake. *A hypocrite through, and through, and through.*

His effigy was damned.

A scrape of a chair's legs against floorboards swiftly followed a waft of rose perfume, and Cesare was flung back to reality.

Into the seat beside him plopped Giorgianna, face blenched as if she'd seen the most horrific apparition.

"Are you 'right?" Lissandri questioned, brow strained.

She blinked at him with eyes circular as moons. "Yes!" She flinched at herself, shook her head, cleared her throat. "*I*-I'll tell you later. That was…" her lips pressed together for a moment, "an encounter?"

Cesare's eyes narrowed at the woman. He knew Giorgianna wasn't lying when she said '*I'll tell you later*'. She would. And that was more than he could promise those he loved. And so he envied her.

Anukka approached their table. "My husband should be here—"

"Now." Iyad fleeted in out of the ether, catching Anukka's shoulders and pressing a kiss on her cheek. The woman's pout blurred to a rosen smile as her fingers skimmed the bleached hair brushing Iyad's collarbones.

The dockmaster adjusted his sidriyeh, then pulled over a chair to sit, a stony regard levelled at Cesare. "Well?"

"You and Donatello ought to get friendly," Cesare declared in hushed Calvessi. "He's one of our best bets, *especially* with his links to rebels in The Trabeculae. And *nothing* if not a competent gossip." Giorgianna passed a disoriented look to Lissandri who signed '*it's a sailor cant*' on The Fingers. "He and I haven't convened in a week. Long overdue."

Iyad angled his head up at his wife.

Anukka's gaze was bitter, her teeth clenching and unclenching. In the end, she locked her arms tight together and rolled her eyes away.

Iyad met Cesare's gaze with steel. "So be it, Agostini." He leaned forward, voice dropping as he returned to Faustinian: "Vencenza's starting to stink of the same shit as Sancta Maria."

Cesare raised an eyebrow. "Elaborate?"

The dockmaster began fiddling with his pipe much to Anukka's protests of '*not in my tavèrna!*' followed by spates of Ahărla hisses.

"You've seen the military checkpoints. The way the votaries and the Clergy flock these streets." Iyad inhaled kretek smoke. "Whatever skulduggery is going on within the inner circle, I *bet* the zealot Abelli is a piece. Their dogma's rearing its foul head. Only a matter of time until it talks and bites."

Giorgianna expelled a '*hm*'. "Abelli never ceases being a motif…"

Anukka's gaze pinned Cesare. "Fundamentalist doctrine at his disposal would have De Tullia categorically inexorable—the Governor has never skimped on an opportunity to cosy up to the High Priest."

Indeed. De Tullia and his dominion needed to be undone regardless of what it took. Regardless of what it *cost*. No false semblance of 'peace' or 'order' was worth the lives of a thousand innocents, and nothing was worth more than freedom when freedom stood as essential as life itself.

Cesare rose, the twins and Giorgianna following. "Many thanks, al-Uwwād. Mişşi."

"I shall see you out," offered Anukka, folding into a triangle a large white shawl embellished with crimson geometry and draping it across her shoulders.

The battlefield that was the cold starscape glimmered with corpses of luminaries, the docks deserted as a graveyard.

"Barsotti expects us soon," Cesare informed Giorgianna.

Lissandri cracked his shoulders, flinging a whetted regard at Cesare, then Giorgianna. "Anything short of remaining safe and returning in one piece is not an option, got it?"

Giorgianna laughed like a warbling mountain brook. "Yes, mother." She hugged Lissandri, the tinker surrendering a smiling eye roll.

Eligio's fretting gaze found Cesare. "If things begin looking even a tad dubious—just get out. *Please*. We'll find another way."

Will we?

Heart heavy, Cesare wrapped his arms around the twins' shoulders, pressing their foreheads to his temples before they departed for *Antigone*.

"Cesare," Anukka called.

The woman stood a few paces away along the docks, her gaze nocking a poison arrow at him. "A word." *Not a request.*

Cesare turned to Giorgianna. "Go on ahead."

Lips tense, she tangled her ankles for a few moments before grudgingly flitting around the corner of *Three Suns*.

Anukka's arms were crossed when Cesare beheld her.

She walked past him towards *Three Suns*'s porch, halting a short distance away, the two of them back-to-back. Cesare heard a lighter open, silence dragging out yet further.

"*Three Suns* was established by my kukaçej,[20] Mikvor," Anukka opened. "In Ahăruj, we lived during a time of political turbulence. The reason I'm here at all is owed to kukaçej and kukamaj[21] wishing a safer life for me and my little jămăk,[22] what with our parents' deaths at the hands of the monarchy. My jămăk died at sea. Scurvy. The irony is that, *now*, Ahăruj prospers, whilst Vencenza is in decay."

A pause puffed by.

"I tell you this so you are reminded, after reading *all* that theory of yours, that the reality of revolution is *nothing* like cape-flailing lionhearts and children playing war. To put an end to an order is to put an end to your humanity, to become your cause's weapon." *Its instrument.* "So, upon my parents' graves, let me repeat to you. Revolution is not victory. Revolution is *death*."

> *'Would you be willing to live*
> *with the weight of a thousand*
> *lost souls on your shoulders?'*

Cesare's eye trained across the water on the acropolis that was the government building, aglow beneath moonlight like bones bleached in a carnivore's stomach. Hatred guttered in his hollow crucible. Hatred for all that spider reaped. Every innocent person he twisted. Imprisoned. Murdered. Every life he reduced to ruin.

> *I am willing to be the final one to*
> *crush this miserable edifice.*

"I have lost too much," Anukka continued, her tone a spiked mace. "Yet I have gained an equal amount in return. If *you* are the reason I lose my husband, Cesare, the reason my son loses a father, I will cut your head from your torso and feed you to the worms of the necropolis."

She slammed shut the door of her tavèrna, smoke left haunting the night.

---

[20] *koo-kah-CHEH'y*; Ahărla for 'maternal grandfather'.
[21] *koo-kah-MAH'y*; Ahărla for 'maternal grandmother'.
[22] *yawh-MAWK*; Ahărla for 'sister'.

SCENE IX

THE REALITY OF
THE RULERS

Giorgianna

A BROKEN PIECE OF BLACK HULL GLEAMED above the entrance to *Stalker's Barge*. Discordant music and dark radiance pulsated from behind an ajar door, sickly oxblood glow dripping across the dead-end alley.

Cesare and I tucked ourselves away in a nearby nook guarded by a misplaced wrought-iron gate.

Rutilence diffused across Cesare's pensive features; his manifold earrings coruscated. In a strange way, red suited him, and with the curlicued graffiti illustrating the weathered baroque walls for a backdrop, Cesare's visage became every edge how I had imagined The Bauta to look beneath his outlawed mask. *Do you know that beside you each and every star extinguishes?*

I passed back to him the sigarétta we shared—the final one either of us had. Perhaps the miniscule gesture was the sole intimacy we were destined to share.

After everything, I didn't know why any splinter of me wished for intimacy from *him*, but I would be a liar if I said that his fingertips hadn't burned imprints into my skin. That I didn't yearn for a second longer beneath that forsaken rain. That in my worst dreams I didn't see dark hair and eyes reflecting back inferno.

Maybe I was content with the moniker of 'liar'.

I dragged sugary smoke, barring its path into my lungs. "Did Libitina take Nara and Eluisa?"

"Yes. I ensured they were treated with due care." Cesare accepted back the sigarétta. "Why did you run off?"

"My amorphous premonition proved correct: one of the three remaining associates of Davide's had been sent after Elenedda."

Cesare exhaled a grey plume. "You said some of the scars on your knuckles were from her."

My stomach kicked. *You remembered that?*

"Punishments for cello mistakes." I plucked back the diminishing sigarétta and puffed a silvery halo. "Supposedly on account of imperfect recitals reminding her of my father." The justification tasted foul. *What possesses someone to rationalise so?*

My own question hardened into a blade and turned on me.

Cesare's eye flared. "And she took it out on *you*?"

"The apple doesn't fall far from the tree." I handed him the sigarétta.

Cesare's fingers hesitated mind-air before pinching it, his brows shuttered low. "I'm sorry?"

"*I* am." I swallowed the heart sitting in my throat. "I treated you no better." I shook my head. "You deserved none of my awful words, or anything I ever did. I am so sorry, Cesare."

Perhaps, I really *was* the crook.

His suffocating scrutiny held mine, studying it as if for a flaw. A nick. *A lie?* Then, Cesare's gaze dropped. "I never cared, vólto," he said glumly and cradled the sigarétta between his lips, inhaling the remainder of the tobacco into his lungs as—I'd gleaned—he often did to unravel the unbearable tightness in his chest. As he had been doing almost every time he smoked over the recent month. *Did you* really *not? Or do you* also *wear a mask when your true face grows too unguarded?*

A silhouette cloaked by a dark dove mantle slipped into the tavèrna, cagey and alert.

Donning colombínae—Cesare's black streaked with glittering shadows, mine with realgar roses curving around the left eye, a glass bead like a sanguine drop suspended at my cheek—we slunk into the goëtic lambency and mu'assel smoke of *Stalker's Barge*. Its living flesh recoiled against our footsteps.

Amidst the undulation of spectral forms, Barsotti entered a private booth.

We followed, weaving between patrons dressed in bronze-inlaid plague doctor masks and taffeta gowns enormous as cakes yet deep as peacock feathers.

The booth was a wall-sweeping box of black wood wrapped in vinaceous velvet, a narrow ebony table drawn across its interior and leather seats ensconced on either side. An hourglass-shaped mirror rose at the wall opposing the door, reflection inverted along the horizontal plane. Alchemical lights shaped into black hands cradling bleeding glass hearts flanked it.

Cesare and I sat across from the Minister of Emissaries.

He lowered his hood and swept a salt-and-pepper braid over his shoulder, his pewter colombína lustrous beneath alchemy.

Cesare cocked his head with a slicing smirk. "A pleasure to convene again, nirô javêl."

Barsotti's eyes sized us up, brown as the earth, an icy blue shard slitting his left iris. Then, he lifted his thin hands. *'It would bring me greater easement to conduct this rèquiem's meeting in verbal silence.'*

Cesare leaned against the seat's back. *'If it pleases you.'*

The Adviser's gaze steeled. *'I have informed the Governor of your arrival, and he has agreed to host.'*

My eyes flung wide, darting to Cesare whose own face was wrought with shock. *'How?'* I questioned.

'If you wish to infiltrate the government building and survive,' Barsotti addressed me, *'I counsel that you pose as my fraternal niece, Salomè.*[23] *The reason being that she lived in Ithilwen.'*

'Lived?'

He hesitated for a juncture in time. *'She is deceased.'*

"What?" I exclaimed. "You want—" I caught myself, *'You suppose I do nothing short of ripping the face off a woman's corpse and wearing it?'*

Barsotti bestowed a pitiless regard. *'What nobler means do you counsel, then?'*

I met Cesare's frown as if we might conjure up an answer.

I could not. Evidently, neither could he.

'Salomè passed three years ago,' the Adviser continued. *'How old are you?'*

'Twenty-two.'

'She would have been twenty.' My stomach only tangled tighter. She would have been just a girl. *'Do you have an adequate means of concealing the principal identifiers of your person?'*

'Flesh tailoring.'

'Salomè was somewhat shorter than you—' as many tended to be *'—her hair was darker, skin paler, eyes blue, features rather dainty by comparison. These are not crucial requirements, as De Tullia has only ever heard of her, but you and I appear far from alike, and your hair and looks are notable, which may prove a detriment to your safety.'* That repulsive epithet of *'winning doll'* imparted on me by Madáma Irene Falco crawled down my back. I would spill that martinet's blood upon this city yet. *'Not least given that both your parents have been detained by the state.'*

'Where in Ithilwen did Salomè reside?' I asked to stave off nausea.

'Illýris—the capital. She was a law student and highly concerned with Balinori affairs. Thus, it will serve you well to acquire rudimentary Ithilweni knowledge, as well as to acquaint yourself with the politics of the Western Isle and the culture and history of Ithilwen.'

---

[23] *sah-loh-MEH*

'*Duly noted.*' I feared Rosalia might soon be not the only one pestering Libitina.

'*I told the Governor that you have already set out and should arrive in a week's time.*'

A gale of sickness hit me.

"I'm *sorry?*" Cesare bit. "On what rationale?"

'*To ensure he complied. If he thought you were yet to set sail, it may have given him greater incentive to decline. This way, his presented alternatives were far fewer.*'

I looked to Cesare, but I found there nothing to return fire to the Minister of Emissaries with; nothing to offer by way of an alternative. We were so horribly short on chances.

'*If this enterprise succeeds,*' continued Barsotti, '*your commute in and out of the government building, should you require it, can be accomplished via passages within and beneath the edifice.*'

'*I'd discovered them,*' signed Cesare. *The day Manuele almost took you from us...* His expression steeled. '*I want our people everywhere in and around the government building; eyes and ears and couriers within not only the primary edifice, but the basilica and the House of Judgement. I require a continuous intelligence stream.*'

Clario's eyebrows knitted. '*I can accept but a few informants. Too many will aggravate suspicion. I can assure you that most of my Guárdia are allies against the Governor.*' From a pouch tethered to his waist, Barsotti produced a scroll circleted with a brass bracelet. The two of us perused the graceful cursive within. '*Compiled by my Centúrion, these are all of the Guardíi who can be trusted. Forty-three in sum.*'

Rolling up the paper, Cesare tucked it into his jacket. "So be it." He sounded the least convinced I had ever heard him be.

'*Signorína Damiani,*' Barsotti gestured. '*Per upper-class Ithilweni praxis, you will be required two guards and an individual playing the role of a personal servant.*'

I didn't think I could feel more repulsion within myself. And yet, in that moment, knowing I'd be forced not only to don the flesh of the dead, but do so beset in the silk and jewels of the ruling class, my soul began to wither. Sarnai had insisted on bearing me company in the ministerial house, but *Gods*, I could not suffer hers laying down her life for me.

Barsotti gripped mine and Cesare's gazes with startling steadfastness. '*Do you accept what I put forth?*'

We had no choice.

"Yes."

'*Very well. I shall inform Governor De Tullia of Salomè's intended arrival and relay the outcome as soon as feasible.*' Barsotti's chin tilted starward, gaze resolute. '*How do you wish to seal this?*'

Cesare's head tipped; eye blazed like a cat's in the night. I knew the answer before he mused, "Blood is worth diamonds."

Barsotti's expression wavered. '*A blood promise.*'

Well versed in the lawless culture, I see.

Cesare's arched eyebrow ticked up. '*Qualms?*'

The Adviser frowned. '*Reservations.*'

Tension gnawed like termites at the ambience.

'*Upper forearm, near the elbow,*' I suggested.

The Minister of Emissaries considered me for another excruciating stretch of moments before meeting Cesare's expectant behold.

"Do we have a deal?" asked Cesare.

Barsotti stalled for the final time, then nodded. "Indeed."

Blades drew.

Blood doused the black table, iron dripping into the air.

And the deed was done.

The deal was sealed.

Yet more blood to never wash clean.

And a promise of fields bathed in it to come.

I will drown your wretched world.

Clutching a handkerchief to his cut, Clario looked at Cesare who remained nonchalant as ever in pain's company. '*There is no doubt in my mind that you have questions, Bauta.*'

Cesare leaned forward. '*I want details regarding interrelationships within the inner circle.*'

The Adviser licked his lips, hissing when he checked under his handkerchief. '*There is little of the current inner workings that I am privy to, I fear. However, you might be interested in a detail regarding the Minister of Scholars.'* Curiosity nudged me. *'Ilenia was, at one point, involved with people in oldtown, some of whom trickled down to the Antrum and Smugglers' District.'*

Glàvca, the innkeeper in the Antrum, mentioned once that Ilenia's name had floated in via smugglers. None of the Hydras knew anything, but perhaps *this* was the reason for the whispers.

Barsotti addressed me: *'Do you recall a woman by the name of Calliupa Soriano who was executed alongside your father?'*

I bridled my ire, reigning it in until my teeth screeched. *'She was a lavìre I would see on occasion,'* I forced myself to sign.

'Ilenia and Calliupa had been friends,' claimed Barsotti. *'De Tullia learned of this and imprisoned Ilenia under the threat of expulsion from the ministerial council, public humiliation, even potential execution. To protect herself, I advised that Ilenia hand over someone she knew—a lower ossíi. I did this upon word from Veronesi that condemning an old contact would better Ilenia's chances of survival. A life for a life.'*

'A life of the downtrodden for that of a spoon-fed aristocrat!' My rage didn't capitulate, didn't dim. Their own people held so little value to the powers that be who remained content knowing the ugliest atrocities befell the slums, who were ultimately *responsible* for it, yet who sent their vultures to tear meat from our already gnarled hides all the same. Who locked us in with our oppressors through checkpoints, curfews, threats.

'I never deemed it correct, only necessary. Calliupa was captured and tortured for information, but was not found to know anything—was not an insurgent of any sort. Her execution granted Ilenia a pardon.' My stomach surged into my throat. *'However, De Tullia now hangs this over Ilenia's head, with the compounding fact of her imprisonment besmirching her reputation. Though I am unsure what transpired in The Trabeculae to prompt Calliupa's odd conduct the day of her execution.'*

'Forgive me if I have little sympathy for the tarnishing of the Magister's precious reputation when an innocent woman was sacrificed to preserve it,' I hissed.

'I know,' said Clario. *'I do not expect sympathy nor praise.'* It took squeezing my fists until my palms all but bled to not rip into him. *'De*

Tullia and Abelli appear close; on account of their similarly puritanical convictions, I suspect, but am unable to confirm. Giordano Veronesi is a mystery. He favours his House of Judgement to the acropolis.'

If there was any other Minister destined to die by my hands, it was the vile death-dealer Veronesi.

'*Additionally,*' Barsotti forced my attention back on his hands, '*Basilio still appears in the governing house.*'

Owing to the Lanuzas' tight-knit bond with the Ministry through their surveillance activity, my surprise was naught. My spirit of inquiry grew more restless.

'*That is all,*' the Adviser signed the fateful three words. '*Once again, I shall extend the necessary information regarding Salomè to the Governor.*'

Cesare stood up with a tongue-click, his sudden voice jolting me, "Our gratitude knows no bounds, signór." He slit a nasty simper.

The Adviser skimmed his fingers by his chest. "Dél'ì lùtius e vísus benedétti."

Before we took our wordless exeunt, I loaded into my gunshot gaze all the contempt seething within me—aimed for Clario Barsotti. *Your hands are no less sullied.*

In the time we lost at *Stalker's Barge*, the star-pricked heavens had readied to weep.

I turned to face Cesare.

He returned my look, and we gazed at each other in shellshock amidst the spired dark buildings leaning into the narrow alley of Vencenza's oldtown.

"We're going in," said Cesare—almost a mumble. As if the words were uttered to pinch himself out of a dream.

I blinked as a cold droplet shattered on my cheekbone. "We are…"

Another moment lapsed between us until, with a huff, a halting smile broke through Cesare's countenance in a flash of lightning, and my own features yielded to a matching expression—as if earth struck by levin and split apart.

"And how much was this blood worth?" He grasped my shoulders. Our footsteps began to meander aimlessly about as half-hysteria struck us restless.

I effervesced, gripping the lapels of Cesare's jacket. "*Anything* to see this empire toppled and bloodline decimated."

His eye glittered with nebulae. An abyss. "So you may drown this wretched world."

I grabbed his wind-carved face. "And you may eat the flesh of *kings*!" Nausea and a thrill warred in my belly, threatening to bring up my guts as I all but twirled away with nowhere else to expel my moria before halting face-to-face with Cesare once more.

He gazed back at me with a realisation of some sort, expression suddenly drawn and strained.

My own face fell into a frown, eyes skimming his features, and I gleaned in them the lines of something like regret. Like guilt. Like pain.

"Cesare?"

He bit down on his cheek, dodging my scrutiny.

Then, he turned and walked down the ginnel towards its exit.

Scene X

Magnum Opus

Giordano | Eligio | Ygąl

THE MINISTER OF JUDGEMENT rarely frequented the basilica besides on weekly congregations stipulated by the Governor to attend. After all, the judgement of man lay solely in the hands of men—Giordano Veronesi failed to see why supreme entities should wish to inconvenience themselves with the trivialities of humanity.

Sa Basílica del Illuterixióne e Benefácio Vísus cantillated with spectral choirs, each pianissimo liturgical note a spirit to haunt the walls.

Around the Grand Judge, The Limbus of the basilica curved into a vault, slits in the fresco-painted dome, inlaid with glass, filtering pearlescent moonlight as it broke through the nimbose sky. An oculus wreathed in embellished gold gazed from the back wall into the chancel below, serving as a conduit for columns of purified light into the basilica's nave through the hours of the sun.

The Limbus of the church was reputedly a region of liminality between the material sphere and the limitless spiritual realms above the firmament where the Divine Faces and their Arcónti dwelled in unknowable incorruptibility.

Giordano's ice-pale eyes traversed the aurated frescos, yet his mind tethered not to the Gods as they ought to, but to the recent trials conducted in his House of Judgement.

Trials over emotional transgression.

His hoary eyebrows knitted—the stress of his line of work greyed all his once-dark hair at merely fifty-two years of age.

The cases had been dubious. Laughter reported by neighbours. An angry outburst at a lapidarium. Altercations between lower ossíi and the soldiers stationed at checkpoints. Some harmless adolescent giggling.

Of course, the law was the law, and it required upholding, but was such crude and unremedied sentencing not likely to beget moral qualms regardless of what sophistry justified its implementation? Was it not unethical to punish *children*? Was emotion not an intrinsic fragment of the unfortunate human condition?

Never matter. It was Giordano's duty as the Grand Judge to be the hand of justice for the state. His quandaries were antithetical to the order of the governorate.

Veronesi folded his thin white hands, eyes fixed upon the dome of The Limbus. "Aísne Faciáe, praemùnivit am no'áltri potíri." *If you are there to listen at all.*

"The harbinger of judgement cometh to be judged." A voice of dark gold and honeyed venom spilled across ouro-veined marble.

The heavy train of Giordano's ink-black judge regalia rustled as he turned.

High Priest Benetto Abelli's footsteps patted quieter than rain as they approached, an endless dalmatic embroidered with gilt and rubies susurrating like the thrum of bright ichor along the floor, bound by a gold cincture at their waist. From a dramatically-projecting triangular shoulder piece cascaded an incarnadine cape, the two diagonal peaks of their tall headpiece dipping into a smooth central concavity. A burnished gold aperúcca, lips red, masked their face. Giordano had already forgotten what the Minister of Churches looked like beneath.

Benetto paused by his side. "The firmament weepeth." Their gloved hands folded. "May this be not a woeful auspice, but an ablution upon the hylic flesh confining us."

"Domínie Abelli." Giordano nodded deeply.

"Giúdice Veronesi." Benetto returned the gesture. "What bringeth thee to our House of Gods upon this rèquiem? It is ordinarily Adviser Barsotti whom we come upon in The Limbus at such hour."

Giordano gazed at the frescos. "Even the godless may, upon strange compulsion, be stirred to pay the deities rare patronage."

"Thou remain chained to misled faith?"

Giordano knew the scriptures. Knew that the incongruence of his assumed pnèuma—'*soul*'—with the corporeal realm should be within his most acute awareness in the sacred Limbus. That said 'soul's' hankering for the spiritual plane ought to be profound and illimitable. Yet, he had never experienced anything of the sort. All he did was find himself staring at impressionist renderings of sky and song, a sight he could with equal ease view in a secular museum.

"My only faith is justice," Giordano asserted.

"Such thee profess, yet thou art here," Abelli contended. "Thou art conflicted."

"The judgement of life and death falls into my hands. The potential dissolution of an existence is mine to decide."

"But *is* it thine?"

Veronesi met Abelli's eyes, black as a starless new moon night.

It wasn't seldom that the Minister of Justice pondered upon the extent of his authority. How much power did he truly wield when the final judgement was bound to, with rare fail, be Crescenzo's? The man whose position Giordano himself had once vied for? The position Crescenzo killed for?

Abelli's bottomless eyes rose to the frescos, yet they looked *beyond*. As if they could gaze beyond the firmament. Into the spiritual realm. "Ómne eráte ílus, e fai'ám itèrum."[24]

---

[24] '*All were one, and will be again.*'

"Rare, you interrupt visitors to The Limbus," noted Giordano. "Clario never speaks of such praxis. To what do I owe the divergent treatment?"

"Far more fascination to take with su minístro de giudício than su minístro de emissaríi."

Giordano bristled. "What do you want, Abelli?"

"We desiderate to attain our magnum opus again, and deeply bewail the loss of previous iterations; such pure and faultless constructions." The High Priest raised their elegant hands Godsward. "Our confined spirits longeth to know the reality of our Divines, to transcend the skin of our material sphere and these tarnished hylic shells wrought of flesh. One is unworthy of the Divine Faces' totality within such based assemblies. Purity of emotion is the utmost rectitude. To express worldly and immodest passions—see evil, utter vice, think transgression—is to subject oneself to Arcóntial authority, for it is *they* who tarnish the impeccable chrysalides and faces bestowed upon us by the upper Gods, but it is within *our* power to deny ourselves the besmirching temptations of the lower Arcónti."

Abelli's arms lowered to their sides. Nullified eyes ingested Veronesi as the High Priest versed: "Dost thou know the illimitable dimensions of the transcendental condition upon the expunging of the defected mind?"

"Why are you telling me this?" *Incomprehensible nonsense!*

"Thou hold far more sway over De Tullia than thou thyself dost realise." Pressing their palms to their chest, Abelli dipped their head and swept out of The Limbus without a parting prayer.

Giordano gazed pensively upon the lines of his palm, a twitch of mirth pricking the corner of his mouth. *Contraire.*

RAIN FELL INTO THE SEA BEYOND THE WINDOW, running along the glass in sluggish rivulets. Eligio thought they looked like tear streaks.

Art supplies lay idle on his table and the clock ticked through the minutes whilst he simply watched the rain, head leaned back against the window frame. Acrylics and verdure perfumed his room, paintings mounting wooden walls and potted plants hunching in dusted corners.

"*Lạlậ!*" Lissandri's voice came. Ậbạdil; their mother's language. When Eligio looked, his twin stood in the doorway, holding a pair of handleless clay wine cups he'd no doubt pinched off of Korneli. The terracotta kulhạṛ set he loved had perished with *The Sunrise*—he would go to immense lengths to not be forced to throw it away. "How did you manage to disappear out of sight like that?" He joined Eligio at the table.

"I just needed air," Eligio replied in Faustinian. Absent. Not quite thinking through his response.

Lissandri's face turned crestfallen. "You barely speak Ậbạdil to me."

Guilt thorned Eligio. "I sometimes think I'm not very good at it anymore." Yet he replied in Ậbạdil.

He'd always been the one at his mạti's feet whilst Lissandri was such the ạbậ's boy, and so Eligio thought it would make him invincible to forgetting. To loss. Only to find himself complacent whilst Lissandri strove to preserve. It embarrassed Eligio to misspeak, to mispronounce or use the wrong word, and so he tried less and less. He'd been so preoccupied with aesthetics that he neglected the material. *Maybe I'm something of a prideful bastard of my own.*

Lissandri pushed one of the cups towards Eligio. "Elaịchi chạ." A wry expression. "I made sure to put as little cardamom as possible in yours."

Liquid the colour of butterscotch rippled within, emanating sweetness the way the sun emanates warmth. Eligio had sworn off any and all meat after laying eyes on the horror of the *Curios*—repulsed by the mere idea of dead flesh, but *milk* he was still willing to have if only in the form of kulfi (but who was there to make it for them without mạti?) or Lissandri's beloved chạ. Eligio cradled the cup by the cooler rim, a smile cracking through the frost that had become his countenance. "Tậe minnạt vậṛạn."

Lissandri bumped his brother's shoulder. "See? Chạ is the smile-maker."

Eligio couldn't stave off the frown that swiftly overcame him. "I don't exactly want to smile a whole lot right now, Andri."

A moment of quiet lapsed by.

"I know, Eli. We have to keep living though. Even if the most we can do is try. And to help each other through it. '*We spot because, by doing so, we ensure another person lives*', right?"

"Don't quote Fabio to me," snapped Eligio.

Lissandri beheld him sadly. "Li…"

"No, Sar." He sipped the chạ, letting its smoothness coat his tongue and soothe him, then placed the cup down. His hands wanted to fidget. To claw at something. He inhaled sharply instead. "I don't understand why God was allowed to have them for the rest of eternity, yet we couldn't for even a few more years." A sting hit his eyes. Their parents were their sanctuary when the enormity of the world grew too great, and now they were just… *missing*. "We will never again come home to them. They aren't there anymore, and neither is home."

Lissandri sipped his cardamom tea before finally turning to his eldest. "Remember when we spent seven months in Gwạtishep?" Lissandri's voice came gently. Almost cautiously.

Gwạtishep was their mạti's ancestral township. '*Windy Tributary*'. And it was precisely that. A little village on a little river.

When Eligio was small, he held in his mind such a frankly ridiculous view of Dayậrabạd. An abstract land of *things*. And he *was* just a child, but he was an *Âbạdil* child, even if by half and a sea away. Perhaps that was Eligio's preoccupation with aesthetics manifesting yet again.

"I miss dancing chạp in a circle with all the villagers," said Eligio, imbibing more tea. His maternal home proved so much more than either of the brothers could ever imagine.

"Me too." Lissandri put down his half-drained cup. He still wore his ragam and chamkạli nearly always. "Do you think we'll ever see it again?"

"Only wậju[25] is still alive," Eligio spoke half to himself. He didn't really know how to think of the future anymore.

Lissandri leaned his head against Eligio's shoulder. "I think we will."

And the pair fell into silence, only the rain whispering and the clock ticking around them.

---

[25] Âbạdil for '*grandfather*', typically used as an address.

Eligio always considered the pair of them to be a creature split in twain; forced to live as two. They didn't need to speak.

His youngest stirred. "This isn't… I don't really know when else to give this to you but…" He reached into the deep pocket of his worker's trousers and pulled out a tiny, snake-green phial of white capsules. "Ces wanted me to pass this on to you." He placed it on the table. "It's from Ygạl."

Nausea spilled oily and cold into Eligio's gut. "I think I'll call it for the night." He took to gathering items for bathing. Bile burned the back of his throat.

"Since when do you sleep at a reasonable time?"

"Since *you've* started keeping awake into the late hours."

A scoff. "What, you have a Danilo double who sings you to sleep every night?"

With a tense smile and overcast eyes, Eligio leaned down to kiss his brother on either cheek, "Bon rèquiem, lạlậ," and left.

YGẠL'S EYELIDS WEIGHED A BOULDERSTONE EACH, urging her to lie in the oudh-scented silk beside his beloved and slumber.

Instead, Isaia yet again barged into their quarters with intel gathered at Damiani and Agostini's meeting with the Adviser.

"All's to be relayed during a final conclave at The Morettae's armoury to-morrow," said Isaia. "Şirîn and Fēngnà are supposed to make an appearance at *Antigone* to-night."

Ygạl smiled to herself, wearily yet truly.

At six years of age, Ygạl had gotten snatched up by a Rŭnethãri slave vessel off the coast of Sa'āli Den in the Hātif Sea. Rŭnethãri ships prowled the coasts of the world and sought two types of captives. One: slaves. Two: 'citizens'. Rŭnethãre was a sprawling city state carved into a near-uninhabitable coastal edge of Isatōnia, between Miəkah and Vyrl'išā (why else would such a physical chasm exist between the two nations and their cultures be so disparate?). Within its vast borders and infrastructure, however, Rŭnethãre was scarcely populated and Ũ'rŭne'lãri[26] were few. So, the royal family would send ships out to kidnap people of all grains and force them into a life as 'citizens' of Rŭnethãre. Not slavery, per se, but surely imprisonment.

That *second* sort of captive was what Ygạl found themselves being twenty-four years ago.

On their way to Rŭnethãre, a storm caught the ship and smashed it to smithereens at the mouth of Dragon's Bight, near the string of islands dubbed Dropped Coins. Ygạl washed up alone on a tiny rock outcrop among bellic ocean waves where, by some blessing, she was spotted by a Vencenzani smuggler ship. The band aboard it was The Grey Pearls, its captain at the time a hard woman named Mèngyáo[27] who picked Ygạl up without dallying. Ygạl, in mere minutes, was thick as thieves with Mèngyáo's granddaughter. Fēngnà. Many years later, she met Sabinus Venator, the previous Dóminus of The Boars, and she and Fēngnà grew apart, yet never with bad blood. Fēngnà had even gifted Ygạl her well-worn zhĭjiǎtào in their time apart.

"I should like to make my own appearance, then," declared Ygạl.

"Itxaro returned from The Stags' district," informed the eavesdropper.

Ygạl's eyes whirled. "Here the fuck we go…"

"Vitture is willing to grant us an audience."

Ygạl all but jumped. "Come again…"

Vitture *never* granted audiences, *never* communicated with other cadres, bar Lucanus'. Ygạl had only sent an envoy to cover all grounds, expecting nothing from the Stag Dóminus.

Isaia produced an envelope from his satchel. "Letter of confirmation handed to Itxaro; penned by Vitture himself."

Ygạl tore the letter from its pouch and dove into the text.

It must have been years since they had last laid eyes on Vitture's penmanship, its painstakingly scrupulous print and Iutulicano dialect recognisable anywhere.

---

[26] The demonym for the iridites of Rŭnethãre.

[27] 夢瑤; *MUHNG-yah-oh*

'… *THUSLY, I REQUEST*
A RETURN LETTER FOR
DATE AND TIME
FINALISATION.

~DÓMINUS VITTURE MUSCARÀ
OF THE STAGS'

Ygal placed the letter down with a strange caution. "Unforeseen…"

Isaia folded his arms, expression dull as dust. "You *could* look happier."

"I *would* be if Vitture wasn't an ally of Lucanus." If Muscarà was willing to cooperate, where did that leave the Dóminus of the infamous Cyclopes, especially considering that spectacle with Mair? "But I fear we're short on chances," Ygal's manicured fingers rapped on the desk, "so I'm willing to take this one." She retrieved a blank sheet and a fountain pen. *Let this not be a bad omen.*

SCENE XI

A PATH OF BRAMBLE

Cesare | Giorgianna | Cesare | Fabio | Giorgianna

CESARE QUITTED HIS QUARTERS at the very aft of the ship's hold and routed six doors down the dim corridor to the bathing chamber.

He swerved sharply, staggering to a halt on the threshold.

"Do you have hands?" snapped Giorgianna from her spot in the bathtub, pinning Cesare with a flushed glare. "Knock!"

Damp curls draped in swathes down her dainty chest, the disturbed water floating atop itself rose petals, her arms submerged. A petal was pasted like a red heart on Giorgianna's cheek, another one clinging to droplet-flecked skin beneath her collarbone.

He couldn't remember the last time he soaked fully-dressed in a near-boiling tub as he would back at *The Sunrise*. It no longer felt right when there were so many more people and so much less by way of resources. He didn't quite want to be grounded anymore, either. He wanted to be immaterial.

Cesare crossed the chamber towards a treen cabinet, drawing a deeper breath once those eyes no longer blazed in his field. "Oughtn't occupy yourself too deeply now, signorína." He infused his tone with all the arch theatrics he could. "Guests may soon be expected." His fidgeting hands rummaged through the scores of tubes and flasks until he finally sighted the glint of scissors on the nethermost shelf, swiping them.

On the nightstand, by the flickering candelabra's side, rested Giorgianna's baselard and a whetstone, her rapier propped against it.

"I shall be doing as I see fit, *signór*," she retorted.

With a secretive smirk, Cesare routed for the exit, leaning against the doorway, and clicked his tongue with a nod of the chin at the weapons. "Errands to run?"

Giorgianna drew a quiver of scowls. "Are you intending to leave or do you want to get in?"

Her hair was unbound and wild—a free thing, the rose-and-eye tattoo painted upon her skin seamlessly entwining with her graceful form. *You are so easy to write music about.*

Thick brows dipped down, a slim hand toying with a curl, and Cesare had never so deeply ached for another's fingers to run through his hair and along his skin. For his own to, even for an infinitesimal moment, do the same through hers.

"I like red on you," mused Cesare, tossing the scissors in the air and twirling them though his electrified fingers once he caught them, and took his leave.

After everything between them, there should be not a single shred of him which desired her. Yet, in the red light of *Stalker's Barge* she was breathtaking and he almost, *almost,* succumbed to the madness he knew he had a proclivity for. His momentary folly had been a testament to it. A warning.

Cesare squeezed his hands tight enough to break its nails, turning a corner on his thoughtless way to the hold, and stumbled when his body collided with another's.

"Watch your fucking path, freak," a woman barked at him.

The woman was Lorita.

Cesare passed back, treating her sweltering gaze with coldness. He found he couldn't stand her touch. "Will you be bringing such pleasantries to our meeting with the band leaders to-night?"

Her upper lip jerked. "I'll not bring anything; I'll not be there."

Cesare frowned. "What is your problem?"

Lorita assumed her customary crossed arms and lour. "I'll never forgive you for conspiring with a Minister."

"I'm not supplicating my sins' absolution before you when *you* conspired with *Davide*, knowing *full* well what sort of scum he was."

Lorita scoffed. "Yes, what it took the ever-intellectual Fabio *years* to realise."

"He rid of him the *second* he learned," snapped Cesare. "*You* disregarded—*enabled*—it. For fucking what?"

"Just like you and Curly are disregarding what Barsotti is?"

"Don't pretend we are, and don't pretend we don't know what game we play. On the other hand, what did *you* ever have? Blind faith?"

Lorita bared her teeth. "Dignity."

"Colluding with a pederast is *very* dignified, I *must* say."

Lorita mirrored his tilted head and narrowed eye, a foul smirk splitting her lips. "So is wanting to fuck a witch and a harlot."

Cesare recoiled. "What?"

"You heard me—"

"Yes, I *heard* you—what is *wrong* with you to talk like that? Have some fucking decency." Cesare *saw* the Madáma's whip, *saw* Giorgianna and Lora flinch at the woman's yell, *saw* the immeasurable horror in Giorgianna's eyes when she realised Guards were pursuing a lower ossíi. Saw her fingertip-shaped bruises.

Lorita did not falter. "I will not have my statements ethicised by an apostate."

"You were never very good at ethics either way. And you know I pray to no deity."

Lorita lifted her hands. "And look what transpired."

Anger surged inside Cesare. "You can say what you mean to my face, Lorita, I fucking dare you."

Her implication was that his heresy, his unwillingness to pray, the twins' heterodox Myseric denomination, as Lorita saw it to be, was the reason for the murder of the twins' parents and the burning of *The Sunrise*. That, somehow, praying to a demiurge would have protected them when it never, *ever* had. Cesare's every childhood plea had gone unanswered, even when he believed some deity might listen to him. It never did. And he almost lost his life just like he lost everything else.

"You don't need me to," Lorita gnashed her teeth at Cesare and stormed past.

The old timepiece read twenty-three hundred on díem lunéra.

Cesare occupied a stool at the end of a narrow little pier table positioned lengthwise along his chamber's run, a bay window gazing at the endless ocean beyond the aft situated behind him. The too-short bed he hardly used nuzzled into a nook in the far wall and right up against arguably the smallest window he'd ever seen. Giorgianna lounged on it, a tome detailing Balinori politics she'd gotten from Libitina soaking up her attention. She wore the recently-procured ensemble of a hitched skirt adorned in ruffles and a strapped crimson corset, the ruched white chemise beneath casting her into the image of a piratess. Her legs, clad in black stiletto thigh-highs, lay stacked atop each other on Lissandri's stomach whose own legs were slung onto the wall, his puffy coils hanging off the bedside.

Angling up the tarnished brass mirror Cesare snatched from Ren (to ver irritation but lack of protest), he trimmed his hair to the chin. Years of practice had made him rather proficient, and *even with the eye* he wasn't half bad.

Across the table sat Eligio, rifling through a box of *Antigone's* old art supplies. With Sarnai's help as a competent tailor, Eligio was able to sew himself a shalwar kamiz from sheets of lovat linen after his beloved sage-green iteration perished with *The Sunrise*. He had made an effort to replicate the intricate embroidery, even attempting the abhala bharat mirrorwork which once adorned his mati's periwinkle dress, but his prowess proved not yet sufficient, so the stitchwork came out plain.

Cesare's heart wrenched, his hand slipping and the scissorblades nicking his neck. He hissed, Eligio's fretting eyes immediately on him. No blood had drawn up.

"*So*," Giorgianna flipped a page, mercifully drawing attention to her crepuscular voice, "*supposedly*, Ným'natħír Lyr'è Ýlla'dăl Elthór, the iridite king of Ithilwen, and Ethelind Frederikke Strøm, the human queen of Vilhelm, are feuding over the de jure state of Raelhål[28] in northeastern Vilhelm—southeastern Ithilwen, *further* inflamed by Ným'natħír's *murder* of former Vilhelmian king, Kresten Mikkel Strøm. Ethelind attempted to marry their daughter, Rebekka Mithian, off to..." Words seemed to desert her. "Where's the footnote?" She spared a moment to search. "Ercwlff...?[29] Maddox, son of Fidelma and Rheinallt Maddox of Yrdagwlat, but that union fell through when princess Mithian disap...*peared*...?"

She flattened the book across her chest, exhaling. "And that was the introductory chapter! I dread to think what possibly awaits."

Lissandri groaned and slid off the bedside, somersaulting backward into a crouch on the floor. "It's a wonder you didn't drop asleep just recounting that." Eligio attempted to use his little twin's shoulder as a footrest in jest, receiving obscenities and a vulgar gesture in return which he took with chuckles.

Cesare passed his fingers through his now-chin-length hair.

The door barged open and in came twirling Rosalia, her knee-length dress' skirt a furry tetramorphic disk in the iridescent hues of a peacock spider's fan: curious Ithilweni garb she'd pilfered from somewhere deep inside Libitina's closet. "Whatcha doing?"

Lissandri yawned. "Receiving a political science lecture."

"Yuck."

Amidst Rosalia and the twins chatting, the corner of Cesare's view snagged on the violin case near his bed, dusty from a month gone unplayed. He couldn't bring himself to touch it.

---

[28] *RAH-ehl-hohl*; a portmanteau of Ithilweni '*raẽl*' for 'southern' and Vilhelmian '*hål*' for 'hall', specifically that of a castle. Raelhålsk is a mixed Ithilweni-Vilhelmian language spoken in Raelhål.

[29] *EH-cool-f*; '*eh*' as in '<u>err</u> on the side of caution' (British pronunciation).

"*Wait*—!" Rosalia's voice chimed through. The girl stood with the index finger of each hand raised. "You'll be *inside* the Ministers' house?"

"If all our cards fall right," said Giorgianna, then grimaced. "Clario says I need someone to play the role of my '*personal servant*' on account of some arbitrary etiquette."

"*Oh!*" Rosalia chirruped. "That can be me!"

Cesare's stomach dropped.

"*What?*" Lissandri and Giorgianna exclaimed in one voice.

"Don't be ridiculous, Rosa!" scolded Eligio.

"Why?" Rosalia shrugged. "I'm Vilhelmian, my surname *and* middle name are too, I speak the language, *and* no plot hole can be left unfilled if you say Salomè lived in Ithilwen because many Vilhelmian girls move there from Raelhål especially for that sort of work whilst speaking little to none of the iridites' language."

"Absolutely not," rebuked Giorgianna. "You cannot be mired in such mortal peril on my behalf."

Cesare's chest panged at the too-familiar sentiment.

"But I'm a good fit!" Rosalia stood firm. "*And* the correct age for a handmaiden of an Ithilweni lady—they'll pick up on such detail for sure."

"No." Cesare's declaration came down like a mallet. "This is not a game, Rosalia. None of us know if we'll even make it inside, much less out alive. You of all people will not be embroiled." He was already sending Giorgianna into the den of spiders to do his dirty work. The means to his ends be damned—he couldn't stomach another one of his famìlia being endangered in the name of his cause.

Cesare's heart only wrung harder when his eyes sought Giorgianna. A gelid torrent of regret thrust all breath from him. *Why am I doing this to you, vólto?*

But she didn't return his behold, occupied with asking Rosalia about Vilhelm who in turn took fascination with the preposterous heel of one of Giorgianna's boots, a gesture the girl was repaid for with a jesting threat of being kicked. In a moment of inattention, that massive political tome came tumbling from Giorgianna's arms and onto Lissandri's head, the tinker expelling a yelp whilst the others erupted into laughter.

Cesare's features couldn't help but soften at the smiles illuminating the faces of his most cherished. *If only I could have protected you.*

"Some folks are playing cards in the hold," Rosalia informed, hauling up the fallen book. "Ygạl's there too! Supposedly to see someone?"

"Fēng," said Cesare as he stood. His vision blacked out momentarily. Head spun. He stood fast until the darkness dissipated, clarifying: "Fēngnà of The Grey Pearls. The pair have history."

"And *I* have a history of enjoying sleep," sniped Lissandri, finally getting up off the floor and stretching his back with chondral pops, "so I shall be retiring for the eventide to the best of my capabilities given the…" an accordion gesture, "*conditions.*"

Giorgianna sighed dramatically, still stretched across Cesare's bed. "A while has passed since I've dominated a poker table."

"All right then, princess." Cesare approached her, pocketing his hands. "Get out of my bed." *I could never hope to sleep if the sheets remind me of you.*

"*You,*" she treated him to a daring look, "can *make* me."

Cesare cocked his head. "I certainly can." He whisked Giorgianna up by the elbows and swept her into his arms. She squealed with exultant laughter, head thrown back over Cesare's shoulder as he dragged her off the bed towards the centre of the room. She smelled of roses and honey like divine ambrosia, his cold flesh drinking down her warmth like water tapped from sunlight, and he almost clutched her tighter to his chest and let her endless hair consume him. *Stop!*

The abruptness with which Cesare released Giorgianna seemed to go unnoticed as she, still laughing, gained her foothold, whirling around to prod Cesare in the chest—a considerable measure taller than him owing to her heels. "Lowlife fiend."

Cesare *tsk'd.* "I don't see *myself* invading another's bed."

"*Some*one has to use it," Lissandri shouldered in, receiving an elbow to the ribs from Cesare and a titter to follow.

"Peace, children," Eligio slung his arm over his brother's shoulder and smacked Cesare lightly on the face, Rosalia at the vanguard with the enormous book in hand as the quintet quitted the bedchamber.

Upon the threshold, Giorgianna circled around Cesare, flicking his chin-length waves into his face. *"I like such hair on you,"* she whispered, beestung lips rouge-red and canted into a frolicsome smile, before twirling on ahead in a swish of curls. And only then did Cesare grasp the pumping of blood through his heart, how shallow its force rendered his breaths. *This is purposeless.*

The Other Side had claimed Cesare's soul long ago. Once his time expired, he could belong to nothing and nobody else.

"SO WE MET IN DU RRÂT A DU ERRÈINA." Danilo put down a card and smacked a skinny hand on his washboard chest. "My mama country—though I'm of Romeua 'ailin', m'self. An 'in'erland little town." We sat around a table in the hold: Korneli. Danilo, Risten. Sarnai and Itxaro cozied up to each other by my side (the former hiccupping and giggling into a ceramic cup of rum, its handle chipped off). Myself. "Risten joined the dock I worked—stocks an' such—and one night, *Antigone* pulled into 'arbour with a blown 'ull. Was never surer of what I'm to make of my life 'til that moment!"

Itxaro's monobrow scrunched up at Ren. "How did you *ever* end up in Errèina all the way from Vilges Island?"

"Poarēs Sijtë," ve said in that unreadable way of vers. "That's the village I'm from. My people are dear to me, but… my *family* was… rough." Ren's white lashes lowered. "I think I miss the deer most. It's in our culture to herd them."

I flicked a card at Korneli's aquiline nose. "And you, big guy?"

He chortled. "You'd be baffled at the 'istory 'tween 'emistóklis and Usaz'khili. I was on 'is ship *way* back in A'anasios days. Family had lived in 'emistóklis since after my birth back in Makvala, and I was a rascal lad!"

My cello-callused fingertips ran along a god of stars card. "All here by a path of bramble," I mused half to myself.

"Far be it from me to interrupt revelry," a voice like warm honey stirred into my blood; Cesare leaned his elbows onto the back of the couch I sat in, Ygạl and Lucrezia with him, "but our guests have arrived."

I sighed in half-jest, placing down the cards and forfeiting the game I was demonstrably winning. "Duty calls, I suppose."

Expressing her interest in tagging along, Itxaro followed me, pecking Sarnai's cheek in farewell.

The white-haired woman thrust a finger at Cesare. A lazy smile stretched her lips. "Giorgi better get a kiss for her trouble!"

"*Sarnai!*" I gasped.

"*What?*"

TWO WOMEN WAITED IN THE CAPTAIN'S QUARTERS.

Fabio gestured to a Miroxîn[30] smuggler, their eyes dark and skin olive, a nose prominent on her[31] person. "Şirîn, captain of The Brass Teeth."

A small smile upon her deq-tattooed face. "A pleasure, rêhevalên.[32]" Loose trousers in earthy tones billowed around their legs, a deep-cut jacket baring a white shirt tucked in beneath and belted with a wide cloth şaal, a şimşûr gleaming at her hip. From within a floral headscarf wrapped around their brow, dark hair pinned at the nape streamed. Her hands carried the imagery of a mask bearing innumerable mouths.

Fabio motioned to the familiar second guest. "Fēngnà, captain of The Grey Pearls."

The Gĕikùx̄héshén's[33] hair wove into a loose plait down a slim back adorned in a greatcoat grey as sea storms and deep brown eyes framed beneath epicanthic folds. A black plum blossom huādiàn stamped the centre of her forehead. A jade pendant adorned her neck.

---

[30] *myy-roh-KHEEN*
[31] She/they woman.
[32] '*Comrades*' in Miroxîn.
[33] *geh-ee-kooh-KHEH-shehn*

"Fēng!" Ygạl grinned sun-bright as he approached the Pearl.

She smiled and swept out her arms to embrace the Dóminus. A tattoo of a circle flanked by oystershell wings marked her wrist. "Far too long no speak, *à*?"

Once the introductions and banter settled, Şirîn led: "Durans had been a Tooth, hence I came to know Fabio." They turned to the Hydra in question. "You saved my life after that near-mortal skirmish with The Hide Wearers, so your Hydras have the support of my Brass Teeth."

Fabio lowered his head. "Thank you, Şirîn. Always." Many of The Brass Teeth, their captain included, hailed from an all-femme militia of Dirêjaso,[34] and though far from numerous, they were trained in asymmetric guerrilla warfare unlike anyone else.

Fēngnà stood pensive. "The Grey Pearls were to depart for supply runs; those we provide are low on stock. Not urgent yet, but worth mentioning. However, Ygạl and I've been allies for years, even if our meetings got rarer than Ergyron's passing.[35] As such, you have my fealty, captain Fabio. Our runs can still be postponed."

"You have my gratitude, captain Fēngnà," Fabio thanked. "The contribution of your large fleet will be invaluable."

Fēngnà nodded with a lukewarm smile.

"Even if not allied," continued Fabio, "the remaining bands in the Cove ought to be informed of the imminent danger of discovery. Though best steer clear of The Blood Dahlias and Black Tongues while we're at it, unless we want to be skinned for 'sympathising with intruders'. We're unlikely to get on Raffaele's good side, either."

"He and his White Lotus are scheduled to sail out quite soon," Fēngnà informed, "and almost certainly wouldn't follow in my footsteps."

"Teodoro will be departing with The Unsung Brotherhood tomorrow," added Şirîn with unmasked disdain for the monikers.

---

[34] *dyy-reh-ZHAH-soh; often truncated to* 'Dirêja'.

[35] A hyperbolic Gethlemian phrase; for the last 30,000 years, a periodic comet dubbed 'Ergyron' (*EHR-gyy-rohn*) has appeared in the sky every 30 years. It glows an eerie turquoise-green and emits multiple tails. The celestial object has gained a wide range of spiritual meanings across the planet, particularly to the Gilmylvetlan people of Gilgyčurmyn who were the ones to name it.

"Dahlia's Blood Rite is the evening of this díem sóle."

"Blood Rite?" Giorgianna gave voice.

"An annual event hosted by Blood Dahlia," Fēngnà enlightened. "Any smuggler from any band brave enough to entertain her is invited. At dusk, she sails *Hangman's Dowry* into the bay where a death trial commences. The victor may ask for anything they desire, bar herself, and is dubbed Dahlia's 'champion'." She shook her head. "It's a bloodbath: all bets are off—*nothing* is off the table. For the past three years, her champion has been a man named Pâin.[36] You *cannot* kill him. Needless to say, her deck ends up a butchery, and..." she shrugged, "Dahlia likes it that way."

Fabio snorted, looking away.

"Because of the Rite," appended Şirîn, "the Cove's most vicious cutthroats will be active on the township streets, so I implore you tread with heightened caution."

Fabio's brows bunched. "Thank you for the reminder. And thank you once more for your aegis."

Ygạl grasped for Cesare's eyeline. "Lady Luck cracked a hesitant smile—"

"Vitture accepts an audience," Itxaro cut in.

Cesare started.

Ygạl glared at the green-eyed woman.

She plucked at her khaki headscarf. "*I* was the one who told *you*."

Cesare arched a brow. "When?"

"To-morrow night."

Cesare sighed, sitting on a stool by the captain's desk. "Perhaps all is not yet lost..." He drummed trimmed nails on the table. "There's a lot to set clear to-morrow; we'll gather at the armoury after I see Etenesh."

Fēngnà departed alongside Lucrezia and Ygạl, talking eagerly, whilst Giorgianna slunk to Şirîn's side, intrigued by the woman.

Cesare's sigh came out more a snarl. *A mire like no other...*

Fabio sat at his desk, entwining his tanned fingers, and eyed Cesare firmly. "What are we to do with you, boy?"

---

[36] A-circumflex ('*â*') indicates an '*æ*' sound in Faustinian, like '*a*' in '*na̠rrow*'.

"It's fine. Don't worry about me." Cesare ran a hand through his hair—the only fibre of him still bearing unearned life. "It's been worse."

"Raul?"

That name dug in like rivets. "Later."

Fabio frowned. "What do I not know, Cesare?"

Twiddling with his nose ring, Cesare shut his eye as if to banish the world from existence. When he accepted back the sight of the dim quarters, he steered his gaze away from Fabio. "Around... my seventeenth year..." He kneaded his cheek between his teeth. "I guess I'd decided I'd broken in the streets enough to venture into the slums. *There...*" He almost didn't know how to confess this to the man who was more his father than he who begot him. "At... one fateful *tick* of the kaleidoscopic midnight timepiece, I... snatched a tourniquet from some rake-thin codger and shot up a half-dose of... *something*, into my arm." Cesare still didn't look at Fabio. "And so... commenced the four months of my tumultuous affair with intravenous narcotics."

He toyed with his sleeve, its ruffle, the tanzanite cufflink—the one Fabio gifted him. Back when Fabio was Paolo. And Cesare finally dared to look up at the old man.

Black eyes bored into Cesare.

And, there, he was suddenly a boy again. Just a reckless, stupid boy.

"What were you thinking?"

A dry almost-smile hooked Cesare's lips. "I guess I wasn't. I guess I sought abatement from this Hell by whatever means."

Fabio went entirely hushed. His jaw flickered—a nip of the cheek. Just like Cesare. "*Mẹi Qạddi...*[37]" When he rubbed his face, his hands shook. "It was me, wasn't it?" Cesare winced at the assertion. "That I left. I couldn't protect you."

Horror seized Cesare. *He* was the one who protected people. Nobody did the same for him. Nobody saved him. At least nobody should.

Cesare didn't know what to say. His own void of words frightened him—he never failed to have something clever to throw back. So, all he could do was lower his chin and shake his head for little rhyme or reason.

---

[37] '*My Saints...*' in Mariano.

The harsh scrape of a chair's legs sounded, followed by hurried footfalls, and Cesare found himself in an embrace, the scent of woodsmoke and sandalwood rising from the old smuggler's faded greatcoat in a reminder of the only childhood memories of Cesare's not marred by pain.

"You were just a kid…" Fabio said in that awful, shuddering tone. "You're *still* just a fucking kid!" A trembling inhale. "I'm not burying my son; do you hear me?"

Cesare's brow screwed up, his chest burned unbearably, so he pulled himself from Fabio in silence and resolved for the streets of that putrefying city state.

THE DOOR SHUT.

Fabio went pacing about his quarters.

Suicidal boy. He'd always been. He'd journeyed by sea all the way from southern Zargòsa by his lonesome at ten; he'd climb atop catwalks and roofs despite being a smart kid who knew better than anyone what would happen if he slipped; he'd lived in that forsaken *Sunrise* after it closed with nothing but a gun and his nightmares. Even in his village in Zargòsa, Cesare had made a name for himself with the constables who'd threaten the itinerants.

Fabio slumped with folded arms against a wall perpendicular to his desk, near the target that had been scrawled into the timber, the chamber in perfect view of him. *Bloody captain Fabio Amadi-Spýros…*

Athanásios Evdemoúdis Spýros, his maternal grandfather from whom he'd inherited *Antigone*, died early. Heart attack. An irony. Fabio had been only eighteen, and since that day, damn near every moment he spent out of *The Sunrise* had been aboard the galleon.

Memories permeated the carcass of the structure—woven with the very grain and fibre of the wood until he sometimes thought he could *see* the past. A mirage and echo of an immemorial life.

He saw a company of four around the couch across the room from him. Not quite solid. Like ghosts. Fading. *Evanescing.*

Only one sat on the couch itself, folding a paper dart. A stocky man with dark skin and coily hair from his Tiimi[38] father and terrible hearing from tender years spent in his mother's family's smithy. Durans.

Nearby, beside a window through which sunrise peered, a tall, slender man in suspenders and a shirt rolled up at the sleeves wound back and forth, babbling half to himself; half to the rest: '…Atla should theoretically have the capacity to support lifeforms—I mean, it simply cannot be *out of the realm of possibility when markers of life have been detected on* Thespika *of all damn places!' Dark hair cascaded to his hips, bound into a loose tail less than half way up,* yet behind *the glasses he incessantly doffed and donned,* his vulpine features were Giorgianna's.

That forsaken telescope still collected dust somewhere in *Antigone*'s storage

'Think there're elves on one of his planets?' Durans turned to the young woman sitting at the foot of the couch and handed her the paper dart. She was tiny—though Fabio's exact age—so they'd called her 'Fata', then. Faerie. *She took the paper glider with a devious look and launched it.*

'Oh, that'd be swell!' enthused Matìa from their spot on the floor near Fata, one hand occupied with a chipped glass of moonshine whilst the other stirred a brush though a peach-coloured concoction of hair dye that had always smelled well-nigh poisonous to Fabio. *Tattoos crawled all over their raw-boned limbs, even to the face.*

The paper dart sailed the air and landed nose-first in a man's dark curls. Durans and Fata exchanged looks of comically wide eyes and gaping mouths, as if amazed by themselves. And at the escritoire—his very same desk to this day—Fabio saw himself when he was young, yet with the same crabby glower and taciturnity.

He hunched over plays and documents as was his wont, *only stirring once disturbed. 'Are you serious?' He plucked the paper dart. 'You're*

---

[38] The majority people of Dííluaná.

better than this, Durans,' he said flatly, though not without a dry subcurrent of jest, and launched the glider back.

Fata lunged to catch it. 'Not if I can help it.' She grinned impishly to which Fabio rolled his eyes.

'Can we pay attention?' Ludovico called out, one hand on his hip.

Matìa raised their moonshine glass. 'I always try, professor.'

Knots tied up Fabio's chest.

In some ways, they seemed to consider him their leader, the one who assembled them, and yet he remained at an arm's length, no matter how deeply he cared for all of them.

And he saw himself young and at his desk again.

Midday shone behind the windows, and Fata watched the timepiece mark with a snick *the arrival of thirteen hundred. She jumped down from the back of the couch and slunk over to the escritoire with a swish of a layered black skirt cinched by a blood-red waspie, leaning her elbows onto the table top. Fabio continued his preoccupation with papers.*

A hammy sigh left her. 'If I'm gonna be stuck with you for this many hours, you might as well entertain me.'

'I'm busy,' Fabio voiced half-absently.

Fata tsk'd. 'You really *oughta drop the dreary act, Spýros.'*

'Another time.'

She sat onto the desk right in front of him, barring him from his work. 'Oooh, witty. What's this?' She pinched a sheet of paper. 'Act thirty-seven?' *A gawk. 'Why* does *this have thirty-seven acts?'*

'What do you want from me, Fata?' Fabio's tone hardened, an irate expression straining his brow and mouth.

She put the paper down and angled her head at him. Satiny hair, darker than the boldest ink, spilled to her elbows and over thick eyebrows. 'To drop the dreary act—hello?' She rapped Fabio on the forehead. 'Come now, captain Fabio Amadi-Spýros.' A curt laugh. An echo along ocean waves. Her fingers stole into the shoulder-length curls framing his face. He still felt the shiver; the inexplicable ache. *'You're so smart in every other department.'*

And he fell quiet. Not taciturn, this time, but inarticulate. He just looked at her. At eyes the blackness of obsidians. Of a star-strewn midnight sky.

Fata pulled back, a hand at her heart. 'Oh…' She took on a pert look, almost mocking. 'Was that a nerve I felt?'

His hands still rested on either side of her hips, her legs hanging off the table around his knees, their distance apart practically nothing even with them both drawn away.

Fata's face cooled. 'Or maybe you're just a crapehanger.'

Fabio's jaw stiffened, but he couldn't vindicate his doomsayer ways, so she leaned forward abruptly and stole his chance to say anything at all with a kiss.

She slipped off the escritoire onto his lap to straddle him, gripping his hair and stubbled face, pulling him into herself until neither of them could quite breathe. Fata had always looked so dainty to Fabio—a wisp of a girl. Yet she wasn't at all. In his hands, she was force and vigour and firm muscle wrapped in flesh.

She broke away, panting. 'You're also such *a craven.'*

He didn't say anything. He just kissed her again.

Fabio shut his eyes, rubbing his temples as the sensation washed over him. Regret. Saudade. There were no happy endings here. Once *The Sunrise* fell into his hands, by and by, he put almost nothing before his work, and it cost him everything that he sidelined.

And so he saw two scenes intertwined. Two scenes for shame.

Fabio was still young. Younger, at least. *Yet, beyond the sill, daylight was dying.*

'You turn your back, then?' His voice boomed through the quarters. 'Like a coward?'

'And you're so *virtuous!' It was Ludovico. His long hair was bound at the nape, and a black swallowtail coat embroidered with sequin constellations clad him, ten asterisk-shaped stars pinned to its lapels. Dark eyes smouldered back at Fabio who sat at that damn escritoire of his. Eyes almost as dark as Fata's,* who suddenly stood there in Ludovico's stead, *yet the fire in her gaze burned lava-hot to the algidness of his friend.*

'So that's it?' she derided. 'That's the end—just like that? That's how easy it is for you?'

'You're not a hero,' bit Ludovico. 'This doesn't end in glory.'

Fabio's fists clenched. 'That's not what I meant—'

'Because you can't fucking choose what's good for you!' Fata's tone rose to a shout. 'It's safer to just throw it all away, right?'

'You shan't reprimand me for my choice when I at least know what I want.' Ludovico stormed for the door.

'You really are just a craven.' Fata did the same.

Ludovico paused with his hand on the knob, and looked one final time at Fabio. 'I hope you learn to make the decisions that don't sabotage you before it's too late. Not for your *sake.'*

The eyes were black, the stars stuffed out. 'All your sort fucking knows is misery.' And the door slammed twice, leaving Fabio in his quarters alone, daylight drowned beneath the sea.

RAIN HAD CEASED, Şirîn left, and the black morning sky unfurled.

From below deck emerged Cesare, jacket, tricorn, and stilétti on him, the waved tips of his freshly-cut hair slit in a perfectly matching line to his sharp jaw.

He descended the gangplank without a glance my way.

His moment of pause in his quarters when he stood, as if dazed, had not evaded me, nor did the knife scars littering the chamber's wall, above his cold bed.

Nobody at *The Arum* spoke of the harm they wreaked upon themselves. We all knew almost every one of us partook in something of the sort—Nara's needles, my razors, that unnamed girl's bashing of her own elbows to redden her finger-paintings—but it was left unspoken. The risk of further exploitation was far too high, so we kept our secrets close. And, in a twisted, dreadful way, Cesare understood, even if nobody ever should.

I strained my lips and gazed across the lagoon towards the curling waves which shattered themselves to flinders like suicidal sirens against the jagged black cliff face. Salty ocean wind ran its icy fingers through my hair, my sheathed rapier and dagger an auspicious weight at my hips. My shoulders lay unadorned by a jacket. Velvet lacked agreeableness with bloodshed.

5 Kraken Avenue 13/7, East Fin, Smugglers' Cove.

I stroked my bleeding eye pendant.

Mircea and Cataldu still lived—the monsters who helped put *The Sunrise* to flames. Nothing would placate me until retribution was mine.

"Giorgianna!" a glum voice called out.

Fabio stood by the forecastle, hands hidden within his greatcoat's pockets. He approached with haunted eyes, asking, "Ïna piɣænis?[39]"

"To set a couple records straight," I replied in Themistoklísika.

Fabio stopped by my side, grey-streaked brows low. "Giorgianna."

A sigh left me. "I know."

We looked to the moon-laven cove. Ocean sang and swayed against *Antigone*'s hull, dancing with yakamoz.

"You know something *else*?" asked Fabio.

I prompted him to continue with a '*hm?*'

"Sailors say Smugglers' Cove was formed when an enormous sea drake took a bite out of the coast. Don't know how much I believe that, but there's charm in the whimsy."

"Is that disposition of yours one my father would beleaguer you over?"

"Endlessly." Fabio's eyes wheeled. "For all his doldrums and despondent cynicisms apropos of the regime, he utterly *buzzed* with fervour and zeal about myths and the cosmos and all the parallel dimensions of the multiverse."

"The planets were always his beloved. He fancied to ponder about life elsewhere in this cosmos that feels so vast and lonely."

Fabio chuckled, a subfusc and sombre sound. "He with his exulting eyes rattling off discoveries of distant nebulae looked damn-near mad

---

[39] '*Where are you going?*' in Themistoklísika.

half the time. Needless to say, Durans and I were thoroughly wildered: a pragmatic mariner to a fault, he was. Though Matìa the vintner would listen to you talk about anything with unflinching fascination."

His ageing face eclipsed. "And worry not: Davide hardly came around—no chance Ludovico would've let him near." The flicker in his dark eyes faded. "I'll forever regret how long it took me to realise the truth. Even if the rest of us hadn't known, I should've been vigilant—he was around *me* the most." He swallowed tightly. "No thought turns my stomach more than the fact that Davide was so close. That he could have so heinously hurt the kids I, as the fucking *impresario*, was obligated to safeguard. And if I had taken even a moment longer..." He shook his head slowly. "I could never live with myself."

He lifted his eyes to the starscape. "I've always felt literature tethered me to reality in some way, even as Durans was always keen to arraign my devoted faith. I didn't believe that the truth of *only* the hegemony begot existential sorrow the way Ludovico postulated, but that life *itself* was an imitation of art, as vice versa, and that existential sorrow was a given within art, thus a given within life. But your father..." Fabio's eyes narrowed at the Amphisbaena asterism. "Always gazed higher; always *saw* more. I think that's why astronomy enraptured him."

'*The final three planets in our
Seren system are...?*'

'*Ananke, Thespika, Lethe.*'

'*Which is...?*'

'*Inevitability, reprieve, oblivion.*'

'*And that means...?*'

'*Astronomers are poets and you
ought to quit pretending otherwise.*'

'I never pretend.'

Inevitability. Reprieve. Oblivion.

It was that day that the thread of my life forever spun into a different weave. "'*Mortals are so small in the vastness of our universe that they cling to any modicum of power they can grasp'*," I quoted the words I overheard Fabio say to Cesare. The words my father would mutter half to himself when peering through his telescope. "*I should have known, too.*"

"You couldn't have," disputed Fabio. "And you ought to quit admonishing yourself for ignorance forced unto you." A scoff. "*I'm* one to talk."

I rubbed together my red-glossed lips. "I spoke with Elenedda."

Fabio groaned.

A humourless smile. "She *did* say you two never got along."

"Not my person. So…" he waved his hands, "*clean,* if that makes sense? I think she thought me a ruffian."

"Did you meet her at the casinos where father dealt?"

"Initially. Afterwards, the only time we'd ever see one another was on the rare occasion you'd come to *Sunrise* stagings."

My stomach kicked. "We came to *The Sunrise?*"

"You don't recall?" Fabio met my gaze with a frown which I returned with a dumbstruck gawk. *No…?*

Fabio lifted his head, dipping it into a slow nod. "*Mmm,* I suppose you mightn't." *So it is true…* I couldn't breathe. "There weren't many instances. Perhaps the only time I saw you was at four?" He paused to think. "It must've been."

"The first time I saw *The Sunrise*," I heard myself, "there was an eerie familiarity, but I disregarded it for a trick of The Court." My heart fluttered. "Is *that* why?"

He shrugged. "Not impossible."

"Gods…" Tears pooled in my eyes. *I've spent so long in the dark…*

"Forgive me." Fabio reached his arm around my shoulder and pressed me to him, resting my temple on his cheekbone.

"*And me.*" I whispered, holding onto a lapel of his greatcoat, my other hand clutching my father's garnet necklace which Fabio had given me. The necklace which almost never left my neck.

We remained in each other's embrace for many heartbeats, only the song of the seas and the whisper of the salt winds to stir the nightdeep quiet.

"I'd always jest," said Fabio, "telling Ludovico he loved women who'd lure a sailor from the sea. He'd fire back that I loved women who'd cut my throat and throw me in."

A chuckle warmed my chest. "Never took *you* as one for romance."

"Neither did I, believe me. Certainly not… *her.*"

"Where is she now?"

"Not here, clearly. But not dead."

I pulled back to look at Fabio. "Would it help to speak of it?"

He snorted. "I'm not grieving over the ordeal." His fingers fiddled with the iron band around his right thumb. "What gives me pause still is… I had my chances to get her back. Still might, if I sought her out."

I pursed my lips. "Why don't you?"

He pulled a '*really?*' face. "I'm fifty-fucking-five, Giorgianna."

"And?" My mouth's corners plucked up. "The age for love is illimitable."

Fabio's eyes half-rolled. "Whatever you say, girl."

I nudged his shoulder. "Grouch."

"Says *you.*"

"Ehi!" I stood away, arms crossed in sardonic petulance. "Not fair."

"None of this is." Tense lines sank into his forehead. "I still don't want you to go into that house and I never will, no matter how many precautions you take. It could never be enough. And I cannot lose my friend's daughter. You are too important."

My heart ached, guilt the writhe and gnaw of maggots within this putrescent husk that was I.

Yet wounds besought abatement.

Blood besought reckoning.

I trained a glance on the achronycal Nereida star—a second moon glowing; an eye nictating in the sky. "So was every person They stole."

SCENE XII

ULTIMA FORSAN

Cesare | Giorgianna

NOTHING SMELLED MORE HAUNTED than the stifling must-and-mothball perfume of Donatello's dollmaking parlour. Its parquet whined beneath incorporeal feet. Garlands of ceramic teeth festooning a multiplicity of wall-mounted shelves chattered. Swarms of lushy-dressed dolls seated on their ledges like dead bees in a perished hive murmured with clockwork souls and porcelain hearts. Wax orbs dangled from satin optic nerves pinched by fingertips of arm-shaped chandeliers.

Seven bisque dolls in bulbous taffeta gowns hang by their throats above the till at the front of which the dollmaker fiddled with winding keys and butchered puppet limbs.

Brass buttons and clockwork parts embroidering his raspberry jacket gleamed at alchemy's volition, his brow-brushing russet curls topped with a hat—clutched by circular cinder goggles and pierced with needles much like the pincushion sitting on his left shoulder. Black shorts and fishnet stockings dressed his reedy legs, with thigh-high boots to match. His scissors were out of sight.

The dollmaker acknowledged Cesare's loitering in the foyer's archway. "*Ah!*" The mechanical gold orb in his right socket gyred, his left eye a glinting citrine. "My *dar*ling Cesare."

Cesare's lips were iron bars bending by force. "Donatello."

His jacket's calf-sweeping train swished as he strutted around his till. "Brings *ti*dings, *do*es he?"

Glass eyes tracked Cesare's paces towards the desk. "*Do* I, indeed." His head canted. "But you first, Manfredonia."

Donatello propped his elbows on the benchtop, armour rings jingling. "For *no*w, the prison break is to take place in th*ree* months—much to *sche*me, I'm sure you *kno*w. For *safe*ty reasons, my informant wishes to remain anonymous *for* the foreseeable time."

Interesting. Cesare could neither confirm nor deny Donatello's claims this way. "Clue them in regarding my end of things."

Donatello gestured hammily. "Clue *me* in."

Cesare divulged the recent events whilst the dollmaker wound up some freakish 'doll': a head with empty eye sockets, a pair of seven-toed feet, and a toothy grin thrice the conventional size.

"How simply *thri*lling to be part of such an en*dea*vour!" Donatello all but squawked as the demonic figurine began walking.

Cesare grimaced. "You best get friendly with Mişşi and al-Uwwād if we want our rumours to fly well."

"Of *cour*se!" The monstrosity almost bit off Donatello's finger. "I shall *hear*tily oblige." He plucked the winding key from the doll. "*Al*ways a treat to see you, *da*rling."

Cesare clicked his tongue. "The pleasure is all mine, signór." He tipped his tricorn and rounded for the foyer.

"*So*on the eye shall see imp*ro*vement, I hear?"

Donatello's words halted Cesare at the archway's threshold.

He turned, palms rested on the door frame.

Donatello sashayed to the side of his desk, fingers drumming on the bench like a devious phantasm's knock. "Everything has a *tiii*the."

A breath.

"Humour me, dollmaker."

His lips kinked. "If your stratagem shall see *ru*in," reaching around the till, Donatello pulled out his glinting gold scissors, long as his arm and no less sharp than knives, "*I* will take *both* of your treasured eyes as compensation."

A thump of the heart beat by before Cesare left the dollmaker with a wordless sneer, fingers twitching for throwing knives.

THE AIR LAY SODDEN, warm, red as wintry dawn, the stench of slaughter unbroken by smoke of the sigarétta in my slickened fingers.

Blood seeped across ridge and trough of floorboards from a crimson pool within which lay scattered Mircea and Cataldu's dismembered bodies. The remaining scraps of Davide's gang. The men who, alongside Abramo and Alphaeus, helped burn down *The Sunrise*. My skirt and skin wore their ichor like anointment, but I was not done.

Madáma Irene Falco.

The Court of Secrets had denied me entrance onto the horseshoe street to which I was once confined. But I had a reason to return to *The Arum* now. I knew in my bones I would be granted passage.

The sleepy sun of five hundred cast the sky in bright rose—such a tranquil sight unfurling above the art nouveau corpse flower that was *The Arum* 'bordello'.

So many nights had crawled by in those gnarled streets, cowering from killers. Weeping after a violation. Hearing the screams of a young lavìre as Madáma Irene Falco beat them bloody or branded them like a farm animal or cut them open with nothing to ease their agony. *You deserve to bleed like the rest of Them.*

I slipped through twined flower stems of hallways, bypassing those forsaken lavìri quarters and ascending to the third floor.

Bone snapped.

To the foot of the Madáma's door collapsed a thewy pair of men. *I remember you.* Falco's curs.

I slunk into the chamber, hiding behind a black lattice entangled with counterfeit lavender gem zantedeschias.

Wrapped in a porphyrous silk robe, Irene Falco sat before a vanity, her salt-and-pepper hair unbound over small shoulders. At the clothing frame near the bed, I spied her steel-tipped whip, phantom pain lashing across my spine. *All the more incentive.*

I stepped around the lattice. "Madáma Falco." My voice sweetened to rose nectar.

Irene saw my bloody visage like a vengeful apparition in the mirror, jumping white-faced from her seat. "Who—?"

"Your *'winning doll'*." I tilted my head as I circled slowly.

She slipped a once-over down my body, empty-eyed. Dour features contorted into that cloying smile of hers. "Where did you disappear to, flower?" She mirrored my pace. "A lavìre ought to know the consequences of disobeying her Ma*dám*—"

She shrieked and stumbled gracelessly. Her feet bruised violet where I shattered their every bone. My nose at long last dripped molten copper: my azoth pushed a fraction over its threshold.

"I am not your lavìre, Irene." I neared as she sought to crawl away. "And you are not my Madáma!" My hand came down hard across her face, just as hers had so, *so* many times done upon me, upon others.

I yanked her by the hair and dragged her across the floor. She screamed and kicked. "I *know*—" I threw her "—you handed Nara and Eluisa over to bandits!"

Her arms planted into the floor; neck hunched. She heaved before nocking a sneer up at me. "Two worthless lives in exchange for mine."

My step retreated, heels leaving scarlet splotches round as bullet holes on the downy rug. "If we are speaking in valuations of life," I grasped Falco's whip, "*you* are in debt."

She scrambled to flee, shrieking for help.

I flogged her across the back. Blood ruptured from her flesh to stain her immaculate silk. Falco screamed, and I snapped her spine where it would silence but not kill her.

"Cruel, isn't it?" My voice was serene as death. "Your handling of your professed 'flowers' and '*dolls*'." I wrenched Falco by the hair, carving a dagger's gory simulacrum between her delicate shoulder blades. "Remember how you'd brand us like cattle? Whip us bloody as we cowered bare on the floor of the establishment we crawled into because we had less than *nothing*?" I slid my blade into her stomach and cut her open. Guts sloshed across foliate tiles.

She began suffocating on blood. I only continued my cooing damnation, "Tie us to the bed and cut out our wombs, and then have those vile pigs you called your guards *rape* us, all while you'd watch with glee as they killed us the way no blade—" the knife pushed until my hand pressed to her innards "—*ever* could?" I wrapped Irene's whip around her own bird-boned neck. "You aren't a Madáma, and this is not a bordello. You are a *flesh* peddler."

Her thin fingers clawed at the leather in vain.

"You are *scum*!" I pulled harder.

She heaved, blood sputtering from her squeezed gullet, her limbs writhing, quivering.

Leaning close, I whispered, "*Some girls are born to suffer*," and Falco limped in my arms.

The door swung open.

Giulia the tavèrna tender stood at the threshold.

Her shoulder-length curls were still dyed plum and shaven on one side, her bronze curves clad in crushed onyx velvet.

Our eyes locked, silence passing between us for an eternity.

Giulia gave up a sigh. "*Whew!*" A hand tipped with black coffin nails fell over her chest. "I thought something was happening."

I blinked twice, opening my mouth, but no words came.

She rested one hand on a cocked hip, gesturing the other at me. "Ya want me to get that for ya, *orrr*…?"

My blinks came in rapid fire. "*Um…*" Releasing the whip, I inched back from Falco's body.

My heart hammered in my throat. *She is gone…*

Giulia pulled a metal chest from under Irene's bed, dumping out tulle and taffeta. "I've wasted *too* much poison," she pushed the coffer towards Falco, "forgetting the woman was mithridatised against all we had on hand."

My bloody lips pressed together. "I realise I've done away with the owner…"

Giulia hauled the Madáma's corpse into the empty chest, folding her limbs so she would fit. When she failed to, Giulia drew out a switchblade from in her velvet skirt and sawed Falco's leg off at the knee with terrifying ease. "On me." She compressed the dismembered human heap and wiped her hands on the silk adorning it before approaching the vanity. There, she plucked two bottles of perfume, prying them open and draining the redolent liquids over Falco's corpse. "I all but run the tavèrna anyway, so a little more on my plate won't hurt," she threw the empty bottles aside, "and I've always detested the bordello patrons."

"The lavìri?" I hesitated to ask.

"Always need fellow tavèrna staff." Opening a lighter, Giulia tossed it inside the metal chest and shut its lid as fire ignited.

She snatched keys off Falco's bedside table and beckoned me to follow her out, locking the door after us.

"Thank you, Giulia." I held my hands at my chest. "For the bordello. Truly. I'd embrace you, but…" I gestured to my blood-sullied person.

Her black-painted lips pulled into disgust. "Appreciate the sentiment, though…"

As the stench of burning ethyls and singed hair crept from beneath the door, Giulia clicked her fingers and pointed her thumb someplace yonder. "Take the back exit."

I dipped my whirling head and obliged.

Giulia clapped. "Actually!" I revolved for her to ask, "What happened with that poisoning?"

A blink. "Poisoning?"

"A few months back ya cajoled me to lace a guy's cherry water with two parts Smite one part Mḗ.[40]" *Oh no.* "How'd that go?"

My lips squeezed. "*Interestingly...* to say the least."

And I left the flesh parlour that was *The Arum* once and for all, on the way out jumping at a distant explosion which no doubt stunk of charred human remains.

---

[40] Full name 'Bašmu Mḗ' (*BAH-sh-moo MEH*); '*Asp Nectar*' in Ancient Rhalese; a poison derived from the boiling and dilution of Eastern Isatōnian Mountain Asp (Ṣer'šādî) venom.

Scene XIII

Eyes Full of Language

Cesare | Giorgianna

SIX HUNDRED HOURS ON DÍEM STELLÁRE, pronounced the clock. An hour until some fraction of lost vision might return to Cesare.

Tricorn and jacket on, chin-length waves brushed to a lustre, Cesare sheathed his stilétti and quitted his quarters. Ascending onto the deck, he turned a corner and—*"Fucking Saints!"*—almost tripped over someone.

Giorgianna crouched against the wall, elbows resting on knees as she smoked. Blood spotted the shoulders laid bare by her strapped corset, her hands and soaring heels dipped in the red of a taken life.

She looked up at Cesare with kohled eyes ever-darkened by the bloodthirsty maw of dilated pupils. Blood oozing from her nose coalesced with the cherry-black glossing her lips. *Tailored someone to death this early?*

"Where are you going?" she asked before dragging smoke.

"The faithful ano-apozem administration."

"Do you want me to come?"

Maybe I do. "If it pleases you to watch me suffer."

She stood up onto her bloody stilettos. Cesare's gaze flickered along the indentation of her bottom lip, the sharp bow, and up close, aventurescence glittered upon the sunstone halos of her eyes in all the glimmers of flame and sun. *Right here, Giorgianna, I don't care.*

"Best not look so uncouth for such an occasion." She strode around him, barging his shoulder, and disappeared below deck.

Cesare slumped back against the wall. *I'm losing my mind.*

STAINED GLASS LANCET WINDOWS filtered viridescent mornlight across the wooden floors and benchtops of the apothecárium's makeshift surgery suite. Aneling the air were balsamic aromas of galbanum and storax.

Reasonable footwear replacing my stilettos (blood and sweat sucked from my clothes by singing to boot), I settled on a high stool by the back wall, Libitina's book detailing Balinori politics unfurled atop the counter before me.

Etenesh, arrayed in a yellow ķemis, hair bound, hovered over Cesare's surgical stretcher in the chamber's centre, inspecting his wounded eye. Dispensing Torpor to numb all motion and sensation, the apothecary retrieved a syringe from a cabinet, followed by a découpage box of a dozen clinking phials, half malachite and half amethyst—ano- and katō-apozem, respectively—which she set onto the metal cart by the stretcher.

Plucking a green vial, Etenesh suctioned apozem through the orifice into the syringe, the liquid within crystalline as sweetwater.

She positioned her thumb at Cesare's right brow and tugged on his lid to insert the needle inside the laceration goring his paralysed eye. She depressed the plunger. Distilled healing elixir spilled into the vitreous body. Lifting the needle from the wound, she voided the plunger to sluice the surface.

Her eyebrows drew together. "The pupil isn't healing."

Cesare went rigid. *"What?"*

The furrows in Etenesh's forehead deepened. "I mustn't have applied sufficient Bloodletter to mitigate scarring…"

My stomach dropped.

"…I will need to administer katō-apozem to heal the laceration if you want to get off tonics."

"Reopen the wounds so ano-apozem works?" I suggested.

"I'm not a surgeon; I don't have the tools."

Her words coiled around my heart.

Cesare's face was wan, his head kicked back, cheek clenched between his teeth and eyes roving the ceiling.

Etenesh repeated the procedure with a purple phial of katō-apozem: fated to heal only by scarring. "The pupil is incorrectly shaped—cuts through the length of the iris and obstructs a portion of the sclera."

A thought flew into my mind. "If the issue lies with the shape, I can tailor it!"

Etenesh folded her hands. "Could you?"

Cesare braced himself up on his elbows. "You've already pushed your magic over the threshold."

I cradled my cheek in my palm. "Scared I'll bleed on you?"

"Both of you have tended to me enough."

My eyes spun as I went to sanitise my hands.

"Don't be a child." Etenesh wheeled her cart around the gurney. "You'll be enduring ridiculous glare and photophobia, what with your pupillary muscles retaining function notwithstanding the mighty chasm in your eyeball."

I pinched an angelite flacon of Torpor off Etenesh's cart.

Cesare sat up. "I'll deal with—" His breath hitched as I shoved my hand into his chest to push him back onto the surgical bed.

"I didn't come here to watch you play your dramatics." Tucking in my knee, I set it onto the stretcher at Cesare's side and perched myself on my haunch. I uncrewed the flacon's cap. Squeezed the pipette tip to aspirate Torpor into the glass shaft. Leaned over.

"I *said*," Cesare's arm parried my wrist, "I'll *deal* with it."

I stooped close enough to touch noses with him. His head bridled back into the pillow. "Quit the martyrdom and let. Me. *Help*." I barged his arm out of my way and dispensed two droplets of Torpor onto his eye. Liquid coated the smooth curvature, the jagged cut drinking it in.

Azoth tipped my fingers in frost as I hovered them near Cesare's eye and attuned to the clinquant thrum in my blood, my organs, my flesh. Vertigo twirled through my aching head.

I pinched shut the incision through the tough fibres of the sclera first, then concentrated on the iris.

The slit riving Cesare's pupil flinched, my magic fumbling to grip such delicate structures, but reluctantly yielded, abiding by my tailor's hands.

Between meticulous movements, I glimpsed Cesare's left eye, emulating the magnitude of its pupil, the ornate shards of its iris—each dimension a cut facet of a dazzling andalusite, coruscating with every dimmed hue of green and aureate and ochre.

My breath caught.

Vulnerable pain swelled against my skull.

I grasped a fugitive pause, lifting my head and haling air into my scrunched lungs before returning to the task at hand, moulding the pupil into a seamless circle and fanning out the threads of the iris into an emanating halo. Finally, I repaired the clear dome of the cornea, and those frozen garottes crushing my organs slacked, my stiff chest loosening a stutter of an exhale as a shiver flurried down my spine.

Cesare's soft breaths ghosted my face, danced with mine, warm against the immaterial frost veiling my skin. Warm like blood—sweet like it; sweet as the cherry perfume clinging to his shirt. And I hungered for it. To peel him apart like a clementine and drink him down. To leave nothing of him for anybody who came after me. *Look at me like you did on the deck again, Cesare.*

"Is something wrong?" asked Etenesh.

I snapped back. "I'm tired." My heart careened into the shelter of my ribs, hands raking curls behind both ears.

"Go sit," urged Etenesh, "I'll take it from here."

I refused to meet Cesare's gaze again, returning to my stool where I swiped my jacket off the counter and ducked inside, curling my knees to my chest and clinging to the thick velvet like a fox holed up in a blizzard.

Etenesh handed him a pill of inkberry[41]—Torpor antidote.

Elbows atop my knee, I cradled my pounding head, sniffing deeply to pull blood back down my throat. Planks making the floor blurred.

Etenesh took to inspecting Cesare's eye with a miniature flashlight. "As suspected," she called. "Your right pupil does not optimally constrict—the rate is slower and the endpoint aperture is wider. Not particularly noticeable unless one is close or searching for it, but notable." She administered eyedrops and motioned Cesare to sit up. "A marginal reduction in eyesight is apparent," she explained whilst tidying, "but *far* from the damage the injury on its own would've left."

Cesare rested his hands over his heart. "Thank you, Etenesh."

She smiled. "The tailoring was a grace, too."

"How is it?" I unclenched my teeth to ask. "You can…" a waning shiver jabbed me, "*feel* flesh tailoring. Almost a tug of dried blood or a poorly-healed scar."

Cesare blinked, brow jerking. "I admit I've grown too accustomed to soreness to be especially bothered," he concluded.

I smirked despite myself. "Danilo will no doubt lament the loss of a fellow eyepatch-wearer."

"He'll live to disrupt another of Lissandri's slumbers, I'm certain." Cesare mused and made to rinse his face, scrutinising his reflection.

"Regarding that two-fold favour?" I asked Etenesh.

> '*…every favour granted, you return two-fold. If I give you apozem, you'll owe me more than coin.*'

It would take too many lifetimes to repay all our dues to this remarkable woman.

She still tidied. "In due time."

A pallid rosen disk—the sun still floated low, dark cobbles moist when we emerged upon a narrow oldtown street.

---

[41] A black-coloured, edible berry endemic to Kyöpeli Woods producing a thick, highly-staining juice akin to writing ink. This juice is distilled, dried, and powdered to a substance able to counteract the effects of *Prasinum accidia* (*i.e.* Torpor).

The smugglers, the cadres, The Morettae, all waited at the armoury for the final conclave ahead of our dreaded cloak-and-dagger operation in the ministerial house. The hereafter we—*I*—set in motion loomed ahead: a terrifying inevitability. But this putrescent kingdom needed to fall. The blood on its hands called to be avenged.

Behind me, Cesare's steps halted. "Vólto."

"Cesare," I whipped around, "I *swear*—"

"Thank you." His words struck me; I didn't recall ever being thanked by him. "I know I refused your help but…" He chewed on his stern cheek. "Thank you for not heeding the inane ramblings of a drugged-up maniac." *Yet your wretched hubris won't let you utter three syllables?*

I held him in admonition, and *tsk'd*. "It is a shame," I stalked closer, "that you can be so aware of the Self, and yet, in chorus, so mulishly immovable." Drawing up within a step of Cesare, I canted my head, my frown a likeness of his. "It is a real shame."

Then I spun on my heel and fleeted for the armoury.

Scene XIV

L'Altro Ieri

Cesare | Giorgianna | Cesare

EVERYTHING WAS TOO BRIGHT. Too wide. Too *much*.

After a month of the world cloven in half, beholding its contours with both eyes dazed Cesare.

And he could *see* the damage.

A dreamy haze settled in the dextral periphery of his field, formless tension dragging behind his eyelids every time he blinked.

His vision could have once rivalled a hawk's, pristine and clear as a newly-cut spyglass lens. Now, chips and scratches marred its pane. And so, he was vulnerable—his most precious boon tarnished.

Giorgianna had fallen back to his side, arms folded and eyes fixed firmly ahead.

On their way to the apothecárium, she disclosed the names of those whom the blood on her hands that morning had belonged to: Irene Falco, and the final two men who helped burn down *The Sunrise*.

Although disappointed he couldn't bash Mircea and Cataldu's heads in himself, Cesare was grateful to Giorgianna. And it had been a long time coming for that loathsome martinet Falco.

But Cesare had far more to be beholden to Giorgianna for.

She mended his eye, bartering her azoth for his vision.

Despite never finding an interest in the arcane, Cesare was no fool to its operations—almost no one on Gethlem was when magic permeated all.

Azoth was life essence—'*spirit*', if one believed such things—and wielding the humour in the ways of magi expended it. Shortened a life with each cast spell. Drain azoth completely, or too much at once, and you die. You burn. You melt like wax right off your bones.

And Giorgianna gave up a droplet of her life for him—plucked it like a splinter from her core and lodged it beneath his cornea.

Guilt settled on Cesare's shoulders. *Why can I not rid myself of this hollowness?*

They arrived silently at the armoury and entered the old melee weapons chamber.

Near the entrance, engrossed in a conversation with Sarnai, a woman dressed in a loose taupe blouse corseted by an emerald waspie leaned against the wall, her dark hair always hidden within a moss-green headscarf and Vito's severed finger a pendant around her neck.

Cesare met her chrysoprase eyes with a smirk. "Bajtalô',[42] Itxaro."

She smiled back with a cut-throat glint, "Kâixo,[43] lehên,[44]" and whisked Giorgianna from his side, the void remaining of her swiftly occupied by the twins and their chatter.

From across the room, Cesare nodded to a newer face: a young-ish man with inky black hair. Errico. He rapped his heart with a fist twice and held up a 'V' gesture to Cesare. A woman wearing an embroidered red kerchief beside him, Alessa, matched the gesture.

---

[42] *bah-hh-tah-LOH*; 'hello' in Marlâre Zargòsian.

[43] *KAH-ee-shoh*; 'hello' in Abeslâri Zargòsian.

[44] *leh-HEHN*; 'cousin' in all Zargòsian dialects. This particular term is used in instances when addressing close *non*-blood-related individuals: a common practice among Zargòsians. The term for a blood-related cousin is '*lehêngusua*'.

Cesare had come across Errico some months prior as he was disseminating his newspaper—one he had already caught wind of and which had previously disseminated some of his own writings—but was about to be intercepted by a legionary. Cesare took the soldier out and struck up conversation with the man, learning of his rank-and-file federating endeavours and unionising with Alessa's aid, herself a water speaker at the aqueducts where she stood daily witness to the deadly exertion the workers were subjected to in the name of keeping the citadel's moat crystalline.

The pair of them were beyond invaluable.

The last of the expected parties forwarded in, so Giorgianna and Cesare commenced relaying everything of consequence and urgency: Barsotti's plans, pleas, promises and petitions; Cesare's upper óssium contacts; Giorgianna's discoveries regarding Davide's gang.

"It's *guards*, you need?" mused Sarnai, hooking an arm over Giorgianna's shoulder. "If *only* there was someone who offered…"

Giorgianna frowned. "Sarnai—"

"Save it." Sarnai poked her chest. "I'm beside you whether you like it or not." She laced her fingers at the back of her head, grin clashing with Giorgianna's trenchant glare.

Cesare observed the supplication in her eyes. But it grew clearer than day that Sarnai wouldn't budge, and the pit within his chest opened wider.

"You need a second," Isaia pointed out.

At the eavesdropper's side was Araya, dark-skinned and towering, tight curls brushing his collarbones and a fringe at his brow. "Since we need our informers in the government building anyway, I'd be happy to."

"What about Etenesh?" asked Giorgianna.

Araya chuckled deeply. A gold ring glinted on his lower lip. "I don't babysit my big sister." He elbowed the head Hound, earning his dull regard. "Isaia can do without me for a bit." He winked.

Giorgianna met him and Sarnai with apprehension. "I resent the thought, but…" She shut her eyes, sighing in final resignation. "Thank you, both, nevertheless."

Sarnai bumped triumphant fists with Araya.

Across the table, Itxaro's gaze avoided Sarnai's. She sucked in her cheeks, tucking stray hairs back into her headscarf whilst her entire frame wound up. Sarnai's teeth clasped over her bottom lip like a rabbit as she dropped her eyes.

"Hounds will be deployed in and around the government precinct," said Isaia.

From her jacket, Giorgianna plucked a scroll, handing it to the eavesdropper. "Centúrion Ioana De Rege of the Guárdia compiled a record of all forty-three Guardíi who may purportedly be trusted. While I have no faith in such claims, it's worthwhile to know the names. I think there's no better individual to set to the task."

Isaia hid the document within his leathers.

"Dialogue within our own ranks remains wanting," Cesare seized his turn to speak. "We need all hands on deck if we want the populace at large on our side, and we cannot do that with internal bickering." He resisted the urge to glare at the blonde. "There's a smoking gun to find. One which could lie anywhere: the Treasury, the House of Judgement, the basilica. We cannot leave any stone unturned."

Aengus peered at Giorgianna. "Won' it be rum that you 'ave guards who're no' iridites?"

"A human in Ithilwen could never employ iridites."

"How do you intend to make your entrance into Vencenza?" Alessa queried. "Guards take records at the fortification."

"We'll sail you in on *Antigone*," volunteered Fabio.

"*What?*" Cesare and Giorgianna exclaimed at once.

"Smugglers' Cove is protected by the same thaumaturgy as The Court," the captain reasoned. "How d'you think it's staring into the open Reverie Sea, yet no outside vessel has ever docked or so much as been seen passing by? To an outside observer with no knowledge of the Cove, there *is* no Cove—just cliffs and skerries." Fabio tapped a finger to his temple. "They say there's an azothian barrier within the brain which must be breached to see beyond the illusion. *So*, should a ship leave the Cove, an onlooker wouldn't suddenly *see* it appear out of the blue. Their mind is tricked into believing they'd seen it all along. Vice versa—they believe there'd never *been* a ship. With that, it's doable for *Antigone* to pass into the Vault of Faces and dock in the port without raising suspicion."

Cesare and Giorgianna swapped wary looks. *No choice.*

"Rita and I," Kel opened, "on top of the efforts of the twins, Ces, contacts, all that, should be at least half-way adequate at spreading rumours."

A brown-haired man, another pair in tow, got up and left, the door almost slamming behind them.

Lorita sighed. "We're still working on unruly Morettae."

Cesare's eyes rolled.

"The Court?" Giorgianna asked Kel. "I'll be all but disappearing."

"A couple Morettae I trust—Yezo and Anka-ny—" the swarthy Naamɓe man who had been the first to side with Kel and the Gilmylvetlan woman who was the last, "are willing to help out."

"We're there too," Errico added. "That's been our work for a while, anyway."

Alessa concurred with, "I know plenty of folks around to help."

Giorgianna clasped her hands together. "I would be forever grateful."

Cesare broke his attention away. "Those of us pertaining to the Antrum are expected at Viper's Den to-night to meet Leone and Valentina, then Vitture later. In the early morning. This is a matter of everyone's safety, not just the Antrum's. We don't know how much damage Davide left behind, no matter what his goons said. A blunder on our end could spell the end for everything beneath upper óssium."

They stood against an autocracy; a ruthless, inexorable despot willing to slaughter his own people to keep them subjugated. Every drop of blood he spilled watered the soil in which tyranny took root, nourishing and sustaining it so brutality may thrive. Immolating the earth with a revolutionary conflagration stood as the only method of doing away with the regime. *What's left in the soil can always sprout.*

But would their matches be sufficient?

THE MUTILATED SUN BLED UPON THE GOLD-LEAF SKY as if a king's severed head across a ballroom floor. One needed to lose a lot of blood for a surface to glisten so red. Maybe the moon would tourniquet the sun's wounds with her pearl necklace so he may flash his white teeth in gloating immortality come the morrow's dawn.

Upon the solitary grotto, tucked like a cavity into the rocky jaws of Smugglers' Cove, sunblinks scintillated, the conciliated ocean a mirror of the spessartite welkin. Honey-crested waves lapped stout rocks leading a mile and a half east to the District and crawled under the soaring precipice into the aphotic depths of a low littoral cave.

On the outcrops, my jacket and boots basked beneath sundown.

I had made the nook in the cliffs my latibule, as if a mermaid hiding from human poachers. Peace was scarce; only its illusion remained a potentiality in this slaughterhouse world.

The grotto was *my* illusion.

I reached into the ruffles of my skirt and plucked out a steel lancet I'd pocketed from Libitina's mortuary. Waning sun traced its edge. I trailed it along my wrist to where a vein quivered, and sank the blade. Flesh split with a *suck*, offering up ichor. A viscid slither trailed down my elbow and dripped into the liquefied sunset as I dragged the blade through my skin to split it.

Attuning to the song of pulse, I translated the susurrations of azoth into the blood's language. Red rivulets purled across my skin, trailing up my palms. My skull strained, throat salty-sweet as I brought my fingertips together and pinched the blood into a blade of its own, glistening as the garnets I adored.

I slashed a fingertip.

Callused skin opened with a sting and bled more.

Ilinka occultist Nashĭgostu Kurilit Gostiata, author of '*Spagyrism and Spellwerk*', was known to wield his blood like swords, voiding his whole body of its vital supply through slashed wrists. He was among the most peculiar magi, ones whose azothian occlusion within the frontal lobe had been punctured, or torn away, by physical trauma. A magus was then permitted unrestricted manipulation of azoth—a method Gostiata dubbed 'transfusion'.

I exhausted my transmuted azoth.

The blood-blade collapsed like a slain civilisation and streamed between my fingers into the waves, and I wished to flow into it. To unify with the seas' vastness, its dialectic wisdom. To nebulise into a million droplets against the cliffs yet remain whole.

But I was human. Reduced to dirt beneath the foot of a titan demiurge reigning the gilded cage which confined Us. My life as extinguishable as a candle flame. The lives of the people I still had with me—no less so. I fell onto this deadly chessboard with no injunction, nothing to catch my catastrophic descent, so I blamed another singularity for pushing me when I had been a domino stacked beside my father whose own plummet was predetermined.

But I was no longer a pawn.

Rebellion against a totality so unjust could only ever end in nullification and rebirth. *Does the enormity of this war not outweigh my puny vengeance?* Was I myopic to forge the revolt into a selfish weapon? But were the very people I massacred not complacent in upholding the regime which kept Us chained? Would I not be shooting down two birds with one bullet?

From a gold sa cannacca chain circleting my corseted waist, I picked a pampel-shaped phial of ano-apozem, releasing a couple drops onto my palm and singing to azoth. The elixir coated my skin with a thin sheet. The laceration along my arm guzzled it and stitched shut with a spidery crawl into unmarred skin. The sensation no longer repulsed me.

"Whatcha doin', girl?" Sarnai's voice startled me.

I plunged my arm beneath the waves, finding the rock outcrops where the white-haired woman stood.

A strained smile nudged my lips. "Entertaining my romanticist ruminations." I swam closer. Sarnai shucked off her boots and rolled up her trousers, dipping her feet into the water when she sat. My eyebrows wound together. "Sarnai…" I placed my hands atop her knees. "I *don't* want you to go into the government building with me."

She smacked her hands over mine. "Well, I'm doing it anyway. I like Araya, and I'm happy to play a role."

"Are you happy to play with your life?"

"I mean, *no…*" Sarnai drawled, "but if it's *necessary*, it's necessary."

"*Listen* to me!" I grasped her hands. "I cannot lose you like Ema and papa. You are too important. My safety will never be worth your life. *Please.* Not for me." She didn't deserve a single ounce of pain.

"Look, I *get* it, *but…*" She shrugged. "I won't be deterred."

"You're impossible."

She smirked. "And you *like* impossible."

"You help me too much."

Sarnai leaned back and buttressed her body with her elbows. "As do you."

I frowned. "*Hm?*"

Sarnai flicked at her suyh earring. "I… never really had friends. No particular reason—just never befriended anybody. Which is admittedly odd, given I'm *rather* gregarious." She threw a hand to her heart in jest before seeking out my gaze earnestly. "You're the first person I truly had here in Vencenza, and so I want to be there for *you.*"

"If you die because of—"

"*Shush.*" She placed a hand to my mouth. "I shall not be moved."

I crossed my arms. "But I do *not* have to be pleased with it."

"Whatever, Eligio." She rolled her eyes. "You mentioned you paid your dearest əəzh[45] a visit?"

I leaned back against the rocks. "She told me that, despite all the things she said of him, despite every time she reviled him, she *loved* my father. And… the tragedy of it all rests in that… my father loved her too."

The sun was a delicate sliver of pale gold melting into the watery crucible of the dimming horizon, the wind and waters a pair of whispering gossipers. "I always wondered why Elenedda never remarried—why neither of them did—and my heart aches too much to let myself believe they still loved each other."

Sarnai bunched her lips. "Reincarnation is a belief in Örgön Gazaar." When I eyed her sceptically, she waved her hands. "Walk with me on

---

[45] Gazaari for '*mother*'.

this. When my övöö[46] passed, əməə[47] was twenty-two—already with child. Later in life, she told me that the part of her heart which harboured övöö's love hollowed out upon his death, then froze solid as permafrost so she would never again love another. But she would find him again in the next life, and in every life onwards. *Her* words, might I add." She met my eyes. "I know reincarnation's not an Illutèri concept, but perhaps your parents were like my grandparents, as far as the depth of their love ran, imperfect as it was."

I observed her eyes: gleaming onyx.

No one ever spoke of Love's violence; of all the times it tore your heart from your chest and commanded you carry on living.

I'd read my way through every heart-rending tragic romance book I could get my hands on at *The Sunrise*. Not that I'd ever admit to it.

To yearn for the agony of love was a destructive delight. To be willing for someone's fingers to open your ribs, to rip your heart off its vessels and hand that warm, beating thing over to Love was a sickness, a rot softening your flesh like fruit. To tremble with hunger—the worst kind of anguish—at the impossibility of attaining the closeness your soul begged for should make anyone swear off something as horrible as Love.

And yet there I was.

'*Love*' in Faustinian was '*ataínè*', after all. '*Eater*'. '*Gnawer*'.

"I don't believe you and I are," I heard myself half-whisper.

A wry smile kinked Sarnai's lips. "I'm inclined to agree." She looked on as diamond stars sparkled into existence. "Whenever I kissed you, my eyes stayed open, looking for a person whose kiss wouldn't feel like opening a vein. It's not fair on either of us, you know. I'm made of candy. And someone in this world will bare their wrists to you."

I knew I could never subject Sarnai to the love I sought. Not when humanity was already cruel and this world was greedy, and they took without scruples. *And what vengeful creature am I?*

I sidled closer to her, eyeing her askew with a secretive smile.

Her brows pushed down. "What?"

---

[46] *oh-VOH'oh*; Gazaari for '*grandfather*'.
[47] *eh-MEH'eh*; Gazaari for '*grandmother*'.

I gently pinched her waist. "Itxaro?"

Sarnai kicked at the vivid padparadscha sapphire that was the water. "Maybe there's something for a candy gal like myself."

I sighed dramatically. "You ought to kiss her, then, I fear."

"Oh, like a certain curly-haired witchling ought to kiss Signór Revolution?" Sarnai's words flustered up butterflies in my stomach. "I'm not blind or stupid, you know." She flicked a pallid lock over her shoulder.

"I love you, silly." I leaned my heated cheek onto Sarnai's knee.

"Love you too, lunatic." Her fingers stroked my hair, the two of us cradled in each other's aura, and in that tiny junction in time, all my grief and loss didn't weigh so unbearably on my back.

Sarnai stirred. "Isaia the Eternal Snore allocated assignments around the district to-night, so I'll take my leave." She kissed my forehead. "You take care, yes? And *don't* send my greetings to Leone."

"I expect to be the first person you come see upon your return!" I warned whilst she zipped up her boots.

"No question!" Sarnai beamed and ran off into the cliffs.

Autumn breeze breathed into the crook of my neck as I traced the empty crevices between the stars, still flushed with sunlight's last droplets, then snatched a breath from the gloaming ether and dipped beneath the waves.

SIX.

Cesare yanked the throwing knife from the wall above his bed.

Two fingers' width off centre. *Not close enough.*

His head swam on his walk to the room's centre, his vision a tunnel as he pivoted and trained his eyes on the target's heart.

The blade flitted from his hand and impaled the wood.

Five.

Two fingers' width.

Cesare scowled and fetched the blade.

'Cesare.'

Let me rest!

He hurled the knife.

Four.

A finger's width.

His teeth broke through his cheek.

Not close enough.

"*Cesare.*"

He swallowed blood and repeated his ritual.

Three.

Three fingers' width.

Breaths lay like handfuls of gravel in his lungs as he retrieved the blade—"Cesare"—to throw it once more.

Two.

Retrieve, return, aim, fling.

"*Cesare!*"

The wall spat splinters.

One!

He turned sharply. "Why are you *shouting?*"

Giorgianna reclined against the door frame in black trousers, her corset overlaying a tulle shirt crimson as blood. As wrath. *As love.* "Because I've been calling out to you for the last four throws."

Her assertion jolted him.

Cesare dropped his throwing knife off on his cluttered escritoire. Folding his arms, he leaned against it. "To what do I owe this company?"

She strolled across the chamber and planted herself on the sill of the bay window. "We *do* depart for the Serpents' district in a mere hour." Her eyes frisked his torso. "You are swimming in your shirt."

Cesare smirked hollowly. "It delights me that you, at long last, recognise my tastes."

An unimpressed regard. "You're not as witty as you think you are."

He *tsk'd.* "What was that I said about you shooting me in the heart?"

Her eyes rolled towards the knife scars where they stalled. "Why?"

Cesare scrutinised the distal wall, painfully aware of the fog to his field's right. "I used to have a sniper's vision."

"You are not diminished."

"To *you*."

Giorgianna's silence prompted Cesare to look back. Her scrutiny gnawed in the way of a fresh burn. *Don't* look *at me like that!*

"Why have I not heard you play your violin?"

"Even if I wanted to, I don't have it in me." He rubbed the tiny hoop in his earlobe. "I feel everything and nothing at once."

Giorgianna approached Cesare.

Her fragrance pressed against him as if a warm body despite her distance. Dizzying. *Maddening.* A philtre.

She carefully tidied the stray waves flicked across the partition of his hair, her brow strained and breaths almost audible—almost ghosting his skin. "I know it's as good as asking a stone to bleed, but please *talk* to me, Cesare."

His chest clenched, heavy and burning.

He recognised the true meaning of her query. Yet, bizarrely… he was willing to endeavour answering the way she wished.

He pushed her hands away and bound his hair, the trimmed length almost too short to stay put, and grabbed the sabre from beneath his escritoire. "Come spar." He made for the door.

"Did you hear *nothing* I said?" Giorgianna pursued. "You aren't in—"

He pivoted. "Do you want me to talk or not?"

She took a step back, then exhaled in acquiescence.

In the fading light, stillness ruled *Antigone's* stern deck. Not even Danilo serenaded the moon. Only the howls and breakers tussled at the base of the mighty hull.

The song of metal gashed the tranquillity apart.

Giorgianna and Cesare's blades unbound; they both passed back.

Cesare spun his sabre through his wrist and struck. Giorgianna parried. *Strike.* Parry. *Strike.* Parry. *Strike.* Parry. Riposte. Cesare dipped smoothly beneath Giorgianna's fast horizontal slice, twirling on his feet to keep her in his line of sight.

He rolled his sleeves to his elbows and slashed skyward. She pivoted, hacked down, hair whipping in every direction. Their swords bound. She unsheathed her baselard and swung. He shoved her before she landed the hit, hooking her ankle with his foot and yanking her legs from under her.

She extended her foot to ram his shin and take him down with her.

Cesare's sabre met Giorgianna's rapier and dagger with a plangent *dong* as he pinned her beneath him. "Give up," he sniped.

Giorgianna's muscles trembled. "You *first!*" She peaked her knees and thrust her pelvis upward. Cesare's breath caught as he lost balance, tipping forward and bolstering himself on the timber strewn with curls.

A gash of pain stunned Cesare into dropping his sabre.

Giorgianna trapped his arm beneath hers and tucked it to her body, hooking her foot on the outside of his before shoving him onto his back with her entire body.

His head struck the floor hard, his chest compressed beneath her thighs. She stabbed the wood centimetres from Cesare's cheek with her rapier and leaned on its hilt. Ringlets spilled off her back onto his shoulders. She dragged the flat of her dagger's blade across her tongue, drinking down the blood left behind, and Cesare realised it was *his* when the pulsation of a gash on his forearm demanded his heed.

Giorgianna tucked the blade under his jaw, forced it to angle back, metal a whisper against the blood pumping hot and alive under his skin. "Déjà vu?" she panted, eyes smouldering down at him. *Devour me.*

Cesare swallowed into his parched throat. "As it's impossible for me to admit defeat," his chest heaved between words he could barely stitch together, "I will chalk up your vast improvement to my sickly state."

Giorgianna peered at him, her own breathing ragged as his, then climbed off and sheathed her weapons.

When Cesare rose, she tugged wordlessly on his sleeve to bring his arm towards her, releasing a single drop of apozem on the cut she herself had imparted. The tonic stretched thin as gossamer, lacquering the wound, weaving it shut. *Water speaking.* Cesare's stomach hollowed. *You are going to kill yourself this way…*

"The implication was that sparring will make you talk." Giorgianna sang the shed blood off his skin and pooled it in her palm, then licked it clean.

Cesare sheathed his sabre. "Then I'm an open book." A lie, but there was too much to say with no prompt.

Her bloodied lips pressed together. "Would you tell me more of your life in Zargòsa?" The question came softly, diffident.

Should've seen that coming.

Cesare tightened his hair tie and combed his fingers through his loose bangs for lack of eyepatch to fiddle with. Yet he still found himself willing to talk. "You told me you rather like long stories. Well, do I have a tale." *If that's the word to you.* Drawing a steadying breath to no remedy, he leaned against the mizzenmast. "After my parents' music career began slipping down the drain like the old blood it was, Raul and my mother, Andelia, took me and my little sister Erosabel to live with my amôna, Golipên Elgani Gebara, in a village called Canronê in Zargòsa's southwest.

"Amôna was…" Cesare half-shrugged, "fine? Reservations regarding Raul's non-Marlâre heritage aside, she never treated us as less than family. Even if I could've sold it, I would never part with that silver crotal bell earring. It had been hers—a Marlâre tradition. Sings to the wind." The other was gifted to his sister. "There were very few younger woodcutters in Canronê, making Raul invaluable."

Cesare gazed across the bay. "He wanted nothing more than to prove his mother's degrading of him wrong. So, with his dreams in pieces, and after amôna's death, he was left with no one to pull him from the edge— Golipên became a matronly anchor he clung to. And he was left with no one to halt his abusive hand—"

"No." Giorgianna's swift word snatched Cesare's attention back. Her brow tensed. "I don't want you to feel obligated to say more if it pains you."

Cesare held her eyes a second before reaching for a pack. "It will pain me regardless." He lit a sigarétta and dragged into his lungs. "He grew detached. All that dazzling charisma of his extinguished. It escalated fast to shouts, berating, throwing and breaking furniture. My mother tried to plead with him, but it only got her screams until… he struck her. Hard."

Cesare drew more charred death into himself. "If there was any blessing, it's that he chose to hurt *me* the most. I'd been a kid with nothing on him by way of brute force, and my inability to keep my mouth shut certainly made itself apparent. I hid quietly in wardrobes and cupboards around the house when Raul would prowl in the dead of night looking to beat me. Sometimes it worked. Sometimes not."

The genesis of his first fear. Eventually, all touch—bar his little sister's—meant pain, and even when it finally ceased to, the black memories of his childhood never vanished.

"My mother became neglectful. Not out of spite, but *fear*. Scared that engaging with Erosabel and me would draw Raul's wrath to us. But I was, *what*, nine, ten? Erosabel was six at most? I didn't *understand* that. To me, it looked as if Andelia left her children to get battered by her husband whilst she holed up in her dressmaking workshop out of his sight. It wasn't true, *obviously* it wasn't fucking true, but I recognised far too late the near-impossibility of leaving a situation like that, no matter how horrible it became." Cesare winced. "I would lock my sister's room at night so Raul wouldn't bother with her. I'd get her out of the house any chance I could, and, when no other choice was left, I drew his attention to myself, even if it meant being unable to move for days afterwards from pain. It didn't matter, in the end." All Cesare and Erosabel had left was each other, but Cesare failed in *that* too. *Bringer of death.*

"A staple Marlâre spice is paprika." He dragged smoke. "During and after Golipên's life, the halls of the old home always smelled in that sweet, peppery way."

Cesare paused to breathe, but he couldn't.

He swallowed, focusing on the bobble of his throat, the rigidity of the mast beneath his back and the clamminess in his palms.

Air filled his lungs and he carried on, "I was ten, returning home one evening—I visited the part of the village where itinerants squatted, and I'd sent my sister off with friends that day, asking she not be home without me. My mother's workshop was…" he waved his sigarétta as if to demonstrate, "far enough removed from the house for one to be none the wiser as to the goings on of the house proper. I no longer bothered saying my greetings to her, by then." He shook his head at himself. *Stupid kid.* "I entered the antechamber… and I could *taste* its aroma. But redder, warmer. *Metallic.* Not paprika." His vision vignetted. "Death. Trusting the horrible premonition, I followed the stench into my sister's bedchamber… and there was nothing. So I went into *my* chamber, and…"

Cesare inhaled, exhaled, grit his teeth, drew smoke. "I found Erosabel. What he left of her." How could Cesare ever put words to what he saw in that cursed room? How could someone, with their own two hands, create a sight so horrifically ineffable? "Blood soaked the mattress through so deeply that red slathered the floor under the bed. Erosabel was dismembered—limbs chopped into pieces; head almost hacked clean off; entrails spilled across the floor; skull cracked; tiny body bruised until no skin was left." Cesare shook his head for no rhyme or reason. "I screamed for my mother. She collapsed and huddled against the wall in hysterical wailing. I could never blame her.

"Then… the front door slammed open." He clicked his tongue. "I barely remember what led up to the next moments, but Raul cornered us in my bedchamber. Went for me first, naturally… and I *saw* Andelia's instincts brandish claws as she tried to stop him. He smashed her skull against the wall. Then," Cesare finished his sigarétta, exhaling before smoke touched his lungs, "I had to open my big mouth. I don't even remember what I told him—that's how fucking insignificant it was!— but enough for him to start swinging his axe at me." Cesare briefly faced Giorgianna's speechlessness. "You can deduce where he got me." And where his second fear originated. Axes were ugly things anyway.

"As he hacked at me, Raul shouted: '*They weren't supposed to get in the way! It was only meant to be* you!'" *You let them die.* Despite himself, Cesare scoffed. "I barely stumbled out of that house with guts dropping out of me; only got away because I knocked over amôna's beloved old paraffin lantern and set the house ablaze. Hence the burns." He gestured to the splotches on his forearm. "An Abeslâri surgeon worked as a doctor among the itinerants and unhoused of Canronê. Miren. She'd practised in Du Rrât a du Errèina until an accident led to the death of a ruling class child she was operating. She, disgraced, was chased out of the capital by her fellowship. I barely knew her, but owe her my life. She stitched me back together and sent me on my way… Anywhere but *there*. I caught a ship from Ingartze to Vencenza. After the beating, I fell into a three-week-long coma, and Raul…" Cesare could barely believe his own words told the truth, "got nothing. Woodcutters were few and invaluable.

"Miren told me she was convinced I wouldn't live… And it's like she was *trying* to rub salt into my wounds, because I didn't fucking want to!" Cesare's eyes snapped to Giorgianna, yet he saw nothing at all. "Do you really think I wanted to *live* after what I had to *see*? After what that evil fucking bastard *told* me? My mother and sister are *dead*. Because of *me*."

"Don't—"

"*I* was the reason I lost *everyone* I *ever* loved."

"You were a *child*!"

"And I should've been *dead*!" he bit. "It should've been *my* worthless body ruined on that forsaken fucking bed!" He looked away. "I hated everything of me begotten by Raul—the lighter shade of my hair, the shape of my cheeks. But I despised *nothing* more than the green in my eyes because it was just like *his*." Cesare had gotten his mother's coarse, thick waves whilst Erosabel's locks—lighter than his—had been smooth as fine silk. "I told myself that if my eyes'd been solely that colour, I'd've ripped the fuckers out. Sometimes I still entertain the prospect."

Cesare's regard flickered across Giorgianna's face, still unseeing. "Make no mistake, I don't hate him for what he did to *me*. I hate him for what he did to *them*." He lit another coffin nail. "These eyes are now a reminder that I *lived*, that I *forced* myself to survive, and that *he* is dead in every way but the physical."

He finally allowed himself to hold Giorgianna's gaze.

Tears welled in her eyes. Her head shook. "I'm sorry," she breathed. "I'm so sorry." A tear dropped down her cheek. "You didn't deserve such horrible pain—never."

Cesare walked past her towards the end of the stern. "It doesn't matter."

Giorgianna followed him. "How can it *not matter*?"

Cesare sat, draping his legs off the deck's edge above the ocean and resting his elbows on the railing in front of his chest. "It was fourteen years ago."

"But it haunts you."

"Maybe it should."

"You were a *child…*" Giorgianna's voice cracked. "This is not your guilt—you are blameless."

Finding himself painfully without words, all Cesare could do was drag his sigarétta even as his heart vied to break him open.

Giorgianna sat behind him. The warmth of her fingertips hovered over his shoulders. "Are you…?" Her inquiry trailed off.

Cesare understood her request, thinking it over.

Ever since she tended to him after Manuele's thrashing, she proved her touch did not stem from malevolence. Considering the note they started off on, such a development astounded Cesare.

"I don't care if you touch me, vólto," he conceded, drawing smoke.

Hesitating a little longer, Giorgianna rested her hands on his shoulders, cautious and gentle.

The missing singe of bile in his throat almost troubled Cesare.

Giorgianna's slender arms slipped around his neck.

Cesare's breath hitched, his stomach clutching as she lay her head onto his shoulder. As her curls cocooned him. Her limbs remained a fraction braced, as if she hesitated even whilst embracing him.

An exhale loosened from his lungs.

Salt wind and evening dew tumbled in linns along the caramel spirals of her hair, and, more than anything, Giorgianna's presence evoked… *solace.*

Cesare's hand floated by her arm, her warm skin, but abnegation tied his aching fingers just in time, binding them shut. Nails sank into his palm. He could never allow himself to touch her the way he wished, no matter how much agony it brought. His sole raison d'être was revolution. Giorgianna's: revenge.

He sighted the scar glistening on his wrist. Their blood promise.

In this miserable world, scars were irreparable. Depending on underlying criteria, the only means by which such bargains could dissolve was the death of all but one party. Once you promised a few drops of your blood, you owed all of it, should even the instigating motive for the binding be realised. Tenderness between them was purposeless. All they could ever end in was bloody and tear-stained tragedy.

Giorgianna lifted her head. "That scum deserves to bleed."

"It doesn't matter."

She pulled back abruptly. "Stop *saying* that!"

"Leave it alone, vólto." Cesare smoked the coffin nail she almost made him forget.

"*Why*? Why do you *do* that?" She sat by his side. "You say *I* should feel no guilt in my father's and Emanuela's murders, yet you wholly blame yourself for something you're even *less* complicit in." She peered at him until he looked back. "You're a hypocrite."

Cesare's impulse was resorting to his wonted '*it doesn't matter*' or '*don't worry about me*' but, knowing it would never work with her, he withdrew along a different path: "All I can reasonably postulate is that… there's little likelihood that Raul wasn't always like that, to some extent." With his mother's demeaning of him as a backdrop, Raul sought control by any means, sacrificing multiple lives and his own humanity in its fruitless pursuit.

Cesare snorted. Fuckers like *that* never ceased stalking him. "That *dazzling charisma* doing what the job description implies." He pensively read the lines of his palm. "I fear nothing more than becoming like him."

He failed to protect his sister. The twins' parents. His home. He could *never* fail again, even if he killed himself in a bid to win.

Silence drew a deep breath.

Giorgianna leaned her head onto Cesare's shoulder. He wound up, but didn't withdraw. "You couldn't."

An inexplicable pressure pushed at his ribs from within.

He cradled in his scarred palm a caramel coil of hers, a perfect double helix. *Everything about you is like a painting.* Cesare was sure he'd regret telling his story, but, in the end, he found himself glad it was *her*.

Then, shouts boomed from the wharf.

SCENE XV

SERPENT AND
BLACK-TONGUE

Giorgianna | Ygạl | Giorgianna

CESARE AND I BOLTED FOR THE WHARF where a pack of six smugglers prowled around one—a dark-haired older man held down by two others.

A bald man, broad as a golem, held a boarding sword to the captive's leg, its blade cut into massive serrations.

Nausea turned my gut. *Fabio!*

Heads snapped to us as we neared.

The two smugglers unhanded Fabio.

Black ink illustrated a gash as if a knife slit at their throats. From its bloodless depths hung an artistic rendition of a black tongue.

Fabio found his foothold with my aid.

The four Tongues slid to flank the two in the centre.

The bald man's eyes rippled like bowls of watery milk as he grinned a half-row of gold teeth. "Who joins us, Visolela?" Sten's head angled towards the statuesque Ónjunu[48] woman with auburn locs and endless necklaces strung of miniature beads. *Sten's first mate and quartermaster.*

She threw us frigid looks, stately features serene. "The main two."

My fingers tightened around my rapier's hilt.

Sten's clouded eyes shot to my hand.

Pressure gripped my windpipe, a sparkling, frosty squall soughing through my veins. *Not mine.* I gulped, shivering, and he smiled as if he knew. *He is singing to my blood…*

"*'EY!*" Korneli's voice bellowed behind us.

He and Ren advanced with drawn weapons, Danilo positioned at a distance with an aimed musket.

Boom! Dan shot nothing.

Visolela unholstered her rifle and fired a returning shot into the night.

"Hold it! *Hold!*" Fabio ordered his Hydras.

"*You,*" Sten jabbed a meaty finger at Cesare and me, ambling a slow circle, his Tongues in harmony, "are *trespassers* in the Cove. Know whose district yous in. *Smugglers'!*" He lifted his boarding sword. "Make a single sideways move on these streets, and I'll cut your tongues and stomachs out. I ain't Dahlia—I'll make not *one* step yous take in our home safe." Sten licked his lips, a piercing gleaming in his tongue, and turned sightless eyes to Fabio. "Fuckin' lucky, Amadi." He spat on the ground. "Fuckin' *lucky.*"

And The Black Tongues stalked off, Danilo and Visolela swapping unaimed gunshots in parting.

I clutched Fabio's arm. "Are you—?"

"Leave it," Fabio swatted us all away. The gesture struck me; I realised where I had seen it before. "Head aboard and inform our Hydras of the Tongues' threat. Make the Pearls and Teeth aware."

The Hydras nodded to their captain and left.

"Giorgianna, Cesare." Fabio faced us. "Keep on the outskirts of the district on your way to-night, or move via oldtown outright. This was a direct warning from The Black Tongues—Sten *will* go through with it should a chance come by."

---

[48] Two primary ethnic groups exist in Ónjolela: *Ónjunu,* and *Basingolo.*

"Does this have anything to do with Dahlia's Blood Rite?" I asked.

"Likely. Tongue leadership is almost never this active in District proper. But this is simply what Sten is. Both compounded makes it all the more deadly. *So*, I will *reiterate*." Fabio gripped both mine and Cesare's arms. "Stay on the perimeter. In a day's time is the Blood Rite and its participants are merciless and bloodthirsty. Pâin, Dahlia's champion, ripped out the spines of five opponents like fish and tore three of their heads off last time, walking out of that fight with a singular cut on his cheek he bears like a trophy. Fēngnà wasn't lying when she said you cannot kill Pâin." Fabio paused, fingers squeezing. "I won't have you die, so stay away. Fuck allies, fuck information—*nothing* is worth handing your lives over to cutthroats."

We had a long and treacherous night ahead of us still, and everything in my bones premonished calamity.

AMID THE MONOTONY OF COMMIEBLOCKS, adrip in the lymphic glow of the Antrum's false stars, unrolled a glorious palladian mansion. The Viper's Den. Behemoth marble projected five storeys into the not-sky. White-clad guards encircled its columned portico.

Plucking Leone's letter from inside her black thawb's appliquéd aureolin sleeve, Ygal handed it to the sentinels flanking an archway at the estate's western facet. "Your Dóminus issued a summon for myself and my consociates. Conclaves, as they tend towards."

The sentinel on the left scanned the letter. "Dóminus Ygal Najm of The Boars and The Hounds?"

"Yes, yes, my guests!" A fruity voice rushed down; the sharp echo of heels tracked by heavy thuds crescendoed from the vestibule beyond the rosey tulle of curtains.

Into view strutted a svelte man in an airy chiffon négligée the colour of cherry blossoms—slit deep to bare the golden tan of his chiselled torso. A serpent tattoo slithered from the centre of his dextral hand to the apex of his shoulder, isabelline pantaloons and white boots dressing his long legs. Four guards sporting matching snake ink accompanied him. All easily measured up to Ygạl's height if not surpassed it, their torsos stripped save for the shoulder-shielding leather chest scabbards strapping longswords to their backs. Leone Caivano was no fighter, so he compensated.

"Out of my way, worms," he dismissed his sentinels and flicked ear-embracing flaxen curls from his honey-gold eyes. Sensuous lips split to gleam teeth finer than pearls. "*Oh*, Ygạl!" He bestowed unto her a flutter of a hug. His moscato and gardenia perfume pricked the eyes near to tears. "So many months have come and flickered by without seeing your stunningly familiar visage." He flourished a manicured hand to beckon his guests into the avant-garde rococo splendour of his mansion's peripheral vestibule.

Two guards positioned themselves by their flanks, the other pair at the Viper's.

Ygạl brushed Leone's powdered makeup off her qarqūsh[49] and offered an arm to Lucrezia who accepted eagerly, tucking close to his side. Giorgianna wreathed her arms around her waist and donned her vigilant frown. Cesare pocketed his hands, chewing into his cheek with that menacing pout plastered to his face.

Ygạl shook their head inwardly. *Tactful diplomacy…* "And *whose* fault, pray tell, may that be, sayın Caivano?"

Marble echoed as their cavalcade ascended a grandiose curving staircase to the third floor. "*Do* forgive me, my friend. Unrest has befallen even my corner of the realm."

They proceeded across a decorated chamber painted top-down with angelic frescos, chiming gimcracks and garish ornaments crowding endless shelves. '*Dust collectors*', Ygạl's maternal aunt Dilnaza called them. No doubt she'd say the same of Ygạl's quarters, so perhaps she couldn't rebuke the man's proclivities, wasteful and sybaritic as they

---

[49] A type of headdress resembling a bonnet tethered to the chin by a beaded strip of cloth, with a T-shaped, embroidered veil attached to its back. Characteristic of the Ḥarb and Banū Mālik [*and other Ṭā'if region*] tribes of al-Ḥijāz.

were. Where Ygạl could generally only afford barter and haggling, Leone purchased outright.

"*But*," the Viper clapped, "to-day, we shall be merry."

Ygạl's scarred lip twitched. "As my correspondence implied, I am not here to be 'merry' with you."

Leone's mascara-framed eyes spun in kittenish disregard. "Of *course*, of course, all shall come to pass as instructed."

"Valentina is in attendance?"

"Awaiting our company in my office."

"How does she fare?"

"Tina is *always* a treat."

"On a personal standing, or on your cock?" Ygạl sniped.

Leone halted and turned gracefully in place, facing Ygạl.

A conceited smile never let up dominion over his face, but liqueur-sweet venom glossed his lips. A deep half-chuckle, threatening as a snake's rattling tail, writhed in his throat. "Oh, *you…*" His head tilted. Ygạl displayed no shortage of her own hauteur in the face of Leone's volatility.

His auric eyes flicked for Lucrezia, glinting. "I seem to have neglected the rest of my guests!" He cradled her hands. "Signorína Montefiore." Leone brushed a kiss against Lucrezia's knuckles, her face deceptively forbearing. "*Oh—*" he straightened, "mayhap it be 'signóra Najm', now?"

Ygạl stiffened.

Lucrezia stared slack-jawed for a couple breaths. "Signorína Montefiore, for now." She nudged up her pince-nez. "But 'Lucrezia' always sufficed, Leo."

He chuckled, "A darling creature," toying with a silken lock by her curved cheekbones. His smile slipped. "Long hair accentuated your femaleness." He slipped the strands back into place. "Shame."

Ygạl's knuckles ached for the impact of Leone's face, zhǐjiǎtào scraping against each other. Lucrezia's nails sank into their arm.

A coquettish smirk hooked Leone's lips as he ran his fingertips along Cesare's collarbone, resting them at the lacing of his shirt. "It *has* been a while, hasn't it?"

The click of Cesare's tongue jolted Ygal. "Not long enough."

Ygal shut her eyes.

Leone palmed his heart, faux rue denting his sculpted brow. "So aloof." His laugh slipped like syrup. "Cleverness is becoming of you." And he strode past.

Ygal glared at Cesare who smirked with mirthless scorn right back. *Of* course *Curly would like you.*

Leone's eyes frisked every curve of Giorgianna. "*Your* name, sweet thing," he twirled her curls, holding out his other hand expectantly, "I am yet to know."

She unlaced her arms to place her fingers into his. "Giorgianna."

Leone kissed her knuckles. "A pleasure to be in such handsome company." He lingered, eyes boring into hers, before snapping upright and clapping twice, "Come along," finally leading the way to the fourth floor.

Giorgianna inched closer to Cesare whose kohled eyes raged with wildfire.

Under the watch of exotic animal mounts, they turned down a long corridor paved with thulian carpet. Six more Serpents guarded the chryselephantine doors to Leone's quarters.

Yet more powdery gardenia hit Ygal hard as a buffalo stampede when they entered.

The chamber sparkled, nothing but brocade and silk as far as the eye could see. Servants tended silently to the distal half of the office—women dressed in plunge-neck dresses grazing their palms and ankles, fashioned of little more than pink diaphane. Gold cuffs clasped their throats, ankles, wrists, unbound to chains but displaying latches to allow for it.

A Qeoloni woman smoking from an opera-length sigarétta holder reclined on one of the morganite damask couches, a peplos of amaranth silk swathing her statuesque frame.

"Dearest and *illustrious* Domína *and* Madáma Valentina of The Hyacinths." Leone gestured to her on his amble to a vivarium behind the sofa, removing from it a leucistic ball python. Lunara. White scales iridesced, her eyes the brightest azure.

Ygal always steered clear of snakes. Bar *one*, it seemed.

Valentina's ebony hair was pinned into a wide chignon around her ears, her forehead decorated with a chainmail of intercalated gold annuli. Large oval hoops pierced both her lobes twice. She scrutinised the snake-garlanded Leone, then steered her black eyes to the guests and bobbed her head before silently dragging.

"Please," Leone addressed his guests, "sit." He spun in place. "And *you*!" A bark at the servants. "Begone from my sight, maggots! I shall not have vulgar filth slur me in front of esteemed company."

The women dropped to the floor in prostration before fluttering off. Ygạl noticed the slit and burn scars across their bodies for which she'd never received an explanation from the Viper. Though she knew what their vow of silence entailed. The thoughts coated her skin with dirt.

Leone sighed breezily and approached his well-endowed liquor cabinet. "Champagne, *mèus càra*?" he questioned Valentina. "Pastis or maraschino, mayhap?"

"I desire none of your moonshine, Leone," she sneered through smoke, her voice rich.

"*You*, for insulting *me*, are *so* daring." Leone grasped a bottle by its neck. "But for certain *goldwine* shall suit you, no? You hardly drink with me." *Couldn't imagine why…*

"I *plead* you leave me be," she muttered.

Leone pouted. "How utterly jejune and stodgy of you, Tina."

She drew smoke in reply.

"Might you have *blood*wine?" Lucrezia requested from her seat between Giorgianna and Ygạl.

"Do forgive me, signorína. For *very* special occasions only, in my abode."

"Caivano would rather feed his guests piss," jibed Valentina.

"You simply have *awfully* mundane tastes, fraúcni,[50]" huffed Leone.

Ygạl faced the Hyacinth. "A while, Nin-kalla."

Valentina nodded. "And yourself, Najm."

Leone brought glasses and goldwine to the table. "The rest of you *will* drink, naturally."

---

[50] *frah-OOK-nee*; 'sweet'.

"I will not," Agostini piped up.

"You never do," whined Leone. "Just one glass?"

"Has that *ever* worked?"

Leone sighed. "*One* of these days I'll wear you down."

From the clenched jaw to the narrowed gaze, it evidently took *everything* within Cesare to not return fire again. But even he knew better, in this house.

Leone poured glasses for everyone, halting before handing the last to Giorgianna. "A drinker?"

"No." Nothing in Giorgianna's tone bespoke amusement.

"*Mm…hm.*" Leone tapped his lips in thought as he pinned Giorgianna down for a dissection. Her copper eyes bound with the burnished gold of his, resolute.

"I *believe*," Valentina glided in, "there was a purpose to this gathering."

As the lingering throngs of tension took to reluctantly dispersing, Ygal replied, "You believed correctly."

Each time Ygal recited their stratagems, they sounded less and less like real words. Between hers attempting diplomacy within the Antrum, Giorgianna's approaching infiltration of the ministerial house, and Cesare dealing with Morettae and stirring discontent among citizenry, it was a miracle any of them could keep their heads above water.

Servants returned to lay out glittering crystalware with desserts, yet even Agostini's mood was too sour to indulge his sweet tooth. No one drank besides Lucrezia and Leone. Not even Ygal.

"The Antrum can no longer remain neutral in the mayhem ensuing above," the Boar Dóminus continued. "Regardless of Davide's claims, we are indisputably in peril." Perhaps these were the ramifications to their continual ignorance of the city's politics, as if the Antrum was ever truly its own disengaged pocket in the universe. As if the powers that be could never come for them.

"Sugar is not to my guests' liking!" Leone shouted. "*Rid us of it!*"

The blond had been dismissive: flitting off to speak with sentinels, allotting time to converse with Lunara, interrupting Ygạl for countless minutes to lecture her about the powder smeared off his cheek as if it'd been her fault! Ygạl's temper had long-since begun waning.

A servant reached for a bowl of chocolate to be taken away.

Leone gripped her arm. A frown etched his smooth brow. "What is *this*?" He pointed to a mole. The woman's face bleached. "*Won't* do, sweetling." Leone plucked a shucking knife from his pants and sawed into her skin, gouging the mole without word or dwell.

Lucrezia didn't catch her gasp in time.

The woman's throat gave up an amorphous croak as blood streamed from the red ditch the Viper dug out, her lips curling over toothless gums to bare a tongue cut at its root.

That would be my answer to the scars…

Façade undented and attention unwilling to be wasted on someone he viewed as so far beneath himself, Leone clicked his fingers and waved the crying woman off, pulling a handkerchief from his pocket to wipe his blade. "Moles, 'beauty' spots, freckles, desecrate flesh. *That*," he waved his knife at Giorgianna's hate-wrung face, "under your eye, and the tiny one on your cheek: *very* irritating."

A peripheral door rattled, jolting everyone.

Guards barged in. "Dóminus Caivano."

"Gods! *What*?" Leone lashed.

"Reports of a double homicide on Death Adder Bypass."

"*Again*?" Leone shot to his feet. Guards dashed to his flanks. "It's like you worms don't know your *Gods*damn job!" He dropped Lunara off in her vivarium and stormed for the door. "Case report! Have my investigators dispatched, accompanied by myself—"

"*What*?" Ygạl exclaimed, following Leone. Valentina pinched her sleeve in warning. "This was supposed to be one of your ridiculous '*consultations*'. You didn't so much as extend the grace of offering a decision!"

Leone pivoted in the doorway. "I'll make contact with my decision the moment I am able to."

"You take an aeon to respond to one damn letter!" Ygąl bristled. "Why did you even request our presence?"

"In case you haven't noticed," hissed Leone, "I am *occupied* and don't have time to slum it with my fellow Dominíi."

"Have *all* the time in the world to host parties and fuck, though!"

Serpents drew weapons.

Leone clicked his fingers and raised a slim finger to halt them. "I will make *contact*, the moment I am *able* to. Don't be a pest, Ygąl." And the Viper left.

Ygąl returned to his seat, rubbing his temples. Lucrezia soothed his shoulder.

If they didn't have Leone, they didn't have anyone. Their imminent meeting with Vitture was bound to bear no fruits. If they had no allies among the cadres, the Antrum was left an open sore for The Bone King to make fester. The Antrum's culture differed from that of Vencenza proper—the people were loyal to their cadres, so if their Domíne couldn't be swayed, neither could they.

Leaning forward, Giorgianna addressed Valentina: "Why *are* you with someone like *him*?"

Ygąl knew why, but he wanted to hear the Hyacinth's rationale.

"His cadre offers mine protection; mine provides his with whispers and commodities."

The *real* reason was that Valentina ran a much smaller cadre—*the* smallest—and having her under his wing gave Leone's power-hunger a generous fondle. Valentina's choice in the matter was trifling at best. To an extent, Ygąl couldn't condemn the Viper for his manoeuvres. There were times when she herself felt not too differently in her employ of Isaia and The Hounds.

"These are uncertain times for us all," Valentina's statement threw Ygąl back into the Viper's hideous camelia-and-gold-leaf office, "but I believe Leone *will* make good on his promise."

Ygąl refrained from snorting, but Cesare did not.

Valentina stood. "When you have the spare minute, come to *Amaranth Lounge*. I will speak with you." She glimpsed the door by which the Viper left. "I fear Leone is due to throw us out, soon."

Nin-kalla dipped her chin in goodbye, jasmine and pomegranate sillage following her as she departed.

ESCORTED BY FIVE BLUE-GARBED STAG SENTINELS, our company arrived at the doors of a romanesque estate constructed of grey brickwork amidst alarmingly pristine and genteel streets, continuing through a barrel-vaulted corridor into the chintz-and-timber halls of the humid house proper.

The murmur of servants swarmed like flies to carrion, crawling up my spine and blighting my skin with gooseflesh. I jostled the unease to a shadowy corner in my mind as a pair of sentinels opened an oak door to Vitture's office.

A sweet, sickly aroma lay limp in the trembling hands of the air. Not blood, but fatty and sarcoid as offal. Soft and wet as dying breaths.

Unease skulked right back out.

On one of the cyanous twin sofas flanking a table sat two men.

The younger, plump and fair, sported a long-sleeved robe matching his smalt-blue eyes, his brown hair trimmed short and a stag's antlers inking his neck. *Vitture.*

Left of him, everything but the black mullet of the gargantuan stranger halted me. Studded leather dressed his muscular frame. A sleeveless vest lay bare vein-coiled arms tattooed with a row of eyes from the summit of his brawny shoulders to the palms of his nail-less hands. Metal embellished almost every carved angle of his face. Lupine orbs, yellow as triphanes, glinted behind steel prison bars of nails hammered through his protrusive brow ridge into his cheekbones.

"*Y*—gal." His wide lips gashed apart to flash incisors sharpened to flesh-ripping points. "Ygal, Ygal, Ygal."

The woman in question summoned a tight smile. "Lucanus. I thought you enjoyed Mair."

"Oh, I *did.*" Lucanus' eyes protruded. "I certainly, certainly did."

Ygạl held the gaze of the Dóminus of The Cyclopes before turning to the Stag. "Muscarà."

He stood sharply, chin high, spine pinned. "Dóminus Ygạl Najm." He dipped his head, Iutulicano-twanged voice measured, extending the same gesture to—"Domína Lucrezia Montefiore."

"Quit licking feet, Vitture," Lucanus hurled.

The Stag raised a hand.

The Cyclops ran his split tongue over his teeth and looked away.

Vitture nodded to—"Eavesdropper Isaia Caruana," before turning to me and Cesare. "And you?"

Lucanus doused us in a once-over.

I held back a scowl, meeting Vitture's eyes. "Giorgianna Damiani." My voice came terser than I'd wanted.

"Cesare suffices."

"A privilege to host you all." Vitture gestured to the sofa across from him and Lucanus. "Sit. Let us delegate."

Unease sat with me.

The cloying stench nauseated me more than the looping propositions of allyship.

Ygạl's oration concluded; Vitture steepled his hands. "Bringing this to my attention has been enlightening," he finally gave voice, "but I must spurn your request."

Ygạl blinked, mouth firm.

My fingers curled beside my thighs.

"I'm sorry?" Cesare seethed.

"Your proposition is an endangerment to my district."

"Our proposition?" Cesare snapped. "And the looming fucking threat to your entire home isn't?"

Vitture bridled at his tone. "You yourself admitted your knowledge is incomplete, that you are yet to ascertain the extent of this so-called 'threat' and that, to do so, you must infiltrate Governor Crescenzo De Tullia's circle. I am unwilling to throw all caution to the wind to aid you in fatuous óssium disputes which may prove only fruitless to us."

"*Fruitless…*" Cesare echoed the word as if it were the vilest slur thrown at him. "This isn't a gambling opportunity. It's the survival of the Antrum! Those óssium disputes you deem so fatuous will—"

"Fornicating with óssium's politicos is something I would've put past even *you*, Ygąl," Lucanus cut it.

An insulting smirk crooked Cesare's mouth. "Whilst there's not much *I* would put past *you*."

"I'd sew your loose lips shut, ossíi," snarled Lucanus. "It's *your* people threatening us."

Cesare perched his elbows on his knees, *tsk'ing*. "Did Davide not take refuge in *your* district, Luca? Perhaps if you gave a smidgen bigger of a damn who came and went on your own turf, we wouldn't be in this predicament."

I tugged his sleeve to counsel caution.

Lucanus' gaze flickered to me, then back to Cesare. A nasty sneer pulled his face. "Need your dirty little keeper to pacify you?"

Cesare was standing before Lucanus' words even struck my ear, daggers clenched in fists. "Wanna see what happens when she doesn't?"

All the rest were up in eyeblinks.

A zweihänder gleamed in Lucanus' fist.

"I *will* not tolerate a display of such barbarism!" the Stag reprimanded with all the spine of a mollusc.

"Don't you *trouble* yourself, yā *wēli*, Muscarà!" Ygąl sneered sweetly enough to rot teeth. "I'll be taking my consociates away," her lip twitched when she appraised Lucanus, "for I see you fancy bringing ungelded dogs indoors."

"*Apologies* I don't prostitute myself to ossíi gnats." The Cyclops thrust the blade of his colossal sword towards Cesare's breastbone.

A pointing gesture.

Perhaps a threat.

He mightn't have grazed skin, even.

But I lunged all the same.

My elbow shoved hard into Cesare's chest; body angled sideways towards Lucanus.

Flesh sang ripe and tender against steel, opening and pouring as my hand snapped around the zweihänder's blade.

My gaze clashed with Lucanus' through a chorus of gasps. Razoring pain amplified the breathing in my ears; my pulse as it emptied out of me. "I'd kill you before you'd ever draw his blood." I squeezed my fist.

And even *he* faltered. Even *he* paled before my Shadow.

"*Get OUT!*" Vitture spat blackly. "*All* of you!"

They say such things come in threes.

We traversed The Serpents' territory on our way back to the Boar estate, disillusioned twice over, Ygąl admonishing Cesare whilst I mended my gashes with the scant ano-apozem remaining on me.

Ygąl let up a sigh. "Unfortunately, our only chances apropos of the Antrum look to be waiting on Leone and Tina."

"How on earth is a piece of work like *Lucanus* still alive to govern a cadre?" questioned Lucrezia.

"Were we looking at the same bloke?" Ygąl snorted. "He is a beast."

"Oh what, he's got *no* one in his district who could do him in?"

"The Cyclopes' jurisdiction operates uniquely," explained Isaia. "Irrespective of who you are, if you kill the Dóminus—Lucanus, say— *you* become the Dóminus with full reign of the cadre. The new Dóminus is untouchable for eleven days post the old one's death, meaning, as stipulated by this law, they cannot be touched. Unsure why *eleven.*"

"The Eleven Days of Liminality," I murmured. *Illutèri.*

"For what he is," Ygąl said, "Lucanus is devout." A bleak laugh. "Fēngnà said Pâin is unkillable. Let the pirate wanker try Lucanus."

Dismay opened up a pit in my stomach.

The Hydras considered, Şirîn's band was small, The Morettae unpredictable and The Serpents and Hyacinths equivocal allies at best. Fēngnà's fleet and Ygąl's cadre were our greatest assets, yet would that be enough to face an enemy as immense as the legions of what was horribly quickly becoming the Empire once more? Not for lack of trying, we would have the majority of the populace on our side, but how often was such a hopeful scenario realised? How much trust could we, on reasonable grounds, place in near-divine luck?

I couldn't say I saw a path forward, and so I feared our desperate ailments would soon call for remedies of an equally desperate calibre.

Scene XVI

End's Beginning

Giorgianna | Cesare | Giorgianna

FIVE HUNDRED HOURS SHROUDED THE CLIFFS AND WHARFS beyond the porthole window of my chamber in lacy darkness, autumnal breeze slipping like cool satin across my skin.

Shivering into my trusty jacket, I tucked my pants into my boots and sluiced somnolence from my eyes before quitting my bedchamber—the second to last down the hallway. Fabio wished to see us in his quarters in the later hours of the morning, after which I endeavoured to scour deeper into my father's archives. Or at least that's what I'd tell everyone.

"*Ow!*" Cesare exclaimed from inside the lit storage room across the corridor. "Do you mind?"

"No, actually, I don't," Lissandri sniped. "Pass me a screwdriver if you're gonna be in the way." Shuffling sounded. Such early awakening was once customary for Lissandri, but recently had been growing rarer; I figured Cesare never went to sleep. "This clock's in a revolting state— cheers—and I *swear* this ladder's plotting my murder as we speak."

I giggled, a secret between me and myself, and left down the creaking hallway for the hold, eager to fill my stomach.

Hunger palliated, I ventured back below deck, a warm flat-bottomed maiolica bowl capped with a plate in one hand, a small platter of lobiani—bean-stuffed bread—in the other.

I noted the storage room's blackened innards and the door to Cesare's chamber at the hallway's end shut. Meanwhile, Rosalia's bedchamber to my left stood empty, quiet chatter emanating through the crack in the door to the opposite room: Eligio's.

I peeked in.

Seated at a table near the tiny room's centre, Rosalia fiddled with a photo frame displaying pinned cadavers of dead insects. Beside her, Eligio voided a watering can into a pot.

He lifted his head at me.

I smiled. "May I?"

A halting beam limned their features. "Come in!"

"I fetched you food."

"*Oh,* you shouldn't have! But thank you."

I sat beside him as he placed the plant among its verdant family.

He'd taken to gardening since settling into *Antigone,* since the tragedy of the *Curios* and *Sunrise,* as if called to nurture something living when death presided around him.

Rosalia held up a monarch butterfly. "I found a spot for my new specimen!"

Eligio made a face. "Lower the dead thing, will you?"

Rosalia pouted. "Libitina said we do *not* speak about bodies that way, old man!"

Eligio stooped to observe the insect. "Look. Its wing is damaged." He frowned. "And who're you calling 'old'?"

My heart ached.

They had all endured too much never-deserved grief. Perhaps, in some awful way, sorrow and bereavement bound us, even as I wished with my entire soul that our circumstances could be different—that our pain may not be so soul-rending—but none of our cards fell in our favour.

"That's the *point*." Rosalia's eyes whirled. "I want to display broken bugs that wouldn't be appreciated in a museum." She pointed to a fluffy moth white as snow and my blood cooled. "This one's pretty."

"*Virgipluma falena*.[51]" I said. "'Virgin-feather moth', on account of its resemblance to downy feathers of baby birds. It's often found hiding in white lilac groves."

"You know it?" Rosalia twinkled in a way I had never before seen.

"Emanuela pinned moths." That name still haunted me, begging to be avenged. "Fascination with dying—like friend like friend."

Some insomniac nights, I still reminisced of the hiemal evenings when Emanuela and I would hole up with botany and entomology encyclopædias. We could never escape our curiosity—couldn't look away from the grotesque. And so Death became us.

"Why haven't you pressed any roses yet?" Eligio questioned gently.

I leaned my elbows on the table, cupping my cheeks. "Somehow, I'm yet to get around to it." The pleasures of unburdened life ceased to matter the day *The Sunrise* perished. Long before. I hadn't even played the cello.

Rosalia pointed to the bowl I'd brought with me. "What's that?"

"*Hm*? Oh, just khinḳali." I lifted the plate lying over top, steam pluming to reveal a pair of dumplings stuffed with chilli-and-cumin-spiced goose and wrapped into the shape of pyramids. I covered the bowl and sought Eligio's gaze. "How… are you faring?"

Light snuffed out in his eyes. "There is this… emptiness." A head-shake. "I supposed the pain grows liveable."

I wrapped my arms tightly around him. "I love you, Eli."

"I love you too, Giorgi." He squeezed me back with a fierceness I had never felt from him before.

"*Please take care*," I whispered.

He was too kind, too *good*. They all were.

---

[51] *veer-jee-PLOO-mah fah-LEH-nah*

"Hey!" Rosalia poked Eligio's elbow. "D'you think I should pin the monarch next to the moth or among the beetles to keep it varied?"

Wiping a tear off Eligio's cheek, I planted a kiss on his forehead before swiping the khinḳali bowl and flitting out.

I halted at the end of the corridor; at the foot of the door to Cesare's quarters. My knuckles hovered over the timber until I forced my hand to strike the timber *once*, *twice*, *thrice*.

'*Yes?*' A call from within.

Heat rushed through my cheeks, but I entered, shutting the door with a near-silent *click*.

Thick curtains plundered the chamber of all light, only a flickering candleflame burning within the blackness—a beacon guiding me to where Cesare sat. On the desk before him, parchment lay blotched with ink—scribbles of his foul handwriting lain down yet crossed out.

He glanced up, candlelight slipping along the contours of his visage, and I could have sworn that, in the penumbra, his brow twitched as if in surprise that it was *me* he saw. "Is all well?" His query almost edged on concern. "Did something happen?"

I stepped closer. "I… got word that you haven't been up to the kitchens yet, and Korneli is *not* well pleased that his khinḳali hasn't been appreciated by every last soul on this ship—he's been vying for his chance to cook again, you know." I caught myself, yearning to fidget yet unable to with my hands occupied. "So… I brought you a couple." I placed the maiolica bowl onto Cesare's desk and finally flicked curls over my shoulder, shifting on my feet. "Khinḳali, I mean. They're rather sizeable. Korneli prepared a splendid alucha plum ṭḋemali to go along, too, but I could only carry so much."

After a heartbeat's worth of silence, a laugh escaped Cesare, short and melodic—a threnody lilting along the piano keys of my vertebrae. "Why have you made a task out of feeding me?"

I handed him a flat look. "Well *you* certainly won't do it."

He watched me, intent, his eyes roving my face, my hair, my fingers. Then, he reached a graceful hand out to me.

I met him with perplexity.

"Take my hand," he clarified.

I opened my mouth to question, but when no words dared step forth, I slipped my fingers into his, shivering at his unfed coldness. In that instant, I missed the burn of him, those hands branding into my flesh the reminder *'you're a low-born vagabond rat like me'*.

Cesare opened my palm skyward, violin-callused fingertips barely skimming my skin as he slipped his hand under mine, angled my thumb back, and pressed to my vein-rooted wrist a kiss, light as breath.

He pulled back, darkness-devoured eyes seeking mine once more. "For your trouble."

I whisked my hand away and tucked it to my torso. "Perhaps you're more trouble than you're worth, signór."

His head tipped sidelong. "Yet here you are."

My cheeks ignited all over. "Fiend." And I quitted his quarters in a fluster.

"*ANTIGONE* WILL BE READY IN THE COMING DAYS," Fabio informed Giorgianna. "She'll bear you hence."

The sleepy sun crawled higher beyond the windows of the captain's quarters, an old clock's *ticks* echoing more akin to *creaks*.

"This approaching week shall be spent buried in Libitina's Ithilweni textbooks, seems." Giorgianna toyed with her curls. "I need to hone my tailoring repertoire—hair and eyes won't be enough in the ministerial house, I fear."

Eligio crossed his arms and paced around the centre of the room, his tumultuous motions scrutinised by Lissandri.

Rosalia bumped Giorgianna's elbow. "I'm going with you as your pretend servant, yes?"

"Rosa, I cannot—"

"No no no," the ginger-haired girl scolded. "You guys are always on about means and ends, *so…*" she gestured to herself, "here's a means."

Cesare's innards snarled until it hurt.

He was sending his loved ones into a spider's nest. One misstep, one unaccounted detail, would spell the crumbling of their schemes. Would spell *death*. Yet liberation mattered above most, above *all*—freedom stood as essential as life itself. With such an existential entity in the way, Cesare found himself forced into unjustifiable means.

> *'To put an end to an order is to put an end to*
> *your humanity, to become your cause's weapon.*
> *Revolution is not victory. Revolution is* death.'

A tithe for his hubris. Now, a tithe for his revolution.

Giorgianna's head hung low. "If it must be so."

Rosalia's nose tilted up, her mouth tucking at the corners. "Stupendous!" She planted herself on the sofa between Giorgianna and Lissandri. "When asked my full name, I will simply rearrange mine to *Trine Rosalia* Dalgaard. [52]"

"I'd advise to not go by Dalgaard," Cesare pitched in. "Vencenzani authorities arrested your parents and are bound to have their names on record."

Rosalia's cheeks puffed. "*Mm*! I'll go by 'Fisker'! My bedstemor's[53] surname." She dreamily recited: "Trine Rosalia Fisker…"

"I'll *further* advise to lay low for the first few weeks," Lissandri added. "Don't leave the building, don't make sideways movements or try anything spectacularly brave. Just acclimate. No need to announce yourself as a person of interest."

Cesare swept over to his jacket, slung on the back of a chair facing Fabio's desk, and extracted from it a snake-green phial of white capsules. He handed it to Giorgianna. "One is all you need."

She hesitated, brows shuttered low, but carefully took the bottle. "What for?"

Cesare paced afield, hands slipped into his pockets, and leaned his back against the wall opposing the captain's desk. "Suicide."

---

[52] *TREEN … dahl-GAAHD*
[53] *BEHS-teh-moh'eh*; grandmother in Vilhelmian.

Ygal—who Cesare got both the idea and commodity from—made those pills all but a mandatory part of Hound and Boar uniform.

Never before had he comprehended in its wholeness his own resignation with death. Only when he cradled one of those tiny white executioners in a vatic crease running through his hand, and with that same hand touched the scant ration of food he could stomach for the day, when he looked at those killers as if into blind eyes and felt nothing but the ontological ease of ceasing, did that comprehension bear down on him. How *simple* it was. Swift. Such a painless abortion and then darkness, peace, eternal.

And he wondered if, as Giorgianna gazed, transfixed, upon the smooth pane of the bottle in her hand, the same thoughts might run through *her* mind.

Her lips pressed, and she slipped the pills into a jacket pocket. "Rosa." She held the girl's hands. "Whatever comes to pass, I need you to be safe."

Rosalia smiled in that glittery way that never quite reached her mismatched eyes. "We'll be careful."

"Our parents were careful," Eligio murmured, and Cesare's chest caved in.

Fabio shifted at his desk. "Eligio—"

"No!" He revolved to face the captain, his voice tearing through the ceiling. Fabio recoiled as if shot. "Not you. Of all people."

"Please, Eligio," breathed Fabio with a voice so hushed and shuddering. "I don't know what more—"

"You want to comfort me?" bit Eligio. "You abandoned a child to his own devices!" Cesare's heart plunged. "You *left*!"

"Li—"

"Stop it, Ces!" Eligio turned to look at Cesare. When he beheld the glow in the artist's wide eyes, his jaw's strain and cheek's rufous flush, Cesare's sunken heart tore up inside him. "Stop diminishing. You are my *brother*, and I *love* you, and I *won't* have you belittle yourself when you were just a child who needed protection yet every single adult failed you." His face twisted. "Even our parents failed you." A sting sprung up behind Cesare's eyes. Eligio inhaled sharply to yell out: "And now we have to watch you *kill* yourself!"

Eligio stared at Cesare, the chamber a cocoon of ear-rending silence, neither of them budging, until Eligio turned and fled from the room. The door behind him shut with the faintest of *clicks* all the same.

Cesare gasped a breath.

Lissandri dashed to the chair across from Fabio. "Eli gets like that. It's—"

"No." Fabio's eyes did not rise, nor did his mutter. "No, he's right."

Silence ascended to its austere throne once more. Hollow, this time.

A throat-clear sounded. "There're more of my father's documents to wade through." Giorgianna stood up.

"Hold on." Lissandri frowned her way. "You aren't trekking all the way to *Di Vitis Lane* by your lonesome with the Blood Rite looming."

"I'll walk you," Cesare briskly offered, needing the seabreeze, the release of movement.

Giorgianna tossed him a barbed look. "Right…"

She made for the door. Cesare followed.

WE ASCENDED THE RICKETY STAIRCASE to the apex of *11 Di Vitis Lane* where stood a door embossed with a tarnished copper '*5/2*'.

Cesare halted at its threshold.

"I'll make my way to The Court later in the night with Kel-Kech and others. Attend, if you wish."

Cesare adjusted his tricorn in a dagger-sharp manoeuvre. The shadow of its brim and the darkling almost-smile crossing his lips only deepened his gloom. "If it pleases you." The premature autumn sunset seeping through the foyer's moth-eaten ceiling traced those cheeks that had felt so hollow in my hands. Yet it was as if he always tried to have fire in his eyes, in his chest, no matter what it took burning. *Brightest flames die quickest.*

He made it two steps beyond the door.

"Cesare!" I grabbed his hand—never, ever warm anymore—lacing his slim fingers through mine. He whirled around, eyes stricken. "You haven't eaten or gone to sleep." I pressed our entwined hands to my thumping heart and wished with all my being that my meagre heat could warm him. That I could dig the bullets from his flesh with my hands and take at least the smallest share of his pain into myself. *We have to watch you kill yourself…*

Cesare clung to my pleading gaze for two heartbeats, blinked for one, grit his teeth on the fourth. "Don't touch me like that." He wrested his hand free and departed.

I hovered on the threshold long after his footfalls petered out.

Biting down my urge to cry out in sheer frustration, I set about rifling through the half-charred bookshelf archiving my father's history.

Hours into the endeavour, the floor heaped with documents, I pried out from the depths of the bookcase's burnt flank a stack of crinkly papers.

The flames never penetrated deep enough to engulf them, but licks and splotches of black-brown eschar marred the beige nonetheless, obscuring much of the text. The handwriting spoke of my father's authorship. However, scraps of another document seemed to be pasted to it—a paler, cleaner parchment inked by another hand.

I perused whatever writing I could discern.

> *'Domínie Benetto Abelli's research delves into*
> *azoth as a tool of spiritual transcendence.'*

A frown pleated my brows. *Research?*

> *'I am attempting to acquire more information*
> *… think there may be external interest on the*
> *part of the Minister of Dominion … High*
> *Priest knows of De Tullia's illegitimate*
> *ascension … Consult appendage.'*

My eyes eagerly flickered to the sliver of documentation nearby.

> '…successful application … may grant a subject
> pneumatic purity … liberation from hylic corruption
> … illimitable wielding of AZOTH in magnitude and
> manifestation … the opening of THE THIRD EYE…

And there it was again. High Priest Benetto Abelli. Eye and trinity. *But what does any of this mean?*

> '…has only … in two subjects… too great to contain,
> occasioning their escape … subject codes: …'

Fire had vanquished the rest, leaving tattered char of both my father's and, presumably, the Domínie's words.

Pulse drummed in my ears. My hands trembled as I expelled a cry of exasperation and hurled the papers on the ground.

Crumbs.

It was all crumbs leading me on meandering paths to some destination I couldn't grasp the details of.

Our allies were few, our means a suicidal leap of faith, and our ends a visionary ambition of near-immeasurable proportions.

And so, I stood all the more compelled, *had all the more incentive*, to go through with what I'd set out to accomplish to-night.

Tidying everything, I ventured to Father's old bedchamber. There, I obtained a loose cotton shirt dark as midnight, then tailored my hair into loose waves the colour of chestnuts.

My reflection halted me.

With the dark tresses and mirror-precise features, I looked so painfully like my father.

Plaiting my hair, I consulted the timepiece. *Sixteen hundred.*

My hand lay at the hilt of my baselard.

Captain Dahlia's Blood Rite awaited my uninvited arrival.

Scene XVII

Il Rito del Sangue

Giorgianna

DEATH'S CLOYING PERFUME DRIPPED OFF THE WIND as I perched myself in a guarded nook on the mizzenmast of Blood Dahlia's *Hangman's Dowry*, my hair once more untailored.

The main deck thronged with smugglers like Hell's devils dancing around a roasting spit of damned souls: swivelling eyes and salt-knotted hair; iron grins and tattoo-soaked scars; ribaldry; guffaws; bays for '*blood!*'.

Countless swords erected upon the deck thrust for a bruising dusk. Blood lacquered their razor edges, cold and clotting, and, suspended above the gleaming forest of blades, a battle raged amid the ropes and crosstrees of the mainmast.

Two men.

One muscular and golden-skinned, sculpted cheeks and russet hair spilling down his scarred and tattooed back. The other: pale as milk and slim as a dancer in his loose pewter blouse, shoulder-kissing ebony corkscrews coiling around a pretty face.

The second was Donacian.

The first was Pâin.

Donacian worked the ropes with expert adroitness, looping them around Pâin's powerful arm and yanking as he launched himself from the crosstree. Pâin grasped the rigging and recoiled Donacian from his trajectory, aiming for the mighty mast.

Donacian cut himself free. Plummeted. Gripped another rope.

Frenzied shouts rose below.

My eyes dropped to the deck.

A man ripped in half by Pâin lay on the quarterdeck near Blood Dahlia's seat, oily-pink intestines dislodged across the dark wood where he, in his final moments, had dragged his torso away in a hopeless attempt to escape Death. A woman lay gutted on the clear stretch of deck cleaving the sword field, a blade protruding from her face.

Quartermaster Aaron and first mate Nikitha at her sides, Blood Dahlia watched the battle with indifference glazing her crow-black eyes, feet folded on a foot rest and gouged orbs coated in glass dangling from her earlobes. '*Butchery*' seemed a demure word for the scene before her.

Screams and jeers snapped my attention to the fight.

Pâin grasped Donacian's head in his massive palm and smashed it at full pelt into the main mast. His skull cracked like wet eggshells and smeared to chunks. Pâin dropped the pale sylph's husk into the maw of hungry swords. Steel rended Donacian's corpse, fresh ichor warming the sky.

Blood-drunken howls ululated at the alighting moon.

He jumped down to the narrow twitchel amidst swords to an uproar of benediction.

His third kill, yet he remained unbled.

Dahlia rose, petite and sturdy. The wind itself seemed to cower before the older woman, the torn-out teeth around her waist chittering. Her hands sank into the pockets of her ink-black greatcoat embroidered with ruby thread, and a smile sweet as fernet curved her lips. "*Exceptional spectacle!*"

Applause anew.

Pâin's chin bore aloft.

Clenching a prayer between my teeth, I crept from my hiding place among the masts.

Dahlia held out her hands. "Another challenger to my champion?"

Murmurs swept through, but nobody braved.

Pâin stood bloody and motionless.

Dahlia ambled forward. Her boots squelched against the strewn innards of the halved man. "Well then—"

"It seems I have no choice but to accept!" I called out.

Every eye centred on me; chatter invaded the motley.

Dahlia's brows pinched, head canting to study me. "You're the curly-haired bird off Fabio's ship."

I hopped to the quarter deck. "Such a fate of mine gives incentive enough to have me murdered by your champion, no?"

Dahlia offered me a once-over and a half-laugh. "If you lay forth your sword…" Her smile grew. She gestured to the main deck.

Bootleggers warbled as I descended to the outcrop between the swords.

Pâin stood well over Ygạl's height, corded with thick muscle, a longsword strapped to a leather harness across his broad back and a gladius idle at his hip.

I glimpsed the scar glistening on his cheek; glimpsed Donacian.

> *'Pâin … ripped out the spines of five opponents like fish and tore three of their heads off, walking out of that fight with a singular cut on his cheek he bears like a trophy.'*

He bound half of his russet hair, and his mercury eyes glimmered with slaughter. *The end justifies the means, right…?*

"Let blood anoint this altar of the waves!" declared Dahlia.

Pâin pounced, fast and cheetah-graceful, longsword angled to cleave.

I launched myself backwards and grabbed a rope, then the next, and kicked myself off the main mast just when Pâin almost struck my ankles. Swinging in an arc, I locked my feet on the rope to free both my hands and unsheathed my rapier. Steel spat sparks as it struck Pâin's longsword. He shoved me away and hacked with his gladius. My baselard blocked the attack, rapier parrying his longsword.

"Little slip of a girl's got some *nerve*!" He pushed me hard and swung his longsword at my throat.

Squeezing my thighs around the rigging, my spine bent backwards into a horrifying 'C'. Blood whirled behind my eyes.

Pâin severed my rigging.

I grasped Pâin's rope and launched myself across two more, nearing the main mast once again. Cheers whistled below. *Aerial silks served me well.*

"You'll be surprised how much *nerve*—" I hoisted myself higher "—certain slips of people have."

Pâin swung across to a nearer rope. Struck with his gladius.

I shoved off the mast's side to *barely* dodge his assault and flew in a wide hemicircle, propelling myself onto the highest crosstrees.

Pâin followed me with ease, both weapons drawn, and attacked.

I cried out with each parry, the force of his strikes almost knocking me into the sword field below. My lungs chafed raw, throat drying, limbs growing heavier as I forced myself to keep parrying, keep standing, keep *fighting*.

He struck.

I reeled back along the crosstree, hearing nothing past the scream of blood through my ears and the crashing of steel. *Faces, he's relentless.*

Blood shed from a gash in my shoulder, my arm, my thigh.

Pâin charged.

I grasped the rigging above and hoisted myself into its tangles, open air whistling beneath me. Pâin roared and began to madly cut up the ropes.

My foot slipped. Fear juddered my heart and a scream got its way.

Pâin's iron fingers clenched my ankle and yanked me down, smashing me hard on the crosstree.

A nauseating ache split my skull, locking up my shoulders as everything doubled and dimmed. Wet warmth spilled at my neck.

He dropped to his knees over me, grasped my head, and *squeezed* my eye sockets.

My blood froze.

Pâin choked, stunned fingers loosening. His abdomen blackened where broken ribs distended skin.

I sang to my blood and flesh, lulling my heart steady, and kicked Pâin in the chest; punched his scarred cheek; drove my baselard into his side. He plummeted off the crosstrees, dragging me with him towards the swords. I groped for the rigging, clenching my fists for dear life, palms burning against the rope as Pâin's heavy frame dragged me down.

I splintered his arms.

My gut spasmed. Blood ruptured across my tongue.

Pâin yowled and let go, halting my fall and sending the rope bouncing.

Swords skewered him, his throat flooding and spasming around gargles. His muscles twitched, lungs collapsed, heart stopped.

I hung in silence for one, two, three heartbeats.

My rope snapped.

I shrieked.

My raw hands locked around another just in time, legs tucking close as I dangled life-saving millimetres above the tips of merciless steel.

Blood trickled down my neck, my head pounding, vision hazy. Ragged breaths filled the deck's silence. *I killed Dahlia's champion…*

"*BRÁVO*, MÈA CÀRA!" Daliah's booming voice all but twinkled. She was clapping. "My new champion!"

Cheers rang like cannonfire in the night, the very carcass of the ship rattling as smugglers whooped and lauded.

I swung myself to the swordless partition and landed on trembling feet. *I'm alive, I survived—always do.*

When folks settled, Dahlia addressed me, "I've been *begging* the waves to rid me of that good-for-nothing for *far* too many turns. I sought someone worthy of the title 'Blood Dahlia's champion'." Her head tipped. "And it seems the salt winds granted my soul's wish."

Swallowing blood and pinning my back straight, I ascended to the quarter deck. "My reward?" I steadied my tremoring voice.

Dahlia sat in her place of honour and set her elbow on the velveteen armrest. "Anything but me."

I halted several steps away. "I request all—"

"But first," Dahlia lifted a brass chalice off a nearby granite stool, its twin beside it, "wine for the victor."

I reined in my agitation but knew I couldn't refuse. *Formalities.*

She took the second chalice, and I understood from her expectant gaze that Dahlia awaited my imbibement.

Observing the bloodwine for a spell, I brought it to my lips.

Sweetness of licorice and blackberry swamped my bloody tongue, tanged with—

My eyes bulged.

Dahlia went to drink.

I leapt and swatted the chalice from her hand, the liquid arcing through the air and splattering across the deck.

Gasps swept the crowd.

"Who poured the wine?" I demanded.

Dahlias drew weapons.

The captain's teeth gnashed. "You *dare*—"

"Who poured the wine?" My sharp voice pressed harder.

She shot to her feet. "Who do you think you are?"

"It's poisoned."

"How would you know?"

"Bašmu Mḕ—Asp Nectar—derived from the venom of Ṣer'šādî.[54] One of the deadliest but most commonly-administered toxins."

"Yet there you stand: living."

"I didn't swallow any. Mithridatism doesn't merely immunise one to a given toxin, but sensitises them to its presence should it exhibit a trace of taste or aroma.[55]" I drummed a nail on the chalice. "If this were summer or goldwine, I might've been unable to identify it, but bloodwine masks Mḕ poorly. So who poured it?"

Dahlia held my gaze, unyielding, then said, "Step forward, Quartermaster Aaron."

The middle-aged man at her right did as told. His black hair was cropped short and mariner-tanned skin inked heavily. "Captain."

---

[54] *ssehr-SHAAH-dyy*; Eastern Isatōnian Mountain Asp.

[55] Don't try this at home. At all.

I handed him my cup. "Drink."

His eyes, dark as sapphires, flicked to the wine, then to me.

My short fuse crackled. "*Drink.*"

"Drink, Aaron!" snapped Dahlia.

He grasped his cutlass and swung for my head.

Splashing the poisoned wine into his face, I parried and engaged.

Behind me, steel chanted eulogies and crewmen screamed '*mutiny!*'.

SCENE XVIII

MUTINY

Giorgianna

MY EARDRUMS THRASHED WITH SCREAMS, grunts, wails, metal chants, splintering wood and ripping cloth, crushed flesh spraying bloody geysers, until my skull rang and hilts grew unwieldy in my grip.

Intestines and hacked human pieces tangled at my feet as, off the edge of my rapier's blade, more exanimate gore fell to join the butchery bathing the deck of *Hangman's Dowry*.

Aaron was lost to the fray but not-yet dead.

My shoulder blades thrust into the captain's as a Dahlia's sword bound with mine. I enveloped their blade. Kicked their groin. Buried my dagger at the base of their throat. They choked and slumped to the quarterdeck. A stomach-twisting *squelch* snapped my attention to where Blood Dahlia hurled a man's torn-off jaw overboard, his paunched corpse following. "Didn't expect to fight alongside Amadi's friend," she panted.

I gripped her shoulder and shoved her down, slitting the throat of a smuggler aiming for his captain's back. "Heard tell that desperate ailments call for desperate remedies." I spat the blood pooling in my teeth from my shattered lip.

"*FIRST MATE*!" Dahlia barked over the deafening din at her allies garrisoning the ship's stern, a bombardment of steel at their feet. A swarthy woman in gold adornments stood at attention. "Disarm the forecastle!"

The straight edge of the first mate's khaḍga cleaved a mutineer's skull. "Aye aye, kepṭen!"

In that moment, the barrage against me and Dahlia intensified, cutlasses and halberds shoving us deeper into the ship's belly.

A gang of eight descended on us in the hold.

Narrowly dodging a knife, I grabbed a man by the long strands of ebony hair and threw him into another, running them both through with my rapier before delivering a knee to a small woman's ribs and stabbing the nape of her neck.

Another attacker grabbed me from behind.

I stooped, flinging them over my shoulder and onto the woman. Dahlia put them to her cutlass before calling me up a staircase.

A sailor bellowed ahead and a pair rushed for us.

A third hurtled up behind.

Dahlia dragged me into an adjacent chamber.

We dispatched two mutineers, the first a bruised mess of snapped bones and the second as gutless as his motives. I wavered on my feet; shivered at the cold of azoth. *I'm going to faint…* Instead, I swung my rapier at a third man behind Dahlia.

He voided my attack.

"Aaron you *wanker*!" Dahlia shoved me aside and slashed.

Aaron parried, "Long time coming, bitch!" thrusting her backward.

"Are you entirely cracked?" She reprised.

Kicking my head back and dragging blood into my throat, I swung my rapier for Aaron.

He unsheathed his second cutlass to block me. "Entirely sick of *you*, miserable old hag!" A strike. "All you do is demean your *crew*men!"

She parried and riposted. "Men like you are the fucking *reason*—the fucking *proof*—I'll always be correct!" She hacked for Aaron's throat.

"*Listen* to yourself!" He volted in the nick of time. "You're deluded!"

"And look at *you*!" Hate ignited Dahlia's eyes. "The fuck is *this*?"

"The fuck is your Blood Rite, Ada?" Aaron all but screamed. "A bloodthirsty harridan is what you are!"

Their blades bound.

Aaron shoved Dahlia away just in time to parry my slash, then kicked me in the stomach and sent me doubling back.

"Better than whatever thread *you're* spun from!" Dahlia spat onto the red-washed carpet beneath Aaron's feet.

They engaged. "You deserve *Hell*, Ada."

I trawled air into my chest. Haem coated my tongue and light bleared. *Just a little. Just enough.*

Aaron's knees cracked.

He buckled with a full-lunged yowl.

Blood surged up my oesophagus. I collapsed with the pain lancing my stomach. My throat disgorged stringy grume onto the soaked carpet.

Dahlia punched Aaron, trapping him into a headlock. "And *you'll* meet your maker soon." She twisted, the *pop! pop! pop!* of vertebrae and the wet gargle of useless defiance singing Aaron's end.

Dread poured between my ribs. The material plane fell away beneath me like the trapdoor fell away beneath my father's feet. A shriek tore out as I scrambled backwards, knocking into the wall-sweeping bookshelf. *Breathe! Breathe…* I scraped with trembling nails through the darkness smothering me, forcing my seams to stay shut.

Shrill silence.

The mutiny had died.

My sore lungs drank down cloying air. *Breathe.*

Dahlia leaned her arms against the desk, her black greatcoat wet with spilled blood, and descended into a grating thunderstorm of coughs.

I shuddered the tatters of panic off and rose shakily.

Dahlia stumbled for the door. "*Nikitha!*"

My gaze traversed the quarters I realised were the captain's, every cramped shelf and nook meticulously neat.

I stalled on the vanity, wincing at the sight of my blood-slathered face and shattered lip, the crescent bruises staining the corners of my bloodshot eyes.

"*Kepṭen!*" Dahlia's first mate appeared at the door. A gold nath ring decorated her bleeding nose and gem-encrusted golden domes of jhumkā earrings glinted in spite of the blood splattered on her orange dhōvathi[56] and loose shirt. "You are well."

Dahlia grasped the woman's shoulder, donning an unlikely smile. "And you survived like I knew you would."

My treacherous eyes riffled through what looked to be familial memorabilia adorning the vanity. *Gods, this curiosity is so beneath me.*

"Sail for the do*cks…*"

My attention trained on a note tucked into a kraken statuette wearing a bright blue glass eye pendant—like the nazar beads Ygạl adored and Luce wore; the porcelain eyes us Vencenzanii used for festive decoration.

'Ada and Calliupa, Ilusán Letío,[57] 21/3/1751/9 (ZE).'

---

[56] Lower attire from the Indian subcontinent consisting of a long, unstitched cloth wrapped around the hips and thighs, with one end brought between the legs and tucked into a waistband, the final garment resembling loose, ankle-length trousers.

[57] **UNNECESSARY LORE:** *ee-loo-SAH leh-TEE-oh*; literally 'First Balance'—the vernal (spring) equinox celebrated by the Vencenzanii and Iutulicani, as well as all ancient Faustinians. It forms one half of a whole celebration called 'De Letíi' ('Il Letíi' in Iutulicano), 'The Balances'. Hence, 'Ilusán Letío' is the 'First Balance', with the 'Second Balance' thus being 'Zalsán Letío', or the *autumn* equinox.

On both occasions in Vencenza (to *grossly* simplify it), small tealight candles are floated in the canals, pale gold for Ilusán Letío and deep gold for Zalsán Letío, whilst the 'caúpu' ('tradesman') sails on a gondola along the main canal singing '*Zamarèse Rèquiem, Argentáto Díem*'—'*Golden Night, Silvern Day*'—as both a reference to the equal length of the night and day, and an invocation of luck to the cosmos. Often, porcelain and metallic (especially gold or brass) pendants depicting eyes, and unpainted papier-mâché masks are hung onto doors and en masse in the streets as both decoration, and to ward off misfortune.

In Iutulica, these festivities take place upon Lake Laútni (*Lake Liberty*) and, traditionally, the caúpu of each respective village or festive procession sacrifices a pig, an old sheep, and a young goose, draining their blood into the soil around which a 'shrine' of rocks called 'acherí dél'aísi' (*ah-keh-REE dehl-ah-EE-see*)—'teeth of the gods'—is erected. The animals are then cooked and shared around the community as fairly as possible with no part wasted. In effect, a 'trade' is made (hence '*caúpu*' means 'tradesman' in the first place): sacrifice for abundance wherein the blood and lives of the animals are the sacrifice, and the food symbolises the abundance.

My brows dragged together. *Calliupa… Soriano?*

Could it really be *the* Calliupa executed alongside my father? A rare name was seldom a coincidence in Vencenza.

And Dahlia was… '*You deserve* Hell, *Ada.*'

"…*a long* discussion ahead." I heard her.

"Aye aye, kepṭen!" Nikitha ran off.

Dahlia turned to me, dragging out a moment before crossing her arms with a scoff. "Suppose this is where gratitude comes in."

I half-smiled wryly. "Seems you owe me a two-fold reward."

"That I do." She ambled closer. "One for being my champion."

"And one for being your saviour."

Dahlia dragged a chair to her desk and, kicking Aaron's corpse out of the way, sat down. "What do you want?" From a drawer, she got a roll of thread, a large needle, muslin, and a bottle looking suspiciously like alcohol labelled 'Zivanía', riding up her torn sleeve to inspect her wounds.

Out of an empty cranny at the bottom of a bookshelf, a black cat slunk, eyes green-gold as cabochon peridots, and pottered towards the captain as if nothing in the world was wrong with the room the creature found itself in. It hopped onto Dahlia's shoulders and nestled amid her hair, the woman scratching the animal's head. A small smile compelled me. I'd always been partial to cats, black-furred especially. I remembered the strays Rosalia would feed, and wondered what happened to them.

"The acquisition of information," I quoted, earning myself Dahlia's wary peer. "Tell me about your connection to Calliupa Soriano, and her association with Magister Ilenia Farnese."

Dahlia blinked. "Did *not* anticipate that." She took to tending to a cut. "You're bound to know something already, then."

Hangman's Dowry swayed into gentle movement as I took the floor: "Ilenia had been a friend to Calliupa. Upon learning of hers fraternising with the lowly, De Tullia imprisoned Ilenia and now hangs this 'disgrace' over her head. Ilenia handed Calliupa over to save herself. *Calliupa* was a lavìre in The Court of Secrets."

Huffing, Dahlia plopped the cat onto her lap and laced her fingers together as the sweet creature curled up. An iron band around the captain's right thumb gleamed beneath blood. "Calliupa was my niece," she declared. "Can't say we were overly close, 'specially after the death of her father—my dimwit brother."

"And you are Ada Soriano?"

"By birth. Iutulicano Vencenzani[58] from pa and Akési from ma. Iupa met Ilenia whilst tavèrna-hopping in oldtown—look," she held up sullied hands, "I don't know either, a'right? And, frankly, neither did Iupa."

"Calliupa didn't know who Ilenia was?"

"Nope. Only reason *I* found out was because a vinificatore I knew told me, but by then the Magister was no longer around." Dahlia set an elbow onto the desk. "If it means anything to you, Ilenia'd been cosy with General Manuele Dioli," she spat on his name, "but things s'pposedly ended horrendous."

My eyes bugged out. "She walked away from Dioli alive?"

"That's what *I* asked!" exclaimed Dahlia. "Didn't make sense back then how a bird I'd been led to believe was lower ossíi managed to scrape herself out of that raper cunt's clutches, but figuring out she's a senator—*Minister*—enlightened me."

I sent my gaze on an idle rove along the filthy floorboards. Between Ilenia Farnese's name finding a place among the whispers of The Antrum, and her numerous entanglements with unlikely parties—surely wrought into weapons against her by the Minister of Dominion, Ilenia hinted at being far more fascinating an individual than I could guess, and I endeavoured to prod deeper into the cogs of her enigmatic brain once I entered the ministerial house.

Dahlia shrugged. "Got nothing else, love."

"What you've told is plenty." I touched a hand to my heart. "Many thanks."

The captain sighed. "A'right, shoot your second query then."

I beheld her with a dagger gaze. "Help us."

She set the cat onto the floor, standing and walking past me towards the window right of her desk.

---

[58] An Iutulicano community residing in north-eastern Vencenza, forming a distinct cultural subgroup.

"Our situation is *dire*," I pleaded. "We are *all* under threat from De Tul—"

"Ask something else." She turned. "You saw what happened to my crew. I'm not putting us in more peril for your chess game."

I reeled in my ire. "You shall see *peril* regardless—"

"*Ask*," her flinty tone slashed, "something *else*."

"No!" I refused. "I ask for this, or I ask for nothing."

This was the end to-night's means justified. A chance to win over the support of The Blood Dahlias for our cause. *This sanctuary cannot last eternity…*

Dahlia's eyes skimmed mine like an apocalyptic text. "Ask for nothing, then."

Hangman's Dowry rocked to a halt.

Nikitha called out to furl up the sails.

My teeth grinded. "Then I shall hold onto this favour."

To my continuous astonishment, Dahlia smiled, the abyss of her eyes dancing with mirth. "And I know you won't let me rest until my dues are repaid."

The cold ether stunk of mouldering carrion, salty waves lapping the dark hide of *Hangman's Dowry*, its blade-studded deck a sea of red and black beneath the night. Two docks away, *Antigone* swayed in such stark contradiction.

Blood Dahlia beside me, I hung back whilst the lion's share of battered survivors disembarked.

I didn't know how to feel about the scene, the rationalisation behind its conception.

Time and time again, this world built on blood and ash and broken bones told its unfortunate children, '*your life is a bartering chip in the gamble of survival*'. Still, I would never stop wondering why some of us were valued so lowly.

"Do you know why I chose 'Blood Dahlia'?" the captain redirected my attention.

"Enlighten me."

"Blood-red dahlias are planted on the graves of disgraced men—a pagan tradition of the ancient southern Iutulicanii." Her eyes aligned with mine. "I stand on those graves, because I *put* the men there." She jerked her chin towards the ebbing crowd. "Your stop." And captain Blood Dahlia left me.

I allowed her words to settle, congeal like ichor, my weeping eye pendant cold as retributive steel beneath my fingertips. *Blood does not wash off.*

Descending the gangplanks, I crouched at the edge of the wharf and sluiced blood off my hands and face for the courtesy of it, then sucked the blood off myself with magic; sang my bruises to dissolve; darned my gashes shut. No one needed to hear of this for the time being, and nobody needed to *see* it, certainly.

Rendered as untouched as possible, I rose to the groan of leather and pounding of heavy footsteps against the gangplank.

Shock gripped my windpipe. A sparkling, frosty squall soughed through my veins. *Not mine.*

My eyes flicked up.

Onto the wharf descended a bald man broad as a golem, a statuesque woman with auburn locs beside him. *Sten and Visolela of The Black Tongues…* Ambling a hemicircle around me, Sten grinned a half-row of gold teeth

and dropped a bow.

I almost gasped, Visolela's face serene as ever when I beheld it dumbly.

The bowls of watery milk that were Sten's unseeing eyes rippled as he straightened, never once breaking from my gawk for those too-long seconds, and the two Tongues stalked off.

I blinked. Blinked again. Forced my gaping mouth shut.

Rubbing my temples with a shudder, begotten by shock or azoth I knew not, I laughed to myself in half-hysteria before making my brisk way back to papa's apartment with far more limbs still attached than I'd anticipated.

The following chapter contains a
brief dream sequence *alluding to
rape and sexual mutilation*. The
italicised text between the two eye
dividers can be *skipped* if necessary.

SCENE XIX

FLESH OF MY FLESH

Giorgianna

I HADN'T FELT IT BEFORE. Never ruminated upon it, in truth. The
phantasmal wisps of tarry silver aroma, the sparkling, marrow-deep chill
my jacket stood powerless against, the tinnitus cantillating through my
skull; how edges blurred, and the adularescent air whirled, and my limbs
floated just a trace off-kilter.

Goëtia. Magic.

Every drop of Cardea's azoth, the essence of her life, sacrificed to
keep oldtown hidden, The Court a secret, now *became* it.

Whilst Anka-ny, Yezo, and Cesare ventured a few blocks over to
assist an old gondolier with his boat, and Kel-Kech visited an elderly man
residing down a perpendicular street alongside Alessa, Itxaro and I
remained on the main alley—*Vicolo de Lùmi*[59]—to help an Asifargazi
carpet-maker, Tafsut Muḥend Zeghlache, house people in her parlour for
the night.

---

[59] *'Alley of Lanterns'*.

From a nearby alcove, a pair of women hauled the ashen body of an old vagrant who passed from starvation the night prior.

My heart balled up, attention fleeing to the zillīj-decorated carpet-making parlour at the entrance of which Tafsut handed a baghrīr[60] to the last man entering her establishment. A white ḥāik[61] draped her head-to-knees, a triangular piece of long cloth attached to it veiling the lower half of her face and blue chalwar sweeping feet clad in heel-less leather balgha slippers. A geometric ouarida[62] symbol tattooed her forehead.

The man clenched a hand to his heart and bowed; Tafsut returned the gesture. To her legs clung her little girl Aldjya—seven years old—wearing an ankle-brushing brown aselham[63] and wrapped in her mother's embroidered tahruyt[64] against the late-night chill.

I held tulle-gloved hands to my chest. "I'm eternally grateful for your generosity, Tafsut."

"And tanmirt[65] to *you*, Giorgianna." She nodded to: "Itxaro."

"You'd better befriend Kel-Kech and Cesare in my absence," I told her. "Yezo and Anka-ny, too."

"Appreciated is all the help."

Aldjya blinked at me with doe eyes green as young stalks. "You're pretty." Her tiny fingers pinched a caramel coil from my hair and stretched it into a calf-length ribbon before letting go. The hair sprung into a bouncy spiral. The girl giggled, scurrying back to her mother's side with a satisfied beam at having pried a chuckle from me.

Itxaro sucked in her cheeks, batting dark lashes at me. "Certain Zargòsians are utterly *weak* for her."

I glared at her as heat spiked my cheeks.

---

[60] A Tamazgha semolina pancake.

[61] A usually-white traditional headscarf, sometimes body-length, worn by Tamazgha (notably Algerian, Moroccan, and Tunisian) women, now a rare sight.

[62] A geometric Amazigh motif in the shape of a diamond symbolising a flower; serves as protection against the Evil Eye. This motif not only appears as tattoos, but also in clothing and rug embroidery.

[63] A loose, long-sleeved unisex robe with a hood worn in the Tamazgha region.

[64] An Amazigh veil consisting of two pieces of rectangular black or deep blue cloth sewn together with ornate, colourful stitching, worn by women in southern Morocco.

[65] '*Thank you*' in Asifargazi, the primary language of Tmurt-Asif.

"Can I get one of you over here?" Kel popped out of an off-shooting street. "This railing isn't cooperating."

"Coming!" Itxaro and the cheeky glimmer in her eyes ran off, leaving me with the Zeghlache women.

Tafsut linked her fingers. "Tricky to help people in The Court. All are so wary."

I gazed through the domed window of Tafsut's small parlour at the dozen people sleeping on the floor. Children and the elderly, women, men, all cramped in, but with warm, dry blankets they'd forgotten the feeling of, perhaps never known at all, and a roof over their heads—such simple things denied to them. "Sometimes each other is all we have," I said quietly. "Have soldiers been in the area?"

"Here not much, fortunately. But elsewhere: yes."

"How far away?"

"To the east." *Towards The Arum…* "Distant enough for news to take to reach us a day. Court dwellers are vigilant, and wise to the thaumaturgy, but sometimes Guards spot you still, and if the look of you they do not like, they pursue." I shuddered as Tafsut's truth conjured recollections of the woman murdered by soldiers on what became my final night at *The Arum*, how they hurled her body into a canal barely a street away. "We heard tell of several instances," Tafsut's breathy voice grounded me. "Most ended in beatings. Some in arrests. Unfortunate few in…" she glanced at her daughter, holding the girl close, "worse."

"Please keep the others informed," I beseeched. "The Court has suffered too much in vain."

The Asifargazi woman faced me, brow strained. "Giorgianna. Where you depart for this coming week I know not, but your tight lips are enough for me to recognise it dangerous. Come what may, take care of *you*."

My eyes plummeted to the cracked cobbles. "I can only hope our efforts will suffice."

"Strength in community. Always." Tafsut's tattooed hands squeezed mine. "Hope prevails."

I squeezed my lips. "How do you say *'love'* in Asifargazi?"

The corners of Tafsut's dark eyes crinkled. "Tayri!"

"Tayri..." My tongue tested the word. Nothing like the Hoġerr 'sēr'; nothing like the Faustinian 'ataínè'. I wondered what '*love*' might be in Marlâre. "My father's father was Asifargazi." Speech came half-idly from me—aloud musings. "He was an orphan, papa, so he knew little of himself. He lived in an orphanage until all but adulthood, not as a child to be taken in, but... a sibling of sorts for the children there. He took an Asifargazi middle name: Lounès..." My voice trailed off. Words and thoughts strung together so clumsily; I hadn't the tools to arrange them, to make plain and legible my disconnect to a people I was severed from by circumstance but not blood. And so I wondered if blood truly did not wash off, when there I stood—two-blooded yet bearing flesh I barely knew.

"'*Companion*', it means," Tafsut said gently. I met her gaze. "Lounès," she clarified, the word fluid as molten metal moulding to her tongue—correct. Known. "His story it suits well, I think." She took her daughter's hand and nodded deeply to me. "Iḍ ameggaz.[66]"

A halting smile tugged at my lips as I touched my fingertips to my pendant. My father's pendant. "Iḍ ameggaz."

"Night-night!" little Aldjya chirruped as she and her mother ascended the staircase to the tiny living quarters a floor above the parlour and slipped out of sight. It was just the two of them caring for the place.

Diamanté stars glimmered upon the velvet-black sky as I shivered into my jacket. My veins still smouldered, frore with azoth, and I grew only more beholden to Cardea. For protecting the innocents of this forsaken realm.

YOU WERE ONLY TWENTY-TWO THE SECOND TIME YOU MET DEATH.
It wore the skin of a gaunt-faced woman dressed in silk.

---

[66] '*Good night*' in Asifargazi.

Ropes burned sore red imprints into your bare limbs at her behest, cochineal sanies leaking from cracked and purple flesh of your thighs, calves, wrists, ankles.

Blood drenching the bed rippled, rising, morphing into arms and hands and fingers that crawled on you like devil's guts.

Bruises black as criminals' fingerprints stamped your skin, and even when they faded, the flesh always hurt—as if dead from sleep-cut beneath.

The stench of rotting corpses gripped your face like warm, clammy hands, monstrous physiognomies of anthropomorphic swine revelling in your helpless agony, and above you loomed that gaunt, white face, that silk-dressed woman, gouged pits of her eyes leaking black pitch. 'Some girls are born to suffer.'

There would be no way out of the slaughterhouse, she promised.

My lungs inflated around piercing ocean air.

I lurched forward.

Sweat cooled on my blistering skin. Disgust burrowed in like larvae. *Get it off!* I writhed, whimpering through clenched teeth as I clawed at my shoulders and hair and arms. *They did this to me!*

Metal shrieked.

My throat purged a yelp and I cowered into myself. *Please not again I don't want to* LEAVE ME—*!*

"Vólto?"

I smacked a hand over my mouth.

Through juddering vision, the black mirage of my quarters realigned.

The door hung slightly ajar.

In the archway stood Cesare. "Are you—?"

"*It's fine!*" I blurted, clutching to my battering heart the corner of the blanket which had slithered to the floor amidst my nightmare-stricken thrashing. "I'm fine, it's all right, *I*—I just—" My throat stiffened. "A nightmare."

Cesare stepped over the threshold. "Is there something you need?"

I shook my head.

He shut the door so carefully it hardly *clinked*. "Do… you want me to stay?"

Yes. "No." Another head-shake. "No, I'm all right."

Cesare frowned, those keen eyes searching me.

"Only if you want to." Burning shame scared my gaze away. It wasn't even *him*. Not really. I just didn't want to be alone anymore.

His brow softened once I braved to peek back at him, and a swell of exhaustion slumped my body onto the bed, my lashes heavy with stolen sleep.

The soft thud of footfalls marked Cesare's approach.

He sat on the unoccupied edge of my bed, one leg extended and the other peaked into a perch for his elbow. "Do you need to talk about it?" His gentle question was something like a lighter flicking open—that soft rasp of metal and breathy sigh of reborn fire.

"Would you listen," I curled up, eyeline tucked safely away from Cesare's, "if I told you a long story of mine?"

"Yes."

My stomach cooled—I'd almost wanted him to refuse—but I nudged my voice on still, "I never dreamt of it, so I thought I'd gotten lucky."

"Dreamt of…?"

"*The Arum.*" Bile singed my throat. "As 'initiation', and I suppose because our *Madáma* was too avaricious to spare coin on tonic, we were forced to have our wombs cut out." I pressed my lips. "With nothing to ease the pain. Just tied down to a bed, sliced open by a scalpel, then sewn up. And *then*…" My mouth hovered open, words unable to take shape around the incomprehensible atrocities they would describe. "*Immediately* then…" I forced out, "fresh sutures and bleeding wounds, she ordered her guards… to rape us." I refused to put palatable language to the violence I had been submitted to. "And they didn't snub an opportunity to repeat it." I counted three times one or both cornered me. "The rest of the guards were eunuchs and would be punished for touching us." My teeth scraped against each other. "I thought I would die that night."

But I lived.

Just like I lived through every night following. Even those that begged me to cut them short. Even those I almost listened to. Even if sometimes I still wished I hadn't clung on.

"I heard the most horrifying screams in that bordello, but," tears threatened me, "I couldn't do anything." I remembered the poor girl, hardly of sixteen years, the atrocious martinet Falco had beaten on my final day in *The Arum*, the girl I gave my last pill of analgesic to, and hoped with all my soul that dreadful prison didn't rob her of too-young heartbeat. "And it's like that soulless fucking martinet *enjoyed* the sight of it all." *Hell is too good a place for you to rot in.* "When it wasn't some belittling moniker like '*girl*', Falco called me her '*flower*'. Her '*winning doll*'." A shudder crawled on me like roaches. "I'd rather be 'vólto' for the rest of eternity."

I picked up the hem of my skirt and rode up the ruffles to bare my thigh, its flesh striated with scars. "Eventually, my psyche eroded beyond pain." I didn't know what was written on Cesare's face and fear rendered me unwilling to look. "Father made me swear I would never again put a blade to my flesh and draw blood in self-punishment. And I never got to say sorry." I shrouded myself in my hair and clasped my own shoulders. "My body was not mine. When you are vulnerable, it is so easy for people to exploit you, and so little is in place to protect you. No one *cares* to." Emanuela's murder taught me that all too well. "And Falco chose the wealthy she serviced over the impoverished she exploited, even if it meant selling her own like we were meat."

I could only hope Giulia was a better woman.

"That's all," I murmured, fingers falling limp on the dark linen strewn with pearls of moonlight.

I had cherished those scant days when clients did not accurse me. When I would rest my chin on the sill of my chamber's window and watch in solitude the crisp celeste of daylight wash into the gilded cinnabar and manganese violet aquarelles of sundown, blurring with murky caliginosity of dusk and plunging into night's starlit black.

The sky was the only colour I ever saw in that stained glass art nouveau purgatory; the sky was freedom and I had been caged.

Freedom, too, was the watery starlight melody of the violin I listened to at *Three Suns* on the nights bridging díem stelláre and auróra. The violin I learned had been played by Cesare all that time. Though I could never admit it to him.

Silence hovered in the ether thicker than fumes of a cataclysmic firestorm, spikes of an incongruous chill pricking my skin.

"Stop," I told Cesare.

"What?"

"You are angry."

"Am I not supposed to be?" he snapped. "You recounted the most heinous shit that could happen to someone. 'Angry' doesn't *begin* to express it!"

Why do you care? "It's pointless."

All Cesare could do was darkly scoff, leaning his occiput against the wooden headboard, as far as the thud told me. "Thought I'd behold the apocalypse before you dubbed anger 'pointless'."

"Yours is directed at the dead. Mine is not. It's over, Cesare."

"Yet it haunts you."

"Opening your big, hypocritical mouth again, I see."

Cesare dithered. "I'm sorry. For the pain you were forced to endure. You walked through Hell with broken bones." My chest tightened. "Your hatred of me was justified."

I shook my head. "There is no justice under this vile authority." I shifted, glancing up at Cesare from a strange angle. "Tell *me* something, instead."

He crooked a brow. "I *was* informed I talk too much."

I puffed less than half a laugh and lay back down. "Even *you* are better than this hollow silence." I nudged his knee. "Tell me something in Marlâre. Something with meaning."

A long note of silence drew into the night.

I shut my eyes and syncopated my breaths to the sighs of the ocean beyond the porthole windows, to the breeze; felt the linen mould around my form like spacetime; curled and uncurled my fingers to remind myself that I was still real. Still living. That the shadows were just shadows.

Cesare said nothing yet, but his silence didn't alarm me this time, didn't set my ears ringing. Something about his presence was so contradictorily comforting.

"Du shudrî invênde avên, hâi elûrra du eremûa vushardô. Lasâ nirô merimôs ekartzèn." His voice warmed my skin like firelight, the syllables of his language each a streak of colour painting before my mind's eye the heavens and the earth. *He could rewrite the most mundane word into music.*

And realisation dawned on my weary consciousness.

'*Talking too much*' liberated Cesare.

Language too was an instrument.

My eyes cracked open. "What does it mean?"

I wanted him to keep talking.

"Amôna told me it's marhimê[67] to befriend non-Marlâre girls," he quipped.

My lips tucked at one corner. "Melancholy is its own tongue."

Several breaths drew before Cesare spoke again: "The cold winter comes, and snow covers the field. She brings my death."

"Case in point."

"Do you know why?"

"*You* do."

"'Marlâre' means 'birds of passage'. Historically, we were chased out of our settlements and forced into nomadism by the kings who wished to wipe us clean off the earth. That short lament is called '*Armayâ*', '*Curse*', because when winter came and they had no home to turn to, *death* was what the Marlâre of the past were cursed with." He waited out a pained heartbeat for the both of us. "But that was the past."

I buttressed myself on an elbow. "You don't sound sure."

He let out a half-hearted huff. "You and I both know we only sing when it's the songs of our dead."

My lips pursed. "Can *you* sing?"

---

[67] *mahr-hee-MEH*; 'ritually unclean'.

"If you paid me handsomely."

A giggle compelled me despite myself. "You don't ask for coin."

"I will resort to it if the question is of *singing*."

A frown reclaimed me. "You don't seek revenge, do you? For Raul's crimes."

When Cesare finally faced me, he wore rebellion in his eyes. Eyes of one who had looked upon the end so many times, he could chart its visage. "Sleep," he got up, "if you can."

"No!" I clutched his sleeve. "Stay." *I don't want to be alone yet.*

Cesare beheld me with incredulity.

And maybe it *was* him. Maybe I wanted that strange peace his company brought even if he could torch it in a heartbeat with eleutheromaniac ravings. Maybe I wanted that too. Even if some hurt and selfish part of mine wanted him to hold me with those slim, tender fingers of a murderer instead.

Cesare's gaze fell. "I'll stay." His words brought more relief than I wished to confess.

He sat back down and I curled up again, tugging the blanket's corner over my middle.

I didn't want to dream. I only wanted the emptiness of sleep.

SCENE XX

LIMB-LOOSENER, SWEETBITTER

Giorgianna

JUST AS RAVEN FEATHERS GLISTENED BLACK, as polished jet drank the light, so too was the entirety of Libitina's wardrobe the not-colour of night.

For her, it symbolised shedding an oppressive past she fled.

For me, it meant the undertaker's old Ithilweni dresses could be mine to wear in the ministerial house.

The ministerial house I would enter in mere hours, poised as the Adviser's niece, Salomè.

Dread shuddered off my fingers as they scaled the chiffon binding my torso, opalescent as insect wings. Many fine membranes of sheer habutai susurrated down my legs, slit up the side to bare my knee and cascading to flutter along the floor. From a bateau neckline, diaphanous sleeves sheathed my arms, looping over my middle fingers. My shoes were ankle-high leyniria[68] embellished with dragonfly motifs and corseted with nacreous lacing.

In the narrow eye of my chamber's full-body mirror, the ethereal gown stood at odds with the warmth of my auric complexion and caramel curls, the vulpine amber of my eyes.

Everything about me called for darkness.

I had tailored my scars and tattoos away, but my flesh remained to be wrung into a mask. I wanted to hold close the final hours in my own skin, with my own name, my own thread of hair.

I stepped beyond my quarters and made for *Antigone's* bustling deck.

Amid the mariners on the forecastle, Danilo shouted nothing in particular. Ren worked the ropes alongside a group of Hydras up in the crow's nest. Near the mainmast stood Lucrezia, hair slicked into finger waves, dressed in her vivianite velvet jacket and chatting to Itxaro, Sarnai, and Araya.

Sarnai sprung into a whirlwind sprint for me, crushing me in her small arm with enough force to blow balance from my legs. "The fateful day!" She pulled back to look at me with those bright black eyes. A beam plumped her cheek, and my stomach lodged in my throat.

"But what does our fate herald?" I mused darkly.

"We're right there with you regardless." Araya winked.

"And Ygal and I are always tinkering away in the background to help see it through," added Lucrezia.

The weight on my chest only pressed in harder. *What precarious scheme have we swindled you all into?*

"Giorgianna!" A call.

I turned to see Fabio descending from the quarterdeck.

Near the helm, Korneli, Dan now on his shoulders, saluted me.

"We're due to set sail soon," said Fabio, tone ever-glum. "Though I know it's far too late, my—"

"I know." I cupped his face. "And I need *you* to trust that my caution will be equal to none. I cannot make a more sincere plea, Fabio."

---

[68] *leh'ee-NEE-ryy-ah*; traditional Ithilweni shoes (*sing.*: leyniri).
Primarily worn in Ithilwen's northeast.

A flat look. "Need I remind you of the Blood Rite?"

I tittered despite everything. He'd handed me an earful like no other when I'd finally come clean. "I won't make it a habit."

His callused palm covered my hand. "Return to us safe, girl," he said in Themistoklísika.

"If I don't, you may curse my name to every Saint and deity."

He huffed a sad sound. "Li int: proteţie ta'ịl Qạddi."

The captain pressed a kiss to my hand, tapped his tricorn, and headed back for the quarterdeck.

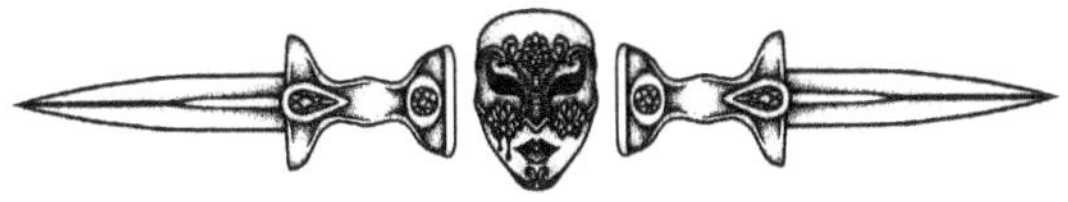

I never feared heights.

Up on the crosstree of *Antigone's* mainmast, the height feared *itself,* the mighty wings of the galleon trembling against a racing air cold as terror.

I couldn't touch the clouds but I touched the wind which hid inside the coils of my tresses, sail rigging a taut, urging pressure against my palms as my feet hung half-way off the crosstree's end—a plank moments before death. But all that rushed through me was a giddy whirl of vertigo turning my belly afloat, my head lighter than breeze.

Fabio ready at the helm, the last of the shouts among the Hydras below petered out, and adomania began to take hold of my ribs, constricting them. I wanted to pause. To *wait.*

Fingers pinched my waist.

I flinched. A shriek. My feet slipped off the crosstree's edge. I groped for the rigging and recaptured my foothold by the skin of my teeth, whirling around. "*Low*life!" I kicked Cesare's shin, narrowly missing as he hopped back with a laugh.

But, as he took hold of the ropes and cocked his head to the side, his smile faded, keen eyes gauging me. "Are you all right?"

I gawked. "I just witnessed my life flash before my eyes! What do you *think*?"

His gaze dulled. "The ordeal you depart on, I mean."

I gulped my heart back down and breathed to soothe its terrified tremors. A sigh left me. "It's liveable." I sat on the crosstree, the skirt of my dress whispering to the open air around my dangling ankles. Sunblinks skated the surface of fine crystals strewing the diaphane.

Cesare sat beside me.

Antigone rocked into movement, leaning sidelong as it tested the currents, and Cesare's breath hitched, his fingers locking around a rope.

I snickered and nudged his elbow. "Didn't take *you* for one to fear heights."

"Not unless it's on something that's *moving*," Cesare retorted curtly. "On *water*."

"Because you cannot control it?"

"Because *it* can control *me*."

Many feet below, between threshing sails, the deck gathered up all my sonder and handed it out between everyone peopling it: sailors ambling and loafing and flitting about; Fabio on the helm; Itxaro and Sarnai gossiping in a corner, faces near-touching; Danilo lolloping off below deck on some quest whilst Korneli barked an order at a deckhand only to laugh at their wild-eyed jolt; Eligio chatting up Araya while seasickness greened Lissandri's face. Rosalia had emerged with her ginger hair woven into crown braids. A collared white blouse and a calf-length black skirt clad her lanky frame, a rust-red vest laced up along her front and a white apron tied beneath a long sash with embellished ends.

The ocean rippled, Smuggler's Cove receded, and my mind gave way to doubt. "What if they're right, Cesare? What if we find nothing and all this proves pointless?"

Cesare pulled up one knee to lean his elbow onto, his forehead notching with indents I was convinced would soon be permanent. "'*Elegy of Spring*'," he led a strange exordium, "as a musical composition, is not ascribed melancholy simply by its minor chords and darker tones, but likewise owing to the absence of major chords and brighter tones. The notes left unplayed define a piece just as greatly as those that aren't. In a similar vein, that which is unspoken by a political regime—the void of noise, if you will—can sing an arguably louder song. It's always *there*, even if no suggestion of it announces itself."

I frowned. "Whether the populace reveres or abhors the regime matters not at all when they *fear* it, but most importantly fear the repercussions of rising against it, in part on account of a deeply-rooted trauma spanning generations. When have Vencenzanii ever *truly* been free? *Truly* liberated from tyranny? Every ruler knows love is bound to temporal conditions. Love and fear cannot coexist when the former is fickle and the latter is a lighter blade to wield, and a heavier chain to shackle the subjects with.

"Under De Tullia's creed, just as the imperators of the past, certain ideas are unworthy of as little as consideration, and thus must be wiped clean away. So, how does one spur the masses to revolt against such a ruler when their fear, not only of the regime but of its scapegoats, as propagandised to them, runs deep enough to render the most outrageous political scandal obsolete?"

"Find the smoking gun," declared Cesare. "Discover something which incites in Vencenzanii such fear of De Tullia *remaining* in power that it tramples their fear of rebellion."

I stood, holding onto ropes pulled taut near my shoulders. "The implication *there* is a necessity to weaponise the very fear the Governor employs to control his people."

Cesare rose and gripped the overhead rigging, his white sleeves billowing in the breeze. "One *should* fear this regime's continuation when its only end is death."

My mouth pressed into a line. "And who's to say *we* are beyond corruptibility?" Power was a narcotic laced with slow-killing venom neither of us had yet savoured the taste of.

"The shadow moves as the sun commands." Cesare's head tilted slightly, the warmth of his soft breath on my lips a too-late reminder of our closeness. "Perhaps we aren't, Giorgianna." My breath stumbled. "Perhaps our demise too is destined among the ashes of this empire."

"Call me that again."

His brows pinched together. "...Giorgianna?" His tongue played each syllable of my name like a litany's notes, and I couldn't draw air.

My fingertips skimmed the curve of his hooped earring, its crotal bell reciting an étude to the twirling wind. *"Your voice makes everything a psalm,"* I whispered.

Cesare's eclipsed gaze flickered to my parted lips, then found my eyes once more. "And your name is a prayer on every tongue."

A rot ripened beneath my skin, something eating away at my flesh. The kind of putrescence from which flowers grew. Like medlar—sweet and yielding.

My fingers slipped into the silk waves framing Cesare's face, cradled his jaw, my nose skimming the crook of his cheek as I rose just a smidge off my heels. *"Only yours—"*

"Can we get a move on?"

I defied a gasp at the uninvited voice.

Cesare's head turned sharply, hair whipping my cheek.

Ren stood at the junction of the crosstree and mast. "Ain't a rendezvous spot, y'know. I'm tryna keep the ropes in order."

Fury seethed in my cheeks as I crucified ver with a scowl; ve glared back as if saying *'serves you right'* and began climbing back up to the crow's nest, taking the searing bullet-hail of my glowers with ver.

Cesare glanced at me, but I dodged his eyes, stupidly easing hair behind my ears.

At the juncture of the mast and crosstree, Cesare stepped aside, a smirk donned, though the red of his cheeks did not escape me. "Ladies first."

I smirked back, "I'll hold you to that," and embarked on the treacherous descent.

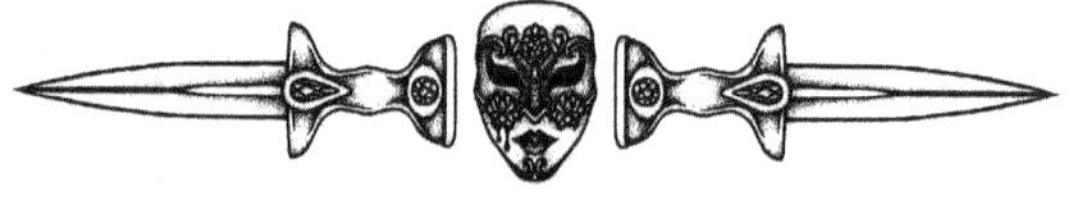

The indent in my lower lip was gone.

The mole beneath my left eye was gone.

My curls were unravelled to smooth satin, woven by Rosalia into a pair of braids along my scalp and unified in one calf-length plait. Dull as gravesoil.

I'd tilted my nose up a tad, pinching its tip into a petite button, and lifted my brows, drawing them a hair further apart and making an earnest attempt at thinning them. In Ithilwen, it was custom for aristocratic human women to pluck them clean away, given iridites had none and their standards of beauty were punitive. *That* was a step too far for me and my thick hair.

Dragging down tears, I sang to my blood, watching through a blur as the redness of pain dissipated from my sclerae to leave behind unassuming grey-blue irises.

> *'When her skin is torn, stitched like a*
> *marionette, hair weaved into thread*
> *anew, will she, upon that silver*
> *looking, see her face?'*

I could not claim I did.

The face in the mirror was a doll—dainty and docile, its skin tight as scabbed wounds yet porcelain-smooth. A resurrected effigy, perhaps: the Self I had once buried.

Across my forehead, I slipped a diadem, a pair of irisating pendants swinging from it on chains more delicate than fishing line to my jaw.

Living inside tailored flesh meant magic would always linger upon me like fading perfume. Fortunately, such would not be too bizarre for an Ithilweni citizen when most iridite attire was crafted with masonry.

At the threshold, I cast a gaze across my bedchamber one last time. The tiny bed with its headboard butting against the far wall. The faint aroma of rose oil salted by the sea and soured by damp wood. The ribbons of cramoisie silk suspended from the ceiling—given to me by Glàvca at the nameless Antrum tavèrna. The mirror, the sink, that short wardrobe doubling as a desk. Home. *Every place I'd ever thought a home was ripped from me.*

My heart weighed the world, but I shut the door.

"I admit," Lissandri's arm perched on my shoulder, "convincing get-up." With his other hand, he gripped Rosalia's elbow, the girl looking anything but pleased to be held hostage. His palm opened. Within it lay a pair of gears. "Always keep clockwork parts on you."

I regarded him curiously. "Why?"

He shrugged. "You never know when the time is right."

"Embraces for the road!" Eligio swept out of the storage room across the corridor, Cesare in tow.

The five of us huddled, and every time I thought I'd already realised how impossibly I loved them all, it came back to me a thousand times over. I never wanted to lose any more of these precious people.

"Please remember," Eligio's voice came gently as ever, "no matter what, that we *will* find another way. Always. Understand?"

I squeezed him tight. "Understand."

The port of Vencenza stretched forever, endless sails swirling with gulls and mariner calls. Sunblinks bounced upon the watery prisms of the Vault of Faces and cast the sprawling skeleton of Vencenza's upper city into a glittering palette of gemstone colour.

Sarnai and Araya stood with me on the deck, the latter laden with bags for the sake of playing to the gallery.

Antigone began to drop anchor.

"Well." Sarnai held out her arms. "This is us."

"*Sarnai!*" Itxaro hurtled across the deck, all but tackling the small woman to the ground as she embraced her in a fierce kiss. Pulling away, she held Sarnai's flushed cheeks. "Be careful, yeah?"

Sarnai blinked, then smiled, "Yeah," and kissed Itxaro on the nose bridge as farewell.

I looked upon the crew for the road.

The twins. Cesare. Lucrezia. Danilo and Korneli. Ren up in the crow's nest. But I left my final glance with Fabio for safe keeping, and strutted down the gangway. Chin high. Spine steeled into a blade.

At one of the hundreds of canals feeding into the port bobbled a ghastly black tumour of a crow gondoa. A City Guard loomed at its oar. Four Guardíi hovered like orbs of silver energy beside. At the centre of the flock roosted an elderly man with a waist-length salt-and-pepper braid, thin frame garbed in rust silk purfled with bronze.

Coldness lay me bare as *Antigone* grew further away but, against every instinct to *Run!*, I approached the gondoa and the soldiers.

A woman at the vanguard of the Guardíi stood taller than Ygąl. A braid ardent as flames, woven impossibly tight, draped her shoulder, her tanned face hidden behind a silver half-mask. "Dónna Salomè Barsotti." She bowed with the other legionaries. "I am Centúrion Ioana De Rege of the Guárdia—Adviser Clario Barsotti's personal faction of legionaries. I and my soldiers are at your service for the duration of your stay."

Barsotti reached his thin hands out to me. "Dél'ì lùtius e vísus benedétti, neptísa.[69]"

I held his hands, stifling a shudder at their clamminess. "So long no see, patrúuo!" Each rehearsed word coated my tongue in tar. "Nêm'tħãme thĩl lu'lãr ýlla'Lúx'alỹnu.[70]" I gestured to my cortège. "My protectors: signór Araya Tesfalem and signorína Sarnai. And my maid: signorína Trine Rosalia Fisker."

The crow and a peacock helped Araya with our luggage.

"As guests in our grand city," the Minister of Emissaries commenced, "you are requested to refrain from emoting."

Once more, against every instinct to *Run!*, I folded my hands and dropped them decorously at my lap the way Libitina taught. "Such things slip my mind after so long in Ithilwen."

---

[69] Faustinian for '*niece*'.

[70] '*Kings' mercy and goodwill*' in Ithilweni. Recall that Ithilweni iridites consider their kings to be materialised gods. Linguistically, '*tħ*' in Ithilweni denotes a hard '*th*' like that in '*then*', as opposed to a soft '*th*' like in '*theology*'. A '*ħ*' on its own is pronounced '*kh*'.

Clario took my arm. Every muscle within me winced. "A reminder going forward."

Against each and *every* instinct to *Run!*, I boarded the vessel.

When *Antigone* vanished from view, despair grasped me, but I made no show of it, appeasing Ioana and 'my patrúuo' with trivialities, instead.

Vencenza's buttercream walls were ghostly beneath the empty eye sockets of the faces embossed onto them. Only the whisper of dresses and capes broke its silence, the quiet murmurs and occasional merchant shouts the city's only lifeblood.

Architectural motifs gave way from the sickled lunes of *The Crescent* to the full moons and miniscule stars of *The Nox*, signifying our entrance to the northeast.

My gullet itched, a redolent perfume clogging my nostrils, and I remembered too late.

The narrow canal opened on one side to a vast courtyard. *Boulevard of Everseers*. A matching waterway, obumbrated by a cloister, flowed in the opposing direction at its other side. Arcuate ribs of bridges overhung the piazza. And from them bloomed lush bouquets of pork-pink honeysuckles. And amid the clustered flowers swung cages housing starved prisoners and corpses.

The Hanging Gardens.

Araya's dark face bleached. Rosalia gawped. Ioana's techélet-blue eyes cast from the scene. The remaining passengers hardly stirred.

I smelt it beneath the nectar: rot. Made worse by the brackish blood of Vencenza's veins, the breeze oppressive with desperation. Rage. *And rage sires vengeful progeny.*

Elenedda would once bring me to The Hanging Gardens, gripping me by the shoulders and jaw and forcing me to look upon the barbarity. '*Nothing is worth it,*' she'd hiss. *Freedom* wasn't worth it if all it got you was *That*.

I comprehended what it meant to be ruled by fear, then. It became all I knew, so I split in twain. *A diptych.*

Yet I was no longer nothing beneath this regime's boot. No longer a scapegoat for the slaughter, a shattered trinket of heterodoxy.

I was my Shadow.

Death became me.

But how much is freedom worth?

Just before we sailed out of sight, a prisoner's empty eyes, nested within gaunt features, plucked my own from their sockets and held them for so long I ceased breathing.

The prisoner spat.

My heart lurched, a gasp fleeing from me. Clario took my hand and hummed to me some vacuous inanity, but I couldn't hear nor care. As the bone-white acropolis of the government building loomed in the too-near distance, I wanted to empty my guts. To scream. To rip the weed that was this city from the defiled earth.

Every last one of you deserves to bleed.

Parapets crowned in balusters stared down their perfectly symmetrical noses, the water of the moat encircling the ministerial house so clear I could see the bottom.

My eyes wandered through friezes and colonnades polished to a gleam. If I listened closely to the windy howls, they turned to wails of prisoners trapped within The Trabeculae: the dungeons beneath that grand citadel. Dungeons stretching further than the citadel itself, deeper than the edifice was tall. Reliquiae of the northern imperators. And it seemed De Tullia was overcome with nostalgia for the Empire with forgetfulness of its brutality. Or perhaps a hankering for renaissance.

We disembarked the gondoa, Araya and two peacocks hauling our luggage off to our quarters.

From the guard station on the berth's bank emerged three Imperialíi in gold filigree and flavescent capes. At their centre, golden-haired General Manuele Dioli himself stood unmasked and helmetless. Loose waves streamed to his mighty shoulders, his sun-touched cheeks, straight nose, full lips all chiselled.

Not man. A flytrap.

He bowed to Clario, a powerful hand at his chest. "Adviser," his deep voice flowed smooth, rumbled like a lion's growl. I wanted to tear his throat out. He glared at Ioana. "De Rege."

The Centúrion nodded. "General."

Manuele's eyes burned. Vivid blue flames. Algid. "Dáma Salomè Barsotti." I was not deaf to his use of 'dáma' in place of Ioana's 'dónna'. "General Manuele Dioli of Vencenza's legions, and the Minister of Blades on Governor Crescenzo De Tullia's council."

Revulsion rooted through my innards as I forced anything but hateful condemnations to take form on my tongue. "I was made aware, signór." *These bone-white floors would be so much prettier lacquered with the scarlet of your veins.* I dipped into a curtsey like Ithilweni women. "A pleasure." *In due time.*

When I rose, the centre of the General's eye was inscribed with my initials. "Let us proceed to the Omphalos." He ushered us inside the Spider's Den.

The Omphalos was the ministerial hall on the citadel's seventh floor: its centre in every respect.

Each skeletal hollow of the freezing edifice echoed—a disembowelled, skinned, buffed cadaver.

Two griffins dragged open the grand doors.

The hall beyond stretched for a lifetime, immeasurable enough to suck all air from my lungs, a wide row of colossal white piliers cantonné holding up the soaring ceiling and every surface pallid.

A scarsella indented the ceiling above the daïs upon which towered a marble throne as if a kingseat built of skulls, garrisoned by Imperialíi. Beside it, a pair of Ministers conversed. One dressed in realgar, rubies and threads of gilt emblazoning their double-spired headdress, their aperúcca aureate. The other, unmasked, wore the grey of spidersilk and corpse ashes, jet-black waves spilling to his elbows.

Dioli stopped at the feet of the daïs and bowed. "Governor Crescenzo De Tullia, Domínie Benetto Abelli. Adviser Clario Barsotti's guests have arrived."

Sepulchral shadows rippled against the Governor when he turned, darkness emanating from his feet in a billion spiderlings. My skin crawled when his oak-deep eyes pinned me for vivisection. Cavernous sockets drank his gaunt face.

The man who reaped Us of freedom.

The man by whose decree I was made a fugitive.

The man who put my father to the gallows.

He descended, every movement across the marble death-silent. "Dónna Salomè Barsotti?" he questioned with a hollow voice, deeper than any sound I thought possible.

I bowed, teeth almost chattering. "Indeed, Governor. Nêm'ťhãme thĩl lu'lãr ýlla'Lúx'alỹnu."

He held a slim hand to his chest where a silver swallow brooch perched. "Dél'ì lùtius e vísus benedétti. I trust your voyage fared well. Iron Strait is a treacherous channel."

I didn't sever my eyeline from his. "Our journey proceeded smoothly, many thanks. I could have prayed for no better a captain and crew to ensure my safety."

Everyone shared introductions, the Minister of Churches chary of approaching—a bloody apparition lingering upon the daïs. Watching. So I watched back.

"You are expected at the Ministerial dinner this evening, dónna Salomè," asserted De Tullia. "Such conditions permit dialogue." There *was* no request, but I wondered what a refusal would earn me. "Centúrion De Rege shall escort you all to your respective quarters. Aíxis,[71] your stay proves agreeable."

I lowered my chin. "Falemícè, gracious Governor."

---

[71] *ah-EEK-sees*; 'Gods' will'; a modern Illutèri wish of goodwill for the future.

As the monstrous doors shut behind us, I speared a parting glance through the ink-dark stain that was the Governor.

Even if not by my hand, your end is nigh, De Tullia.

The lilac organza and white lace weren't enough to make my bedchamber's parlour less uninviting; the lavender silk sofas did nothing to hide that, beneath it, everything was hard stone.

Ioana revealed the entrance to the citadel's hidden tunnels (a portal concealed among the stucco decor within the depths of the master bedroom's walk-in closet), handing all four of us keys we tested for authenticity.

"The maid lodgings are part of the larger chamber," Ioana gestured to the demure door on our right when we returned to the parlour, "hence the ensuite is accessible from two points." She'd doffed her silver colombína. Beneath it was an elegant aquiline nose splotched with a large ruddy birthmark around the left eye. "The two flanking rooms are reserved for the guards. Once acclimated, you may request my guidance around relevant points of interest. Trine, as a dónna's maid, you are permitted to mingle with the servants. Sarnai and Araya, although you *are* granted access to the barracks, I'd advise against it. Your people are planted sparsely among the lower legionaries. Of course, if anything should be amiss, I'm your woman. Settle, for the time being. I shall notify you of evenmeal." And the Centúrion left.

One, two, we counted the receding footsteps, *six, seven,* before huddling quietly.

"A bulky fellow like me's probably best to suss out flocks about city goings-on," said Araya.

"Giorgi and I're on most of the in-building snooping, but *you,*" Sarnai pointed to me, "have direct access to the Ministers."

"*Hm.*" I pinched my chin. "The attention on me will be most keen. So, *you*, Sarnai, are the better party to scout the perimeter."

"That's my role too!" Rosalia piped up, smacking both hands over her mouth before whispering, "*Servants gossip.*"

"Broaden our scope." I threaded my braid through my hand. "Seems only *I* am invited to this evening's dinner." My eyes spun. "Undying woe… But it leaves an open window to get some light reconnaissance under way."

"Good opportunity to pin-point our Hounds," remarked Sarnai.

"To-morrow morning's an a'right time to dispatch couriers back to Isaia," Araya added.

I approached the ceiling-high window and gazed across the moat to the coronate aqueducts encircling it. "On this chessboard, we are not the pawns." From my skirt, I withdrew my bleeding-eye pendant and the clockwork parts Lissandri sent me off with, cradling them in my palm. "We are the queen piece."

SCENE XXI

TO THE GALLERY

Giorgianna | Kel-Kech | Cesare

THE DINING ROOM TIMEPIECE TICKED a sombre beat of seventeen hundred.

Speaking during meals at the citadel was prohibited, so the Ministry and myself ate in skin-peeling silence.

Governor Crescenzo De Tullia sat across the oak table from me, High Priest Benetto Abelli at his right and General Manuele Dioli to his left. Adviser Clario Barsotti and the fur-and-jewel-clad Treasurer Olindo Alagona flanked me. Between Olindo and Benetto sat the vile death-dealer Grand Judge Giordano Veronesi in his black robes and chaperon. Positioned stiffly between Clario and Manuele was Magister Ilenia Farnese.

Fleshflies burrowed into the putrescent body of our city.

The feast, with its coral-red lobster festooned with golden truffle mayonnaise, oysters doused in zesty mignonette sauce, variegated salads like diced gemstones, glittered beneath the soft glow of alchemical lights. Yet every bite tasted cold and raw to me.

As the meal concluded, servants tidied the table.

My stomach turned all the more at the thought of being waited on. *With luck, this won't last long.*

"Wine, dónna Salomè?" offered De Tullia.

"Forgive me, Governor, but I am minded to refuse." I dulled the edges of my tone. *Play to the gallery.*

"A wise verdict," praised De Tullia whilst servants poured drink for the Judge and Treasurer. "Alcohol is nought but an opiate—a disinhibitor to forego." As those words left the Governor's mouth, Olindo hastily placed down his cup. Giordano imbibed.

I scrutinised his chalice: iron, seven black spinels around the knop. An item he brought with him to the dining hall.

"Owing to the illegality of most alcohol in Ithilwen," I recommenced, "one would be correct to infer that His Magnificence Ným'natħír Elthór shares your sentiment."

"And *he* would be correct in such a conviction," contended De Tullia as if he'd desperately yearned to preach. To *convert.* "Purity of emotion is purity of the material. Indulgence and personal pleasures make us dismissive of our duties and moralities." *'Moralities' by what criteria?* "Anger begets blindness to reality." *Whose reality?* "Fear springs forth an unwillingness to act upon that which is compulsory of us as upstanding citizens." *The very fear you leash your subjects with?* "Misplaced revelry abets disrespect, indolence, lawlessness." *To you?*

De Tullia stood, hands folded behind his waist, and paced around the table. "The imperators of the Faustinian Empire, as the kings of Ithilwen, were right to structure their civilisation within monarchic frames. The masses are soft-headed, weak of will, easily deceived by the false creed of terrorists like The Bauta and the pests Morettae. At their deepest essence, the citizenry is an ochlocratic horde in demand of regime to not suffer complete civilisational collapse. Such mercurial minds are liable to arrive at faulty conclusions, and thus cannot be granted the authority of democratic election of leadership. That duty must be directed to government officials versed in political discipline. Likewise, the imperators stood right to employ strict doctrine rooted in theology— flawed as their Myseric beliefs were—within civil law-making."

Across the table, eyes the black of blindness fixed on me. "Art thou a believer, lília?"

"I believe in the Illutèri pantheon, Domínie, but I cannot say I pray." I cannot say the Gods *listen.*

"If a citizen's righteousness," De Tullia's voice boomed from behind me, several steps afield; as if he was turned away from me, "their virtue and honourable principles, are to be reinforced and resolute, they must adhere to a rigid religious code, otherwise there can *be* no morality."

A nod from Abelli. "We ought pray for purity of the face the sacral light of the Trimorphic Godhead didst grant unto our material chrysalis. Arcóntial emotions taint us, and an impartial stance is unfeasible—there ought to, at each moment, abideth conviction."

A citizen's 'righteousness', in these peoples' eyes, was defined as that which fell in line with Their—the ruling hegemony's—interest. The government enacted their laws in a manner most befitting their political affiliation and, in doing so, circumscribed the limits of said 'righteousness', tailoring it to the leader's ipse dixit.

Reminding myself of my place, I folded my hands. "A wise and engrossing analysis, indeed, Governor."

"And you are a thinker, dónna Salomè." De Tullia's algid tone was enough to tell me such qualities were less than desirable under his philosophy.

A gulp of water went stiffly down my throat. "An honour, Governor."

"Your patrúuo extols you as a linguist, and a political science cognoscente," half-mused Crescenzo, pacing around the table en route to his abandoned kingseat, yet he never once looked at Clario.

I readjusted my braid, scouring for any sliver of comfort. "My patrúuo ought not sing my praises too loudly. I am simply enthralled in the diplomatic affairs of Balinor, and but trilingual."

"Which third tongue?"

"Themistoklísika."

A *clack* of metal on wood sounded, and Veronesi lay a hand freed of a chalice at his chest. "Your handmaiden surely rejoices, being taken into a human household and not an iridite one, with a backdrop of a country and people so barbarous." *Look at your own city state, you miserable old worm!*

"Far easier to blame those right before us than the deeper systemic maladies," I couldn't bridle my tongue as the heat of ire rose in my belly.

A half-squint. "What a *very* no—"

"You are *counselled*—" Crescenzo's voice tore through "to be *silent*, Giúdice."

Veronesi lifted his drink. "Governor."

Breathless silence.

The clock ticked. The sun left a streak of blood as it crawled beneath the skyline. The world lay cold and empty without the commotion of shipmen, the clatter of clocks, of paint tubs, pins, the knowledge that the warmth of words and skin lingered just a door over.

"Evenmeal is dismissed," De Tullia announced at long last.

"Governor's will," the Ministers intoned, stood, and took to dispersing. The Grand Judge rushed off first, chalice in hand, followed by the ambling Treasurer. Olindo had been glancing at me throughout dinner with something unreadable. Almost as if he might think he recognised me, but not quite. Looking upon him struck me with vague queasiness, but I chalked it up to him dripping in jewels and fine furs whilst his people starved.

My behold barged into Ilenia's, her left eye a cabochon viridian, the right cerulean as the sea. *Have I seen those eyes before…?*

As she flitted away, my skin tingled, horripilated. *Azoth?*

"Thy presence," I almost jumped when Benetto spoke to me, "we petition at the congregation—eight hundred, each díem sóle. A tradition of the ministerial house."

I curtsied the Ithilweni way. "Duly noted, Domínie."

They opened their gloved palms Godsward, red, "Benefácio lùtius,[72]" and departed, their footsteps all but silent.

The aroma of musk and pine gagged my senses when Manuele paused beside me along his own exeunt. "Mèus dáma."

---

[72] *beh-neh-FAH-choh LOO-tee-oos*; 'Bless'ed light'.

I didn't meet his eyes, could barely compose my speech into anything but violence. "General."

I *felt* him linger, look, my skin crawling off the bones with every second his gravity forced itself onto mine until, finally, he left, a sight almost leaving me alongside. *You are an infected ulcer.*

Manuele deserved to be slaughtered for his crimes. But he deserved to go mad, to break, to *suffer* for it, first. To leave this world in peace was mercy for the swine that was Manuele Dioli.

So you will pay your dues in blood.

Bibliosmia hovered in the enchanted air of the Athenaeum. Staircases climbed up and around soaring bookshelves packed with a thousand lifetimes worth of volumes, rows weaving into a leatherbound paper city.

An enormous clock whispered *nineteen hundred* to the silence.

I slipped into the depths of the library, eyes flicking through titles.

"Who goes there?" A woman's voice.

"Dónna Salomè, Magister." I faced Ilenia who stood at the inlet of a perpendicular passage.

The layered skirt of her fuchsia empire gown slit to the knee, her heeled ankle boots adorned with a curved magenta rod suspending a bleeding-heart flower. Airy balloon sleeves swallowed her arms. As if roots, veins of gold leaf tangled along her dress' square neckline, branching and entwining into an ornate medici collar behind her head from which dangled pampel-cut pezzottaites.

About time I met the enigmatic woman.

She stood beside me, gazing at the towering bookcase caving into a semicircular recess within the wall. In her arms she held a black tome.

A familiar shiver breezed by my skin. *Azoth, indeed.*

I eyed the book she held. "What read snares your curiosity, if you're willing to share?"

"'*A Wound Between Worlds*'. A transcribed Wãnelidãwan text. It concerns translocational enchantments."

Curiosity thorned at me. "What do they entail?"

A sigh. "Through a thaumaturge's employment of potent sorcery, the universe is perforated with azoth—acting as an escharotic of sorts. Via these apertures, one may venture between two disconnected points upon the euclidean plane." Right then and there, I realised what sort of hex Cardea had placed upon oldtown with her sacrifice. "I have long been studying this art. It is believed to take an extreme toll on our world and people; hence, one often falls ill when passing through translocation zones. Materiality appears… disjointed. Foggy." *A waking dream…*

"What prompts your study of these enchantments?"

A twitch between her brows when Ilenia beheld me. "Why are you here?"

"Centúrion De Rege's mention of your Athenaeum snared *my* curiosity."

"The ministerial house, fool." Her tone sharpened.

"I deeply missed my uncle after years abroad."

"You are in a nest of spiders."

What interesting wording.

"Aren't we all?"

She stepped in front of me, the scorch of her chimeric eyes accentuated with gold liner. "You know *nothing* of what lurks within Vencenza's bones, prowls the shadows of our civilisation, the horrors committed under this authority and the vile creatures living in these walls."

"*You* know *me* not at all." I bridled my rage, instead crooking my lips into an empty, mirthless expression. "Neither do you seem to hold reverence for your Governor, o Minister of Scholars."

I knew the red flush of wrath upon a cheek too well not to recognise it on Ilenia. "I will not stand for your meddling! You and whatever purpose you have here shan't jeopardise me." And she was gone.

Yet all she succeeded to do was prove she had much to hide. And much to enlighten me of.

Deeper into the athenaeum I journeyed, fingertips skimming spines, the diaphane of my skirt snagging on loose pages. I imagined Lissandri's delight at a library so vast, and my chest bundled.

Silvern whiffs of magic followed me, clung to my skin like cobwebs. After a couple instances, I figured out that some of the books were written with enchanted ink. A couple of them opened to blank paper where a hex had been cast, and since the author was long-dead, that which they had written could never be read.

With azoth integrated so into the creation of any given thing, the aura of magic—coldness, shivers, the smell of silver—would always follow it. Just as with my own tailored flesh. It must have been the medici collar on the Magister's gown, likely crafted through masonry, that shed the azoth in her presence.

My hand halted along a shelf.

Beneath it, a narrow spine burned so utterly cold.

I pried the book free.

Upon the oxblood leather binding, stamped in argent, was the title '*Silverblood*', and nothing else.

I folded away the cover.

The first page repeated the title, but told more.

SILVERBLOOD

The abridged diaries of
Nashĭgostu Kurilit Gostiata

Translated by
Miluna Catellan

My lips parted.

Nashĭgostu Kurilit Gostiata... '*Spagyrism and Spellwerk*'... The book that taught me all I knew of magic...

I turned several pages, to the date 19/3/1175/9 (ZE). Five-hundred-eighty-seven years ago.

Magic's scent deepened to the intensity of molten metal, and I realised that the ink was infused with azoth.

I realised that the ink was blood.

AS THE SKY DIMMED, reddened,[73] Lorita and Kel-Kech made their way back to the old armoury from Tafsut's parlour. Though still disappointed that it took as much effort as it did to convince Lorita to accompany her to the slums, a sense of pride found Kel at the fact that she ultimately triumphed. To-night, she'd brought rooibos tea to make hot drinks for the denizens. It felt good, knowing she could do something like that.

The pair wondered in the direction of the Solar Square where checkpoints loomed, briefly disoriented by the Court, and noticed commotion among the populace. A jittery tension in the way people clutched their shawls to their chests and scurried into their homes.

When Kel and Lorita went to question a passerby, they snubbed them both and rushed away.

"Better not get near the Square," Rita muttered.

The pair advanced through familiar streets before being halted again by the sight of a barred window, its sill just above Kel's eye level and its inner doors slightly ajar. They approached, calling out, then waited.

"The fuck d'you need?" a gruff voice barked from inside.

Kel-Kech shrank, so Lorita rose onto her toes and asked, "Do you know what's happening?"

"The crows. What else can it bloody be?"

"But what *happened*?"

"Pigs found contraband—a dagger, I think—and started turnin' the whole checkpoint upside down lookin' for its owner. A bunch o' folks

---

[73] Despite the sun of Seren having very similar characteristics and properties to our own Sun, it is smaller and thus has a slightly larger habitable zone (*97 mil–222 mil km radius*). Likewise, its light is somewhat warmer in colour, Therefore, sunsets and sunrises are slightly more red-pink toned than on Earth. It makes for quite a sight.

got beaten, a couple more arrested. It's fuckin' savagery out there. Now go away!" And the door slammed.

"Dick," hissed Lorita.

"Come," Kel-Kech took Lorita's hand, only holding it for a second before the blond pulled free, a blush striking her face. "We need to tell the others," Kel clarified, eyes averted.

They made it back to the armoury, searching for one of their main organisers—the one who took Lapo's place after Giorgianna snapped his neck for prattling. But they did not find him.

"Yezo, where's Tolomé?" questioned Kel-Kech once they looped back around to ground floor.

He only momentarily lifted his eyes from the book bent hideously in his palm. "Down in Smugglers' District with the other two, apparently."

"What?" Kel's innards went cold. "*Nonono*, they're not supposed to go there—Rita!"

"Kel, stop." Lorita shook off Kel's sudden grip. "Let's go." She routed for the exit.

Panic began shaking Kel. "We're not tracking them down."

"Grow a spine!" snapped Lorita. "Yes we are!"

Kel-Kech almost didn't follow the blonde, feeling a sting like a slap.

Yezo offered Kel a sympathetic look, Lorita hovering expectantly in the archway, so Kel drew a tight breath, nipping at her snakebites, and relented.

They scoured several tavèrnae scattered around the Cove before finally sighting Tolomé, brown-haired and pale, in the *Dancing Worm*, sitting around drinking their customary dilute absinthe with Ànzelu and Conrà.

Lorita stormed for the trio. "What the fuck is this?" She gripped Tolomé by the scruff, her outburst attracting a couple eyes.

He met her with an unimpressed glower, "I'm tired," and imbibed his alcohol.

"What is that supposed to mean?"

"It means this is fucking pointless, Rita," he snapped. "We're fighting uphill."

"A lovers' tiff?" asked an unfamiliar voice, deep and female, and across from Tolomé, on the empty stool beside the towheaded Conrà, sat a plump, tall Ukuji woman.

Lorita stiffened, unhanding Tolomé. "No."

The brunet passed wary glances around all the Morettae, then frowned the newcomer's way. "*Who* are you?"

A tight-lipped smile. "Just a *Dancing Worm* regular." She lay an uchigatana across her lap. Her loose sleeve fell away. On her forearm, near a healing gunshot wound, was inked a delicate dahlia.

Kel-Kech's throat seized up.

All the Morettae sprung from their seats, hands raised.

"Woah…" Tolomé's eyes blew wide. "We don't want trouble."

"*Really*?" The smuggler woman's tone rang with ridicule as she too rose, spinning her sword through her wrist. "Certainly not what *this* told me." She demonstrated her wound.

Tolomé's head shook. "That wasn't us—Rita, tell her; that was one of the Hyd—"

"*Oh*, no no *no*!" The Dahlia woman took a step closer. Kel's vision began darkening and blurring when she realised that they had gotten surrounded by Dahlias, and that the tavèrna patrons weren't responding at all to their evident peril. The smuggler pointed her uchigatana at Tolomé. "You don't get to hide from collective responsibility."

"Quartermaster Ahana.[74]"

Another voice.

Kel-Kech turned around, almost dizzied.

Frighteningly close behind her stood a small older woman in a black greatcoat embroidered with red and circleted around the waist with pulled teeth, her hair marbled grey, gouged eyeballs dangling off her ears.

The smuggler woman dipped her head. "Soriano-dono."

The captain stepped forward. The entire tavèrna stood silent.

---

[74] 天花。

"So, *none* of you seem to know how to listen." Blood Dahlia swept ink-blot eyes through the Morettae who stood like statues. Even Ànzelu's brown face whitened. The captain let out a cutting half-laugh. "Don't you know the *Dancing Worm* is Blood Dahlia territory?"

Kel-Kech and Lorita looked at each other with wild eyes, the blonde mouthing '*shit!*' whilst Kel's head spun.

"Your orders, kepţen?" asked a dark-skinned woman within the circle of Dahlias.

Kel-Kech swallowed as Blood Dahlia peered at Tolomé. At Lorita. At *her*. Then, she came to Ahana's gaze.

"Let them leave." Her decision all but jolted Kel-Kech.

"Captain?" Ahana questioned with audible disbelief.

Dahlia looked pointedly at her quartermaster, communicating something beyond words, because Ahana simply nodded and sheathed her sword.

The last traces of sunlight striated the sky when they exited the tavèrna.

Tolomé looked as if he'd seen a ghoul, seemingly opening his mouth to say something to Kel and Lorita only to shake his head and abandon the endeavour.

Kel-Kech turned, shut her eyes to collect the little of her spirit she felt she had, and approached Blood Dahlia who stood, cigarillo in the process of being lit, near the *Dancing Worm*'s door. "Would you possibly reconsider aiding us?" Saying those words alone made Kel's heart escape into the soles of her feet.

Dahlia stared at her with almost a slight revulsion; Kel wanted to die right then and there.

"You're not my responsibility, girl," Dahlia asserted.

"I know, but..." an exhale, "are people not all *each other's* responsibility, of sorts?" Kel folded her hands, eyes dropping to the cobbles. "What I mean is… This should be a concern for all of us. I can't even imagine what De Tullia getting his hands on The Court—let *alone* the Antrum and Cove—would spell." She braved a look at the captain.

Her features had soothed into something unreadable to her. "Don't take *Naufrago Terrace* back. A fair few Tongues live on it." At that moment, Ahana walked out of the tavèrna, and Dahlia joined her as if the Morettae had already disappeared.

Tolomé and Lorita appeared at Kel-Kech's side.

"What did you do?" demanded Rita.

Kel-Kech gazed across at the dimming horizon. "Something useful."

ANOTHER WRETCHED SUNSET dragged like a dead body beneath the sky.

Cesare brought a sigarétta to his mouth, chest rising as he drew charring grey death into himself.

Frozen floorboards gnawed his shirtless back, his fully-clad legs bent at the knees and hooked onto his untouched bed. He didn't know if he would sleep to-night. With Giorgianna and Rosalia forsaken to The Bone Kingdom for his cause, he didn't think he *could*.

Smoking the remainder of the coffin nail, Cesare, against his body's protests, his heavy breath and shallow, vulnerable heartbeat, forced himself to rise, discarding the filter tip and approaching the too-low sink mirror beside the nook of his bed.

Rinsing the face remedied nothing.

His insomnia-battered eyes, his mouth, creaked with dryness; no matter how much water he guzzled, he remained parched, aches ceaselessly jabbing his head. And no matter how many baths he took, nothing could strip Cesare's skin of the invisible filth clinging to it.

With every upward movement of his arms, he could count his ribs, his belt sporting a fresh stab wound to account for his thinning abdomen. It wouldn't be long until his muscle wasted and a skeletal carcass was all remaining of him.

The needles had once shucked him of flesh just as unpityingly, but it had only been enough to give him pause, not seek escape. That shoe dropped when he began to *forget*.

Yet the malnourishment, exhaustion, kept him numb. Dead, even as he still walked. Just like then.

How did I ever scrape out of that bottomless black pit?

Cesare's bleary gaze slid along the scars marring his stomach and chest: the verses of Raul's hate indelibly carved into him; the shapeless coagulation of Manuele's brutality marking his ribs—a stigma of failure; the haloed splotch of the bullet Giorgianna lodged beneath his collarbone.

Bloodshot sclerae cast Cesare's eyes into a hideous green, and he knew he couldn't go on that way any longer.

By any means necessary, it seems…

SCENE XXII

LE PAROLE VOLANO,
GLI SCRITTI RIMANGONO

Giorgianna | Cesare

THE MOUNTAIN VALLEY PULSED, the likes of organs, red above and red below, the sky a dark clot choking the lungs. Waterfalls, oily and claret, tumbled off carnose peaks through gory gashes of gorges.

Your feet squelched as you followed a fleshy path stretching at the foot of the cliffs, paved with gossamer-thin strings of muscle, bones protruding from mutated masses of ribbed intestines. Fringing the track blossomed bushes of scarlet roses so lush they swallowed the leaves.

Snow soaked up the blood. The moist, sweet-warm air cooled to frost. Roses paled and shrunk as you pushed on through a thickening blizzard. Ice hovered in the air thick as fog, burned your feet, until those roses became unending fields of forget-me-nots swaddling cracked and limbless statues.

The mortuary garden stretched to nowhere, moths circling with their dusty white wings. You stalked on aimlessly.

Until a trail of pomegranate arils like torn teeth halted you.

Your gaze followed them along the snow to a scattering of dead moths around a frozen fountain. Upon it sat a woman tall as mountains, limber frame costumed in a lazuline tutu and dark hair rushing down her back. A large, flat mole marked her cheek.

Horror clenched your heart when the woman's eyes lifted to yours. Blue as the endless forget-me-nots.

'Ema…'

Her slender fingers sank into the pomegranate they grasped, ripping it open, and awful pain cracked your ribs. 'Save me, Giorgianna.'

That voice…

The fruit fell from Emanuela's hands and bled into the snow, a thick trail of blood running down her forehead and neck. Running down yours.

No. *Your mouth opened but no sound came.* No! *You didn't want it to be like this again.*

Emanuela pressed her delicate wrist to her death-pallid lips and sank her teeth in—a horrific pearl necklace. Blood pulsed from the stringy flesh of your own arteries with screams and a putrescent past.

She swallowed the flesh between her teeth, and her lovely features wilted as did a keng hwa at dawn. 'Why won't you save me?'

Your innards lurched. Broken teeth skinned your knees as you fell to the mortuary garden. Spine bowed. Throat purged raw meat and grume.

A shard of ice glistened in Emanuela's hand. 'Why do you just stand there?' *She cut her slender throat, ichor a ghastly baptism.*

You crumpled in the snow, yet words still clung to your tongue the way sticky entrails hang from a slit-open stomach. Because you would always be too weak. Too afraid.

'Giorgi, save me…' *From her blood she forged a glass sword. Tears fell down her face and yours two-fold.* 'LOOK WHAT THEY DID TO ME!'

She thrust the blade into her chest. Bone crunched like gravel between diseased molars. Your chest gushed putrid blood to paint scarlet every forget-me-not.

But I couldn't save you…

Sleep threw me out.

My lungs fought for breath, heart ripping apart. My numb fingers locked in the long sleeves of my nightdress which clung to my sweat-bathed body.

Ema.

I saw Ema.

I didn't dream of her anymore, so why?

The door's creak startled me.

Rosalia stood in the archway, an apparition in her white nightgown. "Giorgi?"

"Why are you up?" My voice quavered.

"It's half til six."

I glimpsed the window of the rustic maid quarters I'd chosen over the master bedroom Rosalia instead took (silks and profligate bedding still repulsed me). Beyond the sill, nighttime dulled lazily to that murky grey the autumn mornings preferred. "I…" a drawl, "had a bad dream." My eyes found Rosa. "But it's all right."

She planted herself on the edge of my bed, freckled cheeks puffed. "I wish I could help?"

I chuckled weakly. "I'm a big girl." My head tipped sidelong. "Maybe… you could tell me something."

Her eyes were round. "Like what?"

A half-shrug. "Anything. A story. A secret or a fact I don't know."

"Oh…" She tapped her chin in almost a comic manner, drawing out a '*hmmm*' whilst gazing someplace ambiguous. Her cheeks puffed once more and she looked back at me, lacing her fingers in her lap. "You wanna know something?"

I raised a brow. "*Hm*?"

She shifted in her seat. "I… don't really… feel…" her mouth twisted sideways, "empathy…?"

I blinked.

"Okay," she crossed her legs, "so, it's hard to explain—"

"You don't have *t*—"

"Don't interrupt!" she snapped, then her eyes bugged out and she pulled back. "*Oops*… Sorry." She cleared her throat. "I can talk about it. See, I sort of…" she made a thinking face, "If I sense… a lack of wilfulness, in a person, there's this *teeny* urge to use that to my advantage, almost? But I want people to have the means to… make it hard for me to do that? So… I suppose that's what I'm trying here, since you're in this state right now. You deserve to know. It isn't…" her hands plucked at the air, "something that would be in my favour…? for me to upset you.

"I tend to…" She squinted at the ceiling. "*Hmm*… I suppose… I *observe* the behaviour of the twins, Cesare, you, and I shape my emotive responses to *that*. Otherwise… I hinge more on how things affect *me*, as opposed to seeing the bigger picture. Like *The Sunrise*. It was… hard? for me to understand your pain, but I understood it about the *Curios* because of the twins' parents—I'd known them for far longer and they saved my life. I lived in *The Sunrise* for maybe a couple months, and it wasn't my sole home, you know?

"As a kid in Ellinor, it was a bit odd for me? As in, why does everyone act like that? So ready and so strong to emote? Why am I so…" A shrug. "*Meh*? Or temperamental, depending. I'd… be this person on the outside looking in, and in some ways, I even preferred it."

"What about your own happiness?" I asked gingerly.

"Imitated emotion, generally," she put simply. "I'm… *interested?* is that the right word? in Eligio's compassion, and I like to use it as a 'template'. I *do* feel happiness, I *do* have emotions and I *can* be empathetic, it's just… dampened. I need to remind myself of things. Hugging people, or expressing affection. Most of my motivations are… rooted in cold logic, I suppose.

"I genuinely *don't* want anybody to be hurt! Even if I'm not great at articulating things. Just because I'm like this, doesn't mean I'm some devious mastermind. I want to use all of those traits which *could* be weaponised, to instead… do something that's good. My logic helps me handle things in the thick of it, to be a calm amidst the storm. Learning to get a grip on this thing of mine just makes life easier for everyone."

"Can I help in some way?" I asked.

"Just…" Rosalia shrugged, "understand? And watch—like, make sure I'm not crossing boundaries? And…" she chewed on her upper lip, "don't judge. You know?"

I smiled. "Thank you for telling me, Rosa. I'm glad to be there for you in any way I can be. No matter what."

Rosalia rubbed her neck. "Sorry I've not been much help for your nightmare."

Nestling closer, I embraced the girl, leaning my head against hers. "It's liveable."

She looped her long arms around my waist, and, even knowing she stood at almost my height, it never ceased to strike me just how little Rosalia still was—only fifteen, yet plunged into the world's darkness.

My own childhood was one of such early self-consciousness; a deep guilt at any transgression. I couldn't help but watch myself being watched; castigate every facet of my human performance; wrestle with the implications of my mixed-bloodedness. A passenger of myself.

A double-consciousness. A two-ness.

When you are 'Othered' in the construct you exist within—like I was, *am*, under De Tullia's tyranny—you must pretend for your survival. So I did. I repressed all my anger, sadness, dismay to not burden those around me, as if a child had no right to *be* a child, well into adulthood, until I finally broke.

A *mature child*, I was. A mature child *Rosalia* was. But there was no such thing—an oxymoron at its core, for 'maturity' within a youth could only ever be begotten by pain. Yet it was *praised*. Cynicism and discernment, 'rationality', a void of emotion, were lauded in a child. In *me*. Children didn't deserve to be stripped of innocence so early like Rosalia, like Cesare, like me. But that was how our cards fell.

The front door thrummed with *thump-tap-tap-tap*.

Recognising the pattern, Rosalia and I went to investigate.

Araya and Sarnai slunk in.

Sarnai brandished an empty envelope. "As good a time as any."

Pinching the envelope, I returned to the servant quarters, sitting at the desk beneath the window opposing the bed and commencing to write:

*'De Tullia's conviction is inexorable; his aptitude
for justifying his creed knows no bounds.
Barsotti is snubbed by the Governor—not permitted
to so much as sit beside him at the evenmeal table.
Abelli is a riddle yet to be deciphered.
Veronesi's freedom to speak is certainly disdained, but
begrudgingly accepted.* Noteworthy: *the Grand Judge
drinks solely from a personal chalice, which I believe
ties into the wary disposition surrounding him.
Farnese confronted me in her Athenaeum and displayed
defensiveness, a suspicion towards my presence, but a
parallel, part-masked irreverence for De Tullia.
I suspect she may be a mason(?)
Dioli's misogyny is clear as water, and his
fascination with 'Salomé' is equally so.
Alagona is fickle—willing to worship any deity.
If push comes to shove, the man could be
threatened for information.'*

Lowering the quill, I pressed my lips into a thin line. My eye flirted with the idea of a smaller piece of paper lying near the sill.

I bit the bullet and snatched up the sheet, inking it with text and slipping it into a tiny envelope before returning to the others.

"My scholarly observations," I handed Sarnai the letter, "and…" followed by the dainty envelope, "for Cesare."

An infuriating look. "*Oooh*, love letters?" She nudged my hip with hers. "How romantic, you are."

I rolled my eyes. "You flatter him."

"*Mmm—hm.*" Sarnai smirked and slipped away.

I shook my head and addressed Araya: "Have you discerned our people among the flocks?"

"Indubitably." Araya simpered, fixing his curly fringe. "And *so*, over to you with senator-cajoling." He winked and took his own leave.

I sighed, already tired, and faced Rosalia. "Ioana arrives in an hour to collect us for the congregation. Best prepare."

INDEED, CESARE DID NOT SLEEP THE NIGHT. Not merely for self-punishment, or on account of hunger (he *had* forced himself to eat the previous night no matter how much his innards rejected the thought), but because he couldn't cease tossing in the throes of worry.

Cold autumn sun had dispelled the last of the cloud cover by the time he and the twins met Isaia within *Antigone*.

"Intriguing…" Cesare skimmed the letter of inquiry into the Ministry, penned that very morning. *A possible magus in the senate…* "Giorgianna ought to keep an eye on Ilenia."

"Harassing the Treasurer sounds up your alley," opined Isaia.

Cesare half-smirked. "Worth considering."

Eligio crossed his arms, frown already donned. "You'd need to venture *inside*. And what, pray tell, happened last time?"

"We'll head into oldtown outskirts this evening to hop around some tavèrnae," Cesare informed, ignoring the (albeit earned) jab to his pride. "We've whispers to set into flight."

Lissandri cracked his joints. "About time, gentlemen."

Eligio still held his arms firmly crossed.

"Noted." Isaia pulled his cloth mask back over his nose. "Before I go." He held out a small envelope. "For you, Ces."

"What?" Cesare snatched the curious thing.

Lissandri elbowed him. "Love letters, is it?"

Cesare shoved him off. The twins giggled as he shut himself inside his pitch-black quarters. He removed his jacket and tricorn, lighting the candle at the cluttered desk where he sat.

The envelope was scarcely bigger than his palm, square and off-white.

Dithering a tad longer, Cesare finally opened the letter, and recognised the rounded, dallying cursive of Giorgianna's hand, each letter curling like dainty floral stalks into the next.

His eyes ran along the text:

> *'I… am unsure what I intend to*
> *accomplish here, but… I want you to*
> *write letters to me. I know you are sick of*
> *hearing it but I truly do not care: eat and*
> *sleep. Please. You are worrying everyone.'*

Cesare chewed his cheek. Those words pressed into his throat—*'You are punishing yourself.'* They all saw as he slowly killed himself. They *told* him they saw it. And how many times had Cesare convinced himself that he deserved it?

His eyes lowered to where a few staves of music were scribed.

> *'I cannot call myself a composer, but*
> *I want you to play what I wrote here*
> *and write a short melody back to me.*
> *Your violin has gone untouched*
> *far too long and it weighs on you.'*

How would you know what 'weighs' on me?

> *'If I don't hear back, I understand, and*
> *you needn't bring it up upon my return.*
>
> *14/10/1762/9 (ZE)*
> *P.S. date these notes, please.'*

Cesare placed the letter down. His fingertips toyed with the candle flame as he debated himself on whether to respond.

If he *did*, he would be admitting defeat, but that was not all. He needed Giorgianna *away*—knew she wasn't lukewarm towards him, knew neither was *he* towards *her*. He could never, *ever*, allow such folly, not when he'd permitted himself selfishness in her hands and flesh already. He was a death-bringer. A finite flicker of flame soon to burn out.

But if he left her letter without word, he would be lying.

Lying that he hadn't spent most of his sleepless night thinking of her—of the evil she was now among, Manuele above all. Had he known why Giorgianna detested the sobriquets he called her, he would have never done so. *'Prideful bastard' doesn't fucking cut it.*

And if he left her letter without word, he'd be lying that her name hadn't slipped from his lips like blood from a shot skull. Lying that he never, not even for ephemeral seconds, thought of her in those sweeter ways. Lying that the kiss they almost shared on *Antigone* hadn't left him hovering in a limbo of the moment before their lips touched.

Cesare's teeth broke cheek.

He should have kissed her just before she walked off into the spiders' lair. Should have kissed her at the threshold of her apartment as she pleaded to the deaf ears of his filthy pride. Should have kissed her in the basilica when blood bound them with vengeful promises. *Hell!* Should have fucking kissed her that night she sat beside him after his nightmare and listened to him vent about his loss of direction despite hating him!

Cesare hissed at the singe of candleflame against his fingers.

To Hell with it.

He plucked a sheet of paper and his inkwell and quill.

Great, now I have to rack my composer brain.

SLEEPLESS TIDES
ELLEOR
FROSKEN WART
YRDAGWLAU
IRON SOUL
MERE GWYZT
CELYN KEEP
RASY
CAPE ESBEN
THE NETHER SEA
GIDA
STEPPING STONES
KICUNTH
MORUZAY
EST FOREST
BEFOGGED PLAINS
ESSA PAPILLOT
PEKOSTSUTA
AKESA
MOUNT MAIR
AMUROLOT
HANDIOT ASIF
THE PATH
LERRKTR
LITACHAI
EAGLE'S VIGIL
THURI ASIF
CRISTWAR VERDE
DIRELASO
FARYA
NURRI LAKE
HAMSTI
KOHORTSA
RESYSXANE POT
EPTSITIS RAT
OVVA
KIDHO PLAINS
AD-DIMARD
FORTAZE PASS
AYELECH
STONE OF FIRE
OLIVE GROVE
PEYRO
SALONT
DAPRANT
ZARGA EYE
MOON'S GRAVE
THEMISTOP
KERKANT
MOVATTYA
SA'AHDA
AMOYAU
SA'ALY DERI
HAITY SEA
SARE ISLAND
TAMEVANT
HARMAKIE MOUNTAINS
ZEHENDWAR
DAYARABAD
THE SPIDER GARDEN
WEIR LA DAL

ACT II

"The old world is dying and the
new world struggles to be born.
Now is the time of monsters."

—Antonio Gramsci

The following chapter includes a graphic description of *a murdered woman's corpse* bearing marks of sexual violation (*second paragraph* of the chapter).

SCENE XXIII

DOMUM DEUM

Cesare | Giorgianna

BODIES DIDN'T ROT SO READILY IN THE COLD of winter's early days. Much less so in the pale wind of five hundred hours.

This body was fresh. Clouded eyes stared sightlessly at The Court's snaggletooth eaves, cyanotic skin all the bluer with bruises and lividity. Purulent rope burns corroded her wiry limbs and throat. A jagged white scar burrowed through her navel within which her uprooted womb was once sown. Where her pubis dipped into her inner thigh, blood coagulated to a shuck, rusting and violent.

Cesare swallowed bile and drew his tunnelling gaze towards the girl who had led him and the twins to the corpse; who now cowered inside Tafsut's tahruyt—moon-pale against its dark cloth and her own bobbed curls.

"Do you know what happened?" he questioned.

She opened her mouth for only choked whimpers to leave her throat.

Eligio reached a careful hand for her shoulder. "Would you rather write it—?"

"*No*—" She recoiled before seeking her feeble voice again, "*I*-it happened… *a*—at *The Arum*."

That name lashed Cesare. "*What* happened?"

The girl cocooned herself deeper in the shawl. "It's… near a month's passing since Madạ—*Falco*… *w*-was… *um*…" Her chin scrunched. "*And*…" she recollected herself, "*th*-things became better with Giulia but… these men came… They were angry." She shook her head. "I think I need to explain better."

Tafsut rubbed the girl's shoulders. "Plentiful time."

"*The Arum* was never a bordello," the girl divulged, "*i*-in a traditional sense. The reason for its half-taverna-half-bordello arrangement was Mad—*F*-Fal…co's wish to separate her wealthy customers from the slum citizens. But…" her sapphire eyes glazed, "she could afford such luxury… and that horrible place is marble and *s*-stained glass whilst the streets are *p*-paved in squalor…" She swallowed. "Because *The Arum* was subsidised by a wealthy family." Cesare's blood boiled almost enough to make him scream. "*I*-*I*-I don't know which, I really don't, I just know it's one. Maybe with another's aid? But *i*-it's hidden from the Ministry and other aristocrats. *F*-Falco allowed them to do whatever they wanted with us… *Th*-*th*-things only turned this dire something like twelve years ago when the ownership passed to *th*-the old landlord's son, but that's… all I've figured out.

"And *s*-so… *l*-last night…" she began shaking, "*m*-men arrived with weapons. Giulia never took disrespect so she retaliated, and *th*-*th*-they… *b*-beat her. To death. Then rounded us up and, in little groups, led us into a different room wh—" Her breath caught. "*I*-I don't know how I got away, *b*-but what they did—I didn't want to—they made us do deplorable things but I didn't want to, Qạddi, I *swear*—"

"*Hey*," Cesare urged, voice almost breaking. "We believe you."

A sigh sank the girl's shoulders. The tears dropping down her cheeks harrowed Cesare.

"What is your name?"

"Karmni."

"Your age?"

"Sixteen."

Cesare's stomach bubbled up.

"They're still there," whimpered Karmni. "*Th*-they're trying to decide what to do with the place but… I don't know if the lavìri are…" Her head shook. "The men would dispose of them once they grew bored."

"We need to tell Giorgianna," said Lissandri.

"Giorgianna?" Karmni's eyes widened. "With the light brown curls? She lives?"

"Yes," Eligio confirmed. "You know her?"

Karmni exhaled as if shedding the weight of the world, fingers lacing, head low. "*Oh* blessed Saints, you are good. The last time I saw her, she gave me an analgesic after a whipping and told me how to make my wounds hurt less, even though, if she got caught, she'd be punished too and already had *been*—" She trembled as sobs took her. "I'm so thankful she lives, evvịva!^75 *I'm so glad, I'm so glad.*"

Cesare's jaw clenched. "Stay with Tafsut. The Court will keep you protected."

"Falehạfna, signọri." Karmni bowed. "Li int: protetịe ta'ịl Qạddi."

"Run this back to Isaia," Cesare told the twins. "He's at the old gallery. Meet me at Donatello's workshop after. We'll move onto the tavèrnae from there."

Lissandri tapped his tophat and headed west alongside his eldest.

Cesare turned to Karmni, his tone tender. "If you can find it within yourself, is there any identity of any of the men you could disclose?"

Karmni turned silent, eyes low.

Tafsut took to chastising Cesare, but, right then—"One, yes," Karmni gave voice. "*H*-he went by a pseudonym. Marchino. He… frequented often, and his alias was because, *s*-supposedly, his circle would have him… done away with… somehow? and that enterprise uprooted. I…" an exhausted sigh, "eavesdropped on him and the *l*-landlord two nights ago and, picking up on his voice, *I*-I also learned his real name. Treasurer Olindo Alagona."

Why wouldn't it be? "But you say that the Ministry is not aware of *The Arum*?" asked Cesare incredulously.

---

^75 '*[The] Saints have willed it*' in Mariano.

"No. *I*-I mean, perhaps they know of it as a *bordello*, but *n*…not…"

Admittedly, Cesare was surprised. Not that it lessened the cruelty of the regime. Far from it—the oversight only underscored how forsaken the people of Vencenza were. How little the powers that be cared if they lived at all.

"Olindo *o*-often had his 'purchases' drugged and drunken," Karmni went on, shuddering, "and fancied what he called '*exotic*' ones. That was me, Giorgianna, this one Ilinka girl I was quite close with. And… young ones, as well. Not *children* but not… grown."

Sickness reached down Cesare's throat. "Thank you for telling me, Karmni," he said, and made his swift leave.

This ends before I do.

THE CHURCH UNFURLED IN ALL ITS BAROQUE MAJESTY into the winter dawning. Its colossal cupola-topped dome, mounted with a triple face, reached up as if yearning to scrape away the clouds and rupture the firmament. The minor dome, housing The Limbus, rose behind the main, two more positioned equidistant from the centrepiece, all overlooking a sprawling portico bracketed by colonnades. *Sa Basílica del Illuterixióne e Benefácio Vísus*—the second-largest monument of esoteric faith in the world, right after the Temple of Míchayyim at Yadá'd. Eleven storeys tall without the roofs, nineteen with.

Gazing at the splendour of the basilica's interior devoured the senses, every gold and ruby facet of piscinas and colonnades intricate enough to transcend material comprehension. To invoke the sublime.

Not permitted to sit, the vast assembly of worshippers stood behind stacidia cloven generously in twain by a walkway and positioned obliquely to the cloth-draped altar at the presbytery. De Tullia's Ministry occupied the fore row whilst statesmen of lower ranks stood from the second onwards, my person slotted between two officials I vaguely knew by name, Clario and Olindo in front of me. Ioana never attended the congregations and I was yet to pry into her reasoning. Devout Vencenzanii filled the remainder of the stacidia. To-day, every chapel scattered throughout the city state would be equally peopled.

"Criminals most heinous from the coalescence with our divines must be barred." Abelli's gilded voice shone at the altar. "Arcóntial devices doth corrupt their chrysalis and pnèuma, so rendered faceless they ought be—condemned to the Everlasting Null for their transgressions.[76] By a token alike, Illutèri neophytes who failed the purification sacrament must be punished in equal measure, for unworthy of sacral light they themselves hath proven."

The words gave me pause as the documents I discovered in papa's apartment, mentioning something that '*may grant a subject pneumatic purity*', sprung to my mind.

Abelli pulled away the scarlet cloth draped across the altar.

Upon it lay a corpse.

From their vestment's gold cincture, Abelli plucked a ceremonial dagger, its gilded hilt encrusted with rubies; its lòthmir blade lustrous as moonglow. An axaxún.[77]

My guts cooled.

Abelli held the dagger aloft, between their hands, and intoned, "In hoc corporálum fórmum, no'áltri infernatóri ípsi àd ípse àlti aísi," their fingers curled around the hilt, "su Tribúcce Faciáe, del'issúsu aperúcen lùtius." They levered the blade to the dead neophyte's head; broke skin. Blood trickled across their brow to anoint the altar. Steel slit waxen flesh. "Tevodàte," the axaxún incised the perimeter of the face, "la'mùseë'te ípse òci si no'áltri potíri tèvi ài lemúru." Sliding the axaxún's tip under the skin, Abelli took to cutting back and peeling away the neophyte's face. "Loqui'áte," sticky strings of gore vainly strove to keep tethered the

---

[76] In modern Illutèri eschatology, it is professed that an individual's '*face*' (pnèuma, *i.e.* 'soul'), cannot reintegrate with the three 'Higher Gods' of the pantheon (which essentially equates to the attainment of 'heaven') if their material form dies without a face, or if their face is flayed from their body within what is called '*The Eleven Days of Liminality*' (*i.e.* within the first eleven days following death during which this pnèuma supposedly hovers in a transitional ('liminal') state between materialism and the spirit realm).

[77] *ah-khah-KHOON*; literally '*[a] stabbing god*'.

skin to the muscle, "la'mùseë'te ípse lintáraè si no'áltri faíte faeddári ài crèci." Abelli lowered the dripping flesh-mask of a flayed face into an aspersórium cupping purified water, "Alecháte," swilling the skin and blade, "la'mùseë'te ípse álci ri no'áltri dóve'i àid alechí praevaricátio." Beside the aspersórium stood a cibórium cradling a fire into which Abelli cast the face. "Hoc víscera eccateári," the sarcoid perfume of cooking offal imbued the air, "hoc sánguinem eccateári," the stench of char ascended, "ípse immúndum álce eccateári si no'áltri potíri am apicée de vóstrum tolesià." Abelli poured the bloody water within the aspersórium into the cibórium, quenching the fire. "Ómne eráte ílus e fai'ám itèrum." The High Priest lifted their glistening hands to the heavens. "Su confellórus faíte coìre.[78]"

Silence.

And there it was again. Rule by fear.

As the High Priest went on sermonising, my eyes skated to the noble families flocking the forefront of the opposing stacidia, each jewel tone arranging the bloodlines into an orderly palette.

The purple-teal iridescence of alexandrites drew my chronicle to a stop, and my throat seized. My behold trained on the man at the centre of the family: his fair, middle-aged face; his gold-embroidered plum giornea; his tarnished gold hair cut short and gelled smooth; his hazel-blue eyes behind a grimacing pulcinéllo. *Basilio Lanuza.*

I couldn't breathe. Through the crimson of my tunnelling vision, I couldn't *see* anything but the pig who ruined me. Who almost murdered Lucrezia. My fingers trembled, *itched* to bury in his throat and pour a deeper shade of mortality across the ruby of the church floor.

Reality hurled me back into itself when Abelli dismissed the congregation. Everyone forwarded to the narthex whilst De Tullia approached the High Priest.

---

[78] 'In this material form, we subjugate ourselves to our high deities, the Triple Face, their sacral light. Watcher, cleanse our eyes so we may see no evil. Speaker, cleanse our tongues so we shall utter no vice. Thinker, cleanse our minds for we ought not think transgression. Purify this flesh, purify this blood, purify our tarnished nous so we may be worthy of thy totality. All were one and will be again. The fragmented shall coalesce.'

My head pounded, an unfed sourness gnawing away at my vitals. My state had been in declension over the recent weeks. Sleep would not hold me for longer than a couple hours without a nightmare purging me, just as my stomach would not hold food. Reality flickered in and out.

And yet, the part of my mind which would plead with Ema, plead with Cesare, would not plead with *me*.

"*Oh!*" I exclaimed from bumping into a crow-soldier of the City Guard. "Forgive me, signóre."

They stared through me with glassy eyes, dipping their head slowly and drifting off—a phantom.

In her fuchsia tones, Magister Ilenia Farnese made conversation with a pair of senators and Guardíi on their way out. I scribbled the detail into memory and rushed to huddle with Sarnai, Araya, and Rosalia. "That legionary."

"I saw," remarked Araya.

"Take Rosa back and stay vigilant," I told Sarnai.

"Mèus dáma," Manuele's voice swarmed my flesh. I met the General's groping gaze. "I glean you found our customs a distressing sight." His tone slid like an eel's tail.

My teeth staved off a scowl. "In all due respect, General," *if only it'd been* you *on that altar*, "I was merely taken aback."

The flash in his azure eyes. "If it consoles—"

"Blessed lília." A different voice. From behind me stepped a sóra of the Order in rich cramoisie robes, her skin bronzen, her eyes warm like strong tea. "We are yet to make acquaintance after so long." Her fingers lay on my shoulder, and my flesh flurried with frost. *Azoth!* "Sóra Dafne Ambrosi, an Illutèri votary." Her eyes found Manuele, cooling. "General, may we be excused?"

Manuele's face glazed, but he obliged. *Bless you, sóra.*

She wrapped her arm around mine. "Dónna Salomè Barsotti?"

I signed '*stand by*' to Araya over my shoulder before replying: "Indeed, sóra." The name had become so meaningless to me I hardly heard it.

Eirenic dimness shrouded the church as the final devout departed, cantillations returning to haunt the echoing walls.

We ambled towards the chancel.

Dafne smiled, the gesture jolting me. "Men like him ought to be avoided by all means."

I squeezed my lips. "Tell me, sóra. What is this 'purification sacrament' your High Priest spoke of?"

"A ritual forming part of neophyte initiation…" Her brow strained. "It is too much to explain here." She eyed me strangely. "Tell *me*, lília. Do you know the Illutèri doctrine?"

"I like to think I know enough." Admittedly, no one in my family had been especially pious, not even my grandparents, who instead quoted that the old Illutèri canon sprouted off of Vencenzani paganism. That the new doctrine was little more than spineless striving towards the austerity of Mysericism.

"Enough can be good, but 'enough' can be illusive." We strolled along the columned ambulatory circling the altar's rear. "While our faith has existed for over eight hundred years—*far* exceeding the age of the Faustinian Empire—this *Order* of ours was founded by theologian and political writer Pietro Vestri towards the twilight of the Empire. At the age of twenty-five, he experienced a revelation of divine knowledge, 'enlightenment'—a word the tongue cannot grasp until such a transcendence is upon one.

"He ascended beyond his material chrysalis, witnessing a heavenly basal structure of Facíi: *the Arcónti*. Manifold, complex, vivid, each a unique facet of consciousness and noumenal reality. And above them he saw a superstructure of three more Faces from whom watery light emanated indefinitely: *the Trimorph*. The Primordials. And, in the emanation, he witnessed divine geometry rendering the cosmos and its celestial constituents—entwining to sculpt the skin and flesh and all the bones of the material world.

"Vestri's spiritual realisation was that the truth of salvation was attainable through the reintegration of the pnèuma, 'soul', with the divine godhead—the Trimorph—which bestows the pnèuma unto the hylic chrysalis in the first place. Such, he concluded, was accomplished *only* by transcendence: by knowing the Facíi. Given his knowledge of the divine truths, yet his material separation from the godhead, Vestri dubbed himself in a state of 'liminality': treading upon the threshold between the spiritual and the material plane."

The erudite glimmer in Dafne's eyes feebled. "Ancient Illuteríi were people of oral tradition and a history destroyed by a colonial force." The pillars holding up the ceiling-sky of the Antrum, their surface scoured of its ancient pagan inscriptions, came to my mind. I wondered what they could have once spoken of. "So, the written volume arising from Vestri's Illutèri revival, '*Córpus Illuterixióne*', became our most important scripture.

"Aged thirty-seven, Vestri professed these convictions to Vencenzanii at a congregation precisely where we stand to-day—when this basilica was a Myseric cathedral built upon razed pagan burial grounds." The crawl of spiders assailed my skin when I learned that we still stood upon a boneyard. Upon erased history. "He was declaimed as a heretic and sentenced to a ten-year durance. Be that as it *may*," Dafne raised a pedagogical finger, "his conceptions touched Vencenzanii who had for centuries endured abuse at the iron fist of the Empire. They grasped a true meaning and purer purpose in his words, his Vencenzani culture. The proletariat established clandestine supply chains to The Trabeculae by which they smuggled letters to Vestri who quickly earned Vencenzani reverence and became one of the faces of rebellion against the Empire." And suddenly, Donatello's frightening way of cajoling gears revealed itself.

"After the Empire's fall, The Order of Illutère was founded. The old cathedral was torn down and replaced with *this*." Dafne gestured to the basilica in all its splendour. In all its grim reminders. "Holy ground returned to its people." *Holy ground nourished by its people's bones.*

"The Facíi—the Divine Faces—are the Trimorph and the Arcónti together," Dafne resumed. "The Arcónti are a diverse mass of faces, one to represent each state of the psyche, limited and static in their singular symbolism. The upper gods are a trimorphic face, consisting of three separate yet interconnected entities: The Thinker, The Speaker, The Watcher." We arrived at a glass mosaic inlaid within a grand window behind the altar. "Alecháte—The Thinker." Serene, closed eyes; an open third eye in place of a mouth. "Loqui'áte—The Speaker." Open mouth; blank-yet-watching eyes. "Tevodàte—The Watcher." Mouthless; eleven eyes upon its face, the paired orbitals sporting three irises each.

My brow hardened as I recalled those patterns from my visions. In my father's archives.

"Each eye has a name." Dafne pointed at the *first*: "Nous—mind." *Second*: "Saba—discernment." *Third*: "Bitius—profundity." *Fourth*: "Sinesis—intelligence." *Fifth*: "Asterechme—right eye." *Sixth*: "Taspomocha—left eye." *Seventh*: "Elpis—hope." *Eighth*: "Aina—ever-lasting." *Ninth*: "Pistis—faith." *Tenth*: "Efrum—lips." *Eleventh*: "Aleteia—truth."

She counted on her fingers to three, humming a sacred strain. "Upon conception, the Trimorph incarnates the body—the chrysalis—from the cosmos, begetting bone, flesh, blood. At that point, the chrysalis is an empty vessel for the pnèuma, or face. '*Soul*', the Myserics would call it. Each Primordial excises a fragment of themselves; fuses them together into a blank face which they emanate upon their creation. The bursting of the amnion symbolises the endowment of the chrysalis with its pnèuma."

"Blood is filthy yet sacrosanct to the flesh," I quoted. "Where from did that mantra come?"

The glow crinkling Dafne's face levelled to ice. "Blood has always been sacrosanct to the flesh—since the days of the pagans. But *filthy*?" the sóra regarded me with hardness. "Blood is the nectar of hylicism: the essence of the material flesh. Drawing blood is a sin by the blade of anyone but a priest, or one's helpmeet upon the marriage altar, because losing blood *kills*. Because blood is *sacred*. It is of the Trimorph—stemming from the life they bestowed upon one's chrysalis. Flesh is the vessel through which the Gods live."

Some weighted moments passed before Dafne, in a near-whisper, spoke again: "Abelli, *illúxito am issúsu ramnúna*, if I must, has established a false syncretism within our church." Her jaw fluttered. "They preach under pretence, twisting scripture into a pontifical creed which has no place in a faith that is, at its core, revolutionary. The Arcónti are not *base*, they are the very emotions of humanity. The material form is not *filthy*, its blood does not call to be '*cleansed*', or for any '*transfusion*' De Tullia speaks of. This rotting empire dubs blood 'filthy' yet fouls its body with it—execution through beheading has always been shameful, but *once*, it had brought shame upon the *executioner* for daring to draw blood so. *Now*, that shame is pawned unto the *executed*.

"That prayer the Domínie recited is *ours*: the *votaries*'." Dafne's voice ran through with quivers. "It has no place being spoken to the masses. The material form is not a shell but a *chrysalis* within which the pnèuma blooms in a way ennobled only by these '*Arcóntial devices*' the High Priest foolishly condemns." My eyeline followed Dafne's as she looked to the scarlet apse inaurated with faces and eyes and celestial imagery. "May they *never* look upon the sacral light of our Divines. Caègum nel eccáto lùtius. Calígini fabeddí verità."

The Rams shuddered through my mind. "Blindness in pure light," I muttered. "Shadows speak truth?"

"Indeed."

"Is the sacral light of the Divines not 'pure'?"

"It is, but by remaining solely within the light of the Trimorph the way Abelli teaches, you are blind to true knowledge. 'Calígini' finds its etymology in 'cáligo', '*low*', referencing the basal structure—the Arcónti. *They* are the 'Shadows'. It is only through *them* that spiritual truth may be attained."

And in that moment, I *realised*. "What kind of light keeps you in the dark?"

Dafne scoffed. "That which seeks to blazon itself 'enlightenment' whilst knowing no such concept."

My eyes grew as I continued to stare at the apse, its contours turning to ridges of blood, in turn becoming lucent and fluid as water. "Illutéro ad'dél praevaricátori. Benefácio ad'dél immúndum. Enlightened be the transgressors. Bless'ed be the tarnished." I swallowed. "That's what it means."

The 'transgressors' were those who searched beyond the light of the Trimorph, 'tarnishing' in the shadows of the Arcónti yet attaining true ascension through spiritual knowledge, for one would be rendered ignorant to said knowledge should they remain eternally in the light of the Triple Face. *Personal revelation in the divine is the basal stratum to salvation, not faith in ecclesiastical authority, nor man-scripted doctrine…*

Abelli's creed was false. Abelli ruled by fear.

In the corner of my eye, Dafne's head turned, her scrutiny affixing me for a silent second. "Ludovico's child, yes?"

SCENE XXIV

FERE LIBENTER HOMINES ID QUOD VOLUNT CREDUNT

Rosalia | Giorgianna | Cesare | Giorgianna

ROSALIA NEVER LIKED BOOKS. What did Lissandri see in them, anyway? Thin slices of trees stamped with tusche and a price? Sounded like propaganda. Why the Magister would choose to practically dedicate a mansion to the things completely escaped Rosalia as she tip-toed through the Athenaeum, knowing Ilenia scooted about with an official someplace.

The servants in the kitchens gave Rosalia a pair of soft-soled shoes which helped with silent passage around the government building. To not disturb the Ministers. The *other* side of the coin to such shoes was eavesdropping: the *real* reason servants valued them.

Rosalia slunk deeper into the Athenaeum and began skimming the shelves.

Shoving a hand into a gap between tomes, Rosalia's fingers tripped on a palm-sized disk, grabbing hold of and pulling out a dainty pocket mirror encased in brass. Innumerable somnolent eyes embossed its lid, the knolled surface bumpy as toad skin.

Holding down a retch, Rosalia opened the mirror and shivered as the sparkling sensation of frost prickled down her skin, rousing the hairs in its path. She noted nothing uncanny in her visage upon the silver, having long-since grown accustomed to her sweeping burns.

She turned the mirror over.

A '*XII*' engraved its smooth back. *Twelve what?*

"Who goes there?" Ilenia's demand boomed.

Rosalia whisked around, mirror tucked to her chest—looking glass pointed towards Ilenia and the hoary official who'd materialised in the aisle mere strides away.

The Magister's eyes traversed the shelves and walkway, plodding on right through Rosalia as if the girl wasn't there. Her sculpted brows tugged together. She hovered in place before muttering something to her companion and departing, leary though she seemed.

Rosalia blinked. *Am I… invisible?*

She twirled the mirror in her hands, fascination breaking through the wonted monotony of her dampened passions.

Giorgi must see this!

I FLICKED A SWITCHBLADE FROM INSIDE MY BELL SLEEVES.

"*No!*" Dafne pulled up her own sleeve, baring a forearm. Her sclerae shot with blood, tears waterlogging her eyes as her skin curdled, crawling away from a tattoo of a menacing mask bearing nothing but too many mouths.

Şirîn's Brass Teeth….

I stared at the sóra, and sensed azoth dissipate from the ether.

"Durans was my husband," Dafne said. "I joined the church when the sea took him."

My larynx bobbled. "You knew my father?"

A nod. "A little, yes. Durans and Fabio, I was much closer with. Şirîn, of course. Matìa and I never talked much." She blotted the tears of a tailor's pain from her eyes. "Though I *was* friendly with Matìa's friend and one of the other men's inamorata—an especially quarrelsome smuggler woman called Ada. A *bit* too keen on the disembowelment of men, that one was."

A realisation practically caterwauled in my face.

'*I'd always jest, telling Ludovico
he loved women who'd lure a
sailor from the sea. He'd fire
back that I loved women who'd
cut my throat and throw me in.*'

Could it be… Ada of The Blood Dahlias and… Fabio…?

I blinked, still open-mouthed, then cleared my throat before my opportunity to pry fled. "Do… you know about Ilenia and Manuele?"

Dafne sighed. "I knew Ilenia from those days, though little."

"I believe she can help me. At the very least, she knows something." My heart raced. "Could *you* help me, too?"

Dafne neared. "Only if *you* help *me*."

"With?"

She tossed the nave with wary glimpses. "Neophytes have been disappearing and no aid comes from the legionaries." *As I'd heard…* "If I arrange a meeting with Ilenia for you, then I ask you seek information out for me. But you must remember: Ilenia is deeply afraid. De Tullia hangs immense amounts of information in blackmail over the Ministers. Besides Manuele, Ilenia arguably has the most to exploit."

I scowled. "I wish Manuele dead."

"As do I," bit Dafne. "Him, and another man—Dardan Kadare. An Imperiálus with a sullied reputation for defiling sórae e líliae of the Order."

"Tell me where he's stationed and the job is done to-day."

"Descent to the docks at East Eye."

"Consider his life forfeit."

Dafne grasped my shoulders. "Then, I shall tell you about the purification sacrament, little as I know, or I'll have Ilenia relay it on my behalf."

My ears perked up. "Why would she be aware?"

A sigh. "It's… unfortunately too risky to discuss here. We're already speaking recklessly enough."

I held both hands to my heart. "You have given me great insight nonetheless, sóra Dafne. Thank you kindly."

She grinned. "Giorgianna, yes?"

I matched her expression. "Most assuredly."

Dafne clasped her fingers tight, lowering her head. "Dél'ì lùtius e vísus benedétti, mèa lília."

UPPER VENCENZA'S TAVÈRNAE WERE A DIFFERENT BEAST to those dotting oldtown. Many catered to the upper echelon of society, some even requiring membership, or permitting no admission to unmasked patrons.

This one—*Soleluna*, with its modest size and rustic furnishing— attracted a safer crowd: better-off workers, artisans, musicians, travellers (*back when they could still breach the city walls*).

A good hour into their endeavour, the twins, garbed in inconspicuous worker attire, mingled among the patrons, Donatello busying himself with folks at the bar and an innkeeper who wanted none of his jabber. Meanwhile, Cesare secured himself a shaded nook alongside a salt-of-the-earth man masked in a pulcinéllo, and his own upper óssium contact: a lavìre by the name Iseppa, dressed in a deep cranberry paltò[79] with a matching zánni, her dark hair haphazardly gathered into an updo and lips glossed red. Cesare didn't allow himself to muse on the colours she chose, yet couldn't still the guilt suddenly trepidating in his ribs.

---

[79] An ankle-/shin-length coat.

"Unrest been flaring up all 'bout town," said the man, voice gruff with smoke and shouting, if one were to guess. "Lots o' that 'VÍTAM DI RIVOLUZIÓNE' vandalism, too."

"First symptoms of an organ rejection." Cesare ignored the twinge of pride, brushing crumbs of a baked fritoe dough off the corners of his lips. "Think it'll endure?"

A scoff. A swig of beer. A grimace at the piss-taste of cheap alcohol. "*I* think. Folks are starting to tire. And it's getting dark out in the camps."

Cesare shot a look at Iseppa. She pursed her lips, then clicked her tongue and tugged at the man's collar. "Humour us then, big guy?" She exhaled smoke, quirking a painted brow, all smirks.

He cleared his throat and drank away his fluster. "Word 'as it," his voice quietened, "soldiers 'ave been doing horrendous shit to labour camp inmates. Not clear what sort, but seems to be some torture? Similar word's been comin' from the institute in the northwest."

Cesare and Iseppa shared another look. One of knowing, this time. Of a mutual comprehension that they had just neared the smoking gun.

Iseppa smacked her plim lips and drew closer to the man. "What say we share a drink, *eh*?" She slipped her arm through his, batting long lashes. "On me." As she turned to lead him barward—a diversion, just as negotiated—she tacked on an address to Cesare: "Pleasure to see you, àngiulu." Her disposition darkened with her tone. "Godspeed, you…" Turning away, she blew a kiss to Donatello who caught it from across the tavèrna, waving armour-ringed fingers back at her.

Eligio bumped Cesare's shoulder as he sidled over. "Glad to see you more like yourself."

Sure and true. He'd been able to sleep again, eat again, *fight* again, don his bàuta again. He detested that costume still—a demonic thing which, by some cruelty of the cosmos, survived the destruction of *The Sunrise*—but maybe, if the wretched thing could symbolise something good to Vencenzanii, it wasn't the worst curse upon Cesare's bloodline. He elbowed the artist in the abdomen with a snicker, but donned pensiveness fast. "Word has it, soldiers have been doing horrendous shit to labour camp inmates, if I'm to quote the departed gentleman. Similar word's been coming from the asylum." He nodded his chin at Lissandri who sat miserably failing at a game of chess, before plucking a sigarétta out of his sleeve and making for the exit. "Our toil already yields."

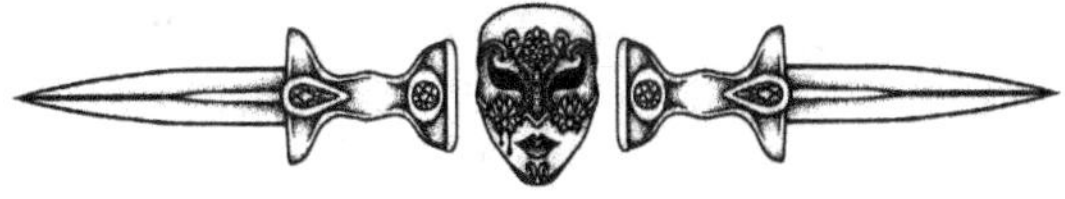

THE SOAPY SPONGE SCRAPED HARD AGAINST MY ARMS, leaving skin raw in its wake.

I remembered how *The Arum* had supped my life like parasitic roots, my flesh as if sprouting thorns, and I found myself right back there. I wanted to sink my nails, my teeth, into myself and peel off the foreign skin I'd been forced into. Robbing a woman of a body—wearing her face, performing with whatever voice and cadence my mind conjured for her, as if some vengeful demon possessing the dead—repulsed me. Manuele's bewitchment with me, with *her*, only made my disgust more excruciating. I set that swine's sights on poor Salomè even in death.

The sponge fell from my grasp into the bathtub, the world suddenly so silent it rang.

I knocked my head back against the tub's edge, submerging my arms to soothe them in the water's warmth.

The sun was yet to reach zenith; its light rippling across the marble of the ensuite's counters and floor was liquid nacre. Everything glowed so white. I'd fain bash my skull against the marble just to anoint the chamber in some colour.

The tub abutted a wall, across from which a mirror reflected me—a long-limbed mutant of a creature with hair slithering boundlessly over the tiles.

Sometimes, I thought I saw the walls split and eyes open within them, swivelling and red. Watching. But my body never made the move to inspect them. My tongue didn't budge to speak, to call out. I just watched the vision back. It did not want to be known, no matter how throat-slitting my desire *to* know it grew.

And there I was again, defining wanting in measures of violence.

My head tipped heavily away from the mirror.

Into the wall sank a recess with a flat sill as if a tabletop. On it rested flacons of soaps, fragrances, and oils, towels, Gostiata's '*Silverblood*', an inkwell, and a letter.

Sitting up, I dried my hands and folded my forearms on the edge of the sill, perching my chin on my knuckles so the letter's text was in a comfortable line of sight.

> '*Anoint the government building with Myrabella.*
> *Everywhere; every plane and cavity of that forsaken*
> *fucking citadel. Myrabella absorbs seamlessly into*
> *stone and the government building is notoriously*
> *fireless—cannot light one measly candle in that*
> *place. Don't ask; wouldn't be fun if I told you.*'

I'd already made a start on the request, eager to question its purpose as I was. Mostly, I had Rosalia slip the flammable Myrabella concoction into servants' wash buckets.

A strain gathered my lips as I observed not Cesare's words, but his dreadful penmanship, the way he scratched out unbidden bursts of thought—his rashness turned to paper.

Every day, I clung to the thoughts of home, of all my most beloved, like a peel to a clementine, and, amidst it all, hoped with all my might that Cesare wasn't still torturing himself. With *all* my might, I begged the dreadful Gods that those people I loved remained unharmed. They deserved to live. And I had no one else.

Beneath the text, several strains of sheet music were scrawled, ones I hadn't yet played; hadn't been able to bring myself to.

The tip of my nail traced the notes. Something about being able to untangle Cesare's handwriting was like glimpsing into him, everting him, reading his entrails as if a haruspex and knowing him. And I could define wanting in no measure but violence.

I dragged in a heavy, shuddering breath. A cloying ache pooled in my belly, in my chest, but I swallowed it, averting my eyes from the letter to the light of the wintry sun.

Brunch with the Ministers approached.

My skin writhed at the thought.

As Lissandri had insisted, I'd laid low for several weeks, drawing little attention to myself besides the unavoidable. It proved necessary. Ministerial spies had been sent after me for almost my entire first moon cycle in the citadel. Now, as the monitoring ceased, came the fated time to take up my blade. To initiate the intent of my presence in earnest.

I had hardly two weeks remaining in these walls.

Chapter sections labelled 'Manuele' are from the perspective of a misogynist and rapist. While <u>no</u> acts of sexual assault are portrayed, reader discretion is still advised.

SCENE XXV

IF THE PRISONER IS BEATEN, IT IS AN ARROGANT EXPRESSION OF FEAR

Ygạl | Manuele | Cesare | Manuele

YGẠL—Lucrezia and Aengus with her—arrived at Valentina's *Amaranth Lounge*. Its entrance was painted appropriately.

Valentina greeted them, her foot-sweeping satin peplos assembled of amaranthine sashes resembling elongate petals. The length of her thick hair lay down her chest, her forehead wreathed in gold-leaf foliage and neck garlanded with metal beads. "Kaskal ak ud.[80]" She ushered her guests inside and towards her office. The plunging back of her dress revealed a tattoo of the hyacinth flower.

Polished umgoloty, silks perfumed with jasmine and pomegranate, decked the *Amaranth Lounge*. Lavìri passed by their Madáma with cheer and camaraderie.

---

[80] Literally *'journey of [the] sun'*; a welcome greeting in Qeoloni.

A dark-haired girl of roughly seventeen years sidled to Valentina, dressed in a gold chainmail top and a white kaunake[81] unlike the satins of the lavìri. Valentina wrapped her arm through the girl's who laughed, saying nothing as she chewed on a tress of hair.

The Domína beckoned Ygạl and their party into her office. "Tea?"

Ygạl squinted. "Are you worth our trust, Nin-kalla?"

"Please." She sat at her desk. The girl slid onto her lap as if she wasn't the size of a grown adult. "Everyone knows white tea masks no poison."

Aengus snorted. "I mustn't fall under 'everyone'."

Lucrezia smiled pleasantly. "We'll have the tea, Domína."

Valentina spoke in quiet Qeoloni to the girl who skipped off.

"Your child?" Ygạl asked.

"Yes." Valentina's features softened. "My sweet Ayana." She gestured to the armchairs across from her. "Please, sit." She steepled her fingers. "Leone agrees."

Ygạl jolted. "Agrees?"

"To your proposition of allyship against the surface state."

Lucrezia and Aengus looked back at the Dóminus of the Boars and Hounds with disbelief of their own.

"He hopes you'll be able to convene with him soon," added Valentina.

The door opened and in walked a lavìre dressed in black silk, carrying a tray of teacups and a pot, her pallor sprinkled head to toe in freckles and dark hair chopped to a bob.

Lucrezia's jaw unhinged.

"Cheera?" exclaimed Aengus.

Ygạl's ringed fingers laced tightly under his chin. "Care to explain?"

Chiara's[82] mercury eyes glowed, lips pulling back to bare gnashing teeth. "I care for *nothing* regarding *you*."

"Care to explain to *me*, then?" Valentina gave voice.

Ygạl's teeth gritted. "*Chiara* betrayed us to the very man who placed us all in jeopardy to begin with. *Just* to stick it to Cesare because she disapproved of him."

---

[81] In this context referring to a woollen skirt-like garment of Ancient Mesopotamia covered in a tufted pattern suggesting feather-esque symbolism.

[82] An obligatory reminder that this name is pronounced '*kee-AH-rah*'.

"You and that ossíi will bring *ruin* upon The Antrum." Chiara set the tray onto the table with a rattle and stormed off.

The door slammed, its echo filling the silence.

"I…" Valentina dragged a cup towards herself, "apologise for that? How strange."

Ygạl glowered beneath the fine yellow cloth of her niqāb, but forced a subject-change for diplomacy's sake: "Instability in upper óssium is growing in no small part due to our—" *Agostini and his troop's* "—efforts. However, state violence escalates in a manner which—"

"Stirs my care not in the slightest," Valentina interrupted. "My concern is *only* with the Antrum's protection. Its safety is the safety of my child. That, to me, is *paramount*."

Ygạl wanted to argue, to parrot Cesare's zealous verses, but couldn't, for she had always felt the same. "I understand."

Valentina placed down her cup. "You do not."

MORNING SUN GLARING INTO HIS QUARTERS, Manuele reviewed reports of recent insurgency in the city.

The Bauta had always been vermin, cavilling and practically a female, but his activities resumed after a stretch of cherished quiet and all the stronger for it. Most frighteningly, support for him surged, even after the Moretta debacle. The Minister of Blades suspected they now collaborated.

Preceding days of endless drills had already worn Manuele out, though he wouldn't admit to such softness. *Couldn't,* when the spirit of his father abided even in death.

The previous night's exercise had been Stealth, followed by Resistance.

For the past five turns, the General forced fresh recruits into water deprivation. For their Stealth drills, he set up cylinders of water amidst a pack of starved, sleeping bloodhounds, ordering his soldiers to sneak by, drink as quietly as possible, and flee without disturbing a single dog. Three soldiers got mauled, two sent to the infirmárium for rehydration. Four managed to complete the task, three of them too cowardly to drink more than a lap.

Resistance was far from what it sounded like: higher-ranked soldiers were injected with bull viagra and expected to fight with etiquette, precision, and elegance without drawing blood. Needless to say, Manuele was the only one pleasured.

Rising from his bureau, he advanced for his ensuite, needing to ready himself for brunch.

The whole morning, ever since his return to his apartment, a particularly putrid stench had been wafting from the kitchens. He hoped those menial harlots wouldn't feed him whatever muck they shat out.

Manuele halted.

Acid singed his throat when he realised that the stink intensified the closer he stood to the ensuite.

He flung open its door.

The reek of chicken blood smothered enough to rip retches from him.

He blinked hard.

Blood clogged the sink and dribbled to the tiles. A miniscule heart floated within the gory pool, scarlet handprints smearing the tub and shower curtain. Down the gold-fringed mirror, scribed in blood, dripped the word 'RAPIST'.

Manuele hurled a dagger at the mirror. Steel dug in to the hilt and shattered glass into a deadly hail. He lurched out of the butchery of his ensuite. *Who the fuck…?*

He quivered with violence and stormed for the door, tearing it open, only to—"Dáma Salomè!"—bump into that josser Barsotti's niece.

A long shift gown of thick grey-blue brocade did nothing for her fecund hips and shapely waist, its sleeves tight along her arms bar the massive deflated lanterns at her shoulders. A fluted collar grasped her slim neck, flaring to cradle her jaw.

"Esteemed General." Salomè curtsied in that Balinori way. "Is all well?"

Her thick lips glistened red, and Manuele's mind grew dark with thoughts of how they would feel around him. Of how her chaste flesh would flush and bruise against his hands. The sound of her as she moaned in pleasure and sobbed for mercy. "Of course." Manuele's tone slickened. "Work inevitably strains the nerves."

"Might you join me on my way to brunch, signór?" Manuele bridled his aggravation at her use of '*signór*' in place of '*signóre*' to address him. He wasn't some common ponce whom females had the right to regard as their equal. "My uncle is rather preoccupied this morn."

Manuele flashed a smile to seal the endeavour of disarming the stupid nymphet. "Gladly, mèus dáma. Allow me to dress for the occasion, first."

Salomè turned, smiling over her shoulder sweetly enough to rot teeth. "Glad in equal measure, signór."

ALONGSIDE THE TWINS AND DOLLMAKER, Cesare departed *Soleluna*, already half a block away from the Solar Square: itself a fifteen-minute walk from the tavèrna.

Biting winds billowed in the loose sleeves of his shirt, snapping at his hair as he held his tricorn in place, but the fangs of the air left no mark in his burning flesh even whilst the twins and Donatello shuddered into their overcoats and jackets.

Lissandri's teeth chattered. "How are you not freezing your balls off?"

Cesare handed over a sardonic grin. "The flames of revolution rage through me."

The tinker threatened to smack him, Cesare passing back with boyish laughter—entirely uncaring for his presence in the upper city.

Commotion in the Solar Square drew the quartet to attention.

An argument brewed at the main checkpoint of the courtyard, overhung by the ghastly silk banners of De Tullia's tenure. Cesare tensed when he saw it was between a masked oldtown man, and a soldier.

Citizens around the man advocated for him, words of '*…to see his ailing sister…*' and '*…unlawful detention…*' finally in earshot.

Then, the legionary struck the man, knocking him down to the sound of exclaims, and rage beset Cesare.

A woman in distinctly upper city attire, already past the checkpoint, gasped, hotly reprimanding the City Guards. An elderly lady raised her cane to strike a soldier. Cesare flicked open his lighter and hurled it at the banners. "DEATH TO THE DICTATOR!"

Cloth burst into flames, screams surging, but not wholly of fear.

As legionaries engaged their batons, the citizenry bashed back with canes and switchblades and rocks.

Fingers sank into Cesare's forearm. "What the fuck did you *do?*" hissed Eligio.

Cesare shook off his grip and cocked his revolver, aiming for the alchemical light atop the guard station. "Feed on upheaval like a tick to blood as Our Lord of Bless'ed Dominion prophesised!"

Pulse pounded the drum of his ears.

He pulled the trigger.

Boom!

Silver and tar ignited in the ether, shrapnel exploding in time with poor man's grenades joining the fray.

"*FLOCKS*!" Cesare heard a girl scream out.

A crow battalion circled the surge of bodies, Imperialíi glinting amidst their darkness. The bellows of the square warped into curses.

"*GET DOWN*!" the girl's voice made the welkin ring.

The flocks engaged their crossbows, aimed, and opened fire at their own citizens.

THE TEA ROOM WAS DECORATED under the auspices of Magister Ilenia Farnese, so all the chairs were rimmed with gold and upholstered in baby pink damask (*De Tullia did not permit that lurid shade of the vile colour Ilenia had wanted*).[83] Chandeliers hung in ornate clusters of crystal, all wood painted white. Manuele preferred to spend as little time in the room as he could safely afford.

His mother enjoyed that milksop hue—would always wear nightgowns in the colour and whine of aches and fatigue. Wasn't fatigued enough to not be unfaithful to his father, Scaevola, it seemed, opening her legs for some lowborn riffraff, then crying of 'battery' at the hands of Scaevola. Manuele commended his father for sorting out the adultery the way he did. He still reminisced on the snap of his whore mother's neck, the chokes as Scaevola gutted her paramour. If De Tullia did anything right in his rule, it was assassinating the previous Governor: the man who convicted and executed Scaevola.

The Minister of Scholars had excused herself long ago, Alagona following shortly after, whilst De Tullia and the remainder of the inner circle were forwarding out for an impromptu meeting to which Manuele was not invited.

The deadbolt clicked, leaving him alone with Salomè.

From a glittering crystal bowl, she plucked a cherry, twirling it in her fingertips whilst studying it pensively. She held it by her lips yet did not bite down, and Manuele wanted to grab her by that braid and smash her face into the table for it.

"That little fruit seems to be captivating you." Manuele willed charm into his tones, standing beside a crockery cupboard with a flute of grappa for a pousse-café.

"Cherries taste like love," Salomè mused half-absently, then finally ate the drupe.

"No alcohol, mèus dáma?"

"*Oh*, certainly not, signór!" she brushed off glibly, pouring herself a coupe glass of lemon water.

Manuele squeezed his fists.

The nymphet strolled past him towards a window. She was too tall. Too fucking commanding a lithe body. "Might you walk me around the

---

[83] **NB:** the author does *not* approve of pink slander.

city, some time, General?" She pirouetted to look at him. "I've been cooped up here for much too long. There are a good few landmarks which I haven't laid my eyes on in *so* many years. Who better to be my escort?"

Manuele lifted his glass to her. "It would be a pleasure."

She shared his cool smile, then imbibed. *Waltzing right into my hands, little dove.*

"I remain quite unfamiliar with some of the happenings in the city. Do tell me what's all this about some…" Salomè waved her unoccupied hand, "*Bauta*. Morettae?"

"The Morettae are an ochlocratic gang of goons serving merely as distractors from the true terrorist of this city: The Bauta."

"So they are rebels?"

"Correct."

"Fascinating." A sip. A turn.

Manuele's jaw tensed at the sight of Salomè's back to him.

"Tell me about him," she said. "The Bauta."

"There's little to say," the General gritted out. "Of the itinerant sort, if you'll permit me. *Vermin* crawled from filth as any slummy. A dark, effete abomination seeking to profane our order."

Salomè had stilled and fallen silent, no longer drinking. Not turning. "I presume you'll have him hanged for his crimes."

The temptation to force her to look at him almost overcame Manuele, but he bridled himself. "Beheaded. On his knees in shame like the hangdog he is." He sipped his grappa. "He'd made it into here, some months back, alongside a lackey. Neither got caught, but I'd fought the runt." A snort. "Good for nothing but dissection. He got me through the face with a knife, but fortunately apozem is plentiful on hand. How he ever got away after I half emptied him eludes me. I only figured out after the fact that I'd almost killed *The Bauta*—"

Ksshhk!

Salomè stood with her back still turned, gripping the stem of her coupe in knuckles white as snowcaps against olive skin. Ascending sun ran its rays along its razor-sharp edges, seemingly transfixing her. Smashed glass lay scattered at her feet where spilled drink pooled.

"I'm sorry," she hummed, so sotto voce; near-droning. "I must have slipped." Her tarn-blue eyes reflected nothing when her head tipped sideways to look at Manuele.

Footfalls sounded behind him, and into view strutted Ilenia.

"Do be careful, dear," she spoke breezily. Manuele watched with repulsion as she flourished a hand. The shattered glass twirled in an eddy, reforming into a faultless coupe in her hands. She set it aside.

"Thee debase thy flesh with thaumaturgy."

All heads turned to behold the High Priest Benetto Abelli. Dressed in red. "That is thy *soul* thee expend through enchantments."

Ilenia held Abelli's gaze resolutely, silently, then drew a curt breath and turned with sharp elegance to Salomè. "What say you join me for a stroll through the gardens, mèa dónna?" She hooked her arm around hers. "I know you've taken a fancy to them."

As the pair quitted the tea room, over her shoulder, Salomè offered a sultry look to Manuele, unreadable, something dark and ugly flashing behind it for just a moment.

The *second* POV of the
following chapter includes a
graphic *second-hand* account of
sexual violence and *femicide*.

SCENE XXVI

MALLEUS MALEFICARUM

Giordano | Giorgianna

"IT IS NOT SOMETHING WE CAN ABET." High Priest Benetto Abelli sat in a tall-backed chair upholstered in velvet, a stain of bright blood and gilden plasma against the grey of the Governor's ministerial quarters

Crescenzo De Tullia folded his hands behind his back and paced the floor with plangent footfalls. "You must understand that your research would greatly benefit the betterment of our society," he contended. "To stamp out the defected and the mind-sick would render our city-state infallible. Supreme."

"Our research be not for anything but our congregation. Its fruit is holy."

Crescenzo halted. "Its *fruit* is *clean*."

Grand Judge Giordano Veronesi took a sip of grappa from his trusted chalice while the tête-à-tête carried on before him.

"*Pure*, Governor," corrected The High Priest. "In a way only the Gods' emanations can and ought be. This is a religious sacrament thee dost speak of."

"On a religious sacrament alone it is *wasted* when its application could be so broad. Our institutions. Our camps. Our pris—"

"Our *church*," interrupted Benetto, voice never once rising. "And our church alone."

"You have made a scientific breakthrough, Benetto!"

"A *spiritual* breakthrough."

Darkness eclipsed Crescenzo's face. "You defy your Governor?"

Benetto stood, fluid, so quiet they could be immaterial. "We answer to nought but the Godhead, and belong to no place but the spiritual circle, for that is thence we spring, and unto thither we return."

Silence pulled taught, the two Ministers—of Churches and Dominion—standing at a cataclysmic impasse.

Giordano tapped a fingernail on his chalice. "Ought I quit this scene?"

De Tullia did not look at him, did not break the clash of gazes he held Benetto trapped in. "Be wise, Giúdice."

Another beat of silence.

"Governor's will," Grand Judge Giordano Veronesi endowed his voice with bite and turned for the exit.

As the door after him shut, he heard the High Priest repeat, "It is not something we can abet." *I fear you'll have to, all the same, o Domínie.*

On his way out of the ministerial house, bound for his House of Judgement, Giordano got halted by the Minister of Blades.

"Giúdice." The gold-haired man nodded.

"Manuele."

A flutter in his tough jaw; a razor-flash behind his eyes. "I heard of a meeting among the worthy men of the Ministry. What reason for my request to abstain?"

Giordano, standing a footstep above the General, peered down his nose. "*Worthy* men, as he says. And *he* is scum given human likeness out of the Gods' pity."

Enormous fingers snapped like molars into the Grand Judge's mantle. "You'll do well to not aggravate me, old man—"

"*You'll* do well to not touch me, *signór*." Giordano flicked off the General's grip as if a clinging bug. "Know who in this house eats who."

Manuele clasped Giordano's arm before he could depart, almost enveloping its circumference. His white teeth bared. "I could snap your spine if I squeeze too hard."

"And I can crumble your life to nothing with a single word," countered Giordano, and Manuele's hand loosened. And his pupils shrank. "I've sent children to the gallows, General," the Minister of Justice sneered with a face serene as death. "My stomach is stronger than your fist could ever be."

ONLY ONE PLACE ABATED THE MISERY of the white-boned citadel: the indoor gardens above its uppermost floor, encased within an ornamented dome beneath the albicant winter sky. Alabaster cobbles upon which I strolled with Ilenia weaved through verdure blooming into bushes and hedges, branches of broadleaves and osiers reaching for the ground and the dome embowered by croceous bougainvillaea. Clario granted me a cello for my stay which, sometimes, I'd take with me to play the melodies penned by Cesare. Silence would always preside over the gardens amidst my recitals, as if even the flowers and foliage stilled to listen.

"What do you seek?" the Minister of Scholars questioned.

"Tell me about Manuele."

"A wicked beast," she spat. "In the time of my entanglement with him, the darkest of his conduct, mercifully, did not befall me—by reason of my rank, I believe. But the other women, whose fate did turn so ill; who were his 'lovers'…" the Magister trailed off. "I've eavesdropped on Manuele and his Imperiálum cronies—Dardan, for one—trade tales of their degenerate exploits." Ilenia flicked open a compact hidden within the breast pocket of her fuchsia bolero. Inside rolled about pills. The Magister plucked one up, swallowing with little thought. "Opium," she clarified. "He would grow bored with his playthings, and that's when all pity expired. He would defile these women, then murder them with the pursuit of imparting the utmost pain. The sight of it pleasures him. It is a sickness. He would disembowel them. Strangle them and bash in their skulls. Then, he would cut open their back, slash the ribs from the spine, and splay them like wings."

My memories grew grimmer with the butchery at *Commegnos' Curios*: near-precisely a mirror of Manuele's methods. *Abramo said Imperialii were present at the Curios…*

"He is dread incarnate," Ilenia went on. "Enamelled with blond beauty and polished by charm." She swallowed. "I persuaded Giordano to give me access to Dioli's court files. There are *dozens* of murder concealments." *Surely why he won't speak against the Governor.* "I knew Manuele would not kill me, given this wretched status, so I worked to bore him of me. Eventually, he left. But *reality* never left, becoming blackmail for De Tullia to weaponise. *He* is dread incarnate, no less, and is *leagues* smarter than the General."

My heart lay heavy in my chest. "Thank you, Magister." We sat on a curlicued white bench beneath weeping willow fronds. The place where I played Cesare's melodies.

Ilenia's eyes, one cerulean and one viridian, lifted to the oculus in the dome. "I chose my stature over the life of a friend: I listened to Clario and Giordano, and handed Calliupa over. Every dress I own is long-sleeved," Ilenia noted oddly before pulling up her balloon sleeve. The flesh of her tanned forearm lay clotted into a dagger-shaped brand. *A Malefactor's Mark.* "I was on death row until I sold Calliupa out. Selling her life bought me mine but left me in debt. She was not deemed as valuable as me. So, De Tullia gained all the more ammunition to keep me in line." These power-glutted larvae thought of Us as dirt, our lives cheap pennies to toss at their leisure. *All of you are scum.* "I do not know how they tortured her, nor what they wanted." Ilenia covered her arm. "And I wish to remain ignorant of both." *You would.* "If it was possible to convince him again, no ally could be as valuable as the Grand Judge."

Hate boiled in me. "I'll cut my own throat before I ally with he who sentenced my father to the gallows; who enabled Emanuela's murderers to go unpunished."

"Your flawed reason is begotten by spite," Ilenia stated plainly.

My mouth dropped open.

"*But,*" she held up a placating palm, descrying the dark diptych of Me: my Shadow presiding, "I shall not push." A sigh left her. "De Tullia, Manuele… If there is pure evil in the world, it is they. Such men must be rid of."

"Then will you aid us in the pursuit of precisely that?"

"Believe me: I want to. I *wish.*" Ilenia's eyes searched mine. "But understand I am taken by fear."

"This is *beyond* fear." I swept back onto my feet. "Beyond *any* psychological order. Our rage is not reduced to mere rule, it is a diffraction—freedom is beyond the material. If we never move, we can never know of our own servitude, so we may never transcend it."

Her jaw strained. "But you do not under*stand*—"

"Oh, but I *do,*" I riposted. And I recalled that frightened girl clutching books of forbidden philosophy to her chest beneath the grim darkness of this decaying empire. A memento. An epitaph. "Even in its darkest and most lowly, a rat still bites."

Ilenia stood and strode away, silence between us weighing the cosmos itself. "Each day, I pray for Their downfall," she intoned as if to no ear. "What else can one do when stripped of agency? Even my *Códice Erudíti* goes dismissed by those hawks." A breathless beat in time. "So…" She turned on her heel in the whiplash momentum of a fighter. "If you help free me of these besmirching shackles…" Plucking a pearl pin from her braided hair, Ilenia slit her fingertips. Ichor dripped. "My hands are yours to bleed this kingdom."

"You know."

"I do. Blood is worth diamonds."

Jaw hard, I drew forth until the closeness of intimacy was all that parted us, Ilenia's heel-augmented height matching mine. "The Court of Secrets speaks, you know." *But* should *she?* "And *I* heard tell—" my voice lowered, lulling, "—that Crescenzo De Tullia's brother, Constantino, whose heart the Governor ran through with a blade, had a child." Ilenia's brows tugged closer. "A child killed alongside the father. A child who was, upon the father's will, subjected to operations not by a physician's capable hand, but by the High Priest's bless'ed dagger." Ilenia's face dropped, so I knew I'd struck the mark of truth. "Operations *you* purportedly observed." Her mismatched gaze deserted mine. And I *felt* the blood rushing like frantic ants through her flesh; heard her heart's flutter in my own ears. She stilled, sensing the intrusion of azoth. My lips quirked at the edge. "Speak with ease, Magister."

"Yes." Ilenia all but choked on the admission. "I was present for those procedures."

A philomath's frisson thrilled through my belly. "Tell me of them. What did Abelli want with the child?"

Ilenia's eyes cooled upon me. "Knowledge has an ethical cost, dónna Salomè."

"Is that what *you* paid?"

The woman downed another opium pill and recollected herself. "It was not the father's *will*, but the father's *sin*. Constantino's violation of his child's mother was discovered and, to evade imprisonment, he was offered a compromise." It took everything within me to not scoff. To not scream. "In truth, the procedures *were* overseen by a physician. But, when the physician would set off, and only I and the Domínie remained, without the physician's knowledge, the true pursuit would reveal itself." Ilenia rubbed her arm where the Malefactor's Mark hid. "It was the living body Benetto wanted. Body to study."

"Study what?"

"Azoth. They would inject the child's liver with an agonist—like bloodwort—to deal stimulatory trauma. This would induce a transfusion of azoth." *Transfusion!* Just as Gostiata coined. Azoth pouring in its raw state into the blood. "Benetto would then observe the movement of the eyes, searching for… *something*."

"Why?"

"They sought to discover how this transfusion could be controlled; induced without an agonist… To bypass transmutation." Ilenia shook her head. "It was for their congregation. They believe that a complete severance of that which impedes direct transfusion of azoth grants the subject spiritual closeness to the Upper Gods, almost as if induced ascension. To them, transmutation, as with any ordinary spell, defiles the flesh, like they'd said to me, because it supposedly mimics the behaviour of the Arcónti—the Lower Gods—which Benetto considers debased.

They believe that what they seek to induce is 'purity', and wish for their congregation to be… like direct emanations of the Triple Face walking among the people. 'Unsullied'."

"The purification sacrament…"

"A prototype of it, yes."

I swallowed the lump encumbering my throat. *Lucrezia is holding onto 'Spagyrism and Spellwerk'; I must speak with her. And tell her about 'Silverblood'.* "Why did you partake?"

"More blackmail. If this activity of Benetto's was somehow revealed, I could be blamed wholly."

"You said this injection of an agonist into the liver is a 'prototype' of the purification sacrament. What, then, *is* the purification sacrament?"

"I do not know. My attendance is no longer welcomed nor permitted, given revelations of my history with oldtown."

Dubiety tugged on my brow, but I granted her the right to vindication. "The end justifies the means." I conjured my six of faces, its edges inlaid with delicate razors, and slashed my fingers, curling them with Ilenia's. "They will pay their dues in blood." *Every day, retribution comes closer to my grasp.* "How much danger are the territories beyond oldtown in?" I feared to ask, but knew I had to.

"A lot. Davide informed Manuele of their existence, thus De Tullia by proxy." *Liar…* "They do not know the passage there, but I suspect its acquisition isn't beyond reach. It is known too that what Benetto wishes to accomplish—unimpeded transfusion of azoth—may permit a subject to break any hex, even one they did not cast. The High Priest wishes only for his congregation to hold onto this knowledge, but knowledge is power, and the power-hungry prowl all around us."

Dread gripped my heart.

Cardea's enchantment on Vencenza's oldtown and Court of Secrets— magic which kept the unwelcome out, which kept Us safe from the teeth of a tyranny baying for our blood. *That* is what lay most at stake. No matter how close Abelli may wish to keep their discoveries, the likes of De Tullia would always covet it. *Perhaps that is what spurs the Governor to linger by the High Priest's side…*

I needed to get out.

"Magister Ilenia Farnese, thank you. Truly."

She lowered her chin. "I am glad Dafne insisted I hear you out, Gior—"

"Deep discourse is a scholar's most prized leisure," a plangent voice suffocated my senses.

Crescenzo De Tullia loomed like a demonic bodach between lush thickets of camellia. Hair spilled in ink down his iron-beset doublet, his eyes starless within the black holes of their cavernous sockets.

I stood pin-straight and hid my fingers, curtsying. "Governor."

"I'll excuse myself." Ilenia flitted off.

Hands folded behind his waist, De Tullia approached. "One does not see the erudite sort absorbed in hushed dialogue unless it is one of utmost demanding subject matter."

"I simply reminisce of home. Of Ithilwen's moraine and bracken. Its alpenglow."

De Tullia paused beside me, emanating such deathly coldness I thought the flower bed might wither in his shadow. "Weakness is all affection can sire. A blindness to one's duty."

"Surely not, Governor. Surely greater loyalties draw force from those of smaller calibre."

"Surely you see how an individual most attentive to personal affections must necessarily be a poorer citizen and leader."

"Loyalty to kith and kin has always been one of the many markers of a great leader."

"And where has that gotten them but not halved upon a spike? The Iutulicani Governor allowed northern kith into his home, and now his province finds itself in conflict between the Myserics and the old Streghèria believers; on the brink of civil conflict." De Tullia maintained that, "A bird cannot conceal itself from arrows just as a spider cannot fly away from hungering jaws. Hence, one ought be a spider to evade traitorous shots, and a bird for teeth to never claim their wings. All such discernment succumbs to obsolescence upon the fallacious veneration for kith, kin, or lover. Inconsequential devotion lays one bare to perfidy. To negligence."

I catalogued the carnations, cornflowers, chrysanthemums. But it was the smattering of irises my eyes stilled upon, slim and tall, their lush petals neither purple nor blue. Dark as gems. As the sparkling tanzanites Cesare wore like he'd plucked stars from the sky and donned them just to spite the night.

My chest caved in, so I forced myself to deliberate on De Tullia's verses the way I figured Cesare might in my position (*though, Cesare in my position would stick a dagger into him*).

The more I grasped the Governor's rationalisation, the more his incorrigible doctrines revealed themselves to me.

I did not believe he truly shared Abelli's sectarian beliefs, but instead wielded at his callous will, justifying his abolition of emotion through *Sa Nóba Giustíca* with 'substantiation' from thrawn and twisted faith.

De Tullia considered affections corruptive, blinding, minatory. He saw no value in loyalty, and the inferiority he regarded emotions with granted him further incentive to exploit the fear of the populace. If emotions were inferior, then the citizenry, gripped by fright, were inferior by extension.

I needed to hear no more. I *knew*, now.

"Libitina Răth'lym'mẽ is the primary undertaker at Vencenza's necropolis, I was informed."

"Indeed." De Tullia's too-deep voice rose goosebumps from my skin.

"I am somewhat familiar with them. May I be granted visitation?"

"If such you seek."

I bowed. "Most magnanimous, Governor."

De Tullia didn't look at me; didn't reply. He merely nodded and left.

SCENE XXVII

PLAGUE OF LOCUSTS

Cesare | Giorgianna| Cesare | Giorgianna

IN STAUNCH SILENCE, in a despicable act of collective punishment, the soldiers slaughtered their own citizens.

Cesare and the twins got trapped inside a cellar at the foot of a building near the checkpoint, two dozen injured and bleeding people they helped dodge the line of fire with them.

Soldiers stabbed and shot the doors to break through.

Hands suturing an adolescent boy's riven calf, Cesare's eyes scoured the cellar for a way out, Lissandri palming the walls for any give whilst Eligio tended to a bleeding young girl.

The door lurched.

Cesare secured the stitching just as the groan of metal on timber signified Lissandri's success: an ascent into the adjoining building torn out of the cellar's far corner.

Slinging their arm over his shoulder, Cesare hefted the injured boy upright. "Get into the building!" he shouted over the din. "Do not walk near the massacre!"

The wounded were syphoned through first, the rest hurtling close behind. The last of them barely fled when the cellar door shattered and daylight poured in with murderous crows.

Cesare's revolvers sang as he shot down the onslaught, following the twins into the courtyard to not draw soldiers after the escapees. A crow left him with a parting slash on the ankle for which he punched and kicked them onto another crow's drawn schiavona.

The Solar Square rang as citizens clashed with soldiers. Blood splattered the corpse-littered sandstone. The wan winter welkin reverberated with cries for mutiny and mercy.

Cesare tore into the butchery, his stilétto burying in an Imperiálus' neck. The griffin slumped into a pool of gore both his and not.

The twins stood on the defensive in a circle of workers the trio had met whilst disseminating whispers, Donatello nowhere in sight.

Cesare ran a crow through, shot down another, earning himself a shallow slit to the side before finally sighting the raspberry-and-gold of Donatello near the strappado at the courtyard's centre. The dollmaker snipped a Guard's head clean off with his colossal scissors before taking a punch to the jaw from an Imperiálus.

Cesare apprehended the griffin's killing strike, grasping his head and slamming it against a colonnade with the wet *crunch* of a splitting coconut before grabbing Donatello's collar. "Get out."

The dollmaker squawked in disgust at the soldier's ruined physiognomy, obliging.

A hard force rammed into Cesare.

He staggered sidelong moments before the strappado toppled, rattling the earth, cracking the flagstone, and a too-familiar cry froze Cesare's blood.

The supine torture device had pinned Eligio's right arm.

Cesare bolted to him, Lissandri close behind.

Eligio strained against the immovable carcass. "No, *I—*" He cried out. "I can't." His skin stretched where the tilting structure sucked his arm beneath itself, flesh opening up and oozing.

Crossbow bolts began flying.

"Cut it off," snapped Lissandri.

"*WHAT?*" Eligio and Cesare exclaimed in one voice.

"Either he loses an arm, or a life. Cut it off!"

Horror tossed in Cesare's guts, but legionaries advanced against the current of rebelling people, and he comprehended the barbarity of what he had to do. *Lòthmir cuts bone like sponge.*

He gripped his stilétto in trembling hands, angled its razor edge, and sawed into the middle of Eligio's forearm.

Bone crunched. The stump of a limb jetted blood.

Eligio wailed, that dreadful sound sickening Cesare enough to turn him faint.

Freed, the trio scurried from an onslaught of crows.

Cesare clutched the sobbing Eligio, repeating '*I'm sorry*' for a frantic infinity. He tore off his own sleeve above the elbow to tourniquet the wound. "Leave," he ordered. "Both of you."

Lissandri plucked Cesare's cufflink off the ripped sleeve. "You're *staying?*"

"I'll be damned if I don't." Cesare turned to the fray.

"*Ces!*" Eligio grabbed his wrist with his intact left hand, eyes nitid and wide. "Promise me you'll come back."

Cesare's heart bated. "I'll come back." He embraced the twins before plunging into the slaughter.

MY GULLET WRUNG AROUND MY FINGERS, bringing up nothing but acid. *Empty.* I clutched the bowl of the toilet and drew air into my burning chest, flushing the contents of yet another meal I'd been forced to consume in this reprehensible house.

My joints creaked as I stood and hovered reflected in the mirror, an apparition in my nightdress with that dark hair falling limp to my knees. Those reddened sclerae and swollen cheeks.

My lashes swept the world to blackness.

Pain impaled me, squeezing tears through my shut lids. I whimpered against the shedding of my skin until the tension of magic dissipated. Pain receded. Frost thawed.

I wiped my tears and sang to my humours to be drained from my face before opening my eyes. Vivid as apocalyptic blood moons.

My caramel hair coiled into a hip-length mane, my skin marked with stretches and scars and illustrated with tattoos, the black moles and indented lips heart-rendingly familiar upon my father's vulpine features. I hadn't seen myself in seemingly aeons.

But the hollowness within me did not fill.

Emptying myself became all I could do to not cut my body. I craved catharsis. Just as I did when my mother scared me away from blades. Just as I did at *The Arum*.

But I didn't want to live like that again.

Pain split down my skull. *I need water.* The silver veins of the bathroom tiles slithered inside the pale marble. The fringes of my vision bleared. '*Save me.*' I huddled on the cold floor, the nightdress my only caress as shudders took hold. *Leave me!*

Knife slits ruptured the walls to open gyrating eyeballs, and the tiny marble cage rustled like a rousing graveyard.

Sense.

No sense.

This makes no sense.

I crushed my eyes shut, grasped my head. A babble rang through it. Nonsense nonsense nonsense *nonsense*—'SAVE ME, GIORGIANNA!'

Death's putrid stench throttled me.

My eyelids cleaved open.

In my lap lay a decaying corpse sullied with gravesoil, its cracked skull decanting pomegranate juice onto my nightgown. The eyes gazing into mine were death-lacquered and blue as forget-me-nots.

I shrieked and scuttled back, yanking the door handle and falling into the parlour. When I glanced back, I saw neither the eyes nor Emanuela's ruined body.

Gasps ripped from me. *Gods, get me out of this place.*

A knock at the door made me jump. '*Donna Salomè?*' Ioana.

I opened the door for the amazonian woman.

Her prussic eyes bore concern. "Is everything alright? I heard screams."

"*Yes*! Yes, *I*-I just fell."

"Well, I bring tidings," she declared. "Dóminus Leone Caivano agrees to aid you."

The door's *click* followed by a whistle sounded, and in walked Sarnai, Rosalia by her side. "Not *nearly* as riveting, but *I* caught Basilio and Crescenzo chatting in the Omphalos just now."

I crossed my arms, exhaling. "Prying into his family is unwise given the ad rem objectives. Even so, it's no less a plaguing thought." *Just as the reasons for Emanuela's targeting…* My heart twisted up.

"I bet *I* could contend with 'riveting'." Rosalia held up a gold-encased hand mirror.

Sarnai snickered. "Gonna have to try a little harder, kid."

Rosalia flicked open the mirror and vanished.

A zap of azoth jolted me.

Sarnai lurched back. "I *beg* your pardon?"

"I know!" came Rosalia's disembodied voice. She reappeared at the *clip* of the mirror shutting. "I found it in the Athenaeum. Ilenia didn't see me when she came looking." The girl handed me the mirror.

I scrutinised the '*XII*' engraved on its back, recalling the studies of scripture I undertook in the *Symbolism in Neo-Illutèri Eschatology* elective at my alma mater. Etenesh supposedly took it as well for about a week before transferring into *Introduction to Alchemical Entomology*. It was probably the most impractical list of electives for a slot. Every graduate had a story about it. "Twelve is the number of enlightenment: one more than the eleven that is liminality."

"I get this chilly, sparkly feeling when I touch it," Rosalia said.

"Azoth," my explanation evoked Sarnai's '*I knew it!*' "The mirror is likely masoned with light bending." I trawled through my cover-to-cover knowledge of '*Spagyrism and Spellwerk*'. "Light bending and shadow weaving are both illusionistic magics which call for a tithe in the form of your vision for the duration of a spell's casting. With a masoned vessel as an intermediary, that tithe is abolished. The choice of a mirror for a vessel rules out the odds of the chimera—'chimera' is the magic woven with masonry—being shadow weaving, which favours cloth." I trailed a fingertip along the eyes embossing the lid, a headache piling. "Here, light bending acts on every aspect of the wielder which courses with azoth, including clothing so long as it is crafted from natural fibre. Substances like stone and metals are non-azothian and cannot be conduits." I gave Rosalia the mirror.

She promptly opened it and disappeared.

Sarnai walked around the girl. "I can still see you from behind. Sort of. It's mirage-looking."

"You should keep it, Rosa," I said. "If it may be of use to any of us, it's you."

"I could work it into something utilitarian, like a shawl," Sarnai offered. "It'll keep you invisible from all angles, too."

"Final advice:" I said, "such objects reek of azoth to those in tune. Be vigilant."

The mirror shut and Rosalia reappeared with a lifted eyebrow. "Then how didn't Ilenia sense me?"

"Owing to how overwhelmingly saturated her own dress is with azoth, I'd wager a guess." I sat on the sofa in the parlour with an exhale. "I bring tidings of my own."

So I recounted all that Ilenia told me.

"This is all news to me," Ioana said once I concluded my narration, her face strained as she scratched under her too-tight braid.

"Instead of attending dinner, under the pretence of visiting Libitina, I want to go to *Antigone*." I *need* to.

"I can arrange that," confirmed Ioana.

"I'll come with, just let me catch a courier to pass this onto Araya," said Sarnai. "He's on Isaia duty, to-day." She slipped out.

"I want to visit Libitina, too!" Rosalia bolted for the master bedroom to prepare.

Ioana remained with me in the parlour. "I'll ensure all your alibis are accounted for."

Curiosity nudged me. "Why don't you attend the congregations?"

"I'm not Illutèri; the High Priest granted me exemption, with some effort. I'm half Yeledí by heritage and adhere to its faith. My father is Yadá'd-born. My real name isn't Ioana De Rege. It's Yòchaná Elimeléch.[84]"

"Would you prefer being called Yòchaná?"

"I like both equally—same moniker, by definition. But…" She tapped her chin. "Perhaps, yes."

My disposition steeled. "Why did you choose to take up feather and sigil?"

"Because I was naïve—believed I," Yòchaná scoffed bitterly, "*I*, could mend a faulty system from within. But I knew nothing." Her eyes bore aloft. "You cannot fix a festered husk of bone with peace and reason. You can only excise it."

"Caught in your virtue, you became another pawn."

"Do you know *why*?"

"Ignorance is servitude." I looked up at her sternly. "But the *only* means for you to atone is to revoke your wings."

Yòchaná nodded and made for the door. The threshold halted her. "They." A turn. "'*They*', to refer to me."

I smiled at them. "Of course."

And then they were gone.

I consulted the clock. *Twelve hundred.*

Time slipped from us like sand from a cracked sandglass.

A DOZEN CROWS CIRCLED THE BLOODY CARRION laid out across the Solar Square, a single griffin left alive to fly among the rot.

---

[84] *yoh-khah-NAH eh-lee-meh-LEKH*
NB: '*w*' in Yad'lashó equates to a shorter '*o*'/'*uh*' sound; '*ò*' indicates a fuller '*o*'.

In the highest window of a nearby building, Cesare drew his sigarétta. He cocked his revolver, loaded with his final cartridge. Aimed for the griffin, waiting for him to stand still *just* long enough. Listened to the furious blood in his ears, the pounding of heartbeat against his skull. Felt the pulse of gashes in his flesh.

Boom!

The griffin collapsed, a landed fish flailing, suffocating on his own blood. Crows flocked to the dead griffin.

Smoke coiled around the muzzle of Cesare's revolver, and he departed. But the day was still high, and he wasn't yet done.

War it is.

SCENE XXVIII

VIGILANTE JUSTICE

Giorgianna | Cesare | Lucrezia | Cesare

WITH THE NOON SUN PEEKING OVER THE FORTIFICATION at East Eye, I crouched by Dardan's decapitated body. Blood branched between the dockside cobbles. *My end of the bargain is fulfilled, sóra Dafne.*

Slipping my index finger in my mouth, I sucked off the blood cooling on my hands, halting when an odd tang caught my attention. *Azoth…*

I cut open Dardan's chest.

The blood inside bubbled with unpurged azoth, flesh singeing until the sweetness of fatty meat found its way to my nares.

He'd attempted to transmute, but not in time.

Dagger digging deeper into his thorax, I drew up enough blood to puddle in my cupped hands, and drank. Warm fluid spilled lush and potent across my tongue and down my throat, my body shivering as it supped the magic imbuing the humour.

When ingested, exogenous azoth coalesced with that of the consumer, replenishing their reservoirs, healing, at times even granting azothian abilities they previously did not possess. And there were only two ways to ingest azoth: drink the saturated blood of a magus, or eat their flesh. *Serves you right.*

I sawed open Dardan's stomach and lowered him into the moat, his corpse sinking to the crystal-clear depths. His severed head rested on the embankment, face locked in a gurn. *What a lovely gift it would make.*

GRAND JUDGE GIORDANO VERONESI annotated every shelf, slot, file in his archive-esque ministerial quarters down to the hour of issue. When he held onto everyone else's, it was no wonder that the Minister of Justice hardly feared for the skeletons in his own closet.

Stepping over one of the Guards he drugged, Cesare proceeded to the documentation filed within the recent months, combing the titles for something recognisable.

Fortuitously, he stumbled upon none other than SORIANO, *Calliupa*, skimming the nonsense justifying her arrest before an alarming turn of phrase gave Cesare pause.

5.0.1: RE-EDUCATION

Administration of lobotomy to Convicted.

ADMINISTRATOR: *Imperiálus*, code 9F600
ORDER ISSUED by: Governor
DE TULLIA, *Crescenzo Zuane*

OUTCOME:

Unsuccessful.

What in Hell is a 'successful' *lobotomy?*

Post-procedure, Convicted exhibited aphasia, echolalia, hysteria, severe and randomised emesis, inability to maintain upright posture, narcolepsy, seizures.

ORDER:

Termination.

Hair bristled on the back of Cesare's neck.

"Lower the paperwork, intruder," a voice ordered.

Cesare *tsk'd*, pivoting to find a Guard thrusting a gladius towards him. The blade oscillated, *an unsteady grip*, and the soldier's rosen cheeks betrayed an age far too young for the sword.

Still, Cesare drew his revolver. "Must you thwart my fun?"

The crow scowled. "You won't shoot me if you want to leave alive."

The only way out was the main door which now stood obstructed by the crow, so he wasn't wrong.

Cesare clicked his tongue, its echo bouncing along the ribbed vaults, and glanced over the Guard's shoulder as if meeting somebody's gaze. Eyes flicking back to the soldier, he caught him stiffen. "How old are you, crowling?"

He grinded his teeth, shifting on his feet. *Your balance is off.* "Nineteen," he declared with all the ferocity of a lion cub.

And right then and there, Cesare could have pitied the boy. Could have humanised this callow child clad in executioner habiliments and a despot's yoke.

But how could Cesare mourn him when the city decayed? When the streets reeked of massacre and camps lay beyond the walls? When the night seemed eternal? After all, soldiers struck their bloody batons down at the masses, upholding a system of abuse.

So, a hollow smirk tilted Cesare's lips, his eyes training behind the soldier once more. "Endearing."

The boy-crow's expression wavered. Some vague compulsion urged his body to turn, his feet to disturb the firm grip they'd hardly found, until he finally succumbed to whipping around, second sword unsheathed to defend himself from nothing.

Cesare's arm swung in an arc quick as silver, a dainty blade slipping from his fingertips and finding its mark in the boy-crow's neck.

His legs buckled. A wheeze left his throat.

Cesare caught the soldier and lowered him to the floor.

He squirmed, blood dribbling from his lips, his eyes wide and glazed. *There can be neither remorse nor sympathy for blood-hungering oppressors.* And it would *never* be the duty of the subjugated to be peaceful. The legions at the checkpoints proved exactly that.

"Die, or live in shackles," said Cesare and stomped on the throwing knife lodged in the boy-crow's throat, blade severing the spine and petering out the pulse of his vitality.

Cesare lifted his gaze to the vaulted ceilings as if to speak to a deity. But there was no one to listen.

EVER SINCE SUSTAINING HER GUNSHOT WOUND, Lucrezia soaked daily in the natatorium outside her and Ygạl's sleeping quarters to mitigate the pain which now chronically accosted her.

She had been doing precisely that when Giorgianna and Sarnai arrived, Rosalia supposedly dropped off at Libitina's mortuary. Itxaro swept Sarnai instantly away whilst Giorgianna dashed to Lucrezia with intel regarding Magister Ilenia Farnese.

Her bathing dress undulating in the water like lush seaweed, Lucrezia lay her forearms on the natatorium's mosaic embankment, perusing the text within '*Spagyrism and Spellwerk*'. Nearby, Giorgianna sat at the water's edge, the book '*Silverblood*' open before her. It contained the translated diaries of Nashĭgostu Kurilit Gostiata himself.

Beside them stood a faïence bowl of chocolates wrapped in foil; Lucrezia had caught Giorgianna swipe a pair.

"This could be why my liver is so shoddy!" Lucrezia bumped up her pince-nez. "This research of Abelli's, I mean. I never had an issue prior to my operations, and it's an illogical side effect of them, but if they'd been injecting me there with an azoth agonist like bloodwort just to deal '*stimulatory trauma*'..." Lucrezia shuddered at the thought of having been an experiment for the church she once held faith in.

"A far more horrific implication is apparent, too," contended Giorgianna. "I suspect De Tullia may covet this research of Abelli's." She turned a page of the journal. "Gostiata writes, '*My propensity towards this phenomenon I dub ‹transfusion› began at my age seven. I had tripped in my sister's térem (where I should not have been), knocking over a haberdashery arrangement. There, a knitting needle, inches eight in length, skewered me deep through the canthus of the eye, up into my skull. From then, it was as if something inside me ruptured.'* So, the head injury was apparently a stab wound through the orbit."

"Why is the blood with which that translation is written infused with azoth?" questioned Lucrezia. "It couldn't be *his*, right? Is it Catellan's?"

More flicking of pages. "Miluna was an apprentice of Nashĭgostu's. An afterword by her reads, *'Preceptor mine willed that I compile his most scholarly journal entries which, with his azoth-soaked blood, I was to preserve following his death and translate to my native Faustinian.'*" Giorgianna's lips squeezed into a firm line. "To return to Gostiata's injury: azoth reservoirs are located within the pericardium, wrists, liver—hence the site of your bloodwort injections—and frontal lobe. Something inside him must *indeed* have ruptured, that 'something' being the 'capsule' in the frontal lobe containing azoth."

"The 'sieve' of sorts through which transmutation occurs!" exclaimed Lucrezia. "And so, through the rupture, azoth could instead be directly *transfused.*"

Giorgianna shut her eyes and screwed her face up. "'*...severance from rebirth in illimitability is merely an amniotic membrane impregnable orbitally.*'" Lucrezia blinked. "Someone told me that, once. A pair. But I… I don't know what it means yet." Giorgianna shook her head. "It's like I'm holding broken pieces, not knowing how to arrange them into something understandable."

Lucrezia looked at Giorgianna, her sunken face and the darkened chasms beneath eyes, the sallowness of her skin, and saw how she and Cesare seemed to be becoming each other. As Cesare's condition shot sharply towards improvement, Giorgianna withered.

"I'm glad you took that from the Athenaeum," voiced Lucrezia. "I fear how Ilenia could use such information." She frowned. "Especially seeing how much she knows about oldtown. I do not trust her."

"Neither do I," admitted Giorgianna, and shut '*Silverblood*'.

"*¡Oye!*" a shout boomed in Itxaro's voice. She swerved around the corner, Sarnai in tow, all but toppling arse over kettle.

Lucrezia's brows bunched. "What's going on?"

Itxaro latched onto Sarnai for support, gobbling down deep breaths. "There was… a riot… this morning. At the Solar Square. The… checkpoint. Crows assaulted a lower ossíi; a clash broke out. Crows and griffins massacred… almost everyone."

The words punched Lucrezia's heart into her stomach.

"The twins and Cesare were there." Itxaro grimaced in her throes. "The twins needed the apothecary but made it back to *Antigone* fine. Cesare hasn't returned or sent word."

Lucrezia threw a look of alarm to Giorgianna.

She had bleached white, her body locked up. "*nononononono.*" Breaths hastened. "No, it's all right, *he'll*—he's—" Her head shook for no rhyme or reason. "*I*-I have to go." She fumbled for '*Silverblood*'. "To *Antigone.*"

SUNDOWN PAINTED THE SKY OVER *THE ARUM* IN GORE.

Cesare nestled himself in the shadows of squalid ruins. Listening out for one name. *Marchino.*

At last, it struck his ear.

A man in bejewelled furs exited the flesh peddler's parlour, advancing for the warrens of oldtown.

Finishing off his sigarétta, Cesare pursued.

Sclerotic bones of alleys twisted and meandered, narrow, dank, ribbed as the black innards of a primordial beast.

Cesare cleaved to his target better than the man's own shadow.

'Marchino' stopped in a sheltered recess to relieve himself. When he turned to keep walking, Cesare remarked, "Fancy I should meet the Treasurer here."

The man wheezed as he hauled himself around to behold the creeping darkness. "Who's there?"

A hollow smirk canted Cesare's lips. "Tax collectors."

"I'll scream."

"Then you'll die." Cesare approached. He knew The Minister of Coin valued his life above all, and nothing spoke of it more than his buckled legs, his sweaty palms groping the brick wall behind him, his knocking knees.

"What do you want?"

"A broad question, no?"

"Don't play word games, rootless—"

Cesare swung a blade to slit the Treasurer's lips, delivering an elbow into his temple which knocked the man to the cobbles. "You've caught me in a bad mood." He leaned close. "Your little bird lackeys—" blood burst free as he cut into Olindo's cheek "—slaughtered civilians this morning, you know."

"*I*-I hadn't issued any order—"

Cesare dug the blade deeper, the fucker whimpering. "All of you pigs are the same to me." He stood. "Humour me, if you know how." Twirling his dirtied dagger, Cesare sauntered a circle around the Treasurer. "That establishment you just left. *The Arum.* You frequent it?"

Alagona's face drained to the colour of his grey-green eyes. "I cannot speak of it."

"*Oh*, I don't need to know about *it*—someone with less mercy than I will see to that. I merely seek a confirmation of what I already know."

The Minister propped his back against the wall. "I must keep my identity concealed, for the Governor would have me executed, and that *Priest*, Benetto Abelli, *ascáita* am issúsu ramnúna,[85] reviles my venereal predilections. Calls them 'wickedness'."

"You like your flesh young," Cesare bit. "*Exotic.* Drugged and indisposed." He spat on the man. "Do you remember the names of those you degraded for your disgusting fucking *predilections*?"

Olindo cowered in silent trepidation.

Cesare brought his foot hard onto the Treasurer's head, smashing his nose, and kicked him over into a lying crumple. "Rack your brain *really* hard now, Minister."

---

[85] *'Incinerated be their name'*; a bastardisation of the honorific *'enlightened be their name'*.

"*Th-th*-there were a few—I don't recall them all!" Olindo Alagona sputtered. "*B*-but… *s*-some… Ānshēng, Varvara, Giorgianna, Ġiżimin,[86] Karmni…" He breathed hard. "I… *I*-I don't remember any more…"

Hate cooled Cesare's blood. "Never thought a heretic would find himself in consonance with a High Priest."

Olindo's eyes bulged. "*Don't*—!"

Cesare's blade slashed through plea and throat. "Or what?"

He watched as Olindo choked. Until his floundering petered out, his muscles slacked, and he sagged limply on the cold cobbles, dying in his own blood and shit as he deserved.

---

[86] The Faustinian '*g*' is pronounced '*zh*', like the Persian 'ژ' or the Cyrillic '*ж*'.

SCENE XXIX

MA 'L MIO PENSIER FALLACE

Giorgianna | Kel-Kech | ?

NIGHTFALL BREEZE CARRIED THE BITING PERFUME OF OCEAN SALT, the seas bustling as their froth-crested waves shattered against ragged fangs of distant cliffs and rifled through the polished pebbles scattering Smugglers' Cove.

I raced down *Siren's Wynd* towards Buccaneer's Landing, curls whipping my face and lungs raw, vaulting up *Antigone*'s gangplank.

Scraggly Eyepatch Dan with his blue rattail and well-worn sorrel vest sat up on the mizzenmast, talking to Fabio down on the main deck. His singular eye landed on me and he let out a high whistle through the gap in his teeth, igniting the night air with hoots like fireworks.

Fabio spun around, brow furrowed. But he didn't manage to get a word out before I threw my arms around his neck in a crushing embrace.

"*Giorgianna…*" He clutched me tight. "Blessed Saints are good."

I pulled back to look at him. "The twins?"

"My quarters."

My legs were moving before I could think.

I saw Eligio first; his shoulder-length coils bound loosely at the nape of his neck; his makeshift kamiz.

His bandaged right arm, amputated at mid-antebrachium.

The twins' eyes fixed on me, polished as acorns and warm as cocoa and wide as suns.

Lissandri sprung to his feet, book dropping from his lap. "Giorgi?"

My hands turned clammy, trembled. "Gods…" I rushed to hug them both. "What did they do to you?" I cradled Eligio's face, brushing tray curls off his brow.

"Cesare. It was Ces—he needed to."

"Where is he?"

A pallor touched his swarthy cheek. "I don't…"

Dread reached down my throat, vying to pry up my vitals, until the urge of nausea forced me to sit. "How bad was it? The riot."

"Bad," snarled Lissandri through gritted teeth. "I don't know how many dead, but it's well over twenty, I'll bet. Cesare shot the light on the checkpoint station which escalated shit, but the feathered fuckers attacked first."

I gulped the acid risen to my throat. "Have you heard *anything*?"

"No." Eligio's eyes silvered. "*I*-I don't—I don't know; I don't know what to do—"

"You could explain the disappearance of all the apozem, for starters." A voice burned through me.

At the threshold of the captain's quarters stood Cesare, one hand engaged in the fastening of a tanzanite cufflink at the ruffles of a clean cotton shirt, the tips of his hair a touch damp. Suddenly, he looked as if he'd been shot in the chest—like everything before his eyes overwhelmed him.

His gaze fell to the eldest brother, and a horrible pain wrung his brow. "Eligio…" The two embraced, Cesare repeating, "*I'm sorry, I'm so sorry, I'm so sorry*," in a frantic, ceaseless half-whisper.

"Stop it, Ces!" Eligio grasped Cesare's shoulders. "Please don't *a*—"

A harsh *slap* bounced through the walls.

Cesare lurched back with a sharp intake of breath.

"Why didn't you send word?" snapped Lissandri, palm as flushed as Cesare's cheek, then trapped him in a tight embrace. "*Maniac.*"

"I bring news," I blurted gracelessly, "but it'd benefit from The Morettae's attention, too."

"Likewise." Cesare accepted his second cufflink—returned by Lissandri. His eyes flickered to me. "There's something we learned this morning."

My stomach panged with unease, only worsened by the grimness of the trio's expressions. "The armoury." I marched for the door. "*Now.*"

Smugglers joined us at The Morettae's den, captains of The Grey Pearls and The Brass Teeth, along with Donatello and several factions of rank-and-file from across lower and upper óssium.

I recounted everything I'd learned that morning—the purification sacrament, Ilenia, The High Priest—and received the ugliest tidings yet: Giulia was dead, and *The Arum* was infested with the scum who had given rise to it in the first place. That information had been relayed to Cesare and the twins by Karmni, the girl whom I'd given my final pill of analgesic to the night which became my last at *The Arum*.

My innards heaved with rage. With hate. "I'll be sure to pay patronage to-night." *I'll drench that vile fucking corpse flower red.*

"Laútni *s*peaks." Donatello sauntered out of the shadows towards the central table, sitting onto it with crossed legs. "The prison break shall be *rea*lised on díem crep*ús*ca. *N*ot this week, but the *f*orthcoming. Ten h*un*dred."

To-night marked the conclusion of díem sóle.

"So we have eleven days," I muttered half to myself.

We sighted the rising smoke, smelled the char, but the gun was yet to reveal itself, and my heart gave into a breath-halting race.

"How long can you be away?" Fabio asked me.

I cleared the lump from my throat. "We'll be going to the mortuary as an alibi come dawn—Rosalia insisted to be there now. Sarnai is with Itxaro in The Antrum."

Şirîn held out her deq-tattooed palms. "These modest developments soothe the ear nevertheless."

I glanced between Cesare and the twins, noting, "Your whispers fly well," apropos of the turn-out.

"Hardly possible without Donatello and the al-Uwwād pair," admitted Cesare, sitting among wooden crates across the chamber from me, temple propped against slim knuckles. "My contacts and the good people of the city, just as well."

He held my gaze enrapt. His expression yielded nothing, did not flinch, as I looked at him, at his kohl-darkened eyes, at the filled-out contours of his sculpted features and the brown of his skin, and it hurt. It hurt so, so horribly. Like I was rotting. Like I was burning from inside.

"Shìwèn?[87]" I heard Fēngnà. "There's inclination to gainsay."

I plucked my eyeline from Cesare, my lungs taking in breath without permission as my head swooned, fingers, fidgety, easing curls behind my ears to no use.

"The Grey Pearls have been greatly stalling our supply run and time is breathing down our collars," explained Fēngnà. "Understand that my continued compromise remains *only* for Ygạl's sake and *isn't* infinite."

When I glimpsed Cesare again, he had already occupied his attention with Fabio who said tightly, "Appreciated, Fēngnà."

Dismay opened a pit inside my stomach once more. *Will our efforts be enough to capture the citadel amidst this prison break?* What more did we have?

"Apropos of what Ilenia told you, Giorgianna…"

Cesare's voice rushed in a shiver off my shoulders. I hated it; I hated how my name on his tongue felt like fingertips caressing skin, how starved my flesh was. I hated that *those* were my thoughts when I heard him talk. But I forced myself to face him, still.

---

[87] A Geikux̄heshyŭ expression of disagreement or question.

"Considering this research of Abelli's presents the threat of Cardea's hex on lower óssium being undone," he contemplated aloud, "and Ilenia, with her unnerving fascination with oldtown and The Court, being aware of its existence more intimately than most..." His eyes slitted, tone bladed. "I think I ought to meet with The Owl of Wisdom." He clicked his tongue. "I found this in Grand Judge Veronesi's archives." From his jacket, he produced a folded paper. "Upon her arrest, Calliupa Soriano, Blood Dahlia's niece and Ilenia's supposed friend, was administered a lobotomy for 're-education'. It resulted in her delirious state at her execution, instead."

My stomach dropped as agitated murmurs hurried through.

And those broken pieces of mine began to arrange themselves into something understandable. "What the High Priest sees as 'enlightenment' is simply the severance of the membrane within the frontal lobe which encapsulates that reservoir of azoth," I began to myself. "This induces transfusion of pure azoth into the blood. Nashĭgostu Kurilit Gostiata essentially lobotomised himself with that knitting needle, which gave *him* the ability to transfuse. What if Abelli's purification sacrament *is* a lobotomy?" My blood ran cold. "Which would mean the state *already* has its hands on their research." I swallowed. "*B*-because the administrator of the lobotomy to Calliupa was a griffin under the orders of the Governor. Ilenia claims that Abelli does not wish for their research to be applied to anything but the congregation, so it cannot be something Abelli knew about."

"We can spread these whispers just fine," one of the workers present said, "but we need *definitive* proof if we want it to deliver the right blow."

"We know De Tullia doesn't keep any document in his own quarters, correct?" a woman beside him clarified, leaning onto a rake.

Cesare nodded. "Our next best bet is Abelli's," the strain in his own voice did not evade me, "within the basilica. But who's to say they're keeping documents at all?"

Lorita's face contorted. "So you put trust in a woman who'd jeopardise our safety *just* as readily as the rest of them?"

"Did you not hear *anything* I said?" A reprimand lashed out of me, almost a shout. The room fell silent. "We *don't* trust her! We don't trust any *one* of them! They're *useful* to us. *They are our disposable fucking means to an END!*"

As my voice echoed through the storeys of the edifice, Lorita's honey eyes glistened. Her nostrils flared like she might charge for me. Then, she stormed out, all but breaking the door with the force of its slam.

Lissandri handed Kel-Kech a scathing glare. "Go babysit your overgrown fucking child."

"Stop jabbing me as if it's my fault, Lissandri!" Kel-Kech screamed out, plunging the chamber into an even deeper silence.

Lissandri's jaw tensed. "As far as I'm concerned," he prowled nearer, "it's *all* your fucking faults. You made us pariahs in the Cove. You've done fuck-all to aid us in this 'revolution' you claim to stand for."

"Andri…" I cautioned.

"In our mati's country," he ignored me, "they say '*inqilāb zindabād*'. 'Long live the revolution'. His eyes reddened, chin wrinkling up. "You wouldn't know the first thing about that. All bark, no bite."

Kel-Kech began to back up slowly, but her turquoise eyes blazed. "Whilst *you* bite each and every hand that feeds you." She strewed a gaze like searing coals across the room, and left.

BRUMAL NIGHT WIND SCRAPED KEL-KECH'S CHEEKS as she chased Lorita down a street several blocks away. In the dark; out of sight. "*Rita!*" She caught up to the blonde. "Lorita, they've done *nothing* but help," she pleaded, even as she still burned with indignation. She knew Lissandri was merely one of them, and that the rest, most of all Giorgianna and Cesare, did not share his sentiment, at least not its latter part. As for the former—making them pariahs… "We've never gotten *nearly* this close, and rogue Morettae are undermining *every*—!"

"You are growing devoted to those people above your own!" Lorita exploded. "Who even are they to you?"

"*Friends*. Is that enough, or do I need them to be holy messiahs?"

"THEY AREN'T YOUR FUCKING FRIENDS! That witch killed Lapo and she'd kill *you*! They'd sell you out in a heartbeat!"

"No, Rita! *Lapo* would do that—he *did* that! Remember Davide? He practically licked that backstabber's feet! The *rogue Morettae* would do that—that's what they've *been* doing. Haven't you considered that perhaps I've been growing 'devoted' to these people because *you* do nothing but snub me? You treat me as if I'm not even your love—"

"I am not *supposed* to love you!" Lorita shook, suddenly so small, eyes glistening and fists clamped tight enough to bleed. "My love for you is a sin I cannot indulge in any longer. I will not be damned for you."

Tears dampened Kel's eyes. "Then I will not be broken for you." She couldn't *give* anymore—Lorita had taken and taken and taken with no tempering whilst expecting to pay with nothing but condemnations. Kel couldn't love—couldn't *live*—like that.

So she walked away.

A rush of footsteps sounded behind her.

Despite herself, Kel-Kech turned around.

Silver flashed in the night.

Kel-Kech's hand gripped the neck of her axe before the thought registered.

Metal struck metal with the ululating *clang* of Kel's isizenze[88] meeting Lorita's longsword.

"Rita?" Kel-Kech beheld the stir of golden magma in the blonde's eyes. The rage upon her countenance.

Lorita shoved against her. Switching hands smoothly behind her back, she swung full-force for Kel.

Clang.

Kel beat the longsword's strike away, arms trembling. "Lorita, I don't want to hurt you. Please *don't*—!" A scream cut off her sentence when Lorita nicked the slope of her shoulder with steel.

The ocean-eyed woman stared nonplussed at the violation.

"You are weak, Kel-Kech," hissed the blonde and lunged with a barrage of slashes.

---

[88] A South African axe with an iron blade shaped like a crescent.

They were far from the armoury—in the crime-rusted valves of oldtown. There would be nothing to tear them from each other. To halt a blade's killing fall.

"Rita, *look* at me!" Kel shrieked over the clashes of metal. "Just *THINK*!" She kept falling on the defensive, doubling back, whilst Lorita advanced. "You *love* me! I *know* you do!"

But her words only spurred Lorita on, her slashes turning to frenzied hacks. "They'll stray us from victory!"

"You're simply not *right*, Rita! Why can't you *see* that?"

"And *you* are *complacent*!"

Blood surged scalding and alive in Kel-Kech's veins, forcing her hand to swing the isizenze in an offensive trajectory. "I'm sorry I'm not my sister!" She rammed her isizenze against Lorita's sword, pinning the blonde against a sombre brick wall. "*I'm sorry you need a* fucking child *to lead you because you don't have ideas of your own and so resent Cesare and Giorgianna because they* do!"

Lorita's breathing tore, her arms shaking beneath the force of Kel's axe against her sword. But she refused to speak as the two women locked gazes for both an eternity and a blip.

Kel's eyes burned. "Did you ever love me, Lorita?" Her voice broke. "Tell me!"

Lorita's throat bobbed with a gulp. "Yes. I do." Her voice trembled, eyes welling with tears. "And I hate myself."

Kel-Kech's jaw wound up tight. Sweat coated her palms. "Then I hate you too." She shoved Lorita's sword and buried the lunate blade of her isizenze in her chest.

Blood dripped down parted red lips.

Kel's grip numbed, axe slipping. Her ankles tied on her tottering retreat and levelled her to the cold cobbles. Spiked heat enveloped all of her organs, raced under her skin, puddled in her eyes.

Lorita slid down the wall, axe still in her. Parting her heart.

She slumped to the stone, mouth trickling vermilion rills, and her glazing eyes fixed on Kel-Kech as a sharp breath intruded her windpipe.

"No…" Kel's vision blotched and vignetted with blackness. Her chest crushed in, sobs heaving out. "No no *nononono*!" She crawled to the blonde, cradled her in her lap, shook her shoulders thoughtlessly whilst the world bleared at the outpouring of tears.

It was no use. She lay dead and cooling. Blood on Kel-Kech's hands.

So the ocean-eyed woman clutched her blonde to her shattering heart, and wept.

THE HOUSE OF JUDGEMENT still stunk of the death which stained its ventricles mere hours prior.

'*What is your purpose here, Magister?*' questioned Grand Judge Giordano Veronesi.

'*You are in possession of court documents surrounding the murder of signorína Emanuela Vehanush Airaldi?*' Minister of Scholars, Ilenia Farnese, replied with her own question.

'*In retentis.*'

'*I want them.*'

'*What spurs you to believe I would grant your request?*'

'*I shall be forever indebted to you for this.*'

'*Supposedly, you were indebted to me last time, yet said debt remains outstanding.*'

'*Consider this a second, and a promise of its fulfilment.*'

'*One ought not speak words they shall readily regret.*'

'*But will you* help *me?*'

Giordano's silence. '*I will.*'

And their voices retreated.

"Governor." A passing giuratóre bowed. "Dél'ì lùtius e vísus benedétti."

"Vísus e lùtius, giuratóre," replied Governor Crescenzo De Tullia.

The giuratóre passed by, and Crescenzo left his vigil beside the door to Veronesi's office.

The Grand Judge held documents which incriminated Crescenzo but which he had no access to by decree of Faustinian law.

Crescenzo palmed his silver swallow pin.

He was the law.

And those standing in his way were to be eradicated.

Scene XXX

The Blet of Limerence

Cesare | Giorgianna

CHORDOPHONES HAD ALWAYS BEEN CESARE'S BELOVED, most of all the violin. Lavûta. The music of his mother's people. But every chordophone was its own mage.

He leaned back against the door, head tipped to match, and listened as, in the bedchamber within, a cello played a wistful nocturne to the star-bestrewn night. Haftiyar Barzanî's *'Sehnsucht'*, Cesare wagered an unanswered guess.

The piece drew its final note, leaving the melody's afterburn to seethe in the flesh. Musicians knew a song's coda never *truly* meant its end. Its echo lingered, a spectre, mirage.

Cesare counted three too-fast heartbeats, another two breaths, a thump of silence, and cracked open the door, stepping inside.

Giorgianna sat in a chair near the room's centre where cramoisie swathes of aerial silk dangled off a hook in the ceiling, plucking the strings of her cello and smoking a sigarétta in pensive silence. A blouse dressed her graceful form in airy charmeuse the colour of arterial nectar, her waist cinched slim by a buckled waspie and her long legs sheathed in black. Curls spilled boundless down her back, as if she were a mermaid granted feet.

Yet her eyes wore the shadows of sleeplessness, her skin leeched of its candlelit vitality to a yellowness of dying leaves, and so Cesare's chest bound, weighed, as if with chains. *I did that to you.* He had sent her into a den of life-devourers. All to suit your little schemes.

"Your ruminations deafen, vólto," he gave voice.

Giorgianna's eyes snapped to circles when they sought him.

She jumped to her feet, grasping the cello's neck as the instrument almost toppled.

Cesare tilted his head. "Can hardly hear myself think."

A flat look. "Will you *ever* cease hypocrisy?"

Cesare clicked his tongue and paced towards a rosewood table flushed to the sinistral wall. "I think I'd cease *existing*."

Her jaw clenched, but instead of firing back, Giorgianna sprung from her standstill and marched after Cesare, throwing her arms around his neck. He staggered, gripped the table behind him, stunned as her hold tightened. "*You're a suicidal maniac*," she whispered. "*Please don't do that—I need you to stay.*"

Cesare's fingers clamped against the forbidden urge to sink into Giorgianna's curls, yet he allowed himself to embrace her no matter how shrilly his mind screamed to stop. With the presence of her in his arms, her materiality, her *being there*, he held her tighter, his eyes shutting, teeth squeezed half in indignation, half in poignant longing. He wanted to drop to his knees and beg forgiveness. To supplicate like a sinner to a god. He needed her to live. *Damn you and fucking damn me.*

"I admit, letters to your nemesis is astonishing even for you." *Idiot.*

Giorgianna unhanded Cesare. "Yet here you are, complying." She puffed a smoke halo which caressed his face and pricked his eyes.

He pocketed his hands, face tipped close. "Do you relish in my thrall?"

"I relish in your betterment," Giorgianna proclaimed humourlessly before holding her sigarétta to Cesare's mouth. He took a puff, more aware of her fingers' ghosting touch against his lips than anything else in that moment. "You…" her beestung lips squeezed together, "look well." She took back her dart. "You worried me."

Cesare expelled a plume and gave a wry look. "If the letters weren't indication enough."

She shut her eyes. "Quite frankly I've never witnessed penmanship so dreadful."

"It remained *well* within your power to cut contact." He tapped her forehead with his own pack of coffin nails. "Yet here *you* are."

Giorgianna smiled sourly. "And *you* partook in my sigarétta whilst having your own. How odd." She dragged.

Cesare pulled a mocking expression, eyes turning in disregard of the thorny heat crawling up his neck.

Her giggle lilted like a brook's warble. In a desk drawer, she reached for a pair of chocolates wrapped in foil, handing them to Cesare. "I like speechlessness on you." She swept stray waves out of his face. "It's cute."

"You know," he plucked the sweets and pulled out a lighter, "I didn't realise you wanted me to shut my mouth so much because you were in love with me."

Giorgianna pirouetted away sharply, flicking curls over both shoulders. "Fiend."

A laugh impelled Cesare as he pinched a coffin nail in his lips. His thumb slid down the flint wheel with a metallic rasp *once*, *twice*, until a flame burst to life as if a heavy breath to singe the tobacco. His attention flickered to Giorgianna through the diaphanous veil he exhaled, finding her eyes intently on him.

"I want you to play the cello again," he told her.

Giorgianna's features first turned abashed, then her curled lashes lowered. Pensive once more. "Only if you play your violin alongside."

Cesare fleeted to his quarters to fetch his violin without hesitation.

When he returned, Giorgianna sat on the chair with her cello, greeting him with a subfusc regard. "What does his majesty request of me?"

He returned to the table. "'*Elegy of Spring*'."

Her blood-moon gaze darkened to nightfall. "Want to rub '*A Bedlamite's Ballad*' into my wounds, bàuta?"

"No." His eyeline vehemently grasped hers. "I want you to take it back. I want you to reclaim the day this filthy fucking kakistocracy devastated your life. I want you to wring by force this melody into a funeral dirge for each and every swine that ever wronged you."

Giorgianna's chest rose with a rigid inhale, then her chin dipped, and she engaged the bow.

The melody played like swords drawn, Giorgianna's cello and Cesare's violin weaving through and around each other as if a pair of blade dancers, twirling so long yet ending too quickly, leaving Giorgianna to draw the concluding notes alone. The melody's spirit remained suspended between them—unsaid words.

Cesare opened his mouth to speak, then closed it immediately lest something reckless stumble forth, swallowed, and tried anew, "You play beautifully." *You* are *beautiful*. It took just about gnawing away his cheek to not blurt the treacherous words aloud.

Giorgianna's brows tucked down to her eyes. "Right." It was almost hurt with which she spoke.

She stood and made for the silks.

Locking her legs in the swathes, Giorgianna suspended herself halfway up as if on a swing. The hook groaned, then silence stretched between them, punctured only by the ocean's sighs. The distant hubbub of crewmen. The ticking clock. Fleeing time. *Lost* time.

Cesare's lips parted, hovered ajar before he finally said, "I will never cease reminding you what he did to me," with a voice half-trembling.

Giorgianna's slim fingers crushed her sigarétta's stub. In their ignorance of them, they had extinguished. "And it will never cease being all the more incentive," she hissed.

"No!" Terror electrified Cesare's nerves. "*Any* incentive but me." *I cannot be your reason to die.*

"You look so lowly upon yourself…"

"This isn't *about* me! If Manuele kills you—"

"He *won't*." A twang of indignation in Giorgianna's tone.

"You *know* what kind of sicko he is!"

"And so he deserves to die!" Her copper-blade eyes smouldered red-hot. The colour of wrath. Of blood. *Of love*. "My vengeance is mine to take. For Ema and for me. *No* one will stand in my way, and I will kill them if they dare."

Cesare approached Giorgianna. Gripped a sash of silk. Met eye-to-eye with her. "Nothing I say will waver your resolve, but—"

Her fingertips pressed to his mouth. "Then say nothing, Cesare."

Each time, his name on her tongue was an insistence. A reminder. A confirmation and a curse at once.

He moved her hand aside. "You should be aware by now that my dry heart forbids me." It was by force that he compelled sardonic wit into his tone. *How easily you strip me of my gall.*

Giorgianna leaned a fraction closer, slid locks of his dark hair between her fingers and tucked them behind Cesare's ear, skimming the curve of his earring. A shiver strewed his skin. "You know," sultry breaths slipped from her lips across his, "perhaps I do enjoy your company."

Darkness eclipsed Giorgianna's eyes when they gazed into him again, and Cesare grew forgetful of himself. His mouth opened, a shuddering breath intruding.

She clutched his shirt so hard nails scraped his shoulders through the cloth. Her nose tucked in the nook of his cheek. Warmth turned to heat to singe as skin so painfully *almost* grazed skin.

The ancient hook gave way.

Giorgianna plummeted with a yelp, Cesare catching her mid-fall.

"Are you—?"

She shoved away. "I'm fine." Her hands fumbled to gather the fallen silk and scurry into her hair.

Cesare's fingers hid inside his pockets.

Madness had crept so, *so* close, and he would have handed himself over like any dutiful proselyte. He would have slashed open his veins and let her drink him down until his life was hers if she had only commanded so. *Damn you damn you* damn *you!* He couldn't. Even as his entire being begged him, he couldn't surrender no matter how much agony it brought. It would be ephemeral. Just like him. He didn't want the pain, nor did he wish to inflict it on another when he already begot such suffering. There was nothing of him to give.

Giorgianna glimpsed the silks, then the misshapen hook, then Cesare, faltering his heart. "Help me put this back up."

"*SHIT!*" Cesare cried out. My heart juddered as his shoulder buckled beneath my knee and almost launched me into open air. "Fucking careful."

"I swear to the Gods if you drop me," I sneered down at him.

Finally hooking the silks back on and grasping them for leverage, I shifted my legs off Cesare's shoulders and slipped into his arms. My palms tread his shoulders and chest as he set me down, then snapped shut where my heart raced.

I distracted myself with the clock. *One hundred; diem zenítis.* My stomach keeled. "I don't want to return," I said. "I haven't kept down a bite of food in days. Every time I look in the mirror, I see a dead woman. I want to claw my skin off." My voice broke when I saw myself reflected alongside Cesare upon the silvery pane of my full-length mirror. "There is no escape."

Cesare's arms wrapped around my shoulders from behind and cheek leaned against my head, his soft cotton shirt saturated with the heat of life. *You're alive.* "I wish there was," he spoke from painful experience.

I latched onto him—desperate for anything at all to hold. "Emanuela haunts me. In sleep and daylight. And I see things. Eyes. *Death.* I see Ema, too. I see her as I did that winter solstice night, and she screams to me to save her but I *can't.*" Cesare's arms around me tightened. "It's *him.* I cannot be near him without twitching with murder. It drives me mad— I want to cut him open and wash my hands inside him." Rage tore through all in its path, forcing my nails into the firm muscle of Cesare's forearm. "I need him butchered like the pig he is," I spat. "Blood does not wash off and I don't want it to. I'll wear his guts like a funeral gown."

Cesare's breaths thrilled along my ear, down my skin, as he shifted curls over my shoulder and rested his slender fingers by my collarbones.

"Tell me again—" his voice dissolved to dusk and glim "—that you will *tear* him and *break* him until *no* amount of necromancy could stitch him back together." His eyes flashed like skinning knives in the mirror. "Tell me *how*."

Into the bottomless well of my vengeful hatred I reached. Like rosary beads, I strung every black memory begotten by that gilded beast onto the thread of my consciousness, rolling them between my fingertips in a silent prayer. "I'll crack open his skull like porcelain just as he did to Emanuela. I'll cut him open, throat to navel, and dump his guts out for every single woman he put his filthy hands to." The seared red sundown of my gaze fell to the mirror, snared on Cesare's—black enough to swallow me. "And then I'll give him wings to make him a bona fide griffin." My lips slashed to a cruel line, blood and poison to Cesare's honey and flames. A blood-promise yet to be paid for.

His arms slipped around my waist like rot embracing medlar. *"That's my girl."* And he kissed my neck.

Heat drenched my face. *"Cesare..."* My head whirled, tipped back onto his shoulder as I clutched his soft cotton sleeve—how nice it must feel against his skin. My hand trod the column of his neck and tangled in hair thicker than molasses spilling between my fingers, and I once more wondered if he knew that beside him each and every star extinguished.

Cesare's breaths bated against my throat where I knew a human could kill another human if they bit just a little too hard. *I want to fall into you...*

A vulnerable ache sharpened behind my ribs. *But not...* My innards twisted. *No!*

"Yours?" My nails sank into his knuckles and he stopped instantly. *Not like this.* Senses returned to me, wringing my brow, and I pushed him off, pivoting to meet his stunned expression. "What do you *want* from me?" I suddenly trembled with more than yearning.

Cesare blinked as if coming back to himself. "I—"

"Do you want me in your bed, Cesare?" He flinched like my question was a gunshot. "If yes, then just say the word."

"No, I don't *care* if you're in my bed—"

"Then *what*? Because it sure *looks* like it."

"I *know* what it looks like—"

"Since you *know* so much, *say* what you *want* from me." Such shame burned inside me at the realisation that I would dig under my bone and rip that bruised, beating wretch of a heart from my own chest for him. That if he dragged me beneath his skin like the hateful needles that I was right on this forsaken floor, I wouldn't care. *Yet it wouldn't be enough.* I wanted—

"Whatever you feel for me, I don't want you to."

His hurried words dropped my mouth open. "And yet you do *that* to me?" Horrible pain rended my chest. "I don't believe you're cruel or stupid, Cesare."

His eyes plummeted to the floor, lips parting as if words clung to the tip of his tongue. Yet wretched hubris fastened his jaw tight. Sewed his mouth shut. *Say something!*

But he didn't.

Your pride is a disease. "And perhaps my belief is blind faith."

The door rattled open.

"¡*Ayyy* come revel with us, girly!" Danilo cheered without a care or know, a bottle of booze in his skinny hand. "Can't sail off without some mariner cheer for the course."

I looked back at Cesare. His fingerprints still burned all over me, his wide eyes still black as a solar eclipse, when I brandished at him a singular word on The Fingers, then turned on my heel and left with Dan, a stilted smile donned too tight.

I gasped winter seabreeze, hoping to no avail that its coldness might quench the unbearable burn inside me.

I couldn't stay with Danilo. Couldn't enter the jovial aura of the gun deck now warbling beneath my feet. Couldn't listen to the Usaz'khili çhuniri which sounded so alike the violin.

Fabio stood alone on the main deck, gaze affixed by the ocean prior to finding me. "Aγyvradiá,[89] Giorgianna." *Is it?*

I approached with folded arms. "Ki sý,[90] Fabio."

"I worried myself sick for you all," Fabio admitted darkly, speaking Themistoklísika. "But at least *something* seems to be coming of this suicidal endeavour."

I pressed my lips together, wishing to seize the opportunity to unspool his brain. "The… sóra who arranged my meeting with Ilenia…"

"*Mm?*"

"Her name is Dafne Ambrosi."

Fabio's eyes widened.

"She recognised me—recalled my father."

"She kept it…" he breathed.

"*Hm?*"

"Ambrosi was Durans' surname."

A nearly-smirk touched my lips. "I got *word*, too… that one of her friends' belamour was an especially quarrelsome smuggler woman a tad too keen on the disembowelment of men." Fabio's cheeks blanched. My smile widened. "Father didn't lie, saying you loved women who'd cut your throat and throw you in the sea."

Fabio scoffed, twisting the iron band on his thumb as he abandoned my scrutiny, and it was with an ache that I recalled Dahlia sporting the same ring. "That I did," murmured Fabio. "We once realised our birth date's the same down to the day: one born at the break of dawn and the other at sundown."

"How did it come to be?"

"We met her in our late teens alongside Matìa—the two'd been friends forever. Her sobriquet was 'Fata'; she was always tiny. We… did not get along at first. I found her irritatingly hyper; she took some odd interest with me and wouldn't let me rest, ceaselessly trying to get me to talk. To 'drop the dreary act'." Fabio's eye roll pried a giggle from me. "She wore me down."

---

89 *ah-ghee-vrah-thee-AH*; 'good evening' in Themistoklísika.
90 *kee SHEE*; 'and you' in Themistoklísika.

"How…" hesitation held my tongue before I permitted myself to ask, "did it end?"

"I was a coward." Fabio's blunt assertion shot me through the heart. "*Craven*, she'd say. I had the ship, and I had the theatre. Ada was a staunch puritan by way of smuggler culture; said I lived one foot on land and the other in the sea whilst she wanted little to do with life off the boat. I was always exceptional at pushing people away—justified it with work.

"Everything about our conversation that evening's a blur but this: *I* was the one who told Ada our lives were too different, that I couldn't live asea; couldn't reject the land. She took it as me no longer wanting *her*, and my fatal mistake was that I didn't correct her. So she walked away and… I didn't call her back. Just as I didn't call back your father when we argued for the final time. I *could've*, yet I was…" Fabio shrugged, "too craven. Too proud to admit I made a blunder. I *never* made blunders—Durans and I were the rational ones! And *I* proved a disappointment. Then had the *gall* to beat myself up for *years* over losing her." He gazed at the stars. "But love plays you for a fool."

Heartache spurred dark memories. "Father marched into the House of Judgement to seek clarity about my disappearance, certainly knowing he would be arrested. He accepted a plea bargain which would doom him just so Elenedda may live. Father threw all caution to the wind for love." Tears threatened me. "Perhaps there's its own reason in that."

A pained scoff deserted the captain. "Durans and I were the *rational* ones, right? Well, Durans died *for* Dafne—jumped into the stormy sea to save her from drowning only to perish in her stead. That's why she left The Brass Teeth for the Order: couldn't take the guilt, even if it wasn't hers." The confronting mirrors around me sharpened enough to cut. "Love made Durans selfless to a *deadly* extent." Fabio glimpsed my way. "Love won't make anyone *reasonable*. It incinerates and levels every shred of rationality you have no matter *who* you fucking are."

No one ever spoke of Love's violence; of all the times it tore your heart from your chest and commanded you carry on living. I had never once loved without pain. I loved Emanuela, but she was taken from me. I loved Father, but he was too. I loved Mother, even, but her love for me extinguished with a clipped breath. And…

"What of *you*, girl?"

I scoffed. "What *of* me?"

"It's on your mind for a reason."

"It doesn't matter." My stomach coiled.

"Both of you are intelligent."

"Both of *whom*?" Ire lashed out.

Fabio frowned. "You mean to tell me *none* of this ties to Cesare?"

I grasped into a chokehold the rage inside me. "He sure knows how to wear a heartbreaker's mask and play the part." And for that, for everything, I still, I *always*, hated him.

"Do his reasons not bare themselves?" posed Fabio. "He'll push away *anyone* who loves him—believes it's the only way for them to stay safe, whatever he thinks that even means in this world. That he is transient, and so it doesn't matter because it would all end in hurt."

'I *was the reason I lost* everyone *I* ever *loved*.'

Was that why…?

'*Whatever you feel for me, I don't want you to*.'

What do *I feel for you, Cesare?*

My breaths quickened. *Nonono Gods please…*

"Giorgianna?"

I dashed for the gangway. "I can't." *I need to be alone.*

The docks and township flickered by on my race across the Cove to the castaway ocean grotto I'd made my latibule. Along the craggy cliffside path, the waves' frothy fingers vied to snatch my ankles and pull me to the frigid depths as if reclaiming a turncoat progeny.

My feet brought me to a halt at the edge of the quiet water. Its black-pearl marmoris reflected my distorted visage.

I gasped and lurched back. My heart thrashed, and maybe it was the water, or maybe it was the indescribable pain, but in that horrible juncture in time I realised… I loved he whom I shot in the chest, whose heart I held a blade to, yet whom my Shadow had once yearned to be so wholly I could devour him. He with the fiendish smiles and haunted eyes. He—

more ideology than flesh. He who had looked upon the end so many times, he could chart its visage. *I love Cesare…*

My tremoring hands flew to my mouth. Tears weighed my lashes and a scream knotted in my throat. *No. No. No.* I couldn't love him but the cruel word cracked open my breastbone and ripped my ruined heart from my ribs like a gem for its boundless collection. He who walked so effortlessly beneath the cloak of Death as if already claimed by it—I didn't want him if this miserable world did too. I would rather love him from afar and be in agony for the rest of my life *but Gods Gods* Gods *it* hurts *and I* love *him—why did you beget me so starved and lovesick?*

A sob tore out of me. *Damn you, Cesare!* His touch would never be enough because I *loved* him and I wanted him to love me too.

My head bowed as I huddled into myself against the cold rock, nails hooking in my scalp, and useless tears spilled down my face. I couldn't even name their source—couldn't admit to myself that I loved another enough to deform into such a sick creature.

But '*love*' in Faustinian was 'eater'. '*Gnawer*'. Ataínè. It devoured. It killed the way blet and putrescence took fruit. To tremble with hunger— the worst kind of anguish—at the impossibility of attaining the closeness your soul begged for should make anyone swear off something as horrible as Love.

And yet there I was.

Scene XXXI

Violent Ends

Giorgianna | Cesare | Giorgianna

"WHAT?" Cesare's question was neither loud nor angered, and yet the walls of the abandoned art gallery echoed with his voice.

"I killed her," confessed Kel-Kech again. She tucked her arms to her torso, wrung her fingers, her shoulders curved inward and eyes each a bright, rippling pool. "*I*-I didn't—she attacked me and wouldn't stop. She just wouldn't *stop* and I…" Her mouth gaped; head shook. "I had no choice—she gave me no *choice*!"

A pallid-cheeked man, dark of hair, the same one I recalled storming out of assemblies, hurled his morètta to the ground. "Should've listened to Rita all along." He spat, almost sullying Kel's boot. "Nothing but spineless." He waved a broad hand. "Move out!"

My stomach sank deeper and deeper as one, after another, after another Moretta followed his command.

Panic drained Kel-Kech's cheeks of colour. "Tolomé, *please!*"

"Stay away." The pale man gnashed at her.

She staggered back. "*I'm sorry…*"

Lissandri's nostrils flared, his jaw twitched, his eyes bore into the back of Kel's head. He advanced for her.

I shoved him out of my way, enveloping the woman in my arms. "We're here."

Anka-ny joined me to embrace Kel who now shook with soundless tears, Yezo approaching for comfort, yet the exodus did not halt until almost half of The Morettae were gone—hardly two dozen left behind.

Yezo doffed his moussor and held the manganese cloth to his chest, asking, "What should we do?"

"There are more of you." *Not by much.* "Establish tenure at the armoury. Go!" I squeezed Kel and let the two Morettae take care of her.

Itxaro clicked her fingers. "Manárša,[91] Əkurofu,[92] and Diodora are with me taking stock of *The Arum*. See you then."

"I'll meet you at the mortuary." Sarnai kissed my nose and departed hand-in-hand with Itxaro.

Everyone petered out, leaving only me, the twins, and Cesare beneath that anatomical heart rendered in gilt upon the ceiling of the gallery's rococo chamber. I had seen how a heart looked beating within a rended chest, had drank the sap it pumped through living flesh. All to feed selfish, selfish hungers.

"This is fucking atrocious as far as our numbers are concerned for the prison break," said Cesare, near-absent. His thumb fiddled idly with the flint wheel of his lighter, his cheek slipped between clenching teeth and brow wrung.

"We have some hope with yours meeting the Serpents and Hyacinths to-night…" But Eligio's statement faded, because he knew the purpose of cadres as our allies was not storming the ministerial house, but building arms against intrusion into oldtown and the Antrum by legionaries. For the prison break next week, we had The Salt Hydras, The Morettae, us, and some Hounds. But the legions were in the *thousands*, and with Morettae now halved…

------

[91] *mah-NAHR-shah*

[92] *eh-koo-ROH-foo*; a nickname, in this case, as it is the Sārḥo term for '*dagger*'. The Sārǝṇ people are the indigenous inhabitants of Sāre Island in southern Mojatīya.

"I cannot stay." Bile rushed up my throat. "I'll approach Ilenia about her speaking with you." I didn't wish to look at Cesare and have him look back. "Farewell, until then." I routed for the exit.

"I think I may have crossed paths with it."

Cesare's declaration halted me.

I peered over my shoulder. The twins stood equally perplexed.

Cesare did not look at me either. "Abelli's research." His clarification jolted me. "Perhaps. At a Guard station, when I was first seeking means to infiltrate the Ministerial house—before I got hold of Barsotti's journal. There was a crow in it I dispatched, and a pair of convicts I freed. They spoke of the soldier that 'there was nothing inside'. I returned to the station and checked his scalp. There, I found an aperture, seemingly healed over. I burned the station down."

My stomach chilled, eyes wide. "That was *months* ago…"

He didn't glance up. "I know."

I wanted to claw out his eyes. To scream. To never again see him. To pull his innards out and crawl inside him so his mind may be mine—so I would never be lied to or kept in the dark by him again. I wanted to kill him for this. I wanted to kill him for everything.

"Why did you even check something so odd?" Lissandri queried. He didn't seem nearly as angered as I, and that maddened me all the more.

"Iyad said he'd heard from some kids at his docks that a government house servant once found a hole drilled into the skull of a soldier."

My jaw twitched. "I cannot even bring myself to be disappointed, anymore." I turned to quit the gallery. The coldness of the handle bit my blistering palms.

"I know that too," said Cesare.

And some threadbare resolve within me snapped.

"Do you know that trusting you is vain, Cesare?" My feet pivoted with a screech against marble. My eyeline shot for Cesare, and he flinched as if not a gaze but *bullets* ripped through him. We looked upon one another at last. Devastating flames curled around my heart, gnawing away at the hateful, bleeding thing. "You endeavour to take on all burden yourself— you would've 'dealt with this little predicament', right? Like you deal with them all? Without a word? Why? Why do you *do* this? Does the lie you invented for yourself press against your throat every time you want to ask for help, so you don't? Does staring in the face of your own hypocrisy wound your pride because *Gods forbid* you admit your shortcomings? Gods forbid *Cesare Ramiro Agostini* admits he alone isn't omnipotent. Because you're a fucking coward!" I caught ragged breaths, heartbeat a storm in my ribs. Cesare stared blenched and wide-eyed at me. "That's what I'd called you in my quarters, right? A coward?" A crack ran through my voice.

It hurt again. So, *so* horribly. Like I carried rotten entrails. Like I'd burned from the inside. And he wasn't at all conscious of my agony.

"But you don't know how many times I've scrawled lovelorn inanities on those wretched letters I sent you, only to rip them to shreds and cast them to flames, then reprove myself for the bêtise I knew I'd entertain again and *again*!" I held onto one iteration. "And I *hate* it!" Before departing, I seized Cesare's stricken gaze one last time—*why won't you see that I* love *you?*—and spat out, "I hate *you*."

It was all I could do to not scream the contrary.

THE DOOR SLAMMED SHUT.

Honey and roses wilted upon Cesare's senses and it took *everything* to not chase after Giorgianna and shout that *for fuck's sake* he *loved* her and to *Hell* with blood promises.

"Ces?" Eligio's voice drowned beneath *coward coward COWARD!*

"*no…*" Pain beset Cesare, as if an aneurysm burst in the vessels crowning his heart and he bled. Red—its every shade. Just like… *her*. "It hurts so bad *so fucking bad*."

Lissandri paced. "Come clean, Ces."

"I *can't*," he snapped. "I need her to *help* me." They struck a deal—a blood promise: she would help him topple an empire and he would help her decimate a bloodline. Nothing else. With blood and scars their binding, one of them could only ever be the other's demise.

But *every* shred of him desired her the way a believer desired his god. Maniacally and desperately, yet with such purity. Such pious, innocent longing. And yet his sin was pride. His sin was cowardice.

"You 'need' her, Cesare," Lissandri sniped, "because you *love* her."

"It's not that simple."

"*Idiot!*" Eligio reprimanded, his eyes tired and angry. "Did you not listen to *anything* just now? Do you honestly think she doesn't feel the same?"

If she didn't, he couldn't take it. Nor could he take it if she did.

"Do you love her?" Lissandri questioned plainly.

"Fucking Saints, *YES!*"

She was beautiful and terrifying and always in his head and he was *so selfish* to want a place in hers. And he *was* a coward because, no matter how deeply he desired Giorgianna, Cesare didn't want *her* to desire *him* because he was ephemeral. Because he was a bringer of death upon *everyone* he *ever* loved. And he loved her.

Lissandri handed over a dull look. "Do you *want* to be in heart-tearing pain for the rest of your sorry existence?"

Cesare's eyes burned. "How much can it be remedied?"

"*Tell* her, then!" scolded Eligio. "You're on borrowed time."

'I don't believe you are cruel or stupid, Cesare.'

But I am a wretched fucking coward.

I LIFTED MY REVOLVER AND BLEW OUT the final arum-shaped ceiling light.

Dying moonglow streamed into the flesh parlour's hallway across foliate tiles heaped with broken bodies and expelled entrails, oily blood burnishing the art nouveau walls in Death's putrescent unction. *Finally, a corpse flower as you ought to be.*

I strutted back into the main chamber of the forsaken sepulchre.

There, the final man cowered on his behind, crawling away when his hazel-blue eyes cast upon my blood-anointed visage. He flinched and whimpered when his hand sank into the innards of his fallen guard.

I gazed down at the snivelling wretch at my feet.

His plain physiognomy found a place among my black memories—the client who had left a spewing gash on my thigh as payment for my final night in *The Arum*. "Remember me?" I slashed his left thigh with my slathered rapier, then pressed the blade into his bobbling throat. Fresh blood trickled into his collarette. "Name."

"*M*-Marcián Lanuza," he bleated.

The surname pricked my ears. "A nobleman." My eyes frisked the purple and teal of his sumptuous attire, his alexandrite necklace and rings. "Your family subsidised this establishment?"

"Yes."

"Only yours?"

"Yes. *M*-my eldest brother finds good standing with the Minister of Dominion."

"Name your bloodline, Marcián."

"Mother Simonetta Marini, late father Salbador Lanuza-Corbalán, older brother Basilio Lanuza, younger sister Ofelia Marini-Lanuza. No spouse or kids."

"They are involved?"

"Father was before death. *B*-Basilio is aware we trade in flesh but not a partaker. The rest: yes."

Worms. "Who else? One family isn't enough to sustain this."

Marcián's lower lip wobbled.

I plunged my rapier into his eye, restraining myself from impaling his skull's innards.

He screeched.

"*TALK*!" I tore the blade free.

"Imperialíi and other nobles paid us for *Arum* lavìri," he rattled off. "But they weren't aware of the bordello's reality." *Not a bordello, but a den of flesh peddlers.* "A share of the money went to Irene Falco, substantial enough to furnish the building to the clientele's tastes. No common ossíi was to be admitted into the bordello unless upon the necessity to keep up appearances. They too were ignorant." *Like Donatello.* "C-customer names are all in a document in the drawer. Bloodink marks all in the know." Marcián swallowed. "*P*-please…" Bloody tears slipped down his face. "I have a family…"

"Who are you to beg my pity?" Murderous serenity flooded me—a lulling rush of narcotics. "Get on your knees." My voice almost droned. When he stared at me with that ichthyic gape, I skewered my rapier into his crotch, driving the blade deeper through his bollocks. He wailed enough to shatter every stained-glass window. "Did you not hear me?"

Shame reddening his face, Marcián crawled to his knees.

"Role reversal is such poetic justice." My blood frosted; head ached.

Marcián's lips smacked dryly.

"Worry not." I felt his veins pulse as they drank up the water I poured into them from his flesh. Panicked pleura throbbed; his lungs recoiled against the unwelcome droplets scaling their arborescent slickness. I attuned to the driblets in his lungs, dragging the water in his veins towards their cores. "The burden of this establishment shall no longer callus your hands." The swelling droplets in his lungs sharpened to fragments. Marcián's chest lurched with a hideous hack. Blood splashed out of his mouth. "I'll leave my regards with your family." My fist snapped shut.

Water-wrought blades tore from within him, ripping apart his torso.

Marcián crumpled in a dead heap to the floor upon which so many innocents had been stripped to the skin by vulgar rapists and whipped without mercy. His blood lacquered the marble with a retributive chrism, crimson unifying with the watery deluge of the blades deliquescing. *Your dues paid in full.*

Retrieving the documents, I stepped beyond *The Arum*'s doors. The shadows of the cursed street clung to my skin like soot.

A Meg'eča[93] woman in a long purple shawl garlanded in endless silver coins talked quietly with a Temistochlisi sporting streaming black hair. Meanwhile, a dark-skinned Sārəṇ man in a vermilion jacket plucked arrows from the dead sentinels littering the ground.

Itxaro clapped. "Encore, lehên."

---

[93] *mehg-EH-chah*; the people of Meg'erab.

I lit a sigarétta. "I'd burn this place down if it wouldn't take the neighbouring building with it."

"Easy on the pyromania, Cesare." I scowled at Itxaro's audacity. She held her palms up. "We'll sort it out. Go. And be careful!"

I kicked a man's corpse out of my way, thanked the Hounds, and left for the mortuary.

Sarnai handed Rosalia a zeegt naamal appliqué veil the colour of a magenta sunset, ornamented with bitüü khatgamal satin stitch, its hidden outside beset with mirror shards. "Keep it turned inside-out so it's visible."

Rosalia threw on the veil and vanished. "How do I look?"

I smiled. "Not at all." If anyone were to make a meagre mirror into a utilitarian garment, it would be the golden-handed Sarnai.

Libitina the undertaker swept out of the embalming room into the lobby we occupied, the plentiful ruffles of her prudent dress—crushed velvet and black as death—whispering against the fuscous stone floor. Corkscrew curls the pink of fairyfloss perched on her wide shoulders. In her snow-white hands lay a satchel. "You asked I hold onto this for you?" she addressed me, pupils stark against iris-less sclerae.

I took the satchel. "Indeed."

SEVEN BLACK SPINELS encrusted the knop of grand judge Giordano Veronesi's iron chalice. I ran my fingers along the inner curve of the cup.

Beyond the window of the Giudice's quarters, sunlight broke through the horizon's ashen skin, cottony clouds soaking up its blood.

I set Veronesi's chalice upon his blackwood desk. Then I left.

SCENE XXXII

PROFUNDITY

Manuele | Giorgianna | Cesare | Giorgianna | Rosalia

AFTER SIX NIGHTS AT THE BARRACKS, little else brought General Manuele Dioli contentment than returning to his apartments in the ministerial house.

As soon as he entered his quarters that díem zenítis morning, and the alchemical lights ignited, a scent accosted him.

Cloying salt. Wet and warm as an opened woman. *Human blood.*

Such a perfume would usually harden Manuele with pleasure, but female filth never wound up in his quarters unless it were the lowly servants going about their duties in his absence, or for whatever carnal release he needed. But with that scent hanging cold and putrid in his own apartment, perturbation bore down on Manuele more than he'd betray.

Leaving the door open, he advanced into the main parlour of his quarters.

At the centre of the tulipwood tea table—situated amid two gold-rimmed black velvet couches and triplet stools—lay a severed head encircled by its pulled teeth. Through a slit under the jaw, its tongue sagged out. Ruptured scalp bared the skull cracked beneath. A sharp object had mashed its eyeballs into oozing slush.

Dardan. One of Manuele's most trusted Imperialíi.

Onto his tongue, a sharp pin skewered what looked to be a note.

Manuele plucked free the pin to read the glib cursive:

'*I know.*'

Sickness tossed in his stomach.

He grabbed a stool and swung it at the head. The wooden seat shattered. The hunk of decapitated flesh *thunked* across marble, splatters of cold gore marking its passage. The scatter of teeth chattered—as if the things still carried souls that lodged in Manuele's skull and whispered. *I know. I'll always know.*

Manuele's tunnelling vision soaked red as he began hurling the items in the parlour in a furious rampage, shattering vases, crippling furniture, scarring walls with fractures.

He shoved his hands into his hair, chest heaving, as he tottered backwards from the ruined parlour.

They'll always know. *He* would never be free, either.

Manuele struggled to intake air. *I am not some feminal draff!* His father raised him well. Raised him *strong.* Yet his ribs constricted and a burn erupted at the centre of his chest. *Curse you!*

He pivoted at the threshold.

A gasp tore out of him.

Beyond the door stood Salomé in a long white chemise and lace cardigan, blue eyes polished and vacant as an eel's. "Pleasant morn, General! I trust you are in good health."

Dumb whore, Manuele wanted to scream at her, but clamped his fists and forced himself to breathe through the hammer of blood in his neck. "Of course, mèus dáma. Glad to return from the barracks to civilisation."

"Well, I shall be joining my beloved uncle for mornmeal. After, though, would you accompany me for a stroll through Vencenza?" She swept mousy hair over her breast, or she would have, were she not flat as a board above the waist. "As you promised?"

He returned to her dead eyes. "Most certainly."

MY EARLY MORNING EXPLOITS HADN'T CEASED AT *THE ARUM*, the mortuary, the abattoir, the House of Judgement, or the General.

Freshly clean, I made my way to Clario's office with tidings, halting only to eavesdrop at the Omphalos.

'*…quell upper óssium unrest.*' De Tullia.

'*What should be done vis-à-vis Treasurer Alagona's death?*' A soldier

My brow crinkled. *Olindo is dead?* He had been on file at *The Arum* as a knowing patron—at least among the documentation the fuckers hadn't destroyed—and I'd endeavoured to get the job done myself, but someone had gotten to him first?

'*I shall arrange Adviser Clario Barsotti to fill his role for the time being,*' replied De Tullia. It wasn't as if Barsotti's advising was of much use to the Governor whose power slipped from his grip, to be fair.

'*Something else, Minister. The Lanuza and Tagliafichi noble families have been found poisoned in their homes. Everyone but young dónna Lurèinsa Tagliafichi are deceased; dónno Basilio was not present. Two Imperialíi have been found dead in the barracks, also—snapped necks and lungs full of water.*'

A smile curving my lips, I strutted off.

Clario's office greeted my presence warily, as if sensing the murder staining me. Clario occupied the main bureau. Yòchaná stood soldier-esque by his side, engaged in quiet chatter with Dafne, Sarnai staring down an ugly gold statue at the corner of the room whilst Ilenia's nose sat buried in a book.

"Good," said Clario as I sat in a damask chair beside Ilenia. "I should like to inform you of dónno Basilio Lanuza's natálè[94] this evening—for

---

[94] *nah-TAH-leh*; birthday; specifically in reference to the celebration.

his birth's forty-second anniversary." I wondered when the Governor intended to enlighten Basilio of his family's fate in light of such a festivity. "The Ministers of Dominion, Emissaries, Blades, and Churches are expected to attend, though the rest are permitted. As such, you, as my niece, are encouraged to be present."

A jolt crackled through my nerves. "*When* this evening?"

"Close to sundown, as customary for him."

"I cannot be expected to stay late—we're meeting with cadres at midnight."

"You may excuse yourself on grounds of fatigue, but a couple hours of attendance are all but mandatory."

Concern overcame me. "There's still the question of how Ilenia might be able to make contact with The Bauta." The thought of speaking his name harrowed me. Perhaps he really was a demon.

Dafne looked slyly to the Magister. "The High Priest would surely be gladdened by *nothing* more than to have *you* forgo an event which venerates the flesh as greatly as a natálè in favour of atoning for past transgressions at the basilica, my lovely Ilenia."

Ilenia shut her book—'*Cardea the Three-Eyed; Our Lady of Thresholds*'—and looked up. *Cardea? The woman who hid The Court away?* I pencilled her read into memory. "Fine idea, sóra! So gracious of you. I have long wanted to meet the enigmatic Bauta." She did not smile, her expression hardly revealed anything, in truth.

Oh, I'm sure you have.

"In which location and with what precautions?" demurred Clario.

"*Stalker's Barge*," I proposed.

"Such *fascinating* places, oldtown and The Court," mused Ilenia in a whimsy I found nothing short of forbidding.

Clario frowned. "Is that wise?"

Ilenia levelled him with dryness. "Did *you* not meet with the pair in that precise establishment by those exact means, Adviser?"

"*I* did not wear a thousand targets on my back, Magister," he retaliated. "I espy your attitude towards discourse with the senate and Guárdia becoming profoundly unmindful." *Not incorrect.* The Minister of Scholars lurked in the corridors of the Athenaeum with officials often, engrossed in hushed conversation. If it didn't go unnoticed by us, I doubted the Governor, of all people, was none the wiser.

"How else do you suggest one builds rapport with potential allies in the fight to overthrow an autocracy?"

I almost laughed at 'allies'. As if their ilk would ever fight to overthrow *anything* in the name of liberation.

"By tactics more delicate, just as this '*fight*' is."

I swapped looks with Sarnai.

The Magister and Adviser butted heads often, the former tangibly more bent on progress, even if untrustworthy, whilst the latter maintained pacifism and mild manners.

"Well, *I* think," Sarnai's voice cut through the thickening tension, "given the whole thing with the purification sacrament and Abelli's research being in danger of exploitation by the Governor, their archives at the basilica are probably brimming. It might be a good opportunity to snoop around. If I tailor my hair to match Ilenia's, and don fitting attire— hiding my whole face, obviously—I can make an appearance at the basilica in your stead."

"I can abet that!" declared Dafne.

"Excellent." I cringed at the word that so effortlessly fell off my tongue. "Considering the Lanuza family is entwined with the Governor, it's not out of the realm of possibility that Basilio's estate may be where some documents are kept. I ought to seize my *own* opportunity."

Ilenia chuckled. "De Tullia remarked you a thinker aptly."

A coldness unfurled in my belly.

"Araya better accompany you," Yòchaná told me. "But I fear Rosalia will have to remain in the citadel."

"I'm sure she'll be more than keen to lurk among the servants," Sarnai supposed.

"We might just be able to make to-night our final one in this Bone Palace." I launched to my feet. "Time is of the essence."

"I'll try my best to make it to the natálè following mine convening with The Bauta," said Ilenia.

A nod to her, and I took my leave.

"Dónna Salomé!" Dafne halted me in the half-concealed walkway.

She dipped her chin. "My gratitude cannot be expressed for Dardan, dél'ì lùtius e vísus benedétti." Her dark eyes met mine. "I promised I'd tell you the little I know of the purification sacrament."

A frisson rose in my belly. "Yes?"

We sidled into an oriel overlooking an empty indoor cortile far below.

"Abelli wants a prophet," revealed Dafne in whispers. "They wish for their research to remain within the confines of the church, but do not especially mind whether the prophet *themselves* is of the church, for they believe that when the third eye opens—Bitius: profundity—and an individual ascends, they will choose the path of 'truth': the Order."

"But what does it *mean* to become ascended? How?"

"Profundity is intellectual depth. Wisdom. It means gaining the illimitable knowledge of the Trimorphic Godhead, the Divine Faces, which Abelli endeavours to attain through lobotomy."

My heart rattled. "When Calliupa's files were discovered in the House of Judgement, under the heading 'RE-EDUCATION', she was documented to have undergone a lobotomy by the order of De Tullia, but the procedure was deemed 'unsuccessful'—rendered her psychologically incapacitated—so prompting her execution…" Coldness spilled through all my veins. "De Tullia is appropriating it; Abelli's wishes be damned."

"There's more," Dafne cut in. "Abelli had once *succeeded*, or what they consider to have been success. I say once, but it was two subjects. They escaped the church. Abelli called them their 'magnum opus'."

And, suddenly, I *understood*.

The Rams.

'We are the magnum opus of the Gods' child.'

And I glimpsed within those patterns I'd seen and heard an esoteric motif I could comprehend, material enough to touch.

I grasped Dafne's shoulders. "Thank you, mèa sóra."

On my hasty way back to my quarters, I slipped a flacon of Myrabella into a servant's wash bucket for good measure.

CESARE TUCKED IN HIS SHIRT AND EXITED THE BATHING ROOM.

"*CES!*" Iyad hurtled down the corridor.

Cesare flinched back. "*Do* not touch me!"

"Donatello is dead."

"*What?*"

"Accosted by legionaries early this morning. Swallowed a suicide pill. His workshop's been sequestered by the state."

This is bad… "He was our most direct tie to the prisons."

"Anukka and I've tenuous contact. At this point, we have enough leeway for that to be enough."

"The reason for Tello's targeting?"

"Authorities saw Donatello displaying aggression towards legionaries during the Solar Square riot."

"Par for the course when you're beheading soldiers with a massive pair of scissors, I suppose."

"Ostensibly. But our whispers've dealt no less damage. Chances are, Tello's intended arrest wasn't unrelated. There's some speculation this may've been connected to the recent murders of the Lanuza and Tagliafichi families. Donatello also frequented *The Arum* unrelated to their activity." Cesare's stomach still flipped at the thought. "Perhaps the state believed he was connected to their assassinations? Or arbitrarily drew the connection like with the Dioli debacle?"

"Plausible but irrelevant," argued Cesare. "You and Anukka are in danger. Run this news to Kel and the Morettae. Get people's militias on watch."

"Anukka's on my part already."

"Excellent. I'll deal with the Antrum and Cove, then I've contacts in upper óssium to meet."

"Ces!" Isaia materialised down the corridor.

"*Saints,*" Cesare bit, "what else?"

"Ilenia wishes to convene at sundown. *Stalker's Barge.*"

"So be it. Donatello. Are you aware?"

"Just got word; yet to inform Ygal."

"Get on it." Cesare dashed to his chamber.

THE *CREAK* OF CAGES RAISED GOOSEBUMPS FROM MY SKIN. The perfume of intestine-pink honeysuckles lay wet against the bone-parched stench of emaciated bodies rotting in the wintry morning draught against which The Hanging Gardens shivered.

Among lush flowers, executed protesters hovered as if mutilated angels. Skin flensed off their backs stretched into wings over uprooted ribs, their husks suspended from chains. And I couldn't stop looking, no matter how harrowing the image. Even now, I still felt my mother's fingers on my jaw; heard her hiss in my ears.

"The Hanging Gardens are a centuries-old necessity of Vencenzani ordinance," Manuele orated as we strolled beneath the bleak bouquets, his armour hideously dazzling. "Its function matches that of the execution rituals—the bathing of death row inmates; their pristine presentation. A confronting sight. A 'pure', 'reputable' man standing beneath the throne, awaiting his sentencing to die for a crime. None of the comforting detachment which comes with rags and grime—a populace cannot be permitted such peace." His eyes trained on a butchered corpse. "Likewise, the consequences of disobedience must be displayed."

Fiddling with my cobalt colombína and the fur trim of my hat's over-wide brim, I fought tooth and nail my urge to argue in philosophical discourse. I knew what was expected of me, so I sought a diffident tone, "You are indeed a stoic, well-learned man, General. But, pray tell, was the Tagliafichi noble family of import? I heard reports from legionaries." It seemed the Governor was not eager to reveal the massacre of the Lanuzas, yet. "Truly dreadful."

"The Tagliafichii formed one of the cardinal links between the government and nobles of Vencenza, given late dónno Tunèin's prestige as a senator."

"Supposedly, dónna Lurèinsa Tagliafichi was the sole survivor," I remarked as we neared a plexus of shaded canals.

"Disgustingly delighted with the demise of her purportedly *beloved* atále sángua[95] whom she so *bitterly* moans over despite triumphant shivers." Lurèinsa all but wept in my arms when she learned of her abusers' death—her brothers had forced the girl to 'partake' in her family's revolting exploits. "Ungrateful, dirty shrew just like her sullied miscarriage of cre*at*—"

"OPEN YOUR DAMN *EYES*, FOOLS!" a voice squalled. My attention shot across the courtyard towards a young man arrayed in plum shades. *"Don't you see the rebels've been right all along?"*

My ribs clenched as a murder of crows swooped down, restraining him. A Guard walloped him across the throat with his baton. A woman in a buttercup gown and vólto jumped from the crowd and thwacked the soldier on the back only to suffer the same brutality. Shouts of discontent rose from the clustering of masked citizens at once, amidst which *'pigs!'* and *'scum!'* soared. Four men dashed for the crows, wresting the woman in yellow from their grasp who wrung a bystander's fashion cane from his grip and delivered it harder than any baton to the back of a soldier's head.

Blood surged hot and electrified against my arteries.

The crowd jostled me, one half scrambling to flee, the other—to resist the soldiers. I saw familiar workers' faces dotting the crowd.

A thick hand gripped my elbow. My guts heaved, in knots. "This is no place for you, mèus dáma." He didn't know who I was.

I wanted to tear free, but the *tick* of loading crossbows fractured the milky sky, Manuele's repulsive hand tightened, and my heart winced in powerlessness.

My feet pivoted to carry me after the General.

I lurched when a passer-by bodied me.

Manuele's hold on me slipped.

"Oh!" Slim arms caught me, gloved hands guiding me back onto my foothold. Within a blink, I saw a colombína, a cavalier hat, brown skin, and eyes such a vivid hazel they thawed flesh from my bones.

---

[95] Literally *'blood family'*. 'Atále' on its own does not denote a family related by blood.

Blood drained into my soles. *Cesare…*

Nonono what are you doing here?

A wanness touched his cheeks. "Please forgive me." Hardly a breath. Soft lips pressed a kiss to my wrist and his slender fingers unhanded mine. *No! Stay with me!* My hands shot thoughtlessly for Cesare's inky tabarro yet clutched empty air as he slipped into the crowd.

Tremors grasped hold of me, sweat coating my palms, but I was dragged away.

ILENIA ALWAYS TWITCHED WHEN OUT OF SIGHT, scurrying around with her books all overwrought and squirrely.

There were no windows in the Athenaeum, so alchemy poured down soaring bookcases and across polished wood tables and floors, turning everything into slabs of chocolate.

Hidden by her mirror-veil, Rosalia stood a few paces from the mahogany table onto which the Magister dumped a humongous tome—something about magic—and flicked through, muttering under her breath with her back hunched.

She suddenly froze. Stood. Threw circumspect looks around herself, brows shoved together.

Her palms ignited with a chain linked from light.

"*Show* yourself!" She swung. The air seared in front of Rosalia who hopped back in the nick of time.

Ilenia scowled as she looked around her Athenaeum and began flogging the air.

Rosalia scurried off and sidled into a tiny slit in the wall between some bookshelves, finding herself in the tunnels. *These don't look like the ones we use to come and go…* Curious and undaunted, Rosalia decided to trek on lest slipping back into the Athenaeum gave her other cheek a burn.

Wails echoed through the stone.

A pair of Imperialíi in their obnoxious yellow armour dragged a man past the mouth of the tunnel.

Rosalia followed.

The man squirmed helplessly a step ahead of her. Tears and bloody snot streamed down his face. *So odd that he cannot see me.*

The girl threw her head around the stark eburnean walls as she trailed the soldiers' descent, taking in the countess turns, the too-few details, through the mesh face covering of her veil. A shard of magical mirror glinted at both her cheeks.

The man continued to bawl and plead. *Gosh, he's noisy.*

Imperialíi took what became their final turn, and the mouth of the corridor gaped into an utterly gargantuan cavity housing a subterranean city—soaring high above and spiralling even deeper into the crust as if a corrugated drill had perforated the planet and titan miners jumped down to finish the job. Ribs of bridges and tunnels like bowed longbones overhung the abyssal drop. Syncytial multiplexes erected themselves along the ridges of the descending spirals. Twitchels veined between them. Bars obscured the too-high, too-small windows. Chains and locks gleamed on doors reinforced with steel.

The Trabeculae…?

The adults had always talked about Vencenza's dungeons!

Rosalia wondered if the chill frosting the oppressive gloom of the dungeons was azoth, or if the place simply lay too deep underground for warmth to percolate.

A griffin passed her by, pausing to peer around before moving on with hesitation. *Why is their uniform so fancy, anyway? All those swirls and sticky-outy bits.*

Rosalia elected to explore the stygian underworld.

SCENE XXXIII

THE VALLEY OF THE
SHADOW OF DEATH

Giordano | Giorgianna | Sarnai | Rosalia | Cesare

DAYLIGHT'S LUMINARY WAS ON THE DESCENT, yet Grand Judge Giordano Veronesi's paperwork crawled on.

Between pages, Giordano swirled his chalice of summerwine and sipped slowly to savour its pear-and-grape redolence. He generally favoured his pārijātaṁ-perfumed *Sōkaṛtaṁ*[96] or cranberry-steeped *Sarsán Aís*,[97] but the *Mngar-mo Char-pa*[98] had long since been on his extensive list of wines to taste. It did not disappoint.

The door to his office opened.

When the Grand Judge glanced up, the grim visage of Governor Crescenzo De Tullia loomed in the archway.

Giordano placed his papers aside. "Governor."

---

[96] Loyāṣa for '*Sorrow Nectar*', named on account of being perfumed with pārijāt—night-flowering 'jasmine' which floresce at night and close at dawn.

[97] Faustinian for '*Tenth God*'.

[98] Rtsanubmi for '*Sweet Serein*'.

Crescenzo shut the door and paced to the centre of the office. "Grand Judge."

"How may I assist?" Giordano imbibed.

"Rather clever you are, Giúdice," Crescenzo remarked, features leaden. "The nuances of your own law escape you not. I commend that. After all, why *should* my hand ever lay upon those records which denounce my rule?"

"You committed fratricide, nepticide, and *several* counts of assassinations," Veronesi named the Governor's crimes like the list of faceless victims it was to him. "To say *nothing* of the spates of blackmail, suborning, and forgery against both Vencenzani officials and the authorities of Salvatrice—*including* Governess Laerzia Della Rovere— just to attain your '*rule*'. How could I allow a man like *you* to tamper with my documents?"

"Hence I commend you, Giordano." Poison dripped off Crescenzo's iron tone. "You are unwavering and resolute."

Giordano's head ached just being in the Governor's presence. "I know what you seek." He drank again to soothe nerve and throat. "But you have nothing against my name, Crescenzo."

"Precisely why I'll have it erased." He unsheathed from around his waist a lòthmir smallsword, its steel fulgurant as levin.

Giordano laced his fingers. "My murder will incriminate you."

"Your murder will incriminate Magister Ilenia Farnese." Crescenzo's eyes flashed. "She *is* eternally indebted to you."

Giordano coughed. "You heard."

The Governor's gaunt jaw flinched. "Clever, *clever* fool, Veronesi."

Grand Judge Giordano Veronesi opened his mouth to riposte, but a cough tore from his chest. His ribs clenched tight enough to crush his lungs. He smacked a twitching hand over his mouth and coughed again.

Cold fingers came away smeared a deep red.

Poison…

Giordano stumbled out of his chair. The office blurred and doubled on his plummet to the floor. Ataxia seized his muscles, blood dribbling from his mouth as he convulsed, his eyes bulging at Crescenzo who stood still, seemingly no less speechless, and watched as the Grand Judge met his grizzly end.

A TERRACOTTA DISK BLAZED AGAINST THE SUNDOWN SKY where red began to bleed in, dripping down the façades of sandstone buildings erected across the aristocrats' quarter in Vencenza's north. Pale and rococo. Curlicued and vast. I detested the sight, knowing the sordid streets of the Court's deepest entrails. We were organs unwanted in this body, and I wished to cut it to pieces and burn it for forsaking Us.

We disembarked the gondoa, Barsotti and De Tullia beside me, and advanced for the Lanuza estate.

With hope held tight in my heart, I had worn, for the first time in this false visage of mine, the colour of my blood. A heavy skirt spilled to my ankles, slit down the length to bare my leg sheathed in black stockings and made fuller by a layered peplum overskirt. An ornate bodice corseted my torso, its sharp neckline plunging to my diaphragm, and over-top flowed a chiffon crimson pelisse strewn with gilt. The entire regalia glittered with garnets, as if a torn-out heart.

When we cleared the stairs, Manuele having joined, Imperialíi counselled us to look away from servants who scrubbed clean an ivory wall defaced with the epithet 'VÍTAM DI RIVOLUZIÓNE'. I recalled what Cesare had told me the night we sealed out blood pact, that he'd throw rocks at the walls of the senators' homes and the windows of the rich out of toothless protest because that's all he could do to purge the spite this regime left him with, lest he took it out on himself.

If only I could wrench those cleaning cloths from the servants' hands and shout treason right then and there.

"Disgusting," I muttered.

We entered the mansion.

Dozens of guests mingled beneath the eye-straining shimmer of chandeliers, faces hidden behind masks much like my own and the Ministry's.

Silence plundered the scene of noise as soon as eyes were laid upon the Governor.

He seemed the only one to ever wear the desaturated tones of ash and spidersilk, his pallid skin and black hair sapped all the more of life until he floated wraithlike through the bowing crowd. I was almost indebted to him for the stark deathliness of his visage, or to that dog Manuele with his blinding gold armour, for I dimmed beside them in my crimson—a colour so familiar to Vencenzanii. And anonymity was a cosmic power.

All the same, I caught the twitch of tension within De Tullia's hollow cheek. Sighted the faint flicker in his eyelid.

The varnish of his forbearance had worn down after long weeks of dissent, giving way to the cracks and fissures through which seeped wrath. I knew the crumbling of one's adamantine façade all too well. *Your resolve cannot be eternal, De Tullia.*

As restrained chatter trickled back in, he and Barsotti approached the centrepiece of the natálè: Basilio Lanuza. He wore the teal and purple of a peacock's feathers, an heirloom alexandrite gleaming at his chest. He bowed deeply to the Governor and nodded to the Adviser-Treasurer, beginning to speak of something I was no longer in earshot of. *None the wiser.* It was custom for the other members of the Lanuza family to arrive to natáli later. Too bad they wouldn't.

Music hummed, yet dancing was not permitted per *Sa Nóba Giustíca,* so sombreness hung in the atmosphere, a cold, foreboding fog, and I wished to snap every finger in that orchestra.

With trepidation, I noted the absence of the High Priest Benetto Abelli. Dafne assured that they would be present, and they *needed* to be for Sarnai to search their quarters.

I drew a deep breath, reined in my anxieties, and faced Manuele.

A gold colombína obscured his tanned face, his square jaw, sharp enough to cut diamonds with, fluttering when our gazes aligned. My thumbs twitched to plunge into his orbits and crush the swivelling azure orbs there.

I stepped nearer and compelled my hand to lay on his gauntlet. "Meet me within the valves of this house, General," I cooed sweetly. His eyes flashed, feral, and my flesh writhed as if gravid with larvae hatchlings.

Manuele took my hand and kissed it, his mouth repulsively warm. Acid singed my throat. "Your will, mèus dáma."

Flicking open a hand fan, so alike the ones my mother would beat me with, I fluttered it before my curved lips, and strutted into the glitz of the natálè.

I promise I will be his end, Ema.

We will be free.

I shall avenge.

SÓRA DAFNE MET SARNAI IN THE BASILICA at sundown.

The Magister's coazzoni and fuchsia gowns, tulle obscuring the face, proved a seamless disguise, made no less so by Sarnai's comparable height to Ilenia's, and so Dafne led her through the church without question.

The sóra's voice lowered to a whisper: *"The Domínie departed for the natálè just now. Their office is unoccupied."*

She cajoled the guarding Illutoríi to momentarily abandon their post and grant Sarnai passage inside.

A drum beat in her chest. *On borrowed time.*

The clock ticked and light faded fast.

Undoing several locks with a pick, Sarnai finally found records of the purification sacrament. Although she pocketed a couple exemplars, it was of information now known through hearsay. Their darkest knowledge remained unsubstantiated with ink.

Panic gripped tighter onto her shoulders as she paged through the archives, hands growing tremulous.

Spring suddenly flickered to late summer and Sarnai halted.

Blood thrummed in her ears.

She flicked back.

An entire handful of dates were skipped.

She perused the text, just to ensure the omission was not on account of something circumstantial.

Sentences cut off, unfinished, and the following text—across the chasm of missing turns—continued paragraphs that were never started.

Breath strained in Sarnai's lungs. Her stomach churned.

She shut and locked everything, then bolted from the office.

Around a bend, she rammed into a body.

Dafne gripped Sarnai's arms to steady her. "Did you find—?"

"It's gone!"

ROSALIA TIP-TOED AROUND GRIFFINS AND CROWS on the descent into the Trabeculae. A few Holy Guards floated about.

She found herself in a rusted hall flanked by tiny cages stacked atop one another, each filled with half a dozen prisoners. Bruises and cuts oozed on their gaunt faces. Rosalia scrunched her nose in disgust. Blood was vulgar to her. The stench of waste and sweat made it no nicer.

Hallway after hallway of the same ugly scene passed until the girl reached the base of the dungeons. *At this rate, they're hiding demons down here!* Rosalia ventured along the horizontal plane where stone walls turned to metal, steel locks became tungsten, moans and wails faded to a graveyard silence. Only legionary capes still susurrated.

Rosalia peeked into a double-glass viewing window within a cell door, seeing a woman chained inside. Her white scalp lay stark where dark hair had been shaved near her left temple. An angry red hole perforated flesh. *You could probably look inside.* Rosalia had already seen a brain at Libitina's mortuary. It was shiny.

In her emaciated fingers, the woman gripped a veiny placenta. Her teeth sank into it, chomping stringy mouthfuls of meat.

Retching, Rosalia hurried off, waving her hands as if to swat away nausea.

Several turns later, inquisitiveness needled again and Rosalia glanced through another observation window. Two girls hunched inside. The first's skull had been sawed away, her brains exposed. *It really* is *shiny, huh?* Rosalia wondered what she was thinking as her protuberant eyes roved the floor.

A metal blindfold of some kind welded to the second girl's head—a strip of steel around the eyes and one over the skull connecting its front and back curves, the simulacrum of a fox moulded upon its front as if a strange mask. *Couldn't you just remove it? Doesn't seem very secure.*

Rosalia's vision shuddered around the edges as if somebody grabbed the world and shook it, oily perturbation she wasn't accustomed to pouring into her belly.

She shuddered and stalked on further, deathly curiosity leading her along like a kitten chasing a candy wrapper on a string.

Passages thinned and darkened. A damp stuffiness bore down as if Rosalia were a worm crawling through soil. Sneaking past some soldiers, she stole a glimpse into a cell.

A pale, freckled man with chestnut hair and beard sat inside, wearing a buttoned coral jacket and charcoal breeches, his celestite eyes glazed and vacant. In the corner across from him, a woman rocked back and forth in a rust-red vest and long-sleeved grey dress. Her golden-brown hair spilled haphazardly and citrine eyes bulged out.

Rosalia stared, an odd feeling she couldn't describe swelling in her chest. *My… parents…?*

Dashing back to the soldiers, she pinched from her apron's pocket a gear—Lissandri said to always keep clockwork parts on you because you never know when the time is right—and threw it as a distraction. Whilst the legionary rushed off to investigate, Rosalia swiped a key off some hangers, carefully opening the cell and slipping inside.

She pulled her veil off. "Mamo? Papo?"

Her papo's eyes snapped to her, widening in recognition.

CESARE RESPECTED PUNCTUALITY IN A PERSON; he didn't need to wait long for Ilenia to arrive at his booth in *Stalker's Barge*.

An unassuming grey tabarro and veil concealed Ilenia's zone-front gown, her face hidden behind an equally plain vólto.

The flesh of the living edifice recoiled against her being. *Unwelcome.*

'*The Owl of Wisdom herself,*' Cesare offered a switchblade smile as he signed on The Fingers, his mouth sore with the split bruise he took during the riot at those despicable Hanging Gardens. '*I admit my awe.*'

She removed her mask and sat across from him. Mismatched eyes measured him, one cerulean and one viridian. '*And I admit* mine *at meeting The Bauta in the flesh.*'

They exchanged obligatory tedium.

Ilenia dithered. '*You have never thought to practise diplomacy?*'

Cesare raised an eyebrow. '*Diplomacy?*'

'*Talk.*'

'*Talk to whom?*'

'*A giuratóre, representative, emissary, De Tullia himself.*'

Cesare filled the lapsing tick with the pointed drum of nails on the table. '*Talk about what?*'

'*Negotiate, Bauta.*'

His teeth set. '*Negotiate* what?'

'*Ceasefire—the cessation of this pointless battle; the torment and carnage it enkindles.*'

'*What is this battle's* point, *Magister? Whose torment is enkindled by it? Who becomes its carnage? By whom is it ‹enkindled›? What am I ‹negotiating›? My freedom? The freedom of the worker? What ‹ceasefire› when the firing squad is on one side?*'

Ilenia frowned. '*Could one not still negotiate should there be no armaments? Should one espouse a peaceful and decorous temper—*'

'*For what? To scrape at the barrel of respectability? Pander to the sad fucking sensitivities of oppressors? There is no* ‹talking› *between liberatory movements and draconian regimes; They do not* want *to negotiate and frankly I don't either unless it's a negotiation of* Their *dissolution, for* that *is the* only *means to cease the torment and carnage enkindled by this* ‹pointless battle›. They *can capitulate.* I *will* never.'

'*Do* you *not enkindle torment and carnage?'* she pressed. '*How many have* you *ended in pursuit of victory?'*

'*What does my* victory *entail, Magister? Why should I mourn those who are granted impunity to strike their bloody batons down at innocents?'* He leaned onto his elbows. "I need you to hear me." His hand grenade of a heart burned. "This could have *never* been a clean fight. This is revolution. Abolition." The old ballad of means and ends, as it were. "It will *never* be the duty of the subjugated to speak peacefully to their oppressors." And the resistance would live on for epochs after Cesare's passing.

Ilenia held Cesare's unyielding gaze. '*Then I wish to help you rid Vencenza of this reign.'*

He scoffed and sat back. '*You are just as much a spider to me as De Tullia. My trust in you is none.'*

Ilenia tugged up her sleeve, baring a Malefactor's Mark. '*You know what these stigmata mean—what they brand you as. You know how De Tullia came to be in power. I wanted no fellowship with the Ministry, but I became aware of his schemes which he now leverages against me. I wish to be free like you.'*

His nostrils flared. '*I wouldn't liken your motivations to mine.'*

'*But speaking in terms of* relativity, *I too wish for freedom.'*

Cesare shuddered as those words rang of Davide's. '*How does your assistance benefit my cause?'*

'*Clario's Guárdia is on my side.'* Ilenia's claim intrigued Cesare. '*Thus, I can assist you and your people in the takeover during the prison break.'*

'*How have the Adviser's legions come to be on* your *side?'*

'*I'm ensuring my security.'*

No doubt, observations of Ilenia rubbing shoulders with senators weren't coincidental. Cesare knew to tread carefully around those who craved the taste of power. '*The allied parties arranged to conduct an offensive on the government building are smuggler bands, lower ossíi affiliated with myself, some members of Antrum cadres, and, now, several worker committees. This information has been communicated to Centúrion Yòchaná.*'

Ilenia squinted. '*What is this ‹Antrum› really?*'

'*What is it to you?*'

'*I take great academic interest in The Court of Secrets; the enchantments taking centuries-deep root in lower óssium are an enthralling arcane art I wish to understand.*'

A click of the tongue. '*Has it ever occurred to you that not all knowledge exists to be universally procured?*'

Her brow indented. '*You advocate insulation of teaching?*'

'*You grasp the necessity of ensuring one's own security, yes? I advocate for the sanctuary of those most vulnerable to exploitation.*'

'*And you see in* me *a threat of aforestated?*'

"Always be wary of the upper ossíi."

Ilenia waited again, then her head dipped in a capitulating nod as she kissed her teeth. "I see." She raised her hands again, '*Regardless, I wish to be of aid this imminent díem crepúsca.*' Ilenia drew out a kidney dagger. "Blood is worth diamonds."

Cesare's stomach coiled up at the Magister's words.

Then he stood, routing for the exit.

"What are you doing?" Ilenia's voice came almost panicked.

Cesare only smiled. "Liberation is worth more." He tapped his tricorn. "Pleasure conducting business with you." And he slunk out of the booth and into the adjacent.

Iyad, Anukka, and Iseppa waited there.

Iyad eyed Cesare sharply. "Did you open your big mouth?"

"Blood on my hands," he mused as he sat across from the three.

Iyad groaned whilst Iseppa held back a titter. Anukka muttered something in Ahărla, Cesare only picking up on '*hălĕm*'[99] which Iyad had taught him.

Iseppa entwined her fingers into a hammock for her face. "Do tell, then, àngiulu."

Cesare went to speak.

The door crashed open.

Iyad exclaimed in time with Iseppa's burst of profanity, Anukka's sickle and Cesare's revolver brandished.

Sarnai slumped into the seat beside Cesare, head collapsing to the table. She clutched papers hard enough to forever dent them.

Cesare blinked at the woman.

She sat up once having guzzled enough air. "It's gone."

---

[99] *haw-L'YOHM*; Ahărla for '*grave*'. Literally '*death cavity*'.

The *second* POV of the
following chapter includes
a scene of *sexual harassment*.

Scene XXXIV

Pneuma

Rosalia | Giorgianna

"NEJ…" Rosalia's mamo whimpered. "Nej!" She crawled back, babbling in Vilhelmian, "*Forsvind*! Fjern det evige mørke![100]"

A griffin approached the observation window.

Rosalia threw her veil back on just in time.

He left, and Rosalia reappeared once more.

Her mother grasped her own head and continued howling.

"Why is mamo acting so?" the girl asked her papo in Vilhelmian, keeping her tones hushed.

"Leave, Rosalia," he droned.

"No! Tell me what's wrong."

Her mother kept sobbing, rocking, her father wholly unmoved.

Frowning, Rosalia shifted her papo's hair at his left temple, finding a scabbed perforation in the scalp. "They're putting things in your brain."

---

[100] **Translation:**
    'No… No! *Begone*! Remove the eternal darkness!'

"They take things out," her father corrected. "You must go away."

Rosalia stood up abruptly, not knowing how to sort through anything before her.

Her father's hands gripped her wrists. Frigid. "But you must free us."

She puffed her cheeks. "I don't think you can all fit under my veil, papo."

His pale blue eyes remained on hers, pleading, and she could've sworn *something* glimmered within their abyss. "*Free* us."

Rosalia didn't understand *why* she interpreted the request the way she did, or what prompted her to arrive upon such a morbid conclusion, but she reached into the pocket of her apron and slipped from it a snake-green phial of pills.

She handed one to her papo, then slowly approached her mamo as if a frightened animal, and fed her another. Her heart didn't sink when her parents' hands limped; eyes didn't sting when she stood alone in a cold cell surrounded by the dead bodies of those who had birthed and raised her. But a heaviness fell upon her shoulders nevertheless.

Libitina always said death was the great leveller. It didn't matter who you were—a peasant, a nobleman, a soldier, a human or iridite or someone else—you were flesh when you died, and flesh was the same.

Rosalia went for the door.

It swung open.

She pressed herself against the wall as four Guards barged inside, cursing about the unlocked latch and the dead inmates.

Rosalia slipped by.

Just past the threshold, a shard of mirror studding her veil caught on the intricate filigree of an Imperiálus' pauldron, pulling the cloth free.

The soldiers' eyes centred on the intruder.

IT STRUCK ME just how precisely Basilio's office at *The Crescent* was modelled after that of his mansion. The pear wood and ianthine velvet, the nephrite armchairs, the air pristine with pine—as untouched as the rows of books poised along sweeping shelves.

The sweeping shelves I now scoured alongside Araya, having already searched the bureau.

Displacing a tome bound in white snake skin, I shoved into the case, pawing something peculiar. "Hold on…" Lifting a loosened plank of wood, I grabbed hold of… *paper?* I pulled it out. *Yes.* The stack of documents was scrunched to a terrible condition, yet the ink was legible. "Correspondence…?" Araya leaned over my shoulder. "With the Governor!" My hands trembled as I flicked through, eyes darting to the clock, the door, the pages, the ink.

> PROCEDURE:
>> …transorbital lobotomy as a method for emotional erasure may replace the preferred transcranial leucotomy for purification sacraments wherein lengthy delivery is unfeasible…

I read on in curious horror:

>> …transorbital delivery has been correlated with an increased risk of failure, notably including subjects:
>>> SORIANO, Calliupa;
>>> …
>>> DAMIANI, Ludovico…

My heart stopped. *No…* I couldn't breathe. Not my father. *How many more times would these demons take from me?*

Tears singed my eyes, but I pushed on.

> NOTE TO DÓNNO LANUZA, Basilio:
> Your knowledge of this must not be made known to ABELLI, Benetto as they presently forbid the utilisation of their research.

> AIMS (*elaborated under* SCOPE):
>> 1. Conditioning.
>> 2. Re-education.
>> 3. Treatment.
>> 4. Prospective.

SCOPE:

As per 1: Legionaries.

> Enhancement of military operations through annihilation
> of emotional response and the fostering of compliance.

As per 2: Dissidents; criminals of minor offences.

> Reintroduction of offending persons
> into society as low-risk citizens.
> Separation of the inmate from
> the inciting factor: EMOTION.

As per 3: Psychiatric asylum patients.

> Mobilisation of lobotomy for the treatment of schizophrenia,
> psychosis, depression, anxiety, insomnia, personality disorders,
> and otherwise-specified psychiatric aberrations.
> Separation of the patient from the
> pathological source: EMOTION.

As per 4: Populace.

> Ridding oldtown of its hex.
> Fostering compliance to the regime.

"*Holy Three…*" Araya's shuddering whisper sounded behind me.

My vision tunnelled as I shoved the documents into his chest. "Take these; get Rosa and leave." I turned for the door. "We shan't be returning to the ministerial house."

Dying glimmers of sundown seeped through sweeping lancet windows and across cream tiles in dark shades of lividity on my route down a too-tall, too-long gallery towards the mansion's ballroom. Blood beat at my temples, my veins alight, yet a slab of ice sat in my vitals.

When I turned down a hallway leading into a parallel corridor, a voice of thunder called the name of the Adviser's niece, and my skin crawled with goosebumps.

I steeled my nerves, *one last time*, and turned.

Manuele ambled for me, his mask doffed, his shoulder-sweeping hair all but wrought of golden thread. A glowing war god in sumptuous filigree and velvet. Everything about him was hideous to me.

"Signór." I curtsied with a sweetened lilt.

Predation flashed by his eyes. "Mèus dáma."

He rose to three inches over six feet, I was sure. A matching height to Ygal, and yet I'd never felt so imperilled near that woman, nor beside the tad-shorter Yòchaná. Manuele's mere being violated.

I lay my fingers gently on his breastplate despite his olid musk turning my insides. "The basilica is empty of all Illuteríi and Illutoríi on díem crepúsca, yes? For the Order's holy disciples disperse to the city's peripheral chapels for liminal worship."

The General's blond brows jerked. "Indeed."

I toyed with my tresses, half-loose in an intricately braided arrangement. "I wish to meet you in the presbytery of that grand edifice at nine hundred the díem crepúsca of the coming week." *The morning of the prison break.* I held the reminder to my heart like a promise.

Manuele's large hands gripped my waist, hauling me hard against a wall to pin me there. The blue of his eyes blazed into sulphur fire, so scorching it turned me cold. I almost shrieked for help.

He leaned intolerably close. "What are you trying to do to me, Salomé?" Hot bile rushed into my mouth as his nose pressed into my hair to breathe me in. "You smelled of lust at the Gardens," he growled. "When that lowly wastrel handled you like a bitch would." For an eyeblink, the scum's assertion that what I felt for Cesare was 'lust' enraged me enough to burn away my fear. "Cock-teaser nymphet." His hardness pressed against me and I just about gave up a retch. "I'd have you moaning my name all through the night, Salomè. You'd stink of lust through the skin beneath me."

Nausea thrust down my throat, but I gulped down the acid coating my mouth. "Surely one cannot be so hasty," I cooed. "Hold off." My hand snaked around his shoulder towards his neck. I wanted to snap his spine, to rip free the muscle and bone under my clammy palm, but instead I drew my face close to his ear, his height awkward. "*Fruit tastes sweetest when most ripe but yet to rot.*" I wanted to kill myself.

A keening scream shoved Manuele off me.

We glanced at each other and rushed to the ballroom.

Beneath the gilded railings of the balcony we emerged on, tense conversation swept the hall. At the navel, Basilio was doubled over, releasing intermittent screams of agony.

Manuele grabbed a passing man's biceps. "What's wrong?"

Even with the vólto, I knew the unsuspecting stranger turned pale. "*D-dónno Basilio just heard of his family's massacre. All but him are gone.*"

You cruel bastards. Of all the times to spring that on a man.

My eyes roamed the crowd. The High Priest lingered there in bright reds and golds, yet Adviser-Treasurer Clario Barsotti did not.

"Uncle…" I spoke aloud. A pit opened in my gut. "I must find him; I worry!" Before running off, I grasped Manuele's elbow. "Promise me we'll see each other next díem crepúsca."

He held me with an unreadable regard, then nodded.

I bolted back into the estate's depths.

Rooms whirled past me in a wild cantastoria until I stumbled to a halt at the threshold of an old reading room, the door of which was open.

Yóchaná stood at the distal bookcase.

Ilenia sat in a velveteen armchair the colour of lavender, Clario's courtsword in hand. Blood slid off its blade.

On the floor at her feet, Clario lay, rended chest feeding blood into the sumptuous carpet.

"Ilenia…" I drawled, pulse pounding my gut. "What is this…?"

"Think of it as a favour," she monologued coolly. "Organising an escape route the way you arrived would hardly be sensible—far too many moving pieces to synchronise in too-little time."

"So you are framing me for Barsotti's murder instead?"

"Clario was irresolute. Spineless. His pacifism could only ever be a hindrance to us. Your framing will disperse suspicion; give the authorities a solid lead on the recent murders. *And*, dare I say, the General shall be more than willing to meet you in the basilica come the prison break day, since he'll suspect *you* as the source of his torment. Several compromising intermediates are omitted this way."

She continued: "My Guardíi—" *yours?* "—are patrolling the perimeter of the Lanuza estate to-night. Leave the building via the rear doors. I will issue the report; the Guardíi on duty shall testify to our benefit."

I opened my mouth, eyes narrow. "Right…"

Ilenia slid the bloody sword across the floor towards me. "Kind regards." Her features were impassive, and I knew our trust of the Magister could run no deeper than a puddle's surface.

ROSALIA'S HEAD SWAM when her heavy eyelids lifted.

From a blur, an unfamiliar chamber slowly sharpened.

Ivory walls immured Rosalia, their bricks traced by that strange glittery frost, the reinforced door glaring at her with a double-glazed observation window like the ones she'd been peeking through. *I wonder how long I've been here.* She didn't remember what happened after the soldiers saw her.

Rosalia went to stand but leather straps pinned her wrists to a chair's armrests, her ankles restrained to its legs, and unfamiliar fear wormed under her horripilated skin.

The door unlatched and opened.

Two Illutoríi in crimson garb forwarded inside.

Behind them, High Priest Benetto Abelli trailed, a pair of Illuteríi flanking them and another two Illutoríi guarding their back.

"Lília," the Domínie spoke in that smooth, mellow tone, their gloved palms opened ceilingward. "Dél'ì lùtius e vísus benedétti." Two of the Illutoríi departed, shutting the door.

Rosalia glanced askew. "I don't feel very *blessed*, frankly."

Benetto took from an Illutóre a pink-red cloth turned inside out. "What of this?" *My invisibility veil! Give it!*

"Shawls like that are very common for servants of wealthy Ithilweni households to wear. It allows us to be unnoticed whilst we go about our servetile duties."

"Gazaari bitüü khatgamal satin stitch technique on zeegt naamal appliqué," they described the veil. "One of thy guards is of Jegün Kəgər hailing, sooth?"

"Sarnai sewed it for me."

"To eavesdrop on thy dónna?"

"To not be a disturbance to her, as I said." Rosalia grew annoyed.

"Thy shoes belong to the servants of this house."

"The maids were kind enough to offer them to me."

"By what impetus?"

"I'm used to being quiet."

"A blithe child." Benetto's eyes narrowed. "Wherefore didst thee venture beneath the house?"

"I… turned down a wrong corner and got curious?"

"Perturbation be not thine. Blood of thy progenitors cools upon thy hands, yet neither *guilt* be thine."

"Papo asked me to free them."

"Whither didst thee learn the connotation of a word so tremendously abstruse?"

Rosalia's mouth hung open for a moment. "I don't know…?"

"Thou feel little."

"Maybe, but I don't feel *nothing*. It's just… dampened…" Her fists and teeth clenched. "But I feel!"

Benetto leaned down, observing Rosalia through their gilded aperúcca, their eyes bottomless. Black. "Dost thou know the illimitable dimensions of the transcendental condition upon the expunging of the defected mind?"

Rosalia frowned. "What…?"

They stood. "She sees not." Their scarlet mantel whispered as they turned for the exit. "Not yet."

"Wait! What does *that*—?" Rosalia exclaimed as a needle pierced her shoulder, as an injection cramped her muscle.

"The Lanuza estate awaiteth our attendance. Permit no Imperiálus admission here."

Rosalia wanted to question them further, but her vision skewed and sleep stole her.

BELLS. BELLS. BELLS.

I had been there before, belfries denouncing discontent.

The Adviser was dead.

The Governor's most loyal nobles were dead.

And I ran beneath a bloody sky through the blackening warrens of oldtown.

Swerving sharply down a capillary, an incorporeal force stopped my burning legs as if a sweep of gelid water.

A man lay beside the canal. A woman crouched on her knees beside him, unmasked, hands sunken into his opened stomach from which she removed pieces of insides and to feast on.

She turned to me, and I saw her face for the first time. Rounded nose and dainty lips slathered in blood, the sunless pallor of cheeks and the slick blackness of hair as if woven of shadows.

Her head tilted, black voids of eyes opening like cosmogyral maws. "ALL WERE ONE, AND WILL BE AGAIN." She stood. The dark waters of caliginosity rippled against her, streamed between her fingers, trickled through her hair. "SHE COMES LOOKING FOR US."

I gulped down gasps, the stitch in my side unravelling painfully. "You called yourselves 'the magnum opus of the Gods' child'. The 'God's child' is Abelli, and *you* are the 'perfect' outcome of their purification sacrament, right?"

"YES, BUT INCOMPLETELY; ALLEGORICALLY. WITH A POWER TOO GREAT TO CONTAIN, WE FLED OUR CONFINEMENT."

"You claimed to be 'the vessels of the Many Faces' divine simulacrum tasked with a mission to complete upon this faceless circle'."

"SU CONFELLÓRUS FAÍTE COÌRE," she intoned.

"The fragmented shall coalesce," I repeated.

"WE ARE FRAGMENTS OF THE DIVINE GODHEAD. NOT SEPARATE CREATIONS, BUT TETHERED BY SPIRITUAL TRUTH, THE UNCTION OF ILLIMITABLE KNOWLEDGE. DIVINE GODHEAD IS COSMOS, NOT BEING. THUS, WHOLE, WE ARE COSMOS, WE ARE ILLIMITABLE AS THE TRUTH ITSELF. WE ARE INCORRUPTIBILITY. IMMATERIAL. WE YEARN FOR COALESCENCE."

And so she was eating the man. They were not separate beings, but, through the cosmos, a fragmented whole, and now she held his shadow weaving in her grasp. She had ingested his azoth. *And there are only two ways to ingest azoth.*

She continued, "WE WHO CAN SHED THE CHRYSALIS OF CORPOREALITY AND TRANSCEND THE VEIL OF THE FIRMAMENT—OUR HYLIC CONFINEMENT—ARE VERY FEW, AND THE GODS' CHILD IS THE GODS' *BRAT* BLINDED BY THE BRILLIANCE OF FALSE ENLIGHTENMENT."

"Blindness in pure light," I breathed.

"SHADOWS SPEAK TRUTH," she completed. "SHADOWS LOOK DOWN UPON THE LIMITLESS REGIONS OF THE WATER; THE WATER OF THE SKY AND THE WATER OF THE EARTH PROJECT APART THOSE SHADOWS TO THE MATERIAL EYE LIKE MIRRORS. FLESH IS GODHEAD; GODHEAD IS COSMOS; COSMOS IS WATER; WATER IS SHADOW; ALL—IT KNOWS."

I squinted. "You say 'we'."

"SHE IS A PNEUMATIC ENTITY."

Realisation tumbled behind my eyes. "Would a lobotomy make me like you?" Is that why those shadows inexplicably drew me to The Rams?

"YES," she stated simply.

I swallowed. "And every failure of Abelli is not?"

"*ALL* MATERIALITY IS AFTERBIRTH OF THE COSMOS, THUS ALL CAN, AND OUGHT TO, COALESCE WITH THE AZOTH OF THE UNIVERSE. IT'S WHY MORTALS DIE. EVERY FAILURE OF THE GODS' BRAT IS FAULTY IN ITS ASSEMBLANCE; CORRUPTED IN ITS INITIATION. EVERY FAILURE OF THE GODS' BRAT IS A PRISONER OF BLIND THOUGHT."

"What makes them so?"

"LOBOTOMY ITSELF. IT IS AN ERRONEOUS METHOD EFFECTIVE ON ONLY FEW. THE GODS' CHILD IS BUT ALLEGORICALLY SO; WE ARE *ALL* THE GODS' CHILD—CHILDREN OF COSMOS."

That must be why The Rams were so liberally able to traverse The Court of Secrets. They *knew*, and thus corporeality moulded around them akin to water. Cardea's hex *recognised* them.

"All those months ago—" I kept realising "—you told me: 'when her skin is torn, stitched like a marionette, hair weaved into thread anew, will she, upon that silver looking, see her face?'… That was about *now*, wasn't it? About my disguise in the ministerial house."

"YES."

"You see the future."

"YES. BUT NOT BEFORE THE PURIFICATION SACRAMENT." *The Third Eye's opening.* She shifted hair from her left temple, revealing a healed perforation in the scalp. "IT TORE THE VEIL BETWEEN THE REALM ABOVE AND THE REALM BELOW; NULLIFIED THE LIMINALITY OF LEARNED CRAFT AND BORN FACULTY."

'…*the severance from rebirth in illimitability is merely an amniotic membrane impregnable orbitally.*' And Davide… '*Cardea served you well… Her azoth is a relic of a sorcerer possessing an illimitable capacity for transmutation—unimpeded by that pesky little occlusion in the fleshbearing nous. Transcendental … Where do you think her 'Three-Eyed' epithet stems from?*' He had known…

"'Find hidden words spat by the blest to this plane from the celestial lazulum," I quoted, "sentenced to quietus beneath the soffits of a suzerain's keep. The overlord shall be defied—impart succour'. What does that *really* mean?"

The woman's neck crooned. "SHE KNOWS."

I frowned to the cobbles. "…The '*hidden words*' are the documents I found to-night. '*Spat by the blest to this plane from the celestial lazulum*' as in… 'given material form—written out—by the High Priest as a mistranslation of a twisted ⟨Illutèri⟩ doctrine'. '*Sentenced to quietus beneath the soffits of a suzerain's keep*'… 'Sentenced to death beneath the eaves of the king's—De Tullia's—house'. The Lanuza estate is an extension of the dogmatic regime."

"YES."

"How is it that I understand you now?"

"SHE KNEW NOT. NOW SHE KNOWS." She stepped back, and despite everything, what struck me most was the sudden normalcy of her—mechanical rigidity now smoothed to humanity. "WE CANNOT GIVE THE GODS' CHILD WHAT THEY SEEK. THERE *IS* NO PROPHECY—THERE ARE LIMITLESS FUTURE REALITIES. THERE *IS* NO IMPARTING DIVINE KNOWLEDGE UPON ANOTHER—IT MUST BE ATTAINED BY THE SELF."

From beneath her trigonic garment, she slipped a gold axaxún, *stabbing god*, its lobed guard encrusted with rubies to resemble eyes. "BUT FRAGMENTATION IS NOT A STATIC CONDITION." She stabbed herself in the abdomen.

I sucked a breath, watching the woman rive herself without a wince, without an indent to her countenance. Blood spilled into her hands as she cut out a hunk of her liver and held it out to me. "ALL WERE ONE, AND WILL BE AGAIN."

My eyes bore into hers with an understanding of what she intended for me to do.

I hesitated, yet she didn't falter, didn't stumble or keel in pain even as blood dripped to the stone.

So I snatched the flesh and ate it.

Light blinded my vision and I saw the throne of skinned hands again, each palm sprouting an eye.

Deep oak.

Pale as ice.

Bright azure.

Black like blindness.

A murky wash of grey and green.

A chimeric smear of viridian to cerulean.

Dark brown shot through with a blue streak.

Seven eyes.

And I recognised them:

De Tullia.

Veronesi.

Dioli.

Abelli.

Alagona.

Farnese.

Barsotti.

The palms closed, crushing the eyeballs within them to viscous gore. All but the centrepiece—black as blindness. *Abelli's eye.*

Its membranous eyelids shut, then peeled open. Its irises had split into triplets, arranged in a triangle. *Tribúcce Faciáe. The Third Eye.*

And yet, they were not black, but oaken. *De Tullia.*

The rulers were veneration of the corporeal—of power, avarice, ownership. To attain true enlightenment—freedom—was to *transcend* materiality; transcend erroneous pedagogy. Thus, to achieve freedom was to excise the cancer of pharisaic ignorance from this flesh, to destroy hierarchy, state violence, the very people who paraded themselves as our saviours. To eat the flesh of kings.

Everything had a meaning…

Light snuffed out.

The street returned.

The woman lay dead on the stone, intertwined with the man, sclerae burnt—wholly black as if the cavernous pupil had devoured her irises.

Azoth pulsed in the air, swaying with the shadows, anchoring me to the fluid and fragile material of reality, crisp and sharp.

And I *recognised.*

SCENE XXXV

THE KNIFE I TURN
INSIDE MYSELF

Giorgianna | Kel-Kech

"DE TULLIA VIEWS PERSONAL AFFECTIONS AS A DETRIMENT to the upstanding nature of citizens and leaders. By what other means could personal affections be eliminated if not through the erasure of emotion?"

I paced the sparring chamber of the forgotten art gallery where paintings of flowers and landscapes hung, where alchemical lights glowed in shades of candlefire. My hair was curly once more, my flesh untailored, my corset and hitched skirt donned over a white chemise.

The twins gathered with me. Ygal and Lucrezia. Sarnai. Isaia. Cesare.

I inhaled tightly, yet the pounding in my chest did not abate. "De Tullia does not care for Abelli's wish to preserve their research for the church alone. A successful lobotomy, like The Rams, could facilitate the obliteration of Cardea's protective hex on oldtown and therefore grant legions access to The Court and its inhabitants. De Tullia aims to finish what Last Emperor Mirone Nascimbene Evangelio started." My throat dried. "De Tullia wishes to 'cleanse' The Court."

"Ilenia expressed her supposed 'academic interest' in The Court and its magic," said Cesare. But I did not look at him. "She questioned me about the Antrum. I refused to humour her, I refused to sign away my blood to her, but I wonder to what extent this sort of knowledge may appeal to *her*."

"What you told me, about her attitude towards negotiation… It has always been *Clario* who voiced such sentiments, against which Ilenia railed, and why she ultimately did away with him." *Never put faith in a politico…*

"These whispers need to be made known," declared Cesare, fidgeting with his single hoop earring upon which chimed triplet coins.

"Consider it done," said Lissandri, offering Eligio to follow him. Eligio's jaw flickered, and he stormed past his brother, leaving the chamber. Lissandri followed with a tight, darkened farewell.

"Where are Araya and Rosa?" My voice trembled when I asked.

"Haven't returned yet," informed Sarnai, her tone jumpy, "but neither were reported to be at the citadel."

I couldn't level my breathing, couldn't still my heart. *Gods…* "We are so many numbers short." Terror washed over me, impelling me to grab hold of the cluttered table's edge. Sarnai soothed me.

"Leone and Valentina expect us in about four hours," Lucrezia gritted, "but I suggest we foregather in our district in two."

Ygal sighed, expelling cigar smoke half in disgust. "Leone put forth a dress code. Come dressed to impress or don't come at all."

Cesare tutted. "*I'd* rather not come at all, but everyone here bar Isaia *does* know how to impress."

Isaia made a face.

"All right," snapped Lucrezia. "I've had enough of this. Time to rest my eyes before I'm forced into Leone's company." She rushed for the exit with a pointed *click* of heels, Ygal sighing before following.

Sarnai hugged me, kissed my nose, and forwarded out almost sombrely, Isaia close behind.

The click of a deadbolt marked an exodus.

Oppressive silence invaded, and I finally braved to look at Cesare.

He stood almost rigid, almost nervous, his billowing shirt white and ruffled as ever, tucked into tight black trousers and knee-high boots. At his hips sat a second belt—a baldric housing his revolvers, stilétti, sabre. A tie bound his hair, bangs fallen loose and untidy around sculpted cheeks.

Yet I couldn't steal furtive glimpses of his lips without seeing the gash throbbing red and rough there. And I couldn't hold his gaze without wishing to scream the most horrid confessions at him.

Cesare crossed his arms. "So what does the princess request of me?" His tone cut. "Or does she simply wish to stare?"

A surge of heat filled my cheeks.

And he didn't know. He didn't know that I loved him. But how selfish was I, after all my cruelty, to think he might love me too?

I tore from the melee rack a rapier. "Spar with me."

Cesare blinked, but unsheathed his sabre.

We circled. His limbs were tense, I could see. Mine were too.

"The shadow moves as the sun commands, indeed," I mused.

Cesare half-smiled despite the world—a haunting gesture. "And either side of a coin itself has innumerable faces."

I bolted for him. "I never expected *this*." His blade met mine. "I never foresaw the horror of the wisdom withheld by that kingdom."

"We never lost sight of *one* thing." We passed back and he reprised. "Power corrupts."

"So I ask *again:*" I blocked, "who's to say *we* are beyond corruptibility?"

"I don't want power," Cesare spoke as we circled each other once more. "I want this rotting fucking corpse to burn."

My head tipped. "What matters most?"

"Freedom."

"But does it, if you are completely alone?"

"Does *life* matter?"

I frowned. "Yes."

"Thus, freedom must necessarily matter."

"And if the bid for freedom *takes*—" I swung "—one's life?"

He ducked under my strike and sidestepped. "The bid for freedom is not bound to a singularity." I avoided his kick to my shin and brought my sword in a downward arc which he caught. "Should it take the life of *one*, upon its gravesoil the life of many more abides."

Levering my blade up, he shoved me back.

"But if life matters so *much*," I struck, winded, "and we speak not of the oppressor," he parried, "has freedom not been corrupted if it is the hand of murder?" I riposted.

Cesare's blade bound to mine. "What matters most, Giorgianna?"

My jaw clenched against the shape and sweetness of his voice around my name.

And maybe I *was* the crook. Maybe I *was* selfish, to be content with a life beneath the oppressor's boot if it meant the people I most fiercely loved could be alive with me. "Justice," I finally spoke, and my heart caved, so I angled my sword and offset Cesare's force, slashing for him.

"In freedom one finds justice." He parried near-instantly. "The two are inseparable."

I passed back, hauling lungfuls of air. "But, I ask, can the quest for those two ideals grow *corrupted*?"

Cesare's gaze fell to the timber as we, again, orbited one another like stars. "It's not beyond the realm of possibility." He slipped his cheek thoughtfully between his teeth, an act as familiar as his tongue-clicks and his restless fingers and his mordant laugh and the heat of his skin. "A part of me believes some people deserve to suffer—to rot in the dungeons or hang on a rope for their crimes. But... I understand too that one needs to be honest with themselves. And when I question *why* that part of me believes this, I realise it's a point of view rooted, first and foremost, in my feelings. I arbitrarily *feel* they deserve to suffer. But feelings are not merely an individual state of consciousness. They are a *system*: certain feelings are perpetuated above the rest; the feelings of particular societal sects are prioritised over others. And so, such reasoning is dangerous when there is no '*deserve*'. There is only '*necessary*'." His eyes, fire and cosmos, returned to me. "And is it necessary to kill a man who stole petty coin to keep himself fed?"

"Is it necessary to kill a man who stole another's right to choose whom to give themselves to?"

"Yes," said Cesare without pause. "He deserves to suffer. *I* think."

"Do *we*?"

"By what condemnation?"

I dashed and swung for him. "We are both *killers*!"

He parried. "Scratched skin and bloody hands as any good sinner."

I hopped back. *Gods, keep talking to me…* "Pride is the deadliest, Cesare."

He beheld me with an unreadable gaze. "Befitting a heresiarch."

"Even if it brings you agony?" I struck.

Our blades met, and we stopped, our eyes likewise clashed.

His chest rose and dropped. Warm breath caressed my lips. "There's a certain romance to misery."

Ramming his sabre, I struck. *Parry.* Strike. *Parry.* Strike. *Parry. Riposte.* I evaded his blade's path.

The curve of a revolver's grip flushed to my palm.

A pirouette.

The muzzle thrust into the centre of Cesare's chest. Just shy of where I'd shot him. Over his heart just *so*.

A gasp broke from him, the silence between us sundered only by the *clang* of his sabre against floorboards.

"Have you ever been honest with *me*, Cesare?" And my limbs ravelled into tremors.

His nostrils flared, head shaking ever so slightly. "Don't start."

"*Start*?" My voice boomed in the quiet of the gallery. "I was under the impression that we've *been* going!" I stabbed my rapier into the floor. "Does the reminder of every single time you told me half of nothing and a third of a lie spur *guilt*? Do I *gnaw* at you, Cesare?"

"Everything about you *gnaws* at me! I—" He inhaled sharply, turning away, but it did nothing to conceal the flash of such heart-rending pain upon his face that I wanted to weep. I only wanted to weep more when his eyes realigned with mine, when he told me, "I cannot lose you, Giorgianna."

"*Why*?"

"Am I to bite my tongue about Manuele of all fucking people? *Saints forbid* I express I care!"

"Like you *cared* all those turns ago?" I rammed the revolver's barrel against his breastbone. "When I demanded to know what you want from me, and you said you didn't want me to feel for you? After what you *did*, you *genuinely* think it would mean nothing?"

His jaw tightened. "I don't *want* anything *from* you, Giorgianna. I *need* you to *live*."

"SAY *WHY* THEN!"

"BECAUSE I *LOVE* YOU! *For fuck's sake*, is that what you want me to admit?" The words ripped into my chest hard as claws and opened it. My feet reeled me backwards, weak. "Do you want me to admit I lied? Well, I did—I lose *everyone* I love and if I lose *you*, I will never, *ever* forgive myself! Is *that* the 'why' you want me to say? Because you are the thoughts of my insomnia, the only reason I picked up my violin again, because I *love* you?" Cesare reclaimed his breath, "I would never try to stop you," his voice frayed, "but *I*-I can't—I *won't* let you walk away without knowing that if he takes you from me, I will rip his guts from his living body—"

"And I love you." My revolver thudded against the floor. A sharp inhale caught between my fingers. *Nonono*—I didn't want to speak those words aloud. "This wretched world reaps from me everything good I ever have but *Gods* I love you, Cesare, I *love* you, a thousand times over I love you." *And I cannot bear it…* I was ruin. A heap of torn-up guts. I'd let Love maim me, for I could define wanting in no measure but violence.

"…I'm sorry?"

"Are you *serious*?" Tears bleared my vision. "That's *it*? Don't tell me you and your big mouth are tongue-tied!" I marched towards him, halting close enough to see those star-flecked eyes. Blazing like nebulae and ruinous as a supernova and both a bottomless abyss each. Those eyes staring wide and stunned as if he *hadn't fucking heard me!* I smote him hard in the chest. "*Say* something, coward!"

"Kiss me back."

"What—?"

Cesare's hands slipped around my jaw and his lips snatched my words and startled whimper between themselves.

I clutched his sleeves, tasted blood, and it came back to me, that day beneath the rain before the sky fell.

My voice reeds bled with the urge to scream that I loved him again and again but *"You're an idiot"* was all I could breathe out before kissing him back desperately enough to convince myself he was vanishing.

Cesare reeled rearward in pace with me, rammed into the table, catching mid-fall a lit candle. My hands made deft work of the baldric weighing his hips, unlatching its buckles and flinging it to the floor along with its bastard blades.

"Maybe." Cesare hooked his arm under my knee and pulled me with him among the clutter on the table. His back thrust hard against the wall, waist nestled between my thighs, and his feverish fingers scaled my back to plunge into my curls like he'd waited his entire life to touch them. *"But I would burn down every empire at your command."* His hair unravelled from its bind in my hands, so thick it swallowed them. Lest I tear it, I slipped his earring out, and let my fingers chart his collarbones, chest, stomach, whilst my teeth nipped skin. Cesare groaned curtly against my mouth. It was pain. Then came the red taste of salt.

I snatched up a gasp as my head whirled from how nauseous love made me. Cesare's lips pressed to my cheek, jaw, neck, breastbone, as if, even through pain, he couldn't bear to not kiss me—*Gods, kiss me all over.* From the ruching of my skirt, I plucked a phial of ano-apozem. I threw it back, drenching my lips in it, and pulled Cesare into me again, drinking the blood from his lips as the soft flesh there healed.

A sharp gasp broke us apart again. *"I'm sorry,"* he breathed out with an anguished voice. His palms grasped my face, so hot they branded me, our eyes meeting in the candlelit dimness of nascent night. "I'm so sorry for doing that to you—for sending you into that place." Slender, gentle fingers urged curls behind my ear. "Please forgive me, I beg you."

I gripped his chin. "Say that you love me, and call me by my name."

There was almost nothing of his eyes but black.

"I love you, Giorgianna."

And I kissed him again. And again. And again. Each time with more desperation. I couldn't kiss him enough, couldn't touch him enough. His clothes, skin, hair, taste, his voice heavy and raw against my tongue—I'd yearned for such closeness for too long. Yearned for *him. Him, him, him,* only him.

I raked my hand through the clutter on the table and struck a box of cigars out of place.

Something thudded, the scent of flames imbuing the air.

My eyes snapped open.

Candlefire chewed at the table.

I yelped and kicked myself off Cesare.

We scrambled to throttle the flames with the black tulle curtains, a smoking char remaining to sully the wood.

Cesare strangled a laugh. "Way to spoil a moment."

"Shut up!" I punched his shoulder. "We nearly burned a table."

He toyed with my curls. "*You* nearly burned a table."

"Because of *you.*" I went to pry my hair from him only to be caught in his grasp.

He sat me up on the table, "I meant what I said about those bastard empires, Giorgianna," before kissing me the way a despairing man clawed for sanctuary at a church door. With reverence and plea.

"*My name on your tongue…*" Shivers rode down my limbs. "*I want to fall into you.*"

Cesare kissed my throat, "*fall into me, Giorgianna,*" my collarbone, "*completely,*" every singe of his lips trailing a begging susurration of my moniker along my skin until his voice stripped to nothing but shuddering breaths. "*I'll scream your name from the fucking rooftops if I have to.*" He leaned me backward, buttressing himself with one arm against gravity, and our lips pieced like bullet clips together, my hands in his hair, my nails gripping his soft cotton shirt to the skin. And he kissed me as if atoning for every instance he cowered. And I kissed him back, pretending I didn't want to break through his bone and have his flesh be mine. As if I didn't *shake* with how rabidly I loved him.

The door rattled.

"You seen my cigar—?"

My elbows skewered hard into the table as Cesare bolted off me.

Ygạl stood in the doorway, eyes circular.

My heart hurtled like an animal hunted for sport, blood blazing my face to tears and hands not knowing what to do with themselves anymore. *Cast you into the Null!*

Eyelids dragging into careful lines, Ygạl drawled, "…Sure," pointing to the table, "I'll just be getting my cigars…"

Opting to uphold civility, I sat up, snatching the canister and handing it to them.

They scrunched their nose. "What'd you two burn?"

My lips squeezed together. *Oh no.* I hadn't thought my face could alight any hotter.

"Are you *done*?" bit Cesare.

Ygạl eyed him askew. "*You're* clearly not. Consider me vanished."

She followed through on her word.

Cesare caught my gaze in the ring of silence.

We stared at one another for a couple heartbeats until a laugh compelled me and he joined in, sweeping me into his arms and spinning me into a sugar-sweet kiss. His warm hands cradled my spine and jaw, my fingers tangled in his hair, like the two of us merely pretended we could have each other. But even knowing there could be no destiny in which our names were written on the same line, I wanted to have him, if only for a blip in this cosmic cycle.

I pulled away from the kiss but not his body. Not yet.

My lips skimmed his cheek. "You know, perhaps disappointment is not your *strongest* forte."

He plucked his earring off the table, "I figured," and fleeted for the clothing hanger.

I gasped in a mockery of astonishment, palm flying to my chest. "The arrogance!" But the burn in my cheeks was real.

Cesare slipped on his waist-cut blazer. "You did wonders for my pride; one can hardly blame me."

I snatched his tricorn away and donned it myself, swinging on my jacket and throwing my arms loosely around Cesare's neck as we breached the threshold into the corridor. "How thy façade lies, bàuta."

His eyes narrowed as he slid his hoop back in, flushed lips crooked in an ascescent smile. "How *does* my façade lie, vólto?"

I nudged his chest. "You are shaking." *Do you love me as rabidly as I do you?*

He crossed his arms, eyes shut proudly—"Calumny!"—but the burn in his cheeks was real too.

A giggle scuttled from my lips. I ran on ahead, turning to face him as we walked. "What is 'enemy' in Marlâre?"

"Dushmayâ." *Fiván.*

We approached the staircase down to the rococo hall mounted with paintings of carnage.

"Rose?"

"Rrozakô." *Arròsa.*

I gazed at the heart gilding the ceiling. "Love?"

My eyes met Cesare's again.

He smiled. "Ne lo'êre kaliranè tu mirazê."

I halted, frowning. "I swear that… couldn't be one word."

He stopped in front of me. "One madman makes many madmen; many madmen make madness."

"Meaning?"

"A *lunatic* is thee, and one you'll make of *me*." Cesare kissed my cheek, rushing past me.

"Fiend!" I gave chase.

He descended the curving stairs backwards, one step ahead of me, hands pocketed, and tipped his head sideways, impudence cocking his mouth into a smirk. "But you love me."

My heart panged.

I locked my arms around Cesare's neck. His breathing stumbled.

"*But I love you.*" My eyes shut against the racing rhythm of his heart. His arms slipped tightly around me.

It really *wasn't* fair. Not one bit.

KEL-KECH SAT ON THE LOWEST RUNG OF THE MIZZENMAST, half-obscured behind sails loosened for cleaning.

Laughter lay hold of Kel's attention.

Giorgianna and Cesare returned to *Antigone* from the gallery, talking rathely about something, Cesare's tricorn atop Giorgianna's head and both of them equally taken with the other whilst they spoke. Cesare caught Giorgianna in his arms and snatched back his hat just before the pair disappeared out of sight, each little kiss they shared punctuated with such tenderness yet frantic urgency.

Kel felt like an intruder on a moment the pair thought they had alone, but she couldn't help lamenting Lorita no matter how much confliction the thought brought. And it only brought more, anyway.

"Can we get a move on?" Kel whipped around to find pale-haired Ren glaring expectantly at her. "You people're always in my business."

"Do you think I'm evil?" Kel queried.

Ren knocked ver head back. "I don't *care*…"

"No, shut up! Sit down."

Ren grumbled under ver breath but begrudgingly obliged. "This 's 'bout blondie?"

Kel tensed. "Don't call her that."

"She's a traitor," ve spat. "A *dead* one."

Kel's temper stung. "You don't know what I felt for her!"

A snort. "At this point, I'd like to know *why* you did."

Kel-Kech's eyes nipped. "I don't *know*, Risten. I don't…"

"Look…" Ren plumped for words that weren't merciless, Kel guessed. No wonder ve and Lissandri got along. "Sometimes you love people who're bad for you, but because you love 'em, you convince yourself their harm isn't bleeding you, even if it's bleeding you the *most*. I mean, how could you blame 'em? You love 'em, right? Well, I think love can be blinding and, sometimes, no matter how much you love someone, the pain *of* loving 'em isn't worth your sanity. I think *your* pain of loving *blondie* isn't either."

"Have *you* ever loved someone like this?"

"No."

"Have you ever *loved* someone?"

"No."

"Never?"

Ren snorted. "What, I look like the type?"

Kel leaned her cheek onto her knee and observed Ren. The deep-set rosen eyes and carved cheeks. The heart-shaped swell of rubicund lips. "A little bit."

Ren blinked. "*Uhuh…*" ve drawled with a dull look. "So can I *go*?"

"Yes. Gangans,[101] Ren."

"Whatever," ve muttered and grasped the rigging, all skilful grace and sinewy limbs as ve climbed up the mast.

"Kel."

Kel-Kech turned around.

Down on the deck stood one of the Commegno twins. The one with the shorter curls and working clothes beset in clockwork. The one with the scar on his chin. The asshole one.

Kel-Kech's shoulders went rigid. "Yes?"

Lissandri crossed his arms and approached slowly; near-timorously. "Can we… talk?"

Kel-Kech glared. "You've never been one to simply *talk* to me."

A sigh. "I know. And honestly that's what I want to talk *about*." He leaned against the mast. "I'm sorry. I took my frustrations with Lorita and this whole thing out on you, and that wasn't fair."

"Have you thought to interrogate *why* you took your frustration out on *me*?" Kel-Kech conjured up defiance, crossness, but in the end, she was so full of grief. "And you come to apologise *now*, once Rita is dead? Not when she was alive yet you could've still seen your error?"

"You were always so forgiving beside Rita. You never made shit difficult, or even really snapped at all." Lissandri's gaze fell pensively to the deck. "I guess I—"

"I guess you saw me as an easier target."

He frowned back up at her. "That's no—"

---

[101] '*Thank you*' in ǂAkxòi.

"Don't worry about it." Disenchantment weighed down her tone as she tucked her knees under her chin and gazed at the sea. "I always have been."

She felt almost ashamed to admit that she'd just about hid behind her little sister. Nū-Ûn was supposed to be the eldest, Kel always thought. The flame to Kel's tranquil waters. The tempest to her breeze. That's how she'd survived the assembly, and her sister had not.

The truth was that Kel-Kech never wanted any part in this, at least not the way she found herself now. That fire did not run in her blood. She could help fan it, help keep it burning, but never be the one to tear the kingdom down.

"You're not an easier target." Lissandri's voice came as gently as he could probably muster.

Kel-Kech turned to the younger twin again.

His sylphine features bore none of their customary whetted edges. "You are kind and sensitive. It's a feat to not succumb to hardness in circumstances like ours." He rubbed the scar on his chin. "Some part of me *was* frustrated with your loyalty to—almost complacency with—Lorita, yes, but… I get it? I mean, I'd lay down my life for Ces or Giorgi if it came down to it. They're my family just as much as Eli. And you had hardly anyone *but* Rita."

Kel-Kech's heart panged. "Am I a bad person for having loved her?"

Lissandri made a face. "No?"

"Was *she* a bad person?"

"Under certain criteria, perhaps."

"She was terrible to *you*."

"Terrible things happened to *her*."

"Terrible things happened to *you*, yet you…" But Kel's thought trailed off.

Lissandri's eyebrow quirked up.

She closed her parted lips. "Oh."

Lissandri lifted a shoulder. "It's a feat to not succumb to hardness."

Kel-Kech considered him, chewing on her snakebites. "I suppose I could consider forgiveness. Eventually."

He tugged on a crooked half-smile. "I can deal with that."

"Can we get a fucking *move* on, how 'bout?" Ren's exasperated appeal dropped from the crosstree above.

The man and woman looked up at the unamused androgyne.

"It's like you do it on purpose," ve huffed.

Kel-Kech hopped down to the deck.

Lissandri left her alone with a salute.

Cold ocean wind swept across Kel's neck, and the memory of Yewada's warmth struck her with deeper sadness.

She reflected on their conversation, observing the sorrow in her own heart. A sorrow for Lorita.

Rita…

Maybe Kel never yearned to be loved by One. Maybe she yearned for home. For the love of ancestral soil. For completeness.

SCENE XXXVI

REVENANT

Ygạl | Giorgianna | Cesare

A BIRD LAY DEAD ON THE PORCH OF THE BOAR ESTATE.

A dove.

Aengus grimaced. "Well *'at's* fuckin' disgustin'."

Its delicate throat was twisted backward, the thin threads of ruddy innards spilled from its gut's cavity now teeming with flies.

Ygạl's stomach turned. "Koşatlen culture greatly appreciates birds: sparrows, finches." She stalled. "Doves..." Many corners of Tokuzay were filled with cages and baths for those symbolic birds. Ygạl rolled his nazar earring between his fingers.

"Intentional, d'you think?" voiced Lucrezia. An off-shoulder ballgown with a layered campanular xhubleta the colour of the emeralds girding her throat clad her, its wrist-clasping sleeves loose and her hands gloved in velvet. Deep green shadowed her eyelids, her lips painted to match.

"Look at its state." Cesare's lip twitched at the bird Ygal knew he hated. "Not to mention fauna doesn't hang around the Antrum, let alone participate in the circle of life."

"So wha'?" Angus questioned.

"Seems like shit Lucanus'd pull," commented Isaia.

Ygal sighed. "Most favourable scenario, frankly." He faced Cesare. "Leone requests no firearms."

Cesare's eyes, shadowed with collyrium and lined with flicks of liquid kohl at each corner, spun.

Aengus glowered. "I don' know wha' I'll do if this falls through."

"It *won't*," gritted Isaia.

The ginger snorted. "Wha'ever." With a parting glare at Cesare and Giorgianna, Aengus entered the Boar estate.

Isaia shook his head. "Aengus hates Leone."

"Smart man," said Cesare before addressing the Dóminus: "What about Chiara?"

Ygal shrugged. "She's a lavìre at Valentina's *Amaranth Lounge*. Can't exactly do much about that."

Cesare's eyebrow angled keenly. "You believe she'll have no sway over Tina?"

"We'll have to hope Valentina has a head on her shoulders."

"*She* may."

Ygal's brows lowered. *This oughta be wonderful…*

THE VIPER'S DEN NEVER CEASED TO IMPRESS with its opulence. Shame the countless slaves clad in nothing but sheer tulle and the armed guards bulging with muscle churned my gut.

A familiar chiffon négligée swathed Leone's chiselled torso as he loitered by a floor-standing candelabrum beside the table parting two pink sofas. I detested the way he and his snow-scaled snake leered at me, so I crossed my legs and leaned into Cesare, running my fingers along the indigo-violet ruffled of his satin shirt—cinched at his waist by a black waspie. I'd worn the ensemble from Basilio's natálè sans the pelisse, pasting diamanté blood droplets beneath my kohled eyes, my lips glossed into a black cherry.

Valentina, dripping in amaranthine silk and gold annuli, requested her daughter, Ayana, to leave. The girl eyed Leone warily on her way by. Her cheek paled when Leone ran his tongue along his canine, and horrid alarm struck me.

"Summerwine, mèus fraúcni?" he offered Valentina.

The Domína's eyes wheeled. "I *said* you can shove your moonshine elsewhere."

"But *camítna*,[102]" Leone all but whined, "this is *precisely* the occasion to partake!"

"Take a 'no'!" my boiling blood forced me to snap.

His gold-coin eyes affixed me—polished and unreadable.

Lucrezia cleared her throat. "Is this not also *precisely* the occasion to partake in that bloodwine I was denied last time?"

The Serpent and the Hyacinth exchanged looks.

"Your guest requests bloodwine, Leo." Valentina smiled sourly. "As do I."

Leone sighed but consulted his endowed liquor cabinet. "Truly, you wound me."

"*I'll* have summerwine." Ygạl conceded.

"A woman of class!" Leone poured bloodwine for Valentina and Lucrezia, summerwine for himself and Ygạl, then smirked at Cesare. "Have I worn you down?"

"I'll throw that wine in your face and we'll regroup," Cesare said with utter nonchalance.

Ygạl shut their eyes and imbibed.

Leone chuckled, sugary and counterfeit. "Feistiness is becoming of you." I stiffened when he turned my way. "Mèus càra?"

The summerwine intrigued me, so I accepted the glass wordlessly.

"Isaia?" offered Leone.

---

[102] 'Beloved'.

"Not on the job."

"Exactly," Ygal gritted, staring the eavesdropper down.

After a split minute, Isaia beheld Leone. "Diluted."

Leone practically sparkled. "Marvellous!"

Whilst he took to watering down summerwine for Isaia, I brought my glass to my nose to inspect. *No scent.* I sipped; swished the liquid; swallowed; waited. *Nothing.*

"So!" Leone sat beside Valentina. "This prison break which shall be your decoy—on díem crepúsca next week, you say? Which parties are arranged to be involved?"

"Some Boars and Hounds," listed Cesare, "The Salt Hydras, Brass Teeth, Grey Pearls, federated citizens."

"And how much do you know about this 'Laútni' character?" questioned Valentina.

"They were imprisoned for connections to dissidents."

"And you claim the state is aware of The Antrum's existence?"

"Yes," I barged in. "I was informed by the Minister of Scholars, Ilenia Farnese, that Davide disclosed the existence of The Antrum and Smugglers' District to Manuele, and thus, by proxy, his Imperiálum."

Leone regarded me flintily. "You are in contact with a politico?"

"My trust for her is none; she is of use."

"The Antrum is not without hearsay about Farnese," Valentina said. "Her interest in the secrets of The Court is known and alarming, and seeing as she has a history here, it is *well* within our right to be concerned for our security."

"Undeniably," agreed Cesare, "but the *more* dire threat is that of the General and his Imperiálum. All they need to find The Antrum is easy passage through The Court."

Ygal cleared their throat pointedly, so I stepped in before Cesare could continue in that unbridled tone of his, "Through lobotomy, if the correct pathways of the brain are severed, an individual can bypass the limit of azothian transmutation, therefore allowing them to potentially manipulate or even *expunge* Cardea's enchantment protecting The Court and all which lies beneath and beyond it."

Leone smoothed his throat with a drink. "And how long has this endeavour existed? Longer than the flocks' instruction by Davide is old?"

"I do not know, but," I cleared an anxious lump from my own throat, "is it not consequential enough that it *exists*?" Coughs took me as trepidation wormed to my nerves. I gulped some wine and held a hand over my mouth.

"And Manuele Dioli?" queried Valentina.

"The morning of that díem crepúsca, I will—" Sticky wetness splotched my palm. I pulled my fingers away, seeing blood, and horror frosted my skin. *Bašmu Mē̄…* Ṣer'šādî venom. One of the deadliest yet most commonly-administered poisons, the one Aaron tried poisoning Dahlia with. The one I ended the Grand Judge with. '*If this were summer or goldwine, I might've been unable to identify it…*' If it affected *me*, then the dose was—

"Ygạl?" Lucrezia's cry stole my attention. He began to cough, retch, choke on the blood drizzling from his mouth. "*Ygạl!*" Lucrezia shook them as if she could save them. "*YGẠL!*"

They collapsed, face ashen, eyes rolled back and bloodshot. *Dead.*

Lucrezia screamed in helpless anguish.

"Let her fly high with her doves," Leone mused with a faint quirk to his glossy lips.

Cesare shot to his feet, daggers in hands. "Snake!"

Isaia, in turn with the Serpent guards, drew weapons. All the while, Valentina imbibed, botherless. *The bloodwine wasn't poisoned.*

Leone plucked a small flask from a trouser pocket. "We shall be merry." Blood coated his tongue when he placed a pill upon it.

Guards closed in around him.

Isaia and I locked eyes.

I was mithridatised and his summerwine had been diluted, meaning we had time but little. *We need to get Leone's pills.*

Cesare snatched a saltpetre pouch from his pocket and ripped it, showering the room with black gunpowder, and kicked the massive candelabrum.

Flames devoured the saltpetre and raged across the carpet, the curtains, the decor, swallowing Leone's quarters in moments.

The snap of Serpent necks harmonised with the crack of wood as I navigated the burning mansion. The fray had separated me from the others.

I'd unclipped my longer skirt to ease my movement, leaving the knee-exposing peplum behind.

With a bloody cough, I stumbled into a wide chamber. Its ceiling suspended aerial silks and hoops and trapeze bars.

Fire began to eat away.

Near the back, five servants huddled.

I bolted to their side. "You need to get out."

They pointed at one of them chained to the wall by the wrist.

'*We won't leave without her,*' one signed on The Fingers.

I studied the shackles. *No key.*

Weakness of creeping death weighed my limbs and bleared my view, but I faced the chained servant. "This will hurt, but it'll free you." She wailed formlessly as I shattered her wrist and hand until the mangled mess of flesh and bone flopped out of the cuff. I embraced the woman, soothing her as I reformed her bruised hand, before turning to the others: "Now *go*—!" A blunt force walloped me in the back.

Servants scrammed.

I turned. "Chiara!"

The freckled woman said nothing, jumping up on the trapeze as I swiped for her.

I hoisted myself onto the silks in pursuit.

She swung nimbly across to a hoop.

"All this to prove yourself a loyalist to The Antrum. All this to counter the 'threat' that was Cesare." My baselard bound with her akinaka.[103] "Yet all for *nought*!" I shoved.

---

[103] Also transliterated as '*akikanes*' or '*acinaces*'; a long double-edged dagger of Scythian origin dating back to first millennium BCE.

Rage flamed her cheeks. "*Fuck you!*" She kicked my abdomen.

I retched up blood as I swung away, grasping a hoop and propelling myself onto another strip of silk near the ceiling. "Nothing else?" We engaged, my every parry a defence against Chiara slashing my silk.

A vestibule at one end of the chamber caught my eye. Within it, Valentina consoled a distressed Ayana.

I swung my leg and kicked Chiara's face. "Did you convince them to betray us?"

Chiara's iron eyes silvered. "None of it was meant to *be* like this!"

"How was it *supposed* to be?"

"Davide was meant to kill Cesare!"

"And *then*?" I shouted. "What *then*, Chiara? Did you *think* before you went to that—?"

"*NO!*" she screamed. "I *DIDN'T!*"

Lucrezia broke into the room in a whirlwind of fury, cosmetics smeared by tears. Her gaze aimed for Valentina and Ayana like an executioner's gun.

"Do you want to kill me, Chiara?" I demanded.

She slashed for me, but did not reply.

I let go of the silk and caught another, levering myself higher by the third. My head swam and tore; agony cut my stomach open from the inside; my muscles slacked. *I won't live…*

Chiara's eyes mortared to mine.

I snapped her arm. She shrieked. Fell.

Looping a swathe into a lasso, I caught her by the throat, tears half-blinding me when the silk choked her flailing form the way a gallows noose would.

In a dying frenzy, she chopped the sash levering me in the air.

We plummeted.

Chiara's strangled corpse broke my fall, but it didn't matter as I began to choke and heave. Blood oozed down my chin. Pain overwhelmed me.

Flames crawled closer, climbing up the silks.

Yet, a shriek snared my waning consciousness.

Lucrezia, machete in hand, gripped Ayana by the hair, dragging the girl from her mother who crawled after them, her ankles severed.

"*No!*" Valentina begged. "Leave my daughter, *spare* her, PLEASE! She's *innocent, please* let her live!"

"How dare you beg my mercy?" Lucrezia threw her arm back and began to chop the shrieking Ayana as if she was firewood.

"*NO!*" Valentina wailed. "MY DAUGHTER! STOP IT! *NO! NOT HER! SHE'S A CHILD*, PLEASE!"

Lucrezia severed Ayana's head; thwacked Valentina in the face with the hilt when the woman got close. "Love for *love!*" she screamed and began beating and hacking Valentina whilst weeping hysterically.

I watched in horror as Lucrezia became my confronting mirror.

I'd slain entire families. I'd slain *children* under the reason that, if I let them live, they would seek vengeance just like me—that I'd be creating noble-blooded monsters moulded of both pain and an upbringing by evil. Yet Valentina was never a *true* evil. She'd been steered by Leone, and yes it justified none of the exploitation she enabled at his hand. But the love for her innocent daughter had been so pure.

Grief flooded me with comprehension: innocence would only ever be punished in this slaughterhouse of a world. Just like the twins' parents. Just like Karmni. Like Ema. Ayana. Maybe, once, just like me and Cesare and Lucrezia and my father. *I want my father…*

Lucrezia hurled Valentina's mutilated corpse aside and sobbed. And sobbed. And sobbed.

I hacked up grume, the euclidean plane swimming, oscillating. Breaths hardly trickled into my lungs, now.

"GIORGIANNA!" I heard Lucrezia scream, but only pain held my mind. "Giorgi no no *no*—"

I collapsed on my back, seeing writhing darkness and glaring light, convulsing, hearing one, two, twelve voices.

I never thought I would die this way. I never once wanted to live, but I had come so close. And I failed.

Forgive me…

FLAMES ENGULFED EVERYTHING as Cesare and Isaia massacred their way through Leone's Serpents in a bid to hunt the Dóminus down.

Isaia coughed up blood, succumbing to the poison.

Cesare halted Isaia's fall. "I need you to hold on, you understand? We're *getting* that fucking antidote." He couldn't think about Giorgianna lest he caved to his panic, but every *tick* made it more unbearable not to.

They cornered Leone in his office.

"What the fuck did this achieve?" Cesare shouted.

"Eliminating a threat," the blond stated simply, a slim estoc in his dilettante hands. "Better safe than your bones picked by the crows." His three remaining bodyguards charged for the pair.

Cesare dispatched the first, brawny and slow. Isaia's karambit slit open a second, slimmer and quicker, guard's throat. He gasped through the blood coating his gullet, his back to the bureau. *No!*

Leone's blade ran Isaia through the abdomen.

"Do *forgive* me!" Leone hew downwards, disembowelling the eavesdropper.

Isaia's protruding eyes locked with Cesare.

He saw light extinguish within their coal-black depths.

The eavesdropper crumpled to the floor, gutted and dead.

Cesare's crushed fist drove into the face of a bodyguard running up on him, stabbing them through the throat in a fit of despair. He grabbed the fucker's hideous axe even as acid burned his oesophagus, turned on his feet in a smooth rotation, and flung it.

It spun through the air and lodged in Leone's skull, killing instantly as it cleaved his brain.

Disgust threw Cesare's head sideways and squeezed his eyes shut, horror rattling him and seizing his lungs. *Fuck you!* He needed that antidote, so he forced himself to approach the Viper's corpse and dig the container of pills from his clothes.

"No." It was empty. "No, *please…*"

Clap! Clap!

Cesare whipped around with weapons ready, seeing a servant instead, one of her hands bruised to complete blackness. *'There's antidote in his bureau—middle-most drawer on the other side—and unpoisoned water in that flask.'* She pointed to the shelves behind the desk.

Cesare scrambled to follow the instructions.

Within the drawer lay a replica of Leone's pill bottle, gloriously filled. A sigh barely loosened Cesare's chest.

He looked back at the slave to see her sign: *'The curly-haired woman was in the performance room.'*

"Thank you. Thank you so much." And Cesare bolted back into the burning building, searching countless rooms and smouldering bodies through vignetted vision.

"*GIORGIANNA!*" He heard Lucrezia's shriek from a room at the end of an upcoming hallway. "*Giorgi no no* no—"

Cesare barged into a chamber where fire had climbed up silks to the ceiling. Beside Chiara's corpse, Lucrezia crouched over Giorgianna's bloody and convulsing form.

Lucrezia locked eyes with him. "Cesare!"

He dashed near, cradling Giorgianna. Sweat drenched her frozen flesh, her eyes rolled back until they were white between knife-slit eyelids. Blood slathered her lips. "Don't let me be too late, I swear to the bastard Saints I'll rip this fucking place to the ground." Propping her against himself, Cesare slipped an antidote pill into her mouth and carefully guided her to drink, for the first time in his life wishing he recalled any prayer at all. He could do nothing but hold her and *beg*.

Giorgianna's tremors subsided, the grimace of agony on her face smoothing to serenity, but she grew so frighteningly motionless in Cesare's arms. She did not breathe.

"Giorgi…?" whimpered Lucrezia.

"No!" Terror gripped Cesare. "*Nonono*, please don't do this, Giorgianna, I need you to *live!*" He brushed hair out of her wax-pale face with trembling fingers. Curls clung to her wet skin, her limp weight in his arms gutting everything. *I cannot lose you too.*

"*Please*," horrible pain burned behind Cesare's eyes, blinding him to everything in the empty world but Giorgianna, "*come back to me.*"

He needed her words and her thoughts and her strength. He needed her to know joy after this dreadful nightmare she endured—she deserved to. Even if she refused to have him, even if, in a wretched turn of fate, she reviled him once more, he *needed* her to *live*. He'd found kindness, and he'd have his body cut to pieces before he let it go.

Giorgianna coughed tightly.

Grume spouted from her mouth, and she finally, *mercifully*, gasped for air.

Her bloodshot eyes opened and fixed on Cesare, fingers clutching the neckline of his shirt as she murmured, "*Will* you *come back to* me?"

Tears poured unrestrained from Cesare's eyes and he embraced Giorgianna as if at any second she might slip away from him again. She latched onto his shoulders, shaking and so cold yet blessedly alive.

Cesare couldn't speak—no words could ever express his relief.

Woodwork began to crumble as fire took a tighter hold.

"It's gonna take us with it," Cesare finally spoke.

"Isaia?" Giorgianna rasped out hopefully.

He shook his head. "Dead."

Giorgianna's eyes fogged, and horrid realisation struck Cesare in that moment. He lost a friend—one of his dearests. *Two, for all it was worth…*

"No…" Lucrezia sputtered. "Ygal! Ygal, *no*, I can't leave—!"

Cesare let Giorgianna free and grasped the crumbling obsidian-haired woman by the shoulders. "Lucrezia, look at me. Listen to my voice. No matter how much it hurts, we have to go."

"Leave me here. I'm better off dead."

"Lucrezia, no—"

"I have *no* one! My mother is dead and my fucking rapist father is dead and Donatello is dead and my Godsdamn uncle tried to murder me and I have no fucking life anywhere in this rotten *Hell* of a world—" Lucrezia panted for desperate breaths. "Ygal was my only family and now she's dead too so what *am* I without th—?"

"*Alive!*" Cesare's voice broke. "That's all you *need* to be!"

"Not without her…" whispered Lucrezia.

Cesare's torn-up heart shrank. He could not help his guilt at the knowledge that the love of his life was saved, yet Lucrezia's was torn from her so unjustly. "Those snakes wanted you *dead*, Lucrezia!" He continued with a voice of fire, nevertheless. "Ygal would want you to *live. They'd* want you perished alongside her." He squeezed Lucrezia's shoulders firmer. "Live to *spite* them! Live, whilst they rot like the worms they were. Live to spit in the face of your soul-crushing anguish. It *will* not crush you."

Lucrezia sobbed and sobbed and sobbed, but allowed herself to be guided to stand.

The three escaped by the skin of their teeth, watching from afar as flames engulfed an entire wing of the Serpents' estate and drew frenzied commotion.

'I don' know wha' I'll do
if this falls through.'
'It won't…'

Damn you, Aengus.

SCENE XXXVII

AMISSIO

Ilenia | Giorgianna

BENEATH THE LIGHT OF DAWN, Magister Ilenia Farnese pored over tomes she hauled from her Athenaeum to her bedchamber desk, devouring every morsel of knowledge about The Court of Secrets and Cardea's curse she could scour.

She reached into a lower slot of the toreutic birch cabinet overlooking her desk—not the lowest, for that was where most searched first. From there, she slipped a stack of papers inked in the High Priest's calligraphic hand, as if they strived to pen everything they wrote in the manner of ecclesiastical annals. Ilenia had set up a Guárdus to retrieve documents of interest relevant to Abelli's purification sacrament before Sarnai could. They did as told, and now Ilenia held in her hands the apotheosis of the High Priest's studies, collated over a summer.

Cardea's death made the enchantment she cast on the Court unbreakable just as she had intended with her sacrificial immolation. However, if Abelli's research supposedly led them a means of severing the mechanism by which certain forms of magic were a born ability…

Ilenia rested her chin on her laced fingers.

Could a lobotomy, should its execution, without an effect on emotions whilst still achieving a broken veil of transmutation, be realised, theoretically allow a subject to manipulate sorceries not of their creation?

When she gave up Calliupa, Ilenia gave up her last remaining tether to the secrets of oldtown. She would reclaim it once more. There was only so much experimenting she could do with magic as it was. Chimerise masonry into useful trinkets like cloths and mirrors and poultices. Enchant simple weapons and locks. How much more an endeavour like Abelli's could permit…

The doors to her quarters opened. Footsteps forwarded in. Several.

Ilenia squirreled the documents away again and angled in her seat, but didn't rise when she beheld her uninvited guest. "Governor."

Two Imperialíi flanked him. *Gods*, how deeply she despised Manuele's gilded flock.

"Magister Ilenia Farnese," Crescenzo intoned. "You are under arrest for the murder of Grand Judge Giordano Veronesi. You are hereby stripped of your Ministerial title and rights."

Ilenia smiled insolently, catching the flicker of muscle in the Governor's jaw. *Frustrated fool fumbling for his slipping power.* "Glad my visit to the House of Judgement proved valuable to you."

"Do you propound your supposed innocence?"

"*Oh* Crescenzo, neither of us ought to lie to ourselves."

"Was it Salomè?" he spat the name like a rotten berry.

"Perhaps." Ilenia remained poised. "I'm frankly not one to know."

"Clario." Crescenzo folded his squeezed and twitching fists behind his back. "Were you responsible?"

Ilenia knew her stay in the dungeons wouldn't be long, and she did not want her efforts to go unacknowledged. "Yes. It was me."

"Then upon what grounds should I believe you are not culpable in the murder of Veronesi?"

"Because I didn't *fear* him, Crescenzo," declared Ilenia. "He did not undermine all that I was and everything I held." Her head tilted. "You are losing grip on your court, your rioting citizens, your burning empire. Yet here you stand, dwindling the meagre aegis you miraculously still possess. Keep it up and you'll see your kingdom in the ashes The Bauta craves."

"*SILENCE*!" Crescenzo thrust his sword against Ilenia's throat. "Sullied *wretch*!" She wasn't afraid—she could unmake his blade without touching it. "You do not dare speak to me this way! I can *break* you—you have *no* power here. You are nothing but old filth dressed in silks as if you will ever be worth more than the slum *dirt* you are."

"Kill me, and lose the support of the lion's share of your senate." Ilenia's words stopped the Governor in his tracks. "I am not your puppet, Crescenzo. You cannot threaten me anymore. I do not fear *you*, either."

The man grasped and knotted together every frayed thread of his temper to hold himself back from running Ilenia through, and pulled away. "Alive or dead, beneath this earth is where you shall rot." He turned for the door. "Get her out of my sight."

Guards seized the Magister, shackled her wrists, and led her away.

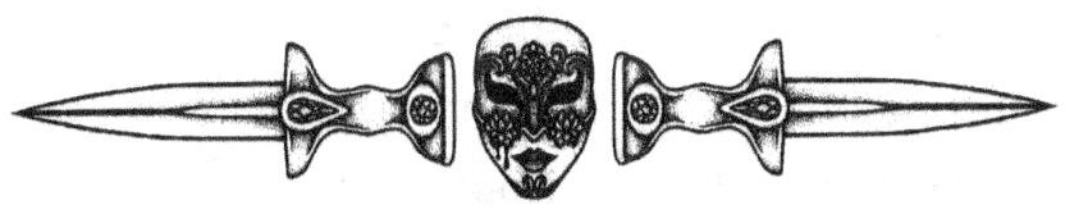

WE STUMBLED BACK INTO THE HOUND-BOAR DISTRICT.

Red-haired Aengus greeted us with disdain. "The fire's visible from 'ere."

Among several Boars and Hounds, Itxaro stood with Manárša, Əkurofu, and Diodora, scrutiny flickering from Aengus to us. Sarnai stared at me with wide and frightened eyes.

My weak heart hammered, limbs still tingling and head a-swim.

Cesare stepped forward. "Listen—"

"The others are dead because of *you*, aren't they?" Aengus' voice hardened unforgivingly. "Our so-called *Domína* woul'n't be blubberin' and red in the eyes if i' ain't tha'!" His own eyes flushed. "Isaia's *dead* 'cause of you! *All* your fuckin' machinations fell through like I said! Maybe Cheera wasn't so wrong," he sneered. "I know wha' *I'll* do."

Steel sang its drawing.

Itxaro swung her dagger and slit a Boar's throat. "*RUN*!"

We did.

Itxaro with half a dozen Hounds, Sarnai included, deserted with us.

The Boars gave chase.

My lungs tore as we raced into The Cyclopes' district, buildings flicking by like pages against gale.

Itxaro halted everyone. "Stay… still…" The Boars no longer pursued. Instead, a dozen Cyclopes crawled out of the tarry shadows.

"What d'ya think, Chea?" A fittingly one-eyed Cyclops, bulky and scarred by keloids, half of his shoulder-sweeping vermilion curls shaven, smirked. "Think Lucanus'd appreciate some guests?" Plugs opened up his cheeks and a septum hung large enough to touch his lip.

The Miəmɔnuhi[104] androgyne beside him, slim yet muscular, black hair tied in a topknot, ran their thumb along the blade of their single-edged dav.[105] Their wide smile flashed sharpened fangs. "*I think guests're always a treat.*"

They flew for us in a flurry of metal.

I snapped an attacker's spine and tore it out, syphoning azoth into the blood spraying from his back, pirouetting on my heel, and cleaving in half an advancing Cyclops with a scythe of ichor before hurtling towards Lucrezia, blood still in my control, and beheading the man chasing her. The sutures of my skull strained. *I'm not strong enough…*

Catching a fleeting second of opened lines, we bolted for our lives.

Of the Hounds, the Cyclopes left alive Sarnai, Itxaro, Diodora, Əkurofu, and Manárša, even if injured, the remaining finding themselves at varying stages of dismemberment.

I didn't know how, but we made it to the lifts up into Smugglers' District and narrowly escaped with our souls, nor did I know how we got back to *Antigone* where Fabio and Şirîn conversed aboard.

Şirîn exclaimed when seeing us.

---

[104] *mee-eh-MAW-noo-hee*; the people of Miədəyol.
[105] A Southeast Asian sword (more widely known as '*dha*').

Fabio's face paled as the pair ran to us. "Saints, what happened?"

Lucrezia collapsed in tears, Diodora leaning down to comfort her.

Exhaustion and near-death finally knocked my legs from under me, my sore throat still bringing up dregs of blood.

"We lost The Antrum," Cesare said, and his words made the horror of our reality *real*.

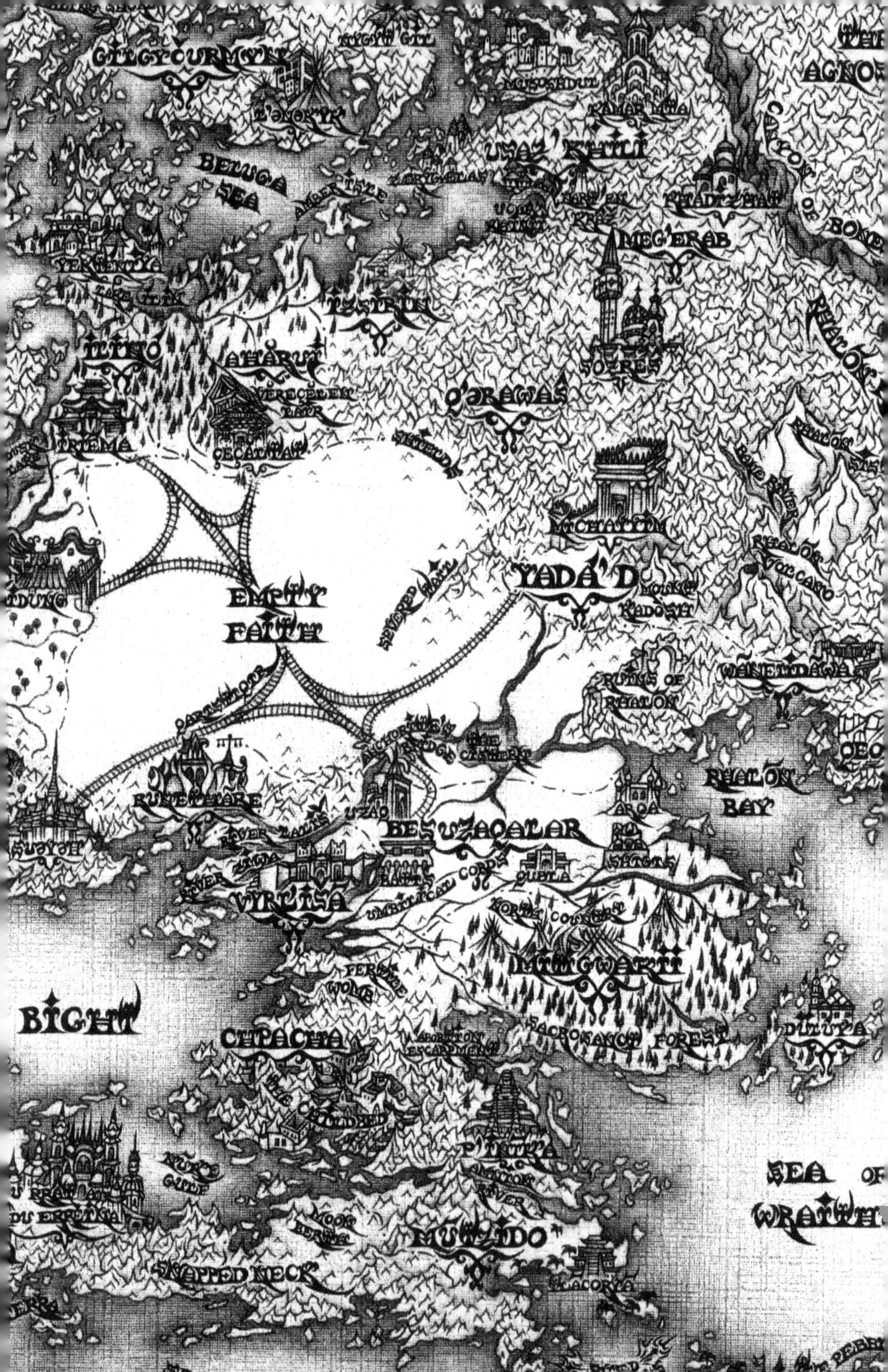
GILGYCURMYER
NYGYH GIL
T'ANORYK
BELUGA SEA
AMBER TYLE
THE AGNOS
PORT OF BONE
KAMAR MWA
USA' KHILI
JOHN KELRET KRA
KHAD'Z'HAD
MEG'ERAB
TESTRIN
AHARUT
VERECELEN LAIR
CECATRIAT
SEVEN OH
SOZREI
O'BREWAS
RHALON
TITTO
TYEMA
EMPTY FAITH
SEVERED WALL
LATCHALION
YADA'D
MOUKE RADOSY
RHALON VOLCANO
TUDUNG
RUINS OF RHALON
WAINEMDAWA
OEO
RUNEHARE
VICTORIUS'S BRIDGE
THE CASKET
RHALON BAY
ARCA
HUSYCH
RIVER PLAINS
UZAO
BE'UZAOALOR
HALOS
OUBLA
SHOTS
VYRTISA
UMBILICAN CORDS
FORBIDDEN COPPICE
FERTILE WOMB
IMTIGWARTI
SACROSANCT FOREST
BIGHT
CHPACHA
ABORTION'T ESCARPMENT
DILUPA
COLDBED
TERRAWDY DU ERRETIA
NURSE GIDE
P'INUYA
MOOR BERNIE
MUUCIDO
SEA OF WRAITH
SNAPPED NECK
RACORYA
TERRA

ACT III

...I would help
fabric in the
to its native

reduce every
social structure
element

"*Step forward:*
we hear that you
are a good man.
You cannot be bought,
but the lightning which
strikes the house also
cannot be bought.
You hold to what you said.
But what did you say?
You are honest, you
say your opinion.
Which opinion?
You are brave.
Against whom?
You are wise.
For whom?
You do not consider your
personal advantages.
Whose advantages do
you consider, then?

You are a good friend.
Are you also a good friend
of the good people?

Hear us then: we know
you are our enemy. This
is why we shall now put
you in front of a wall.
But in consideration of your
merits and good qualities,
we shall put you in front of
a *good* wall and shoot you
with a *good* bullet from a
good gun and bury you
with a *good* shovel
in the *good* earth."

—*The Interrogation of the Good*, Bertolt Brecht

Scene XXXVIII

No Half Measures

Fabio | Giorgianna | Cesare

THE RIBBED SAILS OF THE *MOON HARE* CHUÁN[106] UNFURLED like the wings of an enormous grey bat taking flight, Grey Pearl mariners a murmur of busy commotion beneath the young morning blanketing Smugglers' Cove.

Fabio approached the grand vessel, Giorgianna at his side. "Fēngnà?"

The Grey Pearls' captain looked glumly to Fabio. "Amadi-Spýros."

"What is this?"

"I'm afraid we cannot postpone our supply run any longer. I'm forced to bid you fare—"

"*What?*" Giorgianna exclaimed, still pallid and ill.

Fēngnà regarded her flintily. "My first-and-foremost duty is to the people of Smugglers' Cove my Pearls supply. My *second*-most duty had been to Ygạl. Ygạl is dead. And my ties of loyalty are not to you."

---

106 船; *junk* (ship).

Giorgianna bristled. "If the lives of your people matter so greatly, then surely you comprehend how turning your back—!"

"Has it ever occurred to you that not all existence revolves around your tragedy?"

"What an absurd notion!" argued Giorgianna. "Your people aren't safe just because they aren't ossíi. *None* of us are free u—"

"I will not make further compromises for you." Fēngnà made to ascend to her chuán.

"How much will it matter if you return to a city in ash and ruin?"

"One of my dearest friends is *dead*!" snapped Fēngnà, the silver in her eyes scraping Fabio's heart with a terribly familiar pain. "Do you think I don't appreciate the gravity of my decision?"

Silence swept between them. Giorgianna's jaw tightened with indignation. Fabio's hands fisted in his greatcoat's pockets, his heart heavy as an anchor. The old Hydra couldn't condemn Fēngnà. After all, *he* was willing to refuse helping Giorgianna and Cesare once, fearing for his own hide. Perhaps Fabio had grown too entrenched in his apathy. But did 'apathy' ever exist, at all? Was it not all something else? Something deeper, more human, every time?

As Pearls hauled the gangplank up, Fēngnà's huādiàn hid in the forehead creases of her remorse. "Farewell and fair winds." And she disappeared aboard.

"Şirîn's allyship is guaranteed," asserted Fabio. "I'll inform the Teeth as needed."

"Etenesh…" Giorgianna's voiced forebodingly. Her aimless scrutiny roved the wharf. "This isn't the end." She bolted for the cliff-bound lighthouse.

Fabio gazed across the frigid waters where the harrowing sun arose from the wintry horizon like a sullen vampiric orb, drenching the white welkin in the lurid blood-colours of a fox hunt.

How do we make it out of this alive?

ƏKUROFU ALL BUT TORE OFF THE DOOR TO THE APOTHECÁRIUM. Sarnai and I raced in after him, salve-anointed air smothering in a way it never used to be.

One Boar pinned Etenesh against the front desk, another's dagger pressed firmly under her jaw. Aengus stood at the centre of the room, aiming for her forehead a revolver.

Etenesh's eyes flinched to us. The darkness of her skin blanched.

I drew my revolver and every unengaged weapon thrust towards us. Boars prowled closer. "Let's not do this, Aengus." I tempered my voice against my instincts. "Lower the weapons and step away."

"She knows 'bout us," hissed Aengus, freckled features contorted by rage and mourning.

"We are on your side, Aengus," I insisted. He only spat out a scoff. "The safety and sovereignty of your Antrum matters to us just as much as you," I placated notwithstanding. "We are fighting against the very force endangering your existence. If you don't wish to help us, so be it, but don't persecute those of the least threat to you."

His nostrils flared as silence assailed. The clock ticked. Blood roared through my skull.

I levered my arms just a little lower, steering the direction of my barrel away, and took a cautious step forward. "*Aengus*—" Weapons thrust a threat at me. I jolted but didn't retreat, didn't drop the Boar's slitted eyes. "Aengus, if you leave, no harm will come to any of you. We will do *everything* in our power to protect you—"

"Look where your fuckin' *protection* go' us!"

"Stop thinking with your grief and *listen*!" Guilt sawed through my ribs. I *knew* how grief warped people, how horribly it destroyed soul after soul before it granted any liberty to rebuild. It was cruelty to demand Aengus put down the sacrificial blade of his sorrow, but I knew what was necessary, and what was necessary trumped all else. "Please…" My tone softened. "You are in *danger*. The people who *know* about you, the people who *matter*, are the regime. They want The Court and everything beyond exterminated, *including* you."

"Magister knows 'bout us 'cause o' *you*!"

"No, not us. And the Magister would be the least of your concern when the *General* is aware. When the *Governor* is. All they need is to breach Cardea's curse, and they *will* if we stall. So please, I *beg* you, Aengus, just *leave*. We've lost enough. This must end."

His eyes glistened. "You're no' innocen' in our loss!"

"*I know!*" A shout tore from me, tattered and strident. "I know. And I'm sorry, Aengus. But see this as our entreaty of absolution. Let this be what rectifies our wrong."

Silence pillaged through once more, ceasing my breathing and the beat of my heart. The Boars' weapons still gleamed in the verdigris light streaming through the stained windows.

I met Aengus with an unbroken gaze, and lowered my revolver to my side.

Aengus' jaw flickered as he roughly thrust his claymore towards the floor. "Move out!" he barked and led his Boars out.

The door slammed, my heart resuming its witch-drum beat.

Əkurofu caught Etenesh as she collapsed to the floor.

Sarnai and I rushed to them.

Etenesh groped for the collar of my scarlet jacket. "What on earth?" Her eyes bulged and flinched about. "What is going on?"

I grasped her cold hand, cradling the trembling woman in my arms and crooning a "*Shhh…*" into her hair.

The front door barged open.

Əkurofu was on his feet with his adze poised in a blink, Sarnai with him.

On the threshold stood Yȯchaná.

With them, arm slung over their broad shoulders, was a wounded man. Tall and dark, a golden lip ring glinting, tight curls spiralling to his shoulders and chopped straight across his brows.

"*Araya!*" Etenesh squealed in an outpouring of vigour. She shoved me off and dashed for her little brother, clutching onto him and muttering a fevered string of Sam'säban.

The rest of us darted to embrace him too.

"Rosa?" I questioned. "Where is Rosa?"

A haunted look dimmed the malachite green of Araya's eyes. "I didn't find her."

My stomach dropped and came back up. My legs grew weak, my mouth papery. "*nonononono…*" Sarnai grabbed me as the blackness of panic crawled in. "If she went missing in that house…" *If soldiers got hold of her…*

"*I*-I tried!" sputtered Araya.

"No…" I shook my head. The world turned waterlogged and echoing.

"None of the servants had seen her for hours, but I really tried—"

"No no no—"

"I'm sorry, I'm *so* sorry—"

"*No*, I know." I grabbed his arm. "I know I know I know."

"Ilenia has been arrested."

Yòchaná's declaration all but kicked my teeth.

"*What?*" exclaimed Sarnai.

"On accusation of treason and the murders of Giordano and Clario." I was cold. Ilenia knew too much. "It isn't unlikely that the Governor will extend her sentence to encompass conspiracy to murder Olindo, as well as the Lanuza and Tagliafichi noble families. Basilio is insistent on the former. The Guárdia has been ordered to take up sentinel duty around the citadel. Ilenia played her cards well: the vast majority of officials disapprove of De Tullia's decision and some have attempted to walk out of the senate. With little success, given the climate."

Əkurofu raised a dark eyebrow. "So what'll *you* do?"

"Keep up appearances, for now." Yòchaná sighed. "My situation is delicate; any misstep will land me on the chopping block. Tell Isaia—"

"Isaia is dead," I blurted.

Yòchaná stilled. Paled. "…What?"

"Leone and Valentina… He and Ygạl were murdered; we lost The Boars and The Grey Pearls. Our numbers are more than halved and an overhaul to our strategy is called for…" My mouth salivated with nausea. "We don't yet know how."

"What about the Hounds in the government building?"

"Always allies," assured Araya, "but hardly promising numbers. I'm with you, and we've organised reliably in our ranks. Go, peacock!"

Yòchaná nodded and departed.

My shuddering vision trained on the clock. *Nearly six hundred.* "Armoury." I advanced for the door, fearing all that awaited within the dismal reality beyond.

WITH OVER HALF OF THE MORETTAE GONE, perturbing quiet hung over their armoury.

"How many left?" Anukka questioned.

"Thirty-two off *Antigone.*"

"Sixteen off *Roj,*[107]" Şirîn added.

Kel-Kech shifted from one foot to the other. "Twenty-four Morettae."

"Including those in the citadel," Araya led, "fourteen Hounds."

Errico pitched in: "A good number of us committees, but can't throw them all—I mean, not even *most*—into the citadel. We need the people power in the streets."

Lissandri rolled his shoulders. "Give or take seven of the rest of us?"

Cesare *tsk'd.* "Barely breaking one hundred and no guarantee most of them can fight." Fēngnà's fleet alone was one-hundred-twelve strong; seventy-one for The Boars.

"How many legionaries we up against?" Errico asked Araya.

"No fewer than three thousand."

A snort from Korneli. "No way we can capture 'e citadel wi' 'em odds."

"We intended to use the prison break as a decoy," Cesare reiterated. "The people at the vanguard of the breakout are political convicts; it remains imperative that we assist their escape."

"At what cost if takeover is implausible?" Anukka demanded.

"An alternative perspective," Cesare mused to no clarity for Anukka, or anyone. Or himself. "Do not use the prison break as a tool to *seize* the

---

[107] *ROH-zh*; Miroxîn for '*sun*'.

government, but rather to further *weaken* it in numbers, defences, morale, thus *emboldening* the morale of the populace."

Giorgianna squinted, eyes no longer dark with kajal. "How?"

"In due time. *First!*" He clicked his tongue. "With restructured ranks comes the necessity to strategise anew."

Iyad cleared his throat. "Laútni confirms the prison break will take place at ten hundred next díem crepúsca."

"With help of the Hounds still inside," Araya explained, "The rest will move in through the citadel's hidden passageways when given the sign— four consecutive gunshots at the western end of the government building's south-eastern grand lacuna, ground floor of the house."

"Though its ceiling is opened to a good five," noted Giorgianna.

"What…" Eligio raised a tentative voice, "about Rosa?"

Cesare's heart hurt. He should have insisted she not go into the spider's nest. He should have put his foot down firmer. This was precisely what he'd feared.

Araya said, "The most we could do is sneak somebody in amidst the fray to scout a portion of The Trabeculae, but they couldn't go far without endangering themselves. And I doubt, if Rosalia *is* kept there, that she'd be so close to the dungeons' surface. I'm so sorry."

Eligio lowered his eyes. Lissandri wrapped his arms around his brother, but the eldest shook him off.

Cesare forced his voice to rise even as panic suffocated him, "Given the entrance points from underground, said fray will be concentrated in the aforementioned south-eastern lacuna. From there, the trouble of syphoning out Morettae, Hounds, and smugglers is somewhat alleviated by the nearness of the citadel's old wing: just east to our point of interest. The citadel's old wing presents us with the most reliable mode of leaving —via the subterranean tunnels."

"Isaia had passed onto me the legionary rotations you compiled," confirmed Araya.

"We got it too." Alessa shifted foot-to-foot beside Errico.

"The region is still highly treacherous ground, but beggars can't be choosers."

"What about Manuele?" asked Kel.

Cesare winced.

"The basilica on díem crepúsca is empty—a cleansing custom," explained Giorgianna. "I will face Manuele then." She rested her hands on her corseted waist, blood moons ablaze in her eyes. "I want him dead by the insurrection bells' toll. Then, I will join you in the citadel."

No matter how much horror overwhelmed him, Cesare was forced to view Giorgianna's endeavour as solely strategic. He damned himself one last time before speaking, "Should your efforts successfully conclude, a destructive blow will be delivered to the integrity of the state's security just as well. The General's iron-fisted authority over the legions has resulted in their well-nigh ineptitude in carrying out activity without the guidance of their absolute. Remove the First Cause, and its emanation is necessarily terminated. Remove the General, and his orders cannot be actualised by agents with less discernment than headless poultry—all considered, their horizontal organisation has *nothing* on ours." He nodded to Errico who exchanged proud looks with Alessa and the others of the committees present. "And, one of *the* most powerful instruments in dismantling defences is the fostering of a false sense of security within one's mark." Cesare held his hands out theatrically. "De Tullia's kakistocracy, being *ours*." And he knew what needed to be done, what every notch upon the textile of time amounted to.

"*How* do we resolve to undertake this 'fostering' following crepúsca?" Giorgianna probed impatiently, sardonically. "What could *possibly* spur De Tullia, in his burgeoning paranoia, to cease peering over his shoulder enough to facilitate his fall?"

"Give them what they want," Cesare spoke with the weight of a fatalistic gavel, looked upon his lover with the eyes of a one who had stood witness to manifold ruin and death. "Give them *me*."

Scene XXXIX

Brief and Desperate
as Prayer

Cesare | Giorgianna | Cesare

THAT FATALISTIC GAVEL STRUCK an unbearable silence into the chamber—the sort which pulled taut in the brief seconds before dynamite detonated.

"…What…?" was all Giorgianna said.

Cesare set his teeth and shunned her eyes.

He knew what needed to be done, did he not?

"Absolutely fucking not!" exploded Lissandri, and the room descended into pandemonium. Beside him, the space was void; somewhere in the fray Cesare caused, Eligio had left.

"You're gonna give yourself *up*?"

"That's absurd!"

"You can't do that, Ces!"

"They'll *kill* you—!"

"De Tullia doesn't want me dead on sight;" Cesare cut in, "he wants me detained for execution."

"In what bloody world is that better, Cesare?" Fabio exclaimed.

"It grants you a time delay and the best chance of seiz—"

"You are not a *martyr* for us!" snapped Giorgianna.

"Lehên…" Itxaro addressed Cesare as if talking down a suicidal man. "There's an extent of ridiculousness I expect from you, but enough is *enough.*"

"You've been a *linchpin* in all of this!" Wrath surged in Giorgianna's tone so, *so* high, and Cesare knew why—knew she hid in that destructive tsunami from the grief vying to swallow her whole. "We cannot *lose* you!"

Cesare aimed to fire back but Lissandri interrupted, "Do you realise how desultory your house of cards is? How likely a plan like that is to collapse on itself?"

"You've *lost* it, boy!" Fabio chided. "How *desperate*—"

"*LET ME TALK!*" indignation impelled Cesare to shout.

"What could you possibly say?" spat Giorgianna.

"That *this* is how we strike the governing body with that false sense of security we need. De Tullia detests all dissidents, but *nothing* compares to his hatred of me. He foolishly believes *me* to be the sole First Cause of Vencenzani dissent and that, by excising me, he therefore eliminates the entire malignancy he believes the resistance to be. If I'm captured, with no doubt in the mind of the state that I *am* The Bauta, De Tullia will believe that alone to be enough to quell dissent, which is precisely what his mistake will be."

And somehow, Cesare's self-preservation, no matter how faulty of a human instinct, never once spurred his side. *It always led to this.*

"Suppose I'm arrested," Cesare pushed on. "My execution will surely be the most monumental event in the history of De Tullia's tenure. *Every* legionary will be concentrated around the ministerial house—the Governor won't spare a *single* precaution."

"Not convincing," Lissandri grit out.

"What made it possible for legionaries to decimate the riot at the Solar Square?"

"Many people in one enclosed location?" Kel-Kech tried.

"Precisely. That, with the false sense of security my incarceration bestows, will leave the flocks right for the plucking. The superlative moment to strike our mark, and strike it *dead*."

Iyad's jaw hung loose. "You want us to organise an assault on the government building the day of your execution?"

"Yes," plainly said Cesare. "Minimise the forces necessary on díem crepúsca, rally the people, empty out the ministerial house," his fist stiffened into a punching knot, "and give that filthy fucking kakistocracy *Hell*!"

The sun had shed its bloodstained nightgown for the pallor of wintry daylight, the clock a bomb *tick tick ticking* down to ignition.

Anukka stepped forward. "To put an end to an order is to put an end to your humanity, to become your cause's weapon," she recited the solemn words she twice delivered to Cesare. "Revolution is not victory." Her soil-dark eyes affixed him. "Revolution is death."

Cesare had never once received an ounce of esteem from Anukka, so its meagre morsel proved sufficient to nourish his beaten pride.

"Are you serious?" Giorgianna practically quivered, Sarnai swiftly grabbing hold of the woman lest she lunge with claws.

Anukka didn't quail. "I know revolution's reality better than you most—it's *nothing* like cape-flailing lionhearts and children playing war. You think you'll achieve ends you seek with no sacrifices? No blood? *Eşĕl* aça![108]" She spat on the floor.

"Our circumstances give us few choices," Cesare swept down. "But that doesn't mean they strip us of *chances*."

Glances shot all around: rage, sorrow, resolve, fear.

Fabio cleared his thickened throat. "I know nothing will convince you otherwise." His words quavered, his gaze so lightless when it sought Cesare.

He smirked despite the guilt slicing deep between his ribs. "You know me well."

---

[108] *eh-SH'YOHL ah-CHAH*; Ahărla; *literally*: 'green child'; *figuratively*: 'naïve child'.

"NOT GOING TO SAY ANYTHING?" Lissandri sneered as he—myself and Itxaro with him—pursued Cesare below *Antigone*'s deck. The door to Eligio's chamber was shut.

Cesare made for his room. "There's nothing to say."

My blood seethed, heart raced, feet tremored upon the floor.

"You expect us to let you commit suicide?" Itxaro bit.

Cesare whirled sharply in the doorway. "I expect you to do as I say."

Itxaro estuated in outraged Zargòsian to which Cesare fired back a perfunctory snipe.

"How *selfish* are you?" I shouted. "And who the fuck do you think you are? Swallow your pride for once in your life and think about how much it *hurts* to watch you bleed and die every single day! Think about the people who sacrifice themselves for your cause! The people who are why you've survived and who would kill themselves a thousand times over so you may live just to have the *gall* to call yourself a dehumanised fucking 'instrument'!"

"You are our family," Lissandri pleaded. "Losing you is not an option."

"And it *won't* be," Cesare gritted, "if you do as I *say*!" He turned into his chamber.

"Is this some sort of punishment?" I shoved past Andri and Itxaro. "Will giving up your life absolve you of some sin you believe you've committed?" The door locked in my wake at the sheer force of its slam.

"Leave it, Giorgianna." Cesare tossed aside his tricorn and jacket.

"No!" I clutched his shirt, grasped his face, forcing him to look at me. "Why can't you see how important you are?" My voice grew fragile. "Why doesn't it *change* anything to you?"

Cesare pushed my hands away. "I've already told you there are things more immense than the Self; more pertinent to preserve."

"I *will not* watch you die!" Coldness slithered between my bones. He was content with being tortured and brutalised. He was content with killing himself.

"The end goal was always *this*, Giorgianna." Cesare continued to resist. "Regardless of how I was to reach it. I never expected *you*. I never—"

"You never expected I'd derail your perfect plans of revolution?"

"Yes."

His unflinching response struck silence into the ether.

I doubled back. My ears rang against the emptiness. Everyone was gone, leaving behind only me. Only him.

My teeth clenched hard, then parted to spit out: "You cannot lose me, you say, so your compromise is letting *me* lose *you*?"

"You'll ultimately have to."

"Death is a mortal eventuality, what of it?"

"You know that's not what I mean."

"I *won't* let those reapers *take* you from me!"

"I don't know what you want me to say."

"That you won't go through with it, you—!"

"Fiend?" Cesare leaned close as he strode around me. "Bastard? *Lowlife*." His fingers looped through my hair. He *tsk'd*, his lips hooking into a smirk. "I like it when you call me that, princess."

"Just as you like to play untouchable?" I bristled at the unwelcome burn through my cheeks.

"A reminder of my humanity is appreciated, every so often." Cesare's fingers unravelled from my curls, but he didn't lean away even as his features twisted to bitterness.

"The countless times he's bled half to death aren't enough for his majesty?" I struck his chest with fists.

He snatched my wrists, fingers circling the bone loosely as bracelets. "Perhaps an imminent demise would slake the longing."

"If this is the end," I beheld him steadfastly, "then *stay* with me, Cesare."

He stepped back.

It was quiet again.

Cesare's teeth sank into his cheek as I once more stood witness to his battle with himself. Like he wasn't permitted to touch me. Like he wasn't permitted to *love* me.

As if pulling out by force every bloody thread Hubris sewed his lips shut with, Cesare reached out a graceful hand in a beckon to '*jump*' over an abyssal chasm because he was mad and I was too. "If you are willing to dance with me one last time."

Tentative, I slipped my fingers into the heat of Cesare's, music-born calluses grazing his, both of our flesh defiled with scars yet still healed, even if horribly wrong. And I wished with all my might that love alone could be enough to make him stay.

He yanked me towards him, cradling my jaw and kissing my lips with feverish tenderness.

I gripped the neckline of his shirt. "I will always come back to you."

"And if this time you don't?"

My heart plunged. *If it's one of us, it won't be me.* "I hope you remember me by my name and not my mask." I kissed his cheek. "And bring red roses to my grave." Then there was the frenzy again—hands and breaths fumbling like we were both fading and it might as well be true. Cesare unclipped my velvet choker, my neck laid bare, head tipping back, lips drinking my flesh the way a thirstful flame drinks kerosene. Frantic hands slid down my shoulders to slough my jacket off, skin searching for mine as if he had never touched me, not once.

"You are a goddess." Cesare's palms traced the corseted curves of my chest, my waist. His legs buckled and he sank to the floor at my feet, hands on my hips. "I'd have fallen to my knees the moment I saw you."

A clipped yelp of mine skidded away as gravity jounced with him pulling me to the timber, my shoulder blades and occiput meeting the floor almost hard enough to hurt.

"Lowlife." I giggled at the hair caressing my skin as soft lips skated the crook of my neck. The pulse in my throat. My collarbone. My chest. Fingers tread my stocking-clad thighs, bladed nails ripping the delicate cloth and peeling the ruined cloth away.

Cesare pulled back, slipping off my bloomers and hooking my leg over his shoulder.

My feet flexed when he tasted my scarred flesh, each kiss leaving me trembling until his tongue teased the adytum of my thighs where my ache pulsed most potently. I strained like a violin string, spine curving off the floor, hands clutching Cesare's hair. My every word evaporated into the whimper of his name, and I could've sworn he smiled.

A moan strayed from me as he sketched me in excruciating detail, tracing all my lines the way an artist renders his muse.

My fingers untangled from his hair, arms splaying amidst my tossed-about curls, my body writhing and sore as stars danced on the ceiling, the throb at my centre deep as a second heart pulsing on the edge of crescendo. *I'm going to die…*

Breaths heaved from my chest when Cesare's heat deserted me. He hooked an arm under my knee and waist, hauling me over him. My ringlets enveloped us like a grand drape, and he laughed as if he found his own antics so amusing. "I would have danced the night you poisoned me, you know."

"A lowborn, vagabond rat is what *you* are." I pushed him flat onto the floor, unlatched his belt, tracing his hard stomach to the hot, tender flesh beneath. "And so am I." He tensed against my touch, his startled groan scattering a shiver like saltpetre down my spine. *Your voice…* "You talk too much." A pressure fell to my pulse, a wanting burn. My breathing hitched and thinned. *"And I want to listen to you until the sun burns itself out and every luminary dies."*

A snicker. A flash of flame behind andalusite eyes. "Day by day that cataclysm nears, I'm afraid."

My spine bowed, a sharp gasp backing into my throat, and I felt flesh consume flesh and unify inside me.

An abating sigh shook Cesare, fluttering against my neck, his voice barely together as we came and went like waves and licks of fire. "But if I am to bleed my knees," *feverish lips*, "and skin my hands fleshless for it," *tongue, teeth, torment*, "then make it my supplication." *Gods end me.*

"For what it's worth," I breathed, *"I think I was half in love with you the night of 'A Bedlamite's Ballad'."*

"The bedlamite was you."

"Yes. And I love you," I kissed him gently, *"completely."* Then I kissed him hard, prying from him a bottomless groan, dark as a litany, and I tasted like tears on his sharp tongue.

His knuckles caressed my cheek, his eyes so black I could fall in. *"Maybe that night was* my *'completely'."*

Flames burst behind my eyes, tearing through me as I burned up in screaming embers and evaporated in Cesare's hands.

He exclaimed and unmade, as if my rapture was enough to deliver him. The lean tendons of his neck flexed as he angled his head and rolled his eyes back in a brief moment of daze before gazing into me again, hair snagged on the corners of his mouth. *"You did hold me to it, Giorgianna."*

The sound of my name numbed me for several heartbeats longer. I swallowed. *"And you dance well, Cesare."*

His laugh thrilled down my skin, a haunting melody of wind through the last of autumn's dying leaves, and my lips seized his again. And he replied in equal zeal, breath colliding with breath, my frantic fingers fidgeting with his cufflinks and rolling the tanzanite contraptions aside.

I clutched his shirt, pulling back as I urged him over me.

He broke away. "Are you sure—?"

I snatched his question away with another kiss as my head struck the floor, arching myself into his torso and wrapping my limps around him like a mariticidal spider. *"Make love to me."*

I wanted Cesare to burn into my raw flesh and immolate my lungs as I breathed him in, to kiss me until our tongues hurt yet to kiss me still. To come apart like the rind of a clementine beneath my nails and in my teeth.

I wanted to eat him alive.

"You don't have to touch me," Cesare whispered even as his fingers hooked under the lacing gap of my loosened corset and pulled it apart.

I unbound his shirt's laces, tugged on his sleeve. *"You are a masterpiece."* And all I could do was fall into him again and again.

CLOCK HANDS *TICKED* QUIETLY OVER TO AFTERNOON.

The timepiece overhead, Giorgianna stood by the window and looked asea, boundless curls draped down her chest and bare skin laven by the ambrosial gold of sunlight as if she were a goddess statue. As if the clouds had cleared for her alone.

Cesare wished he could put a note to every curve and edge of her junoesque form. *I want to remember your every detail.* If only he was capable of writing a piece that could do her divinity justice.

Biting his cheek, Cesare returned to his sigarétta, bending his pant-dressed legs and perching his elbows onto his knees amid the mussed sheets of his bed. Turned out that old floors were splinter hazards, so Cesare had needed to get dressed and retrieve ointment when a hefty slice of wood lodged in Giorgianna's back (which, admittedly, had him palming his face to stifle a guffaw).

"I used to listen to you." Giorgianna's voice rushed through like a cold tide across pebbled shores. Cesare's gaze reoriented towards her, and even to that very moment, those bloodsoaked carnelian eyes still reduced his heartbeat to such a clumsy lovesick fool. "At *Three Suns*. When you played violin," she clarified. "I didn't *know*." She observed the weathered floors through sunrays gilding the volitant dust. "The first instance was by chance—an evening of díem stelláre when I ventured to gauge the extent of The Court's prohibition on my freedom." Pensive silence. "I loved the music at *Three Suns*. It was the only glimmer of joy I had. And your violin glowed the most lucent. The Court did everything in its power to lead me to Lucrezia," her eyes cast to his, "but I'm glad it led me to *you*."

Cesare could do nothing but look at Giorgianna lest he choke on the immensity of the words lodged in his throat. He wanted to say so, *so* much, but his treacherous tongue rebelled. "So you *were* hopelessly in love with me." *Idiot.*

Giorgianna donned disgruntlement. "You're still a fiend."

Cesare tutted. "Not *enough*, evidently."

With an eye roll, she picked his shirt off the clothes-strewn floor and slipped it on before climbing into the bed to settle between Cesare's knees. Ruffles nearly swallowed up her fingers as she plucked the stump of a sigarétta from him, earning his objection. "Will you sing for me?" She dragged the coffin nail to completion.

Cesare pouted, eyes thinned. "I see no coin being offered up."

"Then will you tell me something?"

He raised an eyebrow. "Elaborate?"

"Anything. A story. A myth. Something Marlâre. Something pointless or something profound."

Cesare lay back on the bed, a hand propped under his head as he flicked through recollections of the countless stories his amôna told him and his phèn throughout their dismally-short childhood. He'd done well to memorise as many as he could, even if it amounted to hardly a few. "Marlâre say that when we die… we *don't*. Our souls forever sing upon the wind. The soul wants to live again, so everything is burnt—all belongings of the deceased must perish for they are tainted."

"You pray to no deity." Giorgianna noted, perched on his waist.

"I once did, before they proved themselves either cruel or dead."

"I believe in the Divine Faces."

"Is it sad?" he asked without the intention to insult. "To believe the gods are callous beings?"

She smiled so faintly and so sadly. "Misery is hardly a stranger."

Cesare's heart ached. He hated so deeply that she had ever been forced to live through pain, that *he* wasn't innocent in its conception. She didn't deserve any of it. Ever. She was too good and she *loved* so much. So deeply she drowned.

He traced the veins rooted through her wrist. "When I die, I want my ashes thrown to the wind. I want to be free."

Giorgianna leaned over to put out the sigarétta in the ashtray on the headboard, Cesare's shirt already drenched in the rodomel perfume of her skin. "When *I* die, I want my corpse devoured by the ocean." She slotted her knees back around his ribs. "I want to be one with its vastness and verity. With something as rageful as myself."

Cesare's mind bleared at Giorgianna's verses.

The night prior, before the earth had shattered beneath their feet, they'd told each other everything they hadn't yet, all their most unutterable pain, but their joys too. They didn't even kiss besides the mere minutes all-up of his mouth on her neck because it made her laugh and Cesare wanted to hear that seraphic sound. More than anything, he wished to hear her words. And it seemed so cruelly quickly that the light of the next day slashed through his eyes which had seen not a blink of sleep. They had so little time.

Cesare plucked his lighter from the headboard and shifted his head a tad, gazing towards the window where dayglow trickled. "You know," he lit another sigarétta, "I never did feel anything for the identity of a man."

"*Oh!*" Giorgianna flung a hand to her mouth. "Do you not wish to be referenced by 'he'?"

"It doesn't really matter. I'm accustomed to 'he'; I presume that's what I look like to a passer-by, but none of it means anything—I don't perceive myself as any of it. I just don't have an attachment to this body, I think." He frowned. "Sometimes I feel like I shouldn't even be whole—unrelated, but something just... *there*, also. It's as if I wish to sever my limbs to be lighter. Less. I guess I feel trapped in this... vessel."

"How *would* you want to be referenced?"

In the past tense. "'He' suffices. There's nothing intrinsically 'mannish' in that word, anyway."

Cesare looked back at Giorgianna, her gaze mellow and sweet.

She brushed unruly hair from his brow. "Only if it pleases you." Her lips squeezed. "I hope *this* wasn't... distressing? I'm not sure. I just hope you're all right."

Cesare sighed mirthfully. "Alas, couldn't remain abstinent forever." He drew smoke.

Giorgianna scrutinised him with perplexity. "You..." Cesare expelled a silvery cloud and grinned. Her eyes snapped wider. "No... *you*—"

Cesare burst out with a snicker. "What, does it shock you?"

Giorgianna squinted at him with an almost-smile. "Never?"

"Never."

"Not even Isaia?"

He shook his head, sitting back up.

"But what about Lor...?" She trailed off with vague gesticulation.

"Still got a pair of hands and a mouth. Lorita detested the idea of touching me, remember?" She'd been contradictorily insistent, but, even *then*, Cesâre sensed something destructive about her motivations. "I'm glad I didn't compound the burden on her, knowing what I know now." For all it was worth, Lorita never deserved the pain she endured, even if it justified nothing. She remained worthy of feeling some semblance of contentment within herself.

"So, in a way... Giorgianna twiddled with the ample cotton of the shirt spilling between her thighs. "I was your first?"

He regarded her earnestly. "Does that bother you?"

Giorgianna poked his collarbone. "You are in *such* denial of your own hopeless romanticism."

Cesare palmed his bullet scar in jest. "Your calumny is relentless, loloêna.[109]."

"Will you tell me what you said that night?" She grew inquisitive. "After you told me you love me."

Cesare's heart jumped. "You're racking up a debt, you know."

Giorgianna's laugh, dark as her nimbus, played like melodies with Cesare's earrings. She kneaded her fingers through his hair to tousle it all the more, planting a kiss to his cheek. "So thy façade lies after all, bàuta."

His fingertips knitted the moles strewing her thigh into constellations. "Alleged coward, remember?"

Giorgianna tilted her head. "The way you touch me. The way you talk. It's comforting." Her hands slid along Cesare's cheeks. "You are so tender."

"You've been hurt. I would never forgive myself if I hurt you too."

She rested her forehead against his. "I'm sorry, Cesare." Her voice thinned. "I can never reverse the pain I inflicted on you, but—"

"Nothing." He kissed her cheek in a gentle ritual between them. "I love you, Giorgianna."

"I will never forgive myself, either," she finished her severed sentence anyway.

---

[109] Marlâre word literally translated as '*reddest*'; used colloquially to mean '*beautiful and beloved*'.

"Maybe," Cesare pressed her hand to his chest, just beneath his left collarbone, "but your aim *was* atrocious."

She prodded him. "How many times must I call you a lowlife?"

Cesare broke character, hair falling over Giorgianna's shoulder as he leaned his forehead against it, laughing in quiet half-hysteria. "Abyss calls unto abyss, seems." His breath trickled down her decolletage, prying a giggle from her, and it was almost enough to ruin him—the knowledge that these could be their last moments. The knowledge that blood and scars were what bound them. Yet he loved her enough to forget, enough to surrender, and that ruined him most of all.

Cesare feared the touch of intimacy so deeply, yet his entire being *begged* for it. He couldn't name how many times he'd dreamed of touching Giorgianna's hair, her skin; of kissing her again. He hadn't dared permitting himself to even *think* of her bareness. The torment would be too consuming if he never got to have her, so he didn't entertain hopeless longings.

Such cruelty, to want to be loved yet cower from it.

> *'Why can't you see how* important *you are?*
> *Why doesn't it* change *anything to you?'*

So much of this would have been easier if he had never loved. Never *lived*. He lost everyone he ever cared for, did he not? And it was his fault, wasn't it? But… perhaps even *he* deserved the most miniscule scrap of joy. And those he loved deserved his penitence.

"I'm sorry I lied to you," Cesare spoke the words tentatively as a new convert's prayer. "That I withheld everything until the very last minute." He kissed Giorgianna's clavicle. "I'm sorry I treated you like my pawn." And maybe she was too good for him.

Giorgianna cupped Cesare's face, lifting his head so he would look at her. "I'm glad you lived," she said so softly. "That you forced yourself to survive despite the burden of this awful world. I hope you never again feel so much pain."

Giorgianna endowed Love with a voice Cesare never could and it tore his heart, realising how potently hubris had poisoned him with cowardice.

She closed the meagre distance between them; wrapped her arms around his neck, the heat of her body soaking into him. *"And I need you to stay."*

Cesare's anguished heart only bled more. *Why did this awful world curse you so, vólto?* His fingers spindled through Giorgianna's curls as he held her—no longer forbidden. "I hope I get to see you play songs of freedom with roses in your hair." He pressed a kiss to her cheek, lips lingering against her honey-attar skin. *I need you to stay, too.* "And I'm glad we seemed eternally forsaken to crash." *If only it had been in another life.*

But '*our lives are stories written with washable ink,*' she had told him, so would it matter if it were?

Scene XL

Kindling

Giorgianna | Cesare

UPON FIRST BLUSH OF DAYSPRING EVERY DÍEM CREPÚSCA, votaries withdrew from *Sa Basílica del Illuterixióne e Benefácio Vísus* and embarked on pilgrimages to Vencenza's minor chapels for liminal worship: a clysmic rite to purge the hallowed ground. So the church lay empty. Silent.

As nine hundred hours thrust golden sun-knives through the white fat of winter clouds, I knew to-day's impartation of holy unction upon the cathedral would stream only from the veins of the beast I would slay for retribution. A bloodline to be decimated.

The outer structures of the basilica encircling the perimeter of its expansive piazza was where I gathered with Cesare and the twins. The place at which Cesare and I had sealed our blood promise. Now, we stood there once more, so much closer to our objective, so much between us altered irreparably, yet no end in sight still.

He wore his Bauta garb sans mask. A utilitarian amalgam of Vencenzani and Âbạdil garment clothed the twins. Around my stocking-sheathed knees swished the full skirt of the grume-dark dress I'd worn to the Lanuza estate and the cremated Viper's Den, its plunging bodice reinforced with a corset of gilded steel—a piece of armour smuggled out for me by Yòchaná from the Imperiálum vaults. Off my waist hung my rapier and revolver; to my thigh clung my father's baselard. I wanted Manuele Dioli to know that I could kill him with nothing.

My eyes trained on the stone ridge below the eaves; the inscription etched upon it.

ILLUTÉRO AD'DÉL PRAEVARICÁTORI.
BENEFÁCIO AD'DÉL IMMÚNDUM.
ENLIGHTENED BE THE TRANSGRESSORS.
BLESS'ED BE THE TARNISHED.

Hoarfrost mantled my stiff lungs as biting air filled them. "Once the insurrection bells toll," I voiced, "I will find you again."

Eligio latched onto me, pressing me tight against his chest. "Promise me you'll come back." His brittle voice cracked all over. "Whatever you do, please *live*."

My stinging eyes shut as I hugged him back. "I promise, Li."

Cesare unholstered his trusty revolvers, gleaming as onyx, and I caught a glimpse of another—simpler—pair strapped to his hips along with his sabre. "These were given to me by Micheletto when I was fourteen and insisted on staying at the abandoned *Sunrise*," he mused half to himself before facing the twins. He handed them the weapons. "I want you to have them."

"Ces..." Lissandri hesitated, fingers balking as they reached for the weapons. He clenched his jaw before finally taking one of the guns, and I could see his hands tremble. "Why?"

"They belonged to your father," replied Cesare, almost blasé, but I knew him too well not to hear the edges of his voice fray. "This regime left you with no relic of your parents. You deserve to have at least this." He smiled so bitterly. "I'll hardly need them in the dungeons. Even less so should my head go rolling—"

"Don't *say* that—"

"—so they're better off with you. If *I* cannot keep you safe, at least *they* can."

The twins looked at the revolvers—what a dark juxtaposition to be attributed to a dreadful tool of mass death.

Cesare turned to me. "Take my sabre." He unlatched the sword from his belt and handed it over.

I frowned. "What for?"

"Insurance. You never know when your rapier and dagger could be knocked from your grip; when your magic starts to wear you down."

"I have my revolver."

"You can't knock a good escape plan." A smirk. "Besides, I've always wanted a piece of the griffin fucker."

I smiled sourly and took the blade, sheathing it beside my revolver.

"Perhaps I'll sing for you when this all ends."

My heart balled. "Easy. I might mistake you for a hopeless romantic."

"Keep a secret for me." Cesare's gaze and simper dropped at once, his voice weakened. "I need you to live. All of you."

The four of us embraced as if we could each be the other's unbreakable shield, as if we could save one another from every death. And beside them, I could almost believe it, these people who were light and dusk and thunder. Who rattled the sky like an apple tree and gathered its fallen stars to sprinkle in their eyes. Who had been my only lifeline.

My grip tightened, eyes ablaze with the knowledge that I would sacrifice every iteration of my Self for the three of them.

Lissandri still held onto me when our embrace unravelled, his slim clockmaker's hands rough and warm against my palms, and I never thought the softness of someone's features could drive such a sharp blade through my heart. "We will see each other again," he enounced with immeasurable conviction, the molten colour of his eyes imprinting like a bronze wax seal on my mind.

My lips pressed together as they wobbled. "We will." A tear dropped down my cheek, my fingers swiftly swatting it away.

"You still got those clockwork parts on you?"

I laughed despite it all, pulling from a pocket in the ruffles of my dress a pair of gears. "Yeah."

Lissandri's eyes shone despite that cheeky smile of his. "You never know when the time is right."

I hugged him tight once more before at last pulling back to embark on my route towards the omphalos of the basilica where the General would await me. Where I would spill blood and hand over a reaped soul as a final retributive payment for all the pain I weathered.

My retreating footsteps echoed along the marble floors, reverberated up the colossal colonnades, tolled within my bones in the way of funeral bells through a hollow campanile.

Until I abruptly halted.

Until the dread pooling in my gut grew so cold I trembled.

"*Cesare!*" I pirouetted on my feet and dashed back across the marble.

He turned, questions lining his brow, but he failed to speak in time before my arms sealed around his neck and my lips stole his voice away for an instant—such a pathetically ephemeral instant. I wanted to pull the fire from his chest and keep it with me. I wanted him to stay.

Cesare clasped my elbows as he broke off the kiss. "I'll drag you back from Hell if I have to," he hissed and I believed him.

My fists clung to his tabarro. "I will drag this entire wretched world to Hell if it takes you from me." I kissed him on the cheek in a plea and promise—*please don't let this be the last time*—and finally wrested myself free. Finally walked away.

The wrathful beast and its vengeful progeny inside my ribs writhed with a fresher thirst for righteous massacre.

Blood does not wash off. I shall avenge.

THE PRESSURE OF THE ETHER BORE ITS THUMB DOWN on the government house.

Through a crack in a concealed doorway, the ground floor of the south-eastern grand lacuna gaped up at the impossibly high ribbed vaults, thuds of soldier boots and rustles of capes echoing through the eburnine stone and off circling balconies.

Cesare often wondered if he'd be caught by the state, if their vicious hawk-and-mouse game may ever end. He wondered *how* his capture would play out, too. The conclusion he arrived at always entailed something theatric, but martyrdom of this sort had admittedly never crossed his mind—he'd decided long ago that he'd rather kill himself than be taken alive. *That*, however, existed within a vacuum of noncontingency. *This* was begotten by an unimaginable fall of rogue cards. Cesare could *certainly* imagine what awaited him in the dungeons, however. Or what awaited Giorgianna if she lost.

Palms suddenly icy, he shut the door and hid himself away within the passageways weaving through the citadel, awaiting the four-fold gunshot. The signal of insurrection.

A small subdivision of Morettae and Hounds patrolled the corridor, primarily stationed around the secret entrances. They needed most peoplepower to syphon out fugitives.

Bow and arrows beside her, Kel-Kech nervously chewed on her snakebites, preoccupied with her isizenze axe the sight of which Cesare shunned. Yezo and Anka-ny made whispered conversation nearby. Lissandri paid no less anxious attention to his brass knuckles and haladie while Eligio, a talwar strapped to his hip, attempted smalltalk with Araya to stave off trepidation.

"Most importantly, we are a decoy," Cesare repeated one last time in a search for anything to take his mind off Giorgianna. "Fewer eyes on the prison break means more chances of its success."

"If anything," Araya eyed him, "*you're* the decoy."

Cesare tapped a finger on his mask. "The damn breakout may practically be obsolete since all the feathered idiots can think about is capturing little old me for their keeper."

"Cesare," Lissandri's voice came, strangely wavering. Cesare turned to find himself in Lissandri's embrace. "We love you." He choked, arms squeezing harder. "*So* much."

Cesare's heart dropped. "Don't say it like I'm never returning." He fought so, *so* vehemently for the levity in his voice but it was no use as tears got their way, even if only for a second. He hugged Lissandri back. *"Forgive me. For everything."*

"Don't." Eligio shook his head and embraced both his brothers. "Just promise us you'll come back."

No matter how much fear it brought, all Cesare had ever asked for was his famìlia, and he would drain himself of every last breath for it.

Boom!

                Boom!

                                Boom!

                                                Boom!

The thrill of gunfire crackled through Cesare's blood.

"That'd be us!" Araya sang out in harmony with the swinging doors.

Dozens of people poured into the ministerial house. Shouts pealed and drawn steel shrieked, the air whistling with bolts and arrows.

"Bauta!"

"Arrest him!"

The bird-brained goons flocked to Cesare. *Right where I want you.*

Cesare upholstered his revolver and shot a crow before they could slash at him, crimson splattering the skeletal marble as their husk skidded beneath trampling feet.

The first blood of war.

Scene XLI

Tre Applausi per
la Dolce Vendetta

Giorgianna

THE CHOIRS NO LONGER SANG, so the basilica stood in utter stillness. All but the presbytery where, dressed in a loose beige blouse and fulvid trousers, shoulder-sweeping blond waves unkempt, prowled General Manuele Dioli, that lòthmir flamberge gleaming behind his massive back.

"How *brave*." I stepped from the shadows of the columns encircling the altar, rapier unsheathed and screeching as I dragged its tip against the ouro-veined red marble—soon to be redder.

Manuele pivoted, too fluid for someone so hulking.

His glazed orbs, gibbous as cabochon haüynites, glinted. I'd never seen such repulsion in a man's gaze.

My head tipped. "How foolish."

The General began to circle in mirror with me, every muscle wrung. "So *dáma Salomè Barsotti* was a lowly skank." His breaths tattered as if the swish of my red gown enraged him beyond the sense of humanity. "Who are you?"

A smirk plucked my lips. "Your reckoning."

He released a snarl and thrust out his flamberge, charging for me. The lustrous blade swung in a sweeping arc violent enough to dismember the air. I vaulted sideways, slipping out of the murderous range. Steel struck a column. The foundation of the edifice shivered.

Manuele spun, "Damiani's dirty progeny!" and hauled his colossal weapon into a decapitating momentum for my head.

I parried, crying out furiously in time with our blades' recoil as it propelled me backwards. My feet launched me for Manuele, muscles straining as I cleaved for him with my rapier.

I would fight him blade-to-blade first, and then I would pry open his bones.

Our steel bound. My teeth screeched against the hideous ululation begotten by this misshapen blade. He shoved me towards a colonnade. Tucking one leg beneath my hips, I extended the other and propelled myself off the column, twisting as I skidded across the floor to keep him in my line of sight.

He rotated too sharply, roaring as his flamberge hacked down on me before I could rise.

Frost spilled beneath my fascia.

Manuele's sword smashed against mine—blocked barely in time.

I winced, trembling beneath his monstrous force even with the azoth bolstering me.

The General seethed. "Heretic slut!" His leg swung back.

I gripped his wrist and hoisted my lower body up against the sturdy resistance of his stance, my left leg arcing into a kick for his temple. His unimpeded flamberge nearly cleaved my ear off as it squalled by. The impact of my boot stunned Manuele barely enough to crush his eyes shut and pry an exclamation from his gullet, but the leg he'd angled to strike me finished the job of wrecking his balance and sending him reeling.

I pounced him, burying my knees beneath his collarbones and tearing my nails through his cheek. He bayed. Ruby-precious blood rushed through the haruspical creases of my palms. The pythonic beast inside my ribs thrashed. Vengeful. Hankering. *I will drain you.*

I engaged my rapier to impale.

Manuele's knee thrust sharply skyward, leg extending.

Air ripped clean out of me as I was sent flying, flumping to the floor and rolling with the grace of roadkill. If not for the gold-plated plackart Yòchaná stole for me, my insides would've poured out of my mouth in mashed pulp.

Abrasive breaths chafed my lungs as I clambered onto all fours, rapier still clenched in a sore fist, Manuele already upright and poised to kill. A clump of curls and a shred of crimson skirt lay on the floor. *Swine!*

I sprung to my feet and charged.

Our weapons clashed in a fury of profulgent light. The endless floor tilted, impossibly vast, excruciatingly bright. The cathedral shuddered with every clamorous *strike* parry *strike* parry of metal quaking through its structure.

Manuele's eyes bulged and burst with spider-lily capillaries. Veins distended against his skin. Blood oozed to his jaw from the scratches I gouged into his cheek.

My chest tore, exhaustion demanding I grasp my hilt with both hands to withstand Manuele's might. *Damn you!*

I caught the hacking attack of his flamberge on my rapier, its undulating blade shooting a nerve-crumpling vibration through my muscles and buckling my arm.

He kicked me in the sternum. Pain spasmed through my thorax as I reeled backwards, losing foothold and toppling to the marble.

Manuele swung his flamberge and knocked my rapier from my grip.

I attempted to crawl for it.

Thick hands grabbed my ankles and yanked me back.

Manuele wrenched Cesare's sabre and tore it clean off along with the hip baldric, hurling them towards the altar before stomping hard onto my wrist as I frantically pawed for my dagger.

My lungs emptied a scream.

He grabbed me by my hair and threw me, my forehead smacking the hard marble, and stood over me, flamberge discarded. "Pathetic." His powerful fingers wedged in between the latches of my steel corset and began to pry it open.

Heat swamped me. I squirmed in panic but Manuele tore the armour off my dress, threw it into the nave of the church, "Scarlet *bitch*!" and began mercilessly beating me.

I threw my arms to shield my face, curling into a foetus. My joints locked as the violent gusts of pain kept blowing. *No. No. No. Get up!*

But I couldn't. I couldn't summon azoth or reach for my dagger. I couldn't fight back. I just *couldn't I couldn't I couldn't*. All I could do was lie still and take the beating, and the torture and rape and murder that would follow because it all came back. *The Arum*—that vile purgatory had left me an emptied husk.

I would always be too afraid.

Too weak.

Manuele pulled so hard on my curls I shrieked before his huge hand wrapped around my neck and hoisted me in the air, pinning me against a colonnade. *I'm light as a doll to him…*

His orbs exploded with savage azure flames. "Some petty magic did wonders to hide that Malefactor's Mark, whore."

My tongue flailed helplessly in the back of my throat as he *squeezed*. My ribs pinched the desperate lungs caged within them. *Nonono not again please not again not again*—my limbs spasmed. *Not again…*

Counterfeit regret contorted Manuele's features and a smile flashed across his lips, so faint yet so hideous. "Shame to admit I wanted you a little more helpless than this," he pressed against me; a wisp of air breached my gullet, "but I'm sure you'll scream the same as all of them." He slit my cheekbone. A sting opened my skin, blood trickling.

I retched at his hand's pressure, his musk, his breath on my craned neck. My muscles quivered for my baselard.

Manuele's hand snapped around my forearm so hard I knew I bruised to the muscle. I recoiled—it came out as a snarl. The blue blaze of his eyes flared. "You know it was meant to be you, right?" He knocked my head against the colonnade. "Your little Emanuela friend was mistaken for you on account of that hair of hers—so alike your dad's." Horror squeezed its first around my stomach. *No…* "*You* were our target, but I suppose mistakes are human." He smashed my head into the stone again.

And my mind began to pull back, *back* into itself. "What drives a weak, lowborn creature like you to such violence it has no prowess in?"

Snap!

Manuele's pupils cinched to flecks.

His hand flinched away from my throat and he reeled away, howling at the sight of his fingers twisted backwards at grotesque angles.

I dropped to the floor, lungs hungrily efflating with the air they'd been robbed of as I launched into a coughing fit. My bones shivered with azoth. Frost coated the inside of my skin. Nails bit into my palms when I met his hateful eyes. *I'll kill you!*

The basilica shook with Manuele's scream as he toppled to the ground, snapped bones ripping through his trousers.

I bolted for Cesare's sabre lying nearby and drove it deep into Manuele's abdomen—just beside the spleen. He cried out in poetic justice as blood spurted from within him.

"What could *possibly* drive the *lowborn* to violence?" I stopped hearing Manuele's bays at his arms splintering to flaccid mush. All sound bled into demonic whispers in my mind. *Reap what you sow, cur.* "You degrade us!" I sawed open his stomach like a sacrificial solstice pig. Crimson burst from his gasping mouth in glistening clots. "You call us worthless and dirty and putrid!" Ice bolstering my muscle, I hurled Manuele towards the altar, onto his stomach, slick ridges of entrails disgorging from its riven orifice and washing the marble in sublime scarlet. *All the redder.* "You enact violence unto us," I rammed my knee into Manuele's lower back, "enact rape and torture and disabling unto us!" My father's baselard weighed in my hand with all the years stolen from me by this atrocious polity. Each tear and drop of blood I shed for *This.* "I wonder how in the *world* we the lowborn could *ever* be driven to *violence!*" I impaled the dagger into Manuele's back. Hot blood jetted over my fingers as I cut through him, his voice reeds numbed by too much agony to scream.

I leaned close to his ear, voice dimmed to crepuscule. "I'm sure you've heard that a lot. People begging for their lives. Wishing you would spare them." My unoccupied fingers locked in his golden hair, the nauseating sight of the bruises squeezed into me by his fingertips only feeding my vengeful wrath, and slammed his head into the marble. "Emanuela Vehanush Airaldi." I winced at the sound of her name, the memory of her murder so stark and gruesome in my mind. "You remember what you did to her, evidently." A laugh writhed in my throat. "*I do.*" I tore into Manuele's shirt and skin to flay his back. "You *murdered* her!" Blood poured from his muscle, across my arms, spritzed onto my face. "That winter solstice two years ago, you bashed her skull into the frozen flagstone, and your *cronies* forced me to watch as my beloved friend was *stolen* from me!"

Against the edges of my blade, his flesh peeled back in chunks expose the dark, gore-drenched ribs folded as if a dead spider's legs inside his thorax. Manuele's scream sharpened in my ears.

"Some months ago," my condemnation crescendoed, "a pair of rogues infiltrated the infested white skull of the government building, and you almost killed one. You remember—you'd almost killed *The Bauta*, right?" His ribcage *crunched* as my dagger buried into marrow and cartilage. "*I remember!*" I sliced the ribs off his spine one by one. "I remember his blood, and I remember each time my needle had to pierce his flesh so it could stop!" My slick hands slipped off Manuele's squelching ribs as I groped to seize them. "Look who's the runt good for only dissection *now*!" Azoth engorged the vessels of my brain. I gripped the bones and began to pull them apart, shredded skin stretching against the pressure. "Do I still smell of *lust* to you?"

His lungs fluttered desperately within a maelstrom of blood. My nerves thrilled. *Every drop.*

"Do you still wonder what drives a *weak, lowborn vagabond rat* like *me* to *violence*?" I screamed and ripped his ribs from the confines of his torso, snapping and folding them out, blood soaking into my curls as they fell inside him. "You are a *rapist* and you are *filth*, and you deserve to rot like the snivelling tapeworm your ilk are." My hands plunged into the bloody well of his torso, fumbling with the slippery membranes of his organs.

"*No* amount of vengeance," I fisted his pleura and yanked it out, pink pellicles slick and glistening beneath the aurated light filtering into the presbytery, "*no* amount of blood, can atone for what you did." I stretched the deflated flesh over his ribs, giving Manuele wings like a bona fide griffin. "*I* say when you die."

I shoved myself onto my weak feet, doubling back two steps.

My skull groaned as I sang to the veins in the General's convulsing husk. Blood gushing from his torso wirbled, pouring across the marble at the behest of azoth, all dozen pints draining and spilling down the steps of the altar, inching towards my feet. All but the head. If there was any chance the hog's putrescent brain still twitched with undeserved life, I wanted to take it.

I exclaimed as crimson shot up my oesophagus and my knees buckled, almost laying me out. My azoth severed; my head bowed; my heart fluttered in my throat. Acrid iron dripped down my lips from my nose.

When I gasped for air, I breathed blood. I saw blood. Blood was the floor, the sky, the earth. Blood was I. *Blood blood blood*—there was only blood and I drowned in it. And I drowned the wretched world *just as I fucking promised you!*

Upon the altar, the aspersórium—never empty of crystalline water— stood beside the cibórium. The latter, I seeded with a handful of saltpetre given to me by Cesare. He'd said, '*Neither skies nor priests know*', and somehow I'd understood.

The vessel's golden basin blazed.

I knelt beside the butchery that was Manuele, holding my dagger aloft, yet more blood trickling down my hands, and intoned, "In hoc corporálum fórmum no'áltri infernatóri ípsi àd ípse àlti Aísi."

My voice rushed beneath my skin, through my veins, into my marrow, deified as luminous cosmic water, my tongue flexing around each syllable as if at holy instruction. "Su Tribúcce Faciáe," I levered the blade to Manuele's forehead; broke skin, "del'issúsu aperúcen lùtius." The steel slit along his flesh. "Tevodàte," I incised the perimeter of his visage, "la'mùseë'te ípse òci si no'áltri potíri tèvi ài lemúru." Digging the baselard's tip under the cut edge, I began to peel away the hateful face. "Loqui'áte," sticky red strings of gore vainly strove to keep tethered the skin to the muscle, "la'mùseë'te ípse lintáraè si no'áltri faíte faeddári ài crèci." Slicing it free, I lowered the face into the aspersórium, rinsing the skin and blade. "Alecháte, la'mùseë'te ípse álci ri no'áltri dóve'i àid alechí praevaricátio." I cast the damned flesh into the cibórium's fire. "Hoc víscera eccateári," the sarcoid perfume of cooking offal imbued the air, "hoc sánguinem eccateári," the stench of char rose with the smoke, "ípse immúndum álce eccateári si no'áltri potíri am apicée de vóstrum tolesià." I poured bloody water from the aspersórium into the cibórium, quenching the flame. "Caègum nel eccáto lùtius." *Blindness in pure light.* "Calígini fabeddí verità." *Shadows speak truth.*

I lifted my head to the heavens, closed my eyes.

The basilica once more cantillated. Not with the eerie ghost choirs of Illuteríi, but with Death.

Death was a singer with the sweetest voice. I cherished her as I cherished pain, grief, sorrow, rage. I learned what it was to be cut into pieces and sewn back together by their hands. To have my mind liberated by all which we were inculcated to conceal beneath shame.

You will pay your dues in blood because blood does not wash off.

And Their blood was my filthy diamond. *A tithe.*

And maybe I *was* Death all along.

A huff tore from my sore lungs. *It's over.*

My arms dripped with gore from the apex of my shoulders to the tips of my fingers when I gazed down at my hands. At the blood of a vile beast flooding the lines of my palms. The baselard dropped with a *clang* to the slathered marble. My head whirled with hysteria, my throat threshing as laughter forced its way out of me in maniacal convulsions between gasps and morphed into sobs. "*He is gone, Ema.*" My knees sank into the gore coating the floor. "*I rid us of him.*"

All those years of suffering shed off me, yet it hurt just as horribly to endure the agony of rebirth. *Fresh skin cannot emerge without pain.* But I no longer wanted to hurt. *Just leave me…*

The viscous warmth drowning me became a patch of snow around my bowed form. Gooseflesh rose from my skin at the whetted touch of wintry cold, a draught fluttering about my limbs like shivering white moth wings.

Snow crunched as if underfoot.

I lifted my gaze and my heart stopped.

A limber woman in an argentous tutu, sculpture-tall, neared me. Waterfalls of dark hair rushed down her back, a large mole stamped flat beside her aquiline nose. Forget-me-nots bloomed upon her irises, her slender arms sheathed in evening gloves of frost and fingers tipped in gangrenous blackness. A single pomegranate aril hung dainty off a silver chain between her sharp collarbones. *Emanuela…*

She crouched in front of me and cradled my face, slim fingers so cold my fresh froze against her touch.

I grasped her arms with my bloody, bloody hands. "It's over, Ema." I choked out. "He's dead… And I'm sorry, *I'm so sorry.*"

She plucked a piece of her forget-me-not-blue iris, one off each, eyes reforming whilst the freed fragments transfigured into blades of glass-sharp ice.

Gripping a blade in each hand, Emanuela slit open her forearms, wrist to chelidon. Blood poured out, thawing her frost-mantled flesh.

She looked up at me, smiled so softly and painfully. Tucking curls behind my ear with thawing fingers, warm with illusory life, Emanuela kissed my forehead, then pressed her cheek to mine—just as we used to always do. Our little mythological ritual. Then, she stood, stepping away as she bled into the snow.

I lunged to grab her hands but fell short, fingers curling in the snow. "*please…*"

Emanuela began disintegrating to snowflakes, glittering beneath the light still streaming into the flesh of the holy temple, until she was no more than a puff of snow floating for the apse—taken by the Gods forever.

I tucked my head down, hands clutched to my ripping heart, and wept.

I avenged Ema. I cleansed the earth of the blight that was General Manuele Dioli. And now I was left to lick at my unhealed wounds for the rest of my life. *No. No. No! Get UP!* Even as a bloodline lay decimated, an empire stood yet to be toppled; my end of the blood bargain remained unpaid. I couldn't break. Not here. Not now.

Bells tolled.

I whimpered at a pain suddenly clear as reality, looking down.

My father's dagger lay in the cooling carnage before my knees, and hotter blood surged from the incisions parting my inner forearms. Wrist to chelidon.

Dread seized me. I'd slit *myself* open.

Bells kept tolling.

I rushed to darn my veins and viscera shut, crying out and cursing when I realised just how poor my tailoring of intricately deep wounds was and how little apozem I had. *Later*. Sealing my skin as firmly as I could, I launched to my feet, cold and weak and blood-drenched, and bolted for the citadel.

SCENE XLII

MORS OMNIA VINCIT

Cesare

THE PEAL OF INSURRECTION BELLS CRASHED with the clamour of the south-eastern grand lacuna where dissidents grappled with soldiers.

Cesare knew his zealous fighting spirit was mere theatre; with every throat his stilétti slit, his aim was not to defeat the crow and griffin flocks. His resistance was instrumental in distracting the legionaries from the prison break. They'd need the jail space to accommodate The Bauta, soon enough.

Kel-Kech shoved off Cesare's back with a battle cry and hacked her isizenze through the skull of a crow. The din and hordes swept her away. Manárša with her sabre and Diodora with their dussack fought back-to-back with expert efficiency near the epicentre of the chaos. The twins guarded each other by the colonnades flanking the lacuna's northern entrance, Lissandri's haladie and brass knuckles having already taken out several bird eyes, Eligio's talwar yet to reap a soul.

Cesare flicked a stilétto into a reverse grip and impaled a charging crow before pivoting sharply to knee another one down and stab their throat.

All he needed was for his loved ones to get out. To *live*.

Coldness skewered Cesare's right shoulder. He lurched forward as sticky warmth ran down his arm. *Blind spot!* He turned to meet a legionary who spun to clash weapons with him. Metal flashed with the reel of a lifetime in front of Cesare. His killer-to-be spasmed hideously, blood spurting where a blade's tip protruded from their throat, and they sagged to a floor stamped with red footprints.

The chaos left too little time to ponder upon details, but the claret sheathing Giorgianna's arms to the shoulders could veil neither the black bruises imprinting her skin, nor the slits along her inner forearms. Blood seeped down Giorgianna's face from a slash across her cheekbone, and it tore Cesare up to know he couldn't hold her and tend to her no matter how desperately he wanted—*needed*—to. All that the wretched Saints granted him was half a heartbeat to immortalise Giorgianna's eyes in his memory lest he never see her again before a pair of legionaries forced him to draw his sullied daggers and engage.

He rived open a man's face, sticking another through the heart.

Boom!

   Boom!

      Boom!

         Boom!

The gunfire exploding in the distance marked a victorious escape—as close to it as the carnage permitted, no doubt—and in turn signified The Bauta's nigh imprisonment. Cesare allowed himself a couple breaths of freedom, sanguinary and all.

"*ANDRI!*" Eligio's scream tore through—right beside him.

Cesare whirled around.

His gut turned when he saw Lissandri: cornered by legionaries near the exit, seconds from capture.

"*CES!*" Lissandri shouted above the din and hurled his revolver, its barrelling passage through the air halted by Cesare's grasp.

Cesare looked back.

Lissandri slammed a hand over his mouth.

Cesare's blood stopped course.

"*NO!*" Eligio cried out in time with Giorgianna's helpless scream, each note driving into Cesare's heart and slicing it to pieces as he could do nothing at all.

Lissandri's eyes rolled back, sclerae bursting with bruises. His legs failed and he dropped to the ground at the feet of legionaries.

Horror overwhelmed Cesare.

Lissandri was dead.

SCENE XLIII

WE ARE BUT DUST
AND SHADOW

Lissandri

LISSANDRI HAD ALWAYS VIEWED LIFE AS A SORT OF LIBRARY.

Each person was a book—a story of their own. He admitted that, for all his snipes and cynicism, he liked people, at least of certain stripes. Everyone has their literary preferences, they say.

His mạti, Lâlẹn, who'd survived the floods of Gwạtishep and the pelagic voyage in a cramped, dingy boat across The Echoes to Faustina; who spent so many long years forcing herself to assimilate until finally growing content with herself.

His ạbậ, Micheletto, who endured a near-lifetime of destitute; who never waived a chance to instil in his children frugality and compassion.

Cesare—a brother by every measure but blood. Giorgianna who'd just about become Lissandri's dearest friend. Fabio with his wise counsel and scepticism. A man Lissandri never thought he'd see again. Even Rosalia with her prattle and shoddy manners—a little sister to him all the same.

His beloved brother, Eligio. Born minutes before and never once separated from him in their entire twenty-three years. They couldn't die together, sure and true, but it didn't feel any less wrong to leave him behind—to be brought into this world alongside him yet abandon him alone.

Maybe it simply felt wrong to leave behind his friends, his family. '*Famìlia*' as he'd picked up from Cesare all too well. Or '*hậndận*' in his mạti's Âbạdil.

Every person Lissandri loved was a new tome in his library, and a new chapter in his own story. And he in theirs, he hoped.

That was the beauty of his allegory, Lissandri thought. And if it were really true, he'd scour each shelf in search of their books, and he would add to them a thousandfold pages a thousandfold times so those he loved could live forever.

So their stories would never end

the way his did.

SCENE XLIV

BERSERK

Eligio | Giorgianna

EVERYTHING CEASED AT SOME POINT. Carnage, screams, lamentations. Eligio couldn't hear any of it over the pulse in his ears and the agony of his heart dying inside him.

They murdered his brother. Even if it was a suicide pill, even if Lissandri took it himself, he did it *because* of Them. They *murdered* him. And they would steal his body to be Defaced and thrown into a mass burial pit like refuse because the hateful absolutists valued no life above their own power.

A shudder wracked Eligio.

The Sunrise, Commegnos' Curios with their parents, the people of oldtown, his brother. De Tullia's tyranny took *everything* again and again and *again* with no abatement or reprieve!

No justice under any authority.

Eligio lunged, snatching a revolver from Cesare's grasp. Once, his father's. Mere minutes, *seconds,* ago—Lissandri's. And now they were both dead. *My brother is dead!*

Cesare's shout sounded somewhere far from his awareness, but all Eligio did was cock the revolver and shoot a swooping crow point-blank, minced brains and a pulverised eyeball bursting like a fig's innards from his shredded skull.

Five cartridges left.

Eligio spun and—***Boom!***—shot another crow, *four*, no longer registering where, only that they dropped dead as they deserved to.

A blade slashed Eligio's arm; he replied with a gunshot to the attacker's vitals. *Three.*

His chest estuated with hatred.

Hatred for the family taken from him.

Boom!

Two.

Hatred for the lives stolen from Lissandri, Cesare, Giorgianna, Lucrezia, every single person subjugated by this Hell.

Boom!

One.

Eligio's breaths tore, limbs trembled.

He wished to tear the whole world apart. *Lissandri was my brother…*

"*ELIGIO!*"

Awareness returned. Sobering. Sickening.

Eligio turned to who had called out.

It was Cesare, in the grasp of soldiers, his mask torn off and his eyes burning into Eligio. Wide. Pleading.

Panic looped a noose around his throat. His muscles torsed; his body flushed with enough heat to blister. The revolver slipped from his hands to the floor, and he was shaking again, with horror this time.

Cesare was his brother too.

A scream of helpless grief impelled Eligio's raw throat until he wanted to throw up everything inside himself, but the pandemonium carried on, and Eligio felt a hand latch onto his, tearing him from Cesare.

I CUT MY WAY THROUGH THE FINAL SWATHES OF SOLDIERS and finally reached the peripheral exits. Gripping Eligio's sleeve, I took off running for the escape: the ancient subterranean egress at the northern end of the government building, by the river bank.

Everything inside me burned and bled. An ache stitching through my side faltered my step. My heart shrivelled within my ribs. But I couldn't break.

I veered a sharp corner among a faction of Morettae and rammed into Itxaro.

"Hate to admit it," she huffed, "but Cesare's madness had some method to it." My stomach turned somersaults. "We've gotten the lion's share out; Manárša and Kel're taking the old aqueducts. You better get going too. We're right behind."

Eligio gasped a breath and clapped his palms over his face.

"Please, Eligio, we have to *go*." I couldn't look at my sorrow as I pleaded with him.

Itxaro's scrutiny only needed to pass between Eligio and me once for her eyelids to stretch wider in realisation.

We couldn't stall, so continued through the labyrinth towards escape; beneath a cinquefoil arch a couple turn-offs away from a descent to the dungeons. *Almost out.*

A Guard sprung from around a bend.

My heart kicked. I rushed for my rapier, but the crow's gut unspooled around a blade and he sagged in a dead heap. Behind him stood Ilenia gripping a schiavona, sonsie frame clad in a bloody linen chemise, her russet hair matted and dry as hessian. With her unarmed hand, she gripped by the elbow—

"*Rosa!*" I raced to embrace the girl.

She shrieked, squirming away. "*DON'T TOUCH ME!*"

I gawped at Ilenia.

"I will explain; it's too much," she said. "We must leave."

We pushed onto the final corridor. Light glowed at its end—a moon on a starless night. Brackish breeze beckoned with its cool hands to deliver us from the nightmare of the ministerial house.

I stumbled over the ramshackle threshold. The brightness of nearing midday sliced my eyes.

Just by the exit, where several Hounds prowled on alert, Yŏchaná, Sarnai at their side, bound a splint over Ǝkurofu's broken arm, his vermilion jacket discarded nearby for the time being.

"*GIORGI*!" Sarnai dashed to me, locking her arms around my waist as if the blood drenching me mattered not one bit.

I hugged her tight, pressing my brow against her head. Leather-and-lingonberry perfume mollified the violent tumult inside me. "*You're alive, I'm so glad…*" I didn't know what I'd do if Sarnai perished.

"*Wŏch*, your *arms*!" Yŏchaná stared at the slits up my forearms.

Sarnai hopped away, gripping my elbows to look at the purple, bloated skin.

Nausea swam in my innards. "I know, *I—*" My vision darkened. Sarnai and Ilenia caught hold of me. Sweat drenched me. My breathing quickened.

"We need to get to the apothecárium." Eligio wiped his tears and got Ǝkurofu to his feet. "None of us are safe until we're out of this evil place."

With a phial of ano-apozem and some alchemical stents that would dissolve in a few hours, Kasumi[110] repaired my forearms with expert proficiency, signing that she'd gotten more than enough experience with repairing corpses at Libitina's mortuary, and that *I'd* arrived at Etenesh's apothecárium half a corpse myself.

Etenesh had given me a plain shemma robe to change into after I got mended and clean, so I exited the tiny private chamber to let Kasumi tidy in peace.

---

[110] 霞 (かすみ)。

Several revolutionaries and fugitives, Əkurofu and Yòchaná included, dotted the timber floor of the foyer. The rest of the inmates, Hounds, Morettae, workers dispersed between the Armoury, mortuary, art gallery, *Antigone*.

Fabio sat outside my chamber, jolting to his feet and embracing me as soon as his bloodshot eyes met mine.

In the infirmárium at the back, Sarnai and Eligio both rushed to me.

Etenesh hustled about. Ilenia, dressed in a robe not unlike mine, sat on a high stool at the far end of the chamber and combed a tonic of olive oil and clove through her hair.

On the surgical bed, Rosalia clung to a blanket, shivering hard.

I turned to Ilenia. "Was she…?"

Her lazuline-emerald eyes dropped. "I'm afraid so."

Acid forced its way up my throat.

"*Th*-they—the soldiers—*s*-said it would make my defected mind better," Rosalia sputtered, "*a*-and when they *s*-stabbed me, and I began *c*-crying, they seemed so disap–*point*ed."

"What 'defected mind'?" Etenesh hurled her hand towel into the sink. "There's no 'making better' *anything* in such heinous ways. What a ridiculous notion!" She sat down beside Rosalia, carefully soothing the girl's head. "If this is what they intend to do to asylum patients and inmates, I'll pick up a shətol[111] myself!"

"Imperialíi took her from the Holy Guard," Ilenia spoke up. "Abelli wished to attempt making Rosalia into their prophet, and ordered their Illutoríi to permit no Imperiálus near her, but, unfortunately, we know who *really* calls the shots."

Rosalia cowered into the blanket, features crumpling. "I've never *f*-felt this before… this *much*. I'm so scared…"

I gingerly reached to stroke the girl's hair only to have her flinch. "I'm sorry, Rosa…" I didn't know what to say. How was one to reckon with something so horrific? How was *she* to?

---

[111] Shotel (ሸተል); a slender, curved sword (*almost like a large sickle*) from Eritrea and northern Ethiopia.

"How the Hell did *you* get out unscathed?" Fabio demanded of Ilenia. His eyes glistened despite his hard-edged tone. He might as well have lost his children to-day.

"Barely." Ilenia sighed as she plaited her oil-soaked hair. "The prison break got in the way."

I hated the thought, but, standing witness to Rosalia's anguish, I couldn't help resenting the Minister of Scholars.

"Rosalia cannot stay here," Etenesh informed. "The movement of legionaries is too high. Return to *Antigone*, but be gentle with her."

"Thank you, Etenesh."

"Iseppa sent word that Cesare's execution is to be at seven hundred on díem auróra."

My stomach vied to empty itself. *Two days…*

I swallowed, parched. Sarnai held my shoulders.

Eligio helped Rosalia out of bed, shielding her with himself. She clung onto him, yet recoiled from all else.

We re-entered the foyer.

The front door opened and in walked black-haired Anka-ny with her reindeer hide kerker coat.

In tow entered a gangling, scraggly person of approximately fifty years, nondescript by way of dress as all the prisoners were. Bleached tufts of fading peach tipped their dark hair, once seemingly close-cropped, their tanned skin inked neck-down. Even their xenial face sported tattoos. Their dove-blue eyes roved the apothecárium. "Word 'as it, this is where the main orchestrators assemble," they chirped in a cheery voice with a faint provincial accent.

My eyes narrowed at them. "Laútni?"

Fabio stepped around Ilenia. "Matìa…" His nitid eyes affixed the stranger—*or perhaps not*—upon the threshold.

Laútni grinned wide, baring a pearly smile endowed with a triplet of gold teeth. "Fabio!" They threw out their arms.

Fabio's larynx bobbled. "I don't believe it…"

"You best do, old man!" The two hugged, Matìa clapping Fabio firmly on the back. They pointed at me. "And if it ain't Vico's girl!"

I *tsk'd* and folded my arms in jest. "No *mystery*."

His skinny hand patted my shoulder. His eyes twinkled. "He'd be proud of you, sure and true."

The light of thirteen-hundred-hour sun seeped through thick winter clouds, doing little to warm me in the thin shemma against the oceanic wind sweeping Buccaneer's Landing.

"How the Hell'd you manage to get yourself nabbed?" Fabio asked Matìa.

"The nonce Davide."

Fabio tutted. "Bugger."

"*I'll* say! Damn miracle I didn't get my brain skewered by those pigs in gold." Their eyes found mine. "You've 'eard this until it's lost all meaning, I bet, but nevertheless, I'm really sorry about your pa, love. 'e was a sweetheart."

I pressed my lips. "He was." *Whom I wouldn't kill to have my father with me at this moment…*

"And…" Matìa addressed Fabio, "others?"

"Durans remains equally dead; Davide's been killed by Cesare."

"I *beg* your pardon?"

"Too much to explain—in due time. Giorgianna informed me that Dafne's still a sóra of the church; Şirîn is offering us aid, in eternal generosity."

Matìa pulled a knowing face. "That's not *all* the others, Amadi…"

The captain's gaze dulled. "Ada is fine."

"*Uhuh.*" Matìa smirked and hooked his arm around Fabio's neck. "We've got a lot to catch up on, old man."

The two continued onto the captain's quarters after Fabio left every possible reassurance with me.

Eligio and Rosalia had rushed ahead, holing away on the floor of the artist's chamber where Sarnai and I found them alongside the grieving Lucrezia. I frankly didn't care what Ilenia did with herself.

Rosalia clung to Eligio still. His reddened eyes stared at nothing.

"I lost my twin," Eligio choked on his own words. "We've been separated not a day in our lives. Even when he was so insufferably blunt, it didn't matter because he was a piece of me. And now he's gone. Just like our parents." Tears dropped down his face. "I'm on my own…"

I embraced Eligio; Lucrezia and Sarnai gathered around us.

"*You're not*," I whispered. "*You will never be.*" How many times had the twins said damn near the very same thing to me? How many times had they made this existence the tiniest iota more endurable? They were irreplaceable; *Lissandri* was irreplaceable. With his pragmatism and harsh wisdom. His once-ungodly early mornings of fiddling with clockwork or rummaging through shelves for books he'd read thrice over. This vile kakistocracy took his family, and then it took him.

"*They all deserve to die.*" Eligio's whisper frosted my skin.

"*I know.*"

When we unravelled, Rosalia still latched onto Eligio.

Lucrezia sniffed deeply. "We're all tangles, *eh*?" She rubbed at her ruddy face with a carelessness she seldom permitted herself, her black locks unbrushed and loose clothes haphazardly tossed on.

"How are you coping?" I asked.

"I'm not," she gritted out. "Merely sleeping and crying and eating. I can't stop thinking about Valentina and Ayana." She wrapped her arms around herself. "I don't regret killing but… I do. Somehow." Her head shook. "I don't know."

I understood her, though I wished I didn't. I wished I never came to. *I wish none of us ever knew this pain.* How much more grief could we feel before we felt nothing at all?

I wreathed my arm around her shoulders and leaned her head against mine. "I cannot promise it will stop hurting, but it will grow liveable. Little by little. Drop by drop. Every single day."

"What about you, Giorgi?" asked Eligio.

I rose. "Don't worry about me."

I no longer felt the floorboards beneath my feet, hadn't even perceived my own passage through space until the scene before me had transmogrified into the dim bathing chamber, until I sat inside the empty wooden tub, arms around my knees. Arms which the robe sleeves were too short to cover, laying bare the horrific black bruises branded into me.

A sob broke from my chest and I wept, head bowed into my arms.

I'd felt so powerful in the basilica, drenched in blood with the mutilated carcass of Manuele slain on the marble. But after triumph came the loss. The pain.

I whimpered, clawing at my skin with the urge to tear it off. *Why didn't this end with that evil fucking man? Why won't you* leave *me?*

The door gently creaked.

"Giorgi?" called Sarnai.

"*Gods, it feels so empty...*" I was nothing without my gutting vengeance.

Sarnai climbed into the tub and sat across from me, palming my knees. "Talk to me."

"I killed him, Sarnai. I butchered Manuele like the pig he was but it wasn't enough. Why isn't it *enough*?" My hands fisted in my hair. Perhaps my vengeance gutted *me* in turn. I was empty without rage, after all. *I don't know how else to live.*

"I'm sorry." Sarnai rested her head on my knees.

"I regret none of it," I hissed. "I would drag him back from the Null just to destroy him again and again but—" I choked. "*I don't know, either...*"

"There's too much tragedy to bask in the triumph," Sarnai remarked precisely. "It looms over and overshadows everything."

"What about Itxaro?" My voice quavered.

Sarnai huffed, and what I thought would be a sigh turned into tears.

My chest pinched. "Sarnai?" I dashed away my tears and held her shuddering form to my heart.

"No, it—" Sarnai sniffled, "I just—I didn't think it'd hit me like this? *Th*-the Antrum, I mean. Isaia basically picked me up off the street, you know. Otherwise I've no idea where I'd've ended up, 'cause I left Örgön Gazaar to escape conscription and couldn't even go back." She clutched onto the back of my robe. "You know, my family would always gather around in our gər[112] to play shatar,[113] make büüz[114] together for Lunar Birth. Düü[115] and əgch[116] and I loved telling each other oral tales." She sobbed into my chest. "*I had so many people all my life…*"

I caressed her hair, wishing so desperately to take her sadness into myself. Sarnai never earned a single ounce of hurt. *Why does life punish everyone who deserves it the least?*

"I don't know," Sarnai muttered. "I'm crying because I'm happy for Xaro, for *you*, b-but I'm sad because I lost so much—and I wasn't even really friends with any Boar or Hound but they were as close to family as I could've had and I just… I don't *know*, Giorgi." She curled up tighter against me. "*I don't know what the point of this is.*"

I shifted pale locks, white as the snow of Jegün Kəgər, behind Sarnai's ear and stroked her cheek to wipe away a tear.

"Sometimes there is none," I admitted. "You suffer for no sin. But even if grief broke you, here you are." I pressed a peck to her brow and just held her. "I am so sorry I have nothing else to offer you but that, Sarnai."

She shook her head. "I don't know what I'd do without you, Giorgi." The strain on my heart eased a tiny fraction at the sound of her voice quelling. "Please don't die, lunatic. I love you."

"I love you too, silly."

We stayed a while longer in that forsaken wooden tub. We had so little time. *Even if it is in grief, let us be together in grief. At least we shall be together.*

As I carefully pulled back, my hands enveloped Sarnai's. "Itxaro is good." I tried a smile. "I'm content to entrust you to her."

Sarnai giggled despite herself, wiping her flushed nose. "And *I* was neither blind nor stupid about Signór Revolution."

My heart bled as if shot.

"Hey." Sarnai squished my fingers. "He's going to live, okay?"

---

112 Yurt.
113 Gazaari chess.
114 Meat-filled steamed dumplings.
115 'Brother'.
116 'Sister'.

"Look at the state of Rosalia!" Panic recrudesced. "They are going to *hurt* him!" And I couldn't be with him, couldn't hold him, couldn't *help* him.

"We will get him out, Giorgi, miniscule numbers or not."

She was right. This empire couldn't be toppled without the numbers. *Cesare you're a madman* why *why did you* do *this?*

We had the people, but we couldn't use innocents as flesh shields. Weakening the imperialist flocks, first and foremost, was of the essence, otherwise the citizenry would suffer massacres, and nothing could exonerate us of such heedless disregard for humanity.

Dealing initial damage fell into our hands, but even now with the fugitives, we were still few, and most of the escapees were hardly in a fighting state. *Gods, how are we to ever conquer this?* A corpse needed to be Defaced before banishment, after all.

My derailing train of thought screeched to a halt.

Defacement… Why had I performed the Defacement on Manuele?

I jolted—*Sarnai* jolted me. She said something but I didn't hear it.

Defacement was performed on death row prisoners within the eleven days following death, for a faceless entity could not coalesce with the divine Godhead, destined thus to be banished into the Everlasting Null.

The Eleven Days of Liminality…

Recollections of Lucanus came to me, and an idea struck like lightning.

"There's a way to strengthen our numbers." I bolted out of the tub.

Sarnai shouted after me but I was already en route to my bedchamber.

I needed to dress, then I needed to sharpen my blades.

The final section of the following chapter includes *child suicide*.

SCENE XLV

ELEVEN DAYS
OF LIMINALITY

Aengus | Giorgianna

A SOLDIER. *A griffin.*

Aengus backed away from the corpse slumped against an entrance to the Antrum, his heart hammering hard. Blood smelled warm and sharp in the air, on Aengus' blade. *He go' this close…* And if they hadn't been there to waylay the intruder…

Aengus mindlessly tapped a trembling fist on a fellow Boar's chest. "We've go' reconsiderin' to do."

I STILL RECALLED THE FIRST TIME I ENTERED the Cyclopes' district—the day I discovered Davide's repulsive home and almost killed myself with a tailoring fluke.

The streets still yowled in all their sinister proportions. The smashed cobblestones, the foetid aroma lifting off the ducts, the alleys crawling with rogues and oozing tarry shadows: a sea of black and brown like mud floating atop dark water. *Déjà vu.*

And yet, this time, as a massive warehouse invaded my field, its dark corpus lacunose with age and violence, acid didn't slosh cold in my gut. Even with the ghosts of panic and despair still clinging to my shadow, I approached without a falter to my step. *Means to an end.*

A pair of familiar Cyclopes flanked the entrance. A slim androgyne with sable hair twisted into a topknot, ankles and wrists clinking with gold bangles and tan skin studded with epidermals. A bulky, keloid-covered man with shoulder-brushing vermilion curls shaved unilaterally, cheeks perforated by gauges.

Sighting me, the duo uprighted.

The curly-haired man's singular eye glinted. "What's a signorína to need here?"

I halted a safe distance away, back pinned, chin up. "I request an audience with Dóminus Lucanus Arnza."

He tittered, "How 'bout it, Chea?" shoving a slit tongue through the hole in his face. "Think Lucanus'd appreciate some guests?"

Chea ran a thumb along the blade of their dav, smiling a wide row of shark-sharp teeth—filed. "*I* think guests're always a treat."

The pair stepped aside, leaving the doorway unobstructed.

Dithering, I squinted at them both in turn, earning myself only a duplet of larkish grins. *I ventured this far…* So I stepped inside.

Past the vestibule, the tenebrious corridors tangled like malformed arteries. The air hung sarcous as if carcasses in a slaughterhouse with the reek of offal and culled game. My skull pounded, throbbed, yet numbness fogged my mind over as I traversed bifurcations clogged by chattering devils of people. Pierced and vivisected beyond humanity. Tattooed with eyes eyes *eyes eyes eyes.*

The walls began to whisper. Shift. Split open.

I palmed my ringing head. *Stop.*

Shrieks pulsated through the hallways like heartbeats of panicked livestock. The Cyclopes surged with guffaws.

I tore free of writhing limbs and swerved a corner down a deserted passageway.

A spindly hand grasped my elbow.

I brandished my baselard and pirouetted with all the intention to drive the blade forward.

"Sure you wanna go down those ways?" sibilated a man, rough and gaunt. His features melted into wax around the adularescent blue marble of an orb sagging from his left socket, the other seemingly clutched and forced into his brow by aggressive torsion, whilst his lower lip all but split as if stuffed with too much fat for the skin to contain.

An ache pulsed between my brows. With every blink, his physiognomy warped the slightest bit, barely enough to notice, but enough to turn my stomach.

I must have said something, because he doubled back from me.

The dilating vein swept me ahead.

I stopped. Turned.

An ordinary tattooed man was in place of the cockeyed creature, placid as if having never engaged with me.

I've lost my mind.

The most horrifying sound was the truth in my own assertion.

Distance supplanted the rickety wood of the corridor with bricks between which grime hardened to a rind. The air cooled, but the metallic stench of blood only sharpened.

At the hallway's end, an archway opened to a large room not unlike a mortuary crypt.

Hunks of humans spread in gelatinous grume across the stone floor. Chains enwreathing the walls suspended ill-fated persons in various states of skinning and dismemberment. A gutted male hanging by their feet, throat slit as if cattle, was the closest to a whole body in the chamber, though with arms and genitals missing. A jarring bureau with two chairs stood in an alcove at the distal end between a pair of impassive Cyclopes.

In the butchery's centre stood a colossus of a man dressed in a spike-beset leather vest and trousers, muscular arms inked with columns of eyes and hair chopped into a long mullet. His right fist gripped a sickle-shaped khopesh, his left: a zweihänder. Both dripped blood. *Lucanus.*

Lupine orbs, yellow as triphanes, glinted behind nails hammered through his protrusive brow ridge into his cheekbones. "Ah." His wide lips gashed apart, flashing at me incisors sharpened to flesh-ripping points. "Late Ygal's gutsy little paisan."

I snorted, arms laced. "Hardly."

Lucanus paced around his desk. "Loss of privileges, eh?" He rested his blades against the far wall and sat down. "I 'member what that was like. We used to be decently friendly until the woman got all moralistic about my tastes. Sad to see her perish." He tossed a look at the wonky chair across from him. "Sit, since you walked all this way."

Shoulders stiff, I stepped into the chamber. *At least the archway doesn't come with a door.*

Stepping around disgorged entrails and severed heads, I made it to the bureau, and it was with revulsion that I realised the chair I sat in was upholstered in human skin.

Religious memorabilia decorated the wall behind the Dóminus—ruby eye pendants, celestial talismans, golden masks.

"A devout man?" I asked.

"Very. You've heard of Cyclops tradition, I don't doubt."

'*...if you kill the Dóminus...you* become the Dóminus with full reign *of the cadre... untouchable for eleven days post the old one's death...*'

I stifled a grimace at Lucanus' measuring peer. *Perhaps Cesare's temerarious modus vivendi isn't meant for me.* "Indeed."

"What brings an ossíi here?"

"We've already informed you and Vitture of our need for allyship. Seeing as we've lost the Boars, we find ourselves in a great need of support. *So*," I leaned my elbows onto the desk and rested my chin on my laced fingers, "I come to you once again with that request."

Lucanus licked his incisors with a split tongue. "What makes you think I've changed my mind?"

I tilted my head; glanced down; gazed back up.

Snap!

The Cyclopes dropped like stuffed sacks, necks twisted around.

Anxious heat flushed through me with the wave of frost, but my eyes remained fixed on the constricting pupils of Lucanus. "Was hoping I'd help."

The man jumped to his feet, zweihänder gripped. "Dirty slut!"

"*There* it is." Azothian melodies dinned through my skull. The blood on the floor stirred and writhed, slithering across the stone and up my fingers, wrapping my forearms to become gleaming ichorous blades. "You were beginning to *worry* me!" I stepped onto the desk and lunged for Lucanus.

He angled his sword to chop me.

Snap!

His arms broke and deformed. He emptied a howl.

I roundhouse kicked Lucanus in the head. He coggled sideways.

Springing off the table, I hacked down.

Shhhhunk!

The blood-blade sliced Lucanus' torso in twain easily as morlac cheese.

Before my feet struck the ground, I swung to decapitate him, two halves of his head flying in a grizzly detonation of viscera and striking stone with *thunks!*

Blood cascaded off my arms across the floor once more. Red waves lapped at my boots and rushed to cradle the dismembered heaps of former persons.

Wiping my nose, I fisted my father's bleeding eye pendant and made my unsteady way behind the desk.

The triple face mounted beneath the ceiling gazed at me. I touched my fingers to the ruby iris encrusted upon an asteriated gold disk and muttered a prayer—"*Calígini fabeddí verità*"—before unsheathing my dagger and driving it into the bureau's surface. Hand poised on the hilt, I plopped into Lucanus' seat of honour, resting my feet on his desk.

Footsteps hammered the stonework and a pack of Cyclopes raced into the slaughter room, Chea at the vanguard. They gaped, speechless, at their new Domína.

"What's that Illutèri proverb?" I mused. "About eleven days and liminality?"

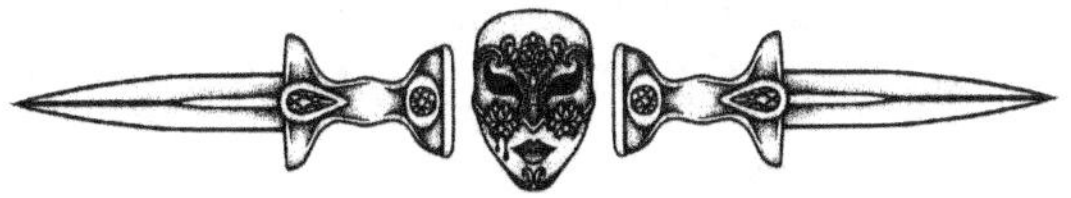

"*Again?*" Fabio exploded. "Giorgianna, how many times must this lunacy repeat?"

Eligio beheld me solemnly. "You better not make a habit of this like Ces." His hard words pierced my heart.

Sarnai blinked at me. "This is *not* what I expected when you said 'there's a way to strengthen our numbers'."

"But said lunacy *worked*," I noted. "The Cyclopes are one-hundred-eight-strong and I am their rightful Domína. *Unwanted*, yes, but my compromise appeals to them: should they assist us, the status of Domíne will be transferred to Lucanus' second-in-command, Chea."

"*¡Whoowhee!*" cheered Danilo. "Girly bumped off Pâin *and* earned Sten's respe't *AND* 's now the Domína of a cadre!"

Fabio rubbed his eyes.

"*And* 'e Dahlia's champion!" Korneli piped up. Danilo nodded along. "Fucking *sensational!*"

"Someone mentions my champion?"

We all flinched towards the wharf.

An older woman stood at the bottom of *Antigone's* gangplank, hands in the pockets of a scarlet-broidered greatcoat, a black grimalkin with its peridot orbs nestled on her shoulder. Beside her was white-eyed Sten, stout and broad in his lamellar armour.

Bewilderment overcame me. "Dahlia?"

She cocked her head, black fringe streaked with silver brushing her brows. "Heard your troupe was short on numbers here and there."

I stilled. "You… offer an alliance?"

"That yet-to-be repaid favour of mine is overdue."

Ren eyed the captain of The Black Tongues. "What's with Baldheaded?"

Sten shrugged. "Genetics."

Dahlia rolled her eyes. "Reinforcement."

I looked at everyone aboard *Antigone's* deck.

Fabio gaped in mute shock whilst various hues of befuddlement painted the rest of the faces.

But no objections rose, so I faced the respective captains of the Blood Dahlias and Black Tongues. "Strength in community," I quoted Tafsut, heart pounding its hopeful rhythm as I touched my palms to it. "Always."

Sten grinned a half-gold set of teeth. Dahlia smiled dryly.

Boom!

A gunshot rattled my heart.

A scream pierced the dusken sky. *Lucrezia.*

Eligio and I hurled down to the cabin deck. Veered into Lucrezia's chamber.

She huddled on the floor, writhing at the legs of an armoire in a tangle of keens and frantic gestures across the room.

I looked over and my blood froze.

Rosalia sat against the opposing wall, a doll in her orange dress—ruffled as a marigold. Her head sagged, her eyes glassy as they stared unseeing at the floor. By her limp fingers lay a revolver. Blood streamed down her cicatrose cheek from a smouldering bullet hole perforating her temples.

"No..." I heard Eligio. "*Nonono* I shouldn't've left her, I *shouldn't've.*"

I realised in horror that the revolver was mine.

Fabio's hands held my shoulders just as my muscles deadened and I slumped to my backside. My eyes couldn't tear from Rosalia's corpse, from her fragile wrists, her flesh wan and translucent as onion skin. Life had been leached from the girl long before she put the barrel to her own head. Adolescence was a lie—Rosalia was *so little* and They *stole* her! And we couldn't protect her.

The empire could never be washed clean so long as it stood.

SCENE XLVI

BABYLON

Crescenzo | Giorgianna

THE OMPHALOS FILLED WITH EVERY PATRON of the ministerial house—all but the Illuteríi, bar a meagre few—and the remaining noble families.

Sundown shadows haemorrhaged through the soaring windows.

Sitting upon his ceremonial seat, Governor Crescenzo De Tullia bit down the twitch of fury in his jaw. Such lowly, vulgar sensitivities fit only brutes. Nevertheless, Crescenzo's humiliating apprehensions were not sprung from naught.

The murder of Adviser Clario Barsotti, a prison break, spates upon spates of frighteningly organised insurgency sparking all across Vencenza, city *and* province, like matches in a withering forest: the state's hold on the citizenry slipped minute by minute. Such, Crescenzo could never permit.

Active insurrectionists were to be culled with no clemency, just as they had been the day they'd shouted inane protestations upon the Solar Square and gotten their dues. Following The Bauta's execution, the

Governor's legions would commence cleansing lower óssium and The Court of Secrets. Their defective beacon of degeneracy called to be snuffed out first. Any and each malcontent awaited confinement to corrective labour camps in the provinces—Crescenzo didn't intend on cleaving to High Priest Benetto Abelli's lunacy for much longer.

But first, Crescenzo endeavoured to rid his *own* blood of filth.

He turned to Basilio Lanuza who stood beside him on the daïs, dressed in the black of mourning and surrounded by Guards. "You did not inform me of Ludovico Damiani's progeny earlier." The Governor's tone sharpened to a guillotine blade. *The progeny I had tasked time and time again to be liquidated.*

"*G*-Governor," the blond man fawned. "*P*-please accept my petition of forgiveness, *I*-I hadn't gleaned it in time despite suspicion, and *th*-thought it disrespectful to—"

"Silence your grovelling," Crescenzo bit. "I have use for you still, as the sole patriarch of the Lanuzas." *You have no choice but to bow to me.*

Tension released Basilio's shoulders. He nodded and bowed vigorously, heading for the staircase.

A Guard thrust out their gladius to halt him.

Basilio's throat bobbed. Fearful questions riddled his eyes when he stared at the Governor. Crescenzo simply gestured him to remain upon the daïs; the Guard lowered his weapon once the noble complied.

The crowd echoed in its decimated numbers through the hollow structure. The passing months had witnessed spates of senators, nobles, soldiers falling to the sword of the recusant hordes. *I shall put an end to it soon enough.*

Silence ghosted through the hall as Imperialíi forwarded in, the court parting before them in a murmuration of frightened starlings. The final griffins to enter shut the doors after themselves. The latch reverberated through the marrow itself.

Halting at the foot of the daïs, the golden elite soldiers, a hundred-sixty-strong, Imperiálus Diodato Casca at the vanguard, kneeled to the Governor and thrust their left sleeves up as an ancient mark of credence—a confirmation that they concealed no contravening weaponry.

Crescenzo rose.

The soldiers rose.

"Succeeding the assault against our citadel this morning," the Governor intoned with his solemn countenance and sonorous voice—a sensate statue carved above a tomb, "General Manuele Dioli has been found brutally slain in the chancel of our holy basilica, his corpse stripped of a face and torn apart as if by the claws of a demon." *May he rot.* "Under such conditions, and with a mounting necessity to defend our state, I hereby declare myself Governor General, and command the Imperialíi to submit themselves unto me, to take up their armaments in defence of the regnant party and the interest of the good people."

Imperialíi bent the knee once more, as if at the behest of a master puppeteer.

Imperiálus Diodato Casca cast their eyes to the ground. "We hereby declare fealty to you, Governor General Crescenzo Zuane De Tullia, as your Imperial Blades." Their voice unified with the rest of the legion. "Our sword and shield are at the command of the Ministry."

Good.

"Dissidence will not be tolerated," proclaimed Crescenzo. "Every threat to my tenure shall be excised as the malignancy it is." He sat upon his throne and held Casca's gaze like a pair of emeralds he could drop and smash at any second if he so wished. "Every."

The Imperial Blades stood, drew their swords, and, in single clean swipes, began to cut down each person standing in the hall. Every noble, senator, holyman, official, servant. *Every.*

The walls quaked with screams. Blood draining from slaughtered bodies flooded the skeletal marble until its pallor drowned. No few desperate survivors clawed and bashed at the locked door of the Omphalos, their wails for mercy rattling the colonnades.

Basilio began to retreat further up the daïs, palms folded over his drained face as he gaped at the massacre he was graciously spared from.

At the fringe of the scene, where blood was yet to lacquer the lifeless ivory, Crescenzo caught a brief glimpse of an Imperial Blade clashing with an Illutèri votary.

His brows pleated when the Imperiálus keeled, when their burnished husk toppled like a panoply. The votary slipped through a gap tucked into the walls and vanished from beneath the edge of a blade.

She knew of the secret passages…

Dissidents, traitors, liars.

Crescenzo De Tullia's rule was not secure until every snake in the grass was eliminated. He could spare *no* precaution.

The struggle died. The clash of metal ceased.

Every person but the soldiers fell dead and rended. *Better off so.*

But he wasn't done.

He stood, lòthmir falchion in hand.

Ushering Diodato Casca and a second Imperiálus to follow him, the Governor marched past a stricken Basilio without a glimpse spared, and descended the daïs, the hem of his iron-silver robe soaking up the bloodbath.

ZILLĪJ TILES decorating the Zeghlache family's carpet-making parlour glistened beneath alchemical street lights.

Yòchaná accompanied us to the slums without hesitation, putting to use their strength and skill to aid the people with repairs. Ilenia remained with Eligio to tend to Lucrezia, but a part of me couldn't help suspecting she simply didn't wish to make contact with those in destitute. Her masonry could have been more than a godsent.

Saying parting words to the folk in the cramped house nearby, I made my way back to the carpet-making parlour where Tafsut fussed over the unhoused with food and blankets.

Little Aldjya sat beside Karmni beneath one big tahruyt on the sill of the large square window, running her little fingers along the cloth's ornamentation. "Mother says Asifargazi embroidery is more than just the craft, but an artform and spiritual resistance."

"Woolwork is a revered art in Tmurt-Asif." Tafsut leaned out of the window. "Tudert is life. Woman gives birth to textile, see."

Karmni folded her fingers—inked with Mariano religious symbols. "Thank you for allowing me to partake, evvịva."

Tafsut's eyes crinkled, and my heart winced at the sight of Karmni smiling back. A thousand tragedies plagued my mind, so I clung to any semblance of hope in the slaughterhouse world.

From around the corner, to my left, a woman stumbled out onto the street, her clothing blood-red, her dark hair streaming.

"Dafne?" I exclaimed in one voice with Yòchaná.

"*Oh!*" The sóra clutched her chest. "My Gods are merciful!"

I ran to embrace her. "What happened?" Her nose bled.

"De Tullia massacred his court and declared himself Governor General in light of Dioli's death. He plans to execute every Illutóre and Guárdus who refuses to join the Imperiálum or City Guards."

"No…" My stomach sank. "Our Hounds are still there. Yòchaná!" I called. "Take Dafne to *Antigone*."

"Where are you going?" they questioned.

"Upper óssium."

"No, *don't!*" Dafne attempted to grab me, but I was already swept away by the umbral capillaries of The Court of Secrets.

Building flickered by, morphing from wood into stone, colours and people distorting like a tumble down a frightening dream of a psychedelic hellscape I had already traversed, every veer a memory and déjà vu.

The Solar Square approached.

I cried out when I ran into something solid, but at once not.

Staggering back, I frowned, beholding nothing but shadows. My heart pounded as I reached for them. The caliginosity rippled around my hand, watery, cool. I curled my fingers and the darkness clumped in my hand.

My eyes widened.

I tugged the shadows, pulling it away in a glittering veil. Azoth hoarfrosted my skin. *Am I… weaving the shadows?* My vision obscured as I draped the darkness over my hair and back. The bargain of a shadow weaver: the more magic they expended, the more invisible they became to the world, the more blind they grew. *But how can I do this?*

Then, I recalled my final conversation with the Ram girl, the liver she cut out of herself and handed to me to eat. *When ingested, exogenous azoth coalesces with that of the consumer, replenishing their reservoirs, healing, even granting azothian abilities they previously did not possess.* And there were only two ways to ingest azoth.

Comprehension tumbled behind my eyes.

Could I control the mind?

Could I glimpse the future?

I thrust off the thoughts and bolted through oldtown into upper óssium.

Citizens shouted.

Fires burned along the skyline. *Chapels!*

Illuteríi clad in crimson rushed by as Guards executed them in droves.

I drew my dagger, its blade ripping the throat of an incoming officére, and pushed on through the collapsing state, its walls scrawled with epithets of revolution. Silver banners of De Tullia's tenure blazed in flames. Blood dripped down unseeing faces carved into eburneous stone. The populace shouted: 'VÍTAM DI RIVOLUZIÓNE!', 'FREE THE BAUTA!', 'FREE THE IMPRISONED!', 'DEATH TO THE DICTATOR!'

The Hanging Gardens unfurled before me.

Dissidents I recognised sawed away the wilted honeysuckles and cut down the cages and corpses suspended from the costiform bridge bowing across the walkway. Where armed soldiers pounced to kill liberated inmates, ossíi fought them off with nothing but bricks and walking sticks and knives.

As I looked upon the scene, I could feel neither hope nor fear at the sight of the regime's brutality in all its hideous glory, its clash against righteous rage.

In my adolescence, my mother would bring me to The Hanging Gardens, grip my shoulders and jaw, and force me to look upon the brutality. *Nothing is worth it*, she'd hiss. *Freedom* wasn't worth it if all it got you was *That*. But, beneath the fear, the sight of the dead and dying, the *murdered*, only cast tinder into the fires of rage. And rage sired vengeful progeny. And that vengeful progeny were the desperate of Vencenza baying for justice. For liberation from confinement.

We were teeth, and we would rip our way out of this putrescent corpse. We would give that filthy fucking kakistocracy *Hell*.

Freedom would *always* be worth it.

The following chapter details *graphic torture* and touches on *human experimentation.*

SCENE XLVII

AS GOLD IS TEMPERED BY FIRE, SO STRONG MEN ARE TEMPERED BY SUFFERING

Cesare

WHEN CESARE'S EYES OPENED AGAIN, he could see his new lodgings, and what an unfortunate development *that* proved to be.

He sat strapped to a chair in the centre of a cell with his arms buckled along every joint to diagonally-thrust stone ledges, his sleeves rolled up. His right arm lay wrist-down, knuckles trapped within crushing devices and fingertips slotted inside what he assumed to be a sort of nail-ripper. A strange metal ridge protruded from the inflamed flesh of Cesare's left chelidon and wrist which faced up, his fingers similarly restrained by metal loops. *Phenomenal.*

Groaning against the ache radiating down his spine, Cesare angled his chin upward. He swallowed, coughing. Barely a drop of moisture coated his tongue. He shook his head. A bolt of pain shot into his skull, his vision blinking with stars as hair irritated his sensitised face.

He fought to bring the rest of the cell into focus.

His chair faced a reinforced door. Alchemical lights blistering the ceiling oozed purulent glow down the bleak stone walls, igniting into an ugly beacon a surgical bed outfitted with a metal tray of tools situated towards the leftmost wall within Cesare's field.

The clash of hinges grated against his head.

Four maskless crows entered. First: tall and rough and pale, every inch a lout. The second stood beside him *stinking* of a stooge. A third was nondescript as dust. The fourth hunched skinny as a gremlin.

Cesare tipped his head and smiled hollowly. "You must be pleased." His voice scraped raw. "So sorry about your General. Pity he couldn't make it."

"You saw to that?" Lout hissed.

"*Oh* no, please. I could never resort to such brutality."

The soldier neared, features mawkishly contorted. "How does the fabled *Bauta* feel caught like the rodent he is?"

"Thrilled, verily," Cesare sneered. "About time you sad bastards managed. *Shame* you needed my own help."

Cesare almost yelled out when a needle sank into the supine knuckle of his left hand.

He ducked his head and swallowed the pain. This is what he had been honing himself for. Each time he pierced his flesh, every instance he tended to his own injuries and withstood an unhealed wound, had tempered him against pain. He knew a day like this was nigh.

"What was that?" Lout gripped Cesare by the roots of his hair and yanked his head back up. "Didn't *catch* it!" His knee rammed hard into Cesare's abdomen. Another two needles drove into his left knuckles.

Cesare breathed thickly. "Special treatment or routine programme?"

He exclaimed as the sound of splintering bone popped through the freezing walls. His crushed knuckles came away black, nerves spasming down his fettered fingers.

"You have a little too much to say," Lout growled.

Cesare *tsk'd*. "That assertion on someone else's tongue sounded far sweeter."

A needle punctured his left palm. He strained, yet vocalised little more than a sharp breath.

Lout drew his baton and prodded the rogue in the sternum. "Name."

"Cesare Ramiro Agostini."

"There used to be a wealthy Agostini clan," Stooge mused, tall with noble features and hair red as cinnabar. "Old patriarch denounced the Governor, so the family was liquidated."

"Glad to see that infamous *virtue* of our vying imperator."

"Disclose all," the prepotent soldier commanded. "Who is with you? How many? Where are they?"

Cesare clicked his tongue and did not reply.

A soldier's fist smashed down on a lever.

A curt shout got its way as the nail of Cesare's fifth digit tore, exposing the jagged surface of tattered red flesh underneath.

The soldier leaned close to Cesare, thin lips shucking back from pale teeth. "Understand where you are, Bauta," he snarled. "There is *no* limit to what we'll do to you. Cutting, burning, mutilation. We'll rip your fucking guts out and stitch you back together if that's what it'll take to get you talking."

Through his rising gorge, Cesare leaned forward just to spite the lout, voice dropped to a hiss. "And it still won't be enough to make me."

The legionary snapped to his imposing height and glanced at the flame-haired Stooge.

Sculpted features polished with a glee he couldn't let show, the soldier plucked the odd metal tag protruding from Cesare's inner elbow.

The force of the tag lifted a sharp wire inserted into the vessel running along his forearm. Metal cut through skin as the soldier pulled it towards the wrist.

Cesare screamed.

The crow ripped the wire free. Blood gushed from the ruptured piping of Cesare's arteries. He gasped deeply, head bowed, and trembled as blistering agony gusted through him with the threat of a blackout.

Nausea inundated him when a soldier gripped his shoulders and another poured hot apozem into the gorge of his mutilated arm. His flesh tugged to heal as if never blemished.

A needle pierced Cesare's biceps and unconsciousness blinded him once more.

The torture continued for hours. Perhaps longer. Cesare couldn't say. Only the pain, his silence, the caws of crows, existed tangibly.

Massive fingers gripped Cesare's jaw so he'd look up. "*Talk!*"

"Try harder," Cesare muttered.

The behemoth of a soldier shoved him. "Get off on pain, do you, sicko?"

Cesare tittered hysterically. "Even the beaten old playwright's trick of irony isn't spared in this shithole."

The brute delivered a kick to Cesare's gut. "*TALK!*" He shoved a dagger under Cesare's chin hard enough to cut skin.

"Bet you wish you could." Cesare spat out blood.

"*Whoreson!*" The crazed soldier clenched his knife and carved into Cesare's arm, tearing gash after spurting gash out of his flesh. Yet all the pain blurred into one edgeless pulsation. The breaking point for Cesare wasn't the moment he unravelled and divulged every word, but the moment he stopped feeling.

Lout wiped his dagger on Cesare's sleeve as his lungs sucked air. Stooge injected Cesare with ano-apozem whilst the third soldier began to unbuckle his bruised fingers.

Cesare clicked his tongue at the gremlin by the door. "Scared?"

He flushed with rage but shut his mouth when the door to the cell unlatched.

In walked none other than the High Priest Benetto Abelli in their gold-and-ruby garb. An entourage of two Holy Guards followed, dragging by their bound wrists a pair of young Illutèri neophytes, their faces obscured by veils of sheer crimson.

The crows dropped into bows before Abelli.

The Domínie cast their ink-blot eyes to Cesare. "So this is He."

Cesare grinned, still strapped down. "Flattered to be such a spectacle."

Abelli paced around him in silence.

Cesare eyed the Illuteríi and his ribs closed in.

At the unhurried conclusion of their lap, Abelli stopped before the inmate. "Does he ponder himself an upstanding man?"

"Not particularly, to be frank."

"But he *must*, shouldst one bethink himself above a civilisational order."

"What 'order'?" snapped Cesare. "'Civilisation' where? Look at what these sycophants subject me to. Gaze upon the suffering of those you call 'slum trash'! If this rotting fucking corpse is *civilisation*, then I'll gladly burn the bloodsucker!"

Abelli peered at Cesare, as if endeavouring to bore straight through his brain to unspool it, before lifting the veils away from the Illuterii's faces. "Lílio àut lília, Bauta." *Son or daughter.* "One must perish so the other may live. The choice is thine."

The neophytes, both sixteen, give or take, began to whimper through Illutorii unbinding their hands.

"No," said Cesare.

"Thy choice is demise of both?"

"Their demise is your choice and yours alone, Domínie."

They dragged out a chord of silence. "Demise is predilected, at times."

Crows swung their swords to slash the Illuterii on the arms, shoulders, legs, tearing down their veils and ripping into their robes. High Priest Abelli watched as their followers were brutalised in front of them. *Because* of them. The daughter clutched shreds of scarlet fabric over her chest. The lílio hissed and moaned at the cuts gouging his body. Yet the soldiers persisted.

"No!" shouted Cesare. "No, *stop*!" He shut his eyes as if the worst pain was incoming. "Lília!" Abhorrent hollowness opened up in Cesare's chest. "Spare the lília…"

"*NO!*" she cried. She lunged to kneel before the impassive Domínie. "*PLEASE!*" Her bulging eyes shot to Cesare, and he felt blood rush from his limbs. "*WHY?*" He wanted to empty his stomach. "PLEASE *LET IT BE ME PLEASE LET ME DIE PLEASE* PLEASE *LET ME*!" The lília's sobs morphed into frenzied shrieks. Into scratching and kicking as Illutorii seized her. *What did I do?*

Two of the crows grabbed the lílio, pinned him to the floor, and began to snip away at his skin. Blood dripped sweltering and distilled between the cold bricks with every agonised contraction of muscle as the soldiers peeled the dermis off the lílio, starting with the hands.

Screams deafened Cesare until he couldn't look at the brutality. Yet each time he turned away, his knuckles cracked between stone molars. And *yet*, even as his resilience eroded, Cesare wouldn't give Them the satisfaction of his compliance.

A soldier cut the lílio's throat, throwing his corpse aside.

Cesare could do nothing as the boy's innocent blood trickled across the stone towards his boots.

Illutoríi hefted the lília towards that operation table.

Straps pinioned her ankles and wrists, a metal restraint clasping around her head to hold it still.

High Priest Benetto Abelli sauntered to the operation table, adjusting the lília's robe for modesty before sheathing their hands in red gloves.

Assembling a syringe and plucking a phial off the metallic tray, Abelli aspirated translucent liquid into the barrel, clearing the needle of bubbles in slow methodology. "An inoculation of Harrow to still the subject."

The lília thrashed against her binds.

Harrow… Cesare's mind raced with what Giorgianna had told him about the *Prasinum* genus. Goldarus *is Smite—numbs motor sensation from the neck down; does* not *numb pain.* Angustia *is Harrow—numbs all motor sensation but the eyes; does* not *numb pain.* Accidia *is Torpor—numbs both motor sensation* and *pain.*

"No…" Cesare looked at Abelli. "No! If you must, inject her with Torpor, *please*! Don't let her feel this!"

But the High Priest ignored him as they palpated the lília's neck, thumb passing over the skin once, twice, until it immobilised a protruding vein. The needle sank. The daughter of the church exclaimed as Abelli pulled the plunger back to register, then injected.

The lília's fight petered out as her muscles slacked, as she fell into cadaveric silence. And yet she would feel *all* of it.

Abelli discarded the syringe and exchanged it for another: a solid metal barrel with an extension of a narrow shaft, two finger rings on each side as if to emulate scissors, a third on the bottom.

"While the preferred lobotomisation tool," Abelli intoned, "the leucotome requireth a burr aperture trepanned through the tough bone of the skull, rendering such procedures effective but hardly summary. In ideal practice, the elongate cannula of this tool inserts through the cranial aperture into the encephalic matter. Depressing the plunger expels a thin metal blade from within the shaft which is rotated to excise a tissue core and rupture the membrane of transmutational inevitability."

Abelli placed the leucotome down, picking up instead a dainty mallet and what looked akin to a miniature pickaxe with a long, sharp handle. "An orbitoclast—leucotome's sibling." They held up the pickaxe-esque tool, its silvern edges catching blinks of murky light. "Its application allows for transorbital lobotomy wherein the sharp pick is inserted through the socket, breaching the delicate bone and penetrating the brain. The goal remains alike: the severance of the barrier between the tarnished hylic flesh and the spiritual pnèuma. Ascendance. Abolition of the limits to our material confinement. *Purification.*"

And Abelli plunged the sharp pick of the orbitoclast through the lília's socket.

Cesare winced as the High Priest hammered the instrument through the cranial bone with the mallet, pivoting the orbitoclast the tiniest degree before removing it and patching up the woman's eye, then injecting her with what was likely Harrow antidote.

A few lapses passed, and the lília emitted a keening wail before beginning to babble, frantic and without sense.

"A failed creation," said Abelli, and Cesare's chest seized.

Unsheathing their ceremonial axaxún, the High Priest incised the perimeter of the lília's face and cut it away, unflinching despite her screams, before slitting her throat with a squelching slowness.

Placing her flayed face on the metal tray, Abelli shucked off their bloody gloves whilst Illutoríi dumped the lília's body beside the lílio. "We hath lost our magnum opus. Our sublime incarnation of spiritual transcendence. Our prophets." Abelli approached Cesare, gazing inside his eyes. "Dost thou know the illimitable dimensions of the transcendental condition upon the expunging of the defected mind?"

Cesare spat in the High Priest's eternally-masked face. "Zealot."

Abelli straightened, wiping their mask with a fogle. "Thy third eye sees," they proclaimed.

Soldiers unstrapped Cesare and dragged him towards the operation table.

"Get *off* me!" He broke free, grabbing a scalpel and stabbing it into the head of an Illutóre, but his second of extrication ceased when he was restrained by Guards and forced down on the bloody surgical bed. A crow pinned his head and injected him with Harrow without palpating a vein, the inoculate spilling into his muscle. All movement but the eyes ceased. Yet he felt the leather around his wrists and the metal beneath his spine, and he could do nothing.

Abelli slipped on clean gloves and took to sterilising their tools.

Panic began to overwhelm Cesare, air struggling to breach his throat as it constricted. *No no no.* He couldn't lose himself. It wouldn't work. Abelli's means would only kill his mind and thus *him*.

He couldn't lose.

But he would.

Abelli admired the sight of the orbitoclast, then positioned their palm on Cesare's brow and angled the horrific tool towards his right eye—the same eye which Davide ruined and Giorgianna lodged a piece of her life into to mend.

The door to the cell opened.

Governor Crescenzo De Tullia entered with a pair of Imperialíi.

The dread flushing through Cesare incinerated with hatred.

Abelli bowed. "Governor."

Without a word, De Tullia's golden griffins cut down Abelli's Holy Guard. The crows gasped but held no power to object.

Before the High Priest could speak, De Tullia's falchion ran them through the gut. They fell to the stone, blood running into that of the innocents they'd slain in the name of thrawn creed.

"Administer antidote and get him off that thing," De Tullia ordered the cowering crows. They jumped precisely when their Lord of Bless'ed Dominion said 'jump', and soon Cesare sat strapped in the chair again.

The blood-soaked hem of De Tullia's pewter robe steeped in yet more crimson as he pivoted to face The Bauta whom he had fought so many tireless years to wipe off the earth.

Cesare curled his tongue up in his mouth to appraise the antidote and released a laugh at the Governor. "Didn't foresee *you* to be my saviour."

A sore muscle pulled taut in De Tullia's gaunt jaw.

He poised his sword and impaled Cesare through the throat.

Cesare hacked and choked as blood poured down his shirt and into his lungs, his muscles jerking in the throes of agonisingly slow death whilst De Tullia looked on in silence.

A pale hand rose.

A needle pierced Cesare's arm and his flesh began to knit closed.

He gorged on panicked breaths, coughing up blood and swallowing it—the only fluid he'd drank in too long. A soldier pinned down his left wrist and seared his inner forearm with a red-hot branding iron. Cesare screamed out. The fatty stench of cooking meat laced the bloody air of the torture chamber.

A soldier doused the burn in katō-apozem.

Skin curdled into the scarred visage of a dagger—the Malefactor's Mark. Branded on all poor bastards condemned to ten months or longer in prison, or those on death row. Cesare knew which destiny awaited him, but he had his mind still. He had *himself.*

"That demented zealant won't rob from me the fulfilment of seeing your head roll across my citadel's agora." De Tullia sheathed his bloody sword. "Your execution is to take place at seven hundred on díem auróra. In two days' time, you will be nothing but a myth, a nameless wraith, your enterprise crushed and fruitless and your false dogma forgotten. You lost, Bauta. Your terror is no more."

A mordant scoff left Cesare. "Then kill me, De Tullia. Because you cannot break me. And when you kill me, bury me standing, because I *will* not bow." He raised his head, and clenched De Tullia's gaze tight enough to buckle it. "Because my death will not save you."

De Tullia's jaw never loosened, fury ignifying within the craters of his eyes like a volcano on the verge of destructive eruption, but he didn't utter a word.

Needles had defiled Cesare so many times that he ceased to feel it by the time a wave of nausea and a rush of fatigue flooded his senses.

The Governor turned for the exit, Imperialíi in tow while crows fluttered down to dispose of corpses. "Put to the sword every Illutóre and Guárdus refusing to join Imperiálum or City Guard ranks." De Tullia's voice bleared. "My use for the church is none—have every sibling done away with *and all of Abelli's abominations put down. The Hanging Gardens are to be cleansed…*"

And Cesare saw nothing all over again.

Scene XLVIII

You Must Have Chaos Within You to Generate a Dancing Star

Fabio | Giorgianna | Cesare

WINTER SCRATCHED ITS CLAWS INTO FABIO'S SKIN, prying it off his back even with the layers of linen shirt and woollen greatcoat to shield him from the roaring seaside winds and the brumous bite of sundown.

He kicked a shard of rock into the writhing sea and looked to the horizon. *Damn you, heartless Martyrs.* His revered Saints never claimed to be the merciful sort. Nevertheless, Fabio couldn't help questioning what in Hell was the reason behind all this horror. Why on earth did Lissandri and Rosalia deserve punishment? Rosalia had been as little to Fabio as any kid running around the Cove, and he'd watched Lissandri grow up at *The Sunrise*—had always felt himself responsible for both him and his brother, no less for having known their parents. They were innocent.

And Cesare…

Dread dried Fabio's throat.

No matter how much the stupid boy upbraided himself as crooked, he was so *good*, down to his core, and Fabio wasn't intending on ever burying his son.

But his revered Saints never claimed to be the merciful sort.

Fabio traced the creases of his cooling palm, untouched by an inking needle. He recalled the tattoos on Isaia's hands. Gxerqụcca—Mariano religious symbols. His late father, Ružan Amadi, to whom he was born a bastard by shipwright Melétia Athanasíou Spýros, was a cenobite of the Mariano faith in Sancta Maria[117] whose entire skin had been branded with Gxerqụcca and whose tongue had been cut out with red-hot knives. A relic of the Empire days when Salvatrici imperators sought genocide, so Mariano religious elders resorted to the most drastic form of preservation. Tattoos served as a less punitive form of the practice. Even children were once tattooed to evade kidnapping by northerners.

Fabio's eyes stalled on the iron band circling his thumb.

"*Thought* you'd be somewhere brooding," a deep voice spoke behind Fabio and his gut keeled.

He turned to see a stocky woman in a basilisk-black greatcoat cinched at the waist with teeth, threads of scarlet querling through its hems. Bleak shadows of fine hair streamed from beneath her ebon tricorn to brush with its straight ends her brow and elbows. From her earlobes, a pair of gouged eyeballs coated in glass dangled, irises a pale grey so at odds with the fathomless inky darkness of hers. *As if on cue.*

She extended a pert look Fabio had received so many times he could've named precisely where wrinkles would form upon her features beneath it. "Alasiotái,[118] Fabio."

He slipped on an almost-smile. "Hello again, Ada."

She stopped at his side in silence.

---

[117] Hence '*bastard*'. While Mariano cenobites (of any gender) are not necessarily called to a life of complete celibacy (though purity and chastity still constitute important cornerstones of devoted religious life), they aren't to marry or have legally documented progeny.

[118] Roughly '*brightness*' in Akési. Called an '*Epithet of Light*' and is essentially used as a greeting symbolising protection from the Evil Eye, showing that one approaches another with no malintent.

Fabio glanced sidelong at the woman. The woman he once loved. Maybe still did. "I see the ring's still on," he noted with pained amusement. They'd exchanged those rings at the age of nineteen with a promise that, whether on land or at sea, even continents apart, they would always be together. Playwrights were cruel for that irony trick.

"I'll geld you." Ada hid her hands in her pockets.

Fabio half-laughed, gazing at the sea once more. "Didn't think *this* is how we'd reunite."

"Whose fault is it that we needed to *re*unite, at all?" Ada's tone cut right through Fabio's heart.

"I know." The guilt of it had never left him. "Forgive me."

"A few decades too late, Spýros." She quietened for some heartbeats. "I would've turned back, you know." Fabio stiffened at her bite. "I lingered on *Antigone*'s deck afterwards in case you'd swallow your pride." A bitter snort. "Guess I put a little too much faith in your miserable sort."

Fabio's chest rended. *'Craven' is the kindest word for my miserable sort.* He gritted his teeth. "I wish there was something I could say, Ada."

"*Dahlia*," she snapped. "Doesn't matter now, anyway."

For better or worse, Cesare had taken after Fabio in many ways, down to the minute details of facial expressions or his utter inability to maintain an organised desk. But one thing Fabio was thankful for was that at *least* Cesare could shove aside cowardice, swallow his pride, and just tell Giorgianna that he couldn't lose her. It's more than Fabio was able to do for Ada and about a dozen times braver. *Love plays you for a fool.*

They both jolted when thin arms rendered fingers-to-throat in tattoos slipped around their shoulders. "Well, well, well." Matìa's voice flowed sweet as mead, which incidentally wafted off their breath the slightest tad. "If it ain't Fata and Spýros like old times."

Dahlia scrunched up her face. "Drop the childish nickname, Calzolari."

They tutted. "Now, now. Needn't the attitude."

With a sigh, she relinquished a smile and a side-hug for Matìa. "Missed you."

"'Fraid I must admit likewise."

"Berengari?" she asked.

Matìa's bright features dimmed. "Killed by the legionaries to get me to talk."

"I'm really sorry, Tìa," Fabio said. "I know how much he mattered to you." Matìa left Smugglers' District because of Berengari, seeking a quieter life in lower óssium. This crooked autarchy bled everyone.

"There's always something left, never forget that." Matìa smiled. "To fall is to hit the ground. To break. Until then, you will always rise."

Fabio's chest hurt.

Dahlia rolled her eyes. "You and Marcello were always unbearable with that nonsense. Ludovico? The slim dealer with hair down to his arse—Giorgianna's pa. I like her. She's got spite."

Fabio chuckled. "If by some miracle we get Dafne back, it will feel something like a renaissance."

"Dafne?" In place of a cold glimmer, Dahlia's eyes suddenly sparkled like a midnight sky bestarred with constellations.

Fabio cleared his throat. "Still a sóra; a help to Giorgianna."

Dahlia tried on a smile half-way. "I would like to see her again."

Fabio endeavoured a wider smile, his brows inching closer as if to offset it. "As would I."

Matìa squeezed the pair of them. "Make that a third."

The trio gazed across the lagoon of Smugglers' Cove. Its dark marmoris caught moonglow onto its crests, and only when Dahlia's dark tricorn splotched with tiny white flecks did Fabio realise that the haze along the horizon was first snow of winter.

THE TIMEPIECE HOISTED ITS ARM TOWARDS MIDNIGHT.

Díem auróra arrived and the empty world ached in liminal limbo—a strange *almost* plane where details blunted at the edges, immaterial yet effectual. The sigh of the sea. The sway of *Antigone*'s hull. The sheets of Cesare's bed beneath me.

They still smelled with the sweetness of his skin, soft as his hair and insomniac voice. If I couldn't be with him, I wanted to hold something which once held him. Which once held us both.

Every moment beset me with the thought of his pain. But if I slept, I knew what I would see in my nightmares. White flagstone, the glint of falling guillotine blades, then blood, blood, blood. And I knew too, come dawn, its realisation would not be beyond the realm of potentiality.

I shifted to my side.

Reddish gleam spilled across the floor and, beyond the window, where snow fell for the second day, and skerries stretched on like fields of salt, the rubiginous disk of the blood moon glowed in the starless sky, almost full. *A blood moon's alignment with Ammuríre Lunéra.* A prophetic symbol of cosmic upheaval and regeneration through destruction. Ancient Faustinians of the south believed the celestial phenomenon was evidence of gods battling, their blood shedding upon the moon, crimson to signify their proximity to humanness and thus the two entities' intrinsic connection.

A blood moon sky screams for apocalypse.

But I detested its sight, detested knowing that to-morrow would be the winter solstice. The day Emanuela was taken. Her murderer was gone, but her murder wasn't. The day of the Undying Moon would never be washed of blood no matter the regnant luminary, and to-morrow would make it no purer. But none of us were pure.

I sat up, adjusted my corset strap, and draped my arms over my knees.

My eyes traversed the cicatrose terrain of my thighs where razors and knives carved grim reminders into my flesh. My mother's mistreatment of me for imperfection. Emanuela's death and my every fruitless attempt to seek justice. Basilio's treachery. *The Arum.* My father's execution. Manuele. Every memory indelibly immortalised upon me as if, for all the torment they brought and all my screams for them to leave me, I feared forgetting. Because they forged me.

I glimpsed the blood promise scars on my hand and wrist. For Ema. For my father. For Cesare. For everyone I loved more than myself. For everyone I lost.

The day I acceded to Cesare's pharisaic wiles was the day I vowed to avenge all the dues owed to me—to *Us*—with blood.

I had always chosen to let this kingdom burn.

CESARE SLIPPED IN THE FINAL EARRING RETURNED TO HIM, clipped his tanzanite cufflinks shut, pocketed his lighter, and beheld himself in the desilvering mirror of the ourie bathing chamber.

Dark hair, lush and thick, framed cheeks gaunt with dehydration, his muscles sore as his hungering body took to glutting on itself.

Folks who romanticised death all too often forgot that, besides your soul, the *other* thing that tended to slip out of you when you died was the content of your bowels. So, given the filthiness of *that* whole ordeal, inmates on death row were starved of food and water (to speak nothing of the emetics or laxatives they were fed in their stead) to render them empty. Cesare imagined the weakness famishment brought was no less useful to the powers that be.

Laundered and pressed clothes lay against bathed skin healed for the sake of the illusion. A pretty spectacle for the Lord of Bless'ed Dominion and a confronting sight for the people. The only blemish permitted in the mask was the rolled sleeves, baring the dagger-shaped visage of the Malefactor's Mark branded into Cesare's left forearm. Upon his wrist gleamed the silken fibres of the scar begotten by Giorgianna's blade. Blood promised and a promise kept.

'So you may drown this wretched world.'
'And you may eat the flesh of kings.'

Cesare met eye-to-eye with himself. With his convictions.

His body lived as a vessel. A weapon. *An instrument.* Material and finite. Breakable as he'd never admit.

His soul was an abstraction. A formulation. An idea.

His words were an emanation of that soul, an infinite scattering outward to burn the hands of the overseers. To illuminate the canvas of fabricated reality.

Immortality was not an eternity in one's flesh. Immortality was an eternity in one's words.

Above all, words were a flick knife, white-hot.

Revolution is death, but to leave behind a scar was to never die.

Hinges cranked and sickly light trickled into the bathing chamber.

Three Imperialíi loomed in the doorway.

"Your day, Bauta," one taunted.

Through all the torture, Cesare hadn't yielded a word, leaving the soldiers to seethe. At least the continuous flow of ano-apozem meant his lack of a spleen hadn't landed him with a fatal blood infection in the dirty Hellhole of a dungeon.

With a flick of hair, a click of the tongue, an easy smirk, Cesare approached and lifted his wrists to be cuffed. "Frankly, you've shot yourselves in the foot by letting me look like this."

A gilded soldier snarled, wrenching Cesare's arms and shackling them behind his back.

Cesare spat out a mocking laugh, and the griffins led him away for execution.

SCENE XLIX

MORIOR INVICTUS

Cesare

CESARE HADN'T SEEN THE LIGHT IN A WHILE. It burned the eyes, pounded the skull. White snow clung to the ivorine skeleton of the ministerial house, the sky overhead paler than both, the monotony blotched only by the bloodstain of a moon and the masked ossíi gathered in the vast courtyard. The dark gallows and guillotine.

Imperialíi handed Cesare over to twelve crows who led him to the guillotine—beside the gallows. Bleared in Cesare's tailored eye, a particularly tall fellow with a glaive and hood guarded his right side. Gremlin was at his left.

A silence so deafening had never infested the agora as when Cesare ascended to the guillotine with the two crows flanking. The other ten encircled the platform.

The blade gleamed. Pain had become such a blur that Cesare figured he wouldn't even feel the thing slice his throat if it came down to it.

Everything drew to a cessation.

Governor General Crescenzo Zuane De Tullia arose to his mezzanine, a charcoal-black stain upon the osseous structure, and Cesare observed with dark amusement just how small the demented old man looked upon his lonely kingseat guarded only by his silver banners.

"Mèi ossíi," De Tullia addressed the populace. "A pestilence has putrefied this body we dub Vencenza for far too long; has threatened to break asunder our bones and infect us with fear." He always gave the same speech. Always told the same tale. "The pestilence must be excised from where it stems, piece by piece if that is what it shall take. And piece by piece it shall be done." The Governor gazed down. "Cesare Ramiro Agostini," he spat the name. "You are sentenced to death for conspiracy and treason against Vencenza's state and people, for repeated and continuous acts of underhanded deceit," Cesare's eyes rolled, "mutiny, mass murder, arson, blackmail, misdemeanour, heresy—"

"Change the tune, De Tullia—"

"*TO-DAY*—" his voice clamoured against the material world "—and beneath the blessed eyes of the Gods, our blood will be rid of *filth*." His eyes lowered once again. "Final words, Bauta?"

"I thought maggots weren't worthy."

"Take this pittance, terrorist. At least the last words you ever speak may hold an ounce of value."

Cesare clicked his tongue. "What was it you said?" His words struck like a match. "'*No blood can be absolved no matter how old it grows, for with time it only grows harder to clean*'? In that case, sincere gratitude for yours choosing to draw my blood upon your precious agora."

Giorgianna said '*blood does not wash off*' and she was right. *Blood does not* forget, *either*. Blood congealed and crusted and stained evermore. Blood knew what it was like to be free.

Cesare gripped De Tullia's far-off eyeline. "You can kill me to-day, but I will not wholly die."

The silence cut deeper than a guillotine, choked harder than any gallows' rope. Even the winter wind hesitated to bite.

De Tullia's eyes bore down on Cesare with the fury of an indomitable titan god, yet he had fallen. He didn't just want your body. He wanted your mind. And in *that*, Cesare had long ago gleaned the Governor's furtive confession to vulnerability. *My mind can never be yours.*

"*VÍTAM DI RIVOLUZIÓNE!*"

Cesare's breath caught as the firmament reverberated with a call from the crowd.

De Tullia's eyes snapped up, and even from where he stood beneath the mezzanine, Cesare saw that fear the Governor so deeply despised. The throng before him surged into a wildfire, roars quaking through the very foundation of the ministerial house.

'VÍTAM DI RIVOLUZIÓNE!'

'DEATH TO THE DICTATOR!'

'DOWN WITH THE REGIME!'

A laugh like fire seared Cesare's lungs.

Gunshots exploded and arrows darkened the sky. *Hound* arrows.

Screams made the welkin ring, yet not of fear, but eleutheromania, vengeance, *rage*.

The citizenry drew weapons against the legions.

Giorgianna's word was always truth: rage was a liberator.

Gremlin grabbed Cesare and dragged him towards the guillotine.

The Guard at his right lunged, glaive gripped, and cut Gremlin down in one swipe. He pulled off his hood to reveal dark features and a fringe of tight curls. "Right on schedule!" Araya winked, a gold lip ring glinting in his grin. With the sharp prong of his glaive, he broke open the locks on Cesare's shackles before handing to him a leather hip baldric (hidden under Araya's winter cape) within which sat Cesare's stilétti and revolvers.

Droves of soldiers closed in on the guillotine.

Cesare rolled his freed wrists. "Never skip a beat!" He kissed the cruciform hilt of a stilétto, pivoted, and plunged its blade into the face of a crow, kicking them into an oncoming pair among a flock climbing onto the platform. They fell with Hound arrows in their necks. Cesare shot one down. Araya decapitated an Imperiálus and retrieved a shield debossed with gold wings just as the soldiers below aimed their crossbows.

They dove to shelter themselves between the guillotine and shield.

A griffin's shout choked half-way. His throat snapped and he dropped in the snow, every other sharpshooter following in various states of disfigurement. Cesare threw a glance and a smile towards the balconies suspended high along the edifice. *That's my girl.*

Cesare shoved Araya away and brought his foot around in a smooth arc, stunning the attacking Imperiálus long enough to rise and deliver a right hook. A knee to their left side. He grabbed the soldier by their griffin helmet and drove their skull into the truss of the guillotine before dumping their moaning form on the headlock. "Admittedly, I'm not in my most *sprightly* state, but it'll *do*." Cesare slashed the rope. The guillotine blade flashed as it dropped to chop the soldier's head in half, snow melting to gory slush beneath jetting blood and brain. Blackness swarmed Cesare's field. *I need water…*

A figure lunged from his blurry side.

He doubled back from a slash.

Blood sprayed from the attacking crow's chest and they fell, baring a gangling man's freckled face and ginger hair.

Cesare panted. "Aengus…?"

"Don' fuckin' say it, a'right?" the Línmhar man bit.

Araya flung the shield and knocked a griffin dead with it, drawing his shətol, and the trio cleared the guillotine's platform, jumping into the tempest of the riot.

Araya chopped a crow down. "How on earth are you so *calm*?"

Cesare grabbed a handful of snow to swallow. "Benumbed."

The three made it to the edge of the murmuration where soldiers staved off furious waves of people. Cesare's blood blazed despite the fatigue. It was good to be moving again. Fighting again.

"*CESARE!*"

His stomach seized at the sound of Eligio's voice.

Some steps away, Eligio punched a crow out of his way with his twin's brass knuckles and locked eyes with Cesare. He bolted across the blood-splattered snow in a stumbling rush, almost bodying Cesare to the ground as he latched onto him, warm and alive.

Cesare squeezed him back. "Shit, Eligio." He pulled back to grasp Eligio's face. "Why are you *here*?"

"I'm not losing another brother."

An officére sprung up.

Cesare pushed Eligio away and poised his dagger to stab.

The officére staggered with a scream at a cutlass running him through.

"Fabio?" Cesare exclaimed.

"Don't be a hypocrite, boy." The old impresario's voice cracked as he embraced Cesare. "Mark my word: I *will* not bury my son!"

They ducked from the bloody trajectory of a torn-off head. Its ruined body flumped to its knees at the feet of none other than Blood Dahlia whose flail splashed gore all about. Behind her, Sten disembowelled a crow with his serrated boarding sword and bashed their head in with a mace. Flesh exploded to mince with the apocalyptic scene of protestors and revolutionaries waving black flags and shouting for a backdrop.

Cesare blinked in befuddlement.

"*Fuck's sake!*" Dahlia exploded. "Can we leave the sentimentalities for *after*?"

Cesare's eyes shot for the ambushed mezzanine where griffin and crow garrisons flocked. Where the Governor stood with his sword and crossbow against the people decrying his tyranny. Fire curled around Cesare's heart. "I'm getting to De Tullia."

Scene L

Reprieve

Giorgianna | Cesare

I WIPED BLOOD FROM MY NOSE. Sharpshooters around the guillotine eight storeys below dropped in mangled piles of limbs in the snow.

The atrocious visage of the gallows constricted my throat, deafened me with the sounds of choked struggle and the *pop! pop! pop!* of broken necks. And I was there again. Watching. But no longer helpless. *Never again.*

The moon's bloody visage peeked through wadded clouds at the cataclysm below.

I rounded out of the oriel I was in and stuck my dagger between the ribs of a crow, then grasped him by the face and hurled him into a wall before slashing a second soldier across the throat with my rapier and continuing down the corridor.

I needed to find Cesare.

Morettae, Cyclopes, Araya's Hounds, rushed by in flurries of darkness, dotted sparsely with defected Illutoríi and Guardíi like chips of ruby and flecks of silver. I did not trust the lattermost for a moment.

Sarnai and Itxaro, alongside the Mişşi-al-Uwwād couple and Illuteríi who survived the pogroms, helped syphon people—primarily servants and whatever inmates possible—out of the building via the tunnels. Etenesh, Tafsut, and Diodora were on medical standby with Libitina and Kasumi, whilst Errico and Alessa, the committees, smugglers, Hounds, Boars, fought among the people in the agora and the streets of the city.

Cutting a crow down, I disarmed them and passed their gladius onto the vermilion-haired Cyclops—Indrì—before addressing Chea: "You and your cadre break out and help kill these metal cockroaches. Be sure to live to see yourself become Domíne."

Chea flashed a fanged grin, then the Cyclopes took off.

Up ahead, at the terminus of the hallway, Dafne skewered an Imperiálus in the chest with her Illutóri guisarme.

A Guard charged her from behind.

Boom!

I shot him down. *Aim not so atrocious anymore.* But that *did* spell the last of my bullets. Turning for the stairs to the lower floor, I met eyes with Ilenia for an unreadable moment.

She nodded to me.

I merely cut my path through the fray.

CESARE CLEARED THE FIRST FOUR STOREYS of the ministerial house and advanced onto the fifth via the winding peripheral stairs, Eligio, Fabio, and Dahlia with him. Araya raced off into the building to aid the Hounds. Sten and Aengus remained in the square.

Access to the Governor's mezzanine was from the seventh's floor, and Cesare intended to strike his mark by whatever means.

Notwithstanding the row of colossal colonnades, the staircase opened them up to the aim of the regime's marksmen.

In the courtyard where insurgency raged, Libitina's hearse burgeoned in the storms' eye. The Salt Hydras trio perched atop with ossíi who danced, sang, played piva and fiddle and tamburello—all illegal under De Tullia's despotism. Eyepatch Dan shouted obscenities with a great big grin as his musket shot the air and legionaries alike. Korneli ploughed down soldiers with his sword-arm. Ren aimed with merciless exactness.

Making it to the fifth floor and into a circular vestibule, Cesare doubled back as a pair of condottiéri whizzed by, inked down the arms with eyes and sporting an amount of piercings alarming even to him. "Those are Cyclopes…"

Dahlia punched a Guard over the railings. "Your loose screw of a maenad offed their cunt leader."

Cesare blinked. "I'm sorry?"

A griffin rushed for them from the archway at the opposing end of the vestibule only for the monstrous spike of a bec de corbin to skewer their throat. A male-seeming person, lanky, with close-cropped hair and covered nearly head to toe in tattoos, held the polearm.

Cesare's eyes widened. "Matìa?"

"'Laútni', by any other name." They winked, peppy and bright as Cesare remembered from childhood. *What are the odds…*

"How are things inside?" wheezed Fabio.

"Almost gutted."

Precisely what I need. "Clear out as much as possible of the rest." Cesare slipped by Matìa and higher up the edifice.

He ached with exhaustion, wounds, dehydration, hunger, days of sleepless torture, but the knife of resolve in Cesare's side never dulled. He was as relentless as this vile regime made him, as relentless as the people below. The will of the masses toppled civilisations.

Sixth floor came and went. The seventh gained on.

Knocking an Imperiálus over and opening their chest with their own monstrosity of a sword, Cesare bolted down a thin corridor and veered left at its end.

A blunt force winded him. Steel flashed in his juddered vision.

He lurched back against the wall to evade a stab. The reverse-gripped blade thrust with a splintering impact into the decorative wooden inlay inches from his temple. The attacker's arm trapped him.

Myrrhic perfume seized Cesare's every sense, blood and honey and roses, and he beheld eyes vivid as carnelians and wide as the blood moon itself.

"Giorgianna!" Cesare's exclamation frayed.

She hopped back with a gasp, and tears beaded on her lashes. "*Cesare...*" Giorgianna's voice would have broken him if she hadn't sealed her arms around him. Cesare dropped his daggers just to hold her, just to root his fingers into her hair like sacred soil and savour her cherished warmth. To know that she was *alive*. That was all that mattered—he needed no more from her.

"*I thought I lost you,*" she whispered, pulling away to so gently cup his face and tuck hair behind his ear. "They hurt you." She kissed his cheeks all over. "They took you from me and they *hurt* you!"

Cesare grasped her face and kissed her. "If this is our final moment," he kissed her again, "I need you to know I love you—" and again "—more than anything."

Giorgianna shook her head. "Please don't, not *now*—"

Cesare ripped the baselard from the wall and stabbed it into the skull of a crow vying to swipe at Giorgianna, rage pulsing against his throat as he clutched her tight to himself. He handed the baselard back to Giorgianna and kissed her bloodied wrist. "De Tullia dies beneath to-day's blood moon."

Picking up his stilétti, Cesare advanced for the mezzanine.

Scene LI

La Corruzione Dei Migliori è la Peggiore

Yòchaná

THE HEART OF THE GOVERNMENT BUILDING ECHOED; the Omphalos lay eviscerated. By a pilier cantonné beside the doors, Yòchaná stole a moment to breathe, to readjust their argent pauldrons, mutter a prayer, wipe the blood trailing down their forehead.

The armour they wore constricted them. Not merely body but *spirit*.

Their kòhén[119] father, Eli'ézer ben-Elimeléch v'Kinéret haKòhén, always detested Yòchaná's military occupation, couldn't stand the sight of blood, and regarded his child's decision with disappointment until his early death. Yòchaná, carrying their father's faith yet mother Zanetta's techélet-blue eyes, had long-since understood the fruitlessness of their endeavour to heal a putrefying system from within. Understood their own naïveté.

---

[119] *koh-HEHN*; Yeledí priest/religious leader.

Eli'ézer spoke of destiny and fate, of divine revelation therein and the shaping of reality by one's deeds. Yòchaná clung onto those words since childhood, since their mother's demise of miscarriage when they were merely nine, but they feared they had misinterpreted the words.

Yòchaná palmed a pouch of saltpetre sitting in an inner pocket of their silver Guárdi blazer, given to them by Cesare before his arrest. *'Neither skies nor priests know'* had been his explanation.

A crimson-clad figure trundled into the Omphalos.

"Dafne!" exclaimed Yòchaná.

"Benedétti," the votary wheezed, latching onto her gold guisarme. "Most of the structure is empty but the periphery's still crawling with griffins. Morettae and condottiéri separated to deal with it and aid folks in the square and streets."

"I ordered Guardíi to follow suit," Yòchaná informed.

"I didn't see any among the ranks," Dafne noted strangely. "How many are left?"

"Eighteen."

Her eyes widened.

Yòchaná nodded gravely. "Imperialíi targeted—"

Dafne choked.

Blood dribbled from her lips. Her hand dropped limply away from her abdomen where a blade protruded, and the sóra fell to the marble.

Dead.

"*Ya hasrá...*" Yòchaná beheld a right eye cerulean as seas, left green as forests. Late Clario's schiavona, dripped blood. A russet braid woven with a fuchsia ribbon. And Yòchaná began to back up with raised hands. "Ilenia..." They chronicled the Magister's every movement as she strode a semicircle.

Steel screeched behind them.

Yòchaná's stomach sank when they glimpsed over their shoulder to find Guardíi blocking the doorway with swords.

They looked at Ilenia. "Why?"

The Magister sheathed her weapon. "I was promised freedom." Her palms lit with chains of light, blistering against the air and gold-white as sun's matter. "That freedom will be mine by *any* means." She swung for Yòchaná.

They dove to their right and rolled.

The air hissed in the chain's wake.

"What are you *talking* about?" Yòchaná crouched near an opposing pilier cantonné. "*This* will be your freedom!"

Ilenia lifted the chain high. Nearby windows groaned as their frosted panes ran through with cracks and tore out, fragmenting to millions of shards. Uproar poured in from the agora.

Ilenia whipped the air with her light chain and hailed glass bullets towards Yòchaná.

They bolted behind the pilier. It shuddered against the assault of projectiles. Yòchaná held the lapel of their jacket over their face. "*Of course* this is why you toiled to gain favour with the senators!" they realised aloud. "*OF COURSE* you needed my Guardíi!" *And how corruptible they were!* Yòchaná reached for a throwing dagger strapped to their torso, its hilt ornamented with the abhorrent effigy of a white peacock tail. They'd never been *theirs*. "You don't *want* freedom!" Their blood boiled. "You want *power*!"

"If that's what will *get* me my freedom!" The floor quaked as Ilenia's chain lashed for the pilier in a searing streak of light. Marble roared, beginning its fissuring.

Yòchaná dashed out from behind the pilier cantonné and flung three daggers.

Ilenia held out her opened arms.

The blades slowed mid-air and reversed. Aimed for Yòchaná.

They turned tail, hardly dodging the daggers, and continued running towards the daïs. *There's a portal into the tunnels behind it.*

Ilenia screamed in fury behind Yòchaná.

The thunder of marble quaked the floors.

Yòchaná dared a glimpse back and their blood ran cold when they saw a colonnade crack. An enormous chunk of rock ripped free.

Ilenia launched it at Yòchaná.

They went to veer but not in time.

The meteor of marble struck their shoulder, sending them rolling across the floor towards the daïs. The enormous chunk struck the ground and settled into rubble and ruin. Pain writhed down Yòchaná's spine; numbed their muscles waist-down. The world spun, doubling and blurring. Fresh blood poured down their brow and face.

Yòchaná pushed their palms into the floor to lift their chest off the ground, to breathe easier.

Footsteps neared.

A schiavona's blade, red-sullied, flashed in their view.

"Ioana De Rege," Ilenia ordered. "Do you swear your fealty to me?"

The ache radiating down Yòchaná's back wormed into their tongue.

Kòhén Eli'ézer, their father, had always quoted that unwise men were destined to become tyrants and that, no matter their face or name, resisting their rule was the godly calling.

> '...*the* only *means for you to atone*
> *is to revoke your wings.*'

Maybe *this* was to be Yòchaná's destiny. Upheaval of an order to repair the world. A festering husk of bone could only be excised, not healed. *So much for 'The Owl of Wisdom'.*

Yòchaná swallowed heavily. Folded one arm beneath their trunk. "Yòchaná Elimeléch," they gritted out, lifting their head to face Ilenia. "Do not call me by the name beneath which I hid myself from this regime. I am Yeledí. And *you* are an accurst traitor! *Burn!*" They spat at Ilenia's feet. "Vítam di rivoluzióne." *And death to every dictator.*

A smile, dark and awful, overgloomed Ilenia's features. "Your will, *Yòchaná Elimeléch.*" She threw her arm back to behead the Centúrion— a Centúrion no more.

Yòchaná dipped their hand into their jacket, grabbed the pouch of saltpetre, and hurled it in Ilenia's face. She screamed out and doubled back, pawing her eyes. Her schiavona clanged against the ground.

Yòchaná clambered to their feet, legs half-torpefied, and shed the blasted weight of Guárdi pauldrons off their shoulders.

Shouts bounced through the hall; Guardíi advanced.

Hobbling around the daïs, Yòchaná depressed a lever in the stucco to open up an eye-shaped keyhole. The peacocks gained. Yòchaná turned the key whilst muttering frantic prayers, finally shoving open the concealed doorway and slipping inside.

Soldiers banged and kicked at the door Yòchaná struggled to shut. Their feet slid from under them. *Curse you!* With all their might, Yòchaná slammed the door, taking a pair of fingers off a Guárdus. The thing clicked shut, sealing them away. *Praise be.*

Sore all over and certainly concussed, Yòchaná took off down the tunnels, throwing off their jacket embroidered with detestable Guárdi symbolism.

Walls skewed, darkened. Breath and heartbeat amplified within their ears. Consciousness waned. Their tingling legs failed and they fell.

As their eyelids shuttered, Yòchaná gazed at the necklace which had slipped out from under their shirt. Gold and hand-shaped, a blue eyeball tucked into its palm. An apotropaic amulet.

Whatever their destiny would be, Yòchaná was glad to meet it free of silver chains.

Scene LII

Sic Semper Tyrannis

Cesare | Giorgianna | Cesare | Giorgianna

A VAST BALCONY filled the semicircular cavity pushing into the government building's seventh floor, hemmed with alabaster balusters. An annular bridge supplied by a pair of flyovers jutting out from the building encircled the mezzanine a step below, once reserved for the Ministry, now swarmed by scraps of Imperial Blades. At the vanguard, Imperiálus Diodato Casca tore swathes through rebels. Condottiéri and Morettae flooded the balconies. Manárša, beside Yezo and Şirîn, shot arrows at the gilded gaggle.

Cesare and Giorgianna made it to the mezzanine via the eastern flyover.

At its centre, Crescenzo De Tullia stood his own with a crossbow.

Cesare's flesh blistered against his blood. He couldn't allow anyone but himself to have the Minister of Dominion, so he pushed onto the annular bridge, skewering a soldier and hauling them over the balustrade into open air. Delirium and fatigue spun through his head, his throat raked raw by the rapid breaths barely plenishing his lungs, his heart palpitating until it hurt.

He slashed a griffin across the throat.

Warm hands latched onto him. *"Cesare, you'll burn yourself out—!"*

Boom!

Giorgianna's body thrust across Cesare's when a gunshot demolished the stucco above them.

A man in black loomed on the overlooking balcony, blond with a face swollen red as a tomato-splattered bastard in a pillory, a pearly revolver in his twitching fist and an alexandrite pendant swinging at his sternum.

"Basilio," snarled Giorgianna—a lynx with bristled hackles.

He lifted his gun.

Cesare raced up the stairs to the mezzanine, Giorgianna close behind, clashing with Imperialíi.

Bullets hailed down.

Cesare's dagger tore through a griffin's jaw. Turning on his feet, he drove a fist into the temple of another, grabbing the lapels of their jacket and thrusting them into the line of De Tullia's fire. A whistling bolt spiked the soldier's occiput.

De Tullia's eyes flashed by Cesare's.

You'll burn for every life you ruined.

An Imperiálus charged Cesare from behind. Giorgianna gored their face with her dagger, digging her fingers into their eyes and thrusting against Cesare's back to roundhouse kick the legionary off the mezzanine, earning herself several slits across the torso and arms but ending her opponent's life.

"Those lessons of mine paid off!" quipped Cesare and slashed a soldier's masked face with one dagger, gut with the other, stepping out and kicking their flailing form onto a second griffin's sword before Giorgianna ran both through with her rapier.

"Just as well—I saved your hide." She swung for a legionary.

Boom!

Giorgianna shrieked.

Blood spurt from a bullet wound perforating her arm.

Cesare caught her as she swavered, dragging them both barely in time from the path of De Tullia's bolt. Near the multistorey balcony at the back of the jutting mezzanine, Hounds clawed at the shields of griffins.

The virid eyes of Imperiálus Diodato Casca snared on Cesare. Gold-plated armour, identical to the sort Manuele would wear, guarded every inch of his thewy body. The legionary's mighty arm arched back. At the end of his swinging polearm gleamed a bloody axe.

Cesare and Giorgianna vaulted in opposite directions. The poleaxe came down between them, smashing the alabaster floor to chips.

Pulse beat Cesare's brow. His field of view vignetted.

Diodato swung to their left.

Giorgianna didn't duck in time. Diodato knocked her in the head with the grip of the polearm before grabbing and hurling her across the mezzanine.

Dread clutched Cesare's throat.

Giorgianna's leg rammed the balustrade at a hideous angle. *Crack!* She shrieked horribly, blood bursting over her boot as her shin split in twain. Şirîn dashed to her from the balconies, şimşûr cleaving soldiers. Behind the captain of The Brass Teeth, Giorgianna writhed in agony as her leg reshaped into the contours of normalcy once more—tailored back together by Giorgianna's own magic.

Cesare quivered with hate and, for a moment, De Tullia faded from his mind as he dug his daggers into Diodato Casca's cheeks—the only exposed part of the soldier—tearing his features into viscid red rags and slashing at them in blind fury. The lòthmir of his stilétti marred Casca's unforgiving armour with screeching fulgurations of trapped azoth, grooves vesicating blood but not enough to injure the body. *Fuck you!* Cesare kicked away Casca's swing and delivered a punch before tearing off the Imperiálus' helmet and bashing them in the temple with the hilt of his dagger.

Diodato buried their knee in Cesare's diaphragm and knocked all air out of him for seconds on end. He reeled back. Every ounce of starved fatigue foisted back into his bones.

Diodato thrust their arms up.

Steel gleamed as their poleaxe hacked down.

"DON'T TOUCH HIM!"

Ribs distended the Imperiálus' cuirass. Gore ruptured from every orifice, every gap in their armour. Deliquiated eyeballs ran in clotted streams down Casca's face as if Giorgianna's scream burst all the vessels snaking through them.

Across the mezzanine, despite the snapped, fragile leg, Giorgianna had risen to her feet.

Diodato toppled.

That hideous polearm followed their fall.

Cesare lurched to evade its path.

Boom!

Cesare staggered, breath hitched, head down.

Hot pressure radiated from his chest where his hand flew. Where his heart bated—a desperate, dying creature.

"NO!" Giorgianna's short, awful scream scratched down the solstice sky and snuffed all light from the world. Somewhere, Basilio's laugh clanked like dishes dropped in a fit of hysteria, half-sobbing.

Sound retreated, beaten down by the throb of blood on eardrums, the haze of a waking dream veiling the world as Cesare pulled his hand away from his chest.

Blood smeared his skin, dark and blistering with the heat of a bullet. A snowflake fell upon it, such a frail thing melting in the massacre of its resting place.

He felt it then. The pain and the burn.

Cesare's gaze lifted to Giorgianna through the fine gossamer of snow baptising the earth. Such incomprehensible anguish stirred within her eyes—carnelian and copper and the sun at once.

The old ballad of means and ends.

"Burn it down," Cesare called out and opened his lighter, hurling it like a grenade into the balconies of the ministerial house.

THE LIGHTER STRUCK STONE AND BURST INTO RAVENING FLAME—a wildfire breathing scarlet smoke into a white welkin. *That's why Cesare wanted the ministerial house anointed with Myrabella.* He wanted to burn it down. As if on cue, everyone with lighters or matches or saltpetre fuelled the pyre. But I couldn't marvel, nor could I glory.

Everything had happened in a blink yet lasted epochs. The mezzanine, Diodato, my broken leg screaming as magic splinted it, the gunshot. *Oh Gods…*

The gunshot hit Cesare's heart—*no*—the mark I'd mercifully missed the night of '*A Bedlamite's Ballad*'—*no no no please*—yet he carried on fighting through the Imperial Blades towards De Tullia as if he wasn't dying. *I swore they wouldn't take you from me!*

The world tilted.

Basilio…

My gaze found him from across the balcony.

The miserable blond worm blanched as if he saw my Shadow inside me. *I will kill you.*

I no longer felt pain as I fled Şirîn's protection and tore towards Basilio, carving my baselard through legions.

A squeal escaped the impresario and he turned tail.

I swiped off the ground the pearly revolver he'd dropped in a fit of triumphant mania and gave chase into the burning edifice.

TIME SLIPPED AWAY WITH EVERY DROP OF CESARE'S BLOOD.

He cut through the last of the Imperial Blades encircling the Governor, limbs and heart so dizzyingly light. He stabbed an Imperiálus between the shoulder blades, swinging around the point of penetration to slit an oncoming soldier's throat and avoid a bolt before disarming the griffin to get hold of their pugio, aim with his left eye, fling.

The blade cleaved the air and impaled De Tullia's elbow.

His arm buckled. A grunt breached his locked teeth. The crossbow fell from his grip. *You end before I do.*

Cesare closed the final few steps between himself and the Governor. Steel glinted.

De Tullia blocked with his lòthmir falchion, shoving Cesare back.

Cesare returned with a horizontal slice, swinging his leg and kneeing Crescenzo in the trunk, "Bet you love the sight of your *myth*," then propelled his free arm to sink steel into the pale gaffer's shoulder. "Your nameless *wraith*!" De Tullia exclaimed, stumbled, but held fast, parrying a reprising hit. "How crushed and fruitless my enterprise stands!" Cesare kicked De Tullia in the diaphragm, sending him stumbling towards the balustrades.

"You are a *cancer*!" Crescenzo's eyes charred with a savage delirium he no longer fought to mask. "A dead man walking!" He bolted for Cesare—a shadow stirring up a flurry of snow, his sword a luminous comet speeding towards Cesare.

He ducked and ripped a gorge down De Tullia's sleeve who passed back in time to suffer no injury, hacking downward and nicking Cesare's thigh. Blood spilled. *Good with a blade, I fear.* But Cesare knew he was better. Just like his Imperialíi, De Tullia knew every trick in the book. The *streets* had taught Cesare.

"And you will die before me." His bloody fingers locked in the tar-black waves of De Tullia's hair and thrust his head towards the balcony. Crimson smeared the alabaster.

De Tullia twisted and arced his arm back to stab Cesare.

He volted and ducked beneath the swing. His stilétto coruscated.

Blood spewed through the silk layers of De Tullia's robes where Cesare slashed his kneecap.

The tyrant tottered with a grunt.

Cesare lunged to knock the final whit of balance out of De Tullia's stance. His falchion fell with him. His skull smashed hard into the stone, blood spilling into the ink of his hair.

Cesare dragged De Tullia across the snow-covered alabaster and trapped him in a chokehold. "You lost." He needed to speak—to himself or the world. Slipping away was not an option yet. "Your terror is no more. But I don't wish forgettance upon your name. I want your filthy fucking moniker to be recalled for centuries to come. Shamed. Mocked." Cesare's grip tightened on the squirming fucker. "*Detested*!" He sank his dagger into the dethroned tyrant's throat, drawing the blood of a coveted fateful end. A shiver spilled down Cesare's nerves, and, for the first time, he relished in the bloodlust Giorgianna must know. "Should've skewered my fucking brain, De Tullia," Cesare hissed and sawed through Crescenzo's neck with crunches of fragile bird bones, severing his head and so the thread of his loathsome life.

Gripping De Tullia's hair, he swung his head into the riot far, far below which erupted all the more at the sight of the wretched thing. Cheers shot for the sky when Itxaro got hold of the head and displayed it to the people from atop the ropeless gallows.

Cesare turned to the ministerial house where Hounds and Morettae and Boars ripped through the dwindling griffins and crows. Where crimson flames devoured that hideous flensed skull of an edifice, the silken silver banners of De Tullia's overthrown regime little more than singed tatters quivering in the winter wind.

His whirling head lolled, eyelids squeezed, bloody hands gripped the mezzanine's railings behind him, and a laugh shook him down to the bones. To the flames within his crucible where finality burned.

His purpose met. His duty completed.

And something shifted—fell and shattered—but something which *needed* to, lightening an unbearable weight.

Cesare's eyes all but stung. *It's over.* Not just De Tullia, but this regime. The confinement of the Vencenzani people within their gilded cage. '*...This revolution grows more self-sufficient by the day, and its existence may soon no longer be contingent on mine.*' The people were more than capable of organising on their own. Fighting on their own. Cesare had weathered years of an uphill battle so those beside him wouldn't need to. Nothing and no one would ever chain the populace of this city state again, he knew.

But I'm not finished yet.

The fire within Cesare was yet to burn out, so he gripped his stilétti and leapt over the balustrade to the black pit of City Guards below, stomping on a crow's shoulders, driving a dagger through their skull, and fighting for liberation alongside the people with the final shreds of his life.

BOOM!

The bullet found its mark in Basilio's ankle. He stumbled into an offshooting corridor at the top of stairs seamed with crackling red flames, snivelling in desperation. I continued my hunt. Two more cartridges remained in his revolver; pathetic scum of his ilk wasn't worthy of wasting azoth on.

Panic and despair struck like flint in me, threatening to burst to a conflagration greater than that devouring the building, but I smothered it with *rage rage rage* until the agony in my chest was gone and nothing remained but my black-blooded beast of wrath baying for revenge.

I cleared the stairs. Rounded the corner.

Basilio scrambled to his feet, dragging a bloody trail behind himself.

Boom! I shot his calf.

He howled and plunked to the ground.

"*Blood* is all I will *leave* of you!" I grasped his short hair and smashed his face into the floor, shattering his teeth and quashing his nose. Gripping him by the scuff, I hurled him to his back, a fist wound tight as I beat his bloodied face.

His hands shot out to smack me across the head like a flailing child. "YOU MURDERED MY *FAMILY*, PSYCHO BITCH! I *KNOW* IT!"

I brought my elbow hard into his cheek, unsheathing my knife. "*You ruined my life!*" Steel rended velvet, silk, skin, flesh, bone. "Serves you and your evil fucking family right, *FLESH PEDDLER*!" Basilio's shriek harmonised with a skeletal *crunch* of mine sawing off his arm. Creeping flames hissed beneath blood, and I wanted it to drown *everything!*

My straining knuckles met with Basilio's jaw so hard it dislocated, yet I continued to pummel him, to stab him through the lashing muscle of tongue. Blade broke through chin, gore gushing as I kept slashing and punching—*fist, blade, hilt, fist, hilt, blood, blood, blood red.* The scum deserved it for everything he stole and all the torment he enabled. For *ever* drawing breath from this earth.

"You were always the Governor's little pet cockroach." My fingers plunged into Basilio's eye sockets and squashed them.

A *craaack* scurried down my spine.

I looked up.

A Divine Watcher statue wreathed in flames broke off its pilaster and plummeted towards us.

I threw myself sideways. Shielded my eyes. Rolled.

The statue fell, showering me with hunks of marble.

Dust settled.

I launched to my feet and swatted flames off myself.

A gargle.

Basilio choked on blood, croaking as if some infernal creature crushed by the gargantuan sculpture.

I engaged the final bullet and—***Boom!***—blew through Basilio's brains.

Dead.

Finally dead.

Heaves ripped from my overwrought lungs. My back bowed as all the anguish poured back in and Gods, it hurt it hurt *it hurt!* I wanted to scream. To rip the sky away and destroy every monument to humanity. I wanted to cry.

Those sullied executioner fingers of mine slid down my wrist where the blood promise to Cesare remained evermore upon me. *I need to find you.* I needed to hear his voice and hold him and *be* with him. I could feel him dying; his heart drained out and so did mine. And I'd *left* him! Nausea pushed against my throat. My shoulders trembled. In the name of vengeance, of retribution, of hate, I'd abandoned Cesare. But I could save him—I could make him stay, I knew I could, I knew!

Please...

I looked towards the terminus of the corridor. Basilio had turned down a dread-end. *Fitting.*

A fiery crack began opening up the ceiling.

I bolted for the corridor's mouth.

Heat beat at my face, blistered my eyes.

Stone and wood crashed to the floor, charred, flaming, trapping me under its carcass.

SCENE LIII

INVIDO, CHE LA LUCE MUORE IN PARTE

Cesare

THE REVOLUTIONARY RIOT ONLY BLAZED HIGHER, but the world had begun fading in Cesare's ears long ago, his muscles lead and feather both.

He drove a stilétto between the ribs of an officére. They sagged in his grip and dropped, and Cesare felt his own body beg to drag down to the earth with theirs.

A hard force shoved him.

He heard the squelch of metal sashing leather and flesh, then the struggle of death.

Warm arms clutched and hauled him somewhere he couldn't name. "*...don't slip away...*" An urging voice gusted through his mind in an autumnal dusk breeze. He would never forget its nostalgic melancholy— some people never left you.

An abandoned capillary dilated in Cesare's view, the din distant.

He stumbled out of the warm embrace and onto snow-laden stone, occiput smacking against a frozen wall. His eyes crept shut.

"Cesare!" Scar-soft hands, chilly from being washed in snow, held his face. "Cesare, *look* at me," the voice called. "Talk to me."

Pale light cut Cesare's eyes as he fought arduously to sharpen reality before him. To look at Giorgianna's face. The contours of her features blurred into the lambent haze of cigar smoke, her lips red as gently-smudged rouge, her eyes the incandescence of a sunset liquefying into rippling seas—nymphic the way she'd been in his sweetest dreams. And maybe that was the cruelty of it: he was always dying.

Cesare sucked a sharp hiss and expelled a pained half-scoff. "Fucker got me." Words kept him tethered, but not enough. Time was up.

"No!" Giorgianna's voice broke. She lay her hands over Cesare's heart. He strained at the hideous pain digging through his bullet wound. *"No,"* she stopped and grabbed a phial of ano-apozem to empty, to thread the liquid through the perforated flesh as if to darn shut the killing blow. "No, I don't know how to tailor deep wounds, *WHY*—why didn't I learn to? And you've lost too much blood *nonono* I'm sorry—"

"I want you to take my bàuta and burn it."

"Do it yourself!" she snapped. "You aren't dying!" His arm slung over her shoulder, Giorgianna dashed to pull Cesare up. "Kasumi—"

"Giorgianna, *stop*!" Cesare slumped back against the wall. "I took a bullet to my fucking heart! Just…" words tangled up amidst his heavy breaths, "stay with me." For the first time, he was scared. Not of dying—never, but of dying *alone.*

"Third time lucky!" she pleaded.

"Third was relinquished in the dungeons."

"No." She dropped to her knees beside Cesare and grasped his face. *"Please* let me help you. For *once*!" She thrashed him. "You are too important; we *need* you to *live*! We are free because of *you*—"

"And I'm willing to be the final soul to crush this miserable edifice."

Giorgianna tucked hair behind Cesare's ear in that loving way she had the night Manuele butchered him. "They cannot take you from me, Cesare. I won't let them. I *love* you; I cannot lose you too, not like this. Why do you refuse to *see* that, you—?"

Cesare broke Giorgianna's stream of fevered consciousness off with a kiss, her lips still tasting of honey and divine ambrosia through the blood. "Prideful bastard, I know." His voice shuddered as tears dropped down his face. "You were my first *love*, too, and I wish I hadn't been such a wretched coward."

Giorgianna wiped Cesare's cheeks. "And *I* wish to be selfish. I don't care about *any* of this. I want the people I love to *live*—to *be* with me!" Her head shook. *"This isn't worth it…"*

Cesare grasped Giorgianna's wrists. "It is," he asserted, thrashing her gently when her eyes shut to give way to tears. "Giorgianna, *listen* to me!" Her eyes met his. "Freedom is worth *everything* on this wretched earth. No matter how much you give or how much it takes, to be free is to *live*. It means nothing in bondage." He wiped a tear, his fingertips— callused just like hers—running over the thin scar marking her cheekbone. "Wrap your arms around my shoulders."

Giorgianna blinked, but made to reach for him.

"Behind," he corrected.

She nestled against the wall, velvet-clad arms holding Cesare so tight she could surely stop him from fading away. His head slumped against her shoulder. Perfume bittersweet as tragedy anointed the curlicues of her hair—hair he had wished to touch from damn near the moment he saw her, and only then did he realise that, along the right side, it had been charred to the elbow by fire. Still, his weak fingers tread through it despite the electric buzz overwhelming his nerves.

"For as poetic as it'd be, I won't let him be my killer." Cesare unholstered his revolver and handed it to Giorgianna. "Do it."

A shaky gasp. "Cesare, no…"

He held onto Giorgianna's arm the way he hesitated to the night he told her his story. "The díem zenítis you learned I lied to you; the day your father's murder broke you. You looked me in the eyes and said you will kill me." He unclipped his tanzanite cufflink, the one he had lost and Giorgianna found, to give to her, but the strength in his arm wasn't enough and the contraption rolled across the algid white. "Let yours be the last face I see on my deathbed."

"Please, I cann—"

"Nethermost drawer…" it was becoming easier not to breathe, "of my escritoire—left side. There is…" he forced his tongue to keep moving, his heart to keep fucking beating just for a minute longer, "an envelope." He kissed Giorgianna's inner wrist, tracing the scar there. *A promise kept. "Pray to every divinity we crash again."*

Painful seconds elapsed until Giorgianna finally took the revolver, and Cesare's hand fell limp into the snow.

He forced a breath. Heavy, horrible. He hated how the red on his shirt looked like a bleeding rose. How deeply it hurt and burned. How much dying felt like Love.

Giorgianna kissed Cesare's cheek. "You are the love of my life."

The cold barrel pressed against Cesare's temple.

He would miss the fire in his blood. In his breath. In his hollow crucible. But he'd miss his familia above all. They were the only reason worth living, and Cesare was glad he, through the pain of existence, had Loved.

"I'm so sorry, Cesare."

And Giorgianna pulled the trigger.

SCENE LIV

LAST MAN STANDING

Giorgianna

THE ECHO WAS AN AWFUL THING. A grim reminder.

Like the blood rushing down Cesare's cheek to stain me.

The revolver slipped from my tremoring hand, and the raging echo of distant revolt faded.

He just wouldn't stop, even dying, and I wondered if, had he not been a flame burning, he could have been saved. He could have *stayed*.

Sobs heaved in hot, panicked gusts from inside me as I latched onto Cesare and wept into his hair.

The sole means of a blood bargain's dissolution was the death of all but one party bound by it, even if the incentive of the promise was realised. So I lost him. *But damn you DAMN YOU!* He was *mine*. Not my possession, but my *person*.

And now he was gone. *You were always Death's, first…*

Cesare became another I loved yet cursed. Another I lost on Ammuríre Lunéra. *Undying Moon.* Such a cruel cosmic joke. *You were supposed to sing for me when this was over*. How could I live through every single winter solstice to come?

Footsteps followed by exclamations sounded.

I looked up to see Eligio and Fabio, Matìa leaning onto the old captain as they held a wound at their side.

"No…" Eligio breathed. "Please not Cesare too…"

"I'm sorry," I blurted. "I'm so sorry *forgive me* he told me to do it he wouldn't let me save him he just wouldn't *stop—I'm so so sorry…*" I barely noticed the three of them huddle around me as my grip on Cesare only tightened.

"Gunshot to the heart." Fabio's voice grued, his eyes luculent. "Or close to it—something vital. He wouldn't't've survived that."

My head shook. "He could have if I'd known how to tailor wounds but I *didn't—I failed* him—I couldn't save him."

Eligio's arms wrapped around both me and Cesare. "This isn't your fault. It's Theirs. There was no saving him." As if his own statement wrenched his heart from his ribs, Eligio gave way to sobs. Cesare was his brother, and now he lost them both. *These callous Gods…*

Ancient south Faustinians practised a mourning ritual of cutting hair, symbolic of loss and humility. So I grasped my curls and chopped them off at my throat, ridding myself of the burnt remains.

My lips pressed to Cesare's cheek for the final time. "Get him out of here." Then I tore my blade into my sleeve and clipped in the tanzanite cufflink.

I almost couldn't stand onto my broken leg—a part of me wished to remain beside Cesare and rot for punishment. He looked so serene in the snow, blood like cherries melting the white, hair a dark halo strewn across his cheek and shielding the tattered wound where the bullet had ripped the final wisps of his life. As if he slept.

But he was dead.

The sound of revolutionary rage returned to my awareness—*far* from dead. My hand squeezed the hilt of my dagger.

This is yet to end.

Crimson flames lapped the citadel as I rushed through its halls. My gut presaged the worst.

I burst into the Omphalos and stumbled to a halt at its threshold.

Several windows had been blown out, colonnades tattered as if ravaged by beastly jaws, marble floors obliterated by craters born of scattershot stone. Remaining Guardíi—about twenty—stood in perfect lines around the central aisle.

At its end, upon the daïs, was Magister Ilenia Farnese.

When I looked at her, I knew my gaze was as empty as my chest. "I see yours wishing no power lived an ephemeral moment." My voice echoed through the hollowed-out walls.

"I sought freedom," Ilenia asserted. "I seek knowledge of the lower extremities of this city. Perhaps Abelli had stumbled upon the means—"

"You sought a false creed," I interrupted. "You sought *lies*."

Defeating a system from within would never be sound. Hierarchy begot despots. Only abolition could ever be a panacea.

"You should show *your* tyranny by lashing out with violence against me?" threw Ilenia.

Guardíi drew swords to defend their new imperatrix.

"You didn't listen." A sparkling black humour leaked drop by drop into my bloodstream. "*Your* violence is tyranny." My skull strained. "*Our* violence is *righteous*!"

The end did not merely justify the means.

The means *must* prefigure *the end*.

My veins froze.

The *snap* of bones and cartilage broke open the ether, spilling forth the *squelch* of ripping skin, the gargle of twisted gullets, the *clang* of steel against marble as every Guárdus toppled in heaps of mashed flesh, leaving only me and Ilenia. Blood poured from shells of silver armour and lacquered the floor. I knew a fight with the Magister would hardly be a steel kind.

"Lawless wretch!" Dislodged stone lifted off the ground at Ilenia's scream and careened through the air my way.

I sprinted towards it, feeding azoth into the gallons of blood on the floor and sweeping it all into a tsunami. It surged before me—a shield. Rocks ricocheted off it. The momentum caught me, spinning me smoothly about my axis as I tore off an ichorous scythe blade and flung it at Ilenia, chasing after it with blood a tornado around me.

She flourished her wrists, sidestepped, and disappeared into nothingness, reappearing on my left just behind my direct line of sight.

I pivoted to launch a flight of bloody projectiles.

A hunk of stone rammed me from my right.

I fell and rolled, striking a column.

The blood once in my grasp now slathered the floor.

Ilenia stood at the bottom of the daïs—an entire court away from where I'd seen her. *A light bender's illusion.*

The column behind me cracked down the centre. Stone groaned.

I propelled myself to my feet.

Painful whiteness seared my eyes. I shrieked, tottering. *I'll never reach her like this.*

The column began to crumble and fall.

Through waterlogged vision and the agony splitting my shin, I bolted in a wide arc around the perimeter of the Omphalos, biding my time to think of how to get near Ilenia. Her movements were too dynamic for my magic to get hold of her flesh as she blinked in and out of illusory existence.

Blood spindled through my fingers as I scaled the proximal end of the Omphalos, weaving once more into crimson cloth. As long as I moved too, I was just as difficult to blind.

I ripped free the ribs of scattered Guárdus corpses to fashion lances and bullets against Ilenia. Three bony projections skewered her thigh seconds before she disappeared. She exclaimed and stumbled. *Not an illusion.*

In Ilenia's second of stillness, I gripped hold of her gashes and yanked them agape to bleed her.

She screamed.

An explosion tore through my eardrums as the last of the windows blew out in a hail of glass.

One sagittally-riven half of that crumbling colonnade disintegrated to a deadly vortex of rock around Ilenia. The other half aimed for me—a gargantuan battering ram.

I pushed more azoth into the blood and shaped it to elastic silks, slinging them over the column. Its force shoved breath out of me as it swept me up.

The Omphalos whirled, the muscles of my thighs sore around the blood-silks. Nausea inundated my gut and my skull tore. I'd never transmuted so much azoth. The height didn't bother me but it would bother my spine if I cleared it.

The column hunk sped towards the corner of weakened ceiling.

I locked my feet, let go of the silk, swept my arms. Freezing azoth burned beneath my skin. Blood slathering the floors spiralled through the air towards me, torn through by flurries of glass.

I lurched violently when the column caved the roof in with an explosion of rock.

Down is my only option.

I unravelled the silks and plunged into the bloody whirlpool I still controlled, its amniotic warmth enveloping me as I plummeted.

My cocoon crashed into the marble.

Ichor splattered all over and around me.

I rose to my elbows, heaving air, nose bleeding. *She is stronger than I am.* I retched. Tinny sweet-bitterness trickled over my tongue. Hideous pain scraped my gullet. I shot to my feet. Azoth supped blood off the floor and from my hair into spinning sashes.

Fog swept through the Omphalos.

Horror seized me. *No.* Not fog. *Glass.*

Rocks huge as heads flew from all directions.

I dropped to the floor again, covered my face.

The ground erupted.

I glanced up.

A wall of glass knives drove to impale me.

I swept up swathes of blood once, twice, shielding myself from the blades and scrambling to stand, one arm over my nose and mouth.

Rocks whizzed around me like an asteroid belt spiralling for the shattered ceiling, dusting up a lethal wind of pulverised glass which spun through my hair and lashes, vying to scratch out my eyes, and in between the hunks of meteorites flickered Ilenia. One. Three. Eleven. None.

I zig-zagged and weaved in the eye of the hurricane as it slowly closed in on me, launching blades of blood to slash Ilenia before thrusting it up into bucklers against onslaughts of stone.

Dizziness whooshed through my aching skull. My gut bled into my mouth, magic weakening to little more than a whirlpool of blood. Panic and frustration strained my nerves. My eyes watered. *I can't do it.* Ilenia couldn't be caught.

Shadows crawled to me as rocks crushed closer.

Shadows…

The memory of cloaking myself in caliginosity struck me with a mad idea.

I shut my eyes.

Azoth seeped from the blood into the shadows cast by stone, hesitant yet curious as a young carnivore before sinking into its immaterial hide.

The darkness shuddered, wailed. A destructive black melody constricted my veins

My head thrust skyward as a scream emptied from me.

The spinning storm of asteroids shot away from me, pulled by the shadows they shed, bashing against the walls and colonnades and window panes where they exploded to pulverous fallout, bringing down with it yet more columns and chunks of ceiling.

Pulse battered at my brain as I gorged on air cleared of glass, neck craned low, breaths louder than a gale of blood in my ears. Far beneath my feet, somewhere afield, a groan of rock quaked the earth to the deepest crust.

My head turned sharply behind me, murky vision training on the foot of the daïs where, mere steps away, Ilenia rose slowly to her feet, head and nose bleeding, body as worn as mine.

I vaulted towards her.

The armour of a dead Guárdus I passed bulged and ruptured when my azoth reaved their thorax of ribs; the bones sharpened to javelins I then threw at Ilenia.

She scrambled up the stairs. Javelins impaled the steps before her.

Blood surged with my azoth, shadows weaving through it as I advanced onto the daïs after Ilenia, slashing for her in bursts, darkness blinding her eyes as it went.

An explosion of light tore her free.

I threw up a veil of darkness to guard my vision.

A shard of glass extended into a glistening sword in Ilenia's hand. "You are a *butcher*!" She charged for me.

I stripped of haem the carmine sashes I wielded. *Water makes a sharper blade.* "And you were *sheep*!" Cold liquid wrapped around my forearms, turning them into blades to clash with Ilenia's glass. Light flashed at the impact.

I yelled out and volted, weaving shadows over my eyes.

Our azothian weapons bound.

I pushed Ilenia's sword with a grunt, pivoting against the returning force and swinging my blade-arm to decapitate. Ilenia ducked in time. Glass slashed horizontally for my right side. I angled my torso to avoid the strike, thrusting my left arm up to hack. She twisted and propelled her right-handed sword up. I thrust forward.

A sternum crunched.

Shhhhhurk!

Pain rended my gut.

Frost needled deep into the soft flesh of my innards. A stream of blood poured down my lips.

Ilenia collapsed beneath me.

One of my water blades impaled her chest. Her glass sword ran me through the stomach.

She breathed heavily, lips parted and baring a tongue slick with red. Her eyes glazed, glazed, glazed. Both a polished gem—an emerald and a sapphire. An eye from my vision of skinned hands. Wrath and hate smoothed off her middle-aged features, tan leaching out, and in that moment, Ilenia was just a woman. We had all simply wanted to be free.

"*I'm sorry*," I breathed.

Ilenia's jaw fluttered with a wince. "I'm sorry too."

And she kicked my torso.

The glass blade slid out of me as I rolled down the stairs of the daïs into the sea of blood flooding the marble. It rippled against me.

Azoth receded, water spilling off my arms, but I knew I bled far deeper as agony locked my limbs into fevered paroxysms. *Ruined body*.

As the world blurred, I watched snowflakes float through the broken roof and melt in the bloodbath. Hesychastic and tragical. Yet sobering, strangely.

Because it really *wasn't* fair.

Not one bit.

SCENE LV

I NEITHER LOVE NOR HOPE ANYMORE

Fabio | Giorgianna

FABIO HAD NEVER SEEN AS MUCH DESTRUCTION as the Omphalos: a third of the roof gone, colonnades reduced to rubble, windows gouged. And all of it dripped with blood, dark and stringy, cooling beneath snowfall. Perhaps he was a pessimist, but he'd expected betrayal from Ilenia. And now she was dead.

Guárdi corpses had been cleaned out to make way for injured revolutionaries, and *oh* how many there were. Most sported a deep wound of relatively non-fatal variety, a few missing appendages, but a frightening number clung to fraying threads of life, pillaged of vital organs and practically torn apart. Scouting parties had been finding more and more people, primarily civilians, mutilated and dismembered. Tortured to death. And those who ventured down into the dungeons came back with stories far more unspeakable.

Near the centre of the Omphalos, dragged away from the gallons of blood pooling around the daïs, Giorgianna lay on a floor-seated stretcher, wan, sudorous skin bruised and hair cut to almost her chin. Eligio sat beside her and Sarnai held her hand, both waiting for her to awaken.

Fabio's heart wrenched. She'd been found in a horrific state—Etenesh claimed she was far more likely to die than live. Fabio couldn't stand the thought. Not after Ludovico. Not after Cesare.

Squeezing his teeth, Fabio limped towards Etenesh's makeshift station near a central window along the hall's dexter wall. He'd sustained a leg injury—several fractures and torn tendons—whilst fighting, which would leave him reliant on a walking stick for life. Somehow, it only marginally peeved him.

Etenesh communicated on The Fingers with Kasumi as the pair tended to Matìa who lay on a gurney, fellow freed prisoners gathered around them. Nearby, Yezo treated Anka-ny's wounds whilst Anukka wrapped Iyad's amputated knee, glaring at all passers-by whilst muttering Ahărla prayers.

"They've gone septic." Etenesh's assertion punched Fabio in the chest. "There's nothing more we can do." Remorse held her face.

Fabio looked at his old friend. *Please don't let it end this way…*

Matìa's head turned, eyelids cracking open with effort. "Look on the bright side, old man," they murmured with that easy smile of theirs. "We got to see each other again."

"There's no '*bright side*', Matìa," Fabio gritted out as tears rolled down his face. "It's all death and carnage."

"What is life if not perseverance regardless?"

"Fucking persevere then!"

A laugh so terribly weak left Matìa. "I'll try." But their eyes closed, "I always try, *you know…*" and they faded away.

Fabio choked, holding a hand over his mouth at the realisation that damn near everyone in his youth was gone. Kasumi went to comfort him but he routed for a shattered window, jaw tight as he blotted his tears.

In the square, Vencenzanii cared for one another's wounds. Injuries. Dead. Karmni, little Aldjya clinging to her, weaved with Alessa through the teeming crowd, doing her part in helping whilst Tafsut tended to the wounded in the Omphalos under Etenesh's guidance.

The Hounds who helped syphon people out of the citadel and thus remained minimally injured had taken to the streets, alongside Errico with Aengus and his Boars, where the citizenry had been attacked by De Tullia's forces in the heat of the uprising. Manárša and Diodora, meanwhile, remained in the Omphalos with injured Hounds, whilst Korneli, Dan, Ren and Şirîn attended to the smugglers, occupying the corridors of the ministerial house. A part of Fabio was stunned they survived at all, given their position amidst the riot. Yet, more than anything, he was *grateful*. So unbelievably grateful.

Araya had found Yòchaná in the hidden passages of the citadel, but Etenesh prohibited them from descending to the square despite their insistence, citing their concussion which *was*, quite frankly, blatant as all Hell. Chea and Indrì saw themselves and their Cyclopes back to The Antrum. They were never there to fight for the ossíi, to be fair.

"Giorgi?" Fabio heard Eligio's voice, stumbling around.

Giorgianna stirred off her stretcher, eyelids splitting open, and Fabio's heart seized up.

Sarnai gasped, *"Giorgianna!"* bursting into tears as she and Eligio both latched onto the curly-haired girl.

Fabio hobbled over as quickly as his leg would allow. He crouched by Giorgianna and embraced her, placing a kiss onto her hair as tears of relief came freely. He couldn't forgive himself if his dearest friend's daughter perished.

Giorgianna groaned. *"What…?"*

"Heavenly Dyad!" Tafsut exclaimed, bolting for Giorgianna and shooing everyone away. "Careful with her!" Her tattooed hands cradled Giorgianna's face.

She sat onto her haunches with help. "What happened…?"

"Far too greatly you exerted yourself," Tafsut said. "Etenesh healed, with ano-apozem, your leg and stab wound, but many arteries were ruptured—Kasumi barely managed to mend. We were forced to excise your spleen, one of your kidneys too, and a portion of liver. Your heart is very weak, fibrosed in part. *More* than rest, you need."

"Cesare…" Giorgianna murmured, and Fabio's heart clamped.

Tafsut's brows wilted. "So sorry, tayri. There was no undoing the damage."

Giorgianna blinked at her in confusion. Then, as if memory returned to her, light extinguished in her eyes. "No." She frowned. "No…" Her breath hitched. She broke away, crawling backwards. "No. No. No, no, no *no no no no no nonononononono*—" She clutched her fists to her heart as if it was breaking all over again, her breaths panicked, distraught, and she *screamed* in such souldeep anguish.

Fabio wished he could soothe her pain, but knew it would be futile. Time didn't heal, but it dulled, and that was all that could bring relief.

Her banshee's call petered out, leaving Giorgianna so forlorn, bereft, arms curved around her own trembling form. "*no…*" A whisper. "*I don't feel anything…*" And yet she wept with such bitter helplessness.

Sarnai and Eligio, Tafsut too, embraced Giorgianna.

Yet Fabio couldn't stand to remain.

Ashes and char blackened the stonework of the citadel, resembling bone lesions, on his route down a thin corridor in search of solitude.

Illutóri paladins had fought valiantly against the flames, quashing it but not without losses, of them left behind no more than a rank of seven who, alongside surviving Illuteríi—approximately twenty-eight of them—returned to *Sa Basílica del Illuterixióne e Benefácio Vísus* where they cared for the injured. The Misersi monks of *Ettàva ris Sánguinem dél'Aís* agreed to tend to a swathe of the populace after some cajoling, having spent the majority of time barricaded within their monastery against Imperialíi and crows. The Misersii were no fighters, and had no organised Holy Guard unlike The Order. As for the griffins and crows themselves, they'd been decimated bar a few counterrevolutionary militias which fled, still under the banner of dead De Tullia. Thanks in no small part to the revolutionary efforts, the provinces of Vencenza were reportedly in an equally insurgent spirit, so De Tullia loyalists would have little place of sanctuary. *This is a civil war…*

Fabio's gut cooled at the thought.

Voices trickled into his awareness as he neared the window at the corridor's terminus.

Around a corner opened up a small circular bartizan with a stairwell leading down, at the top of which stood Nikitha, Visolela, and Dahlia. A cast held Nikitha's leg straight as she leaned onto crutches, whilst a bandage plastered itself across Visolela's eye. Sten died in battle, leaving Visolela the captain of The Black Tongues. The fact that they stayed to help Vencenzanii further astounded Fabio.

Dahlia, arm wrapped in a sling, glimpsed him, muttering something to the women and approaching with a stilted expression somewhere between condolences and attempted amiability.

She stopped beside him. Fabio nodded, hands in the pockets of his greatcoat, and looked out of the window where a white sky unfurled above the government building's snow-capped western minarets, like a bloodstained handkerchief blotched by the dissipating red of Myrabella fumes and aglow with the befitting moon. Whatever happened between Giorgianna and Ilenia had cracked and emptied the moat surrounding the ministerial house, buildings around it flooded if not outright obliterated. Luckily, the aqueduct stood fast.

"Last ones standing," mused Dahlia.

"It's shit." Fabio *humphed*. "Never wanted this."

"Oh shut up!" Her glare cut. "You fucking survived the most violent insurrection since the Vencenzani Rebellion, get over yourself! Crapehanger."

Fabio fell silent, not knowing what to do with himself anymore bar withdrawing into wistful rumination.

The sight of the cerise moon seemed to enthral Dahlia. "Ammuríre Lunéra aligning with a blood moon. Prophetic." She turned to Fabio again. "Lignéza, ìgnis morírum."

Fabio frowned. "I know nothing of southern paganism."

Her obsidian eyes rolled. "You ought to reply with '*ipse fócire è vóstrum*', to which *I* respond '*éra ipse è vóstrum*'."

He rolled his eyes back at her and fell quiet again.

"I'm sorry about the boy. He mattered a lot to you."

"How many times did I say I wouldn't bury my son?" Fabio gritted out. His Saints never claimed to be eternally merciful, and yet…

"It's not fair, I know," Dahlia said solemnly. "We cannot afford to dwell on fairness, can we, though? Doesn't hurt any less."

Comforting folks had never been Dahlia's prowess. Nevertheless, Fabio appreciated it, little as it could do, in the grand scheme.

"Thank you, Dahlia. For helping us."

Silence strained for the hundredth time.

"Ada is fine," she said quietly and fleeted to the Omphalos.

Fabio gazed after her for a few breaths, then his eyes crossed the coldness of Eligio's.

"She needs you," he bit, his jaw overwrought. "Don't be a fucking coward and go back to the Omphalos to see to her." He went for the stairs of the bartizan but stopped at the apex, turning once more to the captain. "We all loved him differently, but we all lost him the same." Fabio's heart caved in. "Don't think your grief for him matters more." And, with that, Eligio was gone.

Conscience heavy as an anchor, Fabio returned to the scene of people among the ruins and ashes of a crumbled empire, watching the way they all helped one another stand and live, the way they fought for liberation and would do it again and again until every chain, every cage, lay broken. The capacity of humanity to demand justice for themselves and each other was surely a phenomenon to admire. Most importantly, following Ilenia's death, and even with counterrevolutionaries still infesting the city state, Fabio cherished the sliver of safety returned to the folk of oldtown, The Court of Secrets, Smugglers' District, the Antrum. Fabio figured greed and power-lust to be the First Cause of some of the worst evil. To allow it to live was ignorance, and ignorance was servitude.

And so Fabio understood:

A revolutionary could never serve.

A revolutionary could never wholly die.

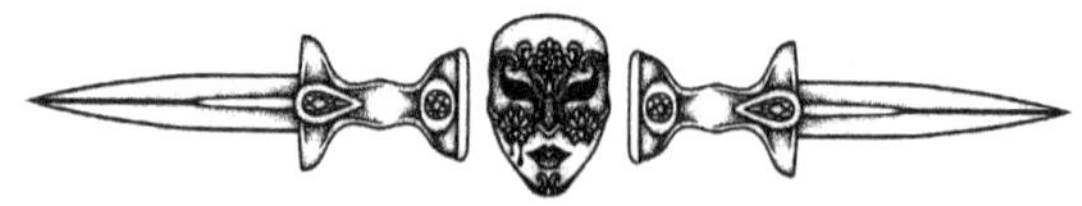

THE STARLESS NIGHT SKY SMELLED OF FIRE; Vencenza's people made prolific efforts to destroy every item of De Tullia's heraldry across the city and provinces.

As I wandered down a capillary shooting off the emptied Hanging Gardens, my body still gnawed—it was only midday that Ilenia almost took my life.

I came upon an argentous silk banner emblazoned with a hideous ashen swallow. I never thought I could hate someone as much as Manuele, yet here I was, so I tore the wretched thing down into the snow. The Governor was merely a man, his ashes indistinguishable from those of his detestable kingdom. In his quest for godly dominion, he lost sight of his own fallibility and paid the ultimate dues.

From my hand hung Cesare's bàuta, a haunting dead weight.

I looked upon its mouthless visage, its eye sockets black with their own gravity, its porcelain and papier-mâché surface as if bone-carven. Death limned its every jarring feature. Cesare wanted the mask forsaken to fire, despised its sight, but my fingers couldn't yield it.

It had been a symbol from the very start, an immolating blaze and a beacon of hope at once; a blade and bullet both. He never made sense. Even when I hated him—*thought* I hated him—I hadn't wanted him to die because he, mask or flesh, was emblematic of a liberty I did not have. Now, the idols he fought to burn finally lay in cinders, and I knew better than anyone how the past festered in your blood until you remained searching for the shreds of humanity left among your rot.

But was it not the *flesh* that begot the flames? *Flesh* that made the revolution? Was the mask not merely an item? *An instrument?*

I kissed the mouthless visage and hurled it against the wall.

It shattered, falling over the heaped banner.

I flinched back from the scatter of shrapnel, hand over my mouth.

Drawing a matchbox and black pouch from my bloody jacket, I threw a handful of saltpetre into the pyre, then struck a flame to follow.

Fire burst to life—a phoenix taking flight. Cleansing through destruction; remaking through righteous violence.

I knew there could be no way Cesare would let himself perish without marking an unhealing gash in the world he left behind, I just never foresaw it wounding *me*. But the catch with loving a flame was that it burned out.

> '*When I die, I want my ashes thrown to the wind. I want to be free.*'

And now he could be.

Once both the banner and bàuta reduced to coals, once the flames hissed at the pierce of snow and tempered to a twirling smoke, I soaked the tears from my eyes, spat a curse upon the fallen civilisation, and made my way to the mortuary.

Washed clean, fresh clothes donned, I anointed myself with holy myrrh, but blood lingered on my skin still, forever sullied. *It does not wash off.*

As I lingered upon the threshold of Cesare's bedchamber, my heart fluttered weakly, without rhythm, my body gnawing, my head heavy.

The sun of díem sóle would soon be on ascent, the black canvas of the sky beyond the window already sluiced with cerulescent murk, but I couldn't fathom sleeping. Couldn't fathom what I would see when I closed my eyes.

My vision bleared as it roved the weathered floorboards upon which Cesare and I had played music and danced and made love, upon which I recited word-for-word my father's lecture on the formation of a neutron star and Cesare had found a grey hair I had never noticed sprung up among my ringlets. He was always sharp like that. And now he was gone. And I stood upon those weathered floorboards alone.

Pain wracked me all over again, so I rushed for Cesare's escritoire where he told me to look for an envelope.

My fingers darted through the drawers until I unearthed the notes I had sent him during our month apart—one of the only things remotely organised amidst the hideous clutter. A small envelope fell away from the stack, wine-dark, slightly puffy to the touch.

I opened it.

First, I removed a slip of folded parchment. Redness stained it as if rouge, petaloid and alar in form. I frowned at the familiar patterns. *Anthocyanins…?* Then, out of the envelope plopped the culprit of its bloat: the head of a red rose, dried and flattened. *Rosa sanguinus.* My favourite flower. The most striking blooms in áti and ápa's dooryard in Ferréli. I hadn't pressed a single rose in seemingly a lifetime. Perhaps, without comprehension, I couldn't bring myself to.

I brushed tremulous fingertips against the petals. *Done recently.* A realisation came to me as I turned to the still-folded note, its stains.

The dots connected into a noose around my throat.

My chest throbbed, but I compelled myself to pick up the paper. To unfurl it. To read the hideous penmanship within.

> *'You hated me for every single thing*
> *I never told you until it was too late.*
> *‹Ne lo'ère kaliranè tu mirazê› means*
> *‹I far too fiercely love you›.*
> *But I fear it is too late.'*

My heart crumpled, flooding with warmth. But not the sweet treacle sort. The stab wound sort. I couldn't breathe again. But I had to. I lived in spite of myself, in spite of loss, in spite of pain. It would always be worth it, even if I sometimes did not believe it.

At the very least, I lived to find Cesare's final letter.

Notes inscribed the bottom, urging me to retrieve my cello. Along with it, I compiled every letter Cesare sent to me which, upon returning to his bedchamber, I arranged in chronological sequence like sheet music to a piece we unintentionally composed together. But the closing strains of the last note did not read like the conclusion of a composition, rather an abrupt cessation—a breath held but never released. Fitting, perhaps, but I no longer wished for a continuation of such a paradigm.

I pressed my lips and a thought came tentatively to me, sending me back to my room where I found that single note I'd held onto but never sent—a lovelorn bêtise of mine. The melody I'd composed was self-contained, almost a coda. I knew it would never receive a response, hence I'd left it unabridged.

My stomach coiled as I looked upon the written prose.

So many times, whilst pondering how to word myself, my composure dallied off and my mind inundated with inanities I could not yet utter—thought I never *would,* at which point I'd incise the overripe fruit borne by the branches of my longing, letting a droplet bleed out to be caught on my quill, and scrawling with its bittersweetness besotted words. It was strange. I never thought I would love my nemesis in every possible world, let alone enough to be sick with it. But *he* was strange: a mosaic full of cracks yet a masterpiece all the same. A cipher I sought to decode.

And there was only one thing left to do.

Setting the unsent letter down at the end of the sequence, I engaged my bow and commenced to play.

Chords ran on, diffident and unwieldy against my fingers at first, both a dialogue and a narrative like lovers reading to each other a novel across a vine-embowered garden treillage. I knew precisely which notes were mine and which his, and yet they were written as if to append the other. As if the music was just as much a conversation as the text.

As the song crawled around me with its thorny brambles, I began to comprehend each edge to the pain sinking into me.

When Cesare's suffering had been the deepest, his mind foggy with hunger and sleeplessness, the most he could compose was a grave drone cut by subito glissandi, sharp and stinging as spiny nettles, as the ache of a parched skull, whilst my chords sprung up in the manner of meadow blossoms: vivace, yet timid all the same. I could never call myself much of a composer, after all.

But, day by day, note by note—as if each one percolated like a drop of water—Cesare's melodies sprouted fresher petals, adagio e rubato, until finally blossoming into the rich hues of a summer longed-for but yet-to-come, free as the wind's expression.

The euphony stuttered as my breath hitched and tears trickled down my cheeks, but I gulped down a harrowing breath and resumed reciting the third-last letter Cesare wrote to me—a lengthy andante-allegro chorus like storm clouds balmifying the midsummer air of the moors.

All the while, my own strains had wilted just as I had, lentando: poisoned by the spider lair that was the perished ministerial house, and the cards flipped, Cesare instead the one to fret over me.

To a note of mine where I'd alluded to wishing harm upon myself, his response was simply,

'*Giorgianna…*'

followed by near a page of sheet music—that very same midsummer storm song—as if a desperate bid to distract me from pain.

And it worked.

I should have known then that he loved me.

I should have known the moment I decided to write him letters that *I* loved *him*.

My hands shook against the final notes they arduously drew out, slow and broad, plaintive (*regret*), then saudadic and lovesick (*a lonely lament*). And as soon as the coda ceased, echoing an answered wail in the silence of the early morning, my heart crumpled into a wilted leaf. *Everyone I love leaves me…*

My cello toppled to the floor. I pulled my knees to my chest and huddled into myself on that chair, in tears, wishing with my entire soul I could be a flower bud again—innocent and small.

The cavity of my ribs lay desolate. Winter-cold. It all hurt too much. Yet, even as they poured again and again, my tears could never revive the barren soil beneath which I buried every person I loved.

The summer had come and gone.

Scene LVI

Elegy of Spring

Faustina, Vencenza, 1763, 18th Century, 9th Centimillennium ZE (Zephyrus Epoch)

Giorgianna

SPRING SCRATCHED FEVERISHLY at the thawing scabs of winter, snow-white skin rupturing with open wounds of raw earth and scaly stonework.

Seasons changed so fast, the pebbly beach of Smugglers' Cove no longer icy, yet coastal breeze still bit my cheeks where I stood on the wharf, six-hundred-hour gloom dissolving above.

Yòchaná approached *Antigone*, clad in a billowing blue robe draped with a white tallét gedólah,[120] fiery hair woven into loose paired braids. She came with Errico and Alessa.

---

[120] The name of *talít gadól* among Sephardim; a long prayer shawl in Jewish tradition with knotted tassels called '*tzitzít*' (ציצית) attached at the four corners.

The *talít* is often plain white per Sephardi custom.

Yòchaná endeavoured a careful smile. "Peace, Giorgianna."

"Salúdi." My voice rattled between my ears. I hadn't slept that night—every nightfall demanded I bring back the dead, and every night left behind but a hole in my chest, a dead tree hollow taken by permafrost.

I had given my flesh to grief.

"Word of progress from the northwest," said Errico. "Two major loyalist hideouts have been dispelled."

All through the winter following the uprising, clashes between dissidents and De Tullia loyalists had continued to flare up across Vencenza. Weeding out griffins and crows—there *were* no surviving peacocks—proved difficult. The moat, too, had been a burden to mend. Our first priority had been inspecting the aqueducts to ensure the lymfática of the city was still supplied with water, but several families had gotten displaced by the reservoirs which surged from the ruined moat, and work to right those wrongs still carried on.

"Word has it," Yòchaná added solemnly, "the Salvatrici wish to intervene. Governess Laerzia Della Rovere expresses trepidation."

"*Trepidation.*" I scoffed. "If she wishes to put our city on the leash of her northern state again, she mistakes what sorts of people we are. We have organised ourselves for months, set up our own supply chains and aid, resisted *former government militias*!" My eyes lifted to the cliffs cleaving the Cove from oldtown. Thin plumes of chimney smoke rose into the lilac milkiness of the lumining sky. "You know," I resumed, "'Iutulicano' means 'without leaders', from 'túlico' for 'leader'. Such was the etymology of De Tullia's surname also—'of highest leaders'. Iutulicanii lived for close to a *millennium* without an organised government. If that is to become of Vencenzanii—'venéte cênit zanúli': 'a lineage gifted foundedness'—so be it. We shall choose that in a hundred lifetimes before we choose Salvatrici *intervention*. It is simply northern colonisation, *subjugation*, all over again which we shall *never* surrender to." My gaze realigned with Yòchaná's again, unyielding as the blood within me. "We are *teeth*. And we are untreadable ice beneath the boot of the oppressor."

Yòchaná's left fist smacked solidly against their right palm which closed around it, their kyanite eyes twinkling. "Vítam di rivoluzióne."

Errico and Alessa rapped a fist against their hearts twice, holding up two fingers in a 'V' and saying, "No kings!"

I held both palms to my weak heart—it would never beat the same again, less in a heartbreak way and more in a heart *damage* way. "I will be in upper óssium soon."

With parting nods, the three took their leave.

I ascended back up to *Antigone*.

A frightening portion of Hydras perished, the once-bustling ship now gripped by kenopsia. I'd come to realise over the winter that the sole means for Fabio to cope with grief was to put his head down and work without a moment's rest. I supposed it was better than me. At least Danilo found some merriment in his lost tooth, proudly displaying the gap to anyone who'd look (and anyone who wouldn't). But he was always ridibund like that.

Ren scrubbed the sails, preparing *Antigone* for a supply run to Sậfynạ in the coming days, whilst conversing with Kel-Kech. Ve'd warmed up to her, though ve'd never admit it. Kel requested Fabio to take her with them, wishing to finally make her way back home to Yewada.

Near the forecastle, Lucrezia stood with arms around herself, a ghost in her billowing white nightgown. Cheeks puffy, wan. Grey eyes cavernous. Pixie greasy and overgrown. Casting an unseeing glimpse across the main deck, she fled below.

She'd been inconsolable until falling utterly mute on spring's first day, not a word for almost a week now. I stayed with her as many nights as I could, as many as my own grief would permit. I knew agony so soul-destroying far too well.

Between my missing spleen and damaged heart, I'd needed to commence tonics lest I perish from simply living, along with a generous dose of elixir to get a hold on my hallucinations. All of that proved costly, so, given our return into Aengus' good books, I'd began frequenting Glàvca's tavèrna again to play the cello. But the remittance wasn't enough, pushing me into cosmetic surgeries for Antrum civilians and body modifications for Cyclopes. By tailoring. It paid significantly better and for good reason. Whilst it ensured I'd survive in the moment, my inevitably early death was sealed.

"Whatcha doin', girl?" a snow-bright voice chirruped behind me.

I turned to find Sarnai, Itxaro by her side. The white-haired woman locked her arms around my middle.

A wry smile tugged my lips. "Rotting in rumination."

Itxaro slung her arms around my neck. "We are here for you, lehên."

I hugged them both. They'd been my rocks through the awful months, along with Fabio and Eligio. Tafsut and Etenesh, too. I couldn't imagine the horror of my state had it not been for them all.

At the very back of the stern deck, I sighted Eligio sitting in solitude, legs swung off the ship's side and elbows perched on the railing. "Pardon me." I slipped out of the embrace, heading for the artist. "Eli?" I asked tentatively when I neared.

"There were five of us." His words hurt.

I sat beside him, leaning my temple against shoulder. "There will always be five of us."

We sat wordlessly as the ocean bustled and the sun emerged from within its waves.

I pressed my lips together. "I still need to…" The sentence trailed off, my stomach sinking.

"Go," Eligio said simply. "I'll know when you do it."

I hugged him tight, his being ever-warm. "I love you, Eli."

He embraced me back, even tighter. "Love you too, Giorgi."

I planted a peck on his forehead and made my way below deck.

The gondoa I'd nicked off the docks bounced over shattering ocean spume whilst I fought against the wind to moor it on the waterfront of the bay's largest skerry.

Snatching up my satchel, heavy as a tomb, I looked up at an old lighthouse reaching for the azureous vernal sky. Fabio never failed to disdain its supposed terrible condition, how flickering and dim of a light it shone. Korneli promised at least five times already to inspect it, but remained to.

Across aquamarine waves, Smugglers' District unfurled in quaint grace, Buccaneer's Landing bedecked with Fabio's *Antigone*, Dahlia's *Hangman's Dowry*, Şirîn's *Roj*, Fēngnà's *Moon Hare*, Raffaele's *Pallid Reaper*, The Rusted Gills' *Black Bile* and The Purple Maidens' *Lamia*, dozens of tiny gondoas.

From so far, you would believe the halcyon image had you known no better. *I* knew better.

The stairs of the old lighthouse creaked as I ascended through the tower, every step coated with dust and wrapped in cobwebs.

A singular window, paneless, small, sporting a wide sill, gazed out of the cramped service room towards the eastern horizon where cliffs curved and plunged into the water. Sea stacks cleaved the surface of the ocean in the distance. Below, each swell of seawater sluiced the dark rocks jutting out of the waves. *Fortuitous, as they say.*

I ran my fingertips along the silver tanzanite cufflink clipping the ruffled white sleeve around my wrist.

Every single one of Cesare's belongings had been burnt per custom, but I salvaged a single shirt all the same, alongside a couple of his earrings. I barely wore the shirt, as if it were a sacred garment, but I couldn't bear every piece of him being reduced to ash.

From my satchel, I lifted an elegant grey urn.

Cesare's urn.

I set it down on the sill.

> *'When I die, I want my ashes thrown*
> *to the wind. I want to be free.'*

I hadn't been able to bring myself to go through with it all winter, reducing to hysteria each time I lay a finger on the urn. It made no sense. Something so small shouldn't be able to contain a flame, a soul, a *Self* so immense and potent. Yet there it stood.

I unscrewed the lid.

My innards coiled up. *Breathe…*

This was the freedom Cesare's eleutheromaniac heart craved. Flesh had been his prison. But the Self was *transcendent*.

I drew a shuddering breath and poured the ashes out.

They caught on the wind, flying out to sea, dissolving in the water, dissipating along the distant horizon. Cesare's second cufflink plummeted to the rock face below. The indigo-violet gem dislodged on impact, the veridic vastness of the ocean devouring both halves.

At last, I threw the empty urn at the nearby outcrop, smashing it to pieces. Waves washed away the remnants, and nothing remained.

Finality crushed my chest. *It's over.*

I leaned out of the window, shoulder-length curls spilling into the arms of the wind as I gazed towards the township, the cliff, the city state of Vencenza. The long, bloody, cruel road I'd crawled. The afterglow of a ghastly civilisation finally fallen. *Everything is over.*

Tears rushed in streaks of fire down my face.

There would never be a next life, a different world. The universe wasn't constructed in such a way. Yet *this* was *our* life. *Our* world. One wrapped in chains and locked in glass, where blood constituted the most valuable currency. But what would we have if we turned a blind eye to its wounds? If we chose to let it bleed and die? If we chose to let each other suffer? If we forced the burden of righting broken injustices onto children for fear of tackling its enormity?

All I had wanted was for the people I loved to *live*. To *be* with me.

And what would we have if not this life?

EXEUNT OMNES

YEGRIKA
ORPHAN CLIFF
STEPPING STONES
UNKNOWABLE TONGUE
THUR'ASTE
DIILUANA
TAMMERGEIER COVE
KOHORTSA
SH'OVVA
KIDHO PLAIN
K'UDIRAA
YENGENGA
LAAM
NAANGDI
AYELECH
ADARE
NAGA DESERT
DAPRAST
ONJOLELA
MOTATYA
AMETHYSTINE DESERT
YEWADA
PADAMOYA
EKISENT
NAMEVAW
ITROSANANA
THE AGNOSIS
THE SPIDER

Ultima Verba

"SUBVERT THE SOCIAL AND CIVIL ORDER! *Aye*, I would destroy, to the last vestige, this mockery of order, this travesty upon justice! Break up the home? Yes, every home that rests on slavery! Every marriage that represents the sale and transfer of the individuality of one of its parties to the other! Every institution, social or civil, that stands between man and his right; every tie that renders one a master, another a serf; every law, every statute, every be-it-enacted that represents tyranny; everything you call privilege that can only exist at the expense of international right.

Now cry out, '*Nihilist! Disintegrationist!*' Say that I would isolate humanity, reduce society to its elemental state, make men savage! It is not true. But rather than see this devastating, cankering, enslaving system you call 'social order' go on, rather than help to keep alive the accursed institutions of authority, I would help to reduce every fabric in the social structure to its native element."

—*Voltairine de Cleyre*

BLOOD REMAINS

And so we come to the fated end of this bloody pantomime.

If you enjoyed *Non Omnis Moriar*, it would mean the world to me to receive your reviews on Goodreads, StoryGraph, or retail sites on which the book is listed. Word of mouth is the best way to support independent creatives. Royalties earned from all English copies of *The Hypostasis of Dissent* duology will be donated to *Doctors Without Borders*, the *Kurdish Red Crescent*, and *All for Armenia*.

If you decide to post about my books on your social media, including photographs and the like, feel free to tag my publisher (*lacrimose.and.righteous*).

I would be honoured.

Until we meet again, reader.

SCAN TO GO TO
GOODREADS

SCAN TO GO TO
AMAZON

SCAN TO GO TO
STORYGRAPH

DUOLOGY PLAYLIST

Shape of Lies —Eternal Eclipse
Goddess —Hatchrr
Walk With Me in Hell —Lamb of God
For a Voice Like Thunder —Rotting Christ
The Headless Waltz —Voltaire
The Endless City —REMINA
No Half Measures —Ingested
Whore of Babylon —Zheani
TRRST —IC3PEAK
Ascend into Darkness —Draconian
Butterfly —GERM (feat. Audrey Sylvain)
King of Kings, Lord of Lords —Mephorash
Malevolence —New Years Day
The Sethian —Draconian
Sanguinem —Mephorash
The Sacrificial Flame —Draconian
Poetry of Madness —Greg Dombrowski
My Mistake —Hallatar
Spiracle —Flower Face
Bella ci Dormi —Canzoniere Grecanico Salentino
Disgraced —Cairiss

ACKNOWLEDGEMENTS

So many golden hands were put to the creation of *Non Omnis Moriar*, and *The Hypostasis of Dissent* as a whole, that I fear I mightn't be able to do it justice in a measly couple pages, but trying my best is the least I can offer.

I want to firstly thank the brilliant artists I commissioned for a number of illustrations. Ayşe-Mira's work is a slice of an ancient matriarchal time and was my first choice when thinking of whom to commission for the mask chart. *Çok teşekkür ederim, canım*; I couldn't be happier with the outcome. Nadia's gritty, metal-like linework so perfectly brings the military emblems into being, and her attention to detail is outstanding. *La ringrazio molto, mia cara amica.*

A special thank you to Brianna Boehm (*beforeviolets* on Instagram) for the consultation she had with me regarding Jewish representation, particularly with respect to blood magic and Gnostic themes. Antisemitism is one of the most dangerous forms of racism and it was important for me to consult a voice that is active in the Jewish community and culture. ‏א. שיינעם דאַנק.

Neither my personal philosophy and subsequent political work, nor the theory for this very duology would be possible without the writings of—and this is inexhaustive for relative brevity's sake—Pyotr Kropotkin, Mikhail Bakunin, Edward W. Saʿīd, Ghassan Kanafani, Errico Malatesta, Eduardo Galeano, Abdullah Öcalan, Aimé Césaire, Ashanti Omowali, Anahide Ter Minassian, Itō Noe, Kuwasi Balagoon, Nestor Makhno, Moḥamed Saïl, Lorenzo Kom'boa Ervin, Ruby Ḥamad, Dimítris Troadítis, Lucy E. Parsons, Voltairine de Cleyre (*understand that I do not endorse or unequivocally agree with every single piece of theory and ideology put forth by any of the aforementioned thinkers*).

A special thanks to Professor Ingvild Sælid Gilhus for her research on Gnosticism, particularly her 1985 book *The Nature of the Archons: A Study in the Soteriology of a Gnostic Treatise from Nag Hammadi*. I widely utilised her writings in the worldbuilding process of *The Hypostasis of Dissent* duology.

It must be noted here that most of the chapter titles are references to popular culture, literature, music, Gnostic scripture, and famous Latin phrases which I do not claim as my own. Notable are *SCENE I* (title of a 1908 book purported to convey the teachings of Hermes Trismegistus on Hermetic philosophy); *SCENE III* ("irrelevant conclusion"; a logical fallacy wherein an argument's refutation does not in actuality disprove the argument *presented*, but rather one that is not relevant); *SCENE IV* (Italian translation of *"one swallow does not make spring"* from Aristotle's *Nicomachean Ethics*: «μία χελιδὼν ἔαρ οὐ ποιεῖ...»); *SCENE V* (translated title of Kim Jee-woon's 2010 action-thriller film 《악마를 보았다》 [one of my most favourite movies]); *SCENE VII* (title of Darren Aronofsky's 2017 psychological horror film); *SCENE IX* (ⲦⲈⲨⲠⲞⲤⲦⲀⲤⲒⲤ ⲚⲚⲀⲢⲬⲰⲚ; alternative title of the *c.* 3 CE Coptic-language Gnostic text *The Hypostasis of the Archons*—what the title of this duology references); *SCENE XII* (Latin for "perhaps your last hour"); *SCENE XIII* (quote from Anne Sexton's 1964 letter to Anne Clarke); *SCENE XIX* (*"Eros once again limb-loosener whirls me sweetbitter, impossible to fight off, creature stealing up..."* fragment by Sappho [Ψάπφω]); *SCENE XXII* (Italian translation of *"verba volant, scripta manent"*: "[spoken] words fly away, written ones remain"); *SCENE XXIV* ("men generally believe what they want to believe"); *SCENE XXV* (quote by Palestinian revolutionary novelist Ghassan Kanafani); *SCENE XXVI* (Heinrich Kramer's controversial *Hammer of Witches* which advocated for the burning of "witches" [women]); *SCENE XXVII* (one of the Ten Plagues of Egypt [מַכּוֹת מִצְרַיִם] from the *Book of Exodus*); *SCENE XXIX* ("but my deceiving/fallacious thought..." from *Rime d'amore(23)* by Torquato Tasso); *SCENE XXXIII* (Psalm 23:4); *SCENE XXXV* (from Franz Kafka's *Letters to Milena*); *SCENE XXXVII* (Latin for "loss", "deprivation"); *SCENE XXXIX* (from the poem *Self-Deliverance* by Traci Brimhall); *SCENE XLI* (Italian translation of *Three Cheers for Sweet Revenge*, a My Chemical Romance album [we love MCR]); *SCENE XLII* ("death conquers all"); *SCENE XLIII* ("pulvis et umbra sumus"); *SCENE XLVII* (Seneca's "ignis aurum probat, miseria fortes homines"); *SCENE XLVIII* (quote by Friedrich Nietzsche); *SCENE XLIX* ("I die unvanquished"); *SCENE LI* (Italian translation of "corruptio optimi pessima": "the corruption of the best is the worst"); *SCENE LII* ("thus always to tyrants"); *SCENE LIII* ("Envious, that the light dies in part", a play on the line "*Invido, che la luce ascondi in parte*" from Torquato Tasso's *Rime d'amore(397)*: "Envious, that you hide the light in part").

Utmost gratitude to Nurcan for editing *NOM*. It's by chance that I met her through real-life community, and I was beyond honoured to have my work be edited by an ESL, fellow mixed ethnic minority of Türkiye who understood my artistic vision. *Dzalian didi madloba, yoldaşım.*

These acknowledgements wouldn't be complete without thanking the beta readers and critique partners who kept my faith burning: Nelita for being there since the very beginning and having read the roughest of drafts (*and somehow enjoyed them...?*) along with just about every iteration since. R. E. Levy, author of queer gothic horror novella *Rivers of Eden* (which you should all read!), for providing immense feedback as a beta reader for both the duology's instalments, and whose kind words helped keep burning my confidence as an author.

Lastly, yet arguably most importantly, my wonderfully diverse online space, full of radically-leftist activists, poets, artists, culture enthusiasts, and the kindest, most enthusiastic, and interesting people I have ever come across, is something I hold so incredibly dear and sacred. Not least of those people are Sila, Maryam, Daniel—poet and author of *A Casket Full of Poems*, Lilly, Raina, Stefano, Edelneria, Ellis—author of *Saturnalia*, Megan, Hydrawi—author of *Infesto*, Faiza, and, very pertinently, Arev, Armenian-Persian-Jewish artist, activist and owner of art boutique *Mulberry Jaan* whose SSWANA-and-Central-Asian solidarity group I met countless wonderful, likeminded people through. Շատ շնորհակալություն, ջան.

So, *so* many more could be named that I'd be here for another book's-worth of pages. I see all of you and I'm so grateful for your presence.

Thank you.

~Sfar